EDGE
OF THE
DREAM

Also by Andrew Rowe

The War of Broken Mirrors Series
Forging Divinity
Stealing Sorcery
Defying Destiny

Arcane Ascension Series
Sufficiently Advanced Magic
On the Shoulders of Titans
The Torch that Ignites the Stars
The Silence of Unworthy Gods
When Wizards Follow Fools
A Brief History of Chronomancy

The Lost Edge Series
Edge of the Woods
Edge of the Dream

Weapons and Wielders Series
Six Sacred Swords
Diamantine
Soulbrand

Other Books
How to Defeat a Demon King in Ten Easy Steps
Death Game Quality Assurance

Arcane Ascension Universe Books by Other Authors
Crystal Awakening by Kayleigh Nicol
Phantom Chamber by Kayleigh Nicol

EDGE OF THE DREAM

THE LOST EDGE ⸗ BOOK TWO

ANDREW ROWE

For the Noel family,
who taught me the magic of words

Cover design by Jason Nathaniel Artuz

ISBN: 978-1-0394-3927-6

Published in 2025 by Podium Publishing
www.podiumentertainment.com

CONTENTS

MAP OF DANIA

A general map of the continent of Dania, with lower detail on the areas outside our protagonist's homeland.

LOCAL MAP

A closer look at the local portion of the map. In the frame story (the Prologue and Interludes), our protagonists begin near the Perfect Stranger, along the coast of the river between Winch and Larkbridge.

In the main story, our protagonist begins in the Court of Rust and Salt on the southeastern side of the map.

MAP OF THE WOODS

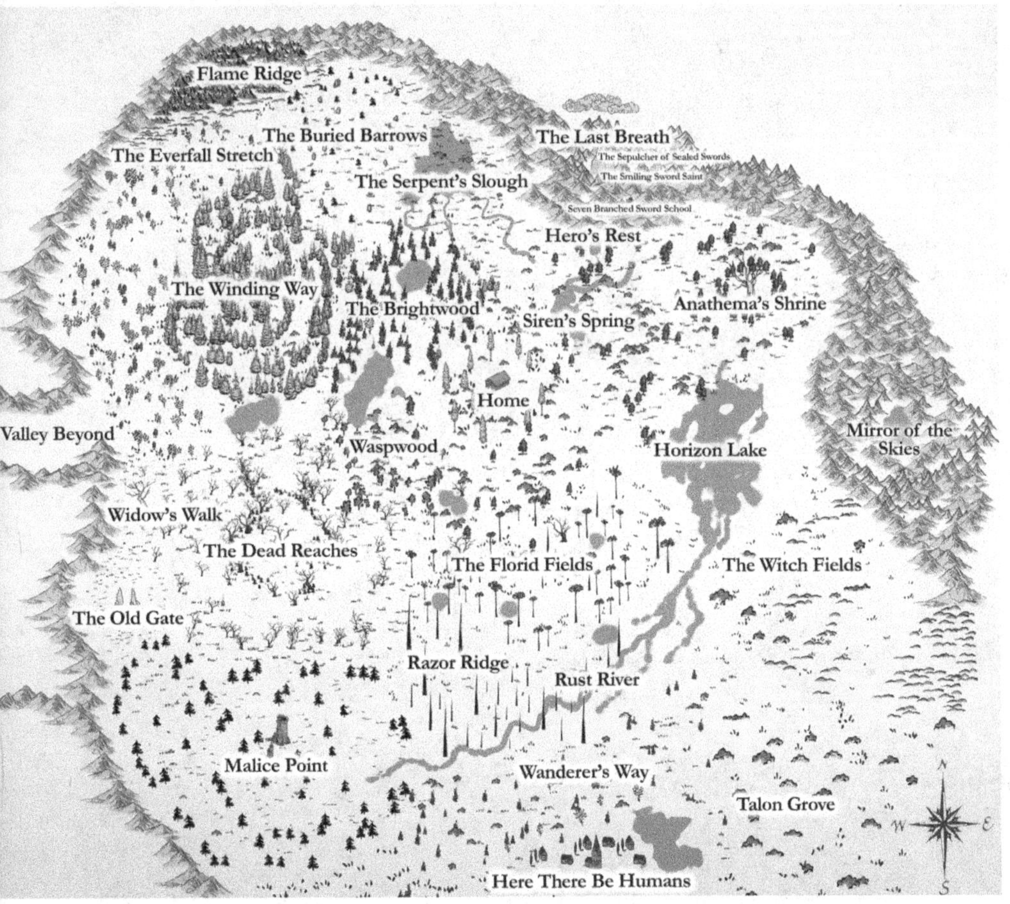

A rough map of the Court of Rust and Salt, though one may doubt the authenticity, given that it was drawn from the stories of an unreliable narrator.

STYLE NOTES

This story contains several Interlude chapters. These chapters are from the perspective of characters other than Edge, the primary narrator, and Edge does not necessarily know about the events that occur in them. The perspective of each Interlude is listed in the title at the start of the Interlude. For example, "Interlude — Thane" indicates that the Interlude is from Thane's perspective.

Some characters within this series communicate telepathically. To indicate this, rather than using quotes, I use different forms of punctuation based on the character initiating the telepathic communication.

I use different types of brackets to indicate telepathy for different characters. For example, <This would be one form of telepathic communication.> [This would be what another form of telepathy looks like.]

This formatting difference is to make it immediately obvious which character is sending the telepathic message without repeatedly using dialogue tags or other indicators. The specific characters in question should be clear once the story actually reaches them.

I use the singular "they/them" for agender and nonbinary characters, as well as characters that have not had their gender determined by the narrator yet. For example, "I didn't know who wrote the note, but they had a peculiar style of writing."

Finally, I use spaces before and after em dashes if they are in the middle of a sentence (AP style). This is purely because I find this style easier to read.

RECAP

SCRIBE'S SCRAWL AND A SWORD'S CALL

Dear Vee,

Since I can't ensure you've actually been hearing what I've been saying, I'm preparing this letter as a redundancy.

My arrival on Dania was largely uneventful, at least at first. No storms or sea serpents on the way, which is surprising, given the reputation of the waters we traveled through. On the ship, however, I began to hear stories that were concerning — talk of an "inquisition" that was hunting sorcerers in the southwest. I've heard them more formally referred to as the "Order of the Cold Iron Chain," which sounds even more foreboding. Conveniently, this was exactly where I was going to be arriving, and the inquisition seemed to have a particular focus on hunting shapeshifters and illusionists.

Auntie always manages to give us such lovely assignments.

From what I could glean from the crew, the inquisition arose in response to some kind of conflict with a local court of "fae" — a term I didn't fully understand before arriving. They're not just a single species with powerful essence abilities like, say, the delaren back at home. Rather, it seems like it's a broad term for creatures tied closely to nature, similar to how the term "elemental" refers to any creature from other planes.

Naturally, I stumbled into that conflict virtually instantly, and through means I couldn't have properly anticipated. Upon arriving in the small town of Winch, I witnessed a young swordsman rescue victims from a burning building, using essence sorcery to leap a tall building in a single bound and slice a fire elemental in half. After his success, he was immediately chased off by the villagers, who had seen a six-petaled mark that he had barely concealed on his cheek under his hood. Apparently, that's a sign of favor from the local fae court, which sparked some distrust among the villagers.

I didn't get involved with him then, but naturally, that didn't last for long. The next day, I was reviewing a local job board and making decisions on what to do next and I saw the swordsman returning to the town with a child he'd seemingly saved from wolves in the nearby forest. That proved more complicated, but again, he was chased away.

I made my way to a caravan stop to head to a larger city, and hopefully far from strange swordsmen and sorcerer hunters. The wagons must have made it . . . oh, a few hours, maybe, before we were waylaid by fake bandits.

Yes, you heard me right. Fake bandits. Auntie's work, or a copycat — their arrows had musical notes carved into the wood. Obviously the Orchestra doesn't usually work so blatantly, so she was clearly sending a message — probably to me, but knowing her, possibly to any number of third parties. Anyway, the swordsman "rescued" me from the bandits and chased them off, but not without a bit of trickery that involved convincing them that they'd be cursed if they waylaid any other innocent travelers. Probably not an issue, given that they weren't, you know, actually bandits — but it was a thoughtful gesture.

After that, I met the swordsman.

I'd initially thought him to be mute, since he wasn't speaking out loud and used a local sign language to communicate, but it turns out he just didn't speak the local human tongue. He did, however, speak Velthryn.

Yes, this sounded alarms for me immediately, but I didn't have any good options. We talked, then agreed to travel together. And he, apparently pleased to talk to someone from Mythralis that he could communicate with, agreed to tell me a bit about his personal story while we walked toward a larger city.

His tale was a long one, so I'll focus on the important parts.

Firstly, his name was Lien — as in the Liadran word you'd be familiar with from Vaelien, Taelien, and so on — but he generally went by the translated name Edge. He was raised in a faerie court but wasn't one of them. I might have jumped to thinking him a changeling, but he didn't call himself that, and his origins seemed somewhat different. He was apparently brought there by someone he called his grandfather when he was an infant.

His grandfather is *probably* the legendary sorcerer and scholar Erik Tarren — or at least someone related to Tarren — so that should give you some idea of Edge's early life and education.

At eleven years old, Edge was involved in an incident where a couple of faeries went to play in a forest outside their own territory. When he helped rescue the faerie children, Edge was offered three boons by what was, according to him, a *faerie princess*.

I'm going to need to take a moment to emphasize just how incredulous I am about the idea that he rescued a faerie princess as a child. Okay. Moment over. Moving on.

This daring rescue resulted in him being marked as a friend of the local fae with a single mark on his cheek — not all six, he got the rest later — and the title "Edge of the Woods." Perhaps more relevant to me, this also appeared to be the event that first led to the rise of the inquisition in human lands, but I'm still not clear on the details.

Also of note is that his rescue was assisted by a strange half-fae girl named Eliree. When he went and found her in the aftermath, he used one of his gifts from the princess (sigh) to get her an invitation as a guest to the local faerie court. Eventually, he'd court her in a very different way, although he's been quite cagey about the details. I suspect this is largely to protect her in some way, but he also seems like he might be ashamed of how he treated her. Which is understandable, I suppose. I wouldn't exactly be thrilled to talk about my own childhood romances, if they existed.

Don't look at me like that, Vee. No, I do not need a boyfriend, or a girlfriend, or anything of the kind. We've been over this. Moving on.

During a three-day celebration for Edge's thirteenth birthday — apparently, three-day celebrations are a local tradition — Edge reached the first level of essence sorcery use while in a role-playing sparring match with his best friend, Ana. Ana was a sword faerie bound to Anathema, an enchanted sword hidden somewhere in a mystical shrine, and Edge's childhood goal was to earn the sword and travel with her.

The power Edge manifested in battle was a rudimentary form of sword essence, which can be used to conjure weapons, perform phantasmal attacks, and similar swordlike things. Yes, yes, I know there's no dominion of swords — apparently essence types on Dania can come in extremely complex varieties, and sword essence is a composite of a frankly staggering number of types of essence.

He also had a sealed power in his right hand, which he believed to be a power related to his bloodline. He would discover much later that this was not the case. Either way, that sealed essence was unusable but slowed his essence development, as his body still attempted to acclimate to it as if it was in use. This led to his essence growth being comparatively slow, and it was why he only had a single usable essence type at thirteen, which was unusual for the local creatures. Well, that and because he was clearly not fae himself. He wasn't human, either, but I wouldn't begin to properly guess at his true nature until later.

With sword essence as his first type, he had achieved the requirements necessary to enter Anathema's shrine and attempt the trials to earn her magic sword. So, he spent some time preparing, gathering herbs and other items, and making himself a new wooden sword to use in combat. Then, he headed to her shrine.

Along the way, Edge visited a few people of note. Firstly, a dragon, if he's to be believed — an ancient and gentle one that had been blinded in battle with a human army centuries earlier. Edge visited the dragon many times over the years, apparently treating the creature like family, reading the dragon stories and bringing trinkets to replenish the creature's long-depleted hoard. He also brought healing water from a mystical spring, hoping that enough of it would restore the dragon's sight, but it had little or no impact.

He also visited the family of the Willowbark Witch, where he stayed the night. Darryl, one of the witches, was a ward specialist and one of Edge's closest friends. Together, they celebrated the second day of Edge's name day, then Edge traveled the rest of the way to Anathema's shrine.

Upon reaching the shrine, he was intercepted by his first love, Eliree, a half-dryad girl. Eliree tried to stop him from the attempt, but he stubbornly refused. He attempted the trials, failed, and was significantly injured.

A quirk of the trials made it so he would lose his memory after each attempt, so he recalled nothing of how he had failed. He tried twice more, growing more injured each time, before Anathema herself appeared and changed the rules on the shrine to prevent him from entering again and getting himself killed. Then, she took him home.

The following day, Edge learned that though he had failed the trials, he had found a treasure map that appeared to lead to a sword. In spite of his grandfather's protestations, Edge set off to a nearby mountain range to look for it, believing that having a real weapon would help him grow stronger, succeed at Ana's trials, and prove to his grandfather that he was ready to leave and see the world.

He traveled the mountains, encountering a few wild animals and a giant spider, until finally he reached the spot on the map — a sword school that was abandoned, but not uninhabited. Echoes, manifestations of past events tied to the plane of memory, appeared at the school periodically, mostly in the form of a few specific students. He believed the echoes to be caused by a breach between planes, which caused power to leak from the plane of memory and other planes into our world.

Pleased by the chance to learn formal swordsmanship, Edge practiced with the echoes while beginning to repair the buildings, where he hoped he would find a metal sword hidden inside. He found no such sword, but he did find a scabbard that had been intended as a name-day gift from one student to another, but had never been given. He took the scabbard and continued to train.

During one rainy day, he discovered a source of sword essence on the mountain. While he didn't investigate it that day, choosing instead to finish gathering essence during the rare storm, he returned later to find another, much more powerful echo — one of someone he called the "Smiling Sword Saint."

Though this sword saint appeared as a woman, rather than a man like our legends say, I'm confident this Smiling Sword Saint was an echo of General Therin Whitestone. You know, Vaelien's old rival, the wielder of the True Blade before its destruction, the hero of the fall of Xixis, all that.

She was also, at least in this form, dangerously unstable. She very nearly killed Edge when he tried to convince her to train him — then again on his second visit, because much like you, he has no idea when to quit.

Eventually, through the use of memory crystals he obtained from trading with Auntie Temper — not his biological aunt, much like you know who — he managed to help the Smiling Sword Saint remember his visits, and gradually, she grew a little more stable. He impressed her with the complexity of some of his homemade sword techniques — honestly, he impressed *me* with the description of them, if they're actually real — and she seemed to agree to train him.

To do so, she manifested a younger copy of herself, who called himself Thane — yes, the younger copy presented as male, that's not a mistake — and Thane helped walk Edge through some swordsmanship training.

The sword saint also convinced Edge that his unilateral focus on sword essence was foolish and that he needed to diversify his essence usage. After some debate, he chose breach essence as his next type to learn. Breach essence was a highly specific essence type tied to tears between the planes, similar to the one that had caused the echoes to manifest. By learning to use breach essence, Edge could more clearly perceive things across planar boundaries. This allowed him to speak to the echoes at the sword school, which were previously inaudible to him, and learn a bit more from them. It also allowed him to create more complex sword techniques, including one that allowed him to strike the points in his opponent's body that generate essence.

After completing this second Dianis Point — that's the local term for the locations in the body that contain essence, and yes, it's tied to House Dianis — he learned the location of the Sepulcher of Sealed Swords, a mountain shrine that held several ancient and dangerous weapons.

He traveled to the shrine with the sword saint, encountering more breaches along the way and seeing events from the past, at least one of which looked like it might have included Auntie, and another that seemingly showcased the eldest student of the sword school being killed by the Blackstone Assassin.

When he arrived at the shrine, he met another person — a gregarious and over-the-top young man with purple hair who called himself Lance Rival. Yes, really. Anyway, Lance claimed to have seen a vision of fighting Edge in the future, so he . . . cooked Edge a meal and jumped off a cliff. Safely, I think. That's . . . yeah. Lance Rival.

Edge finally confronted the shrine, investigating the swords within. After fortunately turning away from several dangerous weapons tied to things like ancient, sealed gods, he eventually realized that the sealed power in his own hand seemed to be tied to a sword deeper underground. He activated a lift, heading down to an underground level, where he met the ghost of one of the former curators of the facility. The ghost was friendly at first, but attempted to trap him in a room where the World's Memory — yes, that magic mirror, the same one Auntie once stole — had been experimented on.

The mirror manifested what appeared to be a nightmare version of Edge. The curator had clearly miscalculated, because the nightmare version of Edge burned his bones, destroying him — and then attacked Edge, of course.

Edge fought at a disadvantage, but after being overwhelmed, managed to break a layer of his seal, triggering a Destiny Dream — a form of dream that occurs when someone reaches a certain essence power threshold and is granted power based on their choices in the dream.

That's where he met a young woman who sounded very familiar to me, and who I strongly suspect will be even more familiar to you.

After a brief battle with that "dream girl," a monster appeared to breach its way into his dream, and he fell into another layer of it — where he found several pedestals representing choices for his destiny. He picked up the last one, the Heartbreaker Sword destiny, but not before attempting to carve letters out of it. He struck it three times, but he was vague to me about his goal. I know a few things he might have been trying to go for, but I won't spoil the fun of speculating about it on your side.

I'm not clear if his sword-altering trick worked, but either way, when he woke up, he was at the second essence level — Torch-level. With his new power, he was closer to being able to match the nightmare in a fight, but still at a disadvantage. With a bit of enviable trickery, he managed to wear the nightmare down with poison and techniques, then destroy it with a glass-cutting knife.

Finally, he reached the sword he'd been looking for on the third level of the facility. It responded to the power he'd unsealed from his hand, and he removed the barriers around it, claiming the sword as his own.

When he left the building, the Smiling Sword Saint nearly stopped him — the sword was apparently so dangerous that even she was concerned. Fortunately, he was able to use the scabbard he'd taken from the sword school to suppress the newly claimed sword's power, and that was enough to convince the sword saint to let him leave.

After that, he headed home to ask his grandfather to tell him the truth about the sword and his own origins.

At that point, Edge stopped his tale — and I made the mistake of asking him some questions about it. This led to him holding me at sword point and taking my earring, which he believed to be a communication device to talk to Aayara Haven. Then, he spoke to the earring—

And, in a bit of brazen boldness, told Aayara that she had something that belonged to him.

EDGE OF THE DREAM

PROLOGUE

SYMPHONY'S SUBORDINATE

It was, in retrospect, somewhat conspicuous to be constantly fidgeting with a single earring.

Of all the things that could get me killed, I wouldn't have expected it to be my complete lack of any fashion sense, but I can't say I'm actually surprised.

Still, Scribe mused, *even if I'm doomed, I suppose I'd better play the few cards left in my hand.*

He watched as Edge inspected the tiny earring, the swordsman seeming pleased as he noted how the base could rotate. There was no trace of nervousness on his face, which was astounding, because he'd just used the device in an effort to contact Aayara Haven, the Lady of Thieves, a legendary demigoddess who was known for being capricious and deadly in her ire.

"The earring *was* in the on position before, wasn't it?" Edge asked. "I'd be a little embarrassed if, after that fantastic evidence exchange between us, I'd made my declaration into an inactive item."

An opening. Good. Gently, now.

"There . . . I think there's been a bit of a misunderstanding between us." Scribe offered his best smile, which was much like a black-market banker offering his best deals. No one was convinced, least of all the person making the gesture.

"Oh? Is this where you tell me that you're not one of Symphony's agents?" The swordsman rotated the earring's base back and forth again, frowning at it. "Or that this isn't a magic item, just a family heirloom of some sentimental value?"

Those were tempting angles and would greatly simplify things if he thought he could convince the swordsman of either, but the man was much more perceptive than Scribe had anticipated from someone with such an optimistic outlook. Calculating minds, in Scribe's experience, tended to come alongside a healthy degree of cynicism, madness, or a mixture of both.

He didn't know the right tool to use for the person in front of him, but he did have a suspicion that one might be more effective than others. "No, you're correct about those points. Scribe is my 'ess' name, and the earring is a communication device. The problem, however, is that you've overestimated my importance."

The truth to start with, and then . . .

Scribe let out a sigh with only a hint of exasperation. "You don't really think that your average Orchestra member is in continuous communication with Symphony herself, do you?"

The swordsman continued fiddling with the earring, every *click* back and forth worrying Scribe that the swordsman would break it. Finally, the swordsman looked up from the item to focus those strange silver eyes on him. "Don't know. Not familiar with your hierarchy. I do recognize when someone answers a question with a question, though."

"No linguistic games intended, I assure you. The earring isn't for talking directly to Symphony."

"Or any of Aayara's other guises?" The swordsman raised an eyebrow. It seemed an improbably common maneuver on his part, especially considering he usually wore his hood up, making the gesture more difficult to see.

"Or any of her other guises," Scribe agreed.

"Well, that changes things, doesn't it?" He reached up, miming pinning it to his ear. "Who was I just talking to?"

Can I . . . No, pretense won't get me anywhere. And besides that, it's not a bad angle to work with.

"My partner."

He gave a quick nod. "And did I send the message properly?"

"You did. It was active, as you expected, and rotating the base does deactivate it."

"Good. Now, are there other ways this device can be used? Perhaps a specific way to send an emergency signal straight to your employer?"

"No. It only has on and off. It's not that complicated."

"How does your partner contact you, then?"

Scribe winced. "She doesn't. Not anymore. I had another earring for listening, rather than sending, but I lost it a while ago, and I haven't been able to replace it."

"There's a story in that, I'm sure." The swordsman's smile seemed sincere, which made it all the more terrifying. "Maybe you can tell me later."

"Maybe," Scribe said neutrally, hoping that there would be a later. The odds that the swordsman would execute him on the spot seemed to be diminishing, but that had never been his principal concern.

Aayara did not take failures lightly, and given where they were going . . . she'd have opportunities to demonstrate her ire if she wished.

That was, of course, assuming she knew about his failure. She wasn't omniscient.

The swordsman's next question was a prescient one. "How do your findings get to Symphony, then, if not the earring? Do you have some other means to contact her?"

"Nothing immediate. Someone will contact me for my reports, rather than me going to her."

"How will they locate you? Scrying magic?"

"Not continuously — that'd be a waste of effort. Periodically, maybe, if that. Certain locations are monitored by her other agents. Someone likely has orders to keep an eye out for me, at which point I'd hand off information."

"In what format?"

Scribe smiled. "Written. My name isn't entirely for show."

"Isn't that a security issue if someone else gets their hands on your papers?"

"I write in a private cipher that only a few critical people know how to read. It's breakable, of course, but not without effort."

The swordsman nodded. "So, I shouldn't be expecting an immediate reply from the Lady of Thieves. Unfortunate. What about your partner? Do they have more immediate means of contacting Aayara?"

"Not that I'm aware of." Scribe groaned. "Again, lost my other earring. I don't even know where she is."

"What would she do if she thought you were in trouble with, say, a swordsman who had discovered your identity?"

Oh, she'd definitely want to come and fight you. Not to rescue me, although she might enjoy rubbing that in my face. She'd just be delighted to see if she could beat you.

. . . Is that what Auntie is trying to set up?

His heart raced at that thought. That was . . . troubling, if it was true. Putting two battle maniacs like them in the same place was a recipe for absolute chaos.

Which was why it sounded like exactly the sort of thing Aayara might have been planning.

". . . I don't think she has the means to get here," he offered weakly, "but she might contact someone to look into things. I don't know. It's been too long since I've seen her; I can't accurately evaluate her resources or behavior."

"Reasonable." Edge flipped the earring back into the on position. "It seems I've made a mistake. If this is Scribe's partner listening, I'd love it if you could relate my message to Aayara if you haven't already. Otherwise . . . we'll be on our way to the local Perfect Stranger along the Lark River. I'll plan to stay there a night if you want to initiate contact." He flipped the earring back into the off position. "Think that'll work?"

Thorns below, I hope not. "It might." Scribe hesitated, then, more out of curiosity than any sort of loyalty, he spoke again. "You . . . *have* to know that you may have just set yourself up for an ambush, right?"

The swordsman's eyes widened in what seemed like genuine surprise. "Oh! That would be lovely! I haven't had a good ambush in months!" He stepped closer to Scribe, who instinctively stepped back. The swordsman frowned at the reaction, then seemed to remember himself. "Oh. Not going to hurt you. And here, as recompense for cutting your ear."

The swordsman reached out his hand. Scribe hesitated, then put his own beneath it.

". . . My own earring is recompense?" He frowned.

"It *was* your earring. You used it to take my story — very clever, by the way, if I didn't make it clear enough — so I took the tool in return. A fair trade, in my estimation. But I did injure your ear in the process, and thus, I offer the earring back in exchange."

The swordsman's . . . logic, if it could be called that, was foreign enough that he couldn't parse it as simply being cultural differences. This wasn't "we kiss cheeks instead of giving handshakes" levels of foreign — it was a fundamentally different worldview.

The worst part was that it was *almost* familiar.

It wasn't that Symphony's games followed the same rules that these fae traditions did. Rather, it was that she had her own inscrutable internal logic, and he had spent the last decade stumbling to follow her steps.

This song was different, but Scribe recognized the dance that was expected.

"I accept the earring as recompense for the physical wound. You must know, however, that you've also wounded my trust."

Edge dropped the earring into Scribe's hand, taking a step back. "Fascinating. I *do* have a tendency to cut deeper than I'd like. What can I offer to regain your trust?"

"Trust is not so simple to rebuild. You can't just give me a trinket for it."

Edge nodded. "Can I offer you an earnest apology?"

". . . That would be a start, I suppose."

"Very well, then. I formally apologize for striking you without permission. In addition, I apologize for the obvious distress I have caused you by demonstrating how easily I could kill you without warning. Finally, I apologize for risking the possibility that Symphony or her agents will harm you now that I have uncovered your allegiance to her."

Scribe blinked. That was a very . . . direct apology for things that were all accurate, but delivering it in such a formulaic style made it sound . . . ritualistic, rather than real.

Still, the swordsman's expression looked sincere as he bowed his head slightly at the conclusion of the apology.

"I accept the apology. I do, however, require two other things to consider the issue closed."

Edge raised his head. "Your trust isn't cheap, is it?"

"No," Scribe said, "it isn't. In my line of work, it can't be. And, if I'm being honest, even with all this, we won't be back where we were before you cut me. This is simply offering you an inroad to begin the process of mending our rapport."

"Humans really are different," Edge mused aloud. "Very well, tell me what you're looking for."

"First, something simple. Do you have anything to treat my cut? I have bandages, but they're a bit awkward for—"

"Ah. Of course." Edge reached into his cloak, causing Scribe to momentarily flinch, but he simply retrieved a potion vial. "Healing elixir. Wouldn't usually spend it on a superficial injury, but in this case, it's more symbolic, so . . . you can use it. Either apply it directly or drink a little. Not the whole thing — this is far too much for that."

"What's more effective?"

"That's complicated. Pouring directly on the wound is usually better, if you really just want to treat one specific cut."

"Pour it for me, then. You know the right amount, and pouring an elixir on myself sounds awkward."

Edge stepped in without any further hesitation, uncapping the bottle, and then put a hand on Scribe's shoulder. "Hold still."

He poured just a bit of the liquid on Scribe's ear, then stepped back, grimaced, and capped the bottle. "That'll start the healing process. It's not instantaneous, but the wound should be closed by tomorrow."

Scribe suppressed the instinct to say, "Thank you," knowing it would be inappropriate in Edge's culture, especially since the swordsman had made the wound. "Understood. As the final thing . . . you still plan to continue traveling with me, right?"

"At least until one of your master's agents intercepts me, at which point I can't make any promises about what I'll do next."

Scribe suppressed a shudder. "Very well. Then . . ." He lifted the earring, then with deliberate slowness, dropped it into a bag on his side. "Continue your story. I'd like to hear what happens next."

"So you can write a report about it to Aayara later?" There was no animosity in Edge's tone, just a simple query.

"I probably will write about it, but that's not the only reason. You left me with many questions, and I don't like it when I have questions without answers."

The swordsman smiled. "On that point we are in absolute agreement. Very well, then. I'll continue the story . . . but not right away. We're minutes from the tavern, and I think we could both use some rest."

Scribe exhaled a deep breath. He was still incredibly anxious, but at least if Edge planned to return to storytelling, the swordsman was less likely to turn and obliterate him at any given time.

They trudged on for several minutes in silence before it finally emerged — a solitary building at the river's edge. It was three stories in height, largely carved out of wood, which gave it the appearance of a classic hunting lodge. A well-maintained stable stood out front, though there were no horses or stable attendants in evidence.

Scribe felt his shoulders tense at the sight of the building, near identical to a half dozen Perfect Stranger taverns he'd visited. It was the kind of familiarity that should have brought comfort and safety. Instead, it made his stomach swim, like seeing your sketchy uncle who always showed up with a smile when his debt collectors were a few steps behind.

"Huh," Edge observed with great articulation. "It's more . . . normal than I expected."

Scribe shot him a look. "What, were you expecting a vast building with gargoyles on the top, thieves perched behind them? Maybe some murder slits for crossbows?"

". . . Maybe at least a couple murder slits?" The swordsman advanced toward the door, strangely casual for someone who was knowingly marching into an organized-crime den. "Honestly, it's mostly the aesthetic that seems off. They couldn't have at least painted it black?"

"I think you might have a romanticized idea of how these things work. This is a place of business. Most of the people there will be ordinary civilians. You're not going to stumble into a band of clichés the moment you go through those doors."

They reached the entrance. Edge pushed the tavern doors open wide enough for both of them to see the interior before walking in.

The tavern wasn't exactly booming with business, but there were several figures inside. A large man was behind the bar, polishing a glass, and he casually glanced toward the entrance as the door opened. A serving girl carried a tray with an implausible number of mugs. A heavily armed group sat at a table with drinks, food, and what looked like a treasure map stretched out in front of them. A single figure stood in the back corner of the bar wearing a hood and cloak, their face completely obscured.

Scribe blinked, taking in the scene.

"Huh. I stand corrected."

They found their way into the tavern and took a pair of stools at the bar. The bartender gave them a quick, appraising look, but Edge wasn't paying too much attention to the threat that he — or anyone else — represented.

He was entirely too excited. "I can't believe someone beat me to the cloak-in-the-corner bit. Do you suppose they'd duel for it?"

"I think it's probably a poor idea to walk into a tavern and immediately start a fight."

"Of course. I should buy them a drink first! What was I thinking?" Edge reached down to his coin purse, but groped only at empty air. "Oh. Right. The hungry bandits."

Scribe sighed loudly, then reached into his own anemic pouch, picking out a few coins, and turned to the bartender. He spoke in the local tongue. "Going to need a couple of rooms for the night. Drinks. And to know if there's a package for me."

"You expecting one?" the man responded, his Caed even rougher than Scribe's, and with a distinctly Selyrian accent.

"Maybe. Um, not sure what the local process is, but you know, loyalty, crystal swords, all that."

The tavernkeep nodded silently, turning away to pick up a couple mugs and set them on the table. He grabbed a bottle of something and started to pour. "Name on the possible parcel?"

"Scribe."

The tavernkeep let out a low whistle. "Don't get many people claiming a name like that around here. Your friend?"

"Just a traveling companion, not a name. Doesn't speak this language."

Edge, apparently realizing he was being talked about, gave a friendly wave and said something that roughly translated to, "Good morning, honored master of eternal drunk house."

Scribe and the tavernkeep both laughed. The bartender gave Edge a friendly slap on the shoulder, pouring more in his glass.

You know what, Edge? Seven out of seven for effort.

Edge looked incredibly excited by his foaming cup of ale, right up until he took his first sip, at which point his expression rapidly changed to perplexed, and then vaguely horrified.

Yep, our ale will do that.

The tavernkeep chuckled again, then reached under the counter. Scribe tensed briefly, worried about a weapon being drawn and the consequences if Edge sensed the same, but the bartender was just pulling open a drawer. He tapped something on the side, shuffled around, and pulled out a single white envelope.

Then, he slid it across the table.

"No package, but this letter arrived for a Scribe."

Scribe eyed the envelope carefully. It was possible he should have waited for Edge to go to bed before asking for deliveries, but on the off chance this had something useful, getting it immediately wasn't a bad move.

It also explained a bit about why the tavernkeep hadn't bothered to do much to authenticate his claims. Not only had he been expected — meaning his description may have been provided — the letter itself would help prove his identity.

After all, if he opened it incorrectly, it would very likely kill him.

The barkeep watched very, very closely as Scribe pulled the letter toward him. Next, Scribe pulled a knife off his belt, setting it on the table. "Cutting board?"

"Sure, why wouldn't that be necessary?" the tavernkeep replied with a smile, retreating for a moment to retrieve one.

In the few moments the bartender was absent, Scribe made a number of hand gestures. These didn't go entirely unnoticed. Edge clearly saw him doing something, and the hooded figure was not so subtly watching them, too.

It didn't matter much. He was just generating a false image over the letter, concealing any text that became visible as he opened it.

The bartender set a cutting board on the bar.

"Thanks." Scribe picked up the letter, set it on the board, then lifted the knife and cut off the right side of the envelope. Then, he lifted and shook it.

A needle fell out.

After that, he rotated the envelope 270 degrees, cutting off one small segment of the corner, then pushed that corner away.

"We're going to need trash for these. Don't touch the needle directly or that corner of the paper. There's a very fragile capsule in there. Too much pressure on it and it'll—"

"I've got it." The barkeep returned a moment later with a trash bin, a couple of glass containers, and a small brush. He expertly brushed the needle and capsule-containing envelope segments into separate containers, then capped them and tossed them in the trash.

Following that, Scribe took a deep breath, then turned over the envelope and carefully cut the entire front off it.

With that segment missing, he extracted the contents — a letter and a single shiny coin.

The letter would show as blank for anyone else, due to his illusion, but the coin was very visible. The bartender's eyebrows went up. "You might not want to flash that around."

"Wasn't expecting it."

A quick movement and it vanished into a sleeve. He took the letter out as well.

"Get rid of the rest of the scraps, if you would. Be careful with the sealing wax, it's—"

"I've got it," he repeated. While the barkeep disposed of the rest of the envelope, Scribe opened the letter.

It looked blank to him as well, which was good and bad. Good because it meant an extra layer of security. Bad because it meant it was high-priority — and implied a sender.

Another quick hand sign for a spell.

Secret Sight.

Colors shifted subtly in his vision. Letters flowed into existence onto the page.

To my darling boy,

Your auntie is so proud of you! So far from home and already making friends!

Scribe pinched the top of his nose. *It's going to be one of those letters, isn't it?* He sighed and read on.

I wish I could just let the two of you play together, but there are chores to be done. To start with, Auntie is going to need you to do some grocery shopping. It shouldn't be too hard in the next town over — you're already heading that direction, it won't be out of your way! You can drop off the groceries back here, or at the next tavern down. List is on the back. I gave you a little something to help cover the expenses. You can keep the change left over.

After that, I've got a much bigger job for you, but you're going to want to make more friends first. After all, it's no fun going on an adventure all by yourself!

Always watching,

Auntie Ess

Scribe briefly checked the "grocery list" on the other side of the letter, then tucked the letter away.

"I'm going to need some rope, a grappling hook, and a much stronger drink."

⁂

The rest of the evening passed relatively uneventfully. Edge made a few efforts at conversation with the people present at the tavern, but the party of adventurers largely ignored him due to the language barrier, and the sketchy character in the cloak vanished almost as soon as Scribe finished reading his letter.

That was a little worrying, but nothing too unexpected in a place like the Perfect Stranger. Everyone had an angle.

Scribe had a couple drinks to be polite, then a surprisingly decent dinner, and finally retired to his own room. Edge, fortunately, managed to find his way to his own bedroom without starting any fights.

As Scribe prepared for sleep, he turned the single large coin over in his fingers. It was a white metal inscribed with the symbol of a musical note — a classic Orchestra favor coin.

He had several of them. Each was personalized, representing a favor from someone specific. He wasn't high ranking enough to have his own yet, but when he did, he knew the design — a glass coin filed with ink.

This one was something any Orchestra agent would have recognized if they had it, though it was near-mythical in rarity.

Not many coins had an audible chime when you lifted and shook them, but Symphony's did.

A favor coin straight from Auntie. People would kill for this.

Maybe I should have stuck with a single room tonight after all.

It took him an hour to properly trap his room's entrances, then another hour before he finally managed to get to sleep.

⊱⊱ ⊰⊰

In spite of his newfound wealth and the risks it represented, Scribe did wake up the following morning.

He was only half surprised to find that he wasn't alone.

But it wasn't a person who he found in his room — just another letter slipped under the door. Fortunately, it hadn't hit any of the trip wires, or he would have had a very loud awakening.

Cautiously, he lifted the letter.

You're going to want to leave fast once you're up. Word travels quickly about coins like that.

When you reach Larkbridge, if you want the coin taken off your hands, go to the local branch and have them send a message for the Ironthorn. He's always buying.

Scribe tucked the letter away. As usual, Auntie's resources carried just as much trouble as the help they offered.

He'd have to decide if it was worth making a deal with this "Ironthorn" or if he should save the coin. If he could keep it long enough, he could give it back to Auntie directly in exchange for a personal favor — and those were often on a scale that could move mountains. Literally.

This Ironthorn probably couldn't offer anything nearly comparable in exchange, but it would reduce the risk of being murdered in his sleep for the coin, so . . . pluses and minuses. Of course, Ironthorn could also be a trap.

For that possibility, at least he'd have an Edge close at hand.

The young swordsman slept in a bit, waking after Scribe had finished eating a mediocre breakfast. Scribe nervously waited for the swordsman to eat, then they made their way out the door and moved back to the road to Larkbridge.

"Well," Edge mused, "that was surprisingly uneventful. Not even *one* theft or assassination last night. I'm feeling a little cheated."

Scribe felt for his pocket, making sure the coin was still there. It jingled menacingly at his touch. "Don't worry," Scribe said. "The day has only just begun."

⊱⊱ ⊰⊰

As they continued down the road, gaining distance from the tavern, Scribe felt strangely comforted by the absence of familiar threats and the drift toward entirely new ones.

"So," Edge said, "were you interested in hearing more of my story today?"

"Definitely." Scribe nodded. It would help take his mind off the dangers that loomed in front of them. And behind them. And, in all probability, all around them. "I believe you were asking your grandfather about the nature of the sword you'd found in the shrine?"

"Ah, yes. He gave me a few answers then. He confirmed that the sword was one piece of a greater whole. He believed that the sword had been left for me to find when the time was right, but that it was too early, in his estimation. The other sealed swords at the shrine were being used for some sort of process to alter my weapon — a process that I'd interrupted before its completion."

"But what was the original sword?" Scribe asked. "If the sword saint recognized and feared it, it had to be around in her timeline and well-known."

"Sure. You already have theories, I'm certain."

"I've been thinking about it," Scribe admitted. "You haven't told me much about the sword's properties, but given that it was sealed away, and clearly associated with the number seven, I'd lean toward the Sae'kes Taelien. It doesn't quite fit the physical description, but you mentioned that it had been modified — pieces had seemingly been added and removed. And given that the God of Swords who wielded it has been conspicuously absent for the last few centuries . . ."

"Were those the only factors in your reasoning?"

Scribe had the distinct feeling he was being tested — again — but he was used to that. His mentor was much the same way. Comparing Edge to her was . . . disquieting, but fortunately, they weren't very similar outside of the verbal prodding and poking that they both seemed to employ. "No. The Sae'kes is known for having an aura that cuts through things that aren't supposed to be able to be cut. Cutting enchantments are probably the single most common kind of sword enhancements, but the Sae'kes specifically is known for cutting things that aren't fully corporeal, or things that are purely composed of essence. Even connections between entities. From what you've explained previously, that may imply that it's built to strike multiple layers simultaneously — something that would also potentially necessitate the many-layer seal on the sword."

Edge gave an appreciative whistle. "I thought about the cutting element of it, of course, but even I wasn't thinking about how that related to the seal. That's a good thought."

". . . But wrong?" Scribe asked.

"Not precisely, but keep going. Anything else?"

"Well, there's your name."

Edge laughed. ". . . It's right there, isn't it? Lien, like in Taelien. I wondered for a time if that was the solution to the puzzle of my origin. Was Lien just short for Taelien? I asked Gramps, of course, but . . ." Edge's jaw tightened in frustration. "He wouldn't answer. Not about my name, or about the sword itself."

"Even after getting the sword? I assumed he'd open up after that."

"So did I." Edge sighed. "He claimed he didn't know for sure. I would have been furious if I wasn't so exhausted. He must have sensed how much it hurt me, so he offered to examine the sword with diagnostic magic and try to figure it out. I was hesitant to let it out of my sight — I felt like there was a chance he'd just take it far away — but I decided to trust him. So, I handed him the sword and went to bed."

"He didn't take it away, did he?"

Edge shook his head. "No, he kept his word. He was still testing it when I woke up the next day. He told me some things right then, largely involving what I'd suspected before. Several pieces had been removed from the sword, and others had been added. As for whether it was the Sae'kes at some point, he couldn't determine that. He suggested taking it to Auntie Temper to have her look at its history with memory sorcery, as well as to adjust the scabbard to fit it properly. So, we went and visited her, and I spent the next three days helping her at the forge. After that, she told me that I'd done enough work to trade for her help, and that she'd send the sword back when she was done testing it and expanding the scabbard to fit it properly."

"Three days? Not weeks?" Scribe asked.

"She wasn't making me anything brand-new this time, just expanding the scabbard and running tests, so it wasn't quite as large of a trade. Moreover, I think she wanted me to get some rest, since I was still in bad shape. And, for a third reason" — Edge gave Scribe a look — "I think she wanted a chance to look at the sword without me there."

"And your name day was coming up, wasn't it? Perhaps she also wanted to give you a gift."

". . . Huh." Edge blinked. "You're right, actually. I was thinking about my name day coming up — it was just a couple weeks out — but I didn't consider that timing might have contributed to her reasoning. That's a good point."

"So, what did you do after that?" Scribe asked.

"Well, I rested for a couple days, then I went back up to the mountains to train. I felt a little naked without the sword, but that didn't stop me from wanting to keep getting stronger. I practiced at the sword school, sparred with Thane, and started working on some technique concepts for testing out my newly unlocked power from my right hand. After all, I was planning to use it very soon."

"For what purpose?"

"Shouldn't that be obvious?" Edge grinned. "It wasn't long before I got the sword back, complete with a properly fitted scabbard and a note with Auntie's test results."

"Which were?"

Edge laughed, then reached into his cloak, shuffling for a moment. Then, to Scribe's surprise, he withdrew a carefully folded piece of parchment and offered it.

Scribe blinked, gingerly accepting the note, and then unfolding it to a dramatic revelation:

". . . I can't read this language." Scribe folded the letter and handed it back.

Edge blinked. "Oh. Right. I might have forgotten that part." He laughed. "Shame, the prop makes the reveal much more satisfying. Give me a moment, I'll translate for you."

Edge closed his eyes, concentrating for a moment, then recited,

Born to be broken,
Made to be unused,
Forged with words unspoken,
Torn apart and fused.

Thrice forged and thrice denied,
This sword of makers' folly tied,
To child born as heroes died,
The final edge of worlds denied.

Bound in chains of fate forgotten,
Sheathed in lies and seven seals,
The blade that rends all things asunder,
The sword that no hand born can wield.

As Edge's eyes reopened, Scribe gave him a dubious look. "You're telling me you just translated that right now, and it still rhymes in Velthryn?"

Edge laughed. "You got me. I translated it in advance. And it's not perfect — the first two lines of the last stanza don't really rhyme with anything else in there. Still, you get the general idea."

". . . Sure. But what does it mean?"

"I had no idea. As it turns out, rhyming prophecies might be fun, but they aren't necessarily *helpful*. Still, I probably would have upset Auntie if I just told her that outright and started asking her tons of questions . . . and, once I had the sword back in hand, I had higher priorities than just asking her for clarity. I finally had a sword — I wanted to try it out."

"Except, of course, that everyone told you it was absurdly dangerous."

"Right." Edge nodded. "So, naturally, I knew the next step was to try it out. Even with the scabbard, I knew the sword would be too dangerous to test sparring with Thane or at the sword school. I needed a place I could test the blade out. One where I could cut loose without worrying about killing someone by accident or convincing the Smiling Sword Saint I was too dangerous to live. So, with that in mind, I began my preparations for another journey to Ana's shrine."

"I can see testing in there making sense, since she could conjure monsters . . . but wouldn't you lose your memories after the visit?"

Edge grinned. "Only if I lost. That day would be my seventh attempt at Ana's shrine, and I wasn't planning to fail. Never again."

CHAPTER I

SEEKING SECLUDED SKIES

Standing atop the highest of mountains, I gazed higher.

The sky was pristine blue and white, unmarred by the wretched smoke of human work. The blazing sphere that cast light into the world filled me with strength. I took a deep breath, drawing in what I could of the thin mountain air.

I inhaled and exhaled a few times, just because the place where I stood was called the Last Breath, and I found the idea amusing. Calming, too. It was a great place to think about my future.

Soon, I told myself. *Just one more test, then I'll get out of this place and finally get to breathe some new air.*

My eyes shifted, focusing on distant sights.

The area just below the mountainside was the primeval woodland that I called home. I looked to the hut where Gramps and I had lived since the days of my earliest memories, then my gaze shifted south, deeper into the woods. The region had remained untouched by human hands for centuries, unless you counted the Willowbark Witch and her children, and no one did. From my high vantage point, I couldn't tell if one of the more distant dots was her house, but I could see the Witch Fields themselves and the Rust River near them.

I looked farther. And beyond, I saw everything.

Ruins of ancient civilizations dotted the wilderness, wrought by humans, fae, and other hands, but largely abandoned. They were long forgotten by most, and even the few adventurers who knew of their existence were wise enough to give them a wide berth.

After all, there were stories of running into terrible monsters in those ruins — even, if one believed it, tales of a blind old dragon.

Wisdom had never been one of my strongest qualities. A smile crossed my lips as I pictured visiting ancient Verthrimax to deliver another healing elixir and some new stories of my own, but that was not where I set my current sights.

I shifted my gaze and felt a smile cross my lips. On the eastern side of the wood stood a strange tree. Not the forest's heartwood, nor the largest tree, but one that couldn't be mistaken for ordinary: the bark was a brilliant cerulean shade with strange white glyphs stretched across nearly every visible surface. At the base of the tree, the roots formed an archway, and that archway was blocked by a door of silvery metal etched with a warning written in a dozen languages.

At the moment, however, neither the shrine nor my home were at the forefront of my mind.

I looked farther still, finding the edge of the woods . . . and beyond it, the sea of humanity. The human towns were sparse at first, only a few of them near the forest's borders. As wood gave way to flat plains and the abundant water of the distant sea, I saw the glittering gems of human ingenuity: cities.

I would see them up close someday . . . but still I looked farther.

Farther until I could see the faint shape of another land: one that on this clearest of days, I thought I might see just barely at the corner of my vision.

It was, if one believed the stories, the lost land of the sky. The home of the Empyrean Empire — and the lost gods. An entire continent that floated just at the edge of possibility. Subconsciously, I reached out, as if to grasp that seeming impossibility.

<Reach too far and you will fall,> came a voice in my mind.

This may have been a beautiful metaphor, but it was also a literal statement. I stood at the precipice of a cliff, and I was not being particularly careful.

I gasped in delight, spinning around and kneeling at the unexpected sound of my friend's voice. I grinned ear to ear and stretched out my arms.

The ancient wolf, his fur a deep gray and his right eye covered by a silvery eye patch, was far too dignified to jump into my arms as a greeting. His smallest pup, however, was a different story. Hinoka gave a cheerful bark as my arms opened and she leapt straight into them. I caught the tiny wolfling and rolled to the ground, laughing and scratching her as she barked and licked my face, eventually finding myself at her sire's feet.

The elder wolf snorted, producing a jet of ice from his nostrils. <Undignified.>

I scratched Hinoka behind the ears, then set her down at her father's feet. "Well, yes. We're kids, and we haven't seen each other in . . . what, three years now? What do you expect, old man?"

<Hmph.> The elder wolf pawed at the ground. <Save that title for your grandfather.>

"So, what you're saying is that you're jealous of us kids, then. Got it." I smirked, sitting up from the ground. "You could just tell me if you want to be scratched, too."

Hinoka barked in agreement. The elder wolf, however, was not so easy to convince. <I would not deign to indulge in such undignified—>

I reached up and scratched the heavy mane under his chin. He went silent, closing his one remaining good eye. An accord had been reached.

We were quiet for a time, simply enjoying the contrast of the sun's bright light and the chill breeze. But as with many joys, it ended too soon.

<We must speak, young one.>

With a sigh, I pulled my hand back. "I suppose so. What brings you home, Uncle Eiji? How bad is it?"

<I come bearing news from distant lands. Human armies are stirring, and in the deep north, there are rumors of a ritual that will bring about the Ashen Lord's return. Something is coming — they are calling it the Second Scouring. We are nearly out of time.>

I brushed my hands off on my trousers, then cracked my knuckles. "Well, then. I'd better tell Gramps that it's time for me to go."

The wolf shook his head in a surprisingly humanlike fashion. <That one is not so swift to move. I fear he will cling to you with the desperation of one who has lost all else.>

I snorted. Eiji was always so dramatic. Not quite "weird door with a creepy poem in twelve languages" dramatic, but close. "He can complain all he wants, but if I clear the shrine this time, he's going to have to acknowledge that I'm ready. And I was already planning to hit it tomorrow."

I felt the telepathic equivalent of a sigh. <It is not yet your name day, child. Were there not rules preventing you from visiting more than three times per year after your first visit?>

Maybe I would have been embarrassed if he'd asked me that sooner, but looking back on it a couple years later, I had no regrets. If I hadn't stepped inside a second time and gotten brutalized by the shrine, I might never have found the map that led me to . . . well, not far from where I currently stood. The sword school, the saint, and the sepulcher.

"Oh, yeah. There were. But, now that I have a sword of my own" — I gestured toward the gigantic sword leaning against a nearby tree — "I convinced Ana to nudge the rules to allow for more frequent resets. It's three times a week now, rather than three times per year, and the rule applies retroactively."

Uncle Eiji turned his gaze toward my sword, then slowly shook his head. <You must be cautious. That sword is no child's plaything.>

"I'm well aware. Shrine constructs are some of the only things I can fight with it without having to worry, though. I'll just have to be cautious not to hit Ana with it when I challenge her — but she knows the risks."

<That scabbard . . .>

"Ah, yeah. Found it in a local sword school. It wasn't large enough to fit the whole sword, but I spent a few days working for Auntie Temper, and in return, she adjusted it to fit the sword properly. Problem is, now the scabbard is too large to wear on my hip, so I just sort of carry it around like this. I wear it on my back when traveling, but it turns out that I can't draw it effectively like that, and it's also . . . kind of awkward. I'd need a differently designed scabbard for drawing it properly, one with some kind of quick release on the side for the sword to slip out, and that would require more extensive modifications."

<A wise decision, to keep that sheathed. But if you only earned it just recently . . . would it not be wise to wait and train with the weapon a bit? Learn to control it better?>

"Maybe, but it's almost my name day, and I thought I'd get myself a gift."

The gigantic wolf snorted. <Ah, yes. I have a gift prepared for you, and I will leave it with your grandfather for the appropriate time. But such frivolities will not improve your odds at completing the tests. Unless you believe a certain faerie will go easy on you?>

I laughed. "Oh, there's no chance of that. If anything, she'll go harder. Neither of us would be satisfied if she held back."

<Then what makes you believe you will succeed?>

I smirked. "I've got a good feeling about it. And, if you're going to insist on practical reasons, I'm Torch-level now. That might give me the *edge* that I need."

<Oh? Reaching a new level is always commendable, young one. Your insistence on using your own name as a pun, however . . .>

I laughed. "Don't you mean *our* name?"

<I am honored that you have chosen to use my name as inspiration for your own. Remember this, though: when a name is used enough, it becomes a part of you. This will be important when you are traveling the world beyond.>

I rolled my eyes at the pseudo-wisdom of his lesson. I'd heard the same thing a thousand times.

Besides, I wasn't denying that my name had meaning. I'd embraced that long ago, just not quite in the way that Uncle Eiji meant. "Anyway, I'm excited for tomorrow. I'm going to finish it this time, I know it."

<That sounds like the type of thing you would say every time.>

I smirked. Absent for three years or not, he knew me too well. "Well, yeah. The air is different every day." I pushed myself to my feet. "So, every day, I take a deep breath — and I plan to win."

* * *

Under the watchful gaze of the stars, when the forest was quiet, I would begin my journey toward the shrine. Before that, I had preparations to make.

I picked up my sword, fastening it onto my back. Then, I reached into a pouch at my side to retrieve an essence-collection vial. I popped it open and activated it, watching as threads of golden essence flowed into the vial.

<I had wondered why you were up here. What *is* that essence? I do not recognize it.>

"I don't know. Exciting, isn't it?" I capped the vial, observing the sphere of gold that had formed within, then tucked it away in my pouch. After that, I turned back to Eiji and gave him a mischievous look. "So . . . it's a long way down, and if things are moving quickly in the outside world, we should get a move on . . ."

<Hmph. It is beneath me, but very well. You may climb.>

I hugged him around the neck. "Thanks, old man!" Then, in a well-practiced motion, I stepped over him as he knelt down and climbed onto his back.

Hinoka barked enthusiastically, and I caught her as she jumped toward me. I'd carry her while her father carried me.

<Hang on!>

He didn't have to ask. I braced with my legs and gripped his fur with my free hand. It wouldn't hurt him even if a jerking motion caused my hand to pull back suddenly: it took a *lot* to hurt the old wolf. I couldn't have pulled out his hair if I tried.

So, it wasn't a bad thing when I gripped a little tighter as Eiji took two steps back, then leapt straight off the cliff.

I gave a hoot of wonder as we flew off the edge, gazing downward in joy as the world flew beneath us — then laughed as we landed in midair, each of Eiji's paws finding purchase in the air itself.

He ran downward at an angle, his paws crackling with electricity and streaming wind with every step. Hinoka barked happily, enjoying the ride as much as I was. She was too young to air walk on her own safely. She could probably take a few wobbling steps, but her brothers and sisters had been eight or nine before they'd learned the technique well enough to use it on their own.

I, of course, would be unlikely to learn it at all. I hadn't honed my essence for that purpose, and I didn't intend to. I'd sharpened my power toward other ends.

Each of Eiji's powerful strides carried us ever downward, until finally, we had neared the forest floor . . . but not quite where I wanted. "Oh, come on, don't take me home! Take me to *the shrine*!"

<Your grandfather will want to speak to you before you begin your latest escapade, young one.>

I groaned. Eiji had saved me climbing time, but if I had to speak to Gramps, it almost wasn't worth it. Picking up my sword had made him more irritable. At first I thought he was nervous that I was going to hurt someone by accident, but I was getting the increasing impression it was more than that.

We hit the ground just in front of the hut. I couldn't see or hear Gramps inside, but even at a distance, I could feel the brightness of his spirit. I knew the feeling of his presence as well as I knew my own face.

Better, really. I didn't exactly look into mirrors often: they were entirely too dangerous. My visit to the Sepulcher of Sealed Swords had been testament to that.

I patted Eiji one last time when we landed, giving him a grudging thanks in spite of his little trick. "Thanks, old man. You staying for lunch?"

<Regrettably, no. Much work remains for the day. I have other messages to carry. Even visiting you was, I fear, something of an indulgence. I hope you enjoy your name-day gift, when it is time for you to receive it. I regret that I cannot stay long enough to give it to you in person.>

"Thanks. It was good to see you both. Missed you."

<Hmph. Such is expected.>

That was the gruff creature's way of returning my remark, and I knew it. "See you later, Eiji." I set Hinoka down, scratching her behind the ear one last time. "And you be good, kid."

I got a friendly bark in reply. She wasn't quite old enough to communicate with me telepathically yet, but I knew she could understand me.

The wolves raced off a moment later, Eiji slowing his matchless pace to allow his tiny child to follow. Even Hinoka was so fast that I would have to push myself to keep up with her normal pace, and I couldn't possibly match her in a race. She was lower level than I was — at seven years, she was only a Candle — but her two essence types were storm and air, which synergized to grant her extreme speed, much like I hoped my own three essences would interact to let me strike with far greater power than was ordinary for my level.

With that, I was left alone . . . well, not alone. I was never alone, not in this forest. But without any telepathic spirit beasts to chatter with and keep me distracted from the conversation that was to come.

The door opened as I approached, seemingly of its own accord. I wiped my boots at the doorway, but that felt insufficient, and I opted to take them off. It wouldn't do to dishonor the wood of the home with muddy booted steps.

Grandfather sat at the central table, not looking up from his book and tea. A teacup sat on the opposite side waiting for me, steaming hot. He must have sensed me coming. He always did.

I walked over but didn't sit down. "I'm leaving tonight. Going to head toward the shrine soon."

"Mm," came Gramps's response. "Sit. Drink."

"I'd rather stand." I picked up the cup of tea and sipped while I was standing. Wasn't right to waste good tea, regardless of the circumstances.

We sipped for a time, then finally, he set down his book and turned his deep gray eyes toward me. They were a darker gray than his robes and hair. I always thought they looked wise and caring, but at the moment, I mostly found his stare to be stifling.

I was a teenager, after all, and very few teenagers cared for excessive scrutiny. I didn't know that from experience — I knew precious few other teenagers — but I'd heard about it in many of Gramps's books.

"You're behind on your lessons," Gramps said finally, setting his cup down with a *clink* that somehow managed to sound as disappointed as his words. His expression was largely neutral, but it didn't matter. The lines of his face, once carved by smiles and laughter, had been rewritten through the last decade of frowns. Even when he held his gaze steady and his expression in check, I could feel the weight of those lines. I knew that he carried a heavy burden, and I was the largest part of it.

He'd never wanted to raise me, after all.

He never would have told me that, but what grandfather wanted to raise their grandchild alone in seclusion? I doubted that was anyone's perfect ideal for a lifestyle, but there we were, and there we had been since the blades had fallen from the lifeless hands of my blood kin.

"Won't matter soon. I'm going to take this one last trip to the shrine . . . then I'm leaving. For good." I set my cup down heavily, letting the ceramic cup ring against the plate.

"Are you, now?" He reached for the teapot, lifting it and pouring more for himself. "Remind me — what happened last time you were this confident?"

I folded my arms. "I already went through all this with Uncle Eiji. Yes, I know I could still fail. No, I don't intend to. And if I succeed . . . you'll let me go, right?"

"Something along those lines, yes." He gestured to the teapot. "More tea, please."

Something along those lines. I wasn't in the mood for his evasive sage talk. I lifted the teapot, a mischievous grin sliding across my face. "Of course, Grandfather. More tea, right away."

A quick swing of my hand sent a jet of tea in Grandfather's direction.

Without the slightest hint of effort, he lifted his cup, his hand moving in a blur. His arm moved with both speed and precision as he caught the droplets of liquid from the air, then rotated the cup slowly in the air to prevent the swishing liquid from slipping over the edges.

A fraction of a heartbeat later, he was setting the cup down. He hadn't missed a drop. Wouldn't do to waste any tea, after all.

A near-imperceptible twitch at his lips signaled his own amusement. "Thank you."

I suppressed a groan.

Grandfather may have been frustrating and overprotective, but there was no discounting his abilities. I had no idea what level he'd managed to raise his essence to — he kept it perpetually suppressed — but I knew he was still leagues beyond me. Beyond virtually anyone I knew, really, save perhaps one particularly ancient dragon and the local faerie queen.

I lifted my own cup in salute for his impressive maneuver, then took a sip.

He gave me a gracious nod, and then his look turned more serious. "It won't be what you're expecting."

This wasn't the line of conversation I'd expected. I raised an eyebrow. "What won't be? I'm well aware that the shrine changes every time. And it's hard to expect much of anything when the tests wipe my memories on every visit."

That was something of an exaggeration — my memories weren't being erased, exactly. More like suppressed. Supposedly it was to maintain the integrity of the testing process, and I'd get the memories of my efforts back if I ever successfully earned the cursed sword at the end of the shrine.

Gramps shook his head at me. "Not the shrine. The world. People."

"I've met people before."

Gramps sighed. "You've met the children of the forest. They are people, yes, and brave and bright ones. It is other folk that worry me."

I shrugged a shoulder. "I've read books. *So many* books."

"And as I've repeatedly reminded you, fiction is fiction, and even 'history' books portray things in a slanted light."

"You mean the world doesn't revolve around shining knights rescuing besotted princesses? Say it ain't so, Grandfather." I tried to let the sarcasm run as deep as I could in my tone.

"It goes a bit beyond the paucity of story tropes in day-to-day life. You will encounter people with behaviors that seem more foreign to you than the strangest of beasts."

I grinned. "All this is making it sound an awful lot like you think I'm gonna win this time."

"Not this time, necessarily. But I am certain that you will someday . . . and you must temper your enthusiasm."

"Only thing I'm going to be tempering is that ancient sword once I've got it free from the shrine. Bet it needs a fresh shine after all the years it's been in there. Might get to put my spiritsharp stone to use."

"I wouldn't overthink your plans for that sword, either. Carrying that blade . . . it is not something I would wish on anyone."

"Pfft." I finished off my tea, setting it back down. "I know, I know. Ana won't shut up about it. Ancient curse, horrible danger, all that. I seem to be in a habit of collecting deadly swords. I'm ready for another one."

"You have grown stronger, certainly. Torch-level is a major milestone, but you still lack flexibility. Yes, you can strike above your level, but that won't help you if your opponent is flying, or simply outlasts you, or . . ."

"I know, I know." I groaned. It was an old argument. Gramps didn't approve of how I was developing my essence. "I'm still working on a ranged sword attack, but the shrine is in an enclosed space. What are the odds of flying opponents?"

Gramps just stared at me. ". . . Moving on."

I sighed again. "Right. Back to the earlier subject. I can handle another cursed sword, Grandfather."

"It is no ordinary curse. Not even a curse at all, precisely. It is more . . . a burden. One you may never be ready to carry." He hesitated. "But we shall see."

Preparation was easy now. I had plenty of practice.

I refilled my increasingly drained gift pouches and warding pouches before fastening them to my belt, but that didn't mean I felt prepared. I was low on a few critical resources, most notably the healing elixir I usually preferred to carry when doing anything dangerous. It still hadn't been quite long enough for me to feel comfortable drawing much water from the Hero's Rest — I didn't want to deplete it so much that the spirits were offended, or worse, that I prevented the pool from replenishing itself. Thus, I only filled a small vial with the liquid rather than the usual full-size potion bottle that I would have ordinarily collected.

There was a good, reasonable argument that I should have just waited a few extra days, trained with my sword in an isolated area where I couldn't hurt anyone, and gone to the shrine when I was better prepared. I had a great counter for that, though:

I didn't feel like it.

Now that I finally had a sword in my hands, I could feel the desperate need to cleave my way forward into my future, to take the next steps into the wider world. To see everything that our planet had to offer, and maybe, if I was lucky, find a few clues to my own past along the way.

Oh, and probably find the missing pieces to my sword. That was important, too, especially if I didn't want it to, say, break my seal open farther if I kept swinging it around without knowing what I was doing. Any usage of an obviously incomplete weapon of phenomenal power was going to be a risk, but with the immortal wisdom of a child, that was a risk I was willing to take.

I packed the rest of my backpack with mundane supplies, mostly things I'd managed to retrieve on my way out of the Sepulcher of Sealed Swords, but also some basics I'd neglected on previous trips, like premade bandages and an herbal poultice. The lack of healing essence didn't mean I was going to completely ignore the possibility of injuries, and I'd learned the hard way that it was better to have something prepared to treat them ahead of time.

Okay, time to go. One last time. Just one last time.

I slung my sword over my shoulder, bade Gramps goodbye, and made the trek to the shrine.

There were no detours for essence this time, no distractions while I stopped to chat with Darryl.

There was no Eliree outside the shrine to distract me, either. That hurt more than I'd expected. While my childhood love had only been outside the shrine on previous visits to discourage me from entering, her absence was somehow a greater weight than her presence had been.

I knew I'd been making mistakes with her, but today wasn't the day for thinking about that. I pushed the weight of her judgment aside and moved forward.

I thought I could feel Ana's gaze on me from time to time, but she didn't appear on my journey. Perhaps she sensed the solemnity of my demeanor, or perhaps she simply didn't want to use up the significant amount of essence required to teleport to me for a conversation.

After all, I was coming for her sword, and she'd need every bit of essence at her disposal if she wanted to stop me.

CHAPTER II

SHRINESEEKER

I paused to look at the stone tablets outside the massive tree that served as the entrance to Ana's shrine. I knew most of the inscriptions well enough to recite them from memory, but a new segment had been added recently.

Beware to tread upon the place that stands beyond this door,
For with each step you take, the walls will close a little more.
This realm is no mere dungeon, no dragon's treasure hoard:
Within it sleeps only a single cursed sword.

The path within is narrow, but follow it you must,
Though your mind may play tricks, this warning you must trust.
Those souls that walk astray are lost until the world is dust.

I liked the style of the new introduction, even if pronouncing "cursed" as "curse-ed" was kind of a stretch. I did wonder about why she'd felt an addition was necessary, though. Was it a clue? Had she discovered something about her own shrine's nature? Or was she just demonstrating a bit of her artistic talent with the words?

I couldn't know until I walked through the foreboding doors that led into the tree.

The rest of the inscription was more familiar. The opening had a somber tone that always reminded me of a grave marker due to the phrasing of the first line.

Here lies Anathema—
Blade of the lost,
Scourge of the wicked,
Bane of all things.

There was a history there, to be certain. One that was alluded to in greater detail in the second tablet, which was the most extensive of the set.

Ware thee of challenges three,
Of steel, and stone, and destiny—
With blade of dark a hero lies,

And with her soul an ember dies.
To claim the blade that once she earned,
Thou must choose the path all spurned,
To seek within and cast aside,
The rage that burns hearts deep inside.
If anger guides thee, turn aside,
Your deepest dreams you cannot hide—
For only one with gentle hand,
Can wield the sword that ends our land.

Classic faerie rhyming, along with elements of mystery and foreboding. I loved this one.

For things like classical destiny shrines, rhymes like these would contain hints to solving the shrine's puzzles. I'd certainly searched for those hints many times over the years. In particular, I'd always been curious if the poem implied that a person was buried with the sword. The usage of the word "hero" in particular had a way of sparking my imagination — could it mean the capital-*H* Hero of legend? — but I tried not to get my hopes up or make too many assumptions.

Was I concerned that the last one hinted that the wielder of the sword would do something terrible? Not really. Faeries loved to write things — and say things, and imply things — that, while literally true, didn't follow their obvious meaning.

So, something like "ends our land" could mean something like "expands the borders of our kingdom" or "is responsible for the name of our court being changed" or "destroys a symbolic representation of our kingdom on a map."

Basically, what I'm saying is that I did a lot of speculation, but it wasn't necessarily going to offer me any meaningful advantage because the poem was almost certainly designed to be misleading.

Now, the last tablet, that was the opposite — nothing flowery, just direct instructions.

Hi! I'm Ana. This shrine is my home, but don't feel the need to take your shoes off at the entrance.

There are some rules, though! ~~Three, to be specific.~~

1. Only those with a completed wellspring with sword essence can enter the shrine. Sorry, non-swordy folks! You can't hope to wield all this without it.

2. No one may enter if they are above Hearth-level. No exceptions!!!

3. There will be risks, dangers, etc. in the shrine. You consent to the risks of taking these tests, up to and including risk of death, when you enter the door. In addition, you consent to have your memories of the shrine's trials suppressed if you fail. This is to preserve the integrity of the trials for future trial-takers!

4. Thrice may thee enter with the passing of each ~~year~~ week.

Addendum: Edge, just because it only says "no exceptions" on the second rule doesn't mean there are exceptions to the other two, so quit trying to sneak in before you have sword essence!

"Three, to be specific" had been scratched out, since she'd retroactively added the fourth rule (or an earlier variation on it) after she'd written the original instructions.

The word "year" had then later been cut through and replaced with the word "week" in order to allow me to reenter the shrine earlier than my next name day. Ana probably could have found someone to reshape the stone to remove the word "year" entirely and allow her to modify it more cleanly, but we both felt this was funnier.

Changing the rules to allow me to enter again early might have felt like cheating under ordinary circumstances, but since she'd made that new rule to limit me in the first place, I didn't feel like it was an issue. In fact, I questioned the need to keep it at all — she could have eliminated it entirely, rather than modifying it — but I supposed some level of moderation was still needed, at least in her mind.

That was fine with me. I didn't expect to need three more tries.

"See you soon, Ana."

I pressed my fingers against the massive door in the base of the tree, watching white light flash over the ancient runes etched into the surface. And, as the doors swung open to greet me, I stepped inside the tree's open maw.

⁂

There's something disorienting about stepping through an open doorway and ending up in a place that looks completely unrelated, at least the first few times you do it. For me, it should have been routine, given the number of previous visits I'd made to Ana's shrine — but without my memories, I couldn't properly acclimate to the process.

The setting itself was a little different from what I'd imagined. No pristine white walls or foreboding doors like in the Sepulcher of Sealed Swords, nor did I find the rough stone I might have expected from the interior of a cave. Instead, my surroundings appeared to be something like a forest clearing, dominated by massive tree roots that created obstacles in the dirt every few feet. There were small rocks here and there, but not a lot of them.

Not large enough to use as platforms, either, I processed gratefully. I wasn't a huge fan of platforming puzzles, and I was glad I probably hadn't run into one right away.

Leaves dotted the ground, which was a bit peculiar, given that there were no actual tree branches up above — only roots were visible from my vantage point.

Roots and . . . movement.

A threat.

I spun immediately on instinct, gauging distance as I turned, and used my off hand to pull Glasscutter off my belt to prepare for an immediate throw.

I barely checked myself before obliterating the poor squirrel. It didn't even look up from the nut it was happily chewing on.

I frowned at the sight, as well as my own response. Cautiously, I fumbled with Glasscutter to resheathe it with my off hand — oddly, I always found attacking with my off hand easy, but I wasn't ambidextrous — and took in my surroundings a little more fully.

Aside from the squirrel, I didn't see any other creatures nearby. That made me slightly more suspicious that the squirrel was an actual threat, but it seemed a little too obvious. Ana obviously knew that any sane person would be wary of a lone squirrel at the entrance of a dungeon, given what powerful spiritual beasts they could be, especially the ones with the ability to steal skills from people. I wouldn't let it get close enough to touch my heart, certainly, but I assumed it was a distraction — or even perhaps some sort of innocent target that was there purely to test if the shrine's entrants would attack a simple animal without provocation like I almost had.

I didn't know how to pass Ana's tests. I didn't know how to avoid penalties, either. I simply had to infer the rules as I went along, and for the moment, that meant I was going to try to avoid jumping to obvious conclusions right away.

I'm still watching you, squirrel.

Aside from the squirrel, the roots themselves were the most obvious potential threats. They were colossal, and some trees and treelike monsters had the ability to move their roots and branches like whips and ropes. If that was the case, one of the smaller roots that was roughly leg width could grab me and pull me down, or one of the larger ones that was torso width could simply bludgeon me into a pulp.

My starting position was atop one of the roots — a particularly large example that was roughly the dimensions of a door but lay mostly flat against the ground. I peered down at it briefly to examine if it might actually *be* a door, but it didn't look like there were any obvious cracks or hinges.

Might just be a safe spot to start on and take in the room . . . or it could be the type of thing where I need to figure out how to move the roots, and something is beneath it, like a treasure chest or passageway.

I resisted the immediate urge to cut through it. It was almost certainly a magical conjuration, rather than a part of the actual tree that housed the shrine, but it looked like healthy living wood. I wasn't going to risk harming a regular tree — or even a conjured one that approximated life closely enough — without a good reason. Instead, I continued my inspection of the area.

A glance back at the squirrel reminded me of something important — it was chewing on a nut. I saw nothing else resembling the nut in the area. Was it some kind of unique treasure I could obtain? A key critical to another part of the shrine? Or perhaps a clue that different types of trees were located in that direction, ones that would have similar nuts? I didn't have enough information to work with, but it was something to think about.

The rocks looked mundane, but that didn't mean a thing. They could have easily been some sort of earth elemental, or maybe a shelled creature that had a rocklike exterior, like conqueror crabs or shale snails.

The leaves were perhaps the most out of place, given the lack of overhanging branches. I ducked down briefly to look at them.

Identical. They're all copies of the same leaf . . . or, no, wait. A few different variants, but in patches. Ana must have conjured them herself. They look like oak leaves, but . . . hm. Is that some kind of sap on some of them?

I leaned closer to one of the leaves, inspecting the sticky substance. It didn't look like much of anything, really — just a few drops of a viscous bright green fluid. It looked vaguely familiar, but I knew a lot of weird bright green fluids, and it could have been many of them.

The easiest tests would be to touch or sniff it, but I wasn't going to do either. Instead, I found a small rock, poked the rock with a temporarily manifested Sword Hand to make sure it didn't immediately animate and attack, and then picked the rock up with a gloved hand. After that, I pressed the rock against one of the leaves.

No sizzling or bubbling, that's good. No reaction at all, as far as I can tell. Huh.

I lifted the rock. The leaf stayed firmly attached.

Oh. Adhesive.

I tested the rock-and-leaf combo against another nearby leaf without the obvious green blobs — it didn't stick. Another test against more of the green liquid ended up with two leaves stuck to the rock, then a third after another test. That was good enough to confirm that the liquid on the ones nearby was what I suspected — a similar adhesive to the one that Ana used on her bandages.

Might be there just to get stuck to someone's boots and be a minor inconvenience . . . or the adhesive could have other properties. A scent that some monsters use for tracking, maybe? Plausible, but I'm not going to test it out. Looks like it's the only liquid on the ones nearby, so . . .

I tossed the rock cautiously into the dirt. It bounced and rolled, but nothing suspicious happened — no sinkholes, no monsters jumping out of the ground to eat it.

Okay. Simple so far. The leaves have adhesive. That's avoidable.

That didn't mean it was the only type of green liquid I'd find on the nearby leaves, of course. Ana was tricky enough that she might create an expectation near the entrance, only to subvert it by switching it out with acid or something later. Similarly, the fact that I was standing on a root now didn't mean that the other roots were safe to stand on, but . . .

I grimaced, estimating the distance to the next root, then the next.

They were almost perfectly placed for jumping.

. . . Ugh. It's a platform puzzle after all, isn't it?

I let out a sigh, gave one last suspicious glance at the distant squirrel, and then began to trace the best routes to jump.

⊱ ⊰

"So, you see, I'm on an adventure, and I would appreciate your guidance, honored spirit beast," I concluded.

The squirrel blinked at me, giving no sign of understanding my words.

. . . Of course, that's what a skill-stealing squirrel would *want* me to think.

We continued to watch each other for a few more moments in silence, like two skilled swordsmen knowing that the other was in range to strike at any time . . . but neither struck. And eventually, as the tension faded, the squirrel seemed to lose interest and went back to perpetually gnawing at its treasure.

Having reached an impasse with the honorable and formidable opponent, I moved on, bowing my head briefly in recognition of my equal. I could see something just barely visible in the distance that looked like a stone structure that I wanted to investigate, so I hopped to the next root in that direction.

. . . Which immediately whipped upward, hurling me straight into the air.

Veking—

A second root swept at me from the ground, this one as wide as my chest and moving at speed. Aggression could be met with aggression, and I doubted I'd be judged harshly for cutting through it, but I froze to question it for too long to draw. Instead, I lifted my still-sheathed sword and blocked. I felt the massive force of impact, but it wasn't enough for me to lose my grip — not anymore. The root hurled me backward and down, but without causing any damage.

I landed in the dirt, rather than on the roots, and steadied my footing. That was, predictably, when things got very bad.

I'd tested for sinkholes with a rock. That had been a good idea, but as it turns out, I weigh a lot more than a single fist-sized stone.

The ground beneath me trembled with a sense that was all too familiar — I'd run the Buried Barrows enough times to know what was coming. I rushed forward and jumped to the closest root before the ground gave out beneath me, only for that once-safe root to animate and lift from the ground just before I reached it. I collided with it in midair, wrapping my limbs around it immediately to ride it as it rose upward, holding on to it like a bucking horse. But with only one free hand — the other was still gripping my still-sheathed sword — I couldn't maintain a good grip, nor could I easily climb.

Maybe a back sheath wouldn't have been such a bad idea after all.

The root lifted until it was nearly vertical, going taut, and then twisted just slightly backward from its original position. This gave me the distinct impression that the root was about to fire me like an arrow — which was, while an amusing image, probably not the best way to traverse the area, especially since it was aiming me back toward where I'd started.

I let go of the root and let myself drop.

While in midair, I reattached my scabbard to my belt — an inconvenience for drawing it later, but a necessary one — then braced myself.

The moment I landed, I was off in a run, the dirt trembling and collapsing beneath me.

As I rushed past the now alarmed-looking squirrel, I jumped over the next root as it swung at me, then ducked the next small one as it flew for my head. Another root, so small I barely noticed it, reached out of the ground and grabbed my leg and then yanked me down. I tripped, falling face forward, but managed to get my hands around the next large root in front of me before the ground collapsed. As the root I was gripping writhed and rose, I held on tight, kicking backward to dislodge the one that remained around my ankle.

My fingers sank into the wood I was gripping, forming cracks. I couldn't tell for certain, but that seemed to make the branch flail more wildly. I didn't let go — there was a vast chasm opening up below me now, one that I couldn't see the bottom of. Another kick dislodged the small root that had tripped me, then I wrapped my legs around the larger root and climbed upward. The larger root lifted up as the previous one had, but rather than simply letting go, I swung myself around to the opposite side of it and kicked off, landing on the still-stable ground behind the root. That stability only lasted for a moment, but I was off in a run immediately, rushing toward my objective:

A tall section of stone that looked like it might have once been a building wall.

I couldn't know for certain that it would be any more stable than the roots, but it was my best bet. So, I ran on, rapidly processing what sort of wall-related threats might be applicable.

An earth elemental, an illusion, another sinkhole beneath it, a wall mimic...

I shuddered at the last one, but when it was close enough, I jumped at the wall segment regardless, using the full force of my Torch-given strength to leap straight atop it.

The wall segment was about as tall as a doorframe and about a dozen feet long, but barely wide enough to stand on. I wobbled when I hit the top, almost bouncing right off it from the force of my landing, but one of my boots stuck in place.

I breathed a sigh of relief — and then processed what had happened and why.

A leaf was stuck to my boot. That leaf had stuck me to the wall. That wouldn't have been so bad — in fact, it might have even been an advantageous stroke of luck — if the other side of the wall hadn't been exactly where the first hive of murder bees was located.

Oh, she made the adhesive smell like honey. That's bad, I realized. *That's really bad.*

The wall had been a fantastic sound barrier. I hadn't even heard the buzzing from the arm-sized bees until after I'd landed atop it. That made for a great bit of ambience as the first several murder bees emerged from below, pausing dramatically.

"Good . . . murder bees?" I tried hopefully.

They flew at me, stingers first. And I no longer had my sword in my hand.

But as my life would routinely teach me — and anyone who got in my way — if I didn't have a sword, I was more than capable of improvising. And that, on this occasion and many others, meant taking what I needed from an opponent.

I didn't even process my own movements. As the first bee came into range, I was reaching out, grabbing a stinger by the base, and then using an entire arm-length bee to parry the incoming assault of the other bees.

After a dozen such parries of midair thrusts from the bees, I hurled the entire bee I was gripping at another one, smashing them out of the air, and then ripped my adhesive-stuck boot from the stone. A hastily formed Sword Hand technique slashed off what I could from my boot, then I was jumping downward, deflecting another pair of incoming bees with the flat of my essence blade. Simply stealing the bee stinger would have been easier, but that would have been fatal for the bee, and they were just defending their home.

I hit the ground on the other side of the wall, already aiming for another patch of stone in the distance ahead — one of several. At this point, I was reasonably confident that I'd find other traps concealed behind the other walls, but my priority was getting away from the sinkholes. Rushing toward monsters could get me injured, but the sinkholes were likely to either end my time in the shrine immediately or deposit me in another part of the shrine that would be less hospitable. Either of those was more of a concern than bees and similar threats.

The bees were, unfortunately, still following me as I ran — either I'd angered them too much for them to abandon pursuit or cutting off the leaf hadn't completely gotten rid of the honey smell that was attracting them. I saw a few other bees rising in the distance from another hive on my right, but I continued running in a straight line, jumping over another root as it lazily animated, then reached the next wall, jumped, and rapidly kicked off it at an angle. The bees weren't quick enough to adjust, half of them slamming straight into the wall with painful-looking results, while others merely reoriented slowly, losing valuable time.

I landed, running and jumping all the way to the top of another wall. That wall trembled, which was never a good sign, and I jumped back off it just before spikes shot out of the top of it.

I landed on a square stone platform next to a single, massive, unlit candlestick. I blinked at the candle. Fortunately, it didn't blink back at me, which was a good sign. Ordinarily, I would have stopped to light it — that was usually a good way to open a passage or something — but the murder bees were still following me. Instead, I scanned the area while I had a few seconds to breathe, finding dozens of additional wall segments . . . and three likely candidates for mostly intact buildings.

I rushed toward the center one, glancing around the area as I ran, taking in a few other important details — more walls that were half sinking into the ground now as the tremors of root movements intensified, at least two more standing candlesticks, and what I'm going to refer to as a horde of murder bees flying in pursuit of me.

I stumbled over another root, but regained my balance and kept running, barely ducking under a single, larger murder bee that had gotten away from the rest of the horde. As it lunged for my back, I side-stepped and grabbed one of the roots as it swung at me, grunting as I planted my feet briefly and swung, using the colossal root to smash the bee right out of the air. It landed with a *fwump*, then buzzed, its wings still moving, and began to lift right back off the ground.

Stubborn. I can sympathize.

I could have rushed to attack while it was down, but that didn't feel right. Instead, I gave it a nod and disengaged, rushing to the massive doors of one of the still-standing buildings in the center of what I was rapidly identifying as some kind of ancient ruin.

The building was much taller than the walls outside, looking like what I imagined to be some sort of palace or temple. This was largely because at that age, I imagined most large human buildings to be either palaces or temples — but in fairness, Ana had the same associations, so it was likely I was guessing correctly if she had built it.

Based on the age and weathering of the stone, though, I wasn't entirely sure this was something that she'd built. She certainly had a mind for artistic work and the time necessary to make something look old, but . . . the way the stone was chipped and worn, and the way the strange still-glowing letters on the door shined bright red, in obvious warning of dangers within, spoke of something that might have predated her role in the shrine.

I couldn't identify the letters at a glance. That was unusual in itself — I wouldn't call myself a polyglot, but I could at least recognize the general style of letters from dozens of different languages. These looked to be some kind of pictographs, but not in a style I was familiar with. Given that they were glowing, I assumed they were enchantment runes of some kind — either that, or there was a separate enchantment designed to create them or make them glow. In faerie culture, letters glowing in red mean something special. That is to say, the same thing they mean virtually anywhere else.

"Don't touch."

Naturally, I wasn't going to let a wall tell me what to do.

. . . Certainly not with a horde of murder bees following me, at any rate.

I raised my hand, wrapping it with a fraction of my power—

And knocked politely three times. It was the nice thing to do.

When the door didn't respond, and neither did anyone inside, I did the less polite thing and reached for my sword belt.

I wasn't sure what would happen if I damaged the rune-etched door. I also wasn't sure what would happen if I drew my sword and actually used it to attack anything — I'd practiced with it by myself just a little bit, but testing it against an ancient ruin would be a new and exciting experience.

So, as the bees buzzed toward me, I drew my sword and made three swift slashes.

I saw the barrier flash as my sword approached — the crimson of ancient power flashing to life — but I didn't feel my sword pass through it. In fact, I didn't feel any resistance from the movement at all.

My sword passed through the barrier and stone as easily as it cut through air.

At first, I wasn't even sure what had happened. I simply looked at the sword without comprehension, briefly wondering if I'd somehow missed the wall right in front of me—

What just—

Then the section of wall I'd sliced fell into pieces.

Oh.

I blinked, lifting the sword and appraising it more closely.

Not bad, sword. Not bad.

With that in mind, I stepped through the doorway.

I didn't realize that the sounds of the murder bees had faded until it was much too late.

CHAPTER III

STATUES AND SECRETS

Right after I cleaved through the wall and stepped inside the room, I scanned the new area for threats.

The room was huge, maybe a hundred feet across, and rectangular in shape, with a cathedral-style ceiling. In fact, "cathedral-style" might have described the room in a more general sense.

The long hall led to a set of steps carved into the stone leading to a central dais. I imagined it was the type of place where an ancient priest might have once spoken to a crowd, back in the days when Dania had gods.

Gods like the ones that stood along the room's walls.

There were four colossal statues along the hallway, each carved with immaculate precision, every detail of their faces and hair impressively life-like. I'd always loved carving things myself, but I couldn't imagine the amount of time it would take to work a thirty-foot-tall statue like those. They were beautiful and foreboding at the same time. Even with my Torch-granted strength, I doubted I could take a punch from something of that size and remain standing.

And only two of them were unarmed.

The first statue was a man kneeling with a gleaming crystal outstretched between his hands.

The second was a robed and hooded woman holding a book and looking up toward the brilliant stars.

The third was a man in an elegant suit with a pair of massive wings, holding a colossal spear and pointing it down at the floor.

And the final statue was a short-haired woman in simple traveler's garb, pointing a bow and arrow straight ahead.

Upon close examination, it looked like the statues might have had color once, but the paint or dye had long faded — thus, they were left plain, without that element of character to hint toward their identities. Fortunately, I didn't need to see the blue in Kelryssia's robes or the red of Caerdanel's hair to know them on sight.

These were statues of the Kelrien Pantheon. Worldmakers, the first generation of gods.

But not the *right* worldmakers.

There was some confusion about why our world had stories about eight different worldmakers rather than the four that were required to build a planet.

Many believed that the two sets of worldmakers were different names or cultural interpretations of the same gods, but . . . they had such vastly different characteristics that the explanation didn't seem to match up.

Obviously, it was also possible that some or all of the legends of the makers could simply be falsehoods or propaganda. There were numerous stories of gods and heroes that were simply myths with no basis in reality, but there were enough stories of these eight entities from completely disparate cultures that it seemed likely that there was at least some basis in reality for each of them. And, of course, there was practical evidence as well. Creatures they created directly. Weapons they'd forged.

Weapons like the Dominion Breaker, the sword that even fate feared.

I absently shifted my grip on my sword as I looked more closely at the statues, pondering their presence.

These four makers were almost never physically depicted on Dania. The Venayan Pantheon for which our world had been named was far more common. Aetor, the Maker of Monsters. Vas Tyer, the Maker of Humans. Cas, the Maker of Machines. The Lost Maker, their name eradicated from records, their face erased from statues. All of these were more commonly depicted in Danian iconography and myth. A shrine to other worldmakers wasn't exactly heretical, given that basically everyone local agreed that the Venayan Pantheon were terrible and virtually no one worshipped them here, but it was *unusual*, much like finding a shrine to the Artinian Ancestor might be on Mythralis.

We had legends of the Kelrien Pantheon, but their physical worship was more central to Mythralian faith. Caerdanel was an exception — she was the Wanderer, known for stepping between worlds with the ease with which I could slip through a door — but the others were more obscure. Statues like this were almost unheard-of on this continent.

. . . Or so I'd been told, anyway.

Okay, that's weird. Those are obviously going to come to life and attack at some point if I'm not careful.

What else can I see before I trigger another hive of murderous monsters?

The statues were impressive, but the ceiling . . . that was breathtaking.

The ceiling was the absolute blackness of the void beyond the world, but within that vast darkness were dozens of brilliant, glittering lights.

Stars. I instinctively reached upward with a hand, the warm light above somehow calling to me, but the ceiling was at least thirty feet up — it would take more than a casual gesture to reach it.

With rope and a grappling hook, maybe . . .

I pondered that, but something else had more of my attention as I looked back down.

The building I'd carved my way into was, so far as I could tell, larger on the inside than the outside. That wasn't *too* surprising, given that the entire area I'd been running around inside looked like it was inside a single tree. I knew that dungeons often were extradimensional spaces, meaning that they didn't actually exist entirely on their physical location on the core plane — they were, at least in part, located on or between other planes of existence.

So, "larger on the inside" wasn't a surprise to me, in itself. I'd been in plenty of other places like that, too, like the witch's house. What I *wasn't* expecting was to find another space like that inside a dungeon — that implied the dungeon was using nested extradimensional spaces inside each other, which was . . . complicated. Not impossible, but complicated.

Don't make assumptions, I reminded myself as I glanced around the room. *It could be something simpler than that. The exterior could have been partially illusory. The interior could also be an illusion. Or maybe I'm not in a nested dimensional space, I was just teleported into a completely different part of the dungeon when I walked through the door. Not every area has to be physically adjacent to one another.*

It didn't *feel* like I'd been teleported when I walked through the door. I realized that I could actually perceive that now, at least to some degree. The breach essence in my Viewing Point made me sensitive to areas where the planes interacted and magical effects that involved moving between them. I'd sensed that when I first entered the tree, but not this specific chamber.

Focusing the power in my Viewing Point, I could see a haze of essence in the air, implying I was still in some kind of liminal space between planes, but it wasn't strong or focused enough for me to gather more information. Perhaps if I had more practice, or more essence of a specific subtype, I could have narrowed down what I was seeing, but for the moment, it was just "big room with essence in the air."

Seems safe enough.

I nodded to myself and took a step forward. *Click.*

Oh, for vek's sake—

The statue of Caerdanel moved, stone arms shifting on joints. She didn't bother to nock an arrow, which made sense, since her bow didn't have a string. Instead, she just pulled back on the air — and a massive stone arrow appeared between her fingers, slotting into a quickly manifesting phantasmal string.

Given that the arrow was about four feet long and thicker than my thumb, it might have been sensible to retreat into the waiting horde of monsters behind me. Instead, I did what I usually did.

I charged.

Lightning burst from the sides of the arrow as she launched it toward me. Less conventional arrow, more ballista bolt, really.

I swung my sword right into it, planning to knock it to the side.

Instead, my sword tore it in half, sending splinters of stone flying. That was undeniably more impressive than deflecting the arrow would have been, but some of those stone splinters caught my arms. I felt a few cuts form, as well as a mild electrical shock from the lightning essence imbuing the arrow. I nearly lost my grip, but trembled through the spasms in my hands, raising it to prepare for another shot.

No such attack came.

The statue shifted again, returning to her previous position.

I took a deep breath, lowering my sword, and took a more careful look at the floor.

The trap panels were more obvious now that I was looking for them. From my current vantage point, I could see at least six tiles that were slightly raised.

Okay. Avoiding those, at least for now.

I pulled the shrapnel that I could see out of my arms but didn't bother to treat the injuries just yet. I didn't know if the room was timed, and I was always concerned about lowering my guard in a room that had humanoid-looking statues.

I'm fine. This is mostly a puzzle, probably. Just need to assess.

Four statues. I know who they represent. We've got a star pattern on the ceiling, which fits Kelryssia. Might be something to that. There's also a strange seal pattern on the ground, which might have something to do with Delsen.

Or . . .

I crept closer to the pattern on the ground, carefully avoiding the raised tiles.

Is . . . that one of the seals for the Buried?

That's . . . odd. They shouldn't be associated with these four worldmakers.

Is that a hint? Something out of place?

I strongly considered slamming my sword into the seal to see if that unlocked something. Because, you know, unsealing ancient evils — even in the context of a scenario like this one — usually wasn't the right solution to a problem.

Usually.

I thought I was genuinely onto something with the seal being out of place with these worldmakers, but it wasn't the only hint. The constellations in the sky were a significant one, too.

What's Kelryssia up to?

I looked at her statue. She was reading a book, which was pretty clearly Kelryssia-like. I couldn't see what the cover said, if anything, due to the position of her hands. And, given how tall the statues were, I couldn't see the text, if any, either.

Not from there, anyway.

Text is often a hint to puzzles. And stone books were still books.

Cautiously, I moved to the side of the Kelryssia statue, avoiding the traps . . . then I awkwardly sheathed my sword on my back, and started to climb up her leg.

Sorry, goddess. Awkward for me, too.

I grabbed her arm to pull myself higher, which surprised me by moving slightly. I released it, dropping to the ground.

Arms are jointed, like the Caerdanel statue. Huh. Okay.

I wonder if they're all poseable?

If that's the case . . .

An idea began to form, but I still needed more information. I climbed, shifting to avoid putting weight on Kelryssia's arms, clambering up her back instead.

Then, from a vantage point sitting on her shoulders, I looked at her book.

In this world both old and new,
I see the paths both false and true,
Eyes forever turned up high,
Guided by the lights of sky.

I paused, looking upward and following her gaze.

Paths both false and true, huh? Astronomy is more Gramps's thing, but I wonder if . . .

There.

I didn't have extensive knowledge of constellations, especially the Kelrien ones. They weren't the same as the ones that I saw in the night sky outside, after all. I'd seen them listed in books, but I didn't have a clear recollection of what they were supposed to look like.

Fortunately, the outlier wasn't only identifiable through obscure astrological knowledge.

One of the stars was *black.*

That might sound super obvious, but it was glowing black in a black sky — it was only visible because it was slightly occluding two of the other stars near it, sort of like a star that was eclipsing other stars.

I wondered if that was symbolic, somehow, but I didn't have the context to say.

Okay. She sees paths both false and true. Stars can be symbolic for paths, so . . . false star, which might be a path forward.

Might be a false path, though, meaning a dead end or a bad path to take. Still want to check it.

Can I get up there from here?

The answer was "no." Not from Kelryssia.

Delsen, on the other hand, had a spear that was thicker than my legs and tall enough that it nearly scraped the ceiling. It wasn't in the right position, but . . .

I climbed back down.

After several minutes of experimenting with rotating statue bits, I figured out that I could rotate not only the arms of the statues, but the bases as well.

Hope this works.

I pointed the Caerdanel statue toward the black star, then hit a switch. She formed a stone arrow and aimed — not at me, but at the sky.

She shot the black star. Her arrow sank into it, lightning flashing in the blackness of the sky before it dissipated. I heard a click.

There we go.

Then I climbed up Delsen's back and spear. I grabbed the stone arrow and fidgeted with it.

As I'd hoped, a circular section of the ceiling rotated as I moved the arrow, exposing a path above.

True? False?

I didn't care. I saw a room above and I was curious. It was time to explore.

I shoved the false star to the side. Up close, I found that the stars were luminous chunks of crystal, each seemingly carved into geometric shapes. I wondered at what type of essence they might contain, but they were so large that I couldn't easily take one with me out of the shrine, and I had higher priorities.

I climbed halfway into the secret room, glancing around for threats — and then tapping the nearby floor, ready to duck right back out of the chamber — before I finally pushed myself all the way inside.

The hidden chamber wasn't quite what I'd expected.

I'd guessed it to be some sort of thematically appropriate challenge. I'd daydreamed of fighting shining beasts while standing among the stars, or perhaps dodging meteors to find my way toward a facsimile of our planet with a hidden key.

Instead, I found an attic.

In retrospect, that was probably what I should have expected in, you know, the top of a building . . . but given that I was in an extradimensional space that very clearly didn't follow the typical rules of architectural construction, I hope you can forgive me for imagining something a little wilder.

On the plus side, the attic wasn't dusty or run-down like one might have expected for a place that was at least thematically supposed to look ancient. I presumed at first that Ana had simply constructed it recently to look old, or perhaps that she was maintaining it herself. It was, after all, a *furnished* attic — one that had a single bed with the covers neatly tucked in, a desk with a statuette holding a sword atop it, a single chair, and a wooden trunk by the bedside.

I narrowed my eyes at the trunk. The trunk, fortunately, didn't narrow any eyes back at me — at least that I could see.

I'm ready for you, hypothetical mimic.

I briefly debated sliding the star back into position to see if anything happened, but decided against sealing off my only obvious means to leave the room.

Sure, I could cut through the floor, but I wasn't some sort of floor-destroying barbarian.

(Walls and doors were completely different than floors, obviously.)

Cautiously, I prodded the floor around me with my still-sheathed sword. When no obvious traps triggered, I frowned around at the room, still searching for threats.

Star Shattering Sight.

With my vision enhanced by my breach essence technique, I scanned the trunk for any obvious signs that it was a mimic. Then the walls. Then the floors and ceiling.

Nothing. No obvious mana structures, no clear weak points that would collapse and bury me or send me tumbling down.

Sometimes an attic was just an attic.

This was something much more, but I wouldn't realize that right away.

I unsheathed my sword, poking the box directly — you can never be too careful — then, when nothing happened, flipped the latch with my sword's tip and pushed the top open from a distance.

No teeth or tongue. Just an empty—

I frowned.

My Star Shattering Sight showed something glowing on the bottom of the box, just barely.

I couldn't see it clearly at a distance, so, grudgingly and cautiously, I approached, first prodding around the box with the sword, then finally leaning close with a deflection-aspected aura surrounding my gloved hand and prodded around directly until I found what I was looking for.

Click.

I jumped back immediately, but there was no trap triggered. Upon further investigation, I found that the bottom — or seeming bottom — of the chest had shifted slightly. When I touched it, the wooden panel slid into the side of the box.

A classic false bottom. And beneath it was treasure more valuable — and more terrible — than anything I could have imagined.

Inside, I found a weathered leather journal and a pen.

Nice try, journal mimic.

I jabbed it. Nothing happened.

Then, after testing the pen and the bottom of the box, I eagerly picked up the journal and opened to the first page.

Runes flashed in my vision. I threw the book at the wall immediately, but fortunately, it didn't explode. Nothing else seemed to happen.

Blinking, I cautiously picked the book back up and reopened it more slowly . . . finding that the text inside the book was glowing brightly under my Star Shattering Sight.

Enchanted text? Huh. Not exploding runes, though. At least not yet. I didn't feel any attempt at a mental effect, either. Maybe it's making the text unreadable?

I tried to read it, but failed. The letters were entirely unfamiliar — and glowing too bright for me to process properly.

After a few moments of deliberation, I flipped through it and observed the same effect on every other page. Half the pages appeared to be blank. Then, cautiously, I disabled my Star Shattering Sight.

The letters ceased to glow but otherwise remained the same.

Hm.

Glancing from side to side, I examined the rest of the room again.

A desk. A chair. A statuette. A bed. The exit. Nothing remarkable, aside from maybe the statue.

I gave the statuette a closer look. It depicted a beautiful woman, perhaps some other goddess, but I couldn't identify her at a glance in spite of an odd feeling of familiarity when I looked at her. She wasn't made of stone like the ones below and had a distinctly different style — rather than looking like an ancient and unknowable being, she looked like a young woman fighting for her freedom.

Where do I know you from?

I found myself inching closer, noting that she wore a dress that transitioned from gold to red, not unlike the color of her hair. The strawberry-blond look reminded me of Ana, but the look on this woman's face wasn't one I'd ever seen Ana wear. She looked fearful, sad, and exhausted — but she still had her silver and gold sword raised up high.

Something about that image tugged at my heart. She looked both a little too real and too familiar for my comfort.

I found myself inspecting the details of how she'd been built, both for traps and out of curiosity. She wasn't made entirely of stone like the statues below — rather, she was largely painted metal, with some bits of crystal in her sword blade. A quick use of Star Shattering Sight showed me that the sword's crystal emanated magic. Oddly, her shoes were also magic crystal, which didn't make a lot of sense to me. Magic swords were common, but gemstone shoes? Those were unusual, at least in my home.

Aside from those magic bits, I noted some essence inside the base of the platform, as well as a visible nonmagical switch of some kind on the base. I also noted that her limbs were articulated, meaning they could be moved either manually or through some internal mechanism. Another puzzle, perhaps.

After a brief search turned up nothing else of interest in the room, I went back to the statue, activated a brief deflection-aspected field around my hand, and flipped the switch.

The sword in her hand lit up like the sun.

I blinked at the sudden illumination, bracing myself for something else to happen. Nothing.

I flipped the switch again. The sun turned off.

On. Off. Test, test.

I sighed at myself.

She's a lamp. A very pretty, weirdly familiar lamp.

I still felt like I needed to do something about her, but her limbs resisted attempts at manual movement, and I didn't want to force them and break something. Presumably something would happen with the internal mechanisms of the lamp if I left it for a while. If not, I could experiment later.

I took a breath. *Okay. Is there anything else to do in here?*

Given that the lamp didn't appear to be in obvious need of rescue, the journal seemed like the obvious puzzle for the room. I quickly searched under the bed, inside the pillowcase, and under the bedsheets. Nothing unusual showed itself. The bed didn't try to eat me.

A few jabs showed that the chair, table, and lamp weren't going to try to devour me, either, so I sat down with the journal and the pen.

Codebreaking wasn't my area of expertise, but it was a classic style of puzzle. It wasn't something I'd anticipated Ana doing, but that just made me grudgingly admire the effort.

Okay. I can do this. Just need to figure out what kind of code it is.

I pressed a switch on the side of the lamp. The crystal flickered on, bathing the room in a light that felt comfortingly like the light of the sun.

Huh. Wonder where she found this thing. Sun essence isn't easy to come by in large enough quantities for enchantment.

I'll have to ask later. For now, it's time to get to work.

I didn't have my books with me, but I was pretty sure that what I was looking at wasn't any foreign language I'd ever seen. I briefly entertained that they were simply unfamiliar letters in Cas or Artinian — those languages had a lot of letters — but while there were some stylistic similarities, these letters appeared to be more . . . formulaic? They were angular, constructed from sharp lines rather than the elegant flowing curves I associated with the calligraphic brush strokes of Cas or Artinian, and they didn't seem to be obviously pictographic in nature.

Hm. Could they be less like letters and more like tally marks?

I played with that idea for a while, but I didn't get anywhere with it — not right away, at least. If there was an underlying numeric system to it, I didn't have enough information to figure it out.

I'd tinkered with a few similar puzzles with Gramps. He liked that kind of thing, although he was fonder of riddles. I leaned toward logic puzzles.

And if I wasn't good at a particular type of problem, I could always cut it into a shape that I preferred.

I couldn't quite turn the situation into a logic problem, but I could handle the component problems with it similarly. Lay out all the options for what type of code it could be — if it was a code at all — and how they would interact. Then, from there, solve.

I took out a page of my own parchment and began to write a grid. I considered using the blank pages in the book itself, but I wasn't quite ready to write inside it yet. I wanted to use those pages for transcribing the encoded pages into a readable format if possible. That might have been the intent from the start, or it might have just been convenient.

After forming the grid, I began to write down a top row of options.

Foreign language.

Rotation cipher.

Keyword cipher.

Mirrored text.

Personal writing style.

Magically obscured text.

Hidden text.

I was confident there were more possible options, but, again, codebreaking wasn't my area. And this was a start. After making the top of the chart, I wrote the same words going down from the top, creating the possibility of each intersecting to create a puzzle. For example, a foreign language and magically obscured text might mean that I had to do something to change the words to make them legible, then translate from there.

From there, I began to narrow it down. I experimented with a couple methods to see if I could reveal hidden text on the seemingly blank pages, using the lamp's light and a briefly lit candle to see if they changed the text, but nothing happened.

I'd heard stories about revealing hidden text with certain types of liquid, but I didn't have anything appropriate on me, and in any case, I wasn't sure I'd want to risk getting the pages wet at this stage.

I activated my Viewing Point again, cycling through different breach essence aspects to see if hidden letters existed on a different layer of the object.

When I hit the Memory Layer, I got *something*, but it wasn't what I expected.

The text on the page vanished . . . then, gradually, began to rewrite itself from the top. I watched briefly in fascination, setting the book down to watch the letters write themselves.

Is this useful? What can I do with—

Stroke order.

I began to rapidly copy down characters on my blank page as they were written, exactly in the way they were written.

Stroke order wasn't relevant in Valian, but it was potentially relevant in languages like Cas and Artinian. If the writer always moved in a specific sequence, like right to left or up to down, hypothetically that could be a clue about the original language of the document.

I found variations in the stroke order almost immediately . . . or, at first, I *thought* I did. The writer was using something like a calligraphy pen, which resulted in distinct shapes at the start and end of each stroke — something that could, in theory, be enough to result in different letters.

After I retraced the process for a few pages, I had enough transcribed onto my own page to use as a starting point.

From there, I began to identify and count the unique letters.

I began from the assumption that the stroke order was irrelevant; there were, so far as I could tell, only about twenty-five unique letters. That was far too few for Cas or Artinian, but a possible match for Velthryn, Liadran, and even a few older tongues like Xixian.

If I considered the stroke order to be relevant, I got about twice as many letters. That made fewer matches than I was familiar with, but it could have matched one of the simplified formats of Artinian that was used for children and foreign words, which had about forty-six characters, in my recollection.

I glanced the book over again, trying to see if there was anything to sort it out one way or another. One stroke order seemed dominant for each symbol. If there was a pattern—

Of course. Capital letters. If this is just Velthryn or something similar . . .

I was eager to test that hypothesis, but I decided to go through a couple more possible secret-revealing methods first. Disabling my Viewing Point technique, I went through my bag for a hand mirror — I'd replaced the one I'd given to the scythe spider a long time ago — and lifted it to the book. As expected, there was nothing unusual in the book, but as I angled it, I saw something metallic glint behind me.

I ducked, hearing something fly over my head, then dropped my mirror and grabbed my still-sheathed sword, standing and swinging around in a single motion.

My opponent manifested fully as I swung, her wild hair aflame and her own sword a sharpened bar of black light. When my scabbard met her parry, I stepped into it and sent a burst of deflection-aspected essence through it, knocking her back a step — almost, but not quite, into the pit that led into the floor below.

Ana groaned, releasing a hand from her sword to sweep it upward, producing a ghostly claw the size of my torso in the air between us. As she moved, the claw moved with her, sharpened nails sweeping for my chest.

In the confines of the attic-like space, I was in too close quarters to draw my sword properly, so I simply applied a Sword Sharpening Shroud to my scabbard with a hint of breach essence flaring along the edges. Then I cut her newly formed claw in half.

She frowned as her technique dissipated, pulling back a fist. I saw a massive hand beginning to form, looking more solid than the claw had.

Nope. Not letting her finish that.

I lunged, swinging my scabbard. I clipped one of the walls with the sword's aura and heard a sound like glass shattering.

The world around me cracked along with it.

The world was in black and white.

I stood, floating in nothingness, approximately the same distance from Ana that I had been a moment before. I felt a hint of relief that she was still present at all, but it didn't last long.

She flickered, there one moment and gone for a fraction of one, then she was back.

What . . . ?

We were alone there. Or . . . mostly alone, at least.

A lonely statuette of a girl holding a sword was lying on what passed for the ground, her blade casting the only illumination in the black-and-white space.

I took a step back cautiously toward the statue, my sword raised in a guard position. At least there was enough space to swing here. I braced my off hand on the scabbard, ready to use it as a lever or to draw the blade if I needed to.

As I moved closer to the statue I felt more . . . stable. More *real*, maybe? Whatever that meant.

Ana flickered back out of existence again. When she reappeared, she was a step farther from me, her sword lowered.

"Uh, Lien? What did you *do*?"

I frowned. "This isn't one of your traps?"

"Nope! Nope nope nope!" She glanced from side to side, obviously concerned, then vanished again.

When she reappeared, I frowned at her. "How is that possible? And to answer your question, I think I clipped a wall with my sword. Not like . . . hard, or anything, just . . . a little?"

"Oh, good. Maybe you only broke reality a *little*, then."

"Hey, don't blame me. You attacked me, what was I supposed to do?"

"Obviously not whatever you did, which clearly wasn't just—"

"Breach essence." I groaned. "I used breach essence to cut through your phantasmal hand thing, and when I clipped the wall . . ."

"You broke a hole in the boundaries of the extradimensional space." She exhaled a breath. "That's bad. This isn't my part of—"

Ana vanished again.

A heartbeat.

She was still gone.

Another.

Another.

And—

She reappeared, looking vaguely ill.

I grabbed her.

"Hey, what's the big—"

I yanked her into my arms, pinning her arms in place, then started stepping backward. She was a fighty thing and had me beaten on dexterity by a massive margin, but in a raw strength contest, I had a significant advantage since hitting Torch.

"Hey, truce, truce!" She tried to wriggle out of my grip, but I held her tight.

"Not fighting. Move with me." I pulled her closer to the statue, standing over it, then pulled her down with me to look at it more closely.

"What are you . . . Are you seriously worried about the sexy lamp right now, Lien? We need to get out of here."

I sighed. "I'm trying to get us safe. I think the lamp is helping. Take a breath here."

She did. She didn't vanish. Neither did I.

"I . . . oh." She glanced up. "Huh."

"I think we're stable here. Wherever here is. Might be best if we're actually touching the lamp, though. If I let you go, will you cooperate?"

"Yeah, but will you? You never accepted my offer."

I blinked. "Oh, right. Terms?"

"Until we get back to my dungeon, no hostilities. Cooperation to figure this out and get back."

"Add an extra three minutes for us to collect ourselves."

"Done and accepted on my part."

"I agree to your terms. Once, twice, thrice, and done."

Ana relaxed. I released her from my grip, but she stayed close, our arms brushing up against each other. I didn't know if that was purely a practical thing to help our stability or if she just wanted to remain in contact out of fear. For my part, fear was definitely a factor, but as usual, my fear instincts didn't lead me toward seeking comfort — my instinct was to cut a hole in the space to try to get back to the dungeon the way I'd gotten in.

Ana's presence was a stabilizing one in a different way than the lamp's — with her there, I wasn't willing to take that kind of risk.

Instead, I awkwardly slipped my scabbard into the harness on my back, then reached for the statue.

"Don't touch her!" Ana grabbed my hand.

I gave her a glance. "What, are you jealous of the lamp?"

"Don't be absurd. I'm definitely not jealous of this lamp."

I blinked at her phrasing. "Wait, implying that you *are* jealous in some other way?"

She wrinkled her nose. "*Obviously.* But now is not the best time to have that talk. I'd like to get back to, you know, reality?"

"I'm pretty sure this is *a* reality. If I got here through breach essence, that implies we've ripped a hole between here and—"

"Another plane, yeah, I know. I don't want to wait long enough to figure out which one it is and what the natural predators are."

When she put it that way, I absolutely *did* want to wait and see what those were, but I supposed that her safety and comfort were the priority. Also, I didn't like the idea of getting either of us stuck here. Fighting extraplanar monsters would be more fun if I had an exit route — I'd get bored eventually, after all.

"Why didn't you want me to touch the statue, then?"

"Did you ever turn off your breach essence technique?"

"Well, not deliberately, but it's on my scabbard, and . . . hm, okay, yeah, the technique essence does flow *through* my hand." I disabled the Star Sharpening Shroud on my scabbard. I didn't think it would be relevant, but caution seemed reasonable when I was stuck in a gaping hole between realities.

"Okay. It's off?"

I nodded. "Yep."

"Good. Now, we touch the statue *together*, okay? It's probably serving as a tether to the shrine, and I don't want one of us to get pulled back alone," Ana explained.

"Got it." We entwined our fingers on one hand, then reached down with our opposite hands touching and grabbed the statue together.

The statue was warm. Strangely warm — enough that it brought the coldness of the place around us to my attention for the first time.

But that was it. Warmth, but no change to our surroundings, no exit from the space that was warping around us and . . .

Was it getting *smaller*?

It's hard to quantify the size of a grayscale extradimensional space, but the air farther away from us seemed to be blurring more, and when I looked at it, it felt like the world around us was *tightening*, while simultaneously *thinning*.

It wasn't so much that I felt like the walls were closing in around us, so much as that *our* walls were breaking, and when they failed, we'd be swept into the endless beyond.

Not an ideal start to my day, to be certain.

As if to emphasize the urgency I felt at the sight, the statue's warmth began to fade.

Oh, that's . . . not a good sign.

"Ideas?" I asked.

"Your breach essence might work, but save it for a last resort if I can't get us out of here. I . . . I've never tried this with this kind of distance before, and

I don't know if it'll work, but I can try to move us back using this thing as an anchor. If it exists in both planes, maybe—"

"Your ley line travel ability. Do you think it'll work?"

I heard something crack around us.

"I don't know. And Lien . . . I'm not used to taking other people with me. I don't know if—"

I squeezed her hand tighter. "Do it. I trust you."

She took a deep breath. Another crack above us. I thought I saw a pane of something glassy falling from above us, something black and wispy creeping in, and then—

"Take us home, take us home, take us home!"

Upon Ana's last word, a burst of sun-bright light flashed from within our hands—

Warmth spread over us even as the world shattered above and below. We plunged down, down, and then—

I felt something yank on my sense of self, and I crashed face-first into solid and endlessly comforting stone.

My only companion was the freezing-cold statue still gripped tightly in my hand.

CHAPTER IV

STABILITY

I pushed myself into a sitting position cautiously, cradling the statue close against my chest. I shivered at the coldness of it. The statue seemed to drink in my warmth.

I couldn't deny her that. I couldn't let her stay cold after what she'd done to help me, after all.

But the statue wasn't my greatest concern.

As I looked up, I searched for her immediately. "Ana? Ana? Are you there, Ana?"

I was back in the attic study, but seemingly alone.

When I glanced around, I saw no sign of Ana, just a still-gaping tear in the stone where I'd sliced through a small section of the wall. The cut was ragged, tearing more than just stone. It had left a gash into something beyond, something that seemed to stretch out farther the longer that I looked into it, that threatened to grab me and pull me back in if I approached, or even looked too closely.

I pushed myself to my feet, wobbling. Ana was still missing.

Which meant I was going back in there for her.

There wasn't any hesitation. Obviously, I should have gone for help, found a way to get Gramps, but if I took too long, I didn't know if—

Ana appeared in front of me, dressed in some sort of heavy work outfit, carrying a sign in one hand and a brush the size of a human being in the other. She slammed the sign into the floor, where it stuck to the stone without sinking in.

It read, "Dungeon Under Maintenance: Authorized Personnel Only."

I took a step closer. "Ana, are you—"

"Hey, no crossing the sign, mister! This is a construction site, you wouldn't want to get sucked into an endless abyss beyond time and space that some careless adventurer made, would you?"

I rolled my eyes, then took a step back. "I'm glad you're okay."

"Same. Now, give me a minute to patch this." She groaned, reaching up gingerly with her gigantic brush and painting over the massive crack. Stone appeared where her brush moved but twisted and distorted, bits of it flaking away and vanishing. The brush's top twisted, too, but remained more stable.

She worked and worked, groaning and sweating with effort, until, eventually, she set her jaw and a flare of blackness ran along her skin and the brush.

When she painted after that, the bricks she formed were solid black and remained stable. Her hands trembled on the brush's grip as she finished that section, and the blackness faded, but she continued to work, painting over the darkness with another layer of ordinary brick.

I waited patiently in spite of the knowledge that our three-minute truce was long ended. This was, in our mutual understanding, a far greater concern than resuming our sparring match.

Her hands were barely able to maintain her grip on the brush when she turned to me, her fingers shaking. "That . . . that was . . ."

"Exciting?" I offered.

"Sure. And absolutely terrifying. I . . . don't think I liked that, Lien."

I wasn't sure if I'd liked it, either.

It had been an adventure, to be certain. A good story. But if Ana had been left behind in that place . . .

I didn't want to think about that.

I didn't like consequences.

"It was pretty scary," I admitted, thinking of the possibility of losing her as I spoke.

It wasn't that I was completely unafraid about the idea of being torn off into some other plane, of course. But it also meant I would be *free*, and . . . there was an appeal in that, even if it wasn't the ideal way to earn my freedom.

I wasn't foolish enough to think I could definitely survive on any other plane of existence, but with breach essence, I had a much better chance than your average person. I hadn't trained to use it as a defensive tool on other planes, but maybe . . .

I shook my head. It was something to think about more another time.

"Were you hurt?" she asked.

I shook my head. "I don't think so. You?"

"No, just . . . drained. And . . . I don't think I fixed that completely. It's stable for now, but . . . can you maybe not use that essence here?"

I took a breath. "You know how much of a disadvantage that's going to put me at. For now, can we formally renew our truce while we take a break for recovery and discussion?"

". . . Yeah. And . . . maybe in a different room?"

"That's fine. Give me a few minutes here without attacking me?"

"Agreed."

I turned back to the desk, picking up the journal and my notes, putting them inside my backpack. Then, after a moment of consideration, I made room in my backpack for the lamp.

Ana stared at me. "You're *seriously* taking the sexy lamp with you?"

"I thought you weren't jealous of her."

She folded her arms. "I'm still not."

"She looks kind of like you, you know." I waggled the lamp.

". . . Looks *more* like a certain princess."

I blinked. "Does she?" I lifted the lamp, taking a look at her. And thinking back to the last time I'd seen her—

I could see a bit of resemblance. The colors weren't quite right, but the way she was built . . . well, the statue was of an older person, an adult. But I could see how there was some resemblance to the girl I'd met during my first encounter with humans, three years earlier.

"Huh. I guess she does look a little bit like the princess, too, but she's got your hair color, and there's *something* familiar about that sword—"

Ana cut me off. "Do you really need to rescue every damsel you come across, even inanimate ones?"

I smiled at her. "Maybe not *all* of them. But ones that have a stabilizing influence on reality? I'm pretty sure this damsel was made just for me."

She muttered something that sounded suspiciously like ". . . maybe a *little* jealous now . . ." but I couldn't quite catch it.

⁂

By mutual agreement, I climbed back out of the room first, through the false star and down onto the statue below. I climbed down awkwardly, unbalanced by the new weight in my backpack, but only slipped when I was close enough to the floor that I handled the impact with little more than an "oof."

Ana had wings. Descending should have been trivial for her. But while she beat those wings during her descent, she was still clutching her gigantic brush, and she had to awkwardly heft the false star back into place to seal that room . . .

Then begin painting the roof to seal the entire place off even more.

By the time she was done, she half drifted, half fell from the sky.

I caught her as she descended faster than she seemed to intend, helping set her down. She gave me a nod, shivering in my grip.

"I think you overdid it," I told her.

"I think I agree, at least in terms of essence use. In terms of doing enough to stabilize that place . . . would you be amenable to waiting here for a few hours without progressing farther?"

I blinked. "Hours? Why?"

"I think this is bad enough that I should go get Gramps, but I don't even have the energy to get to him. If that paint above us starts to crack, I'll need to evacuate us both."

". . . You really think it's that dangerous?"

She nodded fervently. "I didn't design this part of the dungeon. It's from before my time. But I know how dungeon essence works, and I used dungeon essence to try to fill in that gap. That didn't fix it. It's more like . . . I put a bandage on a deep wound. It might heal on its own now, but it's more likely it could just keep bleeding and get worse."

"So, you need . . . what, a surgeon to stitch it together?"

"I don't even know. But if anyone does, it's probably Gramps."

I nodded in agreement. Teleportation magic was one of his areas of expertise. I didn't know how strong he was, but I expected that he was probably in or near the Memory layer. If anyone could fix this, it was probably him.

"Truce terms?" I asked.

"If you agree to wait here for three hours, I will not fight you again until you reach a clearly designated chamber specifically designed for that purpose, or until you leave the dungeon, or until you attack me, whichever comes first."

That was . . . a much broader concession than I expected. That meant no ambushes, which would remove one of her favorite methods of teasing and testing me.

That meant she was taking this *very* seriously.

"You also won't change any puzzles or challenges to be more difficult to compensate?"

"Wasn't even thinking about it. But yes, I agree."

"I agree to your terms, then. Once, twice, thrice, and done."

She offered me a hand. Instinctively, I took it and kissed it.

She blinked at me. "What was that for?"

"Sealing the deal. It . . . seemed significant?"

"I guess it was." She frowned at her hand, seeming uncertain. "I'd better get going."

"Wait. You should stay here and rest a bit first."

She gave me an uncertain look. "Working with you to escape that was one thing, but . . . I'm not really supposed to spend quality time just resting with people in my tests."

"I think we can call this a reasonable exception. Suspend the test in general for the three hours."

"That's . . . no, that's a little too much. But I can spend a few minutes here, at least. Let's sit down?"

We sat down together. "Want something to eat?" I offered. "I have some rations."

"I have food elsewhere. I shouldn't accept anything from you. Technically, this is my home, and if you gave me food and I ate it without offering anything in return, that'd be an inversion of guest right."

I knew that, of course. "Well, you could offer me something, then."

"And give you guest rights here? So you can walk straight through my challenges to the end? Nice try, buddy."

"It was worth a shot."

She smiled, then conjured herself a glass of juice and began to drink. I *still* didn't know how she'd managed to figure out juice conjuration. I took a flask of water from my side and drank along with her.

". . . Would you have actually accepted guest rights if I'd offered, or given you them by accident?" she asked.

I nodded. "I've thought about it before. I'd have accepted, then asked for a tour of the place, walked around to see everything, then asked to leave without finishing the place. I wouldn't want to skip facing the challenges fairly, but it *would* be fun to see everything you've set up."

She gave me a curious look. "But you'd just lose all your memories."

"Sure. Temporarily. But when I eventually win, I'll get all the memories back, and then I'd have gotten to see what an older version of your dungeon looked like. And it'd be more like a behind-the-scenes tour. That'd be kind of fun, wouldn't it?"

"Huh." She took another sip of her juice. "I guess it could be. I suppose I could offer—"

I waved a hand dismissively. "Nah, not today. Too excited. I want to win today."

". . . Seriously? *That's* how you feel after what we just went through?"

I grinned. "Can't help it. I can't leave a fight we started unfinished."

". . . About that. I think might need to add a rule to prevent the further use of breach essence in here."

I froze in mid-drink, putting my flask down. "Seriously?"

"Lien . . . if you do that again, and do more than clip a wall, you . . . you could collapse the entire dungeon. I don't know what would happen, exactly, but it wouldn't be good."

"Sure. And when I walk in here, I don't know what you're going to do to me, either. You could kill me. You could destroy my sword. And you would, given certain circumstances, right?"

"Well, yeah, but—"

"Then isn't limiting my capabilities a little hypocritical?"

She winced. "I can see why you'd feel that way, but I need to design this place for multiple uses."

"And I need to be able to use my full capabilities for a reasonable chance of success. We agreed to specific terms before I walked in. They're the same rules we've used every time . . . unless you routinely change the rules while I'm in here?"

"No, Lien. I haven't needed to."

"But if you can, that really changes the whole dynamic of the place, doesn't it? It would explain why—"

Ana folded her arms. "Are you saying you don't trust me?"

"I'm saying that if you have the ability to change the rules at any time, including in the middle of my attempts, that fundamentally changes the nature of the contest itself. And this can't be the first time I've used breach essence here. In fact, I used it earlier, more than once, for looking at the journal and such."

"Using it for a Viewing Point technique is probably fine. It's attacking with it that's the problem. Weren't you warned about that?"

"Well, yeah, but you know about me and warnings."

She sighed. "You should take this seriously."

"I *am* taking it seriously, Ana. That's why I'm being as clear as possible right now. I'm going to be seriously upset if I can't use one of my essence types. You know how much stronger you are than I am. I'm already at a significant disadvantage."

". . . A lot less than you used to be."

I nodded. "Maybe, but if I have to handicap myself, that gap surges back to closer to what it was. And I'm not going to stop using breach essence outside of here, since I won't know about this encounter, so . . . I'll be continuing to train something I can't use. Obviously that isn't relevant if I win today, which I fully intend to, but . . ."

"I understand. If I do add a rule, I can write it formally outside. You deserve that, at least. And . . . I suppose I can allow any internal use of the essence, not just Viewing Point stuff." She sounded like she was having a hard time even making that concession, but it didn't mean much to me.

"That doesn't really add a lot of other options. Even *I* don't think it's a good idea to use breach essence as a body-enhancement or movement technique."

"I don't know what to tell you, Lien. I can't allow you to collapse my home because you're throwing around dangerous, world-altering essence attacks. *Maybe* if you figure out how to control it better, I'd consider it, but . . ."

"So, you're assuming I'm going to fail this time."

"I . . ." Ana's expression faltered. "I'm assuming you are going to . . . not finish the dungeon this time."

I shook my head, ignoring her phrasing. "That's a little insulting."

"It isn't meant to be. I just, well . . . I have my reasons. There are things you don't know."

"Sure. I can't remember things that happen in here, so obviously I have gaps." I sighed. "This isn't getting anywhere. Adding a sign outside might mean that I can agree to things in the future, but for now, at present, you're putting me at a disadvantage in a challenge after rules have already been established. I want a reciprocal exchange."

"You want me to change the rules on your behalf?" Ana's eyebrow went up. "That's . . . I suppose it makes sense. I could avoid using sword essence?"

"I don't think that's equivalent. My second essence type was breach. In order to be equitable, you'd have to avoid using dungeon essence."

"Nope. Not happening."

"Didn't think so." I considered for a moment. "Okay. What if, rather than an exchange, you reduce the scale of this limitation for this attempt? What if I use a specific breach aspect corresponding to a certain plane, rather than using general breach essence? You know, like memory-aspected breach essence?"

She seemed to consider that. "Do you know if that would prevent what just happened from occurring again?"

"No. I can speculate that it wouldn't cause that effect unless I was using the specific aspect tied to whatever plane we just intersected with, but . . . I don't know for sure."

"Then the answer is still no, at least until you figure that out."

"How am I supposed to figure it out without testing?"

She shrugged. "Once I write up the rule, you can potentially ask Gramps about it, or run tests in similar areas. I'd even consider opening up the dungeon for testing purposes, rather than an actual trial, and creating a separate room for it."

I blinked. "Is . . . that a thing you can do?"

"Sure, technically? It hasn't really come up before, but yeah, I could theoretically let someone inside for something other than the challenge."

"Then . . . why didn't you ever invite me before?"

I tried to keep the hurt out of my voice. I failed.

I don't know if she noticed. Tone wasn't something we always understood with each other.

Her response was simple. "Never occurred to me."

I was silent for a while, just drinking water.

That wasn't great. Quiet made my mind go places I didn't want it to. Thinking about chances I'd missed, mistakes I'd made, setbacks.

Losing the ability to use breach essence attacks in here was . . . more than a little setback. It could add years to my attempts, and . . .

The thought that she could have just . . . invited me inside at any time, just to spend time with her, or play, and she never had . . .

"I should probably go." Ana stood up. "I . . . I don't know how long my patch will hold, and I think I have the strength to get to Gramps now."

"What about getting back here?" I asked.

"Gramps can move us. We'll probably go straight to the room above, though."

"I see." I slipped my backpack off my back. "I'll just work on translating your code, I guess. Unless that counts as progressing?"

"No, it doesn't." She frowned. "It's not my code, anyway. I didn't make that journal. I don't even know what it says."

"Huh." She had mentioned that she hadn't made this part of the dungeon, but I still assumed she'd planted the props there. "And the statue?"

"Not mine, either. But I'd prefer if you don't tinker with those in here further, now that I think about it. They might still be tied to that strange space. I'd prefer if you wait until you take them outside and show them to Gramps before you interact with them more."

I groaned. "Fine." I thought she was being excessively cautious now, but from that, I understood that she was truly afraid in a way that I could never remember seeing. I didn't want to make her feel worse.

I was still frustrated about the change in rules, but it wasn't worth pushing at the moment.

"I appreciate your consideration," she said. "Okay." She took one deep breath, then another. "I'll see you again."

Then she closed her eyes, whispered something, and vanished.

Three hours. I couldn't mess with the journal. Instead, I had a small snack, practiced primary essence compression, and then began to read one of the books I had brought with me.

I couldn't focus. My mind was elsewhere.

By the time Ana reappeared to tell me that I was permitted to leave, I wasn't sure I felt like continuing. Nevertheless, I stood, shook myself off, and refocused.

A handicap? No breach essence?

That was fine. I could have pushed Ana for an exchange, but three hours had been long enough to make me feel more stubborn than hurt.

I didn't need a handicap of my own. If she was going to limit me, that just meant it was time to show off something new.

After Ana vanished, I located the spot on the ground that had a Buried seal.

Caerdanel's arms didn't rotate downward enough to fire an arrow at the ground, but the underworld wasn't her domain. Delsen's arms would have rotated, allowing me to adjust him to punch through the floor with his legendary spear, Cessius. I'd have to find the right trap to trigger to cause him to attack, but that didn't seem too difficult. Just time-consuming.

I didn't bother moving the statue. I was done being patient — I'd do this my way.

I drew my sword from my scabbard, then jammed it into the seal and carved. Sparks flew from the impact. The ward cracked and shattered.

Four titan-sized statues moved in unison, readying weapons. A lightning arrow split the air, flashing toward me, but I tore it to shreds with a Shattering Sword, then hopped over a spear thrust and slashed Delsen's weapon to bits.

When he pulled his spear back, I didn't press the attack, even though I was tempted.

Those gods were long dead. My challenges were those born of other makers — ones that still rested below.

Another cleave tore the floor wide, revealing a dark passage.

I caught another of Caerdanel's stone arrows in my hand, ignoring the burn of lightning against my fingers, and shoved it into my scabbard.

You never knew when a divine lightning arrow might be useful.

Then, with a mocking salute to four ancient gods, I hopped into the darkness below.

When I landed heavily and the monsters began to converge, I met them with a jagged smile and a blade that gleamed with silver light.

CHAPTER V

SUBTERRANEAN

I saw the threats before I hit the ground. Six bat-like koshari, their nature apparent through both their large size and their wings formed from elemental power. Two fire-winged beasts, two ice, two lightning. A classic set. They would use their element to attack from a distance or alter the terrain.

Even as I descended, the first wave of their assault was pouring toward me. I tore through fire and lightning with ease, but the ice froze against my sword's blade, and I had to smash it against the ground to clear the growing frost.

That opened me up to the charge from the next of the monsters — a massive bull-like creature with four horns.

The corridor was about twenty feet wide with walls of carved stone, not unlike what I'd read of des'vahi mountain pathways. Support pillars were present every ten feet or so, holding up the ceiling, which was maybe fifteen feet up.

I jumped behind one of the support pillars, hoping to arrest the bull monster's charge. That technically worked, but not in a "bull conveniently rams the pillar and stuns itself" sort of way like I'd expected. Instead, the moment I got behind the pillar, the bull abruptly stopped and stood up on its hind legs, then began to inhale.

Breath attack, I processed immediately. I charged to close the distance.

My unexpected response was the only thing that saved me from the ambush, as a green-skinned humanoid lashed out from the shadows behind the pillar with a jagged obsidian knife.

Even as the knife missed, the small humanoid was vanishing back into the darkness. That creature, at least, I recognized with a hint of concern — a gen, one of the Buried that was descended from the Frog, the Origin Beast of Poison.

Such creatures were the pinnacle of poison themselves — their skin, saliva, and blood were all hideously dangerous in different ways. There were different types of gen, but I didn't have an instant to think about that, because the bull exhaled before I could finish my charge. The creature's breath wasn't flame or ice like I might have expected, but rather a cloud of some kind of gas.

One of the bats was in the way. It turned to stone as the gas flowed over it, then fell to the ground and shattered.

That's bad, I managed to consider as I rushed straight into it.

I flared deflection-aspected sword essence around me, blasting away the gas as it approached my skin. Then, pushing straight through the gas cloud, I swung my sword across the bull's chest.

I didn't bother to wait to see what happened next. One swing, then I was running beyond the bull, getting as far as possible from the petrifying cloud.

I heard the bull collapse behind me in two pieces, but I couldn't feel any relief. I'd hit something in the ground that made a *click*.

I jumped forward. It was the wrong instinct. A scything blade swung down from the ceiling in front of me, and now I was in the middle of its path.

I swung horizontally, tearing the blade in half and sending a flicker of deflection-aspected essence into it on contact.

The two halves of the severed scythe flew wide. One slammed harmlessly into a wall, embedding deep into it. The other, however, tore one of the still-pursuing bat-like monsters in half.

I laughed as I landed.

Got you!

That was, predictably, where the pit I'd jumped to avoid was actually located.

The ground dropped out beneath me, revealing a pit of gleaming spikes. I slammed my sword into the wall as I fell with the flat side facing up, my arms jarred by the force of the impact, but it wasn't a long descent. Even with my quick reaction, my boots brushed the top of the spikes, and the elementally themed bats were rapidly catching up to me.

Sword Hand.

I pulled myself upward with one arm on my sword, then cut into the wall with my Sword Hand, holding myself in place with that. Then I twisted my actual sword and cleaved upward, rotating it to form a handhold again.

One blade after another, I climbed, but I could hear a scraping sound as the pit's cover began to close above me. I reached for the closing ceiling as I approached. If I could get a grip on it, I could pull myself up—

A blast of lightning struck me in the back. Electricity flowed through my body. It wasn't a strong attack — the bats were Candle-level at best — but it was enough. My fingers slipped free of the stone.

The ceiling closed above me.

. . . And the walls began to close in.

Oh, come on. Are you kidding me?

I'd managed to keep hold of my sword, so I was still hanging suspended over the spikes, just below the now-closed roof. I did what came naturally next—

I punched the ceiling, blasting a hole straight through the stone. Again, then again.

The walls closed faster and faster.

Shatter.

I smashed my fist upward, channeling my Shattering Sword through it. The ceiling exploded into pebbles.

I hauled myself up through it, tearing my sword straight through the stone wall as I climbed.

The frog-like gen was there when I came up. He jumped in with a lunge.

I was in no mood for his antics now.

My free hand caught his wrist, a hint of scabbard-aspected essence forming around my hand to protect myself from any contact poison that might pass through my gloves.

Then, as he attempted to slip back with panic in his eyes, I brought my sword down. It passed through the creature's body with no resistance.

Then, I spun, hurling the rapidly dematerializing half of the gen I was still holding on to into the lightning bat that had shot me while I was climbing. The bat screeched as the body slammed into it, falling to the ground. I walked over, ripped a shattered half of the scythe trap out of the wall, and brought it down on the fallen bat.

The other bats fled after that.

Then, briefly, I was alone.

I cracked my neck, rested my sword against my shoulder, and continued walking down the hall.

All that killing, and somehow, the blade still shimmered pure and clear.

In retrospect, perhaps I should have seen that as a warning sooner than I did.

* * *

There were many types of Buried. Each was, in theory, a form of monster descended from — or at least created by — one of the Origin Beasts. They'd all been sealed beneath the world after their progenitor, the Maker of Monsters himself, had been defeated.

I knew of many types of Buried. Rashan, the eight-legged panther-like beasts with skin that resisted cuts and piercing. Illkain, eye-stealing shapeshifters. Vosh, humanoid serpents of stone and steel.

I'd studied the Buried in depth, both due to Gramps's love of history lessons and my own interest in knowing monsters and their weaknesses. I wouldn't say I was a scholar of the Buried, but I'd like to think that I had about as good of an idea as a professional monster hunter, given the advantages of my upbringing and my close proximity to where the Buried had been sealed.

I had no idea what the creature standing at the end of the tunnel was.

It looked vaguely like some kind of great ape — an orangutan, maybe — except it was about twice as big as it should have been and had about three times too many arms.

Each of the six arms held a colossal sword, and on its massive head, it wore a spiked crown.

"Greetings, great one," I said. "You appear to be the lord of this place. I am seeking pass—"

He threw a sword at me. That was rude. I was talking, and also, that was no way to properly treat a sword.

I swept my own sword to the side, attempting to deflect the sword with the smallest possible movement I could, like Red had taught me.

I'd underestimated the force a twelve-foot ape beast could use to throw a weapon. But more than that, I hadn't expected the magic of the blade that made it weigh more than a hundred times what it should have.

When the flat of my sword pressed against the thrown sword, my blade didn't even nudge it. Before it could skewer me, though, I pushed harder, and the force knocked me out of the sword's trajectory.

I stumbled from the sudden shift, then sensed the sword essence of the blade shift behind me. It had flipped around as it passed me, and now it was spinning as it flew backward toward the ape, like a giant bladed boomerang.

I jumped on top of it, stumbling briefly as I steadied myself, then rode the spinning blade as it flew back toward the ape's hand.

The ape snorted audibly as it reached out for the flying blade.

I leapt off the flying sword and brought my blade down in a rapid swing, straight for the monster's head.

Three swords flashed upward at the same time. One parried my strike, my silver meeting steel, and the other two swept straight at my chest.

I tucked my legs upward, letting one sword pass underneath, then kicked the other in the flat, trying to slam it into its own wielder. The sword flew back as I'd hoped, but only an inch — this sword didn't behave like the one he'd thrown, but the ape was still massively strong, even with a single arm.

I'd barely reached the ground when two other arms were swinging at me. I parried them both with my own, but the force of the blow launched me backward, sending me skidding across the ground.

Six arms. Six swords. I don't know what you are, but I'm going to call you an ashur-ape.

I ducked another swing that came without warning, a single sword that tore through the air above me, in spite of the ashur-ape now standing more than a dozen feet away.

He didn't follow up that attack with another from the other swords, though, and I began to see the puzzle.

Middle-right sword can perform cuts at a distance. Classic air slash technique. Top-right sword throws the weighted boomerang sword.

As if responding to my thoughts, he hurled the boomerang sword again. This time, I didn't try to stop it. Instead, I danced behind it and tried to grab the hilt with my free hand, hoping the enchantments on it would respond to a new wielder and allow me to hurl it back.

I felt *something* as my fingers brushed the hilt, a connection, but I couldn't secure my grip quickly enough before it ripped free. Then I was forced to jump as the ashur-ape swung downward with his ranged-cutting sword, cleaving a broad slash into the ground beneath me.

The cleft wasn't deep, but my ankle hit the side of it, causing me to stumble as I landed.

That nearly cost me dearly as the boomerang sword swung back, right toward my neck.

I leaned back, avoiding the cleave, then raised my own sword in the way before it could swing back around. The next spin of the sword crashed into mine, causing me to trip and fall flat on my back.

I hit the ground hard.

And the ashur-ape moved forward for the first time, leaping straight above me and bringing five swords down at once.

I rolled on the ground, five swords smashing downward in a series of cuts that I desperately avoided. I swung upward at the ape's ankle, but it simply stepped disdainfully over my swing, then tried to bury my sword beneath its heel.

I pulled my sword back before it could, then rolled on the ground and hopped to my feet just in time to catch another horizontal swing from the middle-left sword — which hurled me back, straight into one of the cavern walls.

It knocked the wind out of me. I coughed, falling to my knees. That meant that the next ranged swing ended up cleaving the wall right above me rather than tearing me in half.

I'm losing, I realized.

I grinned, tasting blood on my teeth.

I want more.

I charged.

⁂

A testing swing at the knees, parried.

A swing up toward the face, dodged.

A lunge straight at the chest, deflected.

My hands flowed in a rhythm of movement, my feet shifting as I pressed my assault, but I wasn't making headway. Even with superior technique and speed, I was fighting with one sword against six, and any actual gap in our swordsmanship was less significant than I would have hoped.

Has he been training down here? Are there more sword-wielding monsters?

I didn't have time to consider it in detail.

The middle-left sword swept at me and I had to shift my sword beneath it. Absence of blade was a strategy for avoiding unwanted contact between weapons — such as, for example, when your opponent's sword seemed to discharge a burst of force on contact. When his blade crashed into the ground next to me rather than my sword, stone exploded on contact, leaving a wide furrow.

I lunged in again, trying to exploit the opening, but one sword being in the ground just meant that five were still available. He deflected my sword easily.

I side-stepped his next swing, trying to inch in closer. He was strong, fierce, but sloppy. If I could keep tying up his attacks with the terrain—

Another sword slammed into the ground at my side, and I felt a smile cross my face, right up until strange stalagmites of crimson metal shot up from beneath my feet.

I'd like to say I danced backward or something equally elegant, but really, I half stepped and half stumbled. One of the spikes left a gash along the back of my right leg as I retreated, but I managed to twist to avoid letting it pierce all the way through my thigh as it rose from the ground.

Even so, it was a significant wound, the type that could rapidly turn a fight into a failure.

Like, for example, when his middle-left sword flashed straight at my face.

If I'd been stunned by my wound . . . well, I don't know what would have happened, exactly. In theory, the tests were supposed to nonlethal, but accidents happened. Maybe some ancient magic would have teleported me out the moment the blade brushed my face.

I absolutely couldn't count on that.

Fortunately, I wasn't stunned. If anything, the wound had renewed my focus.

I braced myself, favoring my injured leg, and met that sword with my own.

I knew what would come next, because I'd identified which sword he was using. The swing blasted me back with explosive force, carrying me toward one of the chamber walls.

I braced to catch myself with my good leg, ready to launch myself off the wall and straight into another attack—

But the ashur-ape wasn't going to stop with a single attack at a time. He slammed another sword into the wall. The attack was nowhere near me, but it was the same one he'd used a moment before — top left.

Oh, no.

I slammed my sword into the ground to stop my movement just before the spikes shot out of the wall in front of me. I couldn't completely stop my momentum, and I didn't feel like being impaled, so I swept my left hand upward.

Sword Hand.

I cleaved through the protruding spikes before they could impact me, then heard something shifting to my side—

The ashur-ape was swinging again. Middle right.

Still staggering from a rough landing, I dismissed my Sword Hand and grabbed my sword's hilt with both hands, ripping it up from the ground and slicing through the wave of cutting force. His attack ripped to pieces around me, dissipating harmlessly.

I laughed. This was so much fun!

I gave the ashur-ape a winning smile as I stepped closer, ready for his next move.

There must have been something about that smile, because the ashur-ape took a single step back.

He'd switched to a guard stance. Wary.

Good instincts, but a little late.

I knew how four of his swords worked. Maybe not completely, and four swords wouldn't be the full scope of his abilities. Even if I knew how all six functioned, he might have other powers. But I'd seen enough to change my approach, and long battles of attrition weren't my style.

Sword essence flared around my blade.

He was big and strong, powerful and predictable.

Middle right.

His sword struck out before I could come into reach, this time at a diagonal. I released one hand from my grip, just for a moment, and slammed an essence-bearing fist into the side of it.

The shock wave slammed into the ceiling above me, cleaving deep.

Another step forward.

Top right.

He hurled the boomerang-like sword. I stepped around the blade, grabbing the hilt with my off hand.

Scabbard.

My hand formed a cage of scabbard-aspected essence around the sword's grip. Force carried me a step off my path, but I maintained my grip successfully, spinning along with the sword's motion and stepping out of the way of another middle-right sword swing. Then I slammed the boomerang blade into the cavern wall.

It twitched in place, as if trying to wrest itself free. I slammed a hand onto the pommel, driving it deeper, then stepped forward again.

One step, two. More power flowed through me as I moved into the beast's reach, which in spite of my sword's massive size, still exceeded mine.

Middle left.

I gripped my sword in both hands, then stepped to the side, letting the swing miss. He'd anticipated that and his top left sword was already moving, cleaving downward.

Another side-step, then . . .

Bottom right.

His sword came up at my legs—

Then split into pieces, swarming me from all sides.

I hadn't seen this one, didn't know exactly how it worked, but the counter came instantly.

Deflection.

A burst of omnidirectional deflection-aspected sword essence sent the blade bits flying in all directions, then I was moving, leaping as he thrust the top-left sword into the ground.

My sword came down in a diagonal slash, straight for the ashur-ape's chest.

Got you.

He opened his mouth and inhaled. Fire burned within his jaws, forming a blistering sphere in the air. My eyes widened in surprise, but I struck, even as flames roared out of his jaws.

Shattering Sheath.

My sword came down in a single clean cut.

I landed behind the ape, falling to a knee as my bad leg hit the ground, and slammed my sword into the floor to arrest my fall.

Smoke wafted off my tunic, but that was all that had reached me.

"You fought well, bearer of six swords." I winced and pushed myself to my feet.

The ashur-ape was already vanishing behind me.

I'd only connected once, but with the Shattering Sheath, I'd struck it a thousand times.

I finally found a use for that technique, and I'd won the fight.

It was a shame, though.

I sighed out loud as his swords began to vanish. I reached for the closest one, but it disincorporated between my fingers.

I never did figure out what his bottom-left sword did.

With the ashur-ape defeated, I set my sword down against the nearest wall. Unsheathing it from my back was simply too time-consuming to be practical in most situations, and I wasn't sure when I'd be attacked again.

I inspected my injuries next. Most were minimal — tiny scrapes from shrapnel and bruises from slamming into walls and floors. Nothing new, nothing that would significantly slow me down.

The cut on my leg was the exception. "Gash" might have been a better word, more illustrative of the length and depth of the injury. If I wasn't building up sword essence, that glancing blow might have carved through my entire leg.

Even as it was, it wasn't great.

I didn't hesitate to reach into one of the pouches at my side to retrieve one of the most important things in my possession — my single tiny vial of a healing elixir brewed from the waters near Hero's Rest.

Most of my healing brew went toward Verthrimax and my ongoing efforts to restore his sight. While I wasn't around frequently enough to gather the liquid whenever there was enough to brew, Ana had taken up the task in my absence, and Darryl was the one making the healing elixirs when I wasn't around.

That meant that when I'd started working on this one after my visit to the Sepulcher of Sealed Swords, there hadn't been enough of the essence to collect for a full flask. Just a thin vial, more similar in size to what I used for essence collection.

I poured a bit on the wound, wincing as I felt it stinging on contact, then capped it. I hadn't meant to use much, but I'd ended up pouring about half of it onto the gouge, just to make sure I dripped enough to cover the whole surface.

When I was confident that I'd sealed it properly — I'd made the mistake of not doing that before — I slipped the vial back into my waist pouch.

Such a small amount of the healing elixir wouldn't close the wound completely, but it began to knit together and the bleeding slowed. It would also give me a bit of relief from the pain once the stinging went away.

There was a good chance I'd tear the thing back open completely if I moved in the wrong way. I considered stitching it, but healing elixirs didn't get on well with stitches in my experience. Instead, I applied a heavy herbal poultice, the same thing I usually used on my injuries when the elixir wasn't available. It was a paste that helped accelerate healing on its own, but it also had a consistency that was slightly adhesive, meaning that I was basically gluing the wound shut.

With that done, I wrapped the wound, then tested my leg by pressing it hard against the ground.

I nearly fell over as my vision went red.

Okay, wow. Uh, bad idea.

I took a couple deep breaths, steadying myself, then went to pick up my sword and rested it against my shoulder, polearm-style.

No quick jumps. No rapid movements. No—

Something burst free from the wall to my right. I swung around toward it, slicing it in half before I even thought about it.

Two pieces of the monster fell to the ground, vanishing as I stumbled and landed.

. . . Or, you know, I could just take a break.

I groaned, pulling off my backpack, washed my hands, and had lunch inside the lair.

⊱ ⊰

I pulled my backpack back on, slowly pushing myself to my feet using my now-sheathed sword for leverage. During my meal, I'd come to the conclusion that using my sword as a walking stick was more important for the immediate future than having it ready for a fight. I'd lose a moment to draw, but I was going to continuously hurt myself if I didn't support my leg somehow.

That wasn't the only thing I'd found during my brief pause, though.

While I was eating, I'd noticed something that had blended into the floor — a strangely flat stone that was just where the ashur-ape had fallen.

I dragged myself over to inspect it. It was tough to see in the dark, with only a hint of illumination from the gleaming hilt of my sword and a tiny bit of ambient light with no clear source. I had to lean in very close to see the details, which was often a trap, but in this case, I'd gotten lucky.

It was a coin. A stone coin that had something I couldn't quite make out etched into the surface.

Is that . . . oh, I think that's a picture of the ashur-ape. That's fun. Some kind of text, too, but I can't read it in the dark.

I dropped the coin into my empty pouch, then groaned as I picked myself back up.

Wonder what that's for. Is there a shop in here somewhere that uses weirdly specific coins? Some kind of room that uses the coins as keys? Is it a minor magical item?

Any of those was possible, or some combination, or something different. I didn't worry about it. I'd probably find a place where I could get it identified later.

I continued down the hall in the direction I'd started, still using my sheathed sword as a walking stick. A moment of memory made me miss the stick I'd made for the very first time I'd attempted this shrine, one that was much more suited to this kind of physical support than a colossal greatsword was.

I still didn't know how that stick had been broken. But if I succeeded today, perhaps I'd find out.

The walking was a little easier now that I'd taken a chance to rest and eat.

As long as I don't run into any more challenges that require pushing my leg too hard, I should recover a bit more as I move.

I reached the end of the cavern with no further difficulty, finding a ramp that led up toward a door. I checked it for obvious traps, finding none, and swung it open. Then I let off a string of expletives.

There was no floor in the next room, just an endless black void with two dozen floating platforms above it.

I had, of course, limped directly into a platform-jumping puzzle.

I genuinely considered turning back.

This is something I don't say often. I do not, as a general rule, turn back on things. I overcommit. To people, to ideas, to attacks.

It says something about just how badly hurt my leg was, as well as how much I was not in the mood for whatever special flavor of obnoxiousness the color-coded platforms had in store, that I even contemplated walking back down the hall and trying another path.

Ultimately, the sunk cost won out. I told myself that walking all the way back down the corridor would hurt me in terms of fatigue and chances that re-forming monsters would strike again while I was weakened. Really, though?

It was *mostly* that I wasn't good at turning back, even when I should. If this story has a theme, or you're looking for integral flaws in my childhood self, that's probably a good one to put on the list.

My eyes scanned the room as I slipped my sheathed sword into the harness on my back. I was going to need to jump several times. Jumping with a huge sword on your back is bad, but not generally as bad as jumping while holding said colossal sword. It depends on your center of balance and all that, but in my experience, it's easier to balance a jump — and a landing — with both hands free to wheel frantically in the air while you panic and try not to fall into the abyssal dark.

Not that I did that a lot, mind you. Once, twice a week, at most.

After that, I punched the stone wall.

No, not because I was angry and hurting. Maybe a little, actually. But mostly for the utility of it.

I broke a chunk off the wall, evaluating.

There were twenty-four platforms. That wasn't as common a number in fae culture as three or seven, but it was still potentially deliberate. Even numbers in general tend to have significance to some degree or another, and in the case of twenty-four, it had the extra significance of being exactly twice the number of prime dominions and half the number of deep dominions.

At first, I'd thought there were only a few colors for the bottoms of the platforms. Once I counted the platforms, I realized I was mistaken. There were a few *gradients* of colors. In particular, they were all mixes of black, white, green, and red. In some cases, the tiles had two colors, a split down the middle. Red and green, black and white, black and green, that sort of thing.

There were several ways colors could be associated with dominions. Rethri eye colors, for example, were a common palette associated with the dominions in general. A less common system, however, was more applicable to certain types of elementals and more favored in scholarly circles due to the emphasis on grouping the colors based on dominion "quadrants."

Red, blue, green, and brown were the base colors in the four-quadrant system. Fire, water, air, and stone, respectively. Then, darker and lighter versions for associated primes, going as far as black for death and white for life.

I saw those. I also saw some mixtures of green and red.

Let's hope Ana just was in a painting mood, but . . .

I threw a rock at a nearby platform that showed what looked like a mix of green and red.

I missed.

I cursed, then broke off another rock and threw it. That time it landed right on top, skittered a bit, but stayed without falling off.

Nothing happened. I took a calming breath.

Okay, good. Might just be decorative coloring, or—

A tiny crystal flashed in the center of the platform, then a blast of lightning flashed down from the ceiling to slam directly into that spot. Smoke rose from the surface, as well as the slightly charred-looking rock.

. . . Or there's a delay between something hitting the platform and the trap triggering.

I sighed.

This is going to be an absolute pain, isn't it?

The platforms moved back and forth, anywhere between two feet and six feet to jump between them. Most were on the same level as my starting point, but some floated higher or lower.

They weren't very large platforms — just enough space to stand on, plus maybe one extra pace for movement. Not enough for a running start, but enough that maybe someone slightly larger could stand comfortably. And a walking start was better than a standing one, if only barely.

I threw several more rocks. The next two that successfully landed on the lightning platform triggered it in the same way before — a slight delay, about a second, then the trap went off.

I turned to another platform, more distant, and tried a few throws to break the central crystal, hoping to disarm the trap.

The good news is that I broke the crystal on my second throw.

Nailed it! Looks like I can disarm them that way.

The platform dropped from the sky.

. . . Oh.

I disarmed too hard.

I frowned at the fallen platform.

. . . Guess that route is out. Or . . . a lot more awkward, at least.

More testing, then.

The cycling time as the platforms moved back and forth was greater than that — about three seconds for the full movement. Meaning that if I landed on a platform, and if I wanted to jump before the trap hit me, I didn't have time to wait for the next platform to get into the optimal position.

More rocks while I considered . . . until I managed to land two rocks on the lightning platform only a second or two apart.

The second one didn't trigger the platform.

I blinked. Then I tried again, and again.

The trap has a cooldown period between activations. If I trigger it early with a rock, I can potentially jump right afterward without risking it.

Carrying twenty-four-plus rocks was impractical. But I didn't need to jump on every single platform to make it across the room.

The quickest path was six jumps. That would require one jump that also went *up*, and one jump that went *down*, adding risk.

The next-quickest was eight jumps in a straight line.

Both of those would miss the treasure chest hidden on top of one of the platforms that I could just barely make out, obscured by the movement of other platforms. That one was near the uppermost part of the room, requiring several upward jumps.

And if I looked carefully downward . . . there was one platform that wasn't moving with the rest. It was right up against the wall on the left side of the room, requiring jumping down several platforms, getting ever closer to falling into the void. It was the longest path, requiring twelve perfect jumps, and it led to seemingly nothing of use. Just what looked like an ordinary wall.

It should be obvious where I was going.

I hurled a rock, then surged into motion.

Lightning slammed into the first platform, then I landed, wheeling my hands.

The platform ahead was already moving away, not toward me.

One, two . . .

Throw.

My rock missed, but my cooldown was up.

I jumped just as lightning flashed behind me, then landed on the next platform—

One that was ahead of me, but also a step downward, toward the void.

Light red and green. That means—

I ignored the sound of something moving behind me, hoping I was right, throwing a rock at the next platform beneath me. I didn't get a good look at the colors, but the rock landed. Black flames burst from the square, surging upward.

Then the rock was gone.

I jumped. No waiting on that one. I took a step, judged my distance, then jumped again.

I almost missed. Instead, I barely hit the back end of the platform, then started tilting backward.

I kicked my good foot downward, generating a blade of force from my foot. It jammed into the platform like a spike, steadying me, but that left me wobbling in place when the trap triggered.

Plain green, which means—

A blast of air slammed into me from behind, pushing me forward. I stumbled, but my blade embedded in the platform held. Rather than jumping immediately, I held against the sudden wind, letting it die down . . . then noticed that the next platform wasn't *just* down, but farther away than the others.

Oh. I get it. For this one . . .

I let myself withstand the next couple wind cycles, finding good footing, then, as the next platform came as close as possible, I released my spike.

I braced, seeing the flash of the trap trigger, then jumped.

The blast of wind still slammed into me, just as I'd hoped. It carried me the extra half dozen feet I needed to reach the platform below.

I hit the next platform hard, pain surging through my leg. I dropped the rest of my rocks. They clattered into darkness that was matched by the plain black color of the platform beneath me.

Death.

That's not a great thing to land on.

Deflection!

An aura of deflection-aspected sword essence flashed over me. It wasn't much, but that was about the amount of time I had to brace before the platform's sphere flashed—

An aura of dark washed over me and . . .

Nothing else. I felt a little cold, maybe. My deflection aura flickered slightly, I think? Might have been my imagination.

I frowned.

Defective trap? Just a weaker one? A delayed effect?

Huh.

I waited for it to trigger again, curious.

Yes, I waited for the possible instant death trap to get another try on me.

Once again, I felt nothing when it happened.

I tapped on it with my foot, then shrugged.

Weird.

Might be the deception trap, disguised as the death one? That's possible, I guess, or . . . maybe death magic just isn't very effective against me?

I took my time on that one, resting a bit while what looked like death magic blasted me without any obvious effect.

From there, the next few jumps were significantly easier. Probably because whoever had designed it expected the death magic to be, you know, deadly. Or at least debilitating.

Jump. Close my eyes before the flash of light.

Jump. Deflect a beam of vitality magic with sword essence.

Jump. Ignore the weird voice whispering behind me.

I braced myself, jumped, landed . . . and a burst of flame rippled from below me immediately, without the usual delay.

I still had my deflection-aspected aura on from the death platform. If I hadn't, that might have been the end of my journey, right there. As it was, sword essence wasn't a perfect defense against fire, especially at point-blank range.

My pants caught fire.

I hissed in pain, but I couldn't wait to extinguish them.

The platform beneath me *wobbled.*

I jumped for the final platform, which stood stationary just next to the wall.

I missed.

My legs wheeled in the air. My fingers grasped for the platform.

They missed, too.

No.

A memory of a dream flashed through my mind.

Sword Hand: Segmented Slash.

A blade manifested from my fingers, then split into chain-like segments, jamming into the bottom of the platform. The platform trembled for a moment as my blade sank in. I hit the maximum extension of the chain a moment later, my whole weight dragging on it, but both blade and platform held.

I took a breath, focusing on my essence, retracting the chain and letting it drag me upward. I felt cracks forming as the essence strained to move me, and I braced to cut into the nearby wall, but the chain held long enough for my fingers to grasp the edge of the platform.

I pulled myself up, then patted out the flames on my legs. Fortunately, the burns were minor — more like mild to moderate sunburns. Sword essence contained flame as a component, which gave me a degree of resistance through my secondary essence, but the deflection aura had probably done more to guard me than my inherent defense had.

I debated healing myself further, but I didn't trust my platform to stay steady. Instead, I took a deep breath and steadied myself.

I made it. Phew.

Then the wall leaned forward and tried to eat me.

Aaaaaaah!

I punched the wall in the still-forming mouth, instinctively sending a surge of essence through my fist.

The center of the wall exploded outward, then the remainder of that section of the wall followed, a perfect square of "wall" collapsing into rubble.

"Walls should not eat, Ana!" I yelled. "Walls do not bite people!"

I thought I heard a distant giggle, but it was probably my imagination.

My hands clenched in the air, then unclenched. I kicked one of the bits of the wall, just in case, but it seemed like it had returned to being ordinaryish stone after my counterstrike obliterated the center.

I found another stone coin among the debris. In the better lighting of the room, I could see the image of a hungry wall, as well as the writing on it.

Anathema-Brand Wall Mimic Coin.

I groaned, picking up the coin and putting it into my bag alongside the ashur-ape one.

I took a breath, looked up at the other platforms, still wheeling above me . . . and the gap where the platform behind me had fallen.

If I'd tried to use the chain more, perhaps I could have climbed back up to reach another platform, or even made my way to the treasure box at the top.

Nope. I'm done with this room. Very, very done.

I stepped through the wall into what looked like a tranquil forest ahead.

Looks safe, like a perfect place to rest.

That, of course, meant that, compared to the obvious threats of the last couple rooms, the next chamber would be much, much worse.

CHAPTER VI

SUNDOWN

I stepped into the peaceful glade, momentarily raising an arm to shield myself from the sudden change in the scene. The last room had been better lit than the buried cavern, but this was more like daylight, rather than a moderately lit dungeon room.

I took a breath of the fresh air, marveling at the floral scents. Even knowing how dungeons worked, it was hard to disbelieve my senses. The scents, the sight of the trees and the grass, the way the loam shifted beneath my boots — none of it felt like I was *indoors*.

It was hard to believe that the sun shining overhead was illusory, even if it was strangely pointed, and perhaps a little overly direct in the way that it cast its rays between the boughs of the great trees.

The trees themselves were colossal, some of them nearly high enough to touch the sky. In the distance, I could also see what looked like a mountaintop, which climbed even higher than the trees.

A destination, maybe? Might lead into another cavern-style area.

I took a moment to draw my sword out of my scabbard, given how unsettling the place was, and rested it against my shoulder like a polearm. I secured my scabbard in the harness on my back.

Will have to take this very slow if I'm not supporting my leg while I walk.

When no immediate threats presented themselves, I took a drink from the flask of water on my hip, knowing that breaks were not going to be common or guaranteed once I started moving. Then, I took a closer look at the area, first with my ordinary vision, then with my Viewing Point active.

My ordinary sight took in a couple more details upon more extensive inspection. The strangely shaped sun's rays were casting polygonal bursts of light, all of nearly identical dimensions, illuminating distinct sections of the forest floor.

I am, like, ninety percent sure light doesn't work like that.

Examining those sections at this distance didn't get me anything new, but I intuited that they were likely part of a puzzle, rather than merely serving as ambience for the area.

Each of the lit sections was about ten feet in diameter. Large enough to stand in and move around a bit, perhaps to fight or solve a puzzle. I could see about six of them from my current vantage point at the cave exit.

Maybe I'm only supposed to walk in the light? They seem too far apart for that, though. I suppose a faerie could fly between them, but that looks like . . . thirty feet or so? Hm. I don't think I could jump that consistently or accurately. Maybe if I had a movement technique . . .

I doubted the test would rely on that sort of thing, but having certain "safe" sections of the forest seemed similar to the first challenge, so I couldn't discount it as a possibility.

What else could the light be for?

The rays of light seemed to avoid most of the trees, but when they did pass through the leaves of the forest, some of the leaves gleamed and glowed softly.

Are some of those trees made of glass or crystal? Huh. Could be another puzzle piece there.

I took a closer look at the area with Star Shattering Sight active. The entire sky rippled and wavered ominously a hundred feet above me, beyond the tallest trees. The sight startled me enough that I almost attacked the sky — don't judge me — but I calmed myself as I realized that I was probably just seeing a boundary of the dungeon itself. Unlike the simulated interior areas, this one didn't have a "roof" to obscure my vision, meaning I could see where the extradimensional space ended. That was what I needed to avoid striking with my breach essence if I wanted to avoid another catastrophe — well, that and any other border that might be hidden, like if another was just beneath the forest floor.

If I dug a couple feet, I wonder if I'd hit another boundary of the space, or if I'd hit something like another Buried-style cavern.

I glanced at the ground for weak points, trying to see if there were any obvious pitfalls, but I didn't find any. Similarly, I didn't find any obvious vulnerabilities in the trees.

I dismissed my Star Shattering Sight, frowning.

Where were the challenges? The dangers? Would they appear later?

I felt like I was missing something, but I didn't want to wait forever — the test easily could be timed.

Instead, I advanced. When nothing happened after my first step forward into the forest, I continued at a steady pace until I reached the first section of light. Cautiously, I stuck my scabbard into the light. Nothing strange happened. I reached in with a gloved hand. No extreme heat — the glass-like leaves weren't magnifying the light into dangerous beams — and no other obvious effects.

I stepped in. Nothing.

Huh.

I poked around at the ground for a minute, seeing if there was something like a buried key in the center of the light or anything similar, but I didn't find anything.

I pulled out my hand mirror. The light behaved normally, allowing me to reflect it into a beam in various directions. Illuminating the trees revealed more crystalline leaves, but no obviously hidden switches.

After another minute of testing, I put the mirror back, adjusted the sword against my shoulder, then moved on toward the next light at a jog.

Another quick test, then I stepped in. Nothing unusual.

I took a few more moments to search again, finding nothing but grass and dirt.

Is . . . this just a break between dangerous rooms? A reward for taking the secret passage behind the wall mimic?

I shook my head. It wasn't impossible — dungeons could have rest areas and interstitial regions without threats — but I didn't think I'd gone far enough to warrant that yet. Most likely, there would be something unusual farther ahead, or a hidden danger that was already present. A monster stalking behind me that had started moving shortly after I left the cave, or perhaps something where the scenic setting would create an impression of safety for a while, only to break from that pattern.

The third light stood out to me as a possible change for that. Threes were important.

I tested the light. Nothing felt different. I stepped in, then knelt down to dig for a key.

I'd only been digging for a few moments when I realized something had changed.

Is it me, or is it getting warmer? And . . . a little brighter?

I stood up, glancing around to search for enemies. There was nothing obvious, but . . .

Was that next light always this close?

I turned around, finding that the previous light I'd come from also looked just a little bit closer than it had been. It was subtle, but—

I spun around, and this time I caught it.

The beam of light froze the moment I looked at it, like a kid caught playing with off-limits knives in the middle of the night.

And, much like such a child, the light didn't freeze for long. Oh, no.

Once noticed, the pillar of light bolted. Or, pillars, rather. All at once, the lights shifted and began to converge toward my location, refocusing and beginning to overlap. And as the pillars joined with each other, they brightened—

And the forest began to burn.

Oh, resh it all.

When the sky is trying to murder you, there are certain logical things to do.

Gramps's truism that one should "run, hide, lie, or die" didn't fully apply here, but the first couple options were pretty good, all things considered. But I had a wounded leg, and moreover, I'd never been very good at following directions.

I swung my sword straight through the first beam of light, my blade's aura scattering it. This interrupted the flow of the beam for a heartbeat, but much like you'd expect, it didn't cut the sunbeam.

I wasn't good enough for that. Not yet.

With that failure, the other beams inched closer, and I moved to my next plan — I ran as quickly as my wounded leg could carry me.

Always stay on the path in an unfamiliar place, the wisdom of the fae told me.

The wisdom of the fae didn't have a lot to say about when the path had animated and decided to kill you, which was surprising, given how frequently that type of thing could happen in faerie lands.

There were options on where I could run. The cavern behind me wasn't impossibly far. I also had a pretty good idea of the direction the lights had been leading as a trail before they'd converged.

But backtracking was boring, and if the light was feeling actively murderous, I didn't really feel like following its directions. And so, with the sun burning the trees to ashes in pursuit, I plunged into the depths of the dark.

⁂

I couldn't run very far, but I didn't need to. The lights faded into the distance behind me, ceasing their pursuit rapidly once I'd stepped off the trail into the dark.

Maybe I'd solved a puzzle by choosing the dark, but I didn't think so. Not with all the growling and the glowing red eyes that I could see faintly in the distance around me, watching.

No, I didn't think I'd solved anything by running. I'd simply run somewhere so dangerous that the light itself feared to follow.

What sort of creatures lived in a terrifying place like that? How could I overcome such a threat?

After a few moments of panting and recovering my breath, I took the logical step of turning toward the eyes, waving cheerfully, and saying, "Hello!"

The eyes vanished rapidly upon being addressed. Apparently, the dark creatures of the wood weren't feeling chatty. I hoped I hadn't upset them.

With no imminent danger, I glanced backward. I could see faint spots of light in the distance, but the forest fires themselves weren't visible. Perhaps I'd run far enough that the magical darkness was blocking it out, or perhaps the dungeon had done something to extinguish the flames. I knew there had to be mechanisms for resetting areas after someone had explored them, otherwise the dungeon wouldn't work for repeat visitors, but Ana had always been cagey about how those mechanisms worked.

I spent a bit of time inspecting my leg wound again. I had, of course, reopened my wound immediately, and I needed to rebandage it.

Can't keep running with my leg like this, I'm going to cause more damage.

I resheathed my sword, then went back to using it as a walking stick, prodding the ground in front of me to help avoid roots, rocks, and other things I might trip over. With only the faint silvery glow of my sword's hilt to illuminate the dark, I began to explore.

⊹⊹ ⊹⊹

The darker part of the woods was peaceful at first, but I knew that wouldn't last. Without the overt threat of the sunbeams, there would be something else to make the place a challenge — perhaps the creatures I'd spotted, or something subtler. Something like, for example, the ground collapsing while I was busy looking for the sources of the eyes.

I felt the ground tremble as my sword tapped the dirt, jumping back in alarm. Pain shot through my injured leg as I landed, but I felt the earth shift in front of me. I continued to retreat until I hit a tree and grabbed on.

The tremors continued for some time, but the tree remained rooted in place.

I took several breaths, clinging to the tree with one arm while I prodded at the ground — or, rather, the lack thereof — in the direction I'd been walking.

Gone.

Vek.

I awkwardly clambered around the side of the tree, which seemed to stand at the precipice of a pit now, and prodded at the air with my sword until I hit solid ground.

This isn't working. I can't navigate like this.

Now that I was on steady stone, I took a moment to consider my plan.

Moving randomly in the dark wasn't going to work, especially if there were more pits. It was possible the pits themselves were a route I could follow — maybe they'd take me back down into the caverns of the Buried, in a different location — but that felt like the type of thing that would lead to backtracking, not forward in the dungeon.

The obvious thing, of course, was to get myself a source of light. I had flint, steel, and oil in my backpack — fire starting would be easy. But I had a strong feeling that adding extra illumination to the area would attract unwanted threats, possibly including the killing sky beams from the lighter part of the forest.

Maybe the light traps have reset by this point? I could head back that way and see if they stand still if I avoid them.

It was an option, but I wasn't thrilled with it — there was too much of a chance that they hadn't reset, and if they hadn't, at best I'd be right back to running and reopening my leg wound.

I wasn't out of reasonable options. I could have tried to climb down one side of a pit, then back out the opposite side to proceed from there.

I thought of my hand mirror. When there were puzzles involving light, reflecting it was often a solution. I could have, perhaps, tricked the light beams into focusing somewhere I wasn't, or into carving a path through the dark.

I could have taken a Threatseer Tonic to enhance my senses, using it to help navigate through the darkness safely, avoiding any further pits more easily as I sought a destination.

None of those solutions appealed to me, nor did the other safe ideas that I came up with.

Ultimately, if this trial was supposed to be a representation of who I was, I needed to solve it in a way that suited me.

I wouldn't run or hide. Not for long, anyway.

No, I'd fall back on my first instinct and execute it more appropriately.

If the sun itself was my enemy, I would hunt down and conquer the sun.

I trudged back to the border of the light part of the woods, then moved through the darkness alongside that area. The lights had reverted to their original positions — or, at least, their original spacing. My awareness of the terrain wasn't quite good enough to tell me if they were in exactly the same spots they started, but I saw some trees that I thought I recognized as landmarks, and the relative positions of the light seemed similar.

I kept within the dark, making sure that there were trees between myself and the fonts of killing light. As I advanced, I reached a point where the light split, offering a simple path along what looked like a paved road and a rougher path that led toward the hillside I'd seen from the start.

Perfect.

I followed alongside the second path, keeping to the dark.

I'd been moving for several minutes when I saw the eyes following me from a distance, deeper in the dark woods.

I nodded in the direction of the eyes, acknowledging them, and kept moving. They didn't retreat this time. I wasn't sure if that was a good or a bad sign.

The rough path through the woods gave way to a rocky mountain road, one that felt almost familiar. There was just one problem—

The dark woods ended at the base of the mountain path. There would be no hiding from the sun here.

Well, I'm in too deep now to turn back. I could backtrack, but that would waste like . . . ten whole minutes of my life. Not a chance.

I gave the glowing eyes one last friendly wave.

I heard a distant howl in response — one that drew my gaze up toward the darker parts of the skies. And there, far away, was something I couldn't have seen with the light pollution of the sun at the entrance—

Hidden beyond the clouds was a brightly glowing moon, beautiful and full.

For a moment, I considered abandoning my plan to investigate. Wolflike howling at the moon sounded like a potential way to make some new friends, but I'd set my mind to a hunt, and I wasn't going to give it up so easily.

I stepped out of the darkness and into the comparative illumination of the path. Not directly into one of the sunbeams, of course — just into the brighter area of the forest. I could still see the strangely pointed sunbeams all around, but they seemed to be frozen in place, at least for now.

For several heartbeats, I waited, watching.

Then, with no sign that I'd alerted them, I began to climb the mountain road. As I climbed, I realized that caves dotted the hillside in several locations. Other entrances to this area, perhaps, or exits. Or monster lairs.

I ignored them.

The sun was still shining brightly above — *directly* above — the top of the mountain.

I was just starting to feel a bit confident when I stepped through a beam of light in my path. One of the crystal trees had shed its leaves, and one of those leaves stood at just the right angle for the crystal to refract a line into my path.

I felt very much like I'd stepped through one of those light beams that sets off the magical alarm in an ancient Xixian vault. There was no audible noise, no gigantic doors slamming shut, but I was close enough to see it clearly this time—

The sun itself turning in my direction, angry beams beginning to converge on my spot.

The caves, I processed immediately. *They'd be safe.*

But I was already running, and not toward them. I sprinted straight through the first beam of light, feeling the warmth of it against my skin, but not enough of the beams had converged to burn me to cinders. Within a moment, I was through it, more lights following in pursuit. Behind me, there was no wood to burn on this mountainside—

Instead, as I ran, and more lights focused, the rocks were blackening, and the crystalline trees were being reduced to molten glass.

I reached the top of the mountain with my leg in agony, nearly springing straight off the side as I continued to angle toward the sun.

I'd gauged it just a little wrong, looking from below.

The murderous sun wasn't sitting conveniently above the top of the mountain. Not exactly.

Upon getting closer, I could see it more clearly — a three-meter-wide prism thrumming with power, with hundreds of facets that each created their own rays of blinding luminescence.

More important than the sun's true size and shape, however, was its location. And, of course, the seeming impossibility of reaching that place.

It was floating about twenty feet above a gigantic hole in the center of the mountain, which descended into some other type of cavern below. I could feel blistering heat from that cavern, even as I approached it, but I had no time to search for the source. The strange sun's killing beams were right behind me. And, given the prismatic nature of the sun, others were converging in front of me as well.

I couldn't slow down. I ran toward the sun, my heart hammering in my chest.

I'm here, and I can't reach it. I'd need a ranged attack, and I've never managed to master the art of sending a cutting wave out of my sword. Unless . . .

I charged, raising my sword, channeling essence through it as I moved.

Instead, I pulled desperately from the unsealed power in my right hand, fueling my technique with my sword's rampaging power. Unbridled essence flooded through my body, the silvery aura around my sword blasting outward into a rippling blade three times the length of the weapon.

I laughed.

At least if I die, it'll be after cutting the sun out of the sky.

Let's call this new one . . .

Star Severing Sword.

I brought my sword down, landing hard on the other side of the chasm. I barely managed to jam it into the ground to steady myself before I fell backward, pain surging through my injured leg.

For a moment, I felt warmth on my back, as the sun's accusing beams glanced toward me—

I turned to meet the sun's gaze, my eyes narrowed to avoid the brilliant light, as the glimmering disc slid into two pieces and fell from the sky.

CHAPTER VII

SHOP

I let out a little cheer of victory. What? That's allowed. I'd cut down the sun, okay? I'm allowed to have a good time with that.

After that, I fumbled around for a bit, because I was, you know, almost completely blind. It turns out that cutting down an area's only major source of illumination makes it hard to see. Who knew?

I had light sources with me, of course, mostly in my backpack. Instead of doing the sensible thing and trying to light a torch or something, I carefully turned toward the pit in the center of the mountain, where the sun had fallen.

I had an adventurer's instincts, even then. And by that, I mean that I wasn't planning on going anywhere else until I'd looted the thing that had very nearly killed me.

Looking into the gap, I could see glittering shards of the dying sun. They still glowed brightly, implying that each individual piece held essence, rather than it being an object powered by some kind of core.

That was a good thing. The whole "exploded into bits" part was a bit disappointing, though. Anything made out of solid essence of that size would have been ludicrously valuable. As it was, it looked more like someone had made a prism by connecting flat plates, like a hollow gaming die. Each piece would still be valuable, but there would be fewer pieces, and it was less likely to be as absurdly essence-dense as if it had been a single complete solid.

All that was ignoring the problem — the pit was glowing with something else, too. Heat. At a closer look, I realized that this wasn't just supposed to be a hollow mountaintop. I was basically at the edge of a simplistic rendering of a volcanic crater. It wasn't quite as realistic as the forest, which was clearly by design. There were some segments that visibly glowed with heat, and bits of what looked like molten magma at the bottom, but there were also clear platforms both along the pit and floating in midair.

This was designed to be another platforming segment. Somewhere I could descend, either for treasure or to reach another area. Possibly both.

Another look at my leg, even in the poor illumination, told me that a lot of jumping was going to be a very bad idea. Still, I wasn't quite ready to abandon my loot, so I settled on a middle ground. I found a segment on the wall of the pit without any glowing heat, unslung my backpack, and retrieved my rope, hammer, and pitons.

A few minutes of work later, I had my rope secured on the top of the pit and looped carefully around my waist. I'd fully sheathed my sword on my back — I couldn't carry it effectively while climbing.

I didn't rappel down the side like I might have if I'd been focused on speed. Instead, I climbed downward using my upper body almost exclusively, trying to avoid more damage to my leg or kicking in any segments of the mountain wall that might be less steady than they looked.

The first safe platform on my route wasn't too far down — only twenty feet or so. With my durability, I normally could have just jumped that far without harm, but my injury precluded that. I stopped for just a second on that platform to test if it was the type that did anything strange, like dropping or trying to eat me. Fortunately, the platform itself remained stationary. That would be important if I had to make a quick retreat.

From there, I shifted my rope and kept climbing down farther that way, rather than trying to jump from platform to platform. My rope was about sixty feet, with more like fifty-eight feet of usable length after securing it. There weren't any safe spots perfectly at that distance, but I stopped on another platform about forty-five feet down, tested it for safety, then unlooped the rope from my waist.

At that point, I got to looting.

Each individual shard was about the size of my forearm. They were sharp, irregular in shape, and bright enough that I couldn't look directly at them without blinding myself.

I couldn't tell exactly what mana type they represented or how powerful they were, but if I was right about them being raw essence of any kind — even something as common as light — shards of that size would be tremendously valuable. Each one was probably worth a dozen essence vials in trade, at least. And if they were something more esoteric, like literal sun essence?

Even a single one probably would have been worth a trip into a deadly dungeon. At least for a normal person, under normal circumstances.

I had greater ambitions, but I certainly wasn't going to complain about finding some treasure beyond what I'd originally come for.

There were only a few shards in immediate reach of where I'd lowered myself down, but they were so large that I couldn't carry many, anyway. I shoved three of them in my backpack, then after a bit of hesitation, jumped to another nearby platform to grab one more.

That platform *trembled*.

"Oh, come on." I snatched the one shard of sun, glanced at my options, then immediately jumped back where I came from.

It was a long way down, and honestly, I didn't want to deal with wherever the lava ladder was leading.

I landed back on the safe platform with a stumble and a wince, then shoved the piece of sun in my backpack.

From there, I went fishing.

Not literally, of course. I didn't even have a fishing pole or a spear with me. Instead, I had a very large sword and a somewhat functional technique for extending my reach.

Trying to reach for glowing shards of light with a phantasmal blade extending from a real one wasn't a very efficient gathering method, but I had a very hard time letting go of things when I could see them. And there were two more glowing pieces of the sun just barely out of convenient reach.

My first several attempts just pushed the glittering pieces around, often making further retrieval attempts worse. Eventually, though, I got the hang of thrusting just below the shards, then gently lifting upward. I caught one piece that way, but dislodged the second badly enough that it fell beneath my platform.

From there, I tucked the one I'd retrieved away, then descended just a bit more on my rope, holding my sword in one hand.

It took a lot of fumbling to get the fallen shard to flip back upward onto the platform, but eventually, I got it. My arms were aching almost as much as my leg by the end of it.

I climbed back onto the safe platform, grabbed the sixth shard of the sun, and cut my losses. There was a seventh piece down there somewhere, but I wasn't going to find it. Not right away.

I packed away the shards in my backpack and climbed out of the volcanic crater.

I almost missed the stone coin when I was packing up to leave. As expected, it had a symbol of a setting sun on it.

I frowned at it briefly before picking it up. Something about that symbol bothered me in a way I couldn't understand. Maybe it was just that I hadn't seen the coin when I'd first started searching the area?

It felt deeper, like a memory, but one I couldn't quite grasp. Maybe it had something to do with the memories I'd lost from previous dungeon expeditions. Dismissing the strangeness, I put the coin away with the others.

Then, with stolen light, I gazed ahead toward a new path that led away from the mountaintop. I found that each of the individual sun pieces would focus its brilliance in one direction if held at certain angles, and with that, I could navigate. As I used one to scan the terrain ahead, I gawked at a sight I couldn't have expected.

On the other side of the mountain, there was a *town*.

The town was somewhat less impressive when I arrived. And by that, it was less of a town and more of a facade.

The three dozen buildings I'd seen from the mountaintop? Most of them were wooden structures representing the front of a building, with only shoddy frames for the other three sides to keep them from falling over. Most of them did have rough ceilings of some kind, but it looked like a stiff breeze would cause them to collapse.

I stared mournfully at the sign for a "Ana's Arms and Armor," muttered something about her being a "vile temptress," and stepped back away.

Not even the *door* on that one was real.

As I explored, I realized it was possible that this entire town might have only existed for the purpose of being visible as a landmark from the distance. I'd found a route ahead to another part of the dungeon already, after all — I'd just chosen to avoid it. And it was very possible there had been another viable route back on my original trail, before I'd started messing with the sunlight.

But again, I didn't like to abandon things after I'd found them. I liked searching for clues.

Also, I hated backtracking, and my leg hurt.

So, with all those factors in play, I began to test the doors on each of the obviously fake businesses.

The Inn and Out? Nope. Fake.

Magnificent Magical Menagerie? Super fake.

Find Your Fate and Fortune?

Fa—

The knob turned on the door.

Probably still fake, I considered. *Fortune-tellers usually are. But the building, at least, isn't empty.*

I rapped three times softly on the old wood, then turned the doorknob the rest of the way. A bell rang inside and, instinctively, I dodged to the right — but there was no arrow trap, no immediate doom from my lack of caution.

Instead, a voice came from the inside. "Come in, come on in! Welcome, brave traveler!"

Ana's voice, albeit with her obviously pretending at an older one.

Role-playing? Hm.

A drape of golden cloth covered the entryway. I took a deep breath, stepped forward, and pushed it out of the way to clear my path inside.

I cautiously stepped inside to find the interior surprisingly similar to the dimensions of the humble hut's exterior. I had to duck to get in the doorway and tilt my sword downward to avoid hitting anything on the way in.

I brushed past the silks to find a dark room ahead with a clear light source — a crystal ball sitting on the middle of a table beside a deck of cards.

Ana sat on the opposite side of the table, dressed in elegant traveler's silks but accented by an ill-fitting witch's hat. I wondered if she'd conjured that or borrowed it from one of the witches.

Ordinarily, pretending to be a witch was a pretty terrible idea, given the possibility of offending an actual witch — or worse, amusing one. Given our close ties to an entire family of witches, Ana and I had a great deal more room for leniency than your average stranger. The first time one of the older sisters had found Ana playing at being a witch, they'd taken her away for three days after that to teach her about actual curses.

Not how to cast them, mind you. Just how they worked. At least . . . I was pretty sure of that.

"Come, come! Sit!"

I glanced around the room, but the rest of the interior was concealed behind more hanging silks. No obvious dangers, but again, that was when I needed to be the most cautious.

I approached and sat on a pillow across from Ana as she'd indicated, resting my sword across my knees in a position where I could draw it easily as I stood.

The setup looked straightforward enough. Not all witches were fortune-tellers, and not all fortune-tellers were witches, but there was some overlap. Most forms of fortune-telling were types of ritual magic, and ritual magic was an area where witches excelled.

There are different definitions of ritual magic in different regions, so let me clarify what I mean. In this context, ritual magic means any method of spellcasting that requires a focus — typically an object, but sometimes a set of objects, a person, or an animal — and a set of steps that must be followed with little to no variation. Finally, it must be done with the intent to accomplish an effect.

Let's say that your culture involves giving out a cake on your name day with a set number of candles based on your years of birth stuck in it. The candles are lit. You are expected to make a wish — but one held in silence, not spoken aloud — and to blow out all the candles at once.

If you believe that wish and hold it true in your heart, and you succeed at following the steps, congratulations — you have just participated in a rudimentary form of ritual magic.

Does that mean that something is going to grant your wish?

Probably not, unless there happens to be a wish-granting spirit of some kind that notices your efforts and lends its power toward your cause. That's possible, particularly if you're in an area that conducts this ritual frequently enough that wish essence begins to manifest, then an entity eventually forms from that essence. But one shouldn't count on that sort of thing.

Formal magical rituals involve both the steps above and the expenditure and direction of power to accomplish the desired result. In the case of the name day candle wish, a ritualist might use that process as the foundation for a ritual spell, but introduce additional wish essence into the ritual — perhaps the candles themselves are built with wish essence that they gradually emit, or liquid wish essence is baked into the cake — to ensure there is enough power for the effect.

As for directing the power toward the desired function . . .

I didn't know exactly how that worked. I didn't think just throwing more essence into the process would be enough. There had to be some essence-manipulation component, like how a technique was formed, but it wasn't my area of expertise.

My best guess was that witches had some kind of function within their destiny mark that allowed them to direct the essence used in a ritual toward the intended purpose, regardless of what essence type it was. Maybe they had something like ritual essence or purpose essence as the foundation of their destiny, but I didn't know.

Maybe Ana knew. Maybe I was about to find out.

More likely, though, she was just playing a role of a fortune-teller, and I was about to play the role of "Lien falling into an obvious trap."

Wouldn't be the first time. Probably won't be the last.

From the shadows of her witch's cap, Ana gave me a dangerous smile. "Make thyself comfortable, traveler."

"May I inquire about guest rights while I am here?" I asked.

She scoffed. "You may *inquire*, but you shan't be given such. One can never be safe in the presence of fate, after all."

I frowned at that, but nodded. I could have pointed out that basic hospitality could still exist in the presence of fate, but it wasn't worth the philosophical argument. She was simply telling me the nature of the challenge. "Very well. What services do you offer?"

Ana gave me a look that was probably supposed to be inscrutable and mysterious, but ended up more like she was having a hard time seeing me from under her massive hat. She raised a finger. "For but one coin, I shall read the crystal to see a glimpse into your future."

Another finger went up. "For two coins, I shall look ahead to find a hint of a safe path that you might not otherwise discover."

A third finger. "And for a mere three coins, I will allow you to test your fate against the cards . . . and perhaps find a way to change your destiny."

Without ever taking my eyes off her, I slipped three ordinary coins out of my bag and placed them on the counter.

A vision was fine. A clue sounded fun.

But a chance to test myself against Ana and fate itself? I couldn't possibly refuse.

"Oh, no, no. Not *those* sorts of coins, dear boy." She grinned. "I think you know what I mean."

I sighed and retrieved the three special coins I'd collected up to that point, setting them in front of her. I'd hoped to find something like a weapon shop to spend them in, but I wasn't going to hold the coins in reserve when I had a reason to spend them right in front of me.

Ana grinned at me from across the table.

"Your patronage is appreciated." She swept the coins across toward her and onto the opposite side without even glancing at them, then picked up the crystal ball and set it aside, clearing the space between us. Next, she picked up the deck of cards and set it where the crystal had been, directly in the center of the table.

"Very well, traveler. Let us begin."

* * *

The deck of cards on the table wasn't a familiar one, but that wasn't a surprise. I was familiar with a few different styles of classic fate cards, but Ana preferred to make her own. The tops of the cards for this set showed a single symbol — a black-bladed sword with a crystalline pommel. I couldn't count the number of cards in the deck from the stack, but it looked like a fairly standard number, meaning around fifty.

"I'll shuffle, you can cut the deck," Ana explained. She lifted the cards and began to shuffle them in her hands. My eyes narrowed, already looking for tricks, but it was hard to judge when so few of the rules had been declared.

After that, she set the cards back down. I picked them up, trimming off the top few cards and sorting them to the bottom, rather than doing a standard cut from the middle of the deck. If she was hiding something in the center, hopefully that would move it.

"Very well," Ana said. "Now, quickly, draw your hand."

I reached for the cards.

Ana pulled out a pen.

I cursed lightly, realizing my error, and yanked my hand back to start going through my bags for a quill and parchment. Meanwhile, Ana began tracing her hand directly on the table.

I found my quill and paper, then started drawing my hand, but she was too fast — she finished her outline when I'd barely started.

"I've drawn my hand faster, so I go first," Ana explained, taking seven cards from the top of the deck. I finished sketching my hand out and began to take cards, but she played her first card before I caught up.

"Fortune," she said. "You must now read my fortune."

I nodded, then wrote the words "my fortune" on the parchment and read it aloud.

"Quick, but not quick enough. I play a dragon," Ana said, putting down a card with a dragon drawn on it. The dragon was particularly fierce, breathing fire and flexing a mighty arm. "He burns down your humble peasant village."

Fortunately, by this point, I'd managed to get enough cards to play something in response. "Not so fast." I flipped over a card with a symbol of a treasure box. "Your dragon is distracted by my land's treasure, abandoning your lands to form his lair in mine."

I yanked her dragon card off the table before she could protest, then put it on top of the treasure.

She shook her head. "Poor timing on that. For you see" — she set another card down — "it's collections time."

She flipped her card over. It read "tax collector." With a gesture, my treasure card slid across the table, the dragon still on top of it.

I blinked. *New trick. Nice. Wonder if she's got strings on the cards or if—*

No time to think on this.

I checked my hand. *A princess, a medallion, a knight, a wizard, and a cursed twin.*

"Now, my dragon takes flight again toward your town . . ." She began to shift her dragon forward across the table.

"Dangerous indeed," I said, placing a card. "But fortunately, a traveling knight hears about the rumors of the horrible dragon and even more terrible tax collector and strikes forth to confront them!"

Ana nodded sagely. "An expected outcome, and one the dragon was prepared for. As the dragon descends, he tricks the knight into a dance contest — which was, of course, a trap! Even as the knight dances masterfully, he has danced into his own doom!"

She placed a "Fusion Dance" card on the table. As I watched, both cards flashed brightly, then vanished, replaced by a single new card—

The Blue Eyes Knight Dragon. A truly powerful card, represented by the same dragon picture that had been on the previous card, but now holding a sword and wearing a little helmet.

"Now, as both knight and dragon, my creature is unstoppable!" Ana leaned her head back, cackling gleefully.

"Oh? Is that so?" I leaned forward. "I think not. For there is one form of threat neither dragon nor knight has ever been able to resist. Behold!" I placed a card. "The princess!"

Ana let out a gasp.

"The fused knight and dragon," I continued, "unable to determine if they want to rescue or capture the princess, explode in a burst of internal conflict."

Ana nodded sadly, rubbing at her eyes. "We lose more dragon knights that way."

"And naturally, as the rightful ruler of the kingdom, the princess lays claim to her rightful treasure," I said, sweeping the treasure card across the table. "The tax collector can stay on your side. The princess hates him because he looks at her funny."

"Eminently reasonable. It's a shame, though. Because while she knew not to trust the tax collector, the princess lowered her guard in another way. Behold, the truth!"

She snapped her fingers . . . and the treasure box card opened its maw wide. "The mimic!"

The mimic card stood up, bending over, and began to eat the princess card.

That's no good, I considered. *I'm running out of good cards to play, and — hey, wait, why does she have so many cards in her hand?*

Ana fanned out her hand, showing a dozen cards. When I reached for the pile, she said, "Uh-uh. Only I, the master of drawing, can draw whenever I choose!"

"Well, then. If you are the master of drawing, and thus can draw at will . . ." I shook my head. "You leave me no choice."

"Oh?" She set down another dragon card. And another. "What are you going to do about my dragon army?"

"This." I set down the Cursed Twin card.

She frowned. "I'm not really sure how—"

My hand swept over the card, slashing through letters as I moved.

"Hey, those are my cards! That's—"

She stared at the remains of the card, leaving only four letters in the scratched text: *U Win.*

I grinned at her. "You *did* say that I could cut the deck."

Ana burst into laughter, then flicked her fingers. "Right you are. The card doesn't lie. You win this round, Lien."

". . . This round?"

She winked at me. "Best two out of three."

I nodded sagely. "Then . . . I play this card again."

"That's — ugh, fine! I guess you can go."

And then, with that, Ana vanished in a burst of smoke.

⊹⊹ ⊹⊹

After Ana's departure, I examined the remainder of the fortune-teller's hut. There had to be loot in there somewhere, right? And, of course, an exit.

I found the first of the loot right in front of me, if one could call it that. Most of the deck of cards had vanished along with Ana, but the card that I'd carved myself — the "U Win" card — had remained.

When I picked it up, the card felt . . . heavier. Both physically and to my essence senses. I examined it, wondering if she'd modified it somehow during her departure. Had she invested the card with some kind of power? Or had it, perhaps, already had some that I hadn't sensed earlier?

I tucked the card away. You never knew when you'd need a quick win, after all.

After that, I began a more methodical search. Ana's chair had the next prize — a large key with a design styled after a dragon's head.

Verthrimax, is that you on there? It's a pretty good likeness. And with a dragon . . . this might be the key to the final challenge.

That went into a pouch, too. I stood up to look around.

The door behind me was still there. I opened it, and it looked like it led right back outside into the town. If I wanted, I could rest a bit in what appeared to be a safe location — a rarity in a dungeon like this — and then backtrack to either the volcano or the road that I'd found before the mountain.

The table itself held a few widgets of interest — a crystal ball, the platform for the ball, and the tablecloth. After considering it for a bit, I left all of them there. The crystal ball was pretty likely to just be a prop, rather than an actual divination device, and picking it up showed it to be several pounds. Assuming it was basically just a useless rock, it would be a lot of dead weight and space in my backpack. The platform it sat on was wood painted to look like pewter, which was a weird choice for a fake metal, but Ana probably had her reasons.

The tablecloth was probably just a tablecloth. I lifted it, finding an ordinary-seeming wooden table underneath.

Ultimately, none of that seemed super necessary, so I left it behind.

The shelves were filled with dozens of jars of dubious substances. Most of them were obviously fake, just conjured curiosities. There was, however, a segment with bottles filled with various colorful liquids.

Dangerous. I approached the vials, inspecting them. The bottles were in a wide variety of shapes — some classic slim tubes, a few very broad containers, others so tall they had to be angled to fit on the shelf. One weird twisty one, which probably held something special. *I could take these, but I have no way of testing them completely without an alchemy lab setup.*

There were some very basic tests I could perform without any equipment — by which I mean things like "sniff the contents" — but you really don't want to do that if something might be poison or acid.

Given my penchant for getting hit with bottle-breaking force, just carrying random dangerous bottles would be a bad move. So, I wasn't going to take them without any testing at all.

I picked up the first one, debating if I wanted to do a spot test of each potion on the tablecloth or try seeing how they'd react to my charcoal, when I realized that the bottle had a label pasted to the back.

"The bottle to my left is safe. The bottle to my right lies."

I let out a deep sigh.

You never make anything simple, do you, Ana?

An hour later, I was spot testing something that was probably a healing potion on the table.

A few minutes of careful prodding later, I poured it on my leg, sighing in contentment as my wound finally began to heal significantly.

I can't believe she made the healing potion blue. I feel like there are laws against that. If not, there should be.

With my leg mostly functional again, I transferred the remaining quarter of a healing potion into a metal flask on my belt to avoid the possibility of breaking it in a fight.

Then, I threw a single one of the standard vials — a bottle containing a "rare" essence, if the label logic puzzle was guiding me right — into my bag. Finally, I took the twisty bottle.

I had no idea what that was. None of the logic puzzle bits even pointed at it, and I couldn't resist the mystery.

With my bags filled with more loot, I searched the remainder of the room.

The back door of the building led toward what looked like some kind of foreboding infinite void. That seemed like a good time, but I kept searching a little longer, eventually finding a secret exit through a trapdoor concealed under the central table.

That one led into a *purple-colored* foreboding void, which was much fancier than the ordinary black void. Naturally, I picked my backpack back up, shifted my sword, and began to climb down the ladder toward my next challenge.

***

The purple passage was pretty normal, aside from the unusual lighting. Stone walls, stone floor, sconces holding torches. The passageway was just about wide enough that I could touch the walls if I was sticking my arms out straight in a classic dominance pose.

You don't have that pose where you come from? Huh. Human culture continues to baffle me.

Anyway, about double-arm-reach for the walls. At least, it was that way for the first few seconds, before I picked a direction and took a step.

At that point, I heard a telltale *click*, and it started getting narrower.

. . . This is what I get for resting and letting my adrenaline die down.

I took a breath, glancing toward the ladder I'd descended and the trapdoor that was rapidly shutting itself above me. I could have busted back out and retreated, but nah.

My leg was feeling much better, and I was ready for a good run.

I sprinted straight down the hall as the walls closed in, hearing a couple more *clicks* as I hit the ground in different spots. I ducked just in time to avoid a gigantic swinging rock, hopped over a wall that was emerging from the floor, then formed an instant Sword Hand to cut a hail of arrows out of the air.

As the last arrow shattered, I realized it wasn't *just* an arrow — the middle of the body was a glass tube, containing something that emitted gas as it shattered.

I flipped my Sword Hand around and shoved the remains of the arrow away with the flat of my blade before the gas could fully escape, covered my face with my other arm, then sprinted ahead as gas began to expand in the hall behind me.

The hall was still narrowing, but I was making good time. I could see a distant light ahead — a purple one — and felt confident I was approaching the next area. The area with the light was both taller and wider than the hallway, and it didn't seem to be narrowing. It looked like a safe zone. I thought I could even see a gigantic doorway past the light, but it was tough to make out.

Not too bad of a challenge. I'm almost . . .

I tripped over a brick that was standing out from the rest of the ground. I didn't quite fall, but as I caught myself, I saw the purple light ahead move.

Three things happened rapidly after that.

First, I realized that the purple light wasn't just a simple crystal. It was moving upward as something I could just barely see moved around it, rising from the ground.

Oh, that's not good. That's not a giant light source.

That's . . . an eye.

Second, I realized the end of the corridor being wider wasn't to give me a safe zone.

It was to give the angry cyclopic golem enough room to stand up.

Third, the eye was rapidly growing brighter, with a whirring coming from around it.

That's . . . not a good sound, I processed with infinite cleverness just before the first beam of purple-flavored light tore through the hallway.

There was no time to process and do what most people would call "sane things." Instead, my body moved in that classic Edge sort of way, meaning I threw myself toward the killing light and swung my Sword Hand straight through it.

The beam of light split apart as my blade cleaved through it, sending twin beams behind me to crash into the walls, blasting stone to splinters.

The cyclopic golem and I blinked at each other, seemingly equally surprised that had worked.

Then I charged and the golem, now standing up to a full height of nearly twenty feet, ducked down to pick up something from the ground.

I grinned as I saw it.

A metal glaive, the blade as wide as my chest, and nearly as tall as I was.

Too slow.

I ran and jumped as soon as I reached the area where the ceiling was higher. I couldn't get far enough to swing my Sword Hand in a single leap, but I didn't have to.

I landed straight on the haft of the titanic glaive, right behind the blade.

Thanks for the idea, Gray.

Then I ran straight down the massive spear shaft, allowing the startled golem to lift me as it continued to raise its weapon.

The golem's eye began to flash again as I ran closer.

Nope.

Star Shattering — never mind, I want to keep that thing.

My Sword Hand lashed out, not to shatter the obvious weak spot in the eye like I'd originally planned, but to the side of it. I cut clear through the casing around the eye, pulled up, and tore through the runes that connected the eye to the golem's structure. The eye dimmed, the whirring noise ceased, but the golem kept moving. The statue-like hands released their weapon to sweep a hand at me. I jumped while I still could, getting just enough height to carve a little change in the runes on the golem's forehead.

On to off.

The golem's hand froze in midair.

I dropped toward the ground, slamming my Sword Hand into the golem's chest to catch myself on the way down. Then, with a swing, I hurled myself onto the golem's extended arm.

I stumbled a little on the landing, but stabilized myself with a blade thrust in the shoulder.

And with that, I climbed the inert golem to claim my latest prize — a gleaming purple eye.

Nice.

I hurled it in my bag, but I wasn't done.

I climbed down rapidly, turning toward the still-closing passage behind me.

Where are you . . . ? There.

I found what I was looking for in the ceiling — a massive gear rotating. The mechanism for the trap that was closing the walls.

I released my Sword Hand technique. I might have been able to reach the mechanism by climbing all the way up the golem and cutting into it, but I had a faster method.

I picked up the twenty-foot glaive from the ground, inspecting it.

Looks normal, not magical. Expendable.

Then I hurled it straight into the gears.

With a *crunch,* the gears broke, and the walls ceased to move.

I grinned.

Flawless victory.

With that, I ignored the obvious gigantic door behind me and began to backtrack down the hall.

I had to wait a little while for the gas to disperse, but I used that time to prod the wall, looking for more traps and other items I might have missed.

I found three still-intact glass gas-container arrows, which I shoved in my pack. But the real prize was a single section of the wall that sounded hollow.

Star Shattering Sight.

With my Viewing Point technique active, I could see the areas in the structure that were weak — and it only took a few well-placed strikes to take down that entire wall, leading to another long passage.

. . . I found the button that was supposed to open the wall about a minute after that. Oops.

Anyway, I found another passage, that was the important part.

Backtracking even farther found me another door in the opposite direction. That one, however, just led back to the woods where I'd fought the sun — it emerged in one of the mountainside caves I'd ignored earlier.

So, that left me with two new area options to investigate from this passage. I checked them both.

The gigantic doors led into a room with a Valor-style floor, black and white squares indicating some kind of movement puzzle. I could see another gigantic door on the opposite side from the entrance, but nothing else to indicate the style or details of the challenge.

The hidden passage, however, led to something far more important—

A solid metal door with a massive keyhole in the center and the stylized image of a dragon wrapped around the keyhole.

There was no hesitation. This looked like the end of the dungeon, and while it was a valid adventuring tradition to backtrack and explore every possible route, I wanted to at least get a look at what Ana had in store.

With a gulp, I pulled the dragon-styled key out of my bag and inserted it into the keyhole. There was a rumbling sound, then the door trembled and sank into the ground.

I took a breath as I gazed at the chamber in front of me.

The room was massive, more than a hundred feet across and similarly tall. A single colossal crystal stood in the center, dominating the entire middle section of the chamber. It was the single largest source of essence I'd ever seen, large enough that I couldn't even take in the entire sight from the tunnel entrance. I had to tilt my head upward to get a good look toward the top, more than thirty feet up.

There was a white stone platform with a similar alabaster stairway at the base of the crystal, leading straight to the top.

The crystal was shimmering blue, breathtakingly beautiful, and emanating such powerful essence that I could feel it from the doorway — but it wasn't even close to the most important thing in the room.

No, that was the arming sword thrust into the top of the crystal, gleaming black and gold.

Anathema, I whispered to myself.

I'm finally here.

CHAPTER VIII

SHOWDOWN

I stepped into the massive chamber, eyes searching for threats. That's generally a good idea in a dungeon, with the caveat that dungeons don't always follow the rules you'd like them to.

For example, you'd expect that titanic monsters the size of buildings would be pretty unsubtle and easy to detect before they ambush you. That, however, would only be true if they couldn't appear in seemingly arbitrary locations, like in midair where you'd definitely already been looking.

By the time I'd taken three steps into the room, the door behind me was slamming shut on its own, and glimmering chunks of crystal were beginning to manifest in midair in the center of the chamber.

Now, I know the old truism that you're not supposed to attack anyone mid-summoning or mid-transformation. People put a lot of work into lengthy and elaborate transformation sequences, and it's rude to ignore that in favor of getting in a cheap shot. Moreover, I liked the idea of seeing what my opponent was capable of — it helped add to the excitement of a fight when you saw your opponent doing something powerful and threatening.

That being said, it's *also* rude to underestimate your opponent, and I was keenly aware of what Ana was capable of if left alone.

So, that's all to say that as soon as I saw titanic crystals slamming together in midair to form some kind of gigantic monsters, I unlimbered my sword and attacked with my full strength. Or, rather, I tried to.

My plan was to extend a blade of essence from my sword's tip, much like I'd done to cut the sun down from the sky. But even as I brought my arms down, shackles began to form around my wrists, attached to a phantasmal chain. Something — or, really, someone — yanked on the chain, trying to pull me backward . . .

"Bad move, Ana."

I spun around, interrupting my swing to grab onto the chain. Ana stood right next to the door, just as I'd guessed, holding the other end of the phantasmal chain—

Which I grabbed with one hand and yanked toward me, causing Ana's eyes to widen as she stumbled forward. She was standing at human size, wearing a full suit of gleaming aurum armor — a manifestation of her Golden Raiment technique — but even with the boost to her strength that provided, she couldn't match me muscle for muscle. Not anymore. With access to my own essence, strength was one area I had an advantage over virtually anyone of the same essence level, and Ana was no exception.

She was, however, just as familiar with me as I was with her. While yanking her chain put her into my sword's reach, she anticipated my follow-up, dispelling her own chain before I could use it to try to trip her. I stepped forward to take a swing at her with the flat of my sword — I still wasn't willing to risk cutting her with it when I didn't know exactly how it worked — but I needn't have worried. She vanished well before my blade reached her.

When I turned to face her, she was standing at the top of the stairway that led to her sword. She folded her arms, watching me carefully.

I lifted my sword back to rest against my shoulder, then began to advance on her.

I've never seen her teleport rapidly mid-fight like that before. Is it because she's in the chamber next to her sword and the crystal? That's . . . going to be a pain, isn't it?

My mind immediately raced to teleportation countermeasures. The best one I had available was breach essence, which could disrupt teleportation powers . . . but even as I began to hastily assemble a technique, I remembered that I was expressly forbidden from using it here, on account of the whole "might break reality" problem.

Stupid easily breakable reality. Ugh.

Speaking of things that were easily breakable, I was still looking at Ana when a colossal crystalline beast descended in front of the stairwell, its very landing shattering the floor where its claws met the ground.

It was at that point that I remembered that I had a bit of a tunnel-vision problem when it came to combat, and that when Ana had appeared, I'd somehow managed to forget about the titanic monster that had been forming in midair. Oops.

On the plus side, I recognized the creature at a glance. Four clawed limbs, a gigantic tail with wicked spikes, a pair of wings with a span of nearly half the chamber when fully extended, and jaws that flickered with flame—

On the minus side, it was a *dragon*. A *crystal dragon*.

"Go, my pretty! Destroy him!" Ana shouted, pointing at me.

The dragon didn't need any further urging. Their jaws opened wide, visible sparks flickering as I heard a clicking sound from the back of their throat—

And I ran.

Not away, obviously. This is me. I ran straight toward the dragon's open maw, raising my sword and beginning the technique that Ana had so rudely interrupted.

Star Severing—

I didn't make it in time.

Flames blasted across the chamber, the fire itself glimmering like crystal, which would have been a very beautiful last thing to look at.

Obviously, it wasn't mine. I didn't finish my technique quickly enough to cut the dragon, but I had another moment before the flames reached me, and that was enough.

Sword.

I swung downward, my blade flaring with power as the forbidden essence in my right hand flooded through it, extending my reach. I cleaved straight through the dragon's flames, parting them like parchment. The blistering heat surrounded me as the flames split in midair, the intensity of the heat burning my tunic and skin, but I tightened my jaw and advanced, holding my sword straight in front of me, a flashing blade of essence still overlapping with and extending beyond the silvery surface.

As I advanced through the flame, it slowly guttered out, and I heard the clicking sound from the dragon's throat, followed by a frustrated growl. Then, the massive creature took a single step back, uncertain, and I rushed forward to close the remaining distance between us.

The tail came first, swiping at my legs — or really, my entire body, given the mass of it. I jumped, landing on top of it, and ran straight up the tail toward the creature's back. The dragon spun abruptly, then beat their wings, a gale wind blasting me backward. I landed back on the floor, already running, then ducked a swing from one of the creature's claws. The second claw came faster than I expected, and I barely managed to raise my sword in time—

Not to block, not really. The claw was too massive. But blocking and dodging had never been the core of my style.

When the claw slammed into me, it hit my sword first, which was still flooded with power. The dragon's tremendous mass and strength hurled me straight across the chamber, and I slammed painfully into one of the room's walls with a *crack*.

But when I dusted myself off, groaning and pulling myself to my feet, the dragon was roaring in agony into the air.

Where the dragon had slammed their hand into my sword, their crystalline claw was cracked and broken, blue energy leaking into the air.

I grinned, bracing my sword for another charge—

Except my sword was gone. Or, more accurately, it was on the floor in the middle of the room. I'd lost it when I'd been hurled across the chamber.

And the dragon, while wounded, was looking angry.

My eyes met the dragon's even as they narrowed . . . and, together, we charged across the room to meet each other.

The dragon was faster. That shouldn't have been any surprise, given that they were about a quarter of the room's size, and I . . . wasn't. Also, they had wings beating to carry them farther with each stride. So, I was nowhere near the center when we met, my hands still empty.

When the dragon swung an uninjured claw at me in rage, I'd imagine that they probably were thinking I was no longer a risk without my weapon. Naturally, I chose the moment before they hit me to jam a fist toward their own claw.

Sword Hand.

My essence blade jammed into the center of the dragon's previously uninjured claw. That only slowed their swing for a heartbeat, but that was enough time for me to dance around the claw, at least in part. The wickedly sharp claws drew bleeding lines across my right shoulder as I tried to dodge, but the pain didn't hit me right away. I kept moving, dragging my Sword Hand across the back of the claw and running forward, trying to cleave all the way up the arm as I ran. The dragon jerked back before I could cause too much damage, rearing backward in anguish, but that was fine.

While the dragon recoiled, I dismissed my technique, jumping over a tail sweep that I barely managed to hear coming from behind me, and landed next to my sword.

I ducked, barely avoiding another tail swing that had aimed higher, grabbing my sword and lifting it just in time to hear another clicking sound from behind me.

I didn't hesitate.

I turned, and as the dragon's jaws opened wide, I repeated my technique—

Star Severing Sword.

—and lunged, jamming the extended essence blade right into the back of the dragon's throat.

Then, with a final *click*, flames formed in the dragon's gullet—

"You fought well, and will be remembered."

My sword swept to the left and right inside the dragon's throat. The flames faded as a hair-thin line spread across the creature's neck.

I withdrew my sword, sheathing it.

Then, in two pieces, the dragon fell.

As the pieces of crystal shattered around me, I advanced on the colossal stairwell, ready to confront Ana for the final time. Her expression surprised me—

She wasn't eager. Not braced for the fight. No sword glimmered in her hand.

No. Her expression was one of panic, fear, and regret.

"Lien—" Ana trembled, her hand coming up. "W-wait."

I paused just below her, a little annoyed, but more than that, confused. "I beat your dragon, Ana. If you weren't expecting that, you underestimated me. Now, if you don't have any further challenges . . ."

"It's not that! Wait!" Her sudden intensity stopped me in a way that a sword blade never would have. "I'm trying to listen!"

I blinked.

"Listen to . . . what, exactly?" I lowered my still-sheathed sword, resting it against the stairs.

"Lien . . ." Her eyes were anguished as she turned to me, shaking her head. "We . . . we have a problem."

"What sort of problem?" I asked, dubious. Was this a trick? Another challenge, one that wasn't of a physical nature?

"There's someone outside the shrine. A few someones now, actually, but someone important — they're demanding to come in. They're demanding the sword, Lien."

I shrugged a shoulder. "Then they can get in line."

"That's the problem. This . . . this is the sort of thing that can skip any sort of line. And . . . I think I might need your help to deal with it."

". . . How close am I to finishing this?" I asked.

"I can't tell you that. It's . . ." She shook her head. "I'm sorry, Lien. Ordinarily, I'd never want to ask you to abandon something like this, I know how much it means, but—"

"Is this a test? To see if I'm willing to give the sword up to—"

"It's not," she told me, shaking her head. "There's no reward if you do this, Lien. I'm . . . just asking for your help. I'm sorry. I wish . . ."

I took a step up. Not to attack, but to reach out with a hand, putting it on Ana's shoulder. She must have understood what I was doing, since she didn't dodge or flinch. "Whatever you need, Ana. Always."

Tears welled up in her eyes, then she nodded and pointed. The door to the chamber reopened, but beyond it, I could see a forest glade rather than the previous hall.

I turned around immediately, striding toward the door.

I didn't dare to look back at the sword at the top of the stairs or the crystal. I would do this for Ana, but it was easier if I wasn't reminded of what I was leaving behind.

INTERLUDE I

SCRIBE I

EXITS

As the swordsman continued to walk, he looked introspective, pausing briefly in his storytelling. When the silence persisted, Scribe took a moment to interject.

"That must have been a difficult choice to make, leaving the sword behind like that."

The swordsman took a moment to process what had been said, then blinked, and finally went through a number of complicated expressions. "It was and it wasn't."

"What do you mean?" Scribe asked.

The swordsman took another moment, measuring his words more than he typically did. When he came to his conclusion, it was simple. "The shrine was never just about the sword. Not to me. It was about my relationship with my best friend. Ana said she needed my help. There was never really a decision to be made." He shrugged. "But it *did* hurt. Leaving the sword behind wasn't a hard choice, or even a choice at all. But it hurt."

"I'd imagine. Especially if you felt like you were close to succeeding. I imagine you hadn't ever gotten that close before, but you couldn't even know, could you?"

"No. It was intensely frustrating. But ultimately, I was just a child, and a bit of frustration was a small price to pay. I'd learn soon enough that there were things that were more important than a minor inconvenience."

"Like the threat that the people outside represented?" Scribe asked.

"No," Edge replied, strangely firm. "Like the *needs* they represented."

CHAPTER IX

STRANGERS

I followed Ana out of the shrine, half expecting to black out and suffer memory loss, but I experienced nothing of the sort.

A moment later, we were emerging from a colossal tree through the same doors that I'd entered the shrine through. I didn't worry too much about the fact that we'd come in through a completely different way — teleportation wasn't strange to me, even if I wasn't familiar with exactly how the dungeon's magic worked.

I took a moment to collect myself as Ana walked forward, marveling at the strangeness of being outside and still remembering what had happened inside the shrine. I was supposed to forget everything if I'd failed, and remember every past attempt if I succeeded. This was a third scenario, a middle ground. The exact type of exploit that I'd normally try to find, except in this case, it wasn't intentional.

I had complicated emotions about that, as well as the advantages it might give me in the future, but that was secondary to dealing with the situation in front of me.

We weren't the only ones standing outside the tree.

Four others faced each other, gathered near the doors.

Two of them were largely recognizable to me, more or less, even if they weren't in their ordinary attire.

The first person I noticed was a teen around my own age. Androgynous in a pretty sort of way, lanky, with short and rough-cut crimson hair that was tucked beneath a blood-red cap. Faded gray trousers with hints of white at the bottom, wooden shoes with white socks spotted with red. White shirt, red suspenders. Pouches on a red belt. If the teen had been human, in a human city, the outfit might have looked like something a simple errand runner would have worn. Delivering newspapers or the mail, perhaps, or maybe someone about to start a day of cleaning chimneys.

In the Court of Rust and Salt, a faerie wearing a red cap had a particular meaning. If I wasn't who I was, closely allied with the court, I might have taken a step backward and reached for my sword out of reflex.

Even as it was, as their eyes met mine with a flicker of recognition, I was noticing all the places under the cap wearer's clothes that were just slightly more pronounced than the curves of their body would have produced.

Knives. Many, many knives.

They smiled and winked. I tipped my head respectfully in the presence of a professional, then turned to the second figure.

The second was a tall gentleman wearing a frilly white shirt with large wooden buttons with slightly different symbols on each of them. He wore thick red riding gloves, matching boots, and salt-gray pants. His hair was waist-length and crimson, which was the first feature I'd recognized. The second was the silvery sword on his hip, which had featured in one of the most important incidents in my memory, and wasn't easy to forget even if his outfit and demeanor were different.

Talisian. Wearing the guise of a courtly nobleman. Perhaps his own original identity, before he gave it up? But if he's here in a guise . . .

I turned briefly back to the red-capped fae, processing new information.

Then . . . wait . . . It can't be . . . can it?

But this wasn't the time to reconnect with either of the two people I might have recognized. Instead, I turned to the other two, who they were facing in parlay.

The first was what I'd call a classical courtly fae, wearing pure white formalwear accented with gold gilding, and a red-and-yellow collar signifying fire. His outfit was accented by dozens of gems and jewels, some of which looked like rubies, but others were as clear as glass. His hair was blond with hints of orange toward the bottom, an effect that many faeries had naturally. It was as long as Talisian's red, but splayed out wide, and moved seemingly of its own accord. While the colors suggested flames, giving it a hint of a resemblance to Ana's own hair when she was in a fiery mood, the texture of this man's hair was quite different — more like the feathers of a bird, and splayed outward in a fashion that suggested the movement of wings.

He was large, for a fae, midway past six feet and broad of chest with arms that looked like he would have been at home in Auntie Temper's forge. In spite of that, his features were soft, and his demeanor spoke of a gentleness of heart. His skin was the color of a sandy beach, which spoke to something even more illustrative than his hair about the spectacular rarity of his presence.

This man was fae, yes.

But neither he, nor his companion, was of the Court of Rust and Salt.

And while I did not recognize his companion, I recognized several things about him right away.

He was tall and thin, as fae were likely to be, but in a way that looked gaunt rather than merely athletic. His own long hair was straight and white as parchment, and though it looked as if care had been taken to tame it, the ends were fraying and broken. He wore a tarnished silver circlet on his brow, accenting dark gray eyes that gleamed with a hint of white toward the pupil.

The tarnished circlet alone might have been alarming, as tarnished silver was just as symbolic as rusted iron might be, but it was complemented by something in a similar style with greater impact — a sword on his hip, a near match for the one the Talisian wore, that was similarly tarnished and worn.

More than that, however, I noticed his skin color. As I mentioned before, fae skin colors were broad in variety, and my childhood companions ranged from alabaster to obsidian, with virtually every tone in between, and elemental colors besides.

But there was one skin tone that, among any species, signified more than simple ethnic distinctions — ashen gray, almost as if the natural color of his skin had been bleached away.

Which was, in many cases, exactly what had happened to the Lost Fae of the north, when the Ashen Lord's forces had swarmed across the continent.

I've touched on this before, but it's important enough to recap. When the Ashen Lord came, his armies spread the Ashen Scouring, a miasma of energy that changed creatures and land alike. Animals twisted into fearsome beasts. Plants shifted as well, if they survived. Even the water changed, shining gray in the light of the sun.

Those that inhabited the north fought at first, then fled. Most fae were not so fortunate. Bound to trees, water, and mountains, they were as affixed as the land itself was. There was no retreat.

And so, in the presence of overwhelming force, many courts sealed themselves away, hoping to protect what they could from the ravages of the armies of fiends. Some few survived in those sealed enclaves, but at great cost.

Even with the vast magic that was used to seal the enclaves away, the work that the Ashen Scouring had already done could not be easily reversed. And as the scouring continued to spread all around the sealed places, it worked its way into the roots of trees and the depths of underground rivers.

Those fae that were sealed in those places were twisted by the Ashen Scouring, their colors stolen. Those that survived the change were forced to remain in their enclaves, their health gradually fading as the land itself suffered, unable to leave due to their own wards. While some used their remaining power to call for aid from the other courts, and some efforts were made to provide them with rescue, the majority of the people of their courts were left to die.

The Lost Fae.

I had never seen one in person. It was remarkably rare for one to escape from their own wards. It had happened a few times, historically. Ones who had been willing to brave the dangers of sneaking into the tunnels where the Buried had been sealed, following the passages of the labyrinthine underworld filled with monsters for hundreds of miles to seek an escape. Anyone who had managed such an escape route would have to be immensely determined and formidable.

I saw that in him. When his dark eyes turned to me, evaluating, I held my chin high and met his gaze as best I could.

I knew he was taking my measure, and the measure of the sword essence that flowed from my heart. A moment of pause, then an exchange of nods.

No demonstration was necessary. It was apparent from his aura, his stance. I stood absolutely no chance in a confrontation against that man, but if needed, I would fight him anyway. With that simple exchange, we'd both acknowledged it.

For once, I wasn't eager to try. Not until I understood the strangeness of the scene in front of me.

As if cued by our exchange, Talisian — in his strange noble guise — clapped his hands. "Ah, and there you are, my darling! Anathema, you've grown so much since we last met! Come, step forward, let us all get a good look at you."

Ana danced forward, light on her feet and cautious, staying pointedly equidistant from the two groups. She bowed to the speaker politely, but without emphasis. "My lord, it is my pleasure to greet you at the precipice of my home. Please forgive the lack of more immediate hospitality, I was not expecting any guests."

Her eyes scanned to each of those present, her stance showing her worry. I wasn't sure if she recognized Talisian in the same way I had, but I think she knew this current guise, as his words had implied.

I stepped up behind her, and off slightly to the right, mirroring the way the other pairs were standing. Symbolically, it might have implied superiority on the part of the farthest-forward person in human politics, but fae courts were more complicated, with relationships often reversed or otherwise skewed. In my case, I was standing at the right and back because I was still carrying a reach weapon, sheathed but held against my shoulder like a polearm, and in a position where I could put it to use against the foreign fae if they advanced.

That, too, was silently acknowledged by both of the foreigners, simply with movements of their eyes. No hostility, just understanding.

"No offense is taken at the lack of immediate hospitality, at least on my part. This is an unusual circumstance, as I'm sure our good friends will acknowledge," Talisian said, his stance shifting toward the newcomers.

"We are, of course, aware of the unusual nature of our presence," the broader and healthier of the foreigners said. "And hopeful that we can come to a reasonable accord, in spite of that."

"An accord?" Ana asked him directly. "I believe you have me at a disadvantage, sir. I am not aware of what you speak, nor your nature. Perhaps if you would be willing to introduce yourselves, I could prepare some basic hospitality . . . ?"

Her words were careful, though weighted with caution. I saw a smile of acknowledgment from the wing-haired fae, noting that she had offered to *prepare* hospitality, not to actually give it to them.

"I believe you can offer these people your full guest rights, Anathema," Talisian said, heavy with implication. "They are guests of the court itself and have come a very long way. In one case, among the longest ways imaginable."

A tip of the head from the Lost Fae, who remained silent but turned to the broader fae, perhaps deferring to him.

"Wonderful, we would be grateful for a chance to rest. And to answer the lovely young lady's question, I am, of course, happy to introduce us both. Perhaps once we're seated?"

Ana glanced to me. I remained at the ready, shifting my sword only slightly to show that I was ready to use it. She took a breath.

"Of course."

Then she clapped her own hands, conjuring a table that manifested in between our groups. It was a long, elegant thing, seemingly made from lacquered wood, rather than one of her usual simple constructs.

She took another breath. I steadied her as she wobbled, then pointed again, paling slightly as she conjured six chairs that matched the decor of the table, one at a time.

With that, she gestured to the table. "You may seat yourselves as you please."

The red-capped teen immediately took the one side of the head of the table, seemingly without even thinking about it. That drew a look from Talisian, and perhaps a hint of a sigh. Then, Talisian seated himself to the right side of the teen.

I caught a look of invitation from the teen, eyes moving to the empty chair on their left. My left hand opened in a "wait" gesture. I wouldn't move without Ana being comfortable, even at their prompting.

A bit of annoyance from the teen's eye movements, maybe, but no verbal response. Subtleties were not my strength, but I could tell that I'd made an important choice there.

The Lost Fae sat at the opposite side of the table, mirroring how the teen had chosen that spot, with the broad-shouldered fae at his own right.

That left seats open between the two groups. After a brief pause, Ana took the seat next to Talisian, leaving me to sit exactly where the teen had already indicated. Perhaps they'd already seen where things were going and were giving me an opportunity to secure some sort of advantage by seating myself sooner.

Whatever.

If they were going to play with implications, I could make my own.

I set my gigantic, sheathed sword across the entire table, keeping the hilt near me, easy to draw. And in doing so, I divided the table into segments.

The Lost Fae turned his head to me, speaking for the first time. His voice was deeper than I'd imagined, but not unkind. "A bold decision, abruptly made. Your place was uncertain, your hand now played."

I blinked in surprise. Poetic speech? Rare, but . . .

"No offense shown, no aggression portrayed. I only protect, with the position of my blade."

A thin smile.

"Ah. You seek to guard, our hostility forbade. An understandable declaration, with our positions precisely laid. One wonders, then, if you would stand and take this out of our peaceful glade?"

I placed both hands against the table, preparing to stand.

"Such haste," Talisian said, gesturing for me to stop. "Please, a pause for discourse. We've only just been seated, and our friends have not yet even introduced themselves, as they agreed."

"Nor has hospitality yet been fully provided, as agreed," the wing-haired fae noted.

"I shall have it ready in just a moment," Ana said, strained. She'd pushed herself not only with the fancy conjurations, but before, when we'd been in the shrine.

A snap of her fingers and a carafe of liquid appeared in the center of the table. Then she snapped again, forming empty cups on coasters. She began to pour, as we watched silently, then stood to personally pour drinks at each seat.

I'd put her at a bit of a disadvantage, forcing her to do that. If I'd been a little less aggressive with my posturing, she'd have asked me to distribute the cups and drinks, allowing me to play a part in the hospitality. As it was, I'd chosen a guardian role, which made her do everything herself.

The foreign fae watched her closely, with greater interest than I would have expected for such a simple magic.

But that was nothing compared to when she snapped her fingers again, conjuring a loaf of bread on a wooden board, followed by a small container of salt, which she took a pinch of to dust across the top of the bread's surface.

I could smell freshly baked bread and salt, both scents feeling genuine. And I knew that such a conjuration was a level of complexity beyond Ana's previously demonstrated abilities.

Either she'd picked up a new essence type that she hadn't told me about, or this was some kind of trick. Ley line travel to move bread and salt from an extradimensional storage space, perhaps.

It was quite a demonstration. And from Talisian's darkening expression, perhaps exactly the type of demonstration that Ana should *not* have made.

As she sliced the bread and placed it on newly formed wooden plates, offering a share to each of us, Ana must have sensed that something was wrong, but she didn't say anything more. No one did, not until she was seated again.

"Please, enjoy my hospitality, and the guest rights to this glade. I fear that due to preexisting rules, I cannot extend those same rights to the shrine." Ana's words were careful but important. I saw Talisian breathe a visible sigh of relief at that, and he looked to relax even more when the two foreign fae raised their wooden glasses of juice, intertwined arms in some sort of toast or ritual, and drank from each other's glass in a shockingly coordinated move.

The teen next to me raised their own glass, giving me an inviting look.

Talisian kicked them under the table.

The teen looked startled, almost dropping their juice, then kicked Talisian back. I barely suppressed a laugh at their sibling-like antics, then quickly lifted my own glass.

Ana and I reached across the table to clink our cups together, drinking together. A different gesture from the one that the foreigners had made, but similarly important.

Talisian sighed, pulled the teen's glass out of their hands, tasted it, then handed it back with a silent nod. The teen groaned, then drank from it.

I raised an eyebrow at that gesture. *Testing it for poison? Should I be more worried about this situation?*

No one else seemed to react, so I kept the thought to myself. Then, silently, we each took up a piece of bread and took a bite.

A few moments of silent chewing. The bread was fresh. I saw the Lost Fae's eyes close as he seemed to savor it more than I could have expected.

When they opened, he seemed calmer, but resolved. ". . . My gratitude offered, for this gift outlaid. With this small gift, a debt repaid."

He reached down, and I tensed, but there was no hostility in his movement. He simply pulled up one of his sleeves, revealing a tarnished silver bracelet, and unfastened it from his wrist. I could see intricate letters carved on the inside of the bracelet, perhaps some sort of enchantment runes.

He slipped it off, then placed it on the table and gave me a meaningful look.

With a nod, I lifted the bracelet. Ana frowned slightly, then pulled up her own sleeve. I fastened the silver chain on her wrist.

"Your gift is accepted, kind sir. It is, perhaps, a bit much for mere bread and succor?"

The Lost Fae smiled. "No mere bread, my dear young friend, but the type that helps a hurt heart mend."

Ana put her hand, now wearing the tarnished chain, over her heart. "I'm glad you like it."

She'd dropped the poetry for that reply, but replying to a fae with similar discourse wasn't strictly necessary all the time, it was just a bit of verbal play. By dropping the poetry, she'd made it clear she was being sincere, not just focusing on the wordplay. He nodded and took another bite from his bread, equally meaningful as a gesture.

"With guest rights given and gifts exchanged," Talisian said, "I believe it's time that names are made plain."

"Of course." The wing-haired fae spoke. "You've been more than kind, especially given the unscheduled nature of our visit. Allow me to introduce myself first. I am Lord Oloris Nysarii, the Fires of Purification, Master of Glass and Crystal, of the Court of Sand and Dust."

A court from the eastern side of the continent, I knew. One that had not fully been lost, even in the time of the First Accord, because they had been close enough to the borders of allied lands that they had managed to broker their own deal with the fiends to retain control over their lands, rather than endlessly warring with the fiends who were stretching themselves thin by trying to extend deep into the southeast.

Our court met with them on occasion, but rarely. His presence here was an outlier — most meetings were held in their court, not my home — but not unprecedented.

It was the other who set his bread down, hesitantly, that was the true enigma.

And I knew his name before he spoke it, because I'd heard of him already, in whispers of a growing legend.

The Lost Fae met each of our eyes, then lifted his glass in salute. "In this day of wonders, I greet you plain. I am Valissar Talis, first and last of my name."

Valissar Talis. The man believed to be the youngest candidate ever known for the Talisian Order, the servants of the royal families of the fae courts. Known for a dozen duels with improbable victories against humans, fiends, and fae.

Destined Sword Lord and Questing Knight.

He was here for Anathema, and I was in for a fight.

CHAPTER X

SYMPATHY

"Lord Talis," our own Talisian began, still in his own guise, "I have heard many tales of your exploits. Had we known you would be arriving, we would have made more proper preparations. As you are *no doubt aware*, our queen is not here at present. In the meantime, I can offer you only limited hospitality. You may refer to me as Lord Brine Rosion, or simply as Lord Brine."

I took a moment to appreciate his specific wording. "You may refer to me" was a rare way a Talisian could use a name to identify himself. He never said it was his name, after all. He simply said, "You may refer to me," implying it was his name. Simply using "Lord Brine" was unusual — "Lord Rosion" would be more typical — and that was another tell that something was going on.

Guises could get around a number of fae rules, simply by allowing them to tell stories related to their current nature, but this was a good workaround for a different courtly rule. I approved.

Lord Brine continued to speak. "This little scamp" — he gestured to the red-hatted teen — "is under my tutelage and protection."

The teen gave a feral grin, exposing teeth that looked just a hint too sharp for what humans would consider ordinary, then reached across the table — straight across my sword, in fact — to offer a hand in a humanlike greeting. "Rusty. 'S a pleasure an' all that."

Lord Talis examined the extended hand, then accepted it, and, as both "Lord Brine" and I tensed, gave "Rusty" a simple human handshake. One of a local variety, I think?

He was the type of traveler who made friends and adapted easily, even among humans. That was one of those things that made him rare.

"A humble knight does greet you both, on this auspicious day. I hope my visit brings you hope, not chaos or dismay." He nodded and released Rusty's hand. From the look in his eyes as he shook the teenager's hand, he had some idea of the game that was being played, but he'd chosen to play along.

Among the faerie courts, it's generally polite to play along with any sort of guise you encounter. Faeries engage in guises for any number of different reasons, and without context, it can be difficult to know if you will cause great offense by challenging one.

A teenager like Rusty could be using a guise simply as a game for fun, trying to see if they can convince people of a false identity. This is a common practice among young fae, and one that is encouraged.

Similarly, young fae often use guises to try out a persona to see if it's one that might suit them in the long run. Being able to explore an identity without fear of persecution is extremely important for young people in general, and for fae, guises are a cultural tradition that plays into that need. For some, the role-playing elements of a guise eventually help a young fae find and embrace their true self.

Guises can also be training, especially for fae that have perception-focused essence types. Thus, calling them out on it can be disruptive to their training routine.

Finally, guises can be used for what humans often associate them with — spycraft and trickery. In these cases, interrupting a fae in their guise may save a victim from the fae's attentions, or it may bring upon greater consequences, depending on the fae in question.

As a general rule, you don't want to interrupt a fae's guise without knowing why they're doing it or being prepared for the consequences. This does not necessarily mean you have to play along — there are circumstances under which you may not want to feed into the guise, since that can give the fae power. Simply not acknowledging the guise at all is the most neutral approach, but playing along is considered polite.

There is an important exception to playing along. There are many guises that are designed to be challenged, but only under specific end conditions. Many guises involving layers of secret identities fall into this category, and the more tells a fae in a guise has about an identity beyond what they're playing at, the more likely it is that there's an intention for a big reveal.

This is important to understand because, as I'd already noticed, and Lord Valissar Talis may have as well, Rusty was the type of guise that was designed to be unveiled. It was only a matter of when, why, and how.

"Charmin'. Now, what're ye doin' 'ere?" Rusty asked. It was a bit direct, but that was one of the advantages of a guise with more humble origins — one could ignore some of the frivolities of courtly discourse without offense. It was not expected for a peasant to understand courtly etiquette, after all.

Lord Talis looked to Oloris, who nodded in response to him. Oloris sat up a bit straighter, glancing at those present. "Before we get to that, I believe there are others who remain unidentified here?"

"Hi!" Ana reached across the table to Oloris, similar to what Rusty had done with Lord Talis. "I'm Ana. That's short for Anathema, Bane of All Things, Greatest Weakness, and Dungeon Sword."

"Miss Anathema." Oloris took her hand and kissed it. I felt a twinge of . . . something at that, but I wasn't sure I could identify it. "It is a pleasure to make your acquaintance."

"Thanks!" She offered her hand to Lord Talis next, who gave her a firm handshake.

"Long have I quested, long have I sought — a sword as fine, I have found not."

Ana blinked. "That's . . . really very kind of you, Lord Talis."

"Kindness is not what brings me here, but dire urgency. For hope I walked across the stone, and sand, and sea."

I internally mumbled a little bit about rhyming "sea" and "urgency" feeling a little lazy, but it wasn't like I could do much better.

As if sensing my attention, Lord Talis turned toward me, looking expectant.

"I am called Lien, Edge of the Woods. Most refer to me simply as Edge." I didn't make any physical gesture of introduction. I wasn't operating in a guise, but I was playing a role in this scene. A more minor thing, since I was still operating in my own identity, but while the others were polite and friendly, I was cautious and guarded. I had reasons to be that way, and not just because my test was being interrupted.

I had three ideas of why Lord Talis might be visiting while the queen was away, and I didn't like any of them.

"Well," Lord Brine said, "with all of our introductions given, I believe it would be best if we discuss the reason for this visit."

"Of course," Oloris said with a smile. "As I'm sure you're already aware, my companion is from one of the courts in the north."

No mention of the word "lost," but the meaning was clear enough.

"We are," Lord Brine responded. "It has been many years since I've met with one from a northern court. Is it too much to hope that this visit comes with news of his people's liberation?"

"Alas, the northern courts remain in exile. It was a dire path that Lord Talis followed to reach this place, through the depths of the world."

Oloris's words were simple, but the meaning was clear enough: In order to escape from one of the fae courts that had been sealed behind ancient barriers during the Ashen War, Lord Talis had traveled through the underworld — paths that had once been ancient fae roads but had long been overtaken by the monstrous Buried.

Entering the domain of the Buried was largely considered suicide, even for the most powerful of Skyseekers. The Buried varied in power as much as humans, but it was well-known that the stronger Buried could sense intrusions into their domain — and some among them held strength comparable to or greater than what my mentor had held in the height of her power.

There was no way that even this Lord Talis could have faced such a threat directly, but still, he had risked those tunnels. To do so required a great deal of bravery, but more than that, it required a clear goal. Freedom was perhaps enough of a cause for some, but based on the intensity of Lord Talis's expression, that was not the reason he had come here.

"I would love to hear that story at some point," Lord Brine offered, "but you have both traveled such a long way . . . you are likely to be eager to speak of why you are here."

"For one purpose I came here, and for a noble cause. I seek now to claim this sword, and with no further pause."

There was no question about which sword he referred to. He gesticulated directly toward Anathema.

"Woah, okay, hold on." Ana raised both hands. "This is a little sudden."

"Sudden as it may be to you," Oloris said, "there are old bonds between our lands. Ancient traditions for succor that must be honored."

"A sword ain't succor," Rusty noted. "Even if a Sword Lord might be gettin' stronger with collectin' 'em, they dinnae need to eat 'em."

"Ah," Oloris replied, eyes shining as if he'd hoped they'd make this point, "a sword may not be succor, but one may offer it. In point of fact" — he gestured to the bread on the table — "this one already has proven capable of doing so."

It was at that point that I realized that our hospitality had been a trap. Or, at a minimum, a test.

Ana had given Lord Talis a great deal more than bread when she'd set the table. "Oh," Ana whispered, visibly trembling as she realized what Lord Oloris was about to say.

"As you are no doubt aware," Oloris began, "the fae of other courts did not weather the coming of the Pale King as easily as your own did. It is, of course, a testament to the might and majesty of the Queen of Rust and Salt that she was capable of defending her people with so little loss."

Political talk, my greatest weakness!

Fortunately, I was playing the role of a simple swordsman at the moment, so I didn't need to play that particular game. Not yet, anyway.

Lord Brine nodded in acknowledgment. As he began to speak in response, I saw calculation in his face, and I understood at least some part of it. If he simply accepted that the latter point was true — that we were better off than other courts because of our queen — it might imply our court was in a position to make sacrifices. Disagreeing could potentially insult his own queen, which was obviously unacceptable. "You are, of course, correct about our queen's majesty, and her artful protection of our people. As for the state of our court as compared to the others, well, there are many factors that play into such a thing. Humans have taken much from us in the aftermath of that terrible war, and as you are no doubt aware, our court plays a critical role in the defense of the world against the Buried."

I raised an eyebrow at that, but remained silent. I knew that there were tunnels related to the Buried underneath our kingdom, but the same was true among all the courts, as far as I was aware. Was there some special significance to our court's place? I didn't know, and I didn't like not knowing.

Still, it wasn't my place to speak. I listened. I learned.

Oloris waved a hand. "The wounds inflicted by mortal hands have not been forgotten, nor your role in our people's exodus and sanctuary. Having walked in this beautiful place for even a short time, and having taken part in this generous bounty" — he indicated the remains of the bread, and Ana visibly winced — "it is clear that your people have abundance in a way others may not."

Lord Brine took a breath. "It is true that food is not as scarce as some other resources. If it would please our fellow courts, I would be glad to petition the queen on your behalf, but alas, she is not present. A fact that I doubt you are blind to, given that she currently is meeting with representatives of other courts."

"I would be most grateful if you would pass that message along when the time comes," Oloris replied, "but alas, while we would be grateful for such aid, my boon companion requires something beyond what such grace might solve."

"Though bread helps fight hunger's call, it will not heal the ashen fall." Lord Talis indicated his gray skin, then gave a sad shake of his head. "Through centuries our people hide, with little hope for those inside. With mighty sword in hand raised high, we might breathe in the azure sky."

Ana gawked. I shook myself as I processed his statement.

But it was Rusty who spoke next. "Can't claim to be knowin' all 'bout this sky and such, but I dinnae think that Ana's sword cuts through the Ashen Scourin'."

It probably wouldn't, I considered, *but if my sword is what I think it is . . .*

My thoughts were interrupted by Lord Oloris turning to Rusty to respond. "My companion speaks not of striking down the Ashen Scouring directly, of course. Even if a blade could do such a thing, the scouring would simply spread to fill the gaps, like if you evaporated a bit of fog with flame." He opened his palm, and a pure white flame burned forth, vanishing as he closed his hand. "We have tried, of course. The scouring is not immutable. The elders speak of when the Saint walked the land, purifying regions and sealing others for humans. But we have no Saint, and whatever strange magic she used eludes us. I am a rarity, even among my own people, and wield the power of purification. Even with my own arts, the scouring returns after I burn it away."

Ana and I nodded in understanding, but that did not address the core question.

"What is it that you would want with the sword, then?" Lord Brine asked directly.

"There is but one place within the courts of the north that we know has not been affected by the Ashen Scouring," Lord Oloris explained. "And that place is a destiny shrine. Though I am not an expert on the mechanisms at work, I understand that crystal shrines can create entirely new environments, or adjust the environments within themselves rapidly and completely. Once, our people may have been able to tap the crystals that remain beneath the world, but they remain dedicated to our defense against the Buried. We have tried many solutions, including attempting to duplicate the destiny shrine's crystals, but the magic of the makers remains beyond us. Destiny crystals cannot be moved — not without causing terrible harm by tearing the veins of the world. Even if one could move one, it may be unusable. And so, for centuries, we have failed."

"Through will and whisper words have flown, from deepest depths to farthest throne. Wondrous tales of conjured hoards, born from touch of dungeon sword."

"You . . . think my sword works like a crystal shrine?" Ana seemed to consider that. "Dungeon cores do seem similar, but . . . the sword itself isn't aware like a destiny crystal. I can make simple things with it, but I'm only just learning. I . . . I don't know if the sword could do what you wanted, even if I were to allow you to take the trials."

Lord Talis bowed his head. "We seek no promise, no certainty. Only a chance to live, a hope to be free."

I could see the hurt in Ana's face, the conflict. I could understand why.

It was one thing to deny someone a chance at her sword when they were only seeking a powerful weapon. It was another thing entirely when Lord Talis spoke of using Anathema as a means to feed and free his people.

For Lord Talis, this shrine was not a simple way to prove himself. He was on a hero's quest, one of true importance.

As I realized that, I felt something unfamiliar—

True shame.

Shame that I had not even considered that Anathema was more than sharp edges. And that there were ways that the sword could do great good in this world without ever striking a blow.

Perhaps it was that shame, that hurt, that led me to ask a question. One to defend myself, and my pride, but also one of genuine import.

"You seek it as a dungeon core, and not simply a sword. Are there not other cores, perhaps one not so adored?" I reached out to take Ana's hand and squeezed it tight. She closed her eyes.

"Ah." Oloris took a look at us in a somewhat different light. "What is she to you?"

"She is my brightest morning, my first and deepest scars. She is the blade that walks beside me, the sword that woke my heart."

It was that heart from which I spoke, without hesitation. I saw several emotions flash across Ana's face as her eyes opened, first startlement, then others that were harder to read. She squeezed my hand again, taking a deep breath.

Rusty's response was an even greater mystery. She sat up a little straighter, looking at us as if for the first time, her expression going completely neutral in a way that I found . . . worrying.

Perhaps fortunately, Lord Brine spoke before anything more could happen. "In plainer terms," he explained, "he woke his Heart Point in battle with her. They are still teenagers, but a rivalry was born among them, and such is not an easy thing to sunder."

"A rivalry." Oloris chuckled, but not in a dismissive way. "His words spoke to me of something flavored a bit different, perhaps, but I am not of your court." A breath, and then he shook his head. "Am I to understand that you would have us set aside our request for this budding rivalry?"

"That would not be my place to say," Lord Brine responded, "but it is a factor of importance. I merely wished to clarify."

"Of course." Lord Oloris turned to Lord Talis briefly, then back to Lord Brine. "We understand very well that great steps can be taken in pursuit of a heart's call. This is nothing small. But against the needs of an entire people . . ."

Ana squeezed my hand a third time, then pulled away. "There are rules."

Her voice was barely a whisper, and even that struck my heart hard enough that I felt as if it might crack.

Is . . . she going to let Lord Talis take her sword away? To take her away?

That's not fair—

And for a second time, I felt great shame at my selfishness.

Her sword, her life, her choices. They belonged to her, not to me.

I tried not to let my hurt show on my own face as Lord Oloris looked to her, considering. "We have seen your rules, of course, and would not presume upon you to change them."

"With great respect then," Ana said, her voice a bit stronger, "I do not believe I can help you."

She rose from her chair, walking rather than flying, and indicated the tablets containing the rules. And, one in particular. It read:

No one may enter if they are above Hearth-level. No exceptions!!!

All eyes fell upon it, and though we all understood, Ana spoke next. "Lord Valissar Talis, even in this distant place, word of your strength and deeds has reached us. It is one among these deeds, your own strength having risen into the spirit layer, that disqualifies you."

"There are ways around that," Lord Oloris noted. "In fact, I believe we have a workaround? As you're aware, my friend is a Talis, which means he is a Talisian in training. And as a part of becoming a Talisian . . ."

Ana's eyes widened. "No. I don't want this." She shook her head, turning to Lord Talis directly. "That isn't the way. You don't need to do that. *Please.* Don't."

Lord Talis gave her a soft smile, then shook his head. "Through birth and life this name I wore, with word and deed marked less and more. For trial great, and my people's fate, I am Valissar no m—"

"**Stop.**" I shot to my feet, and though my hand rested in the open air, I could feel my essence go taut. Silver flashed bright in the air, too fast for me to even see—

When I next saw Lord Talis, he'd slid into a combat stance, his right hand outstretched and gripped tightly around a solid pane of silver light. With a grunt of effort and a trembling back, he wrenched and hurled the light upward, where it disappeared into the sky.

Then Lord Talis's eyes narrowed in response, not in anger, but as if he was truly seeing me for what I was for the first time. And, upon seeing my true self, he rested his hand on the sword at his side.

A chill ran down my spine. Not out of fear that I might be harmed, but at what I'd just done. I could feel the tension in the air, just as he could.

"Though your hand sets not upon your blade, I feel the cut of challenge made."

Lord Valissar Talis spoke true—

I did not know how, but I'd struck at him. Not with a sword, not directly.

I'd used the Cutting Remark, or at least a rough approximation of it. It wasn't exactly my teacher's technique, but the effect was close enough. I'd used it without thinking, without meaning, but . . .

Ana raised a hand to her mouth in shock. Lord Oloris and Lord Brine were stunned. For Valissar Talis, however, there was no need for movement, only further appraisal. He waited for what I would do next.

My eyes were locked on his, but in the corner of my vision, I saw something else—

A razor-sharp grin drifting across Rusty's face. At the time, I didn't quite understand why, but even then, I had a foreboding sensation when I saw that expression.

"Well, now." Lord Oloris adjusted his shirt. "This is quite unfortunate. It would appear that the Court of Rust and Salt has violated our guest rights."

Lord Brine finally shook himself, then reacted. "My Lord Talis, forgive us!" He bowed hastily, three times. "This behavior is truly unacceptable, and the child will—"

"Nah." Rusty spoke up. "Not a violation of guest rights. He's another guest, not one of ours."

I blinked, turning to Rusty, appraising. What was their angle?

"Then you would leave us to resolve this in our own way?" Lord Oloris asked.

"Well, I . . ." Lord Brine turned to Rusty. "I still believe an apology is in order from our court, since one of our other guests attacked you without provocation. Please, allow us to handle any punishment on your behalf, since he is another guest, and one that has done us a service."

"No." Lord Oloris interrupted, a hand coming up. "Let the boy speak for himself."

I took a deep breath, considering.

I'd struck from a place of passion, having understood what Lord Talis was planning to do—

The rules were clear. No one could enter the shrine if they were above Hearth-level.

And so, Lord Talis had planned to *abandon his own name.*

For one of the fae, there were few sacrifices that could be made of such significance. As a candidate to be a new Talisian, he had already accepted that he would eventually give up his name to be Talisian — but this act would not allow him to do that.

He would be nameless and deedless, at least for a time. And as a knight of many stories, this sacrifice would be all the greater.

And for a third time, I felt great shame, for I understood the significance of what he was willing to offer for even a chance to help his people—

And still, I stood against him.

There are times in life when there are no simple solutions to right and wrong. Would I stand against someone who sought only to bring clear skies to his people?

Perhaps.

But, though it was my pride that had first caused me to resist the idea of allowing another to attempt the trials, it was not what had made me move in that moment.

It was the subtle slump of Ana's shoulders as she realized the same thing that I had, the faltering of her face. And the knowledge that if given a chance, Lord Valissar Talis would take her away.

She'd told him to stop. She'd made it clear this wasn't what she wanted.

Was my own pride, my own desire, worth challenging Lord Talis's claim, and rejecting his sacrifice?

No.

If it was simply that, I would have set my emotions aside and apologized for my error. Perhaps I would have relied on the protection of the Court of Rust and Salt for the debt that was owed to me, as they'd hinted.

But for Ana's freedom to make her own choices, for her own autonomy, and for the bond between us, I would fight.

"Valissar Talis, great knight and lord, a blow was struck at my accord. My challenge made, the stage is set, I'll speak it plain—

"Now draw. Your. Sword."

CHAPTER XI

SWORD

Lord Valissar Talis did not, in fact, immediately draw his sword.

Instead, he simply stepped forward and appeared in front of me. Then he swept a single finger down.

Rejoi—

I was too slow.

His skin brushed my cheek, opposite of where my own court had marked me, and traced a line across my skin. I felt the sting.

"No duel is needed, no threat of war. For your blow struck, I've returned with more."

I reached up.

They say that when you're cut by a master swordsman, you sometimes don't even feel it. That's only true in narrow circumstances. This was not one of them.

I felt the burn across my cheek even before I felt the wetness. He'd cut me with his finger, so quickly I couldn't even defend myself with a thought.

And before, when I'd attacked without thinking, he'd been so quick that he grabbed my *words* out of the air.

I couldn't fight that.

I wasn't foolish enough to think that I could, even then.

"Well, then. If that's resolved," Lord Brine said hastily, "perhaps we should retire for the moment, and . . ."

"I'm not done." I wiped the blood away from my cheek with a hand, taking a step forward to meet Lord Talis's eyes.

He tilted his head to the side, meeting my gaze with his own, then sighed. And, for the first time, he fully broke from his pattern of speech. "You would insist upon this? I have no wish to harm a child."

"You seek to take away my friend without her consent. That is *harm*."

He took a moment, thinking, then nodded. "You're correct. I owe an apology to both of you for my hasty action — and I grant it now. Will you accept that?"

"I'll accept your apology gladly if you'll agree not to continue in pursuing her sword," I told him.

"I can't do that." He shook his head. "I'm genuinely sorry."

"So am I." I took a breath. "Shall we find a better place for this duel?"

"Wait!" Ana put her hands up. This time, at least, we both listened. "This isn't appropriate."

"Well, we're in agreement about that," Lord Brine said, "but they do seem to be working toward an amicable duel, at least."

"That's not the problem!" Ana marched forward, then physically pushed me away from Lord Talis. I blinked in surprise.

Then she turned toward him, folding her arms. "You can't duel with Lien right now. He has a prior obligation."

I blinked.

Ana pulled out a page from seemingly nowhere. And, of course, I recognized it.

It was a request for a duel between Ana and myself in front of the Smiling Sword Saint.

Lord Talis accepted the page, reviewing it. "It does appear that he has a prior obligation, but there's a section for a date, and it hasn't been set."

"That's right. We need to wait for the queen to get back so she can review it. Of course, she's very busy, so . . ."

Lord Oloris stepped forward. "A hypothetical future duel, while worthy of respect, should not be something that can delay a present duel for an indeterminate period of time. Would you be willing to set this duel aside?"

"Perhaps." Ana shrugged, as if considering it for the first time. She had a plan. I could see that, but I couldn't read what it was. "If Lord Talis was willing to agree to a set amount of time to wait, I would set aside my obligation to this particular duel to allow his to proceed."

"This is not a simple thing you ask for," Lord Oloris replied. "His people are in need of help. You must understand—"

Lord Talis raised a hand, and his companion stopped. "You're buying him time to prepare."

"Maybe." She shrugged noncommittally.

"You must understand that this cause is no game to me. I am hoping to prevent my people from wasting away."

"I know," Ana whispered. "I'm sorry, but I can't let this go forward now."

"A suggestion, then!" Rusty clapped. "Why not let Lord Talis study the sword while he waits? It's not like he's going to be able to use it instantly even if he earns it. Dungeon essence is complicated, especially for things like making food and drink."

Lord Talis frowned. "How long did it take you to conjure such things, young Anathema?"

"I . . . still can't. Not exactly." Ana sighed. "The bread from earlier? I didn't make that with magic. I just . . . made it look like that. I wanted to impress people. I baked it manually, like a human would, then stored it in the dungeon. There are places there where time barely moves, and I can take things in and out of that freely. So, I didn't conjure the bread, I . . ."

"You summoned it." Oloris blinked. "That recontextualizes things. We thought your abilities were . . ."

"Different." Lord Talis nodded. "This is no insult. You were clever to be able to convince us of your abilities so easily. That, unfortunately, also made us more eager to move forward. Still, I have heard of feats such as what you made us believe you were capable of being performed by dungeons before."

"I think it can be done, but . . . I don't really know how. It may require several different types of essence, not just dungeon essence, or far greater mastery."

"And you would allow me to study the sword, and this essence, in exchange for the delay?"

Ana looked at Rusty, then nodded to Lord Talis. "I would."

"Good. Provided we can agree on a reasonable amount of time, I would agree to that."

"Three years," Ana offered. "It is a traditional value, and you can see that as it is right now, Lien is only a Torch."

"Even three years would not be enough for him to reach my level," Lord Talis noted.

"Sure, but he could get closer. Do you accept?"

Lord Talis looked at Oloris, then back to Ana. "I cannot. It is too long to keep my people waiting. Things grow worse by the day. It is not as simple as waiting another three years compared to the four hundred. Something is changing in the lands to the north — something with the scouring itself. I don't know what it is, but I know I must act. Three weeks."

"That's . . . not much time to train. Let us be reasonable. A year and a day?" Ana asked. "He could, perhaps, reach Hearth-level in that time, and it is a traditional value."

". . . It is still too long. Three months."

Ana looked to me. Then, as tears welled up in her eyes, she turned back to Lord Talis and said, "We have a deal."

In a single gesture, she tore the letter from the Smiling Sword Saint in half.

"Three months before the duel." Lord Talis nodded. "But after that, there will be no further delays. I will claim the sword."

"Oh, no, you still can't do that right away." Ana laughed, brushing tears from her eyes.

"What?"

"You see" — she tossed the torn papers aside — "I have a prior obligation."

Lord Talis glanced at the torn page. "You just—"

"Not that one. I've set that duel aside. But you see, Lord Talis, there's another rule you can't cast aside along with your name. There's already a challenge for my sword in progress."

"Your friend was able to enter and challenge, was he not? What outstanding challenges could there be?" Lord Oloris asked.

"Him." Ana pointed at me. "His challenge is still going. He never technically failed his current challenge. I asked him to step outside to see what was going on."

I gawked.

Ana was right. I *hadn't* failed.

"What would you like," Lord Talis said with a sigh, "to set that challenge aside?"

"It isn't actually up to me," Ana said. "He's the challenger, so negotiating stepping aside would be up to him. Lien?"

My mind raced.

If they were acknowledging I had a prior claim, could I just . . . wait, and hold on to that?

It might have worked, but that was a coward's way out. It denied anyone access to Ana's trial, which wasn't fair to her, nor was it fair to Lord Talis, who had come all this way for an attempt. And it wasn't fair to me, either.

I could have offered to enter immediately to finish the trial, but seeing Ana's expression, I got the sense that she didn't want that. I didn't know why. Perhaps I hadn't been as close to succeeding as I'd thought I was?

Or perhaps if I claimed the sword directly, she thought Lord Talis would take it from me by force, since I wasn't a member of the court?

I didn't read him that way, but Ana generally had a better way of understanding fae than I did. So, I followed her lead.

"Since I have an existing claim to Anathema that you ignored by attempting to enter," I told Lord Talis, "you may consider me the injured party for this duel, and thus, I would set the terms. In exchange for setting the terms of our duel, I would set aside the claim to my current attempt to earn Anathema."

"An interesting proposal. Provided you do not delay the start of the duel further, I accept."

"Good." I nodded. "Very well. Lord Talis, our duel will be a threefold duel. Three challenges, each set apart at seasonal increments. Best two out of three for determining the overall winner."

". . . It seems you've managed to get more time after all. Clever. But if I win the first two, we can conclude this early?"

I nodded slowly. "That seems fair."

"And the nature of the duel? Swords?" he asked.

I shook my head. "Even with three months, I can't hope to beat you like that. We will conduct the duel as combat by trial."

I heard a gasp from Lord Oloris. "That could mean *anything*!"

"I'll be reasonable, of course. I suggest a trial, we discuss it. You can refuse or accept it. If you refuse, it's your turn to make a suggestion. Each of us has three total refusals of the trials the other suggests, across all three possible rounds. We will consider our options for three months, then discuss the first trial here on that day and agree to it. Three judges will adjudicate the challenges. Is that acceptable?"

He considered that. "I believe whoever accepts a challenge should be the one to choose the next challenge after the break."

I mentally winced. I'd been hoping I could always be the first to make a suggestion, thus burning through his refusals. "That's fine."

"Good. I accept your terms. Are there any other complications?" He looked to Ana.

"No, that was it. Although each of you will need to pick who will serve as your second and third to help you prepare for the duels," Ana noted.

"Ana," I asked her, "will you be my second?"

"Why, I'd be happy—"

"I'm afraid I can't accept that," Lord Talis interjected. "You are ultimately too close to the issue, Lady Anathema. You would better serve as one of the three judges for the contest."

She sighed. "*Fiiine.* I guess that's true."

I frowned. That put me in a much more awkward spot, but I didn't actually disagree with him. In human culture, there might have been some concern about Ana being unfair as a judge due to her own biases, but fae traditions put so many behavioral and structural obligations on judges that I didn't expect an issue. Apparently, Lord Talis didn't, either. "Okay. Well, if I can't choose Ana, I'll . . . need some time to think about my options."

"I will choose Lord Oloris as my second," Lord Talis noted, "unless you object?"

I shook my head. "No, that's fine. I am, however, counting your refusal of Ana as one of your three refusals for our duel. I never explicitly stated that those three refusals were limited to the options for the contest itself."

"You're quick," Lord Talis laughed. "That's quite clever, but your wording was that each of us has three refusals of trials the other suggested. Your friend is not a trial."

"I could argue that she *is* a trial, believe me." Ana elbowed me, but I continued. "Moreover, her trials are, in fact, the point of the contest."

"True," Lord Talis acknowledged, "but your suggestion was for her as a second, not as a trial. Thus, whether or not she could be considered a trial outside of the contest is a different discussion."

I nodded. "I'll concede that argument and acknowledge that you may begin with all three refusals."

"Wonderful." He nodded. "This might be more entertaining than I expected. I will meet you back here in three months, along with your second and third. I suppose I shall have to find a third as well."

I'd need to find options for both.

I thought of the Smiling Sword Saint immediately, of course — if anything happened, she could step in to protect me.

But that wouldn't be any fun, would it?

And there was something else at play here, more than just the contest on the surface.

As Lord Talis and Lord Oloris departed the glade, Rusty slid up next to me.

"So," they said, "I hear you might need a second. And as it happens, I make an excellent squire."

I looked at Rusty, evaluating what they'd said, and what I'd immediately recognized. If I accepted this offer, things would be much more complicated—

But I only had three months to prepare for my first round, and I needed all the help I could get. Even if it came with an entirely different type of danger. "I'd love to have you."

Rusty gave me a wry grin. "Great! I have some ideas on how to help. I'll see you in a few months."

I blinked. "You're . . . not going to stay and talk strategy?"

"Nah, you can handle that. I'm going to need to go fetch something from Grandmother's house. Now, where did I put my riding hood?"

CHAPTER XII

STEPS

Ana looked distracted as she floated at my side. It was understandable, of course. I had a lot on my mind, but it was her fate that was at stake with our contest. She looked worried. I wasn't sure if I should bother her, which meant that I managed to hold out for at least three minutes before I said something.

We were alone in the glade near the entrance to her shrine now. Lord Brine had escorted the foreigners off to some sort of guest lodgings — perhaps within the inner court, which I had never seen. I wasn't jealous of that, exactly, but I was curious what it was like.

That was much less of a concern than whatever Rusty was up to. I didn't know where exactly they'd run off to, but it hadn't been with Brine. That was odd.

So was virtually any sort of fae talking about a grandmother. And if Rusty was who I assumed . . . well, I wasn't sure I liked the implications of a visit to Grandmother for help.

Ana's silence was almost as foreboding. I took a while to work on treating my leg injury more carefully, then ran out of patience and turned toward her. "What are you thinking about?"

"Oh, Lien." She sighed. "Sometimes it's like I can still hear his voice."

I groaned. "I'm not dead, Ana."

"It sounds so real." She shook her head, wiping faux tears out of her eyes. "Alas, it would seem that I am haunted. Perhaps it's because I never finished that sonnet in his honor."

"A sonnet? Really?" I folded my arms. "Did you even start a sonnet in my honor?"

"Of course, dearly departed soul. Allow me to begin. 'There once was a boy with a stick, his mind was as thick as his — '"

I stepped in front of her. "That's a dirty limerick, Ana, not a sonnet."

She shrugged. "Does it really make any difference to the dead?"

I sighed, rolling my eyes. "What's actually bothering you?"

"I thought I made it clear that I was mourning the loss of a friend, dear ghost."

I stretched out a hand. Ana shifted to her pixie size, then flapped over to it, landing on it and climbing up onto my shoulder. "I take it you don't approve of our strategy?"

"It's more that I'm having a hard time" — she chuckled — "*finding* a strategy."

"We bought ourselves a season. That's a lot of training time. And my master—"

"Is about as likely to kill you herself as she is to teach you anything useful in that time span. So, Lien, you need a plan. A real, clear one. Not vague 'I'm going to be the best at swords by then' stuff."

"I didn't think I was going to be the best, just—"

"Moderately better after a season. Yeah. That isn't going to cut it."

"You're feeling very jokey today, aren't you?"

"It's a self-defense mechanism!" She huffed. "And a you-defense mechanism! Because you're not taking this seriously enough. And yes, you could get hurt, or killed, or both!"

I narrowed my eyes. "You've never worried so much about me being killed before."

"That's because it was me doing it! It's different if *I* kill you, obviously."

I frowned. "You don't want me doing this?"

"I didn't say that." She sighed. "It's just . . . if you got killed trying to protect me, that wouldn't be the proper end to our story."

"It would be a pretty classic ending, wouldn't it?" I asked.

"Classic, sure. But for a different type of story. Not ours. We die together or not at all, okay?"

There was something very serious in her tone. The kind of thing that made me consider before answering, which was admittedly a little rarer than it probably should have been.

". . . Not going to agree to that."

She nodded. "Good."

"Good? You're not mad that I didn't agree to some kind of mutual death vow?"

She leaned forward and poked my head. "No, it's good, because you *thought* about the question and gave a reasonable answer. That's the Lien I need right now. Not the Lien who charges into a lair trying to save the damsel. Which, I'd like to make it very clear, is *not* the role I'm playing right now."

"Understood." I took a breath. "Don't worry, I didn't think you looked anything like a lair."

Ana swatted at me again, but I parried her hand with a single finger. After a brief exchange, I continued. "So, your fundamental problem is my lack of strategy for training over the next few months, right? That's solvable."

"A lack of a plan is solvable. A plan that gets you to where you need to be in order to fight Lord Talis in a season . . . I don't know if that's solvable."

"Well, hammer and forge it with me. We've got the time. And there's whatever Rusty is coming up with, too."

She nodded, looking a little brighter now that we were discussing the ideas.

And that she's playing a role in her own fate, I realized. *She doesn't want to be a helpless damsel — so she's helping give me the plan necessary to win the contest. It gives her some agency. Okay. I can work with that.*

"Well, to start with, the Smiling Sword Saint is still my best resource for combat improvement," I told her. "The sword school is helpful, too, but they drill basics. I need things that are more substantial, like techniques."

"Techniques aren't a bad idea. If you can learn the Sword Saint's Smile . . ." She seemed to consider that, then shook her head. "But that's still sword essence. He's so much higher level than you that he might be able to wrest control over it."

"His destiny." I sighed. "Sword Lord is a direct counter to almost everything I can do."

"Yep. What about your own destiny? Could you do something with that?"

"I . . . have some ideas for that. I definitely plan to work on it, but I don't actually know what my destiny does."

I didn't say "if anything" aloud, but I was thinking it. I hadn't told her exactly what had happened with my destiny, and it wasn't quite the right time. I preferred to focus on more actionable ideas, especially because they were less embarrassing.

"Okay, glad you're thinking about it. But if it might not give you non-swordy powers . . ."

"I need to use other essence types, then. What if I blended something else into that technique?"

"It's going to be hard enough just learning that kind of technique in a few months. You still haven't even gotten an air slash technique to work yet, have you?"

I shook my head. "Nope. No ranged attacks at all. Rejoinder is the closest, but it's still nothing like an air slash, and beyond that, I'd need to learn things like the Cutting Remark as intermediary techniques."

"Didn't you just use the Cutting Remark?" she asked.

"Not intentionally. But . . . yeah, I think so? I can work on that some more. But that's a long way from a true ranged attack, and you saw how easily he stopped it."

Ana nodded. "Yeah. It's pretty much pure sword essence, and as a Sword Lord, he's really good at countering that. He's almost a perfect counter to sword techniques in general . . . okay, let's not focus on that, then. Too many points of failure. You fail to learn one of the techniques, you learn them and can't master them, you learn them and he can turn them against you . . ."

I took a breath. "Okay. What can't he turn against me that I could conceivably learn?"

"Better." She turned around and leaned back against my neck, looking up as she pondered. "Other techniques made from your new essence or breach essence. Or, maybe, internal sword techniques and augments. He *probably* can't manipulate sword essence that's in your body."

I shuddered at the image. "If he could, then he'd probably just be able to make my heart explode or something. Yeah, that'd be bad."

"Right. He *probably* can't do that. So, assuming that, maybe picking up some internally focused augments or techniques wouldn't be a bad idea."

I nodded. "I can do that. A strong movement technique to counter whatever he's going to be doing . . ."

"Teleporting, if he's a Talisian in training."

"That's . . . not an easy one to counter, is it?"

"Nope. Unless you think you can manage some kind of breach-based technique to lock down the whole area, or make teleportation dangerous?"

I took a breath. "That's . . . an idea, I guess. But it might make it impossible to fight. Or, you know, let things leak in from other planes. If I could make it work at all."

"Sounds *amazing*." Her eyes were glimmering as she spoke.

"I'll take that into advisement." I took a breath. "A general body reinforcement technique would be ideal, too."

"Sure. Less of a concern with countering him directly there, although you need to worry about if it's going to be enough to bother using. He's going to be much stronger and faster than you in general. Even a body technique may not be enough to close the gap."

"And if I use a generic sword essence one, he might do the same. In fact, there's a good chance he'll want to use one even if I don't." I shook my head. Ana was right — this wasn't going to be a simple challenge. If I assumed he already had a movement technique and a body-enhancement technique, that put him even further ahead of me than just our levels would indicate.

And if he had access to powers from the spirit layer . . .

I blinked, a thought occurring to me. "Ana. I already have a spirit bond, right?"

"Sure. He's in the spirit layer, he probably has multiple. That's not an advantage for you."

I shook my head. "I wasn't mentioning it as an advantage over him, exactly. I was thinking that it's unusual for my level."

"Most fae are born with one, Lien. I have one, too."

"I know, I know. But mine is a little weird, because I'm not fae — or, at least, I'm probably not. And I shouldn't have one at this level, probably? It's outside of the normal structure. What if we . . . stretched that further?"

Ana blinked at me. "You want more spirit bonds? That's possible, but it's really dangerous, Lien. We've talked about it before. If you wanted to bond to someone strong, even if they accepted, it'd be a subordinate bond — they'd have a lot of control over you, forever. Unless they specifically chose to make it like a family bond . . ." She gasped. "Are you asking me to bond with you?"

"... Uh, no? Hope you're not offended, but no. Not unless I earn the sword, at least."

"I, uh . . . wow, okay." She wiped her forehead. "That's a . . . relief. I wasn't ready for that kind of commitment. We're still young, you know?"

"Weren't you telling me that you were jealous of me sparring with other people earlier?"

"That's different! You're supposed to be *my* rival, not some kind of . . . sword hussy!"

"Sword hussy." I narrowed a single eye at her.

"The title is a work in progress!" She huffed. "Look, this is time to talk about your bad decisions, not my insecurities."

"Right." I barely resisted flicking her off my shoulder. "Moving on. I wasn't talking about more spirit bonds. At least, not to *people*."

She let out an exaggerated gasp. "The swords in the sepulcher."

I nodded. "Every spirit bond gives someone power. With several more, I could punch well above my level."

"But then you'd turn into Evil Mirror Lien! You've literally seen how that plays out! You'd go prematurely gray, Lien! It's not worth it!"

"His hair was really more of a white." Then, after a pause, I added, "It didn't look that bad."

"The hair isn't the main issue here."

"Then you shouldn't have ended with it."

Ana groaned. "Okay. Sheathing that little bit, we'll talk about the more important part — being super evil."

"He wasn't super evil. Just like . . . I don't know, a bit unfriendly?"

"He tried to murder you!"

"You do that all the time."

Ana paused. ". . . I don't actually try very hard to kill you. Most of the time."

"There are times when you do?"

"Look, I have my good days and my great days. Now, back to your terrible plan. It's terrible. Into the junk pile, Lien."

"I'll set it aside." I made a gesture of shelving something. "For now. But I think I was going in the right direction."

"Evil is never the right direction, Lien, unless it comes with enough dark clothing and eyeliner to make it worthwhile."

"He did have a darker outfit than I did."

"Wait, really? Hold on, let me reexamine—"

"Already sheathed and shelved." I pointed toward the forest behind us and an invisible shelf that presumably still held that argument. "So, moving forward. What if I'm not thinking big enough?"

"I don't know, Lien. I feel like I'm always going to be the Ashen Lord in our relationship dynamic. Now, if you feel like conquering a different planet—"

"I don't mean in terms of the evil part, Ana. I mean in terms of getting powers out of their proper sequence."

"Oooh." She snapped her fingers. "You could get the dark eyeliner look permanently with the right power!"

"That's . . . not really my priority."

"Maybe it should be. You're very unlikely to beat Lord Talis in a fight, but if you seduce him—"

"Not doing that."

"I feel like you're taking weapons off the table by saying that, but okay, sure. He does seem to be in a committed relationship already, and I don't know if they're monogamous."

I blinked. I hadn't picked up on the fact that Lord Talis was in a relationship at that point, but Ana always was better at that sort of thing, and she might have had better information. I had another argument, though. "He's also too old."

"Oh. Right, non-fae age ethics." She nodded. "Okay. So . . . you think you could manage to get a shade weave early?"

"I don't know." I shook my head. "It's technically possible. I think the witches have a way, since it's helpful for when the body and spirit don't match."

"I've talked to Darryl about it. He's not actually doing anything fancy like that yet. It's doable, but there are risks. And even if they know how to do it for changing that kind of body configuration issue, it doesn't mean they could teach you how to do it for a combat technique."

"Worth asking, maybe?"

"It might be." She nodded. "But you'd probably need to pick up a relevant essence type if you wanted to do it yourself."

". . . Actually, I was thinking I might not have to."

Ana blinked . . . then processed. "The seal. Are you thinking of breaking more layers of it, then trying to use that as a way to get into your Shade Layer to make a shade weave?"

"Maybe. Or . . . a different layer entirely."

"That sounds really, really dangerous, Lien."

I nodded. "Yep."

"This is great. I can't wait to see how you destroy yourself."

"I thought only you were allowed to kill me?" I asked.

"I'd make an exception if you destroy yourself in a way that's cool enough and I get to watch."

We took a detour on the way home to the Witchwood. We didn't even make it to the house before we found Darryl, who seemed to be waiting for us in the center of a field, surrounded by scarecrows.

He was wearing his traditional pointed hat and pitch-black wizard robes, sitting in midair on top of a floating book. The whole thing looked very impractical and uncomfortable to me, but aesthetics were important to him.

He opened a single eye as we approached. I reached into a pouch on my side, pulled out a vial, and tossed it toward him.

I missed. Pretty badly, in fact. Thrown accuracy wasn't my strength at that age.

Ana flew off my shoulder, rescuing the vial of liquid that was as large as she was, although it very nearly dragged her to the ground when she caught it. With a poof, she shifted to approximately human size, then handed the vial to an amused-looking Darryl.

"A gift, for our safe passage, and any hospitality you might be willing to offer to weary travelers," Ana told him, her voice serious.

Darryl took the vial, lifting it and shaking it, then popped the cap and downed the contents. After he wiped his lips, he frowned. "What was that, exactly?"

"Don't just drink random things!" I told him with a sigh.

"It wasn't random, you gave it to me." He frowned, then reached to his stomach. "Oh, that's a gurgle. Am I in danger?"

I sighed. "It wasn't dangerous, it's just . . . not meant to be drunk in one sitting. It's a rare essence I got I thought you'd like. It's—"

"Alchemy flavored? Weird. I can't usually taste the concept of alchemy." Darryl reached up. "Aaah, now I can smell it, too. Oh, no. Alchemy, why? *Why*?"

"So —" Ana leaned in. "About that safe passage?"

"Fine, fine! Safe passage and guest rights! Do you have water?"

I pulled out a flask.

"No throwing!" Ana glared at me, then walked closer and snatched it out of my hands. Then she fed it to Darryl, and he ran home to the bathroom.

We caught up with him a little later and explained the situation.

"Early shade weave via breach essence, eh?" His eyes were red. His nose? Also red. His hair? Still normal, fortunately. "That's an impressive idea. Terrible, but impressive."

I folded my arms. "There's precedent for it, right? You've been exploring it?"

"I've been exploring gender-affirming shapeshifting, yeah. That's absolutely a valid thing to explore with shade weaves. Thing is, I'd be doing it with shade essence, the essence of . . . you know, shade weaves. You'd be trying to do it by blowing a hole in your shade, then hoping that you could fill that with something sword-shaped."

"No innuendo," I told Ana. "I get enough of that from Dream Girl."

Ana looked annoyed at that remark for some reason.

Wait, is she starting to make crude jokes because of the ones Dream Girl made?

That . . . wow, okay. We have some real issues to work out.

"Moving on," Darryl said, "even if you actually unlocked that layer via breach essence, which I'm iffy on the theory for, it wouldn't let you form a shade weave. You need something that can, you know, weave shades for that."

"Or someone else to do it for me, right?" I asked.

"Technically, yeah. And if you wanted something that's a very standard modification, people can get those early from others. Like, a weave that just makes you generically stronger? Possible. But it's almost always better to make your own shade weaves. And to do that, you need to either get shade essence or wait until you reach the Shade Layer of essence development."

"What about weaving essence?" I asked.

"I . . . uh, guess? You planning to take up weaving?"

"Absolutely not," I told him. "I just like magic theory and wanted to know if it was a thing."

He chuckled. "Right. That's very you."

"What about something conceptually similar to weaving, like . . . forging essence? Could I *reforge* my spirit?"

Darryl blinked. "I honestly don't know. Even weaving essence is . . . well, shade weaving is more of a metaphor for rebuilding the shade, rather than literally weaving anything. So, I guess, if weaving might work — and that's a maybe, I actually don't know — then I guess forging might theoretically work, too?"

I'll save you the scene transition — we talked to Auntie Temper next.

"It's a nay," she said.

"That's it? Nay?"

"I'm not gonna tell ye that it's impossible, lad." Auntie Temper set her hammer aside briefly, to a disappointed "aww" from the little swords and daggers in line for maintenance. "Truly, there may be a way that one such as ye could make it work. But it's nae a wise idea at your skill level, Lien. You'd be best to be waitin' until yer at least at the level to forge yer spirit first, before yer shade."

". . . And if I need strength now?"

"Then find it somewhere deeper." She pointed at my chest with a gigantic finger. "Work on the blade ye've already begun to forge before forging one anew, aye?"

"A blade I've already begun to build . . ." I took a breath, looking to Ana and Darryl. "Oh. I think I know what I have to do."

CHAPTER XIII

STRATEGY

It was strange to come home and find it empty.

I'd been on my own plenty of times, of course, but the hut where I'd grown up was deeply connected with Gramps — it felt wrong not to have at least one of him around at all times.

It felt even stranger to be in a position where I desperately wanted his advice.

Sure, Gramps always thought he knew better than I did about everything, and that grated on my teenage nerves . . . but I also knew he was an expert at all sorts of magic, and I was in a bit of a bind.

Not the sword kind of binding. That would be later, presumably. But the kind of bind where I'd gotten myself into a situation where it genuinely looked like I had no chance of success.

Sure, I'd have some influence over the specific challenges we'd be dealing with, but with an opponent who was at least two full levels above me . . . and had not only one powerful destiny mark but multiple . . .

I was well and truly out of my depth, and I needed to figure out how to even the odds in a comparatively short period of time.

This wasn't to say that I was short on ideas. I had *plenty* of ideas. My sword was presumably an advantage if I could figure out how to use it properly, but with major caveats — it would be less advantageous in a nonlethal challenge, and I didn't know if my opponent would be able to manipulate it with the Sword Lord destiny. If he could, it was a complete counter to anything I could learn in terms of the sword's abilities, so . . . I couldn't count on that as a major edge over my opponent.

And, of course, it was likely he would have a magic sword of his own. He was a famous Sword Lord, after all. He probably had multiple.

Ugh. It's not fair.

I settled down in my bedroom, throwing my dirty and bloodstained clothes off into a pile — Gramps was out, after all — and then going out back to pour a bucket over myself. I didn't have the energy to go out to the healing waters, even though I desperately could have used the healing. And, of course, it was the middle of the night by the time I got home.

After I finished pouring the bucket over my head, Ana was fluttering in front of me.

I stood, dripping, in front of her. "Oh, hey." I waved. "So, I was thinking about options for how to get stronger."

"We should talk about that. And other stuff. But you should probably get dressed. You're soaking wet, and you're going to freeze if we chat while standing out here."

I shrugged. "I don't mind the cold."

"It might be a long talk."

I raised an eyebrow. "Okay." I shrugged, then shook off some of the water and put the bucket down.

You look surprised that was my only reaction to the situation. Fae didn't tend to have much of a taboo about being undressed, and Ana and I were never very modest with each other. A lot of fae weren't that into clothes in general, after all, especially aquatic ones like our naiad friends.

She was right that I was dripping wet, though, so I went inside and dried off. Ana handed me a set of my clothes, and I nodded gratefully as I got dressed, then patted the side of my bed.

She fluttered over, sighed, and sat down. She wouldn't meet my gaze.

"Everything okay?"

She mumbled something incoherent, both because she was clearly still flustered and also because she was currently only six inches tall, then finally turned toward me. ". . . Fine."

"You're being weird," I told her.

"Your *face* is being weird," she replied, as tradition dictated she must.

I nodded fervently. "Yeah, nose is a little big, but I'll probably grow into it. So, what's bothering you? I mean, aside from my huge . . . duel coming up."

"Ugh." She threw her hands up. "If you're going to be like this, I'm just going to go."

I snorted. "Fine, fine. No teasing. Help me out with rapid advancement ideas?"

". . . Yeah, that's fine."

"Great." I resisted the urge to make any more jokes. Ana didn't bluff, at least not outside of card games. And role-playing. And board games.

Okay, she *did* bluff. But not when she said she'd leave if I did a thing. So, I didn't want to push, even though a part of me wanted to.

I didn't understand *why* I wanted to tease her at the time, nor did I really think on it. I was introspective about a lot of things, but my motivations for wanting to fluster Ana weren't the type of thing I was self-aware about.

Anyway, I didn't want her to leave, so I focused on the issue at hand.

"So, sword practice, obviously," I told her.

"Yeah, obviously." She sighed contentedly, clearly more comfortable with this subject matter. "But even if you can beat him in raw skill — which, being fair, you probably can't — it wouldn't be enough to overcome the level gap."

"Know any tricks to hitting Hearth-level in three months?" I asked.

"Not really. How close are you?"

I considered that. It hadn't been that long since I'd hit Torch-level, but I'd probably been close when I'd broken the seal on my right hand, unlocking a fully-formed Dianis Point.

A single completed Dianis Point required six units of compressed essence. That was also the requirement for Candle-level, the first formal level as an essence sorcerer. Most of my friends had been born at that level, but I hadn't hit it until a few years before, during a sparring session with Ana.

Reaching Torch-level required eighteen total essence. So, basically three completed Dianis Points, or you could take one or two Dianis Points and keep making them stronger until you hit the required essence threshold.

I'd been working toward that for years when I went to the Sepulcher of Sealed Swords. If I had to guess, I had probably been within a point or two from reaching Torch — let's say sixteen essence to be safe. Ten sword essence, six breach, since I'd only just made a Dianis Point for breach essence recently.

Then, I'd unlocked a third Dianis Point in the sepulcher. That meant, at a minimum, another six compressed essence.

After that, I'd continued training, but it had been less than a month. I hadn't measured my essence total since then. Gramps had tools for it, but I hadn't bothered recently. "I'm probably at somewhere between twenty-two and twenty-four compressed essence in total," I concluded. "Let's say twenty-two to play it safe. Focusing solely on building primary essence, I managed to make a Viewing Point in six months, which means I was managing a rate of one essence per month."

"Ugh, math. So, that means you're hopeless, right?"

I shrugged. "Wouldn't ever say that. But I don't think twelve to fourteen more essence in three months is a reasonable goal. In nine months . . . maybe. Now that I'm Torch-level, my body will process essence faster. I don't know the math on that, but assuming it's fifty percent faster, that'd mean I could theoretically do something like thirteen and a half units of essence compression in nine months, which is . . ."

"Just about enough. But you'd have to stick with almost exclusively going for primary essence."

I groaned at that. "Might be a necessity. I'll think on it. And ways to get more power faster. Other ideas?"

"Well," she considered, lying on her stomach on the bed to face toward me, legs up in the air. "There's always picking up more essence types."

"Yeah. I was thinking about that on the way home. But three months . . . I don't know. It took me six months to get breach essence, and that was with letting everything else go in the meantime. Even if I choose something immediately, I don't know if my body would acclimate fast enough."

Ana frowned. "What about something similar to what you already have? That'd go faster, right?"

"In theory. Between that and my faster speed from being at Torch-level, it might be doable, but . . . not sure. And even if it did work, something similar might still be something he could mess with using his Sword Lord powers."

"Oh, right. Your main essence is totally useless against him, yeah." She nodded, mostly to herself. "Yeah, so . . . hm. You're doomed?"

"Totally doomed." I sighed, flopping back on my pillow. Ana let out an "oof" as I hit the bed with enough force to send her tumbling. "Sorry!"

She caught herself before she rolled off the bed entirely, then sat up and folded her arms. "Be more careful!"

"I'll try." I lifted my head to look at her. "Oh, and get your shoes off, you're on the bed."

"My shoes are the size of thimbles right now!" she complained.

"Thimbles that have been outside."

"I fly, Lien. It's not the same." She pouted. "But fine. I'll just . . . be cold, over here."

She tossed her shoes off the bed.

I rolled my eyes and reached out with a hand. She looked strangely hesitant, but eventually flapped over and landed next to me. I pulled the covers over us both. She curled up on my chest, lying in a position so that I could talk to her with the blankets keeping us both comfortable.

". . . Better," she admitted.

"Except for the doomed part," I told her.

"Oh, that." Ana paused, thinking. "You could designate a champion?"

I shook my head. "I think that'd undermine the whole affair. I need to figure out a way to win this directly."

"That might just . . . not be possible, Lien."

"I have to try. It's for you, you know."

"Is it?" she asked, suddenly sounding more serious.

I tried to think about that, but exhaustion and injuries weren't exactly helping my level of introspection. "Of course it is. I mean, obviously I like challenges, but it's to help you be free to make your own choices."

". . . Okay." She nodded, seeming like she was holding something back, but I assumed it was still being awkward about the whole bathing thing. It wasn't. "Then . . . what about skipping ahead?"

I blinked. "Skipping ahead how?"

"You've got a spirit bond already, with your sword. Or something like it. We both do. But that's not supposed to be a thing for most non-fae until they hit Regalia-level."

I nodded slowly. "Even non-fae can find spirit-bonding items that let them get a bond earlier, though. My situation is probably like that."

"Maybe? I think you're more like me."

". . . You think I'm a xiphiad?"

She shook her head. "Maybe a variation on one? You're obviously not identical. But I don't think you're a human with a bloodline. Maybe a different type of sword fae, one we haven't seen before."

I took a breath. If I was a fae this whole time, and Gramps simply hadn't told me, hadn't let me feel like I belonged . . .

"Let's not overanalyze that right now," I concluded. "Even if I'm not human, which I'm probably not, I don't see how it lets me skip ahead. Sure, I have the spirit bond with the sword, or something like it, and I could lean into that more, but that's just going to get me more of whatever essence the sword is generating. Maybe I could master whatever abilities the sword has, but that's something he might turn around on me."

"Yeah, if you did something that simple, sure." She shook her head. "But your weird seal is across a bunch of different layers of self, right?"

"Sure. Possibly all of them? I don't know." I frowned. "Wait. You're not suggesting I try to break more layers of the seal early, are you?"

She got a mischievous look on her face. "I *might* be."

I pondered that. ". . . I guess I already half broke another one, and it hasn't killed me so far."

"Wait, you did *what*?"

I blinked. "I thought I told you that. Did I not tell you that I, like . . . overdid it a bit when I tried to break my seal when I was fighting my nightmare self?"

"You may have glossed over that part."

"Huh." I pondered that. "Well, uh, yeah. I definitely did some damage to the next layer. Which would be shade, I guess, if it follows the standard sequence?"

"Assuming the one you damaged was in front of the one you broke and not behind."

I blinked. I hadn't really been thinking of my seal like that, but . . . she was right that layers of self were generally split into two categories. There were the reflected layers that represented your past — your spirit, shade, and memory — and then extrapolated layers that represented the possible futures you could take.

If I had seven layers to my seal, some of them were clearly related to my extrapolated layers as well. And, thinking about it . . . were the seal's layers really in a linear sequence at all?

The core self — that is, my physical body, as well as my essence on the core plane — was connected to every single other layer. Much like the core plane was located at the center of all planes, the core self was the center point of a person.

It wasn't that something like the Memory Layer was farther away in terms of distance or connection than the Spirit Layer, it was just that standard essence growth unlocked access to each layer of self in a set sequence.

There were workarounds for that. It was a known quantity, one I'd even considered before, just a risky one — and one that generally required an essence type directly related to the layer you wanted to access early. For example, someone who picked up shade as an essence type could potentially get access to their Shade Layer early, allowing them to get shade weaves, powers that could be used to permanently make changes to the body. Darryl had considered that, since it was something that could help him with body dysphoria, but he hadn't made a firm decision on it yet.

Of course, I didn't have shade essence, nor any other essence types related directly to specific layers, but . . .

I did have breach essence and a seal. And I was really, really good at breaking things.

"You got a little quiet." Ana poked me with a tiny finger.

"Just thinking about possibilities. You think if I broke through the seal, I could start making shade weaves? Or . . . even memory marks, if I broke into that layer?"

"Maybe. You'd probably need help from an expert, someone who has access to the right kind of sorcery, or someone who is so high level that they'd have access to that layer of self."

"And with that . . . do you think I could win?" I asked earnestly.

"Honestly?" She looked at me. "No idea. But I do think it sounds like your best bet."

"It might be," I conceded. "I'll think about it."

And I did. I was up most of the night thinking about it, in fact, long after Ana had fallen asleep on my chest.

I tucked her into her own tiny bed, thought about it some more, and did some reading. And eventually, I concluded that it was worth asking about, but . . .

I had another idea that night, too. One that was even more desperate, more terrifying. And one that was even more like me.

⊱⊱ ⊰⊰

The next morning, Ana was gone. This wasn't a surprise — I'd been up late, after all, and she was often a much earlier riser than I was in general.

That was probably for the best. I had a big day ahead of me, if I wanted to make any progress toward our ideas from the previous night. I cleaned my clothes from the last night, packed them, ate breakfast, and then set off on the road toward the mountains.

I paused on my path only twice.

First, to clean my wounds in the healing spring, making sure to give proper thanks to the spirits there. It wasn't as taxing on them for me to just wash up a bit as when I actually collected the essence there directly, but I still wanted to show proper gratitude for their help.

Second, I made an ever-so-brief stop at the sword school at the top of the mountain.

When I got there, I saw Red again for the first time in days. And, for just a moment, images flashed across my mind.

I'd seen a vision of her when I'd approached the Sepulcher of Sealed Swords. She'd been just a little bit older than the echo at this school, maybe in her late twenties or early thirties. And I'd watched helplessly as she'd been cut down by a white-haired man.

There was no confusion about who that man was. I knew from the way he'd killed her, the words he'd said, and the gemstone he'd tried to trap her soul in that he had been the Blackstone Assassin. A demigod, son of Vaelien, the God of Time and Fate.

I'd known when I'd first come to the school that the echoes were likely people who had been here many years before. If they were from around the Smiling Sword Saint's time, that meant around four hundred years in the past. Logically, that meant if they were mortals, they'd be long dead.

So, Red being dead wasn't exactly a surprise. Watching her get brutally killed by a demigod was a little different.

I felt my hand tightening as I thought about it, remembering how he'd ambushed her. Demigod or not, he hadn't even given her a chance at a fair fight.

"Something wrong?" Red glanced in my direction as I walked up, lowering her training sword. She must have seen my expression.

I considered telling her. I wanted to tell her.

But she was an echo of the past. If I told her what I knew — what she was, and that she was dead — there was a very real chance that would cause her to twist somehow, or even cease to exist. I didn't dare to take that risk.

"I saw something that bothered me," I managed. I didn't want to lie, but the omission still felt like one.

Her expression softened. It might have been my imagination, but it felt like it was getting easier for me to read her face, in spite of the strange blur effect that prevented her from being fully recognized. "Do you want to talk about it?"

"I do," I told her, "but not yet. I don't think it's a good time."

She walked over and flipped her sword around, offering it to me handle first. "Want to take your mind off it?"

". . . Yeah." I accepted the training sword.

"Great. Fade won't admit it, but she's been excited to spar with you. It's good for her to have someone closer to her age to practice with."

I frowned at that. "How old is she?"

"You know? I can't actually remember right now. Huh." Red shook her head. "Can't be much older or younger than you, though, right?"

". . . You never know."

After exchanging a few jabs, physical and verbal, with Fade, I reminded myself that I had a mission.

While training in the basics was extremely important, if I wanted to make any real progress with my essence development, I wasn't going to do it at the sword school. I hurried up the rest of the mountainside.

It was a lot of walking to do in one day, but I had a plan, and I needed to see it through.

I stepped into an arena that should have been perfectly familiar. It had a habit of repairing itself to the exact state in which I'd first found it, the colossal stone support pillars and wide amphitheater seating restoring themselves to pristine condition with only a day or so of my absence. It should have been the same that day, but as I would learn increasingly as life progressed, my intervention could bring about change even in things that might have otherwise remained in an eternal cycle.

For better and for worse.

In this case, I stepped into the arena gates just in time for something — no, someone — to fly straight past me in a blur of motion.

With my newly augmented Torch-level speed and senses, I was just fast enough to turn toward Thane's form as it shot past me and offer him a cheerful wave as he soared into the distance, eventually crashing into a massive tree with a loud *crack*.

Huh. Training without me. Neat. Concerning, maybe, but neat.

I stepped the rest of the way into the arena, noting more irregularities. The pillars I'd seen collapse so many times from my mentor's deadly body language were standing, but in one case, only barely. Huge chunks had been removed from the base, and now it listed ominously, seeming to await the strong breeze that would finally bring it to an end. An entire section of the seating had been shredded to bits — a section that, I noted with amusement, seemed to be a block that once would have been reserved for a higher social class. I didn't know exactly who had once frequented this arena, but I had to guess that if the elite nobility seating had been torn up, there was probably a reason — conscious or otherwise — for that particular bit of collateral damage.

The damage was interesting, a clear indication of increased persistence for the arena. I'd already known that the Smiling Sword Saint herself had existed beyond the scope of my visits — she'd visited the Sepulcher of Sealed Swords on her own before I had, and presumably knew a great deal more about it than she'd let on when she'd led me there — but the arena had always been static.

Perhaps the sword saint's memories themselves were keeping the arena stable now, or potentially the sword saint's interactions with her own younger self, who was presently dusting himself off with a groan.

More likely, though, I'd caused the change by taking my sword out of the sepulcher.

I wasn't clear on the exact mechanics of how the seal had worked, but it was clearly connected to virtually everything else I'd found in the sepulcher. The other swords were seemingly being used to power the seal on my weapon, and beyond that, the World's Memory — an enchanted mirror tied to the Dominion of Memory, but recently modified to see beyond into other possible futures — was held on the floor directly in between them. Presumably, that mirror was the principal cause of the strangeness related to both memories manifesting in the area, as well as what Lance, the strange man I'd encountered as he was leaving the shrine, explained that he'd happened upon when coming to the sepulcher from the opposite direction. While I'd seen visions of the past on the way there, he'd seen the future.

. . . Had I missed my chance to try that? I'd hoped to go to the route he'd taken to get a glimpse of my own possible futures, but perhaps that wouldn't be possible if the area around the sepulcher was stabilizing.

That was a little disappointing, maybe, but I didn't want to jump to conclusions. It was possible I could still find the destiny-lined corridor he'd traveled, or if that was not possible, I could always make the incredibly unwise decision to tinker with the powerful mirror directly. It had only made a murderous duplicate of me last time — nothing to worry about. What could go wrong?

As I stepped fully into the arena, I sensed another important change. One that sent my heart soaring in celebration.

Sword essence.

It was *everywhere* now — and in a variety of aspects. I could hear the subtle grinding of steel against whetstones, smell the freshly oiled metal slipping into scabbards. I could see the faint luster from a beautiful drawn blade shimmering in the morning air. And, most clearly, I could feel the subtle sharpness of thousands of invisible blades pressed against my skin.

It was wonderful.

I'd known that the seal was probably what had drained the sword essence in the region, but I hadn't been certain that removing the sword would allow the sword saint to generate it. She was, after all, born from memories, not from blades.

. . . But it wouldn't do to underestimate her. That wasn't the first time I'd realized that, nor would it be the last.

She didn't even look at me as I stepped into the arena, instead snapping her fingers and flicking a hand in my direction. A hail of conjured weapons manifested above her and surged in my direction.

It was very much like how she'd greeted me on our first meeting, nearly two years before — but things had changed. I had changed.

And when a cascade of blades neared me this time, and my hand flew out to greet them, I yanked the first sword out the air with barely a hint of resistance. My own essence surged out, covering the stolen sword in my classic Sword Sharpening Shroud, and I shredded the remaining attacks into shrapnel.

"Good morning, Master." I bowed my head just a hint, a flicker of a smirk crossing my lips.

In that moment of lowering my guard, she was straight in front of me, fingers raised and threatening to flick my forehead.

Which, to both of our surprise, I parried.

Her finger resounded as she flicked the stolen sword instead of my skin. I was fortunate that she hadn't been flicking hard — the blade merely cracked, rather than exploding toward my face.

"Huh. You're getting faster, kid." Her other hand landed on my head before I could do anything, and she mussed my hair. "You keep letting this grow out, though, and it's going to blind you in a fight one day."

I growled lightly. "I *like* my hair long."

"Can't say I didn't warn you." She took a step back, looking me up and down. "You look more . . . well, more. It hasn't been that long, has it?"

"Nope. Just a few days since my last visit, but . . . I feel more complete now that I'm carrying this." I tilted my head toward the scabbard on my back.

"Dangerous. Very dangerous, if that thing is already influencing you so much." She eyed the sword with something like wariness, which was not what I ever associated with her expression, but rapidly returned to a more contemplative look as Thane stumbled his way back into the arena. "Think you could kill him if you used that?"

"What? No, I'm not going to—"

"Not what I asked. *Could* you?"

My eyes narrowed. "Could I win a fight with Thane using it? Maybe, once in a dozen times, if I was lucky. The sword is a clear advantage, but I don't know what I'm doing with it, and he's still more than a full level above me. Could I kill Thane with it? *No.* Because I *don't kill my friends.*"

The Smiling Sword Saint folded her arms. "Careful, kid. I'm no faerie, but those words sounded awfully close to a binding oath."

She wasn't wrong. For someone as steeped in faerie culture as I was, specific turns of language were important. Magical contracts generally required a second party to bind with — and, in the cases of greater ones, even a third party to serve as a witness — but there were times when words spoken aloud could be taken as more than a mere promise. An oath, sometimes rendered with a capital *O*, sincerely spoken, could bind someone with their own words. You'd also sometimes hear "vow" used in the context of oaths that only involved one person, but I tended to prefer using the more general term. Most oaths involved things like fealty to a specific liege, but self-spoken oaths were common storybook material, often for purposes like, say, revenge against the Ashen Lord for burning down your family's village, or that sort of thing.

What was the magic that enforced oaths? I didn't know for sure. Scholars often postulated that it was one of the many crystals, perhaps even the same one that offered Destiny Dreams, or perhaps connected with the ancestor of Artinia, who heard their wishes. It was a little creepy to think that something might be listening to every word I spoke, but perhaps it was more that I held some kind of power within that would alert the crystal of a sincerely worded oath.

Regardless of the source, the sword saint was right that I should be cautious, but in that bit of stubbornness, I didn't feel like retracting my words. I didn't double down, either. I just turned, unlimbered my sword from my shoulder, and leaned it against a nearby stadium seating area. "Looks like you've been busy. Could I bother you two for some help with my own training?"

"Sure," Thane replied, cracking his neck. "We have our own training to do, but I wouldn't mind a distraction."

I stepped into the arena and manifested a classic Sword Hand technique to warm up with Thane.

"Don't bother with that." Thane snapped his fingers, conjuring a pair of sparring swords that floated in midair, then tossed me one.

I charged immediately, hoping that my new Torch-level speed would help me catch him off guard, but while he did seem marginally surprised, he was still faster.

To both of our surprise, however, he *wasn't* stronger.

The crack of our blades against each other sent him stumbling back a step. If I'd expected it, I would have taken advantage more easily — as it was, I was sluggish in my opportunistic follow-up strike, allowing him to slide into a sideways stance that caused my thrust to draw a simple line across his shoulder rather than piercing through it.

He barely acknowledged the cut. I'd like to think that was because my strike was so perfect that he didn't feel it, but more likely, he was simply acclimated to more serious wounds and had far better combat discipline than my own. He answered my cut with a flick of his off hand, producing a wide cutting wave. Without room to properly dodge, I answered by cleaving downward through it, as he'd expected.

He closed the gap while my sword was in a downward position, aiming a quick jab at my own upper shoulder. Given that he was still faster than I was, I still didn't have a chance of raising my sword in time. He was expecting me to side-step or something similar, at which point he'd take further advantage of my off-balance state to pursue aggressively — it was a dance that we'd repeated on a hundred occasions, with the script only allowing for minor variations.

But that was before I'd broken the mirror of myself and found an answer that suited me better.

Rejoinder.

An aura of sword essence blasted outward from my shoulder, deflecting Thane's strike and sending a flash of cutting power back in his direction. It was a near-instant counter, one that most opponents would have no answer for—

Except, of course, for the fact that my mirror had learned the technique from the Smiling Sword Saint herself. And Thane was, as different as they currently appeared, a younger version of the same person.

And so, as my technique deflected his strike and sent a burst of cutting power in his direction, he just snorted and performed the exact same technique before it hit him, but, uh, vastly better than mine.

While my version of the Rejoinder technique was a sloppily assembled copy of a copy, his was practiced and honed, effortlessly reshaping the essence I'd thrown at him, repurposing it and sending it back toward me with added power, speed, and precision.

I wasn't exactly surprised he'd managed the counter, but I still wasn't fast enough to do anything about it. The technique cut a long gash across my right arm, which he followed up with a lunge that smashed the sword out of my hand.

Disarmed and dismayed, I stepped inward and rapidly produced another Sword Hand technique with my off hand while mid-motion, effectively trying to punch him in the chest with it. If I landed the hit, I could use a low-powered version of my Star Shattering Sword technique with it to temporarily disrupt his entire essence structure, hopefully weakening him enough to let me get my blade back or find another advantage.

"Nah."

As he spoke the simple word, a wave of cutting force manifested in the air, tore straight through my Sword Hand technique, and bloodied my left hand before it could reach him.

I recognized what had happened — he'd used the Cutting Remark technique — but it was too late to do anything about it.

In another moment, his sword was at my neck. "Round one goes to me."

My eyes flicked to his sword briefly, contemplating if I could grab the blade and reverse my fortune, but it wasn't worth it. I'd get more training in if I paused, treated my wounds, and strategized a little. "I concede. Thanks for the warm-up."

Thane cracked a grin. "Is that your excuse today? Sure. Warm up all you want. The results will be the same."

I smiled in return, but it was more strained than usual.

In spite of what I said, the match hadn't just been a warm-up for me — it was a test of just how much farther I could get against him now that I'd hit Torch-level. Objectively, I knew he was still higher level and better trained than I was, but I'd hoped that reaching my new level would have closed the gap enough for me to feel competitive.

It had been easier to keep up with his movements, to be certain, and from that first strike, I thought I actually had an advantage in strength now — likely a result of the strange secondary essence that was in my right hand.

But without a way to harness my newfound power into real techniques, the advantages I'd gained from increasing my level weren't enough to get me anywhere close to Thane's overall level of combat ability. He had answers to all my established sword techniques, and my other tricks — like the Star Shattering Sword — could only be used under very niche circumstances.

All in all, I still wasn't at his level. Not by a long shot.

. . . And if I couldn't match him, I didn't stand even the slightest chance in my duel.

Thane and I took a brief break, then fought two more practice rounds. After that, the Sword Saint gave us both some pointers on our mistakes — with an emphasis on the *point* part of pointers, since she conjured swords to force us to improve our stances and movements. Finally, after that, she asked me an equally pointed question.

"So, you finally got yourself your sword, and you won't use it. No need to defend yourself, that part I understand, even if it's keeping you pitifully weak. What I don't understand is why you aren't showing off your destiny mark. You made a big deal out of how your people get some fancy dream that gives you a free one, and now you're not even using it?"

I winced. I knew this had been coming, but I still wasn't sure how best to explain it. "Well, I did have my Destiny Dream, or something like it. It, uh, turns out that it might not be the best idea to deliberately trigger your Destiny Dream by breaking a seal on an ancient and mysterious power while fighting a nightmare version of yourself conjured by an artifact connected to a dozen different planes of existence."

". . . When you put it like that, it seems kind of obvious," Thane mumbled.

I coughed. ". . . Anyway, mistakes may have been made on that, or . . . uh, possibly when I rejected all my options to try to carve my own."

"You tried to what now?" the sword saint asked.

"Well, there were swords with, like, letters to represent different destiny marks. So, I eventually picked one up, but rather than using the crystal there to accept it immediately, I cut some of the letters out."

The Smiling Sword Saint stared at me for a moment in absolute silence.

"You . . . tried to *cut the words representing your destiny*?"

"Yes?"

She was right in front of me then, her hand reaching outward dangerously. "That is . . . just . . . mind-bogglingly reckless." She took a deep breath. Was that . . . a tear forming in the corner of her eye? Her hand didn't strike me. Instead, it landed softly on my shoulder. "It's the seventh most beautiful thing I've ever heard."

". . . Oh . . ." I felt a rare surge of pride at my teacher's words. "That's oddly specific, but thanks?"

She leaned in close. "I'm so proud of you." Then she headbutted me, sending me crashing to the floor, my vision swimming.

". . . But you still need to stop letting your guard down."

After picking myself up with a groan, I didn't bother standing, I just sat on the floor and motioned for the two of them to join me. Surprisingly, they didn't protest. Thane just plopped down on the arena stone, and the Smiling Sword Saint reclined in midair, blades forming behind her to form some kind of diagonally leaning sword furniture.

If I'm honest, the floor looked more comfortable, but I respected her commitment to the aesthetic.

"So, you messed with your destiny and . . . what, ended up with nothing?" Thane asked.

I paused, taking a breath. ". . . Not exactly." I pulled the half-shredded glove off my left hand, wincing as that process reopened one of my wounds, and showed off the back of it.

There, reasonably clear in spite of the cuts and dried blood, was the symbol of a destiny mark.

Most destiny mark symbols were straightforward. A pitchfork for the Farmer destiny, for example. Sometimes, you'd have a basic symbol with something else to make it clearer — for example, the Rogue destiny mark just looked like a symbol for a hood, the Thief had the same hood with a symbol of a key inside it, and the Assassin was the hood with a dagger.

There were plenty of sword-related symbols out there, as one might expect with the wide variety of sword-related destinies. The classic Blademaster one displayed three crossed swords of different types, which was understood to represent mastery over a variety of different swords. The Sword Lord destiny was a regal-looking sword with a crown above it. The Storm Fang symbol was a curved sword surrounded by bolts of lightning.

I'd looked at a bunch of pictures of destiny marks and read about them in multiple books, both before and after going into the Sepulcher of Sealed Swords, and I knew two things for certain—

First, my symbol was not anything I'd ever heard described.

And second, destiny marks were supposed to glow in two colors — the symbol's color would be based on the primary elements of the mark, but it would also emanate a colored aura based on the mark's current level.

"Oh, that's not good," Thane remarked, seeing the obvious problem at a mere glance.

My destiny mark was a sword that had been broken in half, and it wasn't glowing at all.

⊹⊹ ⊹⊹

I took a bit of time to explain to them what I'd already learned from reading, as well as conversations with Gramps and Auntie Temper.

"So, as best I can tell, there are a few possibilities. One is that I literally broke my destiny mark, rendering it inactive. There's precedent for that — in fact, I've been thinking about trying to figure out how to make a technique for it, as a variation on my Star Shattering Sword that specifically targets the destiny layer."

The Smiling Sword Saint frowned. That was never a good sign, and I instinctively braced myself with an aura of deflection-aspected sword essence, but nothing visible happened — she was getting better control over her power. "That's pretty niche, kid. You'd have to hit someone directly on the destiny mark to do that, and you'd need enough power to contest the power of the mark itself. You probably wouldn't break it outright in one hit. You might reduce the functionality, but whaling on a single specific spot on someone's body over and over just to limit their destiny mark's powers isn't a great combat strategy. You're better off hitting them the normal way."

"What about using it as a technique against someone who is too high level for me to hurt with normal attacks, to bring them down to a more reasonable level?"

"If they're that strong, why wouldn't they just dodge?"

"Well, maybe they'd just stand there and let me hit them out of a sense that I'm so weak that I'm not a threat — like, you know, you did when we first met."

She was silent for a moment.

". . . Yeah, okay, that was kind of an unusual situation, but I'm not going to say I've never fought some arrogant idiot who gave me the first shot in an actual battle. It's happened. But even if it did happen, your Star Shattering Sword targeting the Heart Mark would almost always be a better use of a first-shot advantage if you get one. It's easier to damage a Dianis Point than a destiny mark and the effect, a Heart Mark is easier to hit than something that could be anywhere on the body, and the impact would probably be greater, too."

". . . That may be fair," I conceded.

I was absolutely going to build a technique for trying to damage or break destiny marks anyway, just in case it ended up being relevant — like, say, in a group combat scenario, or some other niche situation — but she wasn't big on extended discussions. Instead, I refocused on the original point. "So, my mark might be broken, in which case I'd need to figure out a way to fix it, or simply remove it and replace it. There's also the possibility that it's not outright broken, exactly, but incomplete."

"Why would it be incomplete?" Thane asked.

"Two thoughts on that. First, my dream was sort of falling apart around me, and I may not have finished the selection process properly. I'd picked up the sword and cut the letters, which might have been symbol enough to claim my destiny, but there was a selection crystal in the dream, and I didn't have a chance to figure out if there was some specific way I needed to use it."

"And the other reason?"

"I . . . might have chosen a specific destiny name that was, uh, a little ambitious. And when the dream was ending, I heard something like 'requirements incomplete.'"

"That seems pretty direct," the sword saint said. "You're clearly not good enough for whatever you picked. Not surprising, given how weak you are, and that you have a habit of aiming too high. What'd you swing for?"

I coughed, mildly embarrassed.

And then I told them.

I'd made three cuts from the phrase "Heartbreaker Sword," each removing letters to make a single word that stirred the hearts of children and wove works of legend.

There was a moment of deadly silence, followed by the two of them bursting into manic, eerily similar laughter. The sword saint slapped her leg in mirth, causing a shock wave of force to shake the entire arena.

"Oh, kid" — she wiped at her eyes — "I underestimated you. The absolute *hubris* in you. You can't possibly have expected that to work."

I gave the sword saint my best smile. "I didn't know for sure, of course, and it was a razor-thin margin of time to make the decision. But I stand by it — and I don't think that it's quite as poor of a decision as you're making it out to be."

"Oh?" She raised an eyebrow, genuinely curious. "How's that?"

"Because it said, 'requirements *incomplete*,'" I explained, "not that I hadn't met any of them at all. And now, I intend to finish what I started." I cracked my knuckles and uttered the words that many who knew me would come to associate with absolute terror.

"I have a plan."

CHAPTER XIV

SIMULATION

I told the Smiling Sword Saint and Thane the basics of my foolproof plan to finish achieving the requirements to complete my destiny mark.

"Yeah, that's pretty much just suicide with more words." The sword saint let out an exhausted sigh. "And if you're going to get yourself killed, I'd really rather you find a more creative and memorable way to do it. Walking straight back into the sepulcher in your current state and experimenting with an artifact that messes with your other selves is so far beyond reasonable that I'd laugh if I thought your ending would be fun and silly, rather than just incredibly sad."

"You'd be sad if I died?" I blinked, feeling oddly touched.

". . . Well, in the sense that it would deprive me of one of my sources of entertainment. Don't overthink that, focus on the important part, which is the utter insanity of your idea. Even if you managed to make it back to the World's Memory safely — which I have my doubts about — you have no idea what you're doing with it."

I raised an eyebrow. "Couldn't you just walk me back there?"

"Sure, I could escort you back to the entrance. But you've certainly noticed that our area has changed with the absence of your sword — it's going to be even more intense closer to the sepulcher, as memories either fade or solidify into reality."

My eyes widened. "Wait. You think that some of the parts of that memory passage might manifest? I assumed they were too fragile, too liminal—"

"Assumptions like that get people killed. And what would happen if, say, a memory of that white-haired assassin that killed your past-future redhead friend manages to solidify?"

She probably expected me to balk at this idea, maybe experience some sort of fear response. Instead, I gasped aloud. "Do you think she'd be able to beat him in a straight fight if we brought her there?"

"Absolutely not. Her stance was wonderful, and her durability nothing short of heroic, but what he told your other long-dead friend was true. Even in a direct confrontation, the assassin would have won. That's not to downplay your friend's abilities, mind you. She was simply too young, her training unfinish—" The sword saint's expression looked briefly thoughtful.

I grinned brightly at her. "I *could* invite her over here. She seems to be getting more coherent, and I imagine training with you and Thane could only help with that. And, if I'm understanding things right, I think she's your own apprentice's apprentice, so it would be like a grandmaster training—"

"No." The sword saint's voice was quiet but firm. ". . . Not now, at least. And we're getting distracted."

"Isn't distracting you what I'm here for?"

"Cheeky, kid. But you know what I meant. Back to the main topic — your absurd plan. Just getting you to the sepulcher could involve facing the ghosts of a thousand fractured timelines."

My eyes brightened. This was clearly not the expected or desired response.

"Tsk. You're almost as bad as this one." The sword saint pointed at where Thane was sitting on a stump of a now-devastated pillar, eating a sandwich. I had no idea where or how he'd acquired one.

"Leave me out of this," he said, taking another bite. "Only like a *quarter* of my ideas involve fighting other timelines."

"Sounds like a lack of imagination to me." I winked at him. He looked like he was about ready to throw down his sandwich and go another round, but upon lifting his food, he thought better of it. Thane loved eating too much to waste good food.

"That's not even the problem part," the sword saint continued. "Even if you make it back to the front door, the place is probably going mad by now. You took something out of the deepest level of the shrine that was connected to all the treasures on the first floor. The caretaker is dead. Well, double dead. Maybe triple? Lots of dead. Wards are going to start to fail, things are going to be released, and it's going to start falling apart. And before you say anything, yes, it absolutely *does* sound fun. But fun for someone five levels above you, not you."

I groaned. "You could escort me to the mirror, then, and *you* could have fun."

"Too dangerous. Not to me, but to you — and to the mirror. Right now, the mirror room itself is on a separate floor from the dangers. It's relatively contained. But if we reactivate the lift, there's every chance that something slips down from the first floor to the second and follows us. I'm a tremendous fighter, but I don't have access to all my abilities. Something sneaky might be able to slip by me and cause some real harm. Not just to you, but to the mirror itself."

And there it was. The real reason the sword saint was hesitating.

She was afraid. Not of being personally harmed, not of losing me — but of what might happen if the mirror was damaged or destroyed.

Because if the mirror shattered, Thane was very likely to break right along with it.

In a way, I could understand it. Thane wasn't just an alternate version of the sword saint's childhood self — he was, in a strange way, also her own child. Her creation. And they were bonding in a way that made the sword saint protective.

It was sweet, if a bit inconvenient.

I pondered the possibility of bringing someone else with me, rather than the sword saint. Gramps would refuse. He didn't approve of me taking massive risks in general, and this plan certainly qualified as one even in the best scenarios I could think of. Auntie Temper had other responsibilities. Even if Ana was willing to look after the little ones for a time if Auntie Temper left, Auntie wasn't a fighter. She was a powerful memory-essence wielder, and maybe she could do something with that to reduce the risks of traveling to the shrine, but it wouldn't offer defenses against other things let loose inside the sepulcher itself. And given that she couldn't travel through the court — she was still formally banished — I wasn't even sure how she'd get to the shrine. It was a logistics problem and one that didn't even offer a solution.

Uncle Eiji would have been a great option once, but he was constantly traveling, and he'd already left again. I'd consider asking him if he was staying in the area for a longer period in the future, but for now, he wasn't available.

The only others I could think of that might be powerful enough to offer assistance were Verthrimax, the ancient, blind dragon that resided in a lonely tower on the southern edge of the court, and the Willowbark Witch.

Verthrimax would want to help, but he stubbornly refused to leave his hoard unguarded. Even if he did agree to come with me, bringing a dragon to the Smiling Sword Saint's domain was a huge risk, too. I had no idea how they'd interact.

Thinking of introducing those two *did* give me an idea, but not one I acted on right away. It was a longer-term plan.

As for the witch . . . No, as much as I loved her, she'd try to take the mirror out of the sepulcher. Not out of greed, but out of a sense of responsibility. She wouldn't allow something like that to remain unprotected in the middle of nowhere.

Perhaps that last option was the right approach in terms of overall safety — but I also knew she wouldn't let me access it once she had it in her possession. And that was assuming she *could* take it. If she tried to, the sword saint would object . . . and I wasn't sure who would be victorious in that exchange. I didn't like the idea of finding out, either.

". . . You're thinking an awful lot, kid, but there's no point. Even if I got you in there safely, what could you do with the mirror?"

"Get back into the dream," I answered immediately. "The same one I left unfinished. Since the mirror has powers connected to both memories and dreams, I think it might be possible. From there, I can try picking up the crystal that's designed to select my destiny properly and see if that fixes the issue."

She seemed to ponder that. "Even if that was possible — which it might or might not be — do you know how to operate the mirror with that level of proficiency?"

I looked at her. "No. But I think you might. You used it to make Thane, didn't you?"

"That was comparatively easy." She didn't deny it even slightly, which surprised me. "Reentering a fancy Destiny Dream like yours . . . I don't even know if it's possible. It sounds like those dreams are tied to an external power of some kind."

"There are books and notes down in the sepulcher. We could study—"

"Sure, if we had months to sit down there without the place sending murderous monsters to fight us, maybe."

"You could bring them here?"

She sniffed at the air. "I'll think on that. I *do* plan to take care of the memories that are manifesting between here and there, then eventually work my way back to the mirror, but it's going to take time to do it without causing significant collateral damage. But kid, you're starting with the wrong step, as usual. Even if you get into that dream and use the selection crystal thing before the place collapses, do you think the result will be any different?"

"Maybe," I offered. "But even if it's the same, if I'm in contact with whatever controls the destiny marks, maybe I could ask questions, or otherwise find ways to learn what exactly I'm missing. Then, I could leave and enter the dream a third time, once the requirements are met."

"You'd be putting in an awful lot of work for something that *might* help. If you get back in there, why not just pick up another destiny that it's offering you?"

"Because it wouldn't be mine." I shook my head. "And, more practically, it might interfere with the half-complete mark I've already started. But, now that I think on it, maybe I could gather up all the crystals and get several at the same time, if I could figure out how to—"

"Yeah, don't do that. Seriously, kid. Don't."

I sighed. "Fine, fine. But I'm not going to give up on the destiny I carved for myself."

"I wouldn't expect you to. But this is a bad plan, kid."

I frowned. I wasn't good at letting go of anything once I'd set my heart to it, but . . . maybe I didn't need to let go, exactly. ". . . It might be, but it's mine."

"Good on you for sticking with that, then."

I blinked. "Seriously?"

"What, you think I'm going to cast you aside, just because you have a couple terrifyingly risky ideas for advancement? Please, who do you think you're talking to?"

I paused, considering that. "Well, on that note, I do have *another* idea to share."

". . . Of course you do." The Smiling Sword Saint tried to keep her expression neutral. It was a worthy effort, but when her lips twitched, I heard a distant tree falling. At least no one was there to see it, so it probably didn't matter, or something.

"So . . . about my seal." I gave her a sheepish grin.

"Oh, no. Not this again." She folded her arms. "You want to break the whole thing?"

"No, no. That's obviously insane." I paused. "Just like . . . maybe, a strategic part or two?"

She threw up her hands. Gigantic stone pillars rose from the ground, following her gesture.

Huh. That one is new.

I didn't have a chance to think on that demonstration before she spoke, though. "You just don't know when to leave things alone, do you?"

"I really don't." I paused. "But there's a specific idea here, not just arbitrarily wanting to break stuff."

"Fine, fine. Spit it out."

I told her my idea — or, really, Ana's idea — about breaking the seal to try to get access to other layers of self ahead of schedule.

To Ana's credit, the Smiling Sword Saint actually seemed to spend time considering it, which was better than I'd gotten out of *my* idea.

"It's usually considered a bad idea to skip ahead. You're supposed to learn your fundamentals and all that."

I raised an eyebrow. "You don't sound very convinced."

"That's because I'm not. The fundamentals are useful, sure, but I don't think there's any inherent value in having to train in one specific sequence. Lots of different cultures and different types of magic out there. There are certainly people who figure out how to use shade weaves early and it can be fine. But that said . . . just breaking open a part of your seal isn't going to give you what you need to make something like a shade weave, kid. It'll open a door, but you'd still have a mostly empty room on the other side. You'd get some raw power flowing through it, sure, but it would be generic shade essence or that sort of thing."

"Would my rooms be like that, though? Assuming that the sword has some kind of presence on every layer — which I think it does — there could be essence linked to my sword on each. Maybe even enough to make a shade weave, or a memory mark, or whatever that layer corresponds to."

"Yeah, maybe." She tapped her foot on the ground, thinking. The mountainside trembled, rocks tumbling in the distance. "But you'd have no idea what it'd do. You'd just get . . . a mystery shade weave, at best. That should be terrifying, kid. Shade weaves can change your whole body. That's not something you want to just mess with."

"So . . . I shouldn't do it, then?"

She shook her head. "Didn't say that. But assuming your sword has a presence on all seven layers — which is terrifying, by the way — it'd be absurd to just open it up and try to make use of whatever you have on each layer without understanding them. It would make more sense to figure out what the sword's capabilities are for each layer, then unlock the layers you want and build what you want based on that."

I took a breath. "That's . . . going to take some time. I have some notes on the sword, but . . ."

"This is one area where common sense applies, kid. You don't rush through important things like this. It's too important to the rest of your life."

I nodded somberly. I could do more research on the sword, figure out if any of the abilities it had would translate well to things like shade weaves. Gramps could potentially help with that, but he'd be gone for a while along with the fae queen's delegation. In the meantime, I still needed to get stronger. "Then . . . I need your help with coming up with something else to train rapidly. Maybe something to help me get ready for my destiny requirements?"

"I'm not some magic theory scholar. It isn't my background—" She froze for a moment, her eyes narrowing a little. "Hm."

I raised an eyebrow. "An idea?"

"Maybe. Or the start of one." She put her hands together in front of her, closing her eyes briefly. I saw a hint of a glow between them, which faded after a moment. When she reopened her eyes, she kept her palms shut. "This might be a different kind of bad idea."

"Is it the kind that is going to destroy the mirror or kill any of us?"

"No. Well, probably not. But it might make your mark problem worse, or otherwise damage your dream self, if it doesn't work."

"And if it *does* work?"

"It might still cause those problems. But . . . it'll make it more likely you'll be able to do something useful if you reach the mirror in the future."

". . . How?" I asked.

She opened her hands, displaying a newly formed multicolored crystal. Then, without warning, she flicked her wrist at me.

Purely on instinct, I cut the crystal out of the air with a Sword Hand technique I hadn't even felt myself form.

". . . Good reflex. Clearly, you've learned from the best." I caught a hint of amusement in her tone. "But leave the breaking memory crystals to me, kid."

"That was . . ." I glanced down at the shattered fragments of the crystal I'd sliced into pieces.

"Been studying the crystals you've given me. Figured out how to make my own — and then I worked on some upgrades." She snapped her fingers, memory essence flaring as she produced another crystal. This time, she tossed it to me underhand, and I caught it.

Size- and shape-wise, it was just like the crystals that Auntie Temper had given me, but the color was different — a shimmering rainbow of colors, favoring grays and purples. "What is it?"

"A mix between a memory crystal, a dream crystal, and a shade stone." She didn't explain more, but she didn't need to — I could piece it together from things I knew.

"It'll be interactive, like a dream crystal. Based on your memories, like a memory crystal. And it'll have the potential for corporeal manifestations, like a shade stone?"

"You're not ready for that last part yet. This one just uses shade to make the dream more 'solid' — it'll feel like the real thing, and you'll be able to use your abilities more coherently than in something like a dream or a memory."

"Can you make one from my experiences with the mirror, so I can get back into my dream without actually going to the mirror itself?"

She frowned. "You'd let me mess with your own memories and dreams?"

"Sure. I trust you."

She looked briefly like she'd been struck. ". . . Not yet, kid. Maybe at some point, but . . . for now, this is simpler. You can use this crystal for another kind of training. Something to hone your skills for interacting with worlds of dreams. And then, if we make you a crystal of your own someday — or you do eventually make your way back to the mirror — you'll be ready for it."

I felt my hand tighten around the crystal and my lips curl up. This wasn't what I'd asked for, but . . . in some ways, it was better. It wasn't my plan . . . but, if I was honest with myself, it was a better one. One that gave me hope. "When can we get started?"

⊱⊱ ⊰⊰

Three minutes or so later, I was slipping a strange circlet onto my head. It had the crystal I'd been given inserted into a slot in the front, two other crystals in the sides, and one on the back, a piece of what looked like a shard of a mirror. I had to be careful not to cut myself on the mirror shard or get it stuck in my hair, but once I finished slipping the whole thing on, it was surprisingly comfortable.

I deliberately didn't ask if the Smiling Sword Saint had taken a fragment out of the World's Memory to build this thing — I was pretty sure I knew the answer, and she didn't take unnecessary questions well. Also, if I knew the World's Memory had a shard being repurposed for something like this, I'd be obligated to tell Gramps immediately, so . . . I just ignored the obvious, at least for the moment. I was too excited to let something like an ancient artifact being damaged get to me.

I ran my fingers across the circlet, pondering how the Smiling Sword Saint had made it. She hadn't demonstrated any abilities at crafting magical items, although admittedly, she had no difficulty conjuring hundreds of swords that seemed to have magical properties. I suspected those were manifestations of swords she'd previously encountered through some sophisticated application of memory essence — and if that was true, perhaps this was similar, a copy of an item she'd used in her own training in the past.

Or maybe I was looking at it the wrong way. Perhaps she hadn't built it at all. Had it been inside the sepulcher, something designed to interact with the mirror? I wouldn't have been surprised.

I was tempted to ask, but the Smiling Sword Saint responded poorly when I pried into topics outside of what we were currently focusing on. She was growing more humanlike over time, but she was still dangerously unpredictable. If she didn't like my questions, she might take the circlet away . . . and I was far too excited to risk that.

I was going to *fight her past*! I couldn't think of a better way to spend my morning. Or afternoon. Or evening. Or any other time period, really.

I tried not to let my excitement be too obvious, but I failed badly, and I could tell that Thane was a little bothered by my giddy demeanor. Maybe he was jealous? I couldn't tell.

I could ask later. For the moment, I focused on the circlet.

The crystal would have generated a dreamlike vision on its own, but the circlet served a couple different purposes.

The first was purely practical — it let me keep the crystal pressed against my forehead without needing to hold up my hand while in a dream state. Ordinarily, I would have handled it by lying down and putting the crystal on my forehead, but that wasn't foolproof — if I rolled over in my sleep, it could have interrupted the dream.

Second, the Smiling Sword Saint told me that the item was designed to improve the fidelity of any visions created by the crystals. It would feel more real, including more sensory information than a dream typically could. I'd feel a close facsimile of each of my real senses, including things like pain. That, presumably, would help make my training within more relevant to reality.

Finally, the enchantments on the circlet would let the crystal be reused repeatedly in rapid succession, rather than requiring time to recharge between uses. It still couldn't be used infinitely, but the Sword Saint seemed to be under the impression I couldn't hit the limits on it.

Challenge accepted, I thought. Then, following the sword saint's instructions, I spoke a phrase out loud.

"Once again, I draw steel against a world long gone."

I didn't even have a chance to consider how unusually flowery that was before my vision changed and I found myself elsewhere.

⊹⊹ ⊹⊹

I blinked, providing the fade to black that I would have expected from the movement from the physical realm into a place of dreams.

My eyes opened to complete the process of a narratively appropriate scene transition that the artifact had rudely failed to provide and I took in my surroundings rapidly, knowing that danger could — and likely would — be all around me.

I wasn't on an ancient battlefield facing an army of dragons, nor crawling through endless labyrinths beneath the world. I was somewhere far less familiar — a large room with many tables, chairs, and *people*. People eating food. People drinking *drinks*.

This was . . . a restaurant! Or perhaps even a *tavern*!

I chided myself for my previous expectations failing to understand the nuances of my master's strategy. Obviously, I wasn't going to be facing down dragons right away. Everyone knew a proper adventure started in a tavern.

I gazed across the room, taking in the sights around me.

First, there was me.

I was myself. This may seem obvious, but I was fifty-fifty on whether or not I'd show up in the dream as a younger version of the Smiling Sword Saint, meaning something more like Thane.

As it turns out, I was halfway right with both possible answers: I appeared to have my own physical form, but the outfit was wrong and presumably matched the saint's from that point in time. That meant I was wearing a plain white robe tied at the waist with a cloth belt, open-topped shoes without socks (I will never understand the appeal of these), and a slim, single-handed sword in a scabbard of lacquered wood on my left hip.

Ooh, new sword! Nice! Let's see who else we've got around here . . .

Oh, there's the grizzled old veteran. Ah, some sort of nobleman and his bodyguards or attendants. The serving boy . . . probably some sort of disguised assassin? That sounds right. Oh, speaking of assassins, there's someone in a hooded cloak in the corner!

The hooded and cloaked figure must have caught my glance, but they pointedly ignored me, leaning back against the wall with their boots crossed and lifting a pipe to their mouth.

So cool! Except for the smoking. Ick.

Anyway, adventure is waiting, I just have to find it!

I found food first. I already had a plate of it in front of me — it was a bowl of some sort of dark liquid with bits of potato visible and a spoon stuck in it.

Could this be the legendary tavern stew?!

Ana is going to be so jealous.

I took a bite of what I presumed to be legendary stew and it was . . . uh, let's just say that the quality of the food added character and mystique.

I washed it down with something in a mug next to me that was probably alcohol and thus I probably shouldn't have been drinking, but it was a dream, so . . . it didn't really count, right?

Anyway, my vision may have gotten mildly foggier after the first mug, and then the second mug that somehow appeared on the table, and that was when things started to get more interesting.

I heard a *crack*, then looked up from my mug, briefly startled. How'd I let myself lower my guard so badly?

I shook my head, trying to shake off . . . whatever I was experiencing. It didn't really help. Still, I turned quickly toward the sound, seeing what had happened — the possibly assassin serving boy had dropped a tray. Whatever had been on it had crashed onto the ground, spilled, and . . .

Some of it was on the noble's open-toed shoes.

I saw the noble stand. His men stood along with him.

Oh. That's not going to end well.

"Insolent *fool*." The noble's voice rang out across the room. I immediately sobered just a little, my mind coming sharply into focus as the noble reached back.

This is the type of thing where I'd love to say that time seemed to slow down as the noble's hand moved, and that I moved without thinking to stop the blow, but the truth is that time rarely works that way. I didn't even see the noble's hand move, I just heard a *crunch* from the kid's nose and saw him collapse to his knees.

"You have caused me a grave insult, boy. If you should survive this" — he raised his hand again — "you will remember to serve your betters *properly*."

The second time his hand came down, I was there.

I don't remember getting up or my legs moving. Maybe I didn't move — maybe I was operating on dream logic. Or, you know, maybe I was just that drunk.

But I do remember the look of absolute astonishment on that man's face when I grabbed his wrist.

"What . . . is this?" The man stared at me, dark eyes seeming to process my existence for the first time.

"I feel like this might be a trick question, since it's so obvious, but I'm going to go with 'I'm stopping you from hitting a child who is already down.'"

"Are you, now?" He tugged his arm back, then frowned when my grip simply tightened. "My, you're *strong* for a Torch." His dark eyes seemed to appraise me more closely, then. "A brute, then, playing at Skyseeking? Tell me, do you know who I am?"

"Not really. I'm going to go with 'Young Master of the Child Abuser Ho—'"

I'd been a little too distracted by the banter, and, you know, focusing on the guy in front of me in general. I didn't notice the man behind me until the blade sank into my back.

I froze for a moment. Then the pain settled in, feeling . . .

Well, feeling *real.*

The nobleman sighed, slipping his wrist free as I stared at the bit of the sword that had protruded through the front of my chest.

"A shame. You wasted your life to stand up for nothing." The nobleman shook his head disdainfully. "When your spirit is born again, I hope it finds a life with an education."

I let out a hiss. Something as simple as being stabbed to death wasn't going to stop me. I . . . I could still . . .

I took a step forward, trembling in agony, and pulled a hand up, forming a Sword Hand technique. Essence flickered to life around my hand, and . . .

"Remarkable," the nobleman said.

Then he flicked his wrist. There was a blur of force as something smashed into my face, then I was falling, falling, and—

⁂

My vision changed.

I was back in the arena. I blinked rapidly.

Then my hands went to my chest, purely on reflex.

Whole. I was whole.

I shivered regardless, still feeling the echo of blood across my skin.

The Smiling Sword Saint was watching me with something close to concern on her face. Thane, meanwhile, was pointedly ignoring me to look at some kind of large mirror that was sitting between them.

I was too distracted to worry about the mirror.

Huh.

That was terrifying. It felt . . . so real. And I was absolutely outclassed. I have no chance against those people.

Not yet.

I felt a smile crack across my lips.

The Smiling Sword Saint raised an eyebrow at me.

"Once again, I draw steel against a world long gone."

⁂

I was back in the tavern, right at the start of the scenario, just as I'd expected.

I drank more slowly this time, focusing more on the food. When the serving boy came around, I asked for a cup of water next, and he brought me one with a smile.

Then, as I worked on my food, I watched the room, paying a little more attention to the people and the conversation.

Cloak-in-corner guy clearly noticed me noticing him, but he wasn't overtly involved in the fight last time . . . unless he'd been the one who had stabbed me in the back. I hadn't actually seen my attacker.

I was pretty sure I *had* seen the big veteran guy who was draining four mugs of generic dream-tavern alcohol in rapid succession, and that he'd been in front of me when the dream had ended, which meant he hadn't obviously intervened, but he also probably hadn't been the one who backstabbed me.

Aside from him, there were only a few people of note. The tavernkeeper was a large woman who stood behind the bar, perpetually polishing the counter with a rag that couldn't have possibly stayed dry with all the things she was wiping up, but somehow it did.

And then, of course, there was the nobleman and his entourage. Two people with him — I'm going to call them Minion A and Minion B — one of which was a huge bald-headed man, the other was an only *slightly* less massive guy with weirdly beautiful long blond hair that went all the way down his back. Both were armed with thick, curved swords on their hips.

The nobleman himself wore a slender sword like my own, and similar robes, but much higher quality. And, like the minions' robes, they were bright blue rather than white. His in particular also had silver threading on the sleeves, neck, and bottom of the robe. His sword's scabbard was also lined in silver.

Now that I was actually paying attention, I could sense something that felt sort of like sword essence from all three of them. I suspected that meant that it was supposed to *be* sword essence, but the dream couldn't replicate it perfectly, it could just give me the sensation that I was detecting something like sword essence.

And, when I sensed how much of it there was, I realized just how badly I'd misjudged them before.

I'd known that I'd been overwhelmed easily by my attackers. I'd expected from the way that the nobleman moved that he was a Torch-level sword-essence wielder, the same as I was.

Nope.

His *minions* were Torch-level.

The nobleman was Hearth-level, at the minimum, and that meant my chances of winning in a three-against-one fight had gone from low to something approaching zero.

I tried to suppress my smile. Fortunately, I don't think they saw it.

Instead, everyone's attention was soon on the boy who tripped, spilling his dish once again across the noble's shoes.

I stood up immediately this time, as quickly as the noble did — but there were a good ten feet to cross before I could do anything.

Crack.

"Insolent *fool*." The boy's nose broke as the nobleman struck him to the ground.

I took a few steps closer. "That's enough. He's down, you've proven your point."

"And who," the noble asked, "are you to tell me when something is enough?"

"Me? I'm just a humble swordsman with big dreams." I smiled at the truth of my statement.

"You're certainly dreaming if you think your words would sway me."

He kicked the kid. I didn't move fast enough to do anything about it. I heard a *crunch* from the server boy as he fell flat on the floor, then curled up, tears flowing from his eyes.

"Enough." I grabbed him by the collar. "If you want to fight someone, let's take this outside."

"Well, if you insist."

He put a hand on my chest.

I felt a swelling of essence, but it wasn't sword essence, so I couldn't control it. I raised a field of deflection-aspected essence in rapid response, but the blast still hit me like a battering ram, launching me straight across the room, through the back wall, and onto the cobblestones outside.

I hit the ground hard, feeling a surge of agony on impact. That wasn't as bad as the feeling in my chest, though. Something felt agonizingly sharp.

I think that's a rib. That's . . . not supposed to be there.

I coughed. That was all I managed before the nobleman was looming above me.

"Let's begin your lesson."

His foot came down.

But I had seen through his "Nobleman Stomps on Guy Who Is on the Floor" technique before and devised a counter!

Rejoinder.

He stomped right through my essence field. I didn't even cut his shoe.

Not on the first stomp, not on the second, and . . .

By the third, I'm not really sure what was happening, so I can't say.

Pain surged through me with every assault, and then . . . then I was back in the arena.

⊹ ⊹

My jaw tightened.

The Smiling Sword Saint watched.

"Again." I took a breath. "Once again, I draw steel against a world long gone."

⊹ ⊹

The boy dropped a dish.

I was up even before it hit the ground, but it still did.

Crack.

The noble stood, his hand coming up. "Insolent *fool*."

"Wait." I grabbed the nobleman's wrist. "He's just a kid. He made a simple mistake."

The nobleman looked at me, seeming genuinely confused. "A simple mistake from a simple fool deserves a simple response. I'll teach him a lesson. Should he survive it, he will know not to insult his betters again."

"I'm pretty sure he gets his mistake. Don't you?"

I turned toward the child. That was my first mistake. Before the kid could stammer a reply, the nobleman's other hand had caught me in the jaw, hurling me backward.

Fortunately, it had been a simple punch this time. One from a man massively more powerful than I was, true, but without the weight of a technique behind it.

I slammed heavily into a nearby table, feeling a ringing in my ear, the pain from the blow, but . . . that was downright manageable compared to what I'd been hit with last time. A big step up, really.

The sword that nearly gutted me when I turned back around would not have been an improvement.

It wasn't the nobleman trying to cut right to the end of our conversation. Rather, Minion B had drawn his curved blade and taken a swing at me while I was still recovering, which was rude. It wasn't his turn! I was going straight for his boss, and even if I wasn't, the guy who I'd mentally assigned the letter *A* to obviously should have gone before him.

Fortunately, his swing wasn't anything overwhelmingly fast, not like the nobleman's strikes had been. No, it was merely ordinarily fast, the kind that I still couldn't dodge effectively while recovering, but I could respond to with the speed of thought.

Rejoinder.

My essence flared around me, deflecting the sword strike and sending a burst of sharp essence into his arm. He grunted at the blow, as you'd expect from a minion who didn't warrant a speaking part, and then brought the sword back around to slam the pommel toward my forehead.

I ducked, then slammed a fist into his chest, sending him stumbling back in surprise. He wheeled his arms, but caught himself on another nearby table.

Unfortunate. If I'd hit him a little harder, he might have run into that big veteran guy, which . . . could be interesting.

I didn't get a chance to strategize further before he was charging at me again — and, doubly rude, Minion A had drawn his sword and was moving to flank me.

I glanced from side to side . . . then grinned and drew my own sword.

"Now, gentlemen. If we're going to have a disagreement, can we take it outside?"

They responded by charging me from both sides. I laughed, parrying a swing from each of them, then hopped onto a table.

"Hah!" I kicked a mug into Minion B's face, then jumped over Minion A, kicking him in the back and sending him into another table. He crashed into the table, knocking it over, then spun around and hurled something at me.

I knocked whatever it was aside, then braced myself as Minion B charged. I danced between a flurry of his swings, ducking under another hurled item from Minion A with a laugh, and then lifted a mug to parry Minion B's next swing with it.

Harden.

Hardness-aspected sword essence flashed around the mug as his sword sank into it, then I sent a burst of scabbard-aspected over it. He looked incredulous as the sword got stuck halfway through the mug, failing to cut farther . . . and then I *twisted* the cup, wrenching the sword to the side. He moved with it, trying to maintain his grip, and I swept my sword across his forearm, drawing a thin line of blood.

He groaned in pain (as befitting another nameless character without dialogue) and finally released his sword, only to sweep an essence-coated fist in my direction.

I danced backward, laughing and easily dodging the swing.

Now, this was more like it! A true swashbuckling barroom brawl! Maybe this time—

A sword pierced straight through my back.

I frowned down at it.

"Now that's not fair."

The nobleman leaned forward, resting his head on my shoulder. "Life rarely is, especially to a swordsman. Take this lesson to the next life."

"I will." I told him seriously, feeling the vitality already seeping out of me. "Here's one for you."

I slammed my forehead into his nose. I heard a *crack*, a choking sound as he stumbled back, then . . .

I felt something twist in my chest and a brief surge of pain. Blackness.

The arena. Again.

⁂

I clenched my jaw.

The Smiling Sword Saint was watching me very, very closely now. She was only a foot away from me.

"Again," I said simply.

Her only response was silence at first. Then, after a heartbeat, she nodded. "Once again, I draw steel against a world long gone."

⁂

"Insolent *fool*."

My hand caught the nobleman's wrist before it descended.

He looked at me, incredulous. "What is the meaning of this?"

"Wow. That's . . . a really deep question." I paused for a moment. "I don't think I'm old enough to have the answers. But if you'd like, I'll buy you a drink, and we can discuss—"

"I see there's more than one fool here today." He pulled his wrist back. This time, I actually let him — he hadn't hit the kid yet, and I was looking for a chance at dialogue, if possible, not a fight.

I mean, I *wanted* a fight, but I had to at least *try* to talk to him, you know? It seemed like the right thing to do.

Fortunately, he spared us both the awkwardness of having to sort things out through words and chose violence immediately. You can imagine my relief when he turned to his minions and said, "Xiao Min, Xiao Qin, kill these men before I count to ten."

Oh, he made it rhyme! That's—

A sword flashed from its scabbard in a quick-draw technique that was not, well, quick enough.

I caught the flat of the sword with a palm strike, knocking it against a table, then brought my other fist down against the area where the hilt and blade met.

A surge of essence flashed through my hand as I struck. I'd hoped to break the sword at the hilt, but I only managed to . . . maybe bend it a little.

Still, the *clang* that reverberated through the air as I struck sounded pretty impressive, and the shock of his draw being deflected had left Minion B speechless, since he didn't say anything at all about how impressive my counter had been.

Unfortunately, before I could draw any commentary from the other swordsman, or, you know, my sword, something hit me over the back of the head.

I groaned, reaching back to find some kind of black powder in my hair.

I frowned in confusion, turning around, then saw Minion A grinning and raising a hand — which was now burning with fire essence.

Oh. Do they have gunpowder here?

That's . . . real bad.

He stepped forward with a menacing look.

Sword Hand.

I managed one quick cut before he threw a fireball at me.

I threw a ball of gunpowder-dusted hair at him faster.

My hair met the fireball closer to him, which meant that when the explosion went off, I was only hit by the shock wave of force and he was the one that was set on fire. And the remaining cylinders on his belt?

Also on fire.

They didn't explode right away.

I blew in his direction, attempting a suitably dramatic version of the Cutting Remark technique, trying to carry a surge of sword essence across the room to slice the cylinders apart.

It didn't work. As usual, I failed spectacularly at the technique.

. . . But Minion A probably didn't have a chance to realize that, because the moment I blew at him, he stumbled backward and hit a table, which cracked a cylinder, and . . .

Let's just say that if Minion B survived, there'd be an opening for a promotion to a better letter.

I didn't have time to celebrate the combustion. People were vacating the tavern now, given that it was very on fire, and Minion B didn't seem happy about his letter-grade raise. He was charging straight at me with a murderous look (which is not an actual technique name, as far as I'm aware) while the nobleman watched on with a strange and distant expression.

I deflected Minion B's swing with my Sword Hand, drawing my own sword with my other hand and pressing forward in earnest, and then the strangest thing happened—

I had a sword fight with Minion B, and Minion B won.

I stared down at the sword embedded in my chest in shock.

This wasn't supposed to happen. I wasn't supposed to lose to a nameless, unspeaking minion of the villainous nobleman.

"Hmph. You were a fool to challenge Xiao Min, Disciple of the Threefold Blade."

I felt a surge of shock at this additional twist.

Minion B could talk?!

I couldn't handle a twist like that. I lost consciousness immediately.

⁂

Closer.

Better.

Again.

"Once again, I draw steel against a world long gone."

⁂

I fought.

I lost.

I woke.

Again.

"Once again, I draw steel against a world long gone."

⁂

Again.

Again.

Again!

⁂

I blinked awake.

I was back in the arena . . . and coughing for some reason.

"You okay, kid?" The Smiling Sword Saint was even closer, now, only inches away.

I blinked rapidly. "I . . . think so? A little woozy, maybe, but . . . uh. How long has it been?"

"Several hours. Drink something."

I nodded in immediate agreement, grabbing a flask of water from my side and taking a long draw. Immediately, I felt a little bit of the pounding at my temples subside.

Yeah . . . needed that. Has it really been that long? I . . .

"Listen, kid. I don't know if it's good for you to . . . die that many times in a row, like that."

I frowned. "Am I doing that badly?" I asked. "Was . . . was I supposed to win on the first try?"

"Uh, no. You weren't. That's . . . not the issue." The Smiling Sword Saint frowned, looking away. "Look, I think I might have, uh, picked the wrong memory to focus on. We could adjust, if you're not enjoying this one, and maybe pick something out that's a little more—"

"No." It was a simple statement, but a firm one.

"No?" The Smiling Sword Saint's eyebrow went up. "You sure? You . . . you're taking a real beating in there. It's okay to want to stop. You probably *should* want to stop."

"Why would I want to stop?" I asked, confused. "This is the most fun I've had in years."

INTERLUDE II

THANE I

WAYS OF THE SWORD

Thane fidgeted as he sat on the ruined bleachers, watching the massive mirrorlike essence construct that floated in the center. He'd been sitting on his feet long enough that his right leg was falling asleep, but that didn't stop him from twitching his foot constantly, much to the apparent dismay of his older self.

Still, he had to do something. There wasn't any way he could help with what his sparring partner was doing — the Dreamer's Circlet was built for one, after all, and the Smiling Sword Saint had no intention of crafting another.

It wasn't like he ordinarily would have stepped in on anyone else's training exercise even if he could, but this . . . this clearly wasn't going as planned.

His hand tightened as it began again, just as it had a dozen times before.

⊱ ⊰

Edge stood up before the tray had finished falling, but not quickly enough to catch it.

Ugh. Here we go again, Thane thought.

"Insolent *fool*." Zeng Wu's hand went up, and Edge caught it, just like he had the last several times. Thane forced himself to watch, in spite of having seen the results repeatedly now. There were small changes, true, but nothing noteworthy.

"There's no need for violence," Edge said, with eyes that clearly *asked* for just the opposite.

"It is you who dared to lay hands upon me, weakling!" Zeng Wu's other hand moved swiftly, but Edge, having practiced this exchange, managed to mostly move his head out of the way in time. Even a bare brush of his fist across Edge's chin rocked his head back and loosened his grip, which was unsurprising — Zeng Wu was more than two full levels above Edge, a natural prodigy, and a core disciple of the Soaring Sword Sect.

Still, loosening wasn't releasing, and Edge maintained his grip, blinking away the pain and looking little more than irritated. "Do the hand blast thing."

"What?" Young Master Zeng replied. His minions — ugh, Edge's terms had gotten to him — his *sect juniors* were getting to their feet but hadn't drawn their own weapons yet. After all, their senior disciple clearly had this upstart in hand, and it wouldn't do to interpose needlessly.

"The thing where you blast me through the wall." Edge grabbed Zeng Wu's other hand, putting it directly on his chest. "I've been trying to—"

Edge catapulted across the room, slamming through the wooden walls of the building with a loud *thump*.

Zeng Wu dusted himself off, ignoring the now-fleeing serving boy, and walked in the swordsman's wake. Xiao Min and Xiao Qin stood.

"Shall we conclude this business, Young Master?" Xiao Min asked.

"No need. That should have —" Zeng Wu began, only to watch in disbelief as Edge stumbled back into the room, right through the wreckage of the wall he'd passed through.

"No, still too fast," Edge mumbled. He reached up and rubbed his ear, wincing. "Okay, let's get this part over with."

"Xiao Min." The nobleman gestured.

"With pleasure." The outer sect disciple stepped forward, unsheathing his sword, but not even bothering to use his signature blade-splitting technique. Why would he? His opponent was already barely standing, after all.

"Ah, Xiao Min, Disciple of the Threefold Blade." Edge bowed his head in what probably was supposed to pass for acknowledgment but just came across as mocking, given his tone. "Pleased to beat you."

Xiao Min blinked. "Don't you mean pleased to meet—"

Edge surged across the room, faster than Thane had expected, sweeping downward with a newly forged Sword Hand technique. There was a brief exchange of blades, where Edge (as usual) focused with tunnel vision on his opponent, seemingly failing to see Xiao Qin sneaking up behind him.

Edge looked mildly betrayed when he felt the needles hit his back, stumbling forward a step, then Xiao Min's hilt took him in the face.

Edge's eyes flickered as he hit the ground.

"Take him. I have questions," Zeng Wu said.

Well, that was a more interesting ending this time, at least, Thane considered.

Sadly, as with every dream before, it faded the moment Edge's dream body lost consciousness.

⊱ ⊰

Edge groaned, waking briefly again. The Smiling Sword Saint was right in front of him, pushing a flask of water into the boy's hand. Edge took a long draw from it.

He paused just long enough for a moment of primary essence compression, which he'd started working into his rotation each time he failed the scenario.

Thane could tell Edge was drawing in sword essence, but not what aspect he was using, or if he was mixing in anything else. Then, with a determined expression, Edge spoke the words to activate the circlet again.

"Once again, I draw steel against a world long gone."

The swordsman's eyes closed. The scene appeared.

The results were barely different from before.

Edge grabbed Zeng Wu's wrist. Zeng Wu threw an ordinary punch, then when that wasn't enough, a classic Soaring Palm. Edge crashed through the wall, looking mildly dissatisfied. Xiao Min engaged; they had a brief back-and-forth.

This time, Edge managed to land a solid openhanded strike on Xiao Min's face, then side-stepped before most of the needles hit his back. Unfortunately, one was enough, and the paralytic poison worked quickly. He stumbled, deflecting one of Xiao Qin's sword swings, then Zeng Wu knocked the swordsman out with a contemptuous blow.

Thane groaned, starting to stand, but the Smiling Sword Saint stopped him with a look.

Stupid older me. This is pointless.

The next three attempts were no better. The first one was largely the same as the previous attempt, with the swordsman lasting a couple more moments by dodging the needles completely, only to fall to a stronger hit from the young master's Soaring Palm a few moments later.

In spite of that, Edge was grinning like a lunatic when he woke up that time and threw himself back into the dream before he even took a drink.

The next attempt was *worse*. Edge didn't manage to dodge the first punch quite as effectively, and it hurt him badly enough that he barely put up a fight.

The next was back to ending with a second use of the Soaring Palm smashing him straight into the ground.

Edge woke after that attempt, taking a drink. Then he focused, clapped his hands together, and nodded to himself. There was a brief flash of sword essence, so quick that Thane couldn't discern the purpose, and then Edge dived right back into the dream.

For Thane, it was too much. He stood, striding over to the Smiling Sword Saint, and folded his arms.

"This is pointless. It's a waste of time — and by allowing it to continue, you're going to teach him bad habits."

The Smiling Sword Saint turned to him. "Oh? Enlighten me, Great Master."

Thane wrinkled his nose in distaste. "You can be as flippant as you want, you know exactly what I mean. He's *completely missing the point.* He has from the start. He's supposed to be *joining the sect,* not starting a fight with a core disciple!"

"What better way to earn his entrance exam token than to take it off a core disciple's body?"

Thane rolled his eyes. "That would be more compelling if Zeng Wu acted like a core disciple. Those people in there are *caricatures*."

The sword saint shrugged. "We didn't handle the scenario the way he did, so it has to fill itself in somehow. Apparently, Edge's dream mana leans toward extreme personalities."

"You mean two-sigil novel young master stereotypes?"

The sword saint sighed at that. "The cost of a child who has never been to a sect. Even if none of those three have quite the right personalities, their skills seem roughly right, and they're fighting appropriately. That makes the training element of it valid enough for our purposes. I can spend more time making the next crystal a little more accurate."

Thane groaned. "He won't get to another crystal anytime soon. You *know* he can't win that fight."

"Well, not fairly." The Smiling Sword Saint laughed. "But who's to say what will happen after another ten repetitions? A hundred?"

"Winning a fight because you've practiced against someone a hundred times isn't a testament to skill, it's just pattern recognition. And if you haven't noticed, he's not even trying to win. Not really."

"Oh-ho. Enlighten me further." The Smiling Sword Saint reclined on the ground, briefly casting an eye back toward the mirror, but there was no point to either of them really watching. It would be a few more minutes before the fight started, and even then, they both knew how it would end.

"He's just . . . decided to start the fight the same way each time. It's a terrible strategy. If his goal is to save the kid, he should just stop him from dropping the plate."

"And since that clearly *isn't* his only goal?" the Smiling Sword Saint asked.

Thane frowned. "He's being stubborn. Edge is usually the one who is always making weird strategies. If he wants to win, he should be trying novel strategies. Start with an ambush. Insult them from an area that's defensible, like a doorway, so he can fight each person one at a time. Challenge the young master to a duel and take it outside. Any of that would be an improvement. And he has to know that. I've *seen* how he usually fights."

The Smiling Sword Saint nodded, glancing to the sleeping swordsman, then back to Thane. "Do you know what makes Edge worth bothering with?"

Thane paused, considering that question for a moment. The tone had been more serious, enough so that he knew that there was greater significance to it than their previous exchange of words. "The sword. The weird essence in his hand tied to it. He's probably some kind of sword spirit or something, even if he doesn't act like it."

"That's a part of it, true. But I'd begun to teach him before he had the sword — before I was certain of what it was. And I still don't know exactly what *he* is. The seal interested me, but he can do little with it now. In the long term, perhaps he will make it a major part of his power. But if he had shown up to me for the first time with that sword in his hands, and that mark upon him, I would not have trained him. If he was very lucky, I would have sent him away missing an arm and a sword. If not, I would have killed him."

Thane's eyes narrowed. "You would have killed a child?"

"I don't know what exactly he is. I *do* know, more deeply than I know the boundaries of my own self, that he has a sword that *should not exist*." The Smiling Sword Saint shook her head. "So, no. It is not the sword, nor the essence, that convinced me to train the boy. If anything, they served as strikes against him."

Thane wrinkled his nose. "I don't know what to say, then. His physical strength is greater than it should be for his level." He hesitated before saying the next part, even though it was obvious to them both. "He's stronger than I am, purely in terms of muscle. Even more so in terms of striking strength. If he wasn't holding back, he'd be shattering bones when he was punching people of his own level. Maybe even people of *my* level. I don't know how he got that strong, but it's not special or unprecedented. You wouldn't train a dragon who happened to pick up a sword."

"I mean, I might — that sounds like a pretty novel experience. But you're right. He is strong, but that isn't important enough to make him a student. It's probably a species thing, like if he was a dragon, except he's a sword whatever. His sealed essence, whatever it is, probably contributes to his striking strength, too. What else?"

"I don't know." Thane admitted. "It's not determination. We've met plenty of people that refuse to stay down. That redhead from the other sword school beats him there. She seems like she might be your type, too—"

"Stay focused," the Sword Saint growled.

"Right. Courage? I don't think so. It's more he doesn't get scared, since he's, you know, a sword or something."

"You're wrong on that one. He does get scared. He just lashes out when it happens, rather than running. He's learned to resist that instinct, to hold back."

"And is that special?"

"It's unusual, and perhaps noteworthy, but not enough to make him my student. So, why do you think I'm training him? Think."

Thane frowned. "He's pretty good at making techniques for his age. I wasn't around when he first showed that off to you, but you've both mentioned it."

The Smiling Sword Saint nodded. "You're aiming in the right direction now."

"Is that really all it is? I know he's made an unusual number of techniques for his age, but is that really that noteworthy? And what does that have to do with what he's doing right now?"

"Perfect timing. Let's find out, shall we?"

"Insolent *fool*."

Thane watched with minimal enthusiasm, but greater focus. He knew he was supposed to be looking for something new, but Edge had barely been making any forward progress in the scenario. There was no sign that he was anywhere close to winning the fight.

Zeng Wu swung a fist.

Edge shifted his head incrementally to the side, just enough for the fist to pass right by him.

For a moment, they locked eyes.

"Hmph. It seems you have some skill," Zeng Wu said. "Celebrate it in your grave."

Yet again, his hand shot toward Edge's chest with a Soaring Palm.

This time, though, Edge moved faster.

His hand came up closed, flying at Zeng Wu's face . . .

And then he opened his hand, flicking the young master of the Zeng with a single finger.

There was a *crack*, a flash of essence—

And then Zeng Wu hurtled halfway across the room, smashing messily into a table and falling back on the floor.

Wh . . . what?

Thane stared at the mirror.

What the vek was that?!

He turned to the Smiling Sword Saint. She raised a finger in a "shh" gesture, then pointed back at the mirror to where Zeng Wu was groaning and pulling himself from the wreckage of a table.

Edge raised the single finger, looking slightly annoyed, and grumbled something about "aiming for the wall," then sighed and glanced from side to side.

As Xiao Min and Xiao Qin stood and drew their swords, Edge punched left and right at the same time. Twin Sword Hands manifested as he struck, but rather than piercing through their chests, Edge smashed the flats of the swords into the brothers' chests. The two swordsmen flew backward, one into the bar, the other simply falling to the floor.

Edge dismissed the Sword Hand techniques, turning to the serving boy. "You should get clear."

Then he cracked his neck, turning to Zeng Wu, his hand on the sword on his hip. "If you want to continue this, I'll meet you out front."

He turned his back and strode confidently to the door.

. . . That was, of course, a critical mistake. The full brace of poisoned needles hit him in the back before he even had his hand on the door handle.

". . . Oh."

He slumped to the floor, his legs no longer responding.

He barely managed to turn his neck upward as Zeng Wu rose above him. "Take this lesson to the afterlife. No one challenges a Zeng and walks away."

Edge regarded him seriously. ". . . I'll take that into consideration."

Zeng Wu's sword came down. In spite of his words, the young master of the Zeng struck with the flat of his blade.

Thane understood why—

Killing the swordsman would avenge his pride, yes.

But discovering whatever technique the strange swordsman had just used?

That was a prize that even the young master of the Zeng could not possibly ignore.

⁂

Edge's eyes fluttered open . . .

Then he burst into laughter. "Better. *Much* better." Edge must have caught him staring, since he gave Thane a wink, then took a drink. After that, he took a breath. "Once again, I draw steel against a world long gone."

His eyes shut.

Thane turned straight to the Smiling Sword Saint. "Okay, what in all the skies was that technique?"

The Smiling Sword Saint's lips turned up a fraction. Even that minute movement sent enough essence through the air to make goose bumps form on Thane's skin, but he ignored the sensation. "Wouldn't be any fun if I just told you. What do *you* think it was?"

"I . . . I don't know." He frowned, considering. "He barely touched Zeng Wu and he launched him halfway across the room."

"And what else have you seen that does something similar?"

Thane frowned at the obvious answer. "I mean, it *almost* looked like the Soaring Palm. But that technique . . . Edge doesn't have anything remotely like the essence types used in it. He doesn't use motion, air, or anything even *related* to them."

"What does he have?"

"Sword essence, breach essence, and whatever his overpowered mystery essence is." Thane shook his head. "Is his mystery essence related to the types used in Soaring Palm?"

"Not really. But he wasn't using that, anyway. Nor was he using breach essence."

"Then . . ." Thane took a breath. "And he doesn't have any new essence types?"

"Nope. He's starting to work on another Dianis Point, but it isn't done yet. Might get it done by the three-month mark, might not."

Thane struggled with the conclusion. "Then it's a sword essence technique. But . . . I don't know any techniques that use sword essence alone that could do that to a person. I . . . didn't even know you *could* do that with just sword essence."

"I'm not surprised," the Smiling Sword Saint offered. "Neither did I, at first."

Thane stared at the Smiling Sword Saint. ". . . What?"

"It's as absurd as it looked, kid." The Smiling Sword Saint reached out and ruffled Thane's hair in a way that was simultaneously affectionate and deeply disturbing. "In the last . . . what's it been, ten hours? Twelve? I don't know. Less than a day. We've watched our little Edge make a sword essence technique without ever actually raising a sword. He did it without being *awake* for most of the process, and the resulting technique is something that I — a Memory-layer Swordseeker — did not know could be done."

Thane took a deep breath. "But . . . why? *How?*"

"I've been figuring that out along with him," the Smiling Sword Saint said with a hint of fondness. "You were right about something, early on. If he simply wanted to win the fight, he had better ways of doing that. I'm sure he knew that a long time ago. Instead, he was repeating a doomed pattern specifically to experience the Soaring Palm."

"But . . . if he'd just gone through the sect exams, like he was supposed to . . . " Thane offered weakly.

"Sure, he could have gotten there eventually. Do you remember how long the admittance tests took? The ceremony? The days of orientation? Maybe in a few weeks, he would have seen the Soaring Palm for the first time. Of course, this particular memory crystal doesn't go anywhere near that far, but I might have given him others. My idea *was* to let him earn his way into the sect, and to learn from teachers that are . . . more qualified to teach than I am." The Smiling Sword Saint's expression was neutral, but neutral in a way that Thane interpreted as something like annoyance at herself, and . . . maybe a bit of pride? "But he found his own way to learn."

"By being beaten to a pulp? Losing repeatedly, looking utterly pitiful in the process?"

"I think you probably should have learned by now that Edge has a very different sort of pride than ours. It exists, but . . . he would not feel shamed by these failures. To him, each trip through this memory is merely a piece of a puzzle to solve. I had thought at first, as you did, that the puzzle was to find a way to defeat his opponents. Perhaps it was, for the first attempt or two. But from the moment he was struck with a technique, his goal changed. And he would fall a thousand times to reach it."

"That answers the why, I guess. If he thought he could learn a new technique faster by being pummeled, it makes a certain sort of twisted sense. But it doesn't answer the how."

The Smiling Sword Saint was quiet for a moment, contemplative.

Then she asked him one of the simplest questions anyone on the Way of the Sword ever contemplated.

"What is a sword?"

Thane shrugged at the obvious trap question. "There are as many answers to that as there are clouds in the sky."

"Good that you know that. But give me a basic answer — a traditional one."

"Right. A classic, sure. 'A sword is forged for a singular purpose. Unlike the axe, it does not chop wood. Unlike the spear, it is not a tool to hunt. Unlike the hammer, it does not forge as easily as it breaks. A sword is unique among stars and stone in that it is forged for killing alone.'"

"Ah, quoting our old teacher? Wonderful. It's also absolute nonsense, of course."

Thane groaned. "You don't have to tell me that. I already knew it when he said it. It ignores the existence of practice swords, ceremonial swords, ritual swords, fencing foils purely for sport. It ignores curved swords for cutting jungle brush, those weird swords northerners use to chop wood . . . and it's not like an executioner's axe is built for chopping wood. You can use a sword for plenty of things, just like you can use an axe or spear."

"Exactly." The Sword Saint snapped her fingers. "There are *many* uses for a sword. And there are just as many ways of defining the sword itself. I've encountered dozens of different sword schools, each with their own conception of the sword. Their own Way of the Sword, their own essence of the sword. But though I have seen many strange and foreign ways, I have never before seen one quite like *his*."

"You think he's advanced enough to have his own *way*? That's a bit of a claim."

"Not a true way yet, of course. He's just a boy. But, in spite of his age, he has already begun to forge the first part of his blade."

"How? Forging techniques at his age is strange enough, but the steps of his own way . . . he's nowhere near advanced enough for that."

"It's not a matter of advancement. It's about having a different style of thought — and following that thought to its logical conclusion." The Sword Saint sighed. "Had he been raised like we were, with steel in his hands from the time he could walk, he would not have taken these steps — because he would have already been set on a different path. Instead, lacking true guidance, he began to walk his Way of the Sword as a child."

"You're saying he's already made a unique sword style? *By himself?*" Thane asked, incredulous.

"No." The Smiling Sword Saint shook her head. "Not alone. If he had been alone, perhaps he still *could* have forged a path, but his way reflects one other — the sword faerie with whom he trained for so many years."

Thane scoffed. "He admits himself that was more play than true training."

"True. In terms of learning how to fight, it had little value. But in terms of forming his way, it was an invaluable asset."

"How so?"

"For a lonely boy and girl with wide imaginations, it is not so difficult to imagine that a humble stick is a sword. Many children play in such a fashion — but few *dedicate* themselves to this practice as they did. Year after year, as Edge grew, as he forged his essence, he internalized this ideal: in his hands, even a stick is a sword. And now, as he has grown further, he has begun to consider that he, himself, might be a sword."

"That . . . that sounds like the ultimate goal of many sword sects. 'I am the sword' is the kind of thing that ancient masters break and reforge their sense of selves a thousand times to try to reach."

The Smiling Sword Saint laughed. "And he reached it as a child. By *accident.* And then, as we've seen today, he began to reach *beyond.*"

"What do you mean?"

The Smiling Sword Saint gestured as Edge, within the mirror vision, smacked Xiao Min with the back of his hand and launched the minion halfway across the room.

"If you can imagine that a stick is a sword, it is not so far a step to imagine that your body is a sword. For most, it requires unlearning the most basic things we were taught, a complete adjustment of our way and our essence to reduce its rigid nature. For Edge, however, there are no ancient ways burned into him, no assumptions from many generations of training passed down. So for him, it was a small step to say that if his body can be a sword, his opponent's body is also a sword. And so, if *he* is a sword, and his opponent is another . . ."

Thane stared for a moment in absolute awe, processing.

"He's parrying *people.*"

The Smiling Sword Saint laughed in delight. "It's absurd, isn't it? The idea of parrying a person? But you're right — that's exactly what he's doing. Well, a half step from it, if you want to get technical. If he used something like parrying-aspected essence, it wouldn't be knocking them that far. He tried it a few times, and he also tried deflection, but the impact was minuscule. He's using beat-aspected sword essence now."

Thane nodded, finally comprehending what was happening. A parry was a maneuver that was used to deflect a weapon out of position to prevent an attack from landing. A beat was the same type of thing, but more aggressive, designed to knock a weapon out of position, generally to create an opening.

If one could understand a person as a sword, then why *couldn't* you knock them around with a beat, creating an opening in their defense?

It was an absurd sort of logic. The type of thing that no ordinary young swordsman would have intuited.

"That's neat and all, but . . ." Thane shook his head. "It doesn't actually let him do anything special, does it? Now that I know his trick, I could reproduce it. Anyone could."

"Sure. He's been spending time figuring out exactly the right composition of beat-aspected essence to make it work effectively on humans — you could do the same. You'll probably figure it out if he hits you with it once or twice, then be able to use it on him."

"Then . . . I suppose it's unusual he can do that, but what's the point?" Thane asked.

"With just sword essence, his unusual mindset already was leading him to making techniques that most people wouldn't consider possible with that essence type alone. You might be able to match something he makes with sword essence easily enough, but if he can apply that same razor sharpness of mind to making things with breach essence, and his own unique essence . . ."

"He might make something truly unique." Thane nodded. "But is it really a sharp mind we're talking about, or just that he follows a different tradition of his own making?"

"It's both," the sword saint explained. "Without his upbringing, he wouldn't have had an unusual starting point for his ideas and his strange essence composition. But without a certain kind of cleverness and tenacity, he wouldn't be able to use that upbringing to make techniques in an environment like this. How many techniques do you think the average Torch-level swordsman makes?"

"Zero," Thane replied. "But that's because they're learning from others."

"And how many techniques in total do you think the average swordsman knows at Torch?"

Thane frowned. He personally had known several at that point, but when he thought about young new disciples at the sect. ". . . Three or four, maybe?"

"Sounds about right. Thus far, I think I've seen Edge use *seven*."

"That's . . . a lot. But he's got limitations, too. He's awful at ranged and movement techniques."

"True." The sword sage gave a hint of a nod. "His essence skews heavily toward stability, and his philosophy of the sword also limits him as much as it strengthens him. His way is by no means perfect, nor is it even strictly superior to any other. But in all my many years, I have never seen a youth who approaches swordsmanship the way he does."

"Like a master?" Thane asked, raising an eyebrow.

The Smiling Sword Saint chuckled. "No. Not like a master. The opposite, if anything. He approaches swordsmanship like a child who is too stubborn to accept that his dreams are impossible, but armed with the scholarly methods of a sage."

"That's . . . a pretty incongruous combination."

"Yes. I'm looking forward to seeing how it works out."

When Thane looked back to the mirror, he saw Edge losing yet another round. He saw Edge emerging with a laugh, plunging himself back into the fray, throwing himself into another futile battle with reckless abandon.

Thane no longer saw futility in that process. No, as Edge danced between two swings and landed another touch that hurled a swordsman across the room, Thane found himself watching in rapt fascination.

If he could do this *now*, what would Edge be capable of in one year? In five?

If this was merely the beginning of the lonely swordsman's way, where could the end possibly be?

CHAPTER XV

SMASHING STING

I . . . might have gotten a little fixated on using the circlet.

When the sun had begun to rise and I still hadn't eaten more than a few bites of food for the day, the Smiling Sword Saint snatched the circlet off my head after my latest attempt and forced me to eat and hydrate properly. She also made me stand up and engage in a brief real-world sparring match with Thane, which felt weird after hours of being beaten to unconsciousness in a completely different reality.

"You're going to develop bad habits if you develop your style based around a world where there are no consequences for being hurt," the Smiling Sword Saint narrated as I nursed my very real wounds from Thane's beating.

Thane gave the Smiling Sword Saint a *look* when she said that, but I couldn't quite read it. He turned his attention back to me afterward, looking vaguely smug.

He'd probably beaten me more easily than he had before I'd put the circlet on. Part of that was probably the start to those bad habits the Smiling Sword Saint had talked about — I found myself trading hits rather than avoiding them, which wasn't a good strategy in most real-world fights — but another part was that I was just dead tired. I'd been up for close to twenty-four hours. Dreaming with the circlet, it seemed, didn't rejuvenate me like normal sleep did.

The sword saint refused to let me build a shelter nearby. I groaned and asked to borrow the circlet, but she refused that, too.

Before leaving, I spent long enough there to finish my primary essence compression for the day. I'd been doing it in small bits to avoid needing to take too long of a break from using the circlet, but I still didn't feel like I'd done enough for the day, so I had a slightly longer session before I left.

I was working toward building an Advancing Point, taking advantage of the massive amount of sword essence that was now available.

The Advancing Point was located in a person's primary leg — in my case, my right. Building essence in that location helped utilize techniques for speed and mobility. So, the most obvious choices were things like speed essence, agility essence, or essence types that offered teleportation or flight powers.

Using sword essence for that was a little weird, but I had something more complicated in mind. Rather than building an Advancing Point directly out of sword essence, I was using sword essence as a primary component to build something related to it, while also practicing the right actions to try to build a distinct wellspring.

If I succeeded, I'd have something similar and related to sword essence, but skewed toward internal techniques rather than external ones. Even a Sword Lord probably couldn't do anything with sword essence as long as it remained within my body, which meant that things like body-enhancement and movement techniques would be more usable than others. And while my new Dianis Point would contain sword essence as a component, it wouldn't strictly be sword essence . . . assuming I managed to build it right.

I didn't know if I'd be able to finish another Dianis Point in three months, even if it was primarily composed of sword essence, but it would have been foolish not to at least make the attempt.

After finishing my essence compression, I trudged back to the sword school. I tried to join in their own sparring, but Red took one look at me and ordered me to go to bed.

In spite of my absolute exhaustion, I couldn't sleep. The daylight was part of it, but a larger part was that my battles in the scenario made by the circlet — dozens now, maybe hundreds — were still playing through my mind.

Rest gave me more time to process them actively, considering each failure, each individual mistake. I'd already iterated repeatedly throughout the process, but without the ability to jump right into another fight, I had more time to analyze.

I rejected certain obvious solutions, like avoiding the fight entirely or ambushing my opponents and cutting them down before they could react. They weren't bad ideas, exactly, but they didn't accomplish my goals. I worried that if I did anything the Smiling Sword Saint considered "winning," she might move me to a different scenario or take the circlet away entirely.

That was unacceptable. I was still learning. And once I lost at a fight, winning in the future was a matter of pride. I couldn't just skip it now. I'd never get the catharsis of a hard-won victory that way.

So, I'd keep fighting until I won . . . and I was still a long way off from that.

What am I missing? What techniques would let me win?

Hours later, I finally slept, my fingers stained in ink and a journal clutched tightly to my chest.

I don't remember how it started.

I was lying in a field of grass and flowers, three suns shining brightly above me, the smallest of them giving the clouds above a reddish hue. There was no recognition there, but neither was there a lack of it — I was simply there.

And so was she.

She looked much as I remembered, blond hair fading to black at the roots, a smattering of freckles on her cheeks. Gone was the plate armor that had framed her form, however, replaced with a simple white tunic and black slacks. Her spear was missing, too, and I felt some wrongness at that, even in those first moments.

I saw her when I rolled over to my left, moving seemingly at the same time that she had, our gazes meeting, processing, recognizing, and then—

"You."

Dream Girl didn't even bother to get off the grass before she attacked.

I didn't see where the knife came from — there was no obvious source for it; it was just there, and then she was lunging toward me. She was quick, and I didn't have a chance to draw my sword — where was my sword? — before she was above me, knife descending at my throat.

My right arm went up, essence flaring around it faster than I could process. Knife met sleeve and her blade glanced away, leaving only a faint cut on the sleeve and skin. As the impact jarred her arm out of position, I grabbed her wrist tightly, then rolled on top of her, rapidly pushing the knife downward, trying to reverse her own intended maneuver.

I had a clear strength advantage while grappling, and she must have realized that, letting the knife drop before I could pin her with it. When it hit the ground next to her head, it vanished.

Her other arm whipped toward my ear, but we were close enough that the swing was clumsy. The impact made me wince, but it didn't throw me off her. Then I was grabbing both of her arms and pinning her down.

I thought I had her immobile, given my strength advantage, but her face showed no fear or strain, just wry amusement. Her bright golden eyes scanned my arms and bare chest — where was my *shirt*? — and her lips twisted sharply to the right. "Not bad. A little forward of you to pin me down like that. Usually, I'd ask you to buy a girl dinner first, but I might be willing to make an exception for—"

She fell through the ground. Like, literally right through it, as if it wasn't there.

Except her hands, which were still pinned by mine. So, a moment later, I was holding her wrists, but the rest of her body was . . . inside the seemingly solid ground, somewhere?

That was weird enough that I *started* to process the strangeness of the whole situation.

This is . . . oh.

I let go of her hands.

She vanished the rest of the way into the ground, then a moment later, I stood up and deliberately stepped to the side. That put me safely out of the way when the jagged tear appeared in the sky above me, the girl descending from above, now properly armed with her spear, but still lacking her former armor.

She descended in a blur, but I was ready for it, rapidly acclimating to my environment. Rather than trying to find my sword, I simply took a few steps back, allowing her to plunge into the ground and smash her spear deep into where I'd been standing.

I barely managed to dance back as the spear's tip shot upward from the ground beneath me, in spite of her thrust coming nowhere near me.

Not bad.

I flicked my right arm at her without thinking, a crescent wave of cutting force — the same reshing technique I kept trying to make in the waking world and failing — flashing across the field in her direction. She pulled her spear out of the ground and split the crescent with a swing, then twirled it in place, settling into a ready stance as silvery armor slowly began to grow across her body.

"So," I offered, taking a step back and reaching out to my side, beginning to slowly form my sword in my right hand, "we meet again."

"Really? It's been weeks, and that's the best ley line you could come up with?"

I jumped to the side as she lunged again, her speed still exceeding my own. Before she could land her strike, I managed to raise my half-formed sword and swing it upward, knocking the spear to the side. It still brushed against my arm, leaving a small gash. I frowned as I saw my arm bleeding more than it should be from such a glancing wound, but I didn't have time to address it — she was rapidly twisting to sweep at my legs with the haft of the spear. I hopped over the swing easily, but she just brought it upward between my legs in a move that would have been very uncomfortable if I hadn't managed to bring my half-solid sword down to smash her spear into the ground before she finished the movement.

I stepped forward immediately, released my off hand from my sword, and punched her in the jaw.

She was faster than I was, shifting her head to the side, but I still managed to brush my fist against the side of her jaw. She staggered backward and I saw an improbably rapid bruise forming on her cheek. I rested my sword against my shoulder, the weapon's hilt and guard more solid now, but the blade remaining a flickering field of force. I didn't know what was happening with that, but it was still growing gradually more corporeal, and I felt my own coherence growing along with it. "Was hoping to lay you out with that punch, but it looks like I didn't line it up clearly enough."

Dream Girl spat blood, dropped her spear and re-formed it instantly in a different stance, then grinned the most brightly I'd seen yet, the crimson droplets on her lips and teeth only adding to the effect. "*Now* you're speaking my language."

I charged at her, sweeping my sword downward. She blurred to the side, but I adjusted midswing and focused, my sword's half-physical blade extending to a dozen feet in length and leaving a strange gouge in the air as it passed. Dream

Girl's spear flipped into a block, but I pushed into the impact, and the force of it launched her into the distance. I hit her so hard that she flew completely out of my sight, only to reappear right behind me a moment later, already back on the attack.

I spun, trying to guard, but her spear tore a gash in my left shoulder. I grunted at the impact, then swung up toward where she was gripping the spear. She pulled back rapidly, but I'd expected that.

Shattering Sword.

My half-formed blade flashed as a half dozen full copies of the blade appeared midstrike, cutting at different angles. Her eyes widened in response, and she started to vanish in what I suspected was a teleportation technique, but it didn't matter—

I cut straight through the teleportation effect. When she reappeared in the distance, her right arm was bleeding profusely. I'd sliced straight through her silvery armor, too, and there was a jagged rent where my sword's image had passed through it.

I was bleeding, too, and in multiple locations, but I barely noticed. In this space, my pain and injuries seemed real enough, but they only impacted me when I was actively thinking about them. I shifted into a ready stance, the bottom third of my sword's blade now shining silver rather than merely manifested as a conceptual force. I felt like it was more effective now, and that it couldn't have torn through her armor when I'd first begun to form it, but I couldn't say where I'd gotten that impression. In this space, it seemed perception and intuition helped to shape our reality.

As my lucidity improved, it would help me more actively shape my strategy, but I would likely lose some of that intuitive understanding. I wasn't actually sure if that would prove advantageous, but I didn't have a way to stop the process — instead, I simply resolved to use my growing advantages in the best way I could.

That meant more of a focus on my techniques, even if they weren't working quite the way I'd expected them to. And if they were stronger than expected, well, I could use that.

It never occurred to me to surrender, nor to plead for her to do so. The latter might have been my approach for anyone else, but not her. Never with her. A truce, like when we'd confronted that great beast, perhaps — but never surrender.

We'd dance until we couldn't. Somehow, I knew that more deeply than I knew anything else in that place, and my heart slammed in anticipation of the next steps.

"You cut me while I wasn't there," she remarked, absently releasing one hand from her spear to flick her injury with a finger. The wound remained, but her armor sealed itself around the cut. "That's quite a sword."

"Complimenting my sword? That's very forward. Usually I'd ask a girl to buy me dinner first."

"Ooh, he's got callbacks. Tell me if you remember this one."

The ground beneath me trembled . . . and then pitched as the entire world we stood on *lurched* to the side.

I fell as the ground flipped sideways, but I twisted and focused, then began to run upward against the incline as she ran downward toward me, her spear glittering in the light. We brushed past each other in a blur of rapid swings, leaving glancing cuts, and then I was picturing the top of a hill, and it was there, the slope of the grass shifting to allow me to stand straight — just in time for her leap up from in front of me and hurl her spear straight at my chest.

I flicked my still-solidifying sword toward her spear to parry — only for the weapon to duplicate itself in midflight, turning into a hail of a half dozen projectiles.

My sword caught the original, hurling it to the side. That barely mattered when I had only an instant to process the fact that she'd stolen my technique before the others hit me.

But I was more lucid by then, and my sword's growing power was improving my ability to manifest my powers quickly. And stealing techniques reminded me of nothing more than my own style. If I couldn't steal a technique that would save me from her, I'd steal it from someone else, someone I'd somehow reached toward in my past dream. Someone I could feel, near but just out of reach.

Body of—

The last word of the technique was lost to me as she vanished and her spear struck me in the back, piercing straight through my chest.

That one *hurt.*

With a roar, I smashed her remaining conjured spears out of the air with my forearms, silver essence pushing through my veins as I conjured the Rejoinder technique a dozen times in rapid succession, parrying each spear and blasting it out of the air. Then I reached down and grabbed the spear that still protruded through the center of my chest, feeling the metal of the shaft just before the point, and *squeezed.*

The metal crumpled in my grip. Then I twisted it, tearing the top of the spear away, and absently swept my two-thirds–formed sword behind my back, slicing straight through the back of the spear.

When I slowly turned, my chest bleeding fiercely, I saw Dream Girl take a step back and re-form her weapon in her hand—

Only to find that it was still broken and twisted. Her eyes widened, showing something resembling true surprise for the first time.

My heart beat faster seeing that vulnerability. I felt myself smile as I strode forward, raising my sword, now fully formed.

She raised her spear to block. I cleaved right through spear, armor, and the front of her chest.

". . . Oh," she said, blood flowing freely across the horizontal cut. "That's what it feels like."

I took a step forward, stumbling suddenly as I remembered the fragment of the spear still stuck in my chest. Blood was spreading rapidly, too rapidly, from the wound. My vision blurred.

I took another step, trying to lift my sword. She took a step forward, too.

I'd almost reached her when I realized that my sword wasn't in my grip. I'd dropped it. We were even closer when the knife — where'd her knife come from? — slipped from her own fingers.

We stumbled the last steps forward anyway, carried half by determination and half by momentum. When we were close enough to touch, we didn't strike. Instead, we fell against each other, somehow the opposing weight keeping us standing as we continued to bleed and my vision began to fade.

"Think you killed me," she mumbled, finally.

"Think you killed me, too," I managed, every breath bringing more pain. I felt consciousness slipping away, but I gripped it as hard as I could.

". . . A draw, then." Her head tilted up, golden eyes meeting the silver — were my eyes always pure silver? — of my own. "Closer . . ."

I leaned in closer, my breath catching in my chest, her bloodied lips so devastatingly close I could almost . . .

". . . Perfect."

She slammed her forehead into mine with one final smile, then we both fell in opposite directions, hitting the ground together. I barely managed a laugh as I hit the ground.

My fingers met hers as we bled out into the grass and flowers, and together, we died.

I groaned as my eyes fluttered open, blearily processing the mundanity of the waking world around me.

I closed my eyes again briefly, trying to go back to sleep. Not out of exhaustion, but out of a feeling like I'd found something there that was important, only to have it slip right out of my grasp.

Attempts to return to that dream eluded me. This was no surprise — I'd always found sleep to be a most elusive foe in general, and any dream worth pursuing to be even harder to grasp.

With a dejected sigh, I pushed myself into a seated position.

The same girl. Once is a coincidence. Twice is the start of a pattern.

If we get to three times, maybe . . .

I clambered out of my shelter slowly, pouring fresh water over my face, both for cleaning and to shock myself into alertness. As much as I wanted to think about the girl who had beautifully murdered me, pleasant things like that weren't something I could spend the entire day on.

Especially because next time I met her, I wanted a definitive win. And if the bloodstained grin she had given me said anything, I could be certain I wouldn't be the only one training for our next dreaming dance.

I shook myself off, had breakfast, and engaged in a bit of sparring with Grey and Fade. After finishing that warm-up, Red and Green both gave me some pointers. I had another snack, hydrated, and headed off to meet the sword saint.

I'd have to talk to Red about the Smiling Sword Saint eventually, but I wasn't sure exactly how to approach it. Would they get along if I introduced them? Would I be putting Grey and Fade in danger if I put them near someone as volatile as the Smiling Sword Saint?

I'd figure it out later. For the moment, I had training to do.

I reached the arena, sparred with Thane in half-distracted fashion, and hydrated again. After that, I found a shady spot and sat down with the circlet for what I'd been looking forward to.

"Once again, I draw steel against a world long gone."

The world changed, and I began again.

I waited, thinking, planning further. Then, I stepped over at just the right time and grabbed Zeng Wu's hand out of the air before it could strike the serving boy. "The kid made an honest mistake. Let it go."

Zeng Wu's eyes narrowed in rage. "You would *dare* put your hand on me?"

"Yep. Come on, take the swing." His arm pulled back for whatever his own version of the knockback technique was. Always the same angle, or close enough to it.

I did the thing where I angled my head just slightly to the side, allowing his hand to miss. Then, with my other hand, I flicked him in the chest with a finger and manifested my newest technique.

Smashing Sting.

My essence flared into his chest as I released the grip from my other hand, launching Zeng Wu backward. I restrained the urge to cheer as I managed to aim him correctly that time, sending him straight into the wall. He impacted it with a loud *thump*, but I groaned when he failed to fly straight through it.

Not strong enough.

I sighed as I took a step back, narrowly avoiding a draw cut from Xiao Min, then flicked my left arm upward with a flare of deflection-aspected essence to knock aside the first brace of thrown needles from Xiao Qin.

Synchronized Sword Hands: Smashing Sting.

Two blades flashed out from my arms simultaneously and I swept them outward, flats slamming into chests, and bowled both of the Torch-level opponents over.

Then I let the essence fade as I drew the metal sword on my hip, charging straight at the already rising Zeng Wu. He met me by gracefully drawing his own sword in a single motion, and we had a brief exchange before I slashed the wall on my right, tearing a hole.

"Outside. Just you and me," I told him.

"You are not worthy of a duel with me."

He sheathed his sword.

I blinked.

Zeng Wu jerked his head up toward Xiao Min, who was on his feet now, advancing. "Xiao Min, take this arrogant child outside for a lesson."

"Of course, Young Master."

I blinked again. This was not how things usually went. I raised my sword to the wall, preparing to make another cut—

"Don't be a barbarian," Zeng Wu said. "Go out the front door."

". . . Right." I rested my sword against my shoulder, withdrawing a step and deliberately keeping Xiao Qin in the corner of my vision, ready for more poison needles or hurled gunpowder. It never came.

Xiao Min went out the front door. I followed. Zeng Wu and Xiao Qin were right behind me.

I gazed around as the city unfolded around me. I'd been outside before, but generally only for the briefest moments. You know, after being hurled straight through a wall.

The city might not have been tremendous by human standards, but there were dozens of people outdoors, maybe hundreds. Countless buildings in a mixture of architectural styles, but leaning Tyrenian, like the names of the people I'd been fighting with. This particular part of Dania was a melting pot, with Tyrenians, Mythralians, and Artinians all settling close together and mingling. It was why you'd see a broad variety of different names, art styles, fighting styles, and languages. Apparently Valian was the default mercantile language—either that or the sword saint had simply made the memory crystal work that way to allow me to use it more easily.

I was a little nervous about fighting near so many civilians, but they barely seemed to give any of us a glance as I tried to find an open spot. Either the circlet hadn't given them a sense of self-preservation or Skyseekers fighting was a common enough event that they couldn't be bothered to seek shelter.

I found an open spot, a flat area of grass where no one was close by. "Here?" I asked.

"Don't be absurd," Xiao Min said. "Sect disciples aren't going to lower themselves to dueling in a park."

He led the way out of the city, up a serpentine mountain path. We walked a solid mile before I saw it in the distance — a structure atop the mountainside. I took in the triangular-shaped thatched rooftop of the largest building first, then as we approached, I saw smaller surrounding structures and the pristine white walls around it. The walls must have been fifty feet tall, slightly slanted inward toward the top, perhaps as some sort of defensive measure. There were guard towers on the corners of the walls, but those were less impressive than the massive gatehouse at the center. The gate itself was a colossal thing, as tall as the walls, seemingly made entirely of gold. Opulent, impractical, but certainly a statement. I could see faintly gleaming runes all along the gate as we got closer.

As we approached the gate, Zeng Wu took the lead, reaching into his robes to retrieve some sort of badge. He flashed it near the gates and they opened without a word from the guards standing beside it.

"Be grateful," Zeng Wu said. "Not many outsiders are ever allowed within sect walls. It is a great honor, more than you deserve. And it will be your last."

"Will it, now?" I said quietly, less confrontational than I might have been, more thoughtful.

I'd had some time to think on the trail. Only minutes — we moved at a Torch-level pace — and those minutes were ones where I couldn't afford to be too distracted, in case Xiao Qin decided to shove me off the cliff. He seemed like the type.

Or he had *before*, at least.

Had I changed something with my performance . . . or had the Smiling Sword Saint changed the crystal?

I wouldn't find out right away, not without ending the scenario early. And I certainly wasn't going to do that the first time I'd made it this far.

They led me through the gates, then to a raised wooden platform. It stood at about shoulder height, with a small stairway leading up the side, ringed by wooden walls that would be waist height from the stairs.

Xiao Min hopped from the side of the platform onto the top.

Oh. Is that the dueling arena?

I stepped up the stairs. I didn't have any jumping techniques . . . or movement techniques in general. Maybe I needed to work on that.

Perhaps sensing my skepticism at the simple wooden arena, Xiao Min explained. "This is a simple training arena for new outer sect disciples and children. You are not a member of the sect and have not earned the right to be in one of our greater arenas."

"And if I beat you, does that make me eligible for a better arena to fight the others?" I asked.

Xiao Min took the question more seriously. "I am not one of those given a token for the entrance exams. If that is your intent, however . . ." He looked down at Zeng Wu, who was standing aside.

"Were it not for your rudeness, I would have permitted you a chance to prove yourself capable in a spar. If you had succeeded, I would have offered you my token. You are capable for your level, but your insult cannot stand. You interrupted my meal and had the audacity to touch my person. Should you defeat Xiao Min, you will face me next, in this arena. I will waste no further time on you."

I nodded. "I need to beat you both. Got it." I turned to Xiao Min. "Should we get this started?"

"By your leave, Young Master?" Xiao Min asked.

"Begin."

Xiao Min drew his sword and *hurled* it at me in a single motion.

I was surprised enough that I did what my instincts told me, which was to smash the sword straight out of the air with my own. Or, I tried to, at least.

The sword flashed in the air, then *multiplied.*

Xiao Min moved three fingers upward, splayed apart.

My swing caught only air as the three swords shot upward, then spread out.

Then as Xiao Min swept his hand downward in a raking motion, the three swords descending from different angles, all toward me.

He probably expected that I'd be overwhelmed by the assault, thrown off by the novelty of the approach, or something.

But I'd been sparring with Thane for months, and training with the Smiling Sword Saint for far longer.

This might have been his special technique — the thing that made him Xiao Min of the Threefold Blade — but I'd been forged by the cuts of a thousandfold strike.

I braced myself, lowering my stance, and inhaled as I focused my sword essence.

Sword Sharpening Shroud.

My sword flared with power as the three blades descended. Xiao Min adjusted as I swung toward the first incoming blade, but it didn't matter — I stepped forward, leaning into the swing, and smashed the first sword out of the air.

Even as the first sword was shredded by my swing and the remains embedded in the wooden stage, I was spinning toward the second, grabbing the hilt with my off hand and wresting control, then using it to spin and deflect the third sword into the distance. It hit an invisible barrier around the arena, bounced, and landed on the ground.

Then I threw the stolen sword straight at Xiao Min's chest.

He hissed, throwing a punch that glowed with essence, and blew his own sword out of the air, sending it streaking into one of the wooden walls around the arena.

Then, with a snap of his fingers, three more swords appeared in the air above him.

I didn't give him a chance to move them. I charged, closing the ten-foot gap before his swords could descend, and swinging my sword at his throat.

He raised an essence-wrapped arm in panic to guard, but the swing had been a feint. My other hand came up as soon as he blocked his own vision with his movement, and my off hand reached out.

Star Shattering Sword.

I didn't need my sight active to hit his Heart Point with my hand — instinct and practice guided me as my fist slammed into the center of his chest. I felt my essence flow into his body and the cracks form in his heart.

He slumped to the ground, breathing heavily and clutching at his injured chest. My sword settled on his shoulder, next to his neck.

"Next?" I asked, smirking as I turned around.

I'd moved just quickly enough for the needles to hit my chest rather than my back.

"Son of a—"

My knees wobbled. I grabbed the needles, wrenching them out of my chest, but my vision was already blurring.

"I believe it's your turn, Young Master," I heard Xiao Qin say.

"Why, yes." Zeng Wu landed just in front of me. "I think I'll get started right away."

His sword came up. I was unconscious before it came back down.

I tore the Dreamer's Circlet off my head, growling and resisting the urge to hurl it across the arena. "They cheated."

"No," the Smiling Sword Saint said. "You let your guard down. Again."

I hissed. "Are Skyseekers really that dishonorable?"

"No," she said simply. "A few might be, but I never saw someone behave in precisely that fashion. That particular betrayal was, most likely, the work of your own mind."

My eyes narrowed. "Then . . . you didn't adjust the scenario while I was gone?"

"No." The Smiling Sword Saint turned her head to the side just slightly, the mildest movement of negation. "Though I certainly considered it. But you slept last night. You dreamed. And with that, your perspective changed."

"Then . . . I'll never win the scenario as it originally existed?" I felt a strange pang of disappointment at that.

"Edge, the scenario changed every time you entered it. It might have been subtle, but the crystal is always shaped by your expectations. Your only chance to succeed at the original scenario was your first attempt."

I set the circlet down. ". . . Could you revert it?"

"Perhaps. I don't have a technique expressly for that purpose, but I might be able to make one. But I don't think that would be what helps you most."

I frowned. "Why?"

"Because if I reverted the challenge, you'd defeat them easily at this point."

I went silent for a moment. ". . . What?"

"The scenario was not built for the way that you are confronting it. The first versions of those opponents would have been . . . simple. Your first defeat meant that you perceived them as stronger than yourself, which changed the subsequent attempt, and so on. As you've practiced, considered more possibilities, your opponents have adapted further. The challenge is getting more sophisticated. It is not a mark against you that the challenge has changed. It is the only thing that has kept you from overwhelming your opponents. They are adapting, gaining new abilities based on your expectations of what they *might* be able to do."

I grimaced. "I still want to fight the original set at some point."

"Fine. I'll consider that as a reward if you can handle succeeding at this test."

I slowly nodded. I took a drink, took a bathroom break, then sat back down. "Okay. They'll learn and adapt. They'll backstab me, because I expect them to. That means I need to be better. Be faster. Have counters to whatever they do."

"If that's the way you want to approach it," the Smiling Sword Saint said.

"Is there a different way?" I asked.

"Of course," she said enigmatically. "There were different ways from the start. But don't stop now." She gestured at the circlet. "You've just gotten to the point where these fights are getting entertaining."

"Well—" I took a breath. "Far be it from me to deprive you of your entertainment."

Absently, I realized that Thane wasn't around. Perhaps he didn't find the scenarios quite as amusing as the Smiling Sword Saint did.

Or maybe there was something else he'd seen in my last encounter—

Something that gave him some motivation of his own.

I'd find out later, but . . . for the moment, I had work to do.

"Once again, I draw steel against a world long gone."

And thus, I began again.

CHAPTER XVI

STUDY

Days passed as I continued to practice. The Smiling Sword Saint vanished for a time, going off to investigate the road to the sepulcher and the sepulcher itself. I suspected she was doing more than just "investigating," but I was strictly forbidden from following her.

On that rare occasion, I actually listened. Not just because it gave me unrestricted access to the circlet.

Mostly that, though.

"Once again, I draw steel against a world long gone."

After a quick run through familiar introductory steps, I found myself at the entrance of the Soaring Sword Sect. This time, a few minor changes put me in the arena up against Xiao Qin, rather than the others.

Given his penchant for stealth and tricks, I assumed he'd have a much harder time in a straight fight.

When I charged across the arena, deflecting his first brace of thrown needles with a quick flick of my sword and brought it down for an immediate follow-up attack, I realized I'd missed something critical.

Not just that swing. I mean, I missed that, too — largely because he'd blurred and shot across the arena, already readying another handful of needles.

Xiao Qin hadn't just been sneaking up on me through pure stealth before—

He had a movement technique.

I moved to block immediately when he threw his second set of needles, but these moved faster somehow. One of them slipped through my defense, piercing through my sleeve and arm.

I swatted at it like an insect, knocking the needle out of my arm, but the damage was done. My right arm was already going numb.

I tightened my jaw and flipped my sword to my other hand, charging again—

But he was gone, jumping backward in another blur of movement and making another throw.

I swung down on instinct when I saw him throwing something, but checked myself at the last second when I realized what he'd hurled — one of the canisters from his belt. I adjusted midswing, using the flat of my sword to smash it toward him rather than cutting through it.

It's wrapped in flash paper, I realized as the canister arced toward him. *If I'd cut it, it would have ignited the gunpowder.*

I hoped it might explode anyway on the way to him, but I had no such luck. Xiao Qin just caught the canister out of the air with a smirk.

I took a deep breath, trying to fight off the spreading numbness in my right side. I didn't have much luck. I didn't have any antipoison techniques or body-enhancement techniques that might be usable to counter such an ability.

Another problem to solve.

For now, though . . . let's see how this works.

I hurled my sword at him, hoping to provoke another instance of the movement technique.

Instead, he simply stepped out of the way, shaking his head, then tossed his cylinder into the air.

I made the mistake of following it with my gaze—

And then he was in front of me, drawing his own swords from his belt.

This, at least, I had a counter for.

My arms crossed, forming two Sword Hand techniques and parrying both of his initial draws, then I pushed him back with enough force that he stumbled. Now that we were engaged in melee, I had a brief window where I was in my own area of strength. I pushed forward, slashing down with both blades—

And then he was gone, blurring to my side and jabbing at my ribs.

Rejoinder.

A flash of sword essence shined outward as his blade connected. His strike cut through the feeble defense my hasty Rejoinder provided, but the counter-strike portion of the attack worked, drawing blood from his hand.

He winced, and I took that window of opportunity, whirling toward him. He blocked, but that was expected.

Shattering Sword.

Flashing blades manifested in the air as our swords connected, lashing into his arm. He dropped one blade, then kicked off from the ground.

In that moment, I saw it—

There.

The activation of his movement technique.

It was some kind of burst of motion centered around his legs, carrying him straight in whatever direction he was already moving, but with ridiculous speed.

Motion or air essence, maybe? I wonder if I could—

He dropped his sword as he reached the edge of the ring, flicking his hand at me.

A knife flew from his sleeve. Distracted, I hit it without realizing that the blade was made of glass.

The knife exploded into a gaseous cloud—

I coughed once, then my vision went white.

⊰⊱

I woke up, pulling out a notebook, and began to write down what I'd learned.

Movement Technique Notes: Soaring Stride.

Minutes later, I was slipping the circlet back on for my next run.

Days after that, I moved on to my next opponent and my next area of study.

"Once again, I draw steel against a world long gone."

⊰⊱

I stepped into the arena against Zeng Wu himself.

And, for what must have been the thirtieth time that day, I dodged his draw strike, swung my sword across his chest — and heard it *clang* as it deflected harmlessly off his chest.

I'd cut through the silk robes, so it wasn't a protective enchantment on the cloth that was stopping me. Nor was it simply the difference in our levels — he was at least Hearth-level, but that wasn't enough of a difference to stop a sword swing outright.

He wasn't wearing armor under his robes, either. It had taken a few very strange fights to figure that out. Don't ask.

There might have been some specific defensive essence options that could have given someone a perpetually enhanced body strong enough to defend against a casual sword swing at Hearth-level. Maybe if he'd been a disciple of the Solid Steel Sword Saint, that would have been the answer. But I could cut him — I'd done it a few times. Just not when he was paying attention.

It wasn't a reactive defense like my Rejoinder, nor something as rudimentary as my manifestations of deflection essence.

No, it took many repetitions, but I'd found a different answer.

Zeng Wu had something I'd coveted since the first days of my essence training — a body-enhancement technique.

Anyone could throw a little more essence into their body for a rudimentary short-term power boost. That's usually called an augment, and I'd tried using them a few times, simply burning sword essence to increase my strength in the same way that secondary essence did, but in a burst.

I was, in fact, using one at the very moment I'd hit him. For that moment, I was little stronger, a little faster, a little more durable than usual.

It changed precisely nothing. Maybe the pitch of the *clang* was a little higher? Nah, probably not even that.

Augments, as a general rule, don't get you very far. Not unless you're really good at them, at least.

I wasn't.

So, as I dodged backward and barely avoided his counterstrike — which, somehow, cut me in spite of not hitting me — I was working on figuring out something better.

Body-enhancement techniques were just as varied as attacks and utility techniques. They weren't just going to make someone get universally better at everything — they'd have highly specialized advantages.

And his, it seemed, did something *weird.*

As my chest bled from the wound that shouldn't have happened, I felt the lingering traces of sword essence on it, as well as something else I couldn't recognize. I lunged back in, swinging my off hand and forming a Sword Hand, but he simply slapped it out of the way with an open palm—

Or rather, something *around* his palm. I felt it in the brief contact we'd made — more sword essence.

But I couldn't identify the aspect, not in such brief contact. Nor could I tell exactly how it was working, just that he was slapping my swings out of the way with ease.

It didn't seem to matter where I hit him—

Or did it?

Maybe I'd been approaching this the wrong way, focusing entirely on direct attacks.

Star Shattering Sight.

I dodged another swing from him, and this time, I saw it — a brief flicker of a blade that followed behind his swing and pushed beyond it. Not like my Shattering Sword, not exactly.

No, the reason I hadn't been able to see the strikes before was because they weren't there. Not in the physical world, anyway.

It was clear the instant I saw him move with my Viewing Point technique active—

There was a second version of him overlapping with the first. A version of him wearing heavy lamellar armor, a broad-rimmed helmet, and wielding a much longer sword.

I wasn't just fighting Zeng Wu. I was fighting a manifestation of his spirit self, too.

Somehow, he'd built a technique that allowed both of them to fight in unison, striking and defending with both layers of himself at the same time.

That's . . . actually really cool.

Apparently, even jerks could come up with some pretty neat techniques from time to time. I was impressed.

But if he could do that with his spirit . . .

What would I be able to do when I had full access to mine?

No time to get started like the present. Let's see . . .

Sword Spirit Technique, Attempt No. 1.

I raised my sword above my head, concentrating on my seal and the breach essence flowing through my hand. I tried to picture the massive blade that was my true weapon overlapping with the much smaller weapon I held—

Which was a great idea, at least until the moment he stabbed me through the chest.

As it turns out, raising your sword above your head when fighting a very fast opponent is a good way to get dead.

I collapsed, managing one parting swing at him — which missed as he drew backward — before I hit the ground.

Unmitigated . . . success. I cracked a grin as my vision went black.

⊹⊹ ⊹⊹

I'd finally started making serious progress on winning the circlet's challenge, but that wasn't the only thing I was thinking about during those long days. Once I felt satisfied that I'd crack the scenario soon, I retired early one evening to head back to the sword school and begin to work on another project that I had procrastinated on for long enough.

I reclined in my shelter, withdrew the mysterious journal from Ana's shrine as well as a blank one of my own, and began to work.

It didn't take me particularly long to decipher the script. As I'd previously noted, it wasn't encoded in a complex fashion — every one of the unusual letters mapped directly to a Valian one. The author who had written it had simply used an alternate lettering system, one that was so uniform in its style that I suspected it was a personal cipher of some kind.

I wasn't any sort of expert at encoding documents, but I understood that something like a personal letter-replacement system wasn't designed to keep someone who had their hands on the document for a long time from reading it. My suspicion was that it was designed to keep people from casually deciphering it at a glance, perhaps indicating that the writer was working on it in the presence of others, or perhaps that they were concerned about occasional divination magic being used to observe their work.

A more complex code would have been more secure, but a simple letter-replacement system — once memorized — could be written and read just as quickly as "normal" writing in the same language, at least in theory. I didn't know what the learning curve for that looked like, or if the writer of the document had mastered that level of proficiency with this lettering system, but I suspected that the relative ease to read and write in this script was another motivator.

Enough contemplating. Time to read.

Spaces and punctuation didn't seem to differ from the Valian norm, which made things easier. I searched for one-letter words first, since they'd be the words "a" and "I." I couldn't actually determine which was which without context, but "I" was more likely to be the start of a sentence, so I weighted the likelihood of one specific symbol over another for that reason. From there, I skipped two-letter words briefly to try to find "the," given how much it would help to be able to translate letters *T* and *E*. That probably wasn't the most efficient approach I could have taken, but again, not an expert.

That was the most difficult part of the process — trial and error on the first few letters. When I had a candidate for "the," I'd quickly test whether or not the symbol that would make *T* would make sense in other words. Notably, I needed to find cases where the *T* candidate would appear at the start of words, indicating that the word would be "to."

When I was reasonably confident in "the," I also had effectively found "to" at the same time, giving me the letter *O* . . . and you get the idea. I worked through the whole alphabet that way, finding a bit of relief that the author had only used a slight emphasis to denote capital variants on letters, rather than whole different symbols.

Hours later, I had enough to begin to transcribe something.

There are mistakes that are so grand as to define the legends of heroes and empires. I write this in hope that my own story will not be erased, for the legacy of my failure may yet be great enough to eclipse them all.

I felt absolutely delighted at successfully translating the opening. Truly, an auspicious start! I kept working.

This is the story of how I thought to reforge the works of the makers with my own hands. It was not merely the hubris of a hero or the folly of a villain. It was the kind of arrogance that could only belong to a god.

I felt a shiver run down my spine. A work of the makers, reforged?

. . . What were the odds that this was talking about my sword?

Once upon a time, a boy found a sword.

Too simple a start, perhaps? Okay — let's start again.

Once, in the midst of an all-consuming war, a sword of annihilating power fell into the hands of a vicious tyrant. As one might expect, a group of would-be heroes arose to challenge that tyrant, and a particularly skillful and hopelessly attractive young man happened upon a sword that the makers themselves had failed to wield.

And, with the arrogance of youth, he drew that sword and made it his own. He played a role in vanquishing that tyrant, unknowingly assisting in creating the next. For a time, he was seen as a hero, traveling with his friends — his family — and setting things right in the world. Or, at very least, making a good effort at it.

When his master died, he vowed revenge against the man responsible. In retrospect, this was probably his first mythologically significant mistake, if we ignore "picking up the thrice-cursed sword in the first place."

His master's killer became his rival. They raced through the world, through the skies, through the stars, and through worlds beyond for power beyond imagination. They were reborn as gods, and the boy — now a grown man — was joined by his companions and rival in godhood.

I set the journal down briefly. There was no doubt now. This was the story of the Tae'os Pantheon — the seven gods of Mythralis who had risen alongside the Tyrant of Conquered Suns.

The man writing this journal was one of the two apprentices of the Smiling Sword Saint. One of the two who had spent their lives in pursuit of avenging their master.

And, if my suspicions were correct, the two people who were the most likely candidates to be my biological parents.

I took a deep, steadying breath, and resumed my translation.

By now, if you haven't deciphered my identity, I'll be abundantly clear. I've never been much for Tarren's riddles. I am — or at least was — the man once known as Aendaryn, the Sword Saint's Scion, and later, of course, the Seven-Branched Sword Deity. Or, back at home, simply the God of Swords.

I was the leader of a group of seven newborn gods and I had the power of a worldmaker's sword in my hand. I felt invincible, unstoppable.

And yet.

He was better. Always better.

Across hundreds of battles, skirmishes, sparring matches, and true conflicts — he was always my superior. Not just a little, either. Enough that even with the sword, even with six other gods at my side, the best we were able to hope for was a stalemate. And that was without the intervention of his children, who grew stronger by the day. Aayara and Jacinth might not have been worshipped as gods, but in truth, I fear they could have matched most of us individually. When I'd crossed swords with Jacinth before my own ascension, I'd judged him to be a prodigy at my own level, but with a different specialization. As my great enemy's strength grew, so too did his army — his vae'kes multiplying to the point where, if desperate action was not taken, I judged that he would soon be unstoppable.

Kara and I both had our methods of training to try to match him. Some together, some private.

She had long been a member of the Warders — an organization dedicated to maintaining the seals that bound Aetor, the Maker of Monsters. She frequently trained with them in my absence. I remember clearly when she told me she was leaving to attend a Grand Conclave — an international meeting of all the Warder branches. I couldn't have known what would happen when she left.

As a god of another pantheon, and the bearer of a certain sword, I was forbidden from attending. And though I hated to be apart from her, I knew we'd be reunited someday. What was a year, even a decade, in the life span of a god? Better that she take the time to train with her allies and master her abilities, even if that required a time of separation.

I could always sense her from a distance regardless, and send her messages and thoughts with magic. It wasn't the same as being together, but it allowed us to remain close, even if we couldn't touch — right up until we couldn't. Until the day she vanished.

Another deep, steadying breath.

This was . . . not where I'd expected the story to go.

The woman he spoke of was undoubtedly Karasalia, the Impervious Forest Goddess. She was known as a goddess of protection on Mythralis, but not a member of the Tae'os Pantheon for reasons I remained unclear on. Either way, she was, according to most legends, Aendaryn's wife, and the most likely candidate for my mother.

She was a member of some kind of secret order dedicated to the seals of the Maker of Monsters?

What was he talking about?

The moment I sensed her spirit vanish from my senses, I went to the sanctuary of seals, where she had trained. I was ready to throw open the doors, but they'd already been torn off the hinges.

The grounds were devastated. There were bodies everywhere, both of the sealed and their attendants.

Only one man still stood, fresh blood still dripping from his blade.

My rival.

Overcome with fury, I attacked.

When he beat me, he had the audacity to apologize before he left me bleeding in the dark.

I stared at the pages without comprehension.

I'd heard stories of Karasalia's demise before — they were part of the legends I'd heard about Aendaryn's rivalry with the King of Thorns. I'd just kind of . . . assumed it happened later. Much later. Because there was a critical problem if she died at that point . . . assuming I was reading into this journal correctly.

If Karasalia was dead at that point in the story, then who was my mother? Had she given birth during that time period, and I'd been taken away?

That didn't match with what Gramps had told me, but . . . could he be trusted?

Could this story be trusted?

I shook my head. I was jumping to too many conclusions. The story wasn't over yet. Far from it, in fact. I was getting too tired to continue, but I resolved to translate just one more section, then get some rest.

Failure. Another failure. My wife — my love — murdered at the hands of our greatest enemy.

Ria patched me up. She was always the one who shared my enmity the most strongly. I'd loved my master, but Ria loved her in another way, and in a way, her need for vengeance had run deeper — at least until Kara vanished. We were both resolved to find a way to bring an end to things, though we disagreed on the methods.

She wanted to raise an army to counter the vae'kes. I believed that settling things in a more personal way, defeating the master himself, was the proper route. We agreed to take both approaches.

If I was going to defeat my rival, I needed an edge.

I began research I once would have balked at. If I wanted to defeat my rival after he had potentially stolen even a fraction of a maker's strength, I needed a greater fraction of the maker's power myself. And so, I turned to the only thing I had that gave me hope of matching him.

Once upon a time, a boy had found a sword. A sword made to be unused; a weapon so terrible that even makers would flee rather than see it drawn in battle.

The Dominion Breaker.

I took a glance at the sword I'd rested across my knees. I could see the resemblance to the stories of the Dominion Breaker, but it wasn't quite right.

I couldn't wait to find out why.

I eagerly began working on the next page . . . and got complete gibberish as a result.

What? That's not . . .

I frowned at the page, glancing back and forth between my notes and the journal, then sighed in frustration.

You're kidding me.

He changed the code? Now?

It was just getting good!

My stomach growled. My head was aching almost as much as my half-numbed fingertips.

How long have I been working?

Grudgingly, I set my pen down and looked up.

The sun was rising on the horizon.

. . . *Okay, yeah, that's too long.*

I groaned, pulled my cloak over my face, and sighed.

If I was going to beat the circlet's tests later that day, I needed to sleep.

I didn't sleep easily. Not after getting the first taste of that translation . . . and the implications of it.

The journal being in that location, something so close to where I'd been brought as a child. The sword school. The sword itself.

The map I'd found somewhere in Ana's shrine.

These things couldn't be coincidences.

The clustering of two or three of these things on their own was suspicious enough, but the fact that I hadn't been born on this continent — at least, supposedly — and I'd been brought to an area within a boulder's throw of a breadcrumb trail toward the sword I was bound to?

No, this was deliberate. I just didn't know if Gramps had orchestrated it, or someone else.

Perhaps the God of Swords himself.

I wouldn't get answers that day. I wouldn't conclude the circlet's trials to my satisfaction that day, either.

But I kept training, and I kept working on the code.

Day by day, I learned more, both about my own sword and the path of the sword that the Smiling Sword Saint's school had followed.

I wouldn't crack the next section of the code before my duel, but I managed to unravel something more relevant. It had only been a matter of weeks when I set the circlet aside, grinning and laughing, and returned to normal training with Thane.

When the Smiling Sword Saint returned, I told her the news.

"We can move on to the next stage of your memories. I finally won."

INTERLUDE III

THE SMILING SWORD SAINT I

SKILL

The Smiling Sword Saint didn't accept the offered circlet. Instead, she raised an eyebrow. Distantly, she heard trees falling and groaned internally.

At least I've gotten better at making sure the collateral damage isn't right here.

"You expect me to believe you beat Zeng Wu? He's two levels above you, kid."

In truth, she had no idea how long it should take to beat someone two levels up in a duel under weirdly drifting circumstances in a bizarre amalgamation of dreams and memory. If Zeng Wu's capabilities had remained static, it probably should have been sooner, but as she'd watched the fights, Zeng Wu had started pulling out less and less plausible techniques. Ones the real-life Zeng Wu had no business considering, let alone using.

Zeng Wu had never been an expert on creating or utilizing esoteric aspects of sword essence. He'd been talented, yes, and an excellent fighter for his age — but a classic example of their school's style, not the type to run around cobbling together new techniques on a lunch break like some kind of deviant.

But, because Lien was exactly the type of person who *did* make new techniques with roughly the level of effort that one would normally assign to drawing a lewd sketch in the middle of a boring lecture, his dream version of a superior opponent was capable of the same.

The poor boy lacked context so badly that he was overestimating his opponent in a way that took a manageable challenge into an absurd one.

And with that context . . .

The Smiling Sword Saint honestly wasn't sure Lien would ever beat Zeng Wu at all.

"Well, it was a bit of a challenge, but I finally got what I was going for."

Lien looked insufferably smug. It was the kind of thing she imagined got some of the young girls going, but Thane was struggling to keep a straight face in the background, seemingly amused by his would-be rival's attitude. Thane was probably thinking that Lien was displaying a sort of arrogance similar to the stereotypical arrogant young master he saw Zeng Wu as, but this was different.

He wasn't overconfident. He was basking in the glory of a victory he'd already earned.

. . . Supposedly.

The Smiling Sword Saint pushed the circlet back at him. "Show me."

Lien cracked his neck. "Right away, Master."

Her eye twitched.

At least he hasn't started calling me "Shishou" *or something. Small blessings.*

Lien sat cross-legged this time, looking more formal. It would be uncomfortable to sit that way for an extended period, which meant it was his way of saying, "This won't take long."

Implausibly arrogant. He's got something up his sleeve.

"Once again, I draw steel against a world long gone."

She flicked a finger, manifesting a mirrored surface to watch Lien explore the memory. Thane wandered over absently, looking half-bored, like he'd seen this a million times before.

Maybe he had.

She'd been away for a week, after all, dealing with the memories at the shrine. Thane had stayed behind with Lien, continuing to make sure he had physical training in between his bouts against the past. And, of course, staying away from the memories manifested on the road that were strong enough to tear him limb from limb.

Her own erstwhile rival hadn't manifested himself in this reality yet, but other monsters had. Some strong enough to give her pause. If she hadn't managed to advance her own understanding of her abilities to the extent that she had, she might have been hard-pressed against some of those flickers of fancy. As it was, she was exhausted, and watching the boy was a much-needed break.

The scenario advanced to the point where the dish was dropped, and she watched eagerly to see how the boy would finally strike this time—

"Stop." Lien's voice came out before the first punch was thrown.

Zeng Wu turned to the boy, full of disdain, but checking his swing. "And who are you to command me, Junior?"

"It's not a command, exactly," Lien explained. "More like a bit of advice."

"You dare to threaten our lord?" Xiao Min stood up, hand on the hilt of his dao.

"No, no." Lien raised his hands in surrender. "Forgive me, I've made a poor introduction." He bowed his head.

Wait. Is he actually going to follow my original plan? Now?

Are you kidding me?

"Hmph. Bow all you like, it'll just make your head easier to—"

"That's enough, Xiao Min," Zeng Wu said. "I sense sword essence from you, Junior. If you've come to ask for my approval and token, you've approached the subject poorly."

"Oh, it's nothing like that," Lien said, lifting his head back up, a slight quirk at his lips. "I'm not here to ask you for something. I'm here to help you."

"Help me?" Zeng Wu scoffed. "First you dare to insult me by interrupting my discipline of this wretch" — he gestured toward the servant, who was still cowering nearby — "and now you offer me help? You'd best speak *quickly*, Junior."

"It's about your sister," the swordsman said. "I—"

Zeng Wu took a step closer, blurring and reappearing in front of Lien. It was doubtful that Lien could even see the intervening movements, given that he hadn't mastered a movement technique himself.

"You speak of matters that are above your station." Zeng Wu's fingers were at Lien's neck. "Who sent you?"

"No one." Lien spoke, seemingly unconcerned about the sword essence pressed against his throat. "But I've heard things, and I'm very good at getting information. I'd like to make a—"

"Not here. Outside. Come."

Zeng Wu's hand came down, folding his arms in front of him, hands in sleeves. His bodyguards rose from the table as well, following as Zeng Wu left the building.

The servant blinked, glancing from side to side, utterly forgotten.

The Smiling Sword Saint blinked as well.

. . . *What in the world?*

Lien led the way down a street, then turned, the three swordsmen following him. Another street, a left, another, then he knocked on a door three times. "Ox, field mouse, lion's roar."

The door swung open. "In." A huge hand jerked a thumb.

Lien didn't pause; he just made a swift gesture to follow.

Zeng Wu looked concerned for the first time, freezing to glance from side to side, then whispering to Xiao Qin. The bodyguard bowed at the waist, then disappeared down another street.

Xiao Min walked in the door next, followed by Zeng Wu.

A giant of a man smiled through broken teeth at them, slamming the door shut. "You're not the usual clientele, but if you're with the boy . . . make yourself welcome."

Zeng Wu looked deeply uncomfortable, but bowed his head just slightly in acknowledgment, apparently not trusting his words. Understandable, given that he was so out of place, stepping into a smoky room with people who were . . . very much not the type that a young master of a prominent family would typically associate with.

The room ahead was some sort of undercity den, in the Smiling Sword Saint's estimation, or at least the boy's imagination of what one might look like. The smoke was a little thicker than plausible, but the people sitting at half a dozen aged tables with drinks, cards, and dice looked believable enough.

Even she couldn't be sure how much of this was formed from Lien's imagination and how much was the crystal dipping deep into other memories of her past — or the world's own history — to forge a likeness of something she had never truly seen.

Lien found an empty table, pulled up a chair, and then kicked up his feet onto the table's surface. "Sit."

Zeng Wu looked deeply offended, but nevertheless pulled a seat out. Xiao Min stood at his right.

"What is . . . this?" The young master looked from side to side. "If you think you can extort me—"

"Nothing of the kind, Young Master." Lien tapped his fingers on the table. Seemingly instantly, an attendant came by the table, dipping down. Lien whispered in the man's ear. The man bowed three times, low, and then disappeared into a back room. Lien turned back to Zeng Wu. "This clearly isn't your realm, so I'll get straight to it."

"You'd best do that," Xiao Min said. "Or we'll have to skip the pleasantries to—"

Zeng Wu raised a hand. Xiao Min fell silent.

"Please," Zeng Wu said. "Speak."

Lien nodded, looking strangely sympathetic. "Your sister's illness is, as you've long suspected, not a natural one."

What in the spirits' name is he talking about?

Zeng Xiaofan was always pale and cold, but . . .

Zeng Wu's hand gripped the table. "*And?*"

"And I am in a position to offer you a solution," Lien said, hands to the side, open. "For a small price, of course."

"You think to extort the young master?" Xiao Min said. "How dare you?! Master Zeng, we should take this man back with us and break—"

"Xiao Min," Zeng Wu said, "*read the room.*"

Xiao Min looked around, seeming to notice for the first time that cards were no longer in hands, dice no longer rolling. Instead, there was a very large group of very large men surrounding them, none wearing the kind looks in their eyes that Lien did.

". . . Ah," Xiao Min managed. "I see."

"You were saying?" Zeng Wu said.

"A small fee. Something that you will not be comfortable parting with, but that once it escapes you, will likely better your sister's life in the long run, too."

"My position?" Zeng Wu whispered. "House heir? You . . . wish for me to give it up?"

The young master seemed deeply conflicted, struggling.

Lien tilted his head to the side. "Would you, if it would save her?"

Xiao Min glared at Lien but was wise enough not to speak again.

All were silent, every eye on Zeng Wu. No one breathed heavily, in spite of the smoke in the room. Even the Smiling Sword Saint found her breath held in her chest.

". . . I am nothing without her," Zeng Wu concluded, the faintest bits of moisture at the corners of his eyes. "There is nothing I would not give for her safety."

"Young Master—" Xiao Min half shouted.

"Enough!" Zeng Wu hissed. "The choice is made. But beware, house heir or not, if I find out who—"

"It was Zeng Shi, obviously. Real piece of work, that one. And I'm impressed. I didn't ask that one last time. Didn't think you'd go through with it."

"Last time? What are you . . . ?"

"Doesn't matter." Lien tapped on the table again. The server came by, dropping a bag toward the table. Lien caught it in a hand. "I don't want you to give up your position as heir. If you want the cure" — he tossed the bag between his hands — "you're going to need to give someone something."

". . . I don't understand. What else do I have that you could possibly want in exchange for this?"

"You owe a serving boy an apology."

The Smiling Sword Saint buried her head in her hands.

Oh, my student.

She laughed, long and deep, but couldn't allow a smile to cross her lips. The cost was too great.

After all this time, you managed to win, after all.

CHAPTER XVII

SHATTERING SOUL

The Smiling Sword Saint pushed the circlet back toward me, clearly not believing that I'd succeeded.

I showed her my route to victory. By the time I'd taken the circlet back off, she was barely containing her laughter.

"That," she said, "was an amusing approach, but not one that demonstrates your swordsmanship particularly well."

"There are things more important than swordsmanship alone," I said, always enjoying dropping a good dialogue cliché when I could.

"Yes, yes. But I'm your master at swordsmanship — you need to show me your progress with that discipline."

He grinned. "So, you're finally calling yourself my master, are you?"

I think I broke her.

She stared at me for a moment, completely blank, then reached out and silently pushed the circlet back on my head.

"Right, right." I laughed. "Back in I go."

"Wait," she said. "Have you beaten him in swordsmanship before?"

"Oh, sure. Weeks ago. That was the easy part. My last trick was a lot more extensive. Not the most extensive route I've tried, mind you, but—"

She pulled the circlet back off, briefly snagging my hair awkwardly, then pressed a finger against the crystal. It glowed briefly, then she stuck the circlet back on my head.

"This should provide a more adequate challenge, then."

"Uh . . . in what way?"

"Your opponent may have a new trick or two. And, I'd advise against getting overly hurt."

I frowned. "Why?"

"The diminished pain was teaching you some bad habits," she explained, "so I fixed that."

I gulped. "It'll feel like I'm actually dying if I get mortally wounded?"

"Not quite so extreme as that. That kind of repeated trauma can scar someone permanently, or even cause their heart to stop from panic. I wouldn't put anyone through that in training. No, it's still diminished, and it's still a dream — even if I attempted to make it cause full pain, it would be muted by that somewhat. But it will be close enough that you won't want to experience it."

I groaned. "That's going to make some of my strategies a little harder to use."

"I know. That's the point."

I narrowed my eyes. "Fine. Shall we begin?"

"One more thing," she said.

"Hm?" I asked.

"If you fail, this will be your final attempt."

I blinked. "What? You mean . . . you'll kick me out? I won't be your student?"

"Don't be so dramatic. I just mean I'll take the circlet away. If you can't beat him after all this, that form of training is a waste of time. We'll go back to basics."

I tightened my hand. "Fine."

"And, to be clear, no talking them down or completely avoiding the situation," she said. "You started a fight the first time you put on the circlet. It's time for you to finish it. Show me you can solve the problems you create."

"You want to see me solve that fight?" I straightened up.

I cracked my knuckles, pulled the circlet on tighter, and rested my hand on the sword across my lap.

"I hope you're ready. Blink and you might miss it. Once again, I draw steel against a world long gone."

There would be no convenient arenas outside the sect this time, no simple one-versus-one duels.

I'd started this with a messy brawl, and I'd end it just the same.

Zeng Wu pulled back his hand, ready to strike the server, Liao Yun. I knew he was already having a terrible day, working a shift he wasn't supposed to be on. No one deserved the sort of meaningless abuse that he was suffering, but I felt for him, for his sick grandmother at home.

I stepped in between them.

"No."

I didn't grab Zeng Wu's hand this time.

Shattering Soul.

A mixture of several sword aspects, my mystery essence, and breach-aspected essence flowed through my body.

"You don't get to say no to me, stranger!"

Zeng Wu's fist lashed out, bristling with power.

I punched his hand.

Our fists collided in midair, a detonation of essence colliding with essence.

I flew backward, the force of his attack carrying me into a nearby table. I hit it hard, but steadied myself, my hand stinging and knuckles bleeding.

Zeng Wu, on the other hand . . .

Punching wasn't his area of strength.

His variation of his sect's Soaring Palm technique was designed to focus the force into his fist, rather than simply drive me back like the original technique would. He was two levels above me, which gave him a great deal of raw power. I'd felt that power when our hands collided . . .

But it was a mess. Both his punching form and the technique itself.

The Soaring Sword Sect doesn't spend a lot of time teaching how to throw a proper punch. Sure, he had a basic idea of it — he didn't exactly have his thumb tucked into his hand or anything — but their techniques were mostly sword techniques, and the Soaring Palm was designed to be used in a palm strike.

If he'd used the technique as designed, or maybe spent a little more time refining it, given his level, he probably would have been just fine to strike me, even with the new technique active. But he hadn't been training just for this moment. He'd just been angry.

And so, when our fists collided, his own hand wasn't just bloodied — it was shredded, as I'd held a blade on every one of my knuckles. The wounds weren't deep, but the damage was.

My Shattering Soul used breach essence as the core component. While it improved my physical abilities somewhat, like most enhancement techniques due to the inclusion of hardness-aspected sword essence, the main purpose of Shattering Soul was something closely related to my Star Shattering Sword technique. It made my entire body what I'm going to call "ultracorporeal," meaning solid to things that were normally only partially corporeal, like ghosts and other spiritual beings.

Originally, I'd made it as a countermeasure to Zeng Wu's strange technique that manifested a ghostly sword and armor. I had the idea of making myself solid enough that I could disarm him and break his ghost armor, but that was only the starting point. After a few iterations, I found the right combination of essence components to make my body solid to things like star veins, Dianis Points, and the spirits and shades of my enemies.

When I struck someone with the Shattering Soul, the technique would cause a flare of breach essence mixed with my other essence types. If I hit someone just right, that flare of power could damage star veins or Dianis Points, much like my Star Shattering Sword technique did.

And so, when we hit each other in the hand, I was using a lot more than just physical force. His bleeding hand would be easy to mend, but the damage to his Sword Point would hurt a whole lot longer.

He screamed into the air. I shook myself off from the collision with the table, then strode forward, ignoring the murmurs of the tavern crowd. The Shattering Soul was a very potent body-enhancement technique for my level, but it burned through my essence incredibly quickly. I'd need to resolve this fast.

Fortunately, unlike Zeng Wu, I had plenty of experience with fighting without any obvious weapon.

I stepped in as Xiao Qin and Xiao Min began to stand, grabbing them by their shirts, and slammed their heads together. Then I hurled them both backward.

As Zeng Wu screamed and reached for his sword with his good hand, I punched him straight in the jaw.

Smashing Sting.

Zeng Wu flew straight across the room and smashed into the back wall with a *crunch*, sliding down it on impact. I hadn't hit him quite right to send him through it, but that hadn't been my intent. That, I'd found, wasn't the best solution.

Instead, as he groaned and began to push himself up — he was a Signet-level Skyseeker; it'd take more than a punch or two to keep him down — I grabbed him by his neck and lifted him up against the wall.

I wouldn't have used that strategy against a normal person. Too much risk that I'd break their neck. But against him? Well, a Signet-level, sword-reinforced body meant I didn't have to hold back.

My other hand smashed left, then right. Then, having struck him three times, I made sure his eyes were level with mine. "If I ever catch you raising your hand against a civilian again, I'll take it. Understood?"

He nodded fiercely.

I felt the essence behind me just in time to spin and use his body to block Xiao Qin's hurled poison needles. I saw Xiao Qin's eyes go wide as the needles pierced his master's back. Zeng Wu's eyes began blinking wildly — he was fighting off the poison better than I had, given his higher level, but he was still feeling it.

Xiao Min rushed closer, sword drawn, two more hovering behind him.

I tossed Zeng Wu at him. "Take him to a doctor and get those needles treated."

Xiao Min hastily dropped his sword to catch Zeng Wu, shooting me a glower. "This isn't over, stranger. You struck—"

Sundering Stride.

My next new technique sent me halfway across the room in a heartbeat, my hand smashing into his back. I felt the essence in my hand flare, striking his Heart Point.

Xiao Min dropped like a rock, right on top of his master.

Xiao Qin reached for his belt. I pulled a needle out of Zeng Wu's back and hurled it into his chest. His eyes went comically wide as he grabbed it, falling to his knees. Then I stepped over and smashed him across the face.

Then the tavern was silent.

When all three were incapacitated, I exhaled a deep breath, wobbling where I stood, and released the Shattering Soul technique. I'd used it for too long, and my body was going to be sore for a while. That wasn't the biggest problem, either.

Unsteadily, I pushed myself to the bar and ordered a ginger ale, placing the right number of coins on the counter. I'd need it.

My Sundering Stride technique was barely functional, and it left me massively motion sick after using it. If it hadn't been the end of the fight, using the half-formed technique would have been a huge mistake. Even as it was, it was probably a bit of needless showing off, but . . .

It felt good. I knew I had an audience. Both within the room, and beyond.

INTERLUDE IV

THE SMILING SWORD SAINT II

SUBVERSION

The Smiling Sword Saint sat down on a rock, trying not to let her expression shift as she watched the boy lean down next to the bodies of his fallen opponents.

Looting? That's not a bad instinct, I suppose. Doesn't seem like him, but he did defeat them in combat. Taking something as a reward doesn't—

She sighed as she saw him pull bandages out of a bag at his side.

Of course he's treating their wounds. Why was I expecting otherwise?

There was something stranger than that, though, if perhaps more interesting.

The scenario hadn't ended with the fall of Lien's three opponents. And he hadn't pulled the circlet off, either.

He'd met her requirements, technically. Sure, she would have preferred to see some superior swordsmanship, rather than what looked like a barroom brawl. But she'd gotten smashed and had a few bar fights of her own — as long as he could actually survive them, she didn't care if he used his sword or not.

She *did* care about the quality of his techniques.

That movement technique was awful. There are so many aspects that are better, and whole other essence types that are better for movement. The Soaring Sword Sect has several, why isn't he—

Oh, right. I haven't taught him any of the sect techniques. I . . . maybe I should get on that.

"I don't know what you're thinking, exactly, but to confirm, you're a terrible teacher," Thane said cheerfully.

She flicked a finger in the boy's direction. He raised both arms in front of himself and conjured a pair of phantasmal blades to block the burst of essence she'd thrown at him, but it blasted him out of the arena.

"This only proves my poiiiiiiiint—" he said as he was carried off into the distance.

She suppressed an eye roll. The kid was right, she wasn't much of a teacher. But apparently she'd managed to train a couple successful folks in her other life, so . . . maybe there was hope there.

She could fake it until she learned, right?

The Smiling Sword Saint turned her eyes back to the mirrored surface in the air that displayed Lien's progress, finding that he was no longer bandaging his victims. Instead, he was handing a pouch to the serving boy and telling him to take the rest of the day off.

Oh, good, he's giving away my past self's money. And probably getting the kid fired.

She let out a sigh, a gale wind manifesting in the trees around the arena. She heard Thane let out an alarmed noise in the distance as the winds pushed him around.

Maybe not the latter. I suppose even the owner of that shop probably would realize it's better for the kid to be long gone when the wounded young master wakes up. Hopefully the other staff won't be victims of their frustration.

The restaurant staff had been watching the exchange, of course. So, it seemed, were most of the patrons.

Lien finished the bandaging, then picked himself up, still wobbling a little as a result of his horrible motion sickness–making technique, and then stumbled his way over toward the hooded and cloaked figure in the back of the tavern.

Huh. Is he going to pick another fight, this time with the sketchy guy in the shadows?

"Good day, venerable elder," Lien said, bowing his head low. "I'd like to begin your test, please."

. . . What?

The cloaked and hooded figure was silent for the moment. Then he leaned forward just enough for the Smiling Sword Saint to see a dangerous expression crossing his lips.

She tensed in spite of herself. Lien wasn't ready for an attack at that close of range, and he—

The cloaked man bent his head back and barked out a laugh. "What gave me away, young man?"

"Venerable Master, this one has long studied the art of looking mysterious while sitting in the back of a public house or eatery. And while you have truly mastered the ambience necessitated by the role, it's entirely too hot for a hood and cloak, not to mention the wrong region for that type of attire. Simply put, Venerable Master, you're *too* conspicuous. It's almost as if you wanted people to notice you and ask questions. And given that sect trials are today . . . it was a bit of a leap, but a hidden master watching prospective candidates was not out of the question."

The Smiling Sword Saint felt her jaw sliding downward as the hooded figure pulled his hood back, revealing a white-bearded man. He had the classical features of a martial arts master — his long beard trimmed to a point, his eyebrows long enough to serve as knives, and his long hair immaculately accented by a Tyrenian-style hairpiece.

That . . . wait, no. Was someone actually doing that during my sect trials?

She had a vague recollection of someone doing that in the restaurant, but . . . a hidden master?

Did he just imagine that, or . . . is this a detail that I completely missed?

"Oh-ho-ho, a hidden master, is it?" The old man clapped his hands together. "And I suppose a hidden master should be impressed that you've beaten down three men trying to eat?"

"No, Venerable Master, but I imagine a hidden master would be interested to see a nobody defeating a core disciple."

A hint of a smile as the old man reached up and stroked his beard. "Hmm? Is that what just happened? To me, it seemed as if a few foolish children had a play fight. Nothing to worry over, but also nothing to be impressed by."

"Indeed, Venerable Master, it is not worthy of your notice. But I would hope that, perhaps, my recognition of your nature might be enough to warrant taking your test?"

"Hmph. Presumptuous of you, child, but as a fellow who appreciates the Way of the Mysterious Stranger, I will permit it."

The hidden elder pulled a single coin out of his bag.

Not a bronze coin, like the ones that the Outer Sect disciples carried, that would allow someone to stand in line for the Outer Sect trials.

Not a silver one, like the one that Lien had chosen not to take from the garb of the defeated young master, that would allow one to skip that line and give them the prestige necessary for a shot at the Inner Sect.

Not a gold coin, like the one the Smiling Sword Saint had earned herself, by participating in a test given by the young master's uncle after being introduced by them.

No, it was a pitch-black coin with flecks of white, like the night sky dotted with stars.

She had never seen its like before.

What have you gotten into, my student?

The old man flicked his hand, and the coin disappeared into his sleeve.

"The test will be dangerous. Very dangerous indeed. Still interested?" the old man asked.

"Oh, yes." Lien cracked his neck. "When do we begin?"

"Oh-ho-ho. You already have."

He clapped his hands.

And then, with a wave of disorienting movement, Lien was standing in the middle of a different part of town.

The kid steadied himself — barely, since he was still motion sick, probably more so now that he'd been teleported — and took a look around, then frowned, and reached down to find a scroll tucked into his belt.

He carefully broke the seal on the scroll, unfurling it and reading over it with surprising speed. The Smiling Sword Saint only caught the beginning—

In a place where cousins rust,
And peasants go to wash off dust,
A spring of clearest—

"Wishing well," Lien muttered, then took off at a run.

The Smiling Sword Saint gawked.

"That was faster than usual," Thane said, taking a seat on the rock next to her.

She turned and pulled a twig out of his hair. It was unseemly, and if he was a younger her, he needed to look proper. "What do you mean?"

"It's always a riddle at this stage, but it's different every time."

"Ah," she said, putting things together. "He's done this before, then?"

"He's certainly tried." Thane scoffed. "He failed this first step a few times. Couple of the riddles were based on Tyrenian idioms he didn't recognize, like a certain distant mountain."

"And other than that?"

"Even after he started to solve them, he ran out of time early on, since he didn't know the town. Now? After a week of practice?"

Thane waved back at the mirror.

Lien was already at the side of a wishing well, staring at the surface with an inscrutable expression on his face.

It was only a few moments later that his hand darted in, like he was trying to seize a fish before it could react — but what he dragged out of the water was neither fish nor coin, but a black-and-white key.

He took off again at a jog, ignoring the stares of a few of the civilians nearby.

The Smiling Sword Saint frowned. "What just happened?"

"It's a box key for one of the local banks. Figuring that out was one of the easier steps, but he went to the wrong bank the first couple times. Got beaten up by bank enforcers."

". . . Why would bank enforcers beat up someone for bringing the wrong key?"

Thane scoffed. "I think in the scenario Lien imagined, the 'bank enforcers' are other sect disciples playing roles in the test, kind of like those guys who are about to jump him in the alley."

"Wait, who—"

Three cloaked figures ambushed Lien as he ran through a narrow alley, two jumping down behind him from a rooftop and another seamlessly appearing from being camouflaged against a building wall by the color of his hood and cloak.

Lien didn't slow down; he simply charged straight after Camouflage Guy, ducked a lazy punch, then grabbed the man by the cloak and shoved him at the other two ambushers. While they tripped over each other, Lien laughed and kept running.

"That's the first group," Thane said. "The one in the clearing ahead is a lot tougher, so he usually . . ."

Lien grabbed a loose brick from one of the nearby building walls, wrenching it free with surprising ease, and pulled out a piece of paper from behind it to tuck into his belt. Then, as he reached the edge of the alley, he hurled the brick across the street with surprising grace, straight through a window.

"Hey, over there!" came a voice.

Lien waited one second, then another, then sprinted out of the alley and to the right. Two sect disciples charged straight past him, going the opposite way, toward the shop.

"It can't be that easy," the Smiling Sword Saint mumbled.

"The note Lien picked up says which shop to target. Apparently they're an important asset to the sect, and thus, the disciples are pledged to their protection. Those sect kids are going to be bowing and scraping to apologize for the brick. They'll clean it up, fix the damage. Lien made sure of that on one of his runs."

The Smiling Sword Saint shook her head. "Waste of time."

"He doesn't like the idea of someone getting hurt because of him, especially commoners. But the shop owners are rich retired Skyseekers, and it gets cleaned up, so I guess this distraction gets a pass," Thane explained.

The Smiling Sword Saint shook her head.

He's a good kid, but he's going to waste his talent if he keeps worrying about every little thing.

Still, there was something heartwarming about seeing him rounding another corner, two more disciples yelling for him to stop, as he laughed gleefully and hopped over a waist-high fence that seemed to stymie the disciples that followed him.

Circlet simulation needs some work if those are slowing people down, she considered. *They could just hop over like he did.*

Lien finally slowed down as he approached a bank, breathing heavily, and wiped his forehead with the back of his hand before stepping inside.

"Good day, young man," an obvious sect disciple wearing a business suit in the sect's colors greeted him. "How may we assist you today?"

"Key . . . to . . . box," he groaned, out of breath, lifting the key.

"Of course, we're happy to help with that. Right this way."

Lien staggered after the disciple. Another disciple came by and offered Lien a glass of water, which he sniffed at — presumably checking for poison — and then downed in a single extended gulp.

"Th . . . thanks." He handed the glass back to the stunned disciple. "Needed that."

Then he kept following the first disciple to the vault room.

"Do you remember your access number?" the disciple said.

"It's one-eight-four-four-seven-three," he said.

The Smiling Sword Saint blinked.

"It's on another paper he finds inside his shoe; it's been there since the start of the test," Thane explained. "There was an obscure clue related to it in the paper behind the loose brick."

"*Why* is the test like this?" the Smiling Sword Saint asked out loud, but rhetorically.

Thane answered regardless. "At first, I thought it was because he expected it to be. But then, after my own third attempt, I realized that the old man is there and runs the test this way, even if Lien isn't involved."

". . . Wait, what?" The Smiling Sword Saint turned to her younger counterpart. "You did this, too?"

"Of course I did. You've been gone for a week, and Lien has to sleep sometimes."

"How hard was it?"

Thane smirked. "Why? You thinking of giving it a try?"

The Smiling Sword Saint folded her arms. "Don't be ridiculous. A test at this level is beneath a Skyseeker of my power."

"It's fine, I won't tell him. But you have to solve the riddles on your own."

". . . As if I'd need help from one of you."

"And handle the fights with our strength from back then," Thane added.

"Are you challenging me, Junior?" the Smiling Sword Saint asked, a hint of an edge to her tone.

"Nah." Thane shrugged. "But after seeing this, I doubt you'll be able to resist the urge to do better than he does. I should know."

"And how did that go?"

". . . I haven't had as much practice as he has yet. He had a several-day head start."

The Smiling Sword Saint scoffed. "Excuses." She turned back to the viewing mirror, finding Lien digging through various items in the bank box before pulling out a note, what looked like a useless pebble, and . . . maybe a chew toy for some kind of animal.

"This is going to take a while, isn't it?" the Smiling Sword Saint asked.

Thane shrugged. "That depends on how long he lasts against the three-headed dog this time."

Several hours later, an exhausted and bleeding Lien staggered up a road, barely managing to move with the freshly bandaged tooth marks on his legs.

The old man was standing just in front of the sect gates, having abandoned his hood and cloak in favor of classical sect-elder robes. He watched with an inscrutable expression as Lien approached.

Lien came within a sword's length of the old man, then fumbled around inside his own robes, looking momentarily confused, before finally locating something. He pulled out a silver chain with a large black-and-white key on the end, setting it down, then fished through his bag and pulled out a black-lacquered wooden box with a white lock.

After that, he retrieved the seemingly ordinary pebble, inserted it into a hole in the back of the black-and-white key, then pushed the key into the box's lock.

Finally, he lifted the box-and-key combination, then offered it to the old man. "I . . . believe this belongs to you."

"Open it yourself," he said.

Lien nodded, turning the key in the lock. There was one click, then another. Lien looked vaguely alarmed, hurling the box just before several needles exploded out of tiny holes in the side.

An aura flashed across his skin, deflection-aspected sword essence protecting him from the few needles that came close by. The box landed on the path, spilling open, and revealing . . .

A seemingly empty box.

Lien groaned, watching the box from a distance, then approached and prodded it with a Sword Hand technique. After a moment, he bent down cautiously, then lifted the box with a glove of deflection-aspected essence formed around his hand. He poked around inside, eventually finding a latch, unveiling a false bottom, and pulled his head back to avoid the gas trap that triggered as soon as he opened it.

After shaking the box out, he found a piece of paper at the bottom, inside the hidden portion.

He tossed the deadly box aside, lifted the tiny piece of paper, and unfolded it.

This paper is poisoned. If you can reach me before it takes effect, the coin is yours.

Lien raised the paper with a laugh, still holding it in fingers shielded by deflection-aspected essence, and walked over to the elder, offering the paper. "The last bit of poison was a bit excessive, don't you think?"

"Perhaps," the elder said, "but I would like to make sure that my personal disciples are always ready for another challenge, even when the danger seems to be gone."

The old man reached into the sleeve of his robe. Lien tensed, shifting immediately into a defensive stance.

The old man smiled, pulling out his hand to display the black-and-white coin between his fingers. "You've earned this."

He flicked his wrist at Lien suddenly, but Lien was ready. He caught the hurled coin, tucking it away in a pouch at his side, then handed the old man the poisoned paper.

"So, I am to be your personal disciple, then?"

"Don't be foolish, boy," the old man said. "That coin was just to earn yourself the right to stand in line for the placement test. You'd better hurry," he said. "The sun is setting, and the sect entrance exams are about to begin."

CHAPTER XVIII

SECT SECRETS

After defeating my original opponents, I kept the circlet on a bit longer, indulging myself in other elements of the scenario that it had created. The most important of these was earning a coin to take the sect entrance exams, which was clearly what the Smiling Sword Saint had intended me to do with the circlet in the first place.

I wanted to impress her, so I made sure to do it in a fashion she wouldn't expect.

I'd picked up a great deal of information about the city, the sect entrance exams, and other elements about the sect while the Smiling Sword Saint was away dealing with memories manifesting around the Sepulcher of Sealed Swords. I made use of that knowledge to get myself an unusual coin that would allow me to take a more difficult version of the sect entrance exams and potentially earn a place as a core disciple or personal disciple of one of the elders. There was, however, a critical problem—

The memory crystal ended the moment the first stage of the exams started.

If I wanted to actually take the exams, I'd need the Smiling Sword Saint to make me another crystal that included a different segment of her memories.

"Well," I asked her, "was that a good enough display of my talents for you?"

"You certainly have a talent for finding strange ways to handle simple problems," she told me, but in spite of her deflection, I was pretty sure she was impressed. "I will allow you to train more in this fashion, under one condition."

I frowned. "What sort of condition?"

Perhaps I'd overdone it a bit and she wanted to give me a handicap in the future? Or maybe she wanted me to spend less time with the circlet, to share it with Thane more?

"You must never use that butchery of a movement technique again. After the third time you used it, you were making *me* motion sick just watching it." She sighed. "What in the world inspired you to use deflection-aspected essence as a means of propulsion? Why not just use lunging-aspected sword essence?"

". . . There's a lunging aspect?" I asked.

She put her head in her hands, shaking with laughter, tears, or both.

I decided to take that as a good sign.

For the next couple weeks, I went back to normal training while the Smiling Sword Saint began working on preparing the next memory crystal for my use. She assured me that she could have made something functional immediately, but given my performance in the last test, she wanted to make sure that the sect entrance exam was "something special that reflected my student's personal style."

I wasn't sure if I should be flattered or terrified by that.

As I continued to train, I also periodically went back to the journal I'd found in Ana's shrine, tinkering with decoding the next section. Unfortunately, this one wasn't a simple one-to-one letter translation, nor did it simply take the previous code and add a letter rotation like I'd hoped.

It turns out I didn't have a lot of patience for sitting and attempting decoding for long periods of time, especially when hitting people with swords was a better option. I briefly considered passing off the journal to Gramps — decryption was much closer to his skill set and area of interest — but as a point of pride I decided I needed to do it myself.

When I finally did, it was surprisingly simple: the alternate letter system had been layered on top of a keyword cipher. Once I applied the keyword-based rotation, it translated easily . . . but it was a lot more time-consuming to translate than the first part.

Still, that made it all the more satisfying when I got through it. Or . . . it should have, if not for some of the content.

The first part was much more enjoyable than the ending.

The idea behind it was simple. The original Dominion Breaker was intended to be a physical deterrent to foreign gods with the ambition to strike against the world of Kelrien. Not an altogether absurd notion, given that the Sun Eater was already posturing to begin his assault on Rendalir, or perhaps he'd already begun his conquest. Records of the timeline for that era are shoddy at best, and while I'm sure Tarren could reconstruct the events with that mirror of his, he's always had higher priorities — or kept his knowledge to himself.

So, with the threat of a rampaging worldmaker destroying planets, the Kelrien Pantheon forged the Blade That Cannot Be Wielded. A remarkable sword, the first and only known weapon that was successfully bound to one of the fathomless dominions — and the most dangerous of them. It is no exaggeration that the offensive power of the sword was theoretically limitless. The principal function of the weapon — the one for which it was named — was locked behind four phrases, one held by each of the Kelrien worldmakers, to prevent the sword's power from being abused. One can only speculate as to what the "Dominion Breaker" function was, as it has never been used. Delsen, one of those first four worldmakers, was killed before the weapon saw battle. When the Sun Eater did strike, the sword's full capabilities could not be utilized.

Of course, the four-part password wasn't the only problem. The sword was made as a symbol, not a practical weapon. While a project of great power and complexity, the great efforts and sacrifices to make the weapon were simply to allow the sae dominion to be utilized in the first place. It was, so far as I can tell, effectively what we'd call a dominion-bonded weapon with a single function, rather than a more complex dominion-marked weapon with several features — at least at that point.

When the Sun Eater invaded, a hurried effort was made to actually make the sword useful. This obviously failed. Caerdanel added a component — a crystal of her own creation — to allow the sword to be harnessed to a limited degree, then brought it to battle. She failed, of course. The Sun Eater was injured, but without the full power of the weapon — or, indeed, even the slightest bit of practice actually using a weapon tied to a fathomless dominion — Caerdanel was killed. It is a testament to the power of the weapon that the injury she struck, even without any practice, was enough that the other surviving worldmakers were able to force the Sun Eater's retreat.

I paused, drawing in deep breaths. There was no doubt now. I knew this story, though it hadn't been told in quite the same fashion. The creation of the Dominion Breaker — and the fall of the sword's makers.

But some details were new . . . and important.

What . . . what is a fathomless dominion?

I could guess from context that it was something beyond a deep dominion, but . . . I hadn't heard that specific term before, and something about it sent shivers down my spine. *The sae dominion . . . that's the rethri word that's used as a prefix for the Sae'kes. "That which annihilates," or something along those lines.*

Is there an actual dominion that simply has the function of . . . obliterating everything? And . . .

Is that what I've been using?

I thought back to the way the Smiling Sword Saint had looked at me when she'd seen the sword . . . and, for obvious reasons, her reaction began to make more sense.

Should a power like that even exist?

I kept reading, enraptured by the story.

In the aftermath of the Sun Eater's retreat, the sword was taken by one of the two remaining makers — Kelryssia. She began her own works, her own crystal, with the intent to suppress some of the sword's power and make it more viable to be wielded in a fashion analogous to a normal weapon.

With the knowledge that the Sun Eater might return, or that other threats might emerge that warranted the blade's use, they entrusted the sword to a mortal paladin order that would look over it, holding it until someone worthy was chosen to wield it. It would remain a weapon of last resort.

History has shown us time and time again that a weapon designed as a last resort will always be used.

When I claimed the Dominion Breaker, I chose to honor the makers . . . at least at first. I used it sparingly, only against opponents that could truly be a threat to the planet as a whole. The Sun Eater's children. The Origin Beasts. Threats that even a so-called god might not stand against with their power alone — at least, not with any guarantee of success. So, I'd use the Dominion Breaker to skew the odds.

Each time I came a razor's width from meeting my end, I knew that the sword might not be enough to save me in my next encounter. And, with each mistake made, my regrets reminded me that the sword's power was not meant to be mastered.

And I was never satisfied with anything less than complete victory. Over my foes, or over my blade. There was little difference.

And so, as my great enemy's power surged, I approached my contemporaries with a plan — to mark the sword as our own symbol, to change it significantly enough that it could be used regularly, and to use it to strike down our enemies without fear.

Hubris, like I said. But that was only the beginning.

We chained the sword's power behind seven runes etched into the blade, suppressing it enough that I could learn to harness it with my own. It would not have the full potency that the original sword did, but such power was irrelevant if it could not be harnessed.

With the newly named Sae'kes Taelien in my hand, I would write a legacy of victories over legions of implacable foes — all, save one.

Perhaps if I had stopped there, my story would be written with a different hand, and my legacy a brighter one.

Makers, forgive me. I was a fool.

Even one enemy left unconquered was one too many.

I set the journal down for a time, flexing my hand in the air as I gave it a break from transcription and considering what I'd been reading.

So, the Dominion Breaker is the same weapon as the Sae'kes Taelien, the famous sword of the Tae'os Pantheon. That's not a massive surprise, but it does recontextualize some things. It's also not clear if this is being told chronologically; I don't know if he made the initial changes to the sword before or after Karasalia's disappearance. It probably doesn't matter right now, though. The important part is that I can confirm that the God of Swords made direct and deliberate modifications to the sword — but the resulting weapon still doesn't look like the one here.

I knew I'd told myself that I'd stop after one more section, but . . . this was too important. My fingers and my mind ached from the exertion of translating so much text, but I kept reading.

After Kara vanished, I turned to my greatest weapon — the sword and the lie that I'd adopted as my personal symbol — with increasing desperation.

I had held the sword for years in its present form, mastered the sword's use beyond any previous wielder, and I'd begun to chafe at the bonds that we'd placed upon it. And I'd begun to question the foundation behind those alterations.

I tinkered with removing the runestones, one at a time, and attempting to harness the power of the sword with fewer restrictions. I made some progress with this, but it was too little, too slow — even without the runes, the sword was fundamentally limited by three other measures: two gemstones created by the makers who had briefly held it, and of course, the four-phrase binding that would unlock the last of the sword's power.

Our runestones. Two gems. Four phrases. Seven seals, seven layers between myself and the sword's full power.

In my ambition, I began to remove them all.

I stared at the sword at my side — the obvious gaps in the pommel and hilt, the shape of the blade that had been clearly altered from the stories of the Dominion Breaker.

It seemed that the writer had gone through with his plan . . . at least in part. But while those seals had been removed . . .

I frowned, turning to the next page to read farther, hoping for some answers—

And found a different code.

With a deep sigh, I set the book aside. I was too tired to start translating something entirely new, and I'd need sleep for the following day.

It was only three days before my first duel with Valissar Talis, and it was finally time to go home.

⁂

The journey home was an easy one now. The creatures of the mountain were no longer the threat they had been on my first trip up the mountainside, due to both my strength and my knowledge of their habits. And so, I found myself taking a leisurely pace down the mountain, worrying about something else entirely.

Was I prepared for my first duel?

The answer was obvious. No, I wasn't. I couldn't be.

I couldn't claim I'd spent those months optimally, but I hadn't wasted them, either. I'd improved my core sword skills, practiced my existing techniques extensively, started work on a new Dianis Point, and created multiple new techniques. I'd trained with my new sword, too, and broken the first cipher in a document that I was now confident related to the same weapon. One day, I hoped that would help me harness the sword's secrets.

Purely from an objective standpoint, it had likely been the most productive three-month period of my life. There were ways I could have potentially wrestled more raw power out of that time frame, if I'd risked trying to unlock another layer of self early or sought out a different destiny, but both of those routes would have involved significant risks of long-term consequences. In the long run, I suspected I'd made a reasonable choice for my training, even if it hadn't been strictly perfect.

But the truth remained — I wasn't ready. Three months had never been enough time. It hadn't even been enough time to finish the Advancing Point I'd started.

That didn't mean I felt hopeless. Instead, my mind turned toward options for the duel itself. It wasn't the first time I had considered them, of course, but now that I'd completed my training period, I could revisit what was available to me with better context.

I couldn't hope to defeat Valissar Talis in a duel. What sort of contest could I win? And, perhaps more importantly, what could I win that he would not suspect me capable of winning?

We would both be suggesting dueling options, with a limited number of denials across the three rounds of the contest. I'd likely need to use at least one of my own in this round, unless I suggested something he'd consider an easy victory right away . . . which he might refuse anyway, since offering him what appeared to be an easy win would be suspicious.

I also needed to consider whether or not any suggestions I made, or any suggestions of his, would be something that would tax my strength or injure me in ways that would prevent me from succeeding in future rounds.

So, what could I do with the resources and skills I had available and the training I'd just completed?

I made a list on the way home. It was, like the life of a mortal, depressingly short.

CHAPTER XIX

SERVANTS' SCORN

I found someone waiting for me at the edge of the court's territory. This was nothing new, but the figure wasn't quite who I'd expected.

The beast towered over the nearest trees, watching me approach from the mountain path. Her fur was the white of snow, splotched with dark patches of freshly drawn blood. It did not escape my notice that the dark spots were most pronounced near her jaws and claws.

There was no recognition in my eyes for this particular wolf, but I approached her calmly in spite of the colossal essence I felt emanating from her, and the threat in her watchful eyes. I knew the figure astride her well, after all, and I recalled our last conversation.

The wolf growled as I stepped to the threshold of faerie lands. I raised a hand in greeting, showing politeness rather than supplication. I didn't particularly mind gestures like bowing, as such actions had never wounded my pride. I wouldn't overly lower myself here for a different reason — this was a wolf, and I wasn't prey to wolves. It wouldn't do to give the wrong impression, especially since I knew what was likely to come next.

"Come closer, child. You have a strange scent about you."

The titanic wolf's voice boomed out from the forest. I took a few casual steps forward, feeling the spirits in the air shift as I crossed into the lands of the Court of Rust and Salt, then paused and waited.

The wolf dipped her titanic head down, the size of it large enough to engulf me in a single bite if she chose. Then she sniffed at me, her nose close enough that each breath stirred the wind around me.

"Is that . . . Eiji's smell about you? My, my . . . come closer, so I can better look at you, child."

I couldn't get much closer without risking being bitten in half in an instant, but I stepped closer regardless. I understood the reason.

I'd spent enough time with the great dragon Verthrimax to understand when I was greeting someone ancient and powerful but very nearly blind.

The old wolf's eyes narrowed as I came closer, failing to completely focus. They didn't have any obvious injuries over them like one of Eiji's eyes did, but this wolf was, I suspected, even older. I wondered if my technique of gathering the healing waters for gradual restoration of sight would be helpful to this ancient creature, but I did not know her well enough to approach it. And while

I did not have a wolf's talent for scent, I could smell the stench of death on this ancient creature's jaws.

I would approach her with kindness, but I would not be unprepared.

"My, my. What a strange mark you have there, child. Is that the mark of a princess's promise? Come closer, let me have a taste . . ."

I tilted my head to the side. "I think that's quite close enough, ancient one."

The wolf took a step back, the movement of her single paw sending up a wave of leaves, then lowered her head. There was a rumbling as the forest began to *tremble* for hundreds of feet around us, birds ceasing their song, and even the tinkling of the kodama bells going silent.

Then the wolf's head rose, not to howl, but in a tremendous, booming laugh. The sound of it sent a vibration across the wood, shaking trees and shattering rocks. I felt a chill across my skin.

The wolf turned to regard me again, eyes seeming brighter than before.

"A pity. You do not run away, but neither do you follow." The wolf's head lowered back down to level with me. "Would you lead a pack, then, one day? Or run as a lone wolf might?"

"I think I'm too young to make that sort of choice," I responded, "but for the moment, while I might not run with a pack, I do have a family. And I am headed home."

"Hmph." The titanic wolf let out a snort. "You refused my third request, so you may not ride on my back. But you may walk alongside me for a time."

With that, the colossal wolf turned away. And, without any questions asked, she began to take tremendous strides toward my own home.

I sighed. I'd already been walking for miles.

But it wouldn't do to fall behind. Not when the wolf had made such interesting statements about my role.

We ran for a time before I heard a whistle from astride the beast. The creature slowed, and I slowed along with her.

"Grandmother," a whispered voice came from the top of the wolf's back, "I think you can leave it to me from here."

"You always think I can leave it to you," the titanic wolf drawled into the air, "but fine, fine. It's not like I wanted to see the old man, anyway." She snorted a wave of air that froze the tree in front of her solid. It was, perhaps, good that I hadn't tried to run ahead.

I blinked.

Was this ancient wolf being . . .

What was the word Fade had used? *Tsundere?*

"There, there, Granny. You'll be able to see him later if you want. For the moment, I have private business with the boy."

They let out a light cackle. Once again, the trees around us trembled. "Private business between teenagers? You're right, I want nothing to do with that. Off with you."

The colossal wolf lowered her head all the way to the ground . . .

And a figure closer to my own size slid down the fur just a bit too fast.

"Eep!"

Instinctively, I stepped out in front of the figure and stretched out my arms, catching them before they fell straight onto the rocky ground.

I *almost* managed it gracefully. The corner of a bright red cloak smacked right into my face, obscuring my vision as my hands reached outward, and the sliding figure slammed into my chest, sending us both tumbling to the forest floor.

I'd hit the ground in this forest enough times that it felt a little like coming home. With sword essence reinforcing my body, a collision with the dirt wasn't much of a threat, and fortunately, I hadn't landed on any large rocks.

The real threat was the one above me. Not the wolf, who I could hear already departing the scene with colossal steps.

No, it was the figure who had landed right on top of me, who slowly and deliberately shifted atop me, almost as if they didn't want to leave their position. Gingerly, they shifted the crimson cloak off my face, and my eyes met with Rusty's.

"My hero," they said, tipping their red hat and giving me a wry grin.

I let out a groan. The words didn't sink in just then. In fairness, I'd just finished a run with a massive wolf after a several-mile hike.

My heart was beating fast for other reasons, too.

We froze in that moment for a time, my eyes meeting with ones of warring azure and crimson, then another voice broke our reverie.

"Hi, Li — aaahh!"

Ana appeared in the air next to us. "I'll, uh, come back when you're not busy!"

I opened my mouth to speak, but Ana had already vanished before I managed any words.

For a moment, I thought I saw a satisfied smile on Rusty's face. Then they took a breath and finally pushed themselves up from atop my body. "So," they said, "three days. We've got a lot to discuss."

We approached the small hut where I'd lived my early life together with my grandfather, but Rusty paused near the garden outside, looking strangely hesitant.

I blinked, then understood. This was not a common situation for me, but not one without precedent, either. "I offer you an invitation to my home for this one occasion, along with guest rights and safe passage."

"Kind of ya." Rusty nodded, tipping their cap, then took a tentative step into Gramps's domain.

I approached the door, turning the handle. As usual, it wasn't locked. There wasn't a need for such things there.

"Hm." Gramps stood in the doorway as the door swung open. "Now, this is an occasion. We are not usually in the habit of having guests, and certainly not ones without my prior permission given."

I folded my arms. "Given the circumstances, I didn't think you'd mind. I'm sure you're aware of my pending duel?"

"Yes, yes. I've heard all about it. Come, sit. I'll prepare tea for all three of us."

I stepped in. Rusty was . . . more hesitant. So, I took their hand and guided them inside.

"There's a cloak rack here—" I pointed to a wooden pole with several protrusions out the side. It wasn't pretty, but I'd carved it myself, and I was proud of that. "If you want to hang your riding cloak, or your hat."

"The cloak, sure." Rusty removed their cloak, revealing a different outfit than I'd last seen beneath it. I know that might not sound like anything significant, but I was operating under the assumption that Rusty was using a guise, and it took a greater degree of sophistication than most teenagers could manage to change outfits while in a guise. Now, I hadn't seen Rusty actually make the change, so it's possible that the transformation could have occurred any time in that three-month period, but still, it was a degree of commitment that I hadn't expected.

Or, alternatively, Rusty just looked like this all the time. But I didn't think so.

I had some suspicions on who I was dealing with right from the start, but unveiling a guise wasn't always to my advantage. If Rusty had a particular game they were playing, it was better to figure out that game before casting it away. I was much more likely to earn a reward for cleverness in that way, rather than the ire of a game spoiled early.

So, I helped Rusty put their cloak on the rack and inspected the new outfit briefly for tells. Rusty wore crimson-dyed leather armor this time — greaves, bracers, a breastplate, and a gorget. Their red cap this time was solid leather as well, secured with a strap on the bottom to keep it in place. I could see the bottom of a white gambeson beneath the armor, which would help give some protection to the areas that weren't armored, and offered padding to prevent chafing beneath the armored sections.

In other words, they were dressed for combat. Perhaps leaning into the squire part of the role.

I didn't see any obvious weapons to accompany the armor, but with my sword essence, I could sense something beneath it.

"Like what you see?" Rusty offered me a smile.

"And what I can't see." I gave them a wink. I was, of course, talking about their concealed weaponry. What else would I be talking about?

They blushed. "That's . . . very forward of you."

It was around this time I realized what I'd implied and decided to ignore that knowledge entirely, doubling down. "I find that directness is well served in situations like this. Now, can I help you with anything to be more comfortable while you're a guest here?"

"I, uh, that's okay. I don't think there's anything I specifically need." Rusty was stammering a little, so I pulled out a chair for them, then went to help Gramps with tea.

Gramps leaned in. "Aren't you already entangled with a tree?"

"First off, that tree wanted to take a break. And no, I don't want to talk about it. Second, this isn't like that. They're my second for the duel."

"And is that *all* it is?"

"That's more than enough for me to worry about right now."

"Reasonable," Gramps mused. "I'll look forward to seeing how long things *stay* reasonable."

I sighed, bringing tea back to the table, placing some in front of each of us. Then, I went and retrieved a loaf of fresh bread and some salted butter. Fortunately, Gramps was always baking, even when I wasn't around. Bread and salt were very direct forms of hospitality, but I needed to be confident that my statement of guest rights was properly fulfilled.

I cut the bread and buttered it, then brought it to the table and set it beside the tea. "I offer you this to fulfill my offer of hospitality."

"How very traditional of you. I accept." They seemed to have recovered quickly from being flustered, and now they were inspecting the inside of the cabin with interest. "Where is the rest of it?"

I blinked, thinking. Was . . . there some kind of offering I'd forgotten? I looked to Gramps, but he was still busying himself with food preparation and didn't reply.

"I don't know what you mean," I admitted. "If you want more food, I'm happy to see what we have available?"

"No, not the food. This is fine, I'm not particularly hungry. I mean your home."

I blinked. "Oh. I suppose I could show you my room and the tool shed?"

I walked them around for a moment. They looked strangely perplexed.

"I don't understand," they said finally.

"You don't understand . . . what, exactly?"

"You've . . . lived here?"

"Sure." I nodded. "For most of my life."

". . . Oh." For a moment, a range of emotions flashed across their face, but I couldn't read exactly what they meant. "It's very nice."

They said it in a way that sounded like, "Your patch of dirt is, of course, a very nice patch of dirt."

And while their glamor didn't overtly crack, that exchange did bring me a hint of greater understanding. The kind of knowledge that might bring embarrassment to a child.

Was my house . . . small?

I'd . . . never really considered that. It was just home. My loved ones had grander places, of course. Anathema had a magically constructed dungeon inside a colossal tree. Verthrimax had his colossal tower.

When I thought about it, even the ruined buildings of the sword school were physically larger than our hut. And the closest thing I'd seen to another hut like it, well . . .

The witch's family had their own hut, but it was some kind of extradimensional space, much larger on the inside. Perhaps that was what had led Rusty to believe my own home would be larger, if they had visited the witch?

For the first time, I think, I looked at my humble home and wondered if, perhaps, I should have been embarrassed to be hosting someone there.

Then I brushed that errant thought off like the dirt they'd made it sound like. "Doesn't really need to be elaborate. We have what we need to live a good life."

And that was true.

But it did make me wonder about why a seemingly humble fae would have the impression our home should be much larger. What had they been expecting, and why?

"Of . . . course," they replied, seemingly lost in thought.

We finished our tea and bread, then got to business.

"So, the duel," I began.

"The duel," Rusty replied. "I can see that you've been training."

I nodded. I wasn't sure what they were seeing, exactly. My essence, perhaps, or freshly scabbed cuts on my face and hands from swordplay. "I've developed some new techniques."

"You can do that?" They blinked. "I didn't think people our age could make techniques."

"Seems to be a talent of mine. I had help, of course."

"Of course," they replied, seeming relieved. Perhaps assuming that the "help" was the primary source of my technique knowledge. "I spoke with Grandmother while you were away, and she was kind enough to offer some tools for you to use for the duel if needed."

Now that was interesting. "Grandmother. That was the name of the grand wolf I ran with earlier?"

Gramps turned to look at us for this part of the conversation.

"It is a mere fragment of her name. For she is as old as the winter snow," Rusty offered. "But more of her name must be earned, and now is not the time for such tasks."

"Of course." I nodded. "I am pleased that Grandmother has offered help, and that you went to get it."

That was about as close as I could get to an expression of gratitude without saying "thank you" to a fae creature in a disguise. They acknowledged it with a nod.

"Three gifts. None need be returned later, though I will likely return them if you do not need them."

Rusty laid out three objects on the table in front of me.

A silvery necklace with a single bright green jewel on it, shaped roughly like the number nine in Velthryn writing.

A simple hand mirror.

And a circular metallic case.

I examined each of them on the table. "May I ask what each of these is used for?"

That was my polite way of asking, "These are enchanted, right?"

"Of course." Rusty nodded. "Three gifts, each with three boons. I will tell you one of each."

Rusty tapped a finger on the necklace. "Water this *tama* three times — not too close together — and it will grow. Wear it during this time, and until it reverts to its original size, it will protect you."

"What is too close together, in this context?"

"Usually you would want to water it once per sun, or once per moon, or once per season, or once per year. The longer the time between waterings, the stronger it will be. Meaning that if you want to use it for this duel . . ."

"I should start today." I nodded. "But it'll be stronger if I wait and use it for the last trial. Fresh water or salt?"

"There is meaning to both. Neither will harm the jewel."

I nodded. "What will it protect me from?"

"I don't know. Grandmother didn't say." They looked unbothered by that revelation.

I wasn't big on blind trust. So, I had three days to figure out what exactly the necklace actually did, but without appearing rude.

In any case, a necklace that protected me was potentially very useful, unless the protection it offered was from something completely worthless . . . and that wasn't likely. Powerful fae often enjoyed playing tricks, but offering worthless gifts wasn't like them. More likely, I'd need to do something to figure out how to make the gift useful, and if I didn't, it would be my own fault for failing to utilize my advantage.

"Do you know anything else about it?" I asked.

"The colors match yours," they said.

I blinked. That was true, for the most part. I did wear a lot of green, and my eyes were often silver. And my sword was as well, of course. "Huh. A good gift, in that regard."

"Yes," Rusty said. "The others are as well."

"I suppose the mirror is also silver." I gestured to it. "Is this the sort of mirror that reflects someone's true nature?"

Rusty smiled. "What fun would that be? No, give something to yourself in the mirror, and they'll give it back to you later."

"Huh." I blinked. "When will they give it back?"

"When you need it," Rusty said, as if it was obvious.

". . . Right." I nodded. "Okay. Useful. And the container?"

"It's a compass."

"What does it do?" I asked.

"It points north," Rusty explained helpfully.

I'd been expecting something a little more . . . wizardy. But it was still potentially useful. I didn't own a compass. "These all sound like they could be helpful."

"'Course they are. Now, let's get to talkin' strategy . . ."

For three days, I hosted Rusty as a guest. We only had one bed of my size in my bedroom, which meant that I slept on the floor.

I got the sense that I could have offered to share my bed, but that would have led to some very different complications that I wasn't ready for. *Possibly* including more duels.

During the first day, I went to the Rust River. There, I watered the *tama* necklace for the first time. I felt someone watching me while I did it, but I wasn't sure who it was. I didn't think Rusty had followed me, but that didn't mean anything.

I suspected that Talisian was watching me from a distance on multiple occasions, but I never saw him. I just sensed a hint of distant sword essence that felt like him, just out of sight.

On the second day before the duel, Darryl arrived to help us prepare. Rusty was my second for the duel, but the fae didn't only have a second — Darryl would be my third. He ended up sleeping on the floor along with me while we strategized, which was nothing strange for us. We'd been sleeping on floors together since we were small children.

I got the sense that Rusty was jealous of that, too.

I could have watered the *tama* again that day, but I decided against it. If I waited longer, I'd have a strong tool for the second or third trial, and I suspected I'd need it more at that point.

Finally, on the last day before the duel, Ana showed up again. She couldn't really help us prepare in any meaningful way without it being a sign of favoritism, but I was happy to have her around.

Being with Ana helped make things feel a hint more normal — and helped remind me of the stakes.

On the final morning, we rose together and made our way to Ana's tree.

It was finally time to discuss our first duel.

CHAPTER XX

SETTLING SCORES

We met in the glade just outside Ana's dungeon entrance, just as we had before. The trees surrounding the grove in a circular pattern gave the area the feeling of an arena, though we had yet to decide upon a challenge.

That would be the second step. The first was, of course, formalities.

Darryl met us at the entrance to the glade, falling into line three steps behind Rusty, who was, in turn, three steps behind me.

Lord Valissar Talis approached from the opposite side of the glade, Lord Oloris following three steps behind him . . .

And behind them, the first strike of the battle, in the form of a person.

Eliree, my once love, twice denied, thrice ignored.

I drew in a sharp breath as I saw her. There was an instant feeling of betrayal at her presence there, standing alongside my opponent. She met my gaze and held it without shame, striding along with him toward the center of the glade, where a table had been conjured for us to meet.

It was only when Rusty's hand settled on my shoulder that I realized that I'd stopped moving. I tensed at the touch, then forcefully exhaled a breath and resumed my movement.

Rationally, I could understand any number of reasons why Eliree might have taken the position that she did. Lord Talis had minimal options on who to approach for a third. Most court locals would be unlikely to agree to aid him, since I was ostensibly defending Anathema, a faerie of the local court. The politics of siding against Ana would not be in his favor.

So, who else would be an option? Other outsiders and guests. How many of those were there?

Aside from Gramps, there were vanishingly few. Auntie Temper might have counted, perhaps, but she was banished — she would not have been able to participate in the contest. Travelers like Eiji, perhaps, who were not quite members of the court . . . but those were few, and still so closely tied to the court from a political standpoint that they would be nonoptions.

I had already chosen a witch. Asking one of the other witches would have been an interesting balance, but they weren't likely to be inclined to agree.

Bringing in a human from outside would have been tantamount to an act of war. Other fae courts were far too distant. Perhaps he could have made the journey if he'd been unoccupied, but Lord Talis had been training in Anathema's dungeon, learning how her sword and essence worked — and thus, leaving would have lost him a significant opportunity.

So, who was left?

I should have seen it. I should have anticipated it.

I had no idea what they'd offered to get her to agree. From the dark expression on her face as we approached the table, they might not have needed to offer anything at all.

After all, *I* hadn't asked her. I hadn't even talked to her since I'd accepted the contest.

In retrospect, that was a pretty significant mistake. Fae didn't operate on the same time scales that humans did, but like me, Eliree wasn't fully fae. That had brought us together, once.

Now, it seemed my inaction had torn us apart.

Lord Brine was already present at the table, standing to Ana's right. To Ana's left was a third figure, one who wasn't familiar to me. They were androgynous, wearing a long robe consisting entirely of pale white feathers. Similar feathers stuck out from above their ears, and I couldn't tell if those were a part of their body or some sort of accessory.

I couldn't tell what type of fae they were at a glance. There was a wide variety of birdlike fae in the world, and several types in our specific region. They had a kindly look, which made me lean toward something like a swanmay, but early impressions of fae were often deceptive.

Ana opened the conversation as the two groups approached, giving me little time to think. "Welcome to my home. I am the first of your three judges, Anathema. To my right is Lord Brine, and to my left, Master Feather."

I raised an eyebrow at the extremely generic title for the third figure, but it wasn't a major issue. Lord Brine was a guise, so it wasn't all that unusual for another judge to be using some kind of guise as well. I didn't know if that guise would be relevant to judging the contest or not.

It was probable I should have been thinking more about that, but I was a little distracted. I missed a good third of the introductions looking at Eliree, who had the grace to look straight back at me, her expression betraying nothing about the reasons for her presence.

Ana continued her explanations. "And finally, we have our thirds for each duelist. Darryl, son of the Willowbark Witch, and Eliree, personal guest of Princess Discardia."

I gave Ana a quizzical look at that last part. I hadn't heard Eliree referred to in that way before. It was true, of course — I'd used one of my boons with the princess to get Eliree an invitation to the court, all those years ago — but I hadn't heard it phrased quite like that.

Ana gave me a look like she'd been offering me some kind of *hint*. I frowned, holding on to that line, but I couldn't immediately unravel it.

"Now, it is time to begin the discussion of our first challenge. Per our previous agreement, the duel will consist of three challenges, each separated by three months. Each duelist will have the right to three refusals of proposed challenges. These refusals are maintained across challenges, and thus, early refusals will still be relevant later. After the basics of a challenge are decided, the judges will discuss the details, which will then be explained to duelists before the challenge begins. Is this understood by all parties?"

A series of agreements.

"Good. Once a challenge has been completed, we will wait a season before the next duel and meet back at this location. At that point, the person who *accepted* the previous challenge will propose the next duel. Is that understood?"

"Excellent." Ana nodded. "Does either party wish to withdraw from the challenge?"

"No," I replied immediately.

"I must decline that offer now, my acceptance was a solemn vow," Lord Talis said. Apparently, he was taking this seriously and had gotten back into verse.

"Very well. Prior to discussing the contests, tradition dictates that the seconds and thirds from each side should be given a chance to speak to the opposing side, attempting to convince them to decline the duel and seek another form of restitution. We will begin by having each duelist speak privately with their opponent's second."

I nodded. I'd known this was coming.

I wasn't worried about talking to Oloris Nysarii.

Eliree would be another question entirely.

***

We stepped formally away from the meeting table, then retreated to opposite, semi-isolated parts of the glade to talk.

Oloris Nysarii had a sympathetic look on his face when we found a place to talk. "For what it's worth," he said, glancing toward Eliree, "this wasn't my idea."

I raised an eyebrow, wondering at his strategy. "I'm not sure thinking it was Lord Talis's idea to recruit my . . . Eliree makes things any better."

"*Your* Eliree? Interesting slip there." Oloris gave me a conspiratorial look. "But to clarify, it wasn't *his* idea, either." He waved a hand dismissively. "But enough of that. We have business to discuss, don't we?"

I pulled my eyes away from Eliree for a moment, looking back to Oloris. He still had a friendly look, but I could see the cunning in his features, too. I couldn't afford distractions . . . and maybe that had been his intent? Exploiting an obvious weakness?

Maybe there was more to it, but I couldn't read him. Perhaps I should have spent more time studying my opponent's ally rather than focusing exclusively on training. "We do have business. I could save you some trouble, though. I have no intention of withdrawing from the contest at this time."

"Of course, of course." He waved a hand dismissively. "For formality's sake, I have to ask, however. Between us, I think Lord Talis is impressed by your dedication to your friend. Were you to withdraw, perhaps we could come to some sort of arrangement that serves all of us. He is soon to be a Talisian, and when he ascends to that mantle, he may be in need of a squire . . . one who would travel with him, of course, and with the sword as well."

I blinked.

Was . . . that an actual solution?

As long as Ana and I were together—

I turned to her, as if to ask, and I saw the sorrow on her face. She wasn't looking at me, and she was hiding it well, but . . . she was nervous. Exhausted. She wore the best of masks, but I'd known her forever. I could recognize them all.

What Oloris proposed may have given me everything I personally wanted, but it did not change the fundamental nature of why I'd challenged Lord Talis in the first place.

Ana's fate, her sword's wielder . . . those were her choices. She'd made it clear that Lord Talis facing her challenges and taking her away was not what she wanted. Traveling with them both would let me stay with her, true, and perhaps even eventually claim the sword . . . but no, the foundational problem remained. Ana's freedom.

But I wasn't so arrogant that I thought I could know Ana's mind completely, and a failure to communicate was probably why my former lover was on the opposite side of the battlefield. With that obvious failure looming in front of me, I made the choice to do better with this one.

"I'd like to ask Anathema her opinion on your suggested course. She is, after all, the focal point of this contest."

"Eminently reasonable. May I accompany you and listen?"

I didn't know his angle there, but I couldn't find a strong justification to refuse. "I have no objection."

"Excellent," Lord Oloris replied, a hint of humor on his face.

I headed to Ana. He walked by my side, rather than behind me in deference. I wasn't honestly sure whether or not that was impolite, since he wasn't the duelist I was up against, but it wasn't relevant enough to comment on.

"Anathema, Lord Oloris Nysarii has a proposition, and I would like your opinion on it."

"Please, go ahead." Ana looked curious but concerned.

I explained the proposal. She listened attentively, then took a breath, looking at Lord Talis, then to me.

"While that proposal is very reasonable, it does *not* resolve my own concerns."

"Understood." I nodded. "In that case, Lord Oloris, I cannot accept your solution."

He'd likely been trying to bait me into *refusing* the proposition. My language, however, was not technically a refusal — it merely was a lack of acceptance. That may sound like a meaningless distinction to you, but in faerie culture, it was like the distance between twilight and dawn. They may look similar at certain moments, but they were moving in opposite directions.

It wasn't likely to have been effective — I'd already been denied when trying a similar trick earlier — but every possible attack was something I needed to be aware of and counter, even if it wasn't likely to work. It was always possible I was missing a hidden layer, after all.

"Very well. Thank you for the consideration and candor." Lord Oloris gave me the kind of smile that acknowledged an opponent had made the right move and bowed slightly. "I believe that ends my role in this round, as it were. Shall we wait here?"

We waited. Rusty and Lord Talis returned a moment later.

"We were unable to reach an agreement," Rusty reported. "Such a shame. A *shame* . . ."

I didn't know what Rusty had suggested, if anything. We hadn't discussed that beforehand. Which, in retrospect, was another mistake.

I took a breath. I knew what was next.

"Duelists, given that your seconds have not been able to sway your opposition, it is now time to speak to your opponent's third."

Eliree and I stepped away from the table in unison, almost like the beginning of a dance.

Then, together, we retreated from the glade.

When we were alone, I folded my arms. "Why?"

It was a simple question. At times, however, there were no simple answers.

"Is that really what you want to discuss right now?" Eliree asked me.

"It's what I want to discuss. But you're correct that it isn't what we should discuss." I sighed, my shoulders slumping. "Do you have a proposal for me?"

"What a choice of words. Perhaps I should have asked *you* that question, once. Before it was . . ." Eliree shook her head. "You should surrender. You can't beat him. You know that."

"Be careful, Elle." My tone was firmer, more aggressive than it probably should have been. "You've just made three declarations that could be proven false."

"Have I really earned such enmity that you would use that against me?" I saw the hurt in her eyes, and it only made my blood burn brighter. Wasn't *she* the one betraying me, then and there?

I took a breath, then another, then a third. And, after a moment, I repeated an earlier question. "*Why?*"

She must have seen something in my expression then. "It's complicated. But I'm not doing it to hurt you."

I nodded slowly. "You're hurting me regardless."

"I know."

Another breath.

"I'm not going to surrender," I told her firmly.

"I know that, too."

I gave my once love a final look. I saw her hurt, and once again, I walked away.

⊹⊹ ⊹⊹

There was no agreement made by Darryl and Lord Talis, as expected. And thus, with that formality behind us, we met once again on our own sides of the table.

"Please, be seated," Ana instructed us.

I sat across from Lord Talis. I didn't leave my sword on the table this time — it wasn't needed. Instead, I simply set it down next to me, on my right side, between myself and Rusty.

That wasn't meant to be symbolic. Perhaps it still was.

Darryl sat down on my left, Eliree across from him, and Lord Oloris across from Rusty.

"With our duelists present, along with their seconds and thirds, we may formally begin the proposal of challenges for this combat by trial. Per our first meeting, the first challenge will be proposed by Lien, the Edge of the Woods."

This, at least, I'd had plenty of time to think about prior to the contest, and I had strategies in mind.

If I proposed a challenge and my opponent refused it, he would have the next proposal, and so on. There were multiple possible approaches to this situation. If I proposed something that was too obviously to my advantage, he'd just refuse it outright, then likely counter with something similar, reducing my own number of refusals.

If I proposed something that seemed too much in *his* favor right away, he might refuse that as well, purely out of suspicion.

If we reached the point where I ran out of refusals in this first stage of the duel, I'd have none left for the second duel, where he would be the first one to propose a contest. If that was the case, he'd basically have an automatic victory, because he could propose something I couldn't compete in, like demonstrating an essence type he had that I didn't.

So, ultimately, my intention was to try to figure out something that he might accept, but where I would have an unforeseen advantage. I'd thought of several cases like that ahead of time, but many of them were logistical impossibilities.

I'd settled on a few options, and I had to hope he'd accept one of them before I ran out of my own refusals.

"I propose a duel of swords to seven points — between our dream selves."

Lord Talis looked briefly taken aback, then furrowed his brow, genuinely appearing to consider the suggestion. He turned to Oloris, who shrugged—

Then to Eliree, who shook her head.

My hands tightened under the table as Lord Talis turned back to me. "A cunning challenge of might and skill, and one where blood is never spilled. Of great wisdom is this idea born, and to reject it, I must mourn. Though compelled to give this thought a try, by advisor's wisdom I must deny."

Well, that's my best chance down, thanks, Elle.

I didn't look at her. I couldn't.

She'd clearly known what I'd been training for. She'd likely been watching from a distance. I didn't know how much she knew about my capabilities, but probably more than anyone aside from my teachers and fellow students.

This was a genuine problem, but one I had no immediate solution for.

Ana clapped her hands ceremonially, drawing all our attention. "Lord Talis, you have now used one of your three refusals. It is your turn to make a suggestion."

He nodded seriously to her, then turned to me. "Deep within the forest's heart lies a place of deepest dark. A treasure hidden deep within, by judges wise and royal kin. A race to claim a buried jewel, the first to raise it wins."

I raised an eyebrow at that. I knew of many dark places within the forest, but not one that met that description. "Please allow me to consult with my second and my third."

I turned to Darryl. He shrugged. "No idea."

"Rusty?" I leaned over to them.

"Think 'ey wants to go straight into one of the Buried caverns. Not a good idea. Even if you could handle it okay, we'd be riskin' too much by opening a doorway. He wants you to refuse this one, but you should, anyway."

I turned back to Lord Talis. "I must respectfully refuse."

He nodded, then gestured to me.

Ana spoke next. "Lien has used one of his three refusals as well. Lien, it is your turn."

I did like the core theme of Lord Talis's idea. Was there a way I could use it to my own advantage?

I conferred with my team, then spoke an idea. "A forest filled with winding ways, with mists where one can be lost for days. Within that wood are targets placed, three goals to take away."

The poem was clear enough for someone with my upbringing, and hopefully for his as well. I referred to the Winding Way, a specific part of the Court of Rust and Salt that was an ever-shifting labyrinth of trees, traps, and terrors.

His team conferred. Lord Oloris spoke next. "We will accept this, so long as you accept the last two lines of his own previous suggestion apply to your challenge."

I thought back.

The implication was that the judges would hide the goals . . . apparently along with support from the royal family? That was the most questionable part, but I couldn't object to it. Especially given some of my suspicions.

"If that's the case, it would still need to be three goals, and those would be the same as the 'buried jewel' he mentioned. These would not necessarily be literal jewels, but treasures placed by the judges at their discretion. Is that agreeable?"

"It is," Lord Oloris agreed, faster than I expected.

I looked to Rusty first. They gave me a lengthy, exaggerated wink.

I turned to Darryl. He turned to Lord Talis. "Would we be able to provide advice and support before the contest begins?"

A brief conferral of looks on the other side, then Lord Talis simply nodded.

Darryl looked to me. "It's not perfect for your skill set, but it's honestly not slanted too far in his favor, either, as far as I can tell. Have you already been through the Winding Way, Lord Talis?"

"Never have I gone that way, nor heard of it prior to this day."

That was interesting. He'd only just learned about it, but he'd be willing to accept it?

That implied he had some way around it, perhaps one suggested by Eliree, which made it a likely trap. As part tree spirit, it was probable she had more insight on the forest than most, perhaps including a way to navigate it more easily. She might have even wandered through it before, but with the way the forest changed, and the judges being the ones burying the treasure . . .

"I want to ask what 'royal kin' would mean before we move forward," I asked.

Lord Brine spoke up, surprising me. "Lord Talis proposed that part of his own suggested contest to the judges ahead of time, and we spoke to a representative of the royal family. They agreed to allow any part of the forest to be used for the contest, but only if a member of the royal family was allowed to observe the location the treasure was buried and approve of it."

That was simultaneously both eminently reasonable and suspicious. Had Lord Talis made a deal with the royal family to intervene in a challenge in some way? Or was he simply getting permission to avoid future problems?

Beyond that, I had to be worried about the implications of my own suggestion in that context.

Aside from that, there was another thing the Winding Way was famous for—

Once, ancient fae had lived in passages underneath this entire court and far beyond. They had traveled underneath the hills to distant lands, both of mortals and other fae. Those caverns were forbidden now, for they had been used to imprison ancient and terrible monsters. The Buried.

And the Winding Way was said to be one of the areas where the ancient seals on the Buried were closest to the surface. The mists and forest labyrinth were, according to some, a defensive measure to prevent any Buried that escaped from making it deep into the court before powerful fae could find them and intervene.

Had I accidentally suggested *the same challenge* that I'd just refused?

I didn't think it was identical, but if he was expecting some sort of advantage related to the Buried's tunnels, I might have accidentally still given him that advantage.

I had to hope that the only reason for royal involvement was to prevent any "buried treasure" from being lost during the challenge. That didn't sit well with me, but I didn't have a better answer.

I considered the situation carefully. I still had two refusals, and I could have probably argued that I wanted to amend my own challenge suggestion . . .

But running through the woods to find buried treasure?

That sounded very much like how I'd lived my entire life. Even if he had some sort of hidden trick, I thought I could handle it.

"I think we're both in agreement." I turned to the judges. "Lord Talis?"

"I accept your trial," he said.

Ana clapped her hands. "The trial has been set. You have one day and one night to prepare. We will meet again here at tomorrow's dawn, whereupon transportation will be provided to the forest's entrance. Rest well tonight. Tomorrow, your battle begins."

CHAPTER XXI

SECRETS

I walked and talked with Rusty on the way home that night. Rusty stayed the night as a guest, helping me prepare.

That was strange, but something else was stranger — Gramps missing again.

There probably was a clear explanation for that, but he hadn't left any sort of obvious note or anything.

What are you up to, Gramps?

I shook my head. I couldn't worry about him right at that moment.

I left *him* a note that night, explaining a bit about my situation, and that I planned to go back to training after the first round of the duel.

Then I got what little rest I could.

In the morning, Rusty was gone, and Darryl was brewing potions in the kitchen. Neither of those was particularly alarming, but Darryl up early and doing things to prepare made me feel less prepared.

There were so many last-minute ideas on what I could do, what I could have done prior to the match. Things I'd missed. But there was no time, and so I had a small breakfast, some tea, and then grabbed my things and headed out.

The Winding Way didn't have just one entrance, but Ana appeared when I was midway there and pointed me toward where we'd be meeting. She was wearing all black clothes that morning, which wasn't unprecedented, but it wasn't her typical aesthetic.

"Black? Is that a 'mourning my death' joke?" I asked.

"No," Ana explained, "it's something else."

She didn't clarify and vanished a few moments later. I kept walking.

Rusty met us a little bit later, just before I arrived at the entrance. They'd changed their outfit as well, but to a familiar one — they were wearing their long riding cloak, the one I'd seen them wear when they'd been with the titanic wolf. I thought I saw fresh wolf hairs on the cloak, too.

"You've been busy," I told them. "What have you been up to?"

"Oh, had a bit of midnight business. Nothin' *strictly* against the rules, you understand." They gave me a wink. "Especially since we hadn't set all the rules yet. Hard to break the rules before they exist. After that, well, I still did want more rules, so I had a predawn meeting with each of the judges to talk 'bout terms. Lots of little stuff to settle. Lord Oloris did the same."

I nodded. "Was Lord Oloris present for your midnight business as well?"

Rusty shook their head. "Didn't meet the qualifications."

I raised an eyebrow. "Care to elaborate on that?"

"More fun if I don't." Rusty rummaged through their pockets, frowned, then eventually pulled something out — a folded piece of ancient-looking parchment. "Don't let other eyes fall on this. 'Side from mine, 'course."

I took the parchment, unfolding it, and briefly gawked.

It was, apparently, a map of the Winding Way. "This is . . ."

"Shh. Less talk, more walk." They waved me ahead. "Study it, but not too hard. If you study too hard, it won't help."

I wasn't sure what that meant, but I looked the map over as we walked, noting routes. "North, west, south, west . . ."

"Not out loud, either. Shh." Rusty's finger went to my lips.

"Fine, fine." I looked the map over further. "Can you explain the symbols, at least?"

There were several different types of symbols on the map, but no legend to explain them. I was pretty sure the skulls were either traps or monsters, but the swords could have been either combat or treasure . . . and the X marks could have also been treasure, or possibly indications of places I shouldn't walk. And there were other, stranger symbols, too, including writing in another language. Artinian, maybe? That was a little strange — the people at the sword school spoke Artinian, but I wouldn't have expected it on a fae map.

Was this connected with that original map I'd found, all those years ago?

I pushed that thought aside, watching Rusty as they responded to my question.

"You'll get some hints on what the symbols mean when you get the instructions. But in general, you're after the same thing you always are."

Meaning . . . oh, swords. Right.

"Now, hand the map back," Rusty told me.

I turned to them, confused. "I can't hold on to it?"

"No. Never bring a map into the Winding Way."

I frowned at that, but handed the map over. I thought I had a pretty good memory of the locations on it, at least.

We arrived at the entrance to the Winding Way a few minutes later.

The forest was thick here, overgrown. There were cobblestones of a human-made path leading all the way up to an opening between two titanic trees — this place was close to where a human and fae settlement had once existed, long before the wars had torn them apart.

Beyond the trees, I could see only fog. It was very much like the fog that had blocked my path to the sword school in the mountains, and I wondered if there was a connection there, too. Was there some sort of deliberate magic keeping people away from both locations?

I'd learned to navigate the fog in the mountains easily enough, but I couldn't be sure the same tactic with my scabbard would work here, especially since there wasn't just one destination. I remembered from seeing the map earlier that it had icons for three different swords on it. Three different goals.

When everyone had gathered, Ana appeared between us. "Good morning, everyone. The contest has been set up. Beneath the surface of the Winding Way, three swords are hidden. Your objective is to obtain at least two of them, then escape from the woods. The person who leaves the Winding Way with the largest number of swords from the forest wins."

Immediately, I had several tricks in mind based on the wording of the objective. Ana said that the person who exited the woods with the most swords won, so I could walk in and craft more swords, then—

"Only the three swords that were placed there yesterday by our judges, and approved by a royal representative, will count toward the total," Ana continued. She gave me an apologetic look, seemingly reading my idea immediately.

That was the one problem with having Ana as one of the judges. She knew how I'd think about this.

The rules discussion continued for some time, providing several other criteria. We did, for example, need to enter the Winding Way. I suspected that rule was for my opponent, not for me, but I wasn't sure exactly how he would have worked around it. Some sort of sword-summoning ability, perhaps?

"Finally, your second and third may not enter the Winding Way during the trial itself, nor may they interact with the swords after you have entered the woods until the trial is concluded. Are all those rules clear and accepted by both parties?"

We stated our acceptance.

"Good." Ana clapped her hands. "Then we'll begin after a countdown of three. Three . . . two . . . one . . . go!"

Lord Valissar Talis vanished instantly, leaving a gaping portal in the air behind him. I cursed, rushing the portal, but it closed behind him before I reached it.

Then, as I ran toward the two trees at the end of the road, the trees shifted, leaning down at diagonals to block my path. Vines rose in the ground between them, barring the entrance.

I spun, finding Eliree standing right where she'd been, her hands outstretched toward the trees. She gave me a sad smile.

Nothing had been said about the second and third interfering with the combatants before they got inside. They weren't allowed to attack the duelists, but interfering with the forest? That wasn't expressly disallowed.

When I looked for Lord Oloris, worried that he was going to do something similar, I found him already gone.

Wonderful. This is great.

Darryl walked over to me, shaking his head, then handed me a potion bottle. "Drink."

I accepted it and quaffed it immediately. My vision swam for a moment, then . . . clarified. Everything looked just a little sharper.

He handed me two more vials. "Drink the second one when you get near the next entrance, then the third if you get hurt."

I took them, tucking the third potion away, then broke into a run.

I'd seen the map. I knew where there were other entrances. I was, unfortunately, already running out of time.

⁂

Mist washed over me as I rushed toward the southern entrance to the Winding Way, unstoppering the second potion that Darryl had handed me. I wrinkled my nose at the smell — one had to wonder if Darryl's constant tea consumption was a way of compensating for how his potions often turned out — then chugged it down.

Contrary to the scent, the flavor was . . . almost nonexistent? It tasted mostly like water. I blinked, coughing briefly as I made the mistake of trying to drink while moving rapidly, then . . .

The mists around the forest were gone.

Or . . . not gone, exactly. Just sort of . . . translucent? I mean, mist is usually translucent, unless it isn't. But whatever the potion was doing was letting me see through the mist much more easily. Given that I didn't know how the mist itself worked, I didn't know what the potion was doing, but it was going to help a lot if the mist wasn't going to be limiting my visibility.

Thanks, Darryl.

I rushed through the tree line . . . and promptly remembered that the directions I'd been given to avoid getting lost were applicable to entering from the east side, not the south.

I did, however, remember what I'd seen on Rusty's map. And some more esoteric instructions they'd given me.

Follow the wind. Or the directions, if needed.

I didn't have any magical way of following the wind itself, but I could see leaves blowing here and there. The forest was also lit by some sort of ghostly lights, which shifted subtly in the breeze. I wasn't sure if those lights were some kind of enchantment, or if they were actually tiny, fiery faeries, or something more esoteric like *onibi*. I kept a respectful distance in case they were the latter — *onibi* weren't likely to be friendly, even with the marking on my cheek.

I checked my compass briefly, making sure I was properly oriented. The map I'd looked at had a compass on it, so I could use my own compass to figure out which way I needed to go, at least in theory.

Thinking back to the map, I considered what I'd seen for the options.

There had been three icons on the map representing swords. One had a little symbol like a rock beneath it, another a river, and a third . . . some kind of dragon?

Oh, I'm definitely going for the dragon sword.

It wasn't the closest, but closest was relative when the entire forest was shifting, anyway.

I ran to the north, dodging as two hedges shifted at my sides, trying to entangle me. Without the potion to see through the mist, they'd have surprised me easily — the movement of the labyrinth brush was almost silent. It was kind of eerie.

In spite of seeing that, I nearly missed the vine that started to wrap around my right leg. I kicked it. The vine *yelped*, then pulled away.

"Sorry," I whispered. "Can't slow down."

I heard a *shh* noise from the vine, which sounded almost like it was telling me to be quiet, then it slunk away.

Huh.

In spite of being native to the forest as a whole, I wasn't very familiar with the flora or fauna — it had been forbidden for me to go here. That hadn't stopped me from peeking my nose in with Ana once or twice, but the Willowbark Witch or Gramps had always found us almost instantly and dragged us back out.

So, while I had an intellectual understanding of some of the mechanics, I was still briefly startled when I saw an entire part of the eastern forest seemingly . . . run away?

It seemed like that segment just . . . split off from the rest of the woods, including the area with the sword that had the rock icon next to it. That was bizarre, but I didn't know what it meant. I also couldn't worry about it, given that I was heading for the obviously superior (by virtue of being more dangerous) dragon-looking icon.

I was starting to think about why it was important not to carry a map inside this part of the forest. This entire region was designed as a labyrinth to prevent monsters from escaping.

If one of them even gets up to the surface . . . well, what are the odds of that?

Predictably, that was when I heard some shuffling in the bushes to my right.

I reached for my sword on my back. There would be no playing around with monsters that escaped from the underworld.

Ribbit.

I blinked as the bushes shifted again, then something hopped out. It was the size of my hand, green and yellow.

Oh, it's just a little froggie. Nothing to—

Ribbit.

The bush trembled.

Then a geyser of acid thicker than my torso sprayed out from the mouth of a second frog — one that wasn't in that bush, but in a completely different one to my right side.

Once again, the potion saved me. I could see the attack coming clearly, which the frog creature probably hadn't expected. I danced backward, avoiding the surge, then rushing straight for the monster—

Which was a frog, but a humanoid one, standing on two legs and a foot taller than I did. They weren't wearing any clothing, but they carried a pair of black bone knives in their hands.

The creature hopped backward immediately as I rushed forward, hurling one of the bone knives. I drew my sword and deflected the knife in a single motion—

And then the frog was right in front of me, jabbing while I'd briefly moved my arm in front of my own face.

I twisted to the side, avoiding the jab, then kicked forward, sending the frog tumbling backward. They hit the ground and rolled, then leapt straight upward from the ground, opening their mouth and croaking.

There was no acid this time, just a bloodcurdling sound that sent a shiver down my spine . . .

And a tremor through the ground.

I leapt forward just before the dirt opened beneath me into an enveloping chasm, which continued to spread. I kept running to outpace it, turning only briefly to deflect a second hurled knife that I'd sensed through the essence within it alone.

My dream training had saved me there. I'd gotten so used to having needles thrown at my back that my sense of sword essence had stretched, allowing me to detect similar weapon essences.

Unfortunately, as the knife tumbled into the chasm, the frog creature disappeared into the distance, too. I was tempted to pursue it — the creature was a potential threat to the forest if it got out — but I couldn't prioritize that. I didn't even know if the creature was real or purely created for this challenge. In either case, we were being observed by powerful fae. If the monster was an actual threat, they wouldn't escape. Not without a way to navigate, at least.

I gave one last suspicious glance around, trying to figure out which way the creature had fled . . . and quickly lost my sense of direction. I pulled out my compass, but the needle spun around in a circle.

Wonderful. So much for going north.

I closed my eyes and let out a deep, deep sigh.

Great. Just great.

Then I shook myself off and began to follow the wind.

Following the wind was a more difficult prospect in a place where it didn't obey the ordinary rules of how wind was expected to work. At times I'd follow a breeze, only to find a leaf seemingly blowing in a circle. Other times it would lead me into a solid wall of foliage, which might have been fine for certain types of faerie creatures but that I absolutely did not have the ability to handle without dealing harm to the bushes. And, if there was one thing applicable to the outside that would be true here as well, I absolutely did not want to make the forest itself angry.

So, I meandered a bit until I found what I was looking for — or, something close enough, at least.

A pristine, perfectly pure lake.

There was nothing draconic in sight. I had, fortunately or not, managed to follow the wind to a different target.

Well, it's still a sword. Assuming Lord Talis didn't get here first.

I walked to the water's edge. The icon on the map had shown water, and the instructions had been that the swords would be hidden, so . . .

It's probably underwater, isn't it?

I paused, closing my eyes and focusing my sense of sword essence. Immediately, I could sense several powerful sources of sword essence — more than three — like beacons within the woods.

Some were moving rapidly. My best guess was that those were whatever swords Lord Talis already had in his possession, from this forest or otherwise. Some were moving more slowly. One was static.

The one right in front of me . . . well, that was moving toward me at a brisk pace.

I opened my eyes to see a blade piercing upward from the water's surface. After that, a stately arm was exposed, pushing the sword upward, as if offering it.

Well, that's simple enough. Except that it's, you know, an obvious trap. It's not like there are women who just live in lakes and distribute swords. Not for free, at any rate.

"Hello!" I called out. "Person of the lake, are you offering that sword to me?"

A song called out to me from the water. The moment I heard the musical tones, I felt myself stepping closer to the surface of the water, without any conscious thought on my part.

That was dangerous. Very dangerous.

I took a better look at my surroundings.

The lake was an almost perfect circle, surrounded by a section of wet rocks. Beyond that, the rocks gave way to the forest where I stood — or, where I had stood. Even in the moments I'd considered my surroundings, I'd unconsciously stepped just a little closer to the lake's edge.

Immediately realizing that, I stowed my sword in my sheath and started shuffling through my bag. I didn't have ear wax on me, but I had a scarf and extra socks. I quickly tied the socks together around my head, then wrapped the scarf around them and tied that on, hoping it would keep them in place.

As that dampened the strange song, I stopped moving toward the water.

"Hello again! Your song is lovely, but I can't come swimming right now. I'm here for a hidden sword. If it isn't too much trouble, maybe you could come out so we could discuss a trade?"

There was a pause. Then, even with the padding over my ears, I felt a laugh.

A tall woman, clad in a regal dress made of leaves and lichen, stepped out of the lake. She held a blade in her hand that shimmered white in the light and a pommel in the shape of a crown. The magical aura of the weapon was so thick it was almost palpable. When I gazed at it, I could see raw potential reflecting on the surface. Something about it called out to me, and I felt like if I could just claim it, I wouldn't even need to worry about collecting the other swords.

If all I had was this, I could defeat Valissar Talis in every contest. I could finish Ana's trials with ease; I could prove my readiness to Gramps. I could go see the world, visit the crystal shrines. I could defeat the Sun Eater, and the sealed Ashen Lord, and the King of Thorns, and the Maker of Monsters. I could look into its reflection to see my past, and my future, and find my family, and—

I frowned.

That . . . wasn't right, was it?

And when had I gotten so close to the sword? My fingers were outstretched toward it, only inches from the blade.

When I pulled my hand back in surprise, I saw my reflection move within it, strangely skewed and distorted.

Why were my eyes gold?

With great effort, I slid my hands into my belt, holding them in place, and focused my senses on the weapon.

It was an absolutely beautiful thing. There was no question that it was magical. Formidable. It was exactly the type of sword I'd dreamed about when I was young, one that would help me defeat any obstacle—

Which, of course, wasn't what I was looking for at the moment. Nor was it in any way realistic. Sure, a powerful-enough sword could help me fight, but . . . seeing into my future? Finding my family?

Finding the one item that could solve so many problems at once was a child's dream. Even if such a thing existed, simply being handed it all in one gesture wouldn't make the slightest bit of sense.

Upon closing my eyes, I remembered the rules of the contest. Three swords had been hidden in the Winding Way the day before.

This was not one of them. I knew that because I didn't sense even a hint of sword essence from it, which expressly was part of how we were supposed to find our goals. And, more than that, I knew it because this sword had almost certainly been formed from my own dreams of what a magic sword would be.

I took a deep breath, steadying myself, and bowed. "Greetings, great spirit."

"My greetings, young one. I have waited for one worthy to claim this gift." She lifted the sword aloft, causing it to shimmer, as if gleaming from the light of a hidden sun. "Should you choose it to accept it, I will grant you this boon to aid in your journey."

She turned the glimmering weapon in her hands, one hand on the blade, another still on the hilt, and offered it toward me.

I noticed that she didn't even call the item a sword — perhaps it didn't look like one to her. Just an object of unformed dreams. Or maybe she could see a sword but didn't know what a sword was. I wouldn't have been surprised by either.

"I hope you haven't been waiting too long," I told her.

She nodded solemnly. "Ages in the eye of the mind, akin to the time it takes for water to boil when placed upon a blaze."

So . . . just minutes, if she's being literal with that time comparison.

. . . Or it's possible she doesn't know how boiling water works. I could see a spirit like this trying to boil water without a pot.

So, either this item probably came into existence when I walked into the woods, or it could be something eternal and timeless that has just taken a specific form now that someone is here to claim it. Or some mix of the two, maybe?

I let out a chuckle. "And this sword . . . what is it, exactly? What does it do?"

She paused for a moment, taken aback by the question. Then, straightening her back, she spoke solemnly. "This is Maximum Ultima Godslayer. Even I do not know its true powers."

. . . Oh, no. Did I name a sword that when I was like . . . five?

The truth was that I'd probably named it a lot more recently than that, which made it worse.

A sword that could solve all the problems in my life just by having it. Maximum Ultima Godslayer.

Even then, rationally understanding that what I was looking at was a fiction made form, I was tempted by it.

I let out a small, embarrassed cough. "That's really nice of you to offer, but I'm looking for a different model. Maybe one that's similar, but a little older?"

She looked startled once again. "Oh! Well, I'm not very good with time, but someone did leave a similar-looking widget with me some time ago. Would you like to come see it?"

Even the diminished sound of her voice was more dangerous this close. I felt myself taking another step closer, frowned to myself, then shook my head. "I'm not much of a swimmer. But if you're willing to trade the sword, I'd be happy to offer you something extra if you'd retrieve it for me."

"Oh? You want to give me things? That's strange. People don't usually do that, except when they do." She gave me a quizzical look. "What will you give me?"

My knees trembled at her words, but I stayed in place. Barely.

I'd spent a lot of time in this forest. Naiads, nereids, sirens. I'd met plenty of them. None of them had tried to tempt me with a sword before — that seemed almost unfair. But I'd heard more than one siren-like song, and I had a limited ability to keep my wits about me.

More than that, I had plenty of things to trade, and some prior experience with what aquatic fae often enjoyed.

I pulled out some acorns filled with honey. They were a classic for most faeries, and the closest thing to a general currency I tended to use in the forest.

I started with an opening bid of three acorns. We bartered from there, ending up at a total of six acorns, three silver coins, and a single tiny sword that I'd carved out of stone for future use in a gaming miniature. Trading a sword for a sword felt like an appropriate symbolic deal for the weapon itself, and the rest were essentially a labor cost for sending the sword siren off to retrieve it for me.

With the deal completed, I waited as she plunged back into the water.

A moment later, I saw something strange happening. A section of the lake began to ripple and shimmer. I felt myself wandering closer against my will, then . . . I saw the frost on my breath. I felt the chill in the air.

And finally, I saw the entire surface of the lake freeze solid.

My eyes widened in alarm and concern for the lake spirit, but only a moment later, a hand tapped the ice from below, shattering a section of it. Then, not even shivering, the lake spirit pulled herself out of the hole in the icy lake, frost in her trailing hair.

She held a colossal sword of ice in her hands, stretching them out in front of her. "Is this more like what you were looking for?"

I sensed the sword essence instantly, then grinned. "Yes. I think it is."

"How wonderful! I hope it helps on your quest." She offered it toward me, then frowned. "Oh, but be careful. It doesn't do too well on land."

I took a moment to put on some heavy gloves from my bag, then accepted the sword. Even with them, I could feel the ice magic seeping into my fingertips in the few moments I held the weapon.

We finished our trade smoothly. I found myself standing on the frozen lake itself when we'd completed the trade — I'd walked onto it without being consciously aware — but I managed to retreat smoothly after accepting the offered sword.

I was very fortunate the water was solid. If she'd brought me a different kind of weapon, I might have drowned. I tried not to think too much on that.

I'd made excellent progress. I had my first hidden sword.

Unfortunately, I *also* had a time limit. The sword was already melting.

No faerie trial was ever simple.

⊱⊰

As I ran back into the forest, following the wind, I unsheathed my own sword. Then, cautiously, I sheathed the ice sword in my scabbard.

The magic of my scabbard's essence worked to preserve the phantasmal weapons of the sword school longer than they'd normally last. I had to hope that it would do the same for the ice sword.

With that, I started running with my usual sword held against my shoulder, like one would carry a polearm. As dangerous as my blade was, I knew from experience that neither the sword's metallic edge nor its magic would cut me. I assumed that was because of either my nature or the spirit bond I had with it. Either way, it meant I didn't have to worry about accidentally cutting myself . . . just my clothing and other possessions. And my surroundings.

Running with the sword slowed me down a bit, but I still made a good pace. Good enough, in fact, that I arrived at the second sword while Lord Valissar Talis was still there.

I caught sight of him as a colossal creature of stone crashed through the forest, stumbling with the swordsman atop it. He had both of his hands on the grip of a sword that was plunged into the creature's shoulder, with only the hilt and a small section of the blade exposed.

The monster he stood atop was like a walking hill, standing nearly as tall as the trees. From the dirt that caked the creature's lower body, I instantly processed the trap that Lord Talis had triggered. This sword had likely looked like it'd simply been thrust into a stone, but it had actually been stabbed into the body of a massive earth creature. From the look of it, I guessed it was some sort of elemental that hadn't been harmed by the sword and had simply agreed to hold on to it for the test.

Lord Talis was gripping the sword with both hands and trying to stay steady on the creature's back as it rumbled through the forest. I could sense the sword essence from the weapon, meaning that he'd found the real one, not a fake . . . and I could see that the sword was gradually starting to slip free.

I had a few options. I could try to climb the creature and contest Lord Talis directly for the sword. I could try to incapacitate the elemental somehow, or perhaps offer the elemental a trade, like I had with the lake faerie.

But I could also sense the wind shifting, leading in another direction—

And I really, really wanted to find the dragon.

In that rare occasion, my interests were aligned with the practical. I had very little chance in a direct physical contest with someone as powerful as Lord Talis, and I didn't need to have one to accomplish my goal.

As soon as I sensed the direction of the wind turn, I checked my sword sense, confirming another sword was still present in that direction—

Then I turned away from the battle and ran as fast as I could. Not out of fear, but opportunity.

Several minutes later, I found myself breathing heavily. My sword arm and shoulder were sore from the awkwardness of how I was carrying my weapon — it couldn't cut me, but it could still bang against my arm when I took a bad step here or there.

I found myself at the entrance of a cavern cut into the side of a hill. This was, under ordinary circumstances, exactly the type of thing I'd want to avoid in a place like this—

From the soft purple glow that emanated from the cavern's entrance, it resembled many of the darkest tales I'd heard about entrances to the underworld.

Several lines of water stretched out from the mouth of the cave, like the many heads of a serpent, branching into the forest. I stepped across the first of them, then reached out with my senses. As I'd expected, I could sense a sword ahead, somewhere within the cavern.

I looked up as I approached the cavern entrance, noting how the stalagmites and stalactites at the cave's entrance looked an awful lot like fangs.

The cave isn't the dragon, is it? Two rocklike monsters feels a little too samey.

Still, I may as well check.

I reached down, picked up a rock, and tossed it into the cave entrance—

And instantly, the cavern's jaws snapped shut.

Then, as the ground trembled, I realized too late that the rivers next to me were beginning to rise and solidify.

Oh. I've made a terrible mistake.

This wasn't a repeat of the last challenge — it was, in some sense, a combination of both. The cavern wasn't a dragon. It was just one head.

The entire forest moved around me as seven rivers rose, forming long, serpentine necks.

I hadn't wandered into the mouth of a dragon.

No, I'd managed to find myself standing among the heads of a hydra.

CHAPTER XXII

SERPENT'S SWORD

When the rivers began to lift themselves off the ground and coalesce into a gigantic monster, my typical instinct would have been to attack as quickly as possible, before the monster finished forming.

In this rare circumstance, however, the sheer scale of the monster — and the extent to which I'd made a mistake — was enough to leave me simply stunned. Which was probably good, in retrospect, because attacking something of that scale without a plan was not the wisest course of action.

Fun, maybe. But not wise.

Maybe this is a case where I need to paint a clearer picture of scale.

See that tree over there? It's probably thirty feet tall, if I had to guess. Several times my height, obviously, and wide enough that my sword couldn't carve through it in one swing, even if it was still.

Every one of this beast's necks was probably six times that length, and at least a few times the width. That doesn't mean it was standing 180 feet in height, exactly, since they weren't just pointing upright. The river necks, as well as the solid stone one, were all coiling around like snakes from a slowly forming central body. And watching me, obviously.

So, if you were thinking, "maybe he was too small to notice and could sneak away," nope. I must have triggered something when I'd gotten as close as I had, either a physical trap or simply moving within the perception of the monster.

That didn't leave me with a lot of good options. I was getting more confident in my fighting abilities, but I was still Torch-level. This thing was big enough that it could snack on things the size of taverns.

I had a colossal greatsword specifically for fighting titanic monsters like this. In theory, massive swords were specialized toward fighting huge creatures. In this circumstance, I didn't have the knowledge necessary to apply that advantage properly. I was confident my sword had powerful magic, but I still had precious little idea on how to use it.

And so, when the monster's heads finished forming, I fell back on a different one of my usual techniques.

"Greetings, powerful spirit." I bowed my head. "I seek safe passage through your land, as well as a sword within it. Please accept this humble off—"

The stone head roared into the air, the sound of a rockslide down a mountain, and I had my answer. The ground trembled beneath me, and even as the creature's first head descended, the half-formed body of rock beneath it began to lumber forward. It didn't have fully formed legs, just towers of stone and water that sort of shapeshifted to approximate walking. Distantly, I could see something that looked like more legs behind it at first, but that I eventually realized was actually a number of tails that seemed to help keep it steady.

That thing is going to obliterate the landscape if it attacks. The trees—

I glanced behind me briefly. The trees were much, much more distant than I remembered . . . and seemed to be slowly shifting away farther.

Is . . . the forest itself running away?

I sighed.

Apparently, the forest had better instincts than I did, because when I saw that monster coming toward me, I went back to my default.

I ran. Not away, but straight toward it.

If I'm giving myself credit for anything here, it's that my action caught the mountain-sized land hydra — which was actually probably some sort of nature spirit, or genius loci, by the way — off guard. It actually stopped moving briefly, enough that I was able to close a good amount of the distance between us before it reacted.

Unfortunately, when it did, the hydra chose a course of action I didn't have a good countermeasure for. Rather than trying to bite me, like a true hydra might have, it simply swept one neck — hundreds of feet long, taller than my full height, and thicker than my body — across the ground.

There was nowhere to dodge but up. I mean, or down, if you could burrow. I couldn't do that. A second head loomed nearby, just sort of waiting for me to make the obvious move and jump into the air.

I have many flaws as a fighter, but taking the obvious move is rarely one of them.

I braced myself, sword out, and concentrated.

Shattering Soul.

The neck slammed into me. If it had been the stone neck, it probably would have broken most of my bones. Fortunately, this one was made of water, and rather than being fully solid, it was being held together purely by prodigious shaping ability — meaning that what hit me was a wall of water, like a tidal wave, rather than body-pulping force.

The power of the water striking me was enough that it would have bowled me over, but instead, I passed inside the neck briefly, then it kept moving beyond me, circling back up into the air.

I dropped to the ground and it passed through me entirely, my sword still held in a death grip. That's not the wisest way to hold a sword in most circumstances, of course, but I wasn't trying to attack, just to avoid dropping it.

Release Shattering Soul.

As the neck that had struck me rose back up, I tried to steady myself. I was soaking wet and the blow had winded me, but I looked up to see exactly what I'd hoped—

Just a bit of water leaking from the neck, where it had passed over my sword and body.

Just tearing a physical hole in a creature like this wouldn't do a thing. It was basically keeping itself together through pure magic — or, in specific, likely a combination of applying essence-shaping and higher-layer techniques from spirit and shade.

When I'd activated my body-enhancement technique, I'd done it with the knowledge that it made me corporeal to multiple layers of self at once. I was drawing mostly on breach essence, which flowed across my skin and on the surface of my body, then sword essence and my own personal essence flowed within me to increase my physical abilities. The technique was designed to let my body damage star veins and Dianis Points in my opponents, or to hit things like ghosts with my bare hands.

What I was fighting wasn't a ghost, but it was an inherently spiritual being. And while I couldn't hope to fight something on the scale of that monster directly, if I could punch enough holes in its soul, I might be able to render it incapable of holding itself together long enough to get the sword and get out.

That was the idea, at least.

I felt pretty good about it right until it opened the central, stony mouth and roared, forming a conduit of earthy green light within its jaws. I didn't know what that was going to be — bright green wasn't a typical breath-attack color I was familiar with — but I was pretty sure it would kill me if it hit me directly, so I doubled down on my classic strategy and broke into a sprint, running straight toward the thing.

When the monstrous head came down, it unleashed a beam of light that was wider than an ancient tree. When the massive font of energy hit the ground where I'd been standing moments before, plant life burst from the forest floor. Trees began to shoot upward like spikes, following the beam's path, and vines began to snake their way across the dirt, following me as I ran.

Oh, some kind of accelerated growth beam. That's . . . not great. If it hits me, I'd probably age several years in an instant. Also, I'd probably die.

Fortunately, the creature's head was slow and ponderous, and it moved without finesse. When it finally got close to me, I jumped to the side and made the beam miss, then quickly ran off at a different direction, angling toward the hydra's half-formed legs.

Got one good chance at this.

I raised my sword as I got close, then focused my essence, remembering the technique I'd used to cut the sun from the sky—

Star Severing Sword.

A blade of obliterating essence extended from the edge of my sword, vastly lengthening my reach, and I swept it straight through one of the colossal creature's legs.

It stumbled, falling to what might have been one knee if it had knees—

But it didn't fall.

Then, a second neck hit me from behind, sending me tumbling to the forest floor.

I hit the ground hard, rolling, losing my grip on my sword. I'd hit something hard enough that my forehead was bleeding, which was never good. I was half blinded by the time I pushed myself up. My sword was a few feet away—

And the creature wasn't giving me a chance to go for it. It was still unsteady on its half-formed legs, but another neck was sweeping toward me rapidly.

My eyes settled on my sword, but I didn't lunge for it. That approach clearly wasn't working.

Instead, as the neck swept down on my location, I drew the other sword from my scabbard and flooded my own essence into it.

Let's see what you can do.

As the neck approached, I hurled the ice sword straight through it, then shifted my stance to ready myself.

Just as I'd hoped, a massive section of water froze solid as the sword passed through it, far wider than the blade of the sword itself—

Then, as that section approached, I slammed my fist into the ice.

Star Shattering Sword.

The entire frozen section of the neck exploded, severing it from the rest of the body. The remainder of the water whipped past me harmlessly, and the hydra's stone head roared upward into the sky in sudden fury.

That wouldn't buy me much time. A spirit of the land like that wouldn't be significantly hurt by losing a single "neck" — that was just a projection of its power, not the creature's true body. I might have caused it real harm by damaging a portion of the creature's spirit, but it was so colossal that it wouldn't be lasting or significant harm.

Which was good, in the sense that I didn't actually want to hurt the land spirit. It was also bad, since if even something on that scale couldn't do it real damage, my chances of fighting it seriously were basically null.

I didn't try. I used the moment where it collected itself, trying to re-form the severed neck, to gather up both of the swords, then started running toward the creature again.

I could sense the power of the sword the creature held more closely now that I was getting close — and I could tell that it was somewhere toward the back, not the front. So, as the creature recovered, I used the ice sword again as I ran between the pillars that served as its legs, then swept the icy blade straight through a section where one of them was mostly water. When that leglike construct froze, I slammed my fist into it, causing the creature to stagger.

It almost fell onto me. I had to pull out my admittedly terrible movement technique to blast myself forward with enough speed to get behind the hydra before it toppled into what would have been a sitting position for any ordinary creature.

Then, I pitched over and fell to a knee behind it, losing my balance. My teacher had been right — it was a terrible technique. The motion sickness cost me key moments.

It was during those moments that I first saw the sword, a colossal Artinian-style two-handed sword more than ten hands long, thrust into one of the creature's eight massive tails. The cross guard was carved into the style of a cloud, with the blade resembling a jagged bolt of lightning. For an instant, it was nearly in my reach as the creature shifted to try to turn around toward me—

But I was too off-balance to reach it, and then that tail rose up toward the sky.

I coughed, cursed, and swapped swords. My ice sword had been rapidly melting, and I didn't know how much sword I'd need for it to count as a success when I exited the area.

Before the creature could fully turn, I leapt forward onto the sword-bearing tail, then began to run straight up it. When the tail turned too far upward for me to continue running, I plunged my sword deep into it, holding the blade at a horizontal to keep it from sliding.

Then, I held on for dear life as the colossal tail thrashed in the air.

I was lucky I hadn't eaten much that morning.

When the tail finally stopped thrashing, it lowered into a stable position, nearly horizontal to the ground. I pulled my sword out of the tail, then stood on wobbly feet. The creature's heads were still whipping around in the air, trying to get toward me, but it couldn't quite reach all the way around to its own back, and its legs were seemingly still not fully re-formed.

One step. Two steps.

My legs wobbled as I stumbled forward unsteadily on the slowly moving surface of the tail, passing my sword to my off hand as I prepared to reach for the embedded weapon's grip.

I was perhaps thirty paces away in a straight line from the sword when a portal appeared over the tail and Valissar Talis dropped out of it, landing on the opposite side at an equal distance.

Oh, no you don't.

I rushed forward, once again activating my shoddy speed technique—

And fell right off the tail.

I can blame any number of things for that. The tail moving, the technique itself being shoddy, my injuries.

But in that moment, it was not Valissar Talis who outmaneuvered me. He didn't need to.

When I tumbled off the tail, I knew I'd just defeated myself.

I didn't stop when I landed on the ground, of course. I looked upward, hoping that perhaps he'd made a similar mistake, or that there was another objective—

But no, he simply strode down the tail calmly, as if it was unmoving, and plucked the weapon out without the slightest hint of effort. Then, with a simple nod to me, he vanished into another portal.

My hands tightened. The hydra settled back down against the ground, then returned to its original state, rivers and stone.

And so, I didn't even have a monster to challenge. I was just alone.

My mind raced. My hands trembled.

Was there another solution? Another sword hidden that I could find, to even the odds?

But as my mind searched for solutions, my senses found no answers. Every single bit of sword essence I could detect was now either on me or outside the Winding Way, presumably with Lord Valissar Talis.

I'd lost my footing. I'd lost the second sword.

And the truth was clear—

I'd lost this round, too.

⊱⊱ ⊰⊰

In spite of being near certain there were no other solutions, I didn't give up easily. I wandered through the Winding Way for some time, knowing that Lord Valissar Talis had already left and wasn't likely to return.

I met other creatures there, offered trades. I considered making other weapons, but I knew that solution wouldn't work.

I found nothing. And so, eventually, I left the glade.

"Both duelists have exited the Winding Way," Lord Brine pronounced. "What swords have each of you retrieved?"

"You can go first," I told Lord Talis.

He nodded amiably, then drew a weapon from his hip. "In forest deep with leaf and loam, a sword once laid within a stone."

"Ah, yes," Lord Brine replied. "The Sword in the Stone Elemental. Wonderful. That's one."

Lord Talis gestured to me.

I didn't really feel playful enough for rhymes, but I forced myself. As painful as it was, I knew we had more rounds to go, and long-term plays were important. "In waters deep, a spirit sings. With guile great, a gift she brings. But beware her gifts, they wear a guise. Judge them not, with just your eyes. Within the lake, the true sword lies."

"Oh, how impressive. You met with and successfully uncovered the truth behind the Lady of the Fake." Lord Brine gave me a nod. "That was, perhaps, the most difficult of our challenges."

I tried to feel a bit of pride at those words, but it felt hollow.

The difficulty wasn't what mattered. I gave a nod to Lord Talis.

"In deepest glade, a spirit wise. A beast with heads that reached the skies. Its voice was thunder, its claws the rain. Among all creatures, this beast did reign. While opponent fierce did stand and fight, I stood alone while out of sight. And when I found the creature stunned, I knew that young Edge would run. Though his victory was close at hand, I knew that he could barely stand. And so, with guile and surprise, I appeared atop this spirit wise. And with great speed, we raced among the skies."

He raised the sword aloft, and I heard the crackling of distant thunder.

"The Sword in the Serpent is yours." Lord Brine nodded. "And with it, victory in this contest. Unless your opponent has any additional swords he wishes to display?"

I shook my head. I'd once again considered crafting swords on the way out of the Winding Way, but I knew they wouldn't count, and my search for any additional hidden swords had been without success. "No. I believe I've only earned one point to my opponent's two. Thus, that would make him the victor of this particular round. Good match, Lord Talis, and well fought."

"My opponent is gracious in his defeat. Well fought. You nearly had the victory. I will look forward to our next round." He broke from his pattern of speech to say that, which I appreciated.

"I will as well." I took a deep breath. We bowed together ceremonially, then departed in opposite directions from the glade where we'd met.

Ana appeared next to me a few moments later. "Hey, Lien. You did really well back there, even if you didn't win—"

"Not now, Ana." I shook my head. "Thank you, but . . . I don't think I want to talk."

Her expression sank. "Oh . . . okay. What do you need?"

"To break something."

INTERLUDE V

SCRIBE II

STORIES

The swordsman turned his gaze to Scribe as he walked, shaking his head. "Made a lot of mistakes that day. I still sometimes think back to that first round of the duel, wondering what things I could have done differently to win."

"I have some questions regarding the trials, if you don't mind," Scribe noted. "Three questions, in fact."

"Oh?" The swordsman grinned. "Exactly three?"

"Well, with possible follow-up questions."

"Sounds wonderful." He dipped his head amiably. "Please, go ahead."

"Did you ever figure out if that frog-like Buried you ran into was real?"

"Oh, good question. Yes, I actually told the judges about it, and they just sort of laughed. Conjured monster, nothing more. They were quite insistent that the chances of a Buried actually escaping the underworld were minimal." The swordsman grimaced. "Story for another time there. But that particular one was just a test. I *did* have to go back in there later. Was a little more careful with my things on the next trip."

"Follow-up: How exactly did Rusty get a map with the sword locations on it?"

The swordsman grinned. "Going to need to leave that one to your imagination. It's not my secret to tell. I did leave some clues, though."

"Okay." Scribe nodded, thinking. He didn't have an immediate answer on that, but it might come to him later. "A second question. The lake spirit. You turned down that first sword she offered. What would have happened if you'd taken it? Would it have reverted to some other form upon leaving the Winding Way, or simply vanished?"

"Oh, no. It *was* a real sword, and a powerful one. Just not one of the swords that would have counted for the purpose of the test — because, as I speculated at the time, it didn't exist before I approached the lake. Therefore, it wouldn't have met the judges' criteria. And if I'd accepted it, she wouldn't have given me a second item."

Scribe nodded. "So . . . she conjured the sword for you, as a test?"

"In a manner of speaking." The swordsman considered for a moment, seeming uncertain. "I suppose the chances of you ever encountering her are low enough that I can say a little. The spirit of that lake is one of the oldest and most powerful of the fae in the entirety of the court. But she doesn't know that."

"What do you mean?" Scribe adjusted his glasses. "Are you referring to her isolation from the rest of the court, being in the Winding Way?"

"That's a component of keeping her safe. There are others. I'm going to trust you with a secret, Scribe. If you choose to use it for harm, there will be consequences."

Scribe gulped. For a moment, he considered just revoking his question, but curiosity still pulled at him too strongly to resist. "I have no intention of abusing any of the knowledge you're giving me."

"Good. Because that woman is dear to me, as are many of the creatures of my home. She is under my protection, though even I don't know if she would actually need it." He shook his head. "She is known as the Lady of the Fake. She is a spirit of innocence, of quests, and of imagination."

Scribe blinked again, processing that. "Imagination? Like Ana?"

"Yes. I believe I mentioned this once before, but Ana is something of a throwback to ancient fae who embodied concepts related to creativity. They are vanishingly rare in the modern day, at least in our court. My hope is to find others within some of the lost courts, but that's a different discussion."

"So, when you approached, she conjured something that was . . . based on those essence types, I suppose a sword that resembled your quest?"

Edge nodded. "You're on the right track, but it isn't exactly that. Shortly before I approached, she would have sensed me coming, then found that sword among her belongings. She would have no recollection of where it came from, but she would sense that it was a part of my quest and that her role was to present it to me."

"Huh." He blinked. "But it was a trap, in some way?"

"Not precisely. I expected a trap at the time, because she has a voice like a siren, which lured me toward the object of my desire. At the time, I thought she was planning to drown me. A lot of naiads and similar creatures have instincts to do that. Kelpies, too, which pretend to be horses, then drag you underwater when you try to ride them. I was thinking she was like that at the time, but I was wrong. The trap was simply to uncritically accept a gift she offered, which appeared to be the objective of my quest, but wasn't."

"But it was still a magical sword, just one that was created too recently to count for a point in the test?"

"A magical sword in the same sense that one of Ana's conjured swords was, rather than being something made by a blacksmith. It wouldn't function to generate more sword essence, for example, unless someone like me used it for long enough that the world recognized it as a sword. It would have magical powers, but they would be . . . vague."

"Vague?"

"The Lady of the Fake's powers conjure something that approximates the desires of whoever is questing for them. Something that could solve *all* your problems, if only you had it." He shook his head. "The thing is, no one object can reliably solve all your problems, no matter how powerful it is. And using an object like that as a shortcut to solve one thing will often create other problems. In my case, I knew I was looking for some kind of hidden sword that would probably have magical powers, but I had no idea what they would be. Thus, the sword's properties would be like those of a dream of a magic sword — potentially powerful, but unreliable and inconsistent."

"That still sounds incredibly useful. Could you focus such an item by having a clearer goal?"

He nodded. "Sure. But there are consequences to using such a thing. As a powerful object of externalized dreams, the more you use one, the more those dreams become part of the item — and less a part of you."

"So, it's like a cursed weapon. It could betray you by using an unpredictable power, or take away your goals as you work toward them." Scribe frowned. "Perhaps before you even reached the conclusion you were looking for."

"I suppose that's one way it could end up. I've certainly had dreams of cursed weapons — that blade ending up like one would have been quite appropriate. An interesting suggestion. Do you have experience with a cursed weapon?"

"Not directly. I just heard a lot about a weapon sort of like that growing up. Go on."

"Not much more to say about the sword she offered, really. Not yet, at least. It's more relevant later."

Scribe raised an eyebrow. "Wait. With those risks, you went back for it?"

"Of course I did. Once I had a better idea of what it was, and who she was. I wasn't going to let a magic sword sit around at the bottom of the lake, beyond the Door of Discarded Dreams."

"The what now?"

Edge grinned. "Another story."

Scribe sighed. "Understood. What would have happened if someone's quest was for something other than an object? Like . . . if they encountered her while trying to save a princess, or to have a child to save a broken marriage?"

The swordsman's look was somber. "That's . . . another reason it was a good thing she was in the middle of the Winding Way when I met her. In a time when humans were closer to our lands and she roamed other bodies of water, encountering the Lady of the Fake often had tragic results."

". . . Oh." Scribe frowned at the implications of that. "Right. I had a third question."

"Good. Let's move on, then. What was it?"

"Trying to . . . oh, right. How in the world were you supposed to fight that hydra spirit?"

The swordsman laughed. "I imagine the idea was to have both of the other two swords from the contest. As I observed, the ice sword was an excellent counter for the water component of the genius loci. The Sword in the Stone Elemental was very likely similar, but with abilities geared toward manipulating stone rather than water. We were probably expected to confront the final challenge together, if we'd each obtained one sword around the same time."

"As a means to . . . what, force you two to make amends?"

"Part of the narrative of a combat by trial often involves each participant learning to respect the other, with hope for a nondeadly resolution to the contest. My suspicion is that the judges deliberately built that challenge with the idea that we would help each other."

"Which . . . I suppose you did help him, inadvertently."

Edge grimaced. "I certainly did."

"Could you two have beaten that monster in a fight, if you'd worked together?"

The swordsman laughed. "Absolutely not, if it was trying. Even at Valissar's level, even with two swords above our level specifically geared toward fighting it, we would have had no chance if the genius loci was actually intending to fight us. Something of that level could batter a small army of essence sorcerers. They were an adult playing with children. I imagine the judges had convinced all three of the sword-holding spirits to participate in the contest in advance. That doesn't mean it was risk-free, mind you. Fae contests can be deadly. If that spirit had fallen on top of me, I'd probably be dead."

"I'm impressed you performed as well as you did, considering your opponents."

Edge shrugged. "Really, my successes can largely be attributed to my second and third. Without them, I would have been wandering blind through the mist. That, by the way, would have made the Lady of the Fake much more dangerous, if I'd found her at all. Being able to see clearly with the potion helped make it obvious the first sword she offered me was a little . . . too much."

"Still, I don't think I could have done anywhere near as well, even given your advantages."

"Well, likely not, but that's not your fault. It wasn't a contest you would have picked, nor were the prizes tailored toward you."

"I suppose." He didn't think he could have handled any contest of the kind, but that wasn't worth saying. Instead, he took another approach. "Do you think that's why you failed? Should you have picked a different challenge?"

"There definitely are other contests that I had a chance of winning. Too many permutations to think about in much detail, but that doesn't stop me from daydreaming. I think about smaller things related to the contest, too, and around it. If I'd spent more time specifically focusing on making a better movement technique, could I have reached that third sword before Lord Talis did? Probably. Would I have been able to make it out of the forest with two of the swords? Probably not. I'd have done better, yes, but there's a good chance that would have just led Lord Talis to trying to teleport a sword away from me or something similar."

The swordsman took a breath before continuing. "Knowing that didn't stop me from dwelling on that particular failure, or on others. If I'd spent the night before talking to Eliree, would she have closed that first forest entrance, or would she have found some way to skew things to my advantage instead? It's difficult to say."

"Seems she had an obligation to the team she was on. They might have decided on what she was going to do in advance."

I nodded. "Very likely. But perhaps she would have left an opening for me, or warned me about that strategy, if I'd sought her out. There . . . were options. There are always options."

Maybe for him, Scribe considered. But he didn't say that out loud. Instead, he asked a question. "So, you've decided to talk about Eliree again?"

The swordsman shrugged. "You called me out on tailoring my tale, and you were correct. The reasons, however, weren't quite as simple as what you stated. I had other reasons not to want to talk about her."

"Such as?"

"I was embarrassed." The swordsman laughed. "Maybe 'ashamed' would be a better word. I didn't navigate my first relationship with perfect poise and purpose. I don't think anyone does, but it was messy, and I didn't want to get into all that much detail about it. I far prefer to talk about the adventure parts."

"And in this case?"

"She was part of the adventure. Leaving her role out would be a disservice to both her and the story." He paused in his step, then turned toward Scribe entirely. "That said, I will say this. Eliree remains dear to me, as do the others I spoke of. If you, or anyone else who is listening, used my story as a means to seek out and harm those I care for, I would take that very, very personally."

Scribe felt the hairs on the back of his neck rise. For just an instant, there was a gleam in the swordsman's gaze, and he felt as if he had a sword pressed up against the center of his chest, ready to pierce through his heart.

Then the swordsman blinked. The phantom sensation of the sword vanished, gone as quickly as it had appeared. Edge smiled as his eyes reopened, laughing and clapping Scribe on the shoulder. "But enough of that dire talk! Are you enjoying the story so far?"

Scribe gulped. "I . . . am, yes."

It was an honest answer.

It was the little flashes of danger *outside* of the story that worried him.

What dangers awaited at the story's end?

He tried not to think too hard on that as they continued to walk.

CHAPTER XXIII

STOP

In the aftermath of the duel, I sat down with my second and third to discuss what had gone wrong.

"I think the fundamental problem is that you agreed to the wrong terms," Rusty explained. "You should try ones that let you win, instead."

I groaned. "It's never that simple."

"Clearly not. But I've seen you do better than this before. Use your cunning more, fight harder. Perhaps because you thought more was on the line."

I turned to Rusty. "When?"

They shrugged a shoulder. "A while ago. Don't worry about it."

I frowned. It was another hint, but one that I didn't dig into right away. I wasn't in the right state of mind. "Darryl, any feedback, aside from 'plan better'?"

Darryl said it clearly. "Not so much. You really do need a better contest. Also, maybe just to keep improving. He's just kind of better than you."

I nodded. I wasn't insulted. A little hurt, maybe, since I wasn't in the best frame of mind after losing the match . . . but a part of me had expected to lose. Maybe even appreciated it, in a strange way?

I didn't *like* losing, mind you. I'm generally very competitive, but I'd looked up to Valissar Talis when I was younger. I'd heard stories about him, and now having seen him in reality . . . he'd lived up to those stories.

People usually didn't. Or so Gramps always told me — I didn't have enough experiences with strangers to say. So, when I'd met Valissar Talis, I'd sort of expected to be disappointed about the legend measuring up to reality.

So . . . I didn't like losing. But I *did* like that Valissar Talis was a worthy opponent. I just had to work on being a worthy opponent *to him*.

Rusty, however, had more to add. "Can't be thinkin' that he's just 'better' in all ways. That's losin' talk. He's older, yeah, more experienced. Got strong destinies, better essence. He's a better swordsman, handsome, and charming—"

"Are you eventually going to get to the point where you talk about where I'm better?" I asked.

"You're very brave." Rusty patted me on the arm.

". . . Didn't Lord Talis travel through hundreds of miles of Buried tunnels just to get out of his sealed court?" Darryl asked.

"Oh, yeah. Guess he's pretty brave, too." Rusty shrugged.

I sighed. "I actually do think there are things where I'm better, in the sense that I've had hyperspecific training he's unlikely to have."

"Played the dream duel card too early," Darryl noted. "Now you can't . . . Wait, can you just keep asking about that?"

I blinked. "I guess. I don't think we set a rule against it."

"It would look a little weak." Rusty shrugged. "But it wouldn't be an expected tactic."

"I'm fine with looking weak. Sometimes that's the best way to pull off a win. But . . . let's talk about some other options, too."

"Right. Well, seeing as you did end up doing a bit of sword fighting . . . you might want to work on that."

I closed my eyes. "I always do."

⁂

Before leaving, I confirmed that I didn't need to return the ice sword to the Lady of the Fake, or give it to the judges. It was a small consolation for my loss, but apparently I could keep the weapon . . . at least for as long as it lasted.

While my scabbard was helping sustain the sword, I needed the scabbard for my primary weapon. I could lug my sword around unsheathed for a while, but the Smiling Sword Saint had clearly disapproved of using it without some sort of way of limiting the sword's danger.

After a few moments of frustration at the problem, I realized I already had a solution. I pulled out the mirror that Rusty had given me. I hadn't used it in the contest itself, but it still could be useful.

It was a little large for a hand mirror. When I raised it, I could see my own reflection clearly, but the world behind my mirrored counterpart was a blur, like you might expect the world to look with grease on your spectacles. I tried to clean the surface out of instinct, but nothing changed.

Must just be how it works, I considered. *Not that strange, really.*

It got a little stranger once I unsheathed the ice sword to pass it through the mirror as Rusty had instructed — and my mirror counterpart, rather than retrieving an ice sword of his own, simply stretched out a hand to accept it.

I hesitated. He raised an eyebrow at me.

"You'd better not run off with this. I've had enough issues with mirror copies of me already."

My mirror image soundlessly laughed, then gave a "come on" gesture.

You know what? I've seen much weirder, and I'm too stressed to deal with this.

I sighed. "Take good care of this for me." Then, I passed the ice sword into the mirror.

The mirror's surface rippled like water as the ice sword's pommel passed through the material. The mirror Edge took hold of the grip once that was through, then pulled it the rest of the way into the mirror.

Then, with a last nod to me, he walked off a small way with the sword and began a basic warm-up routine.

Huh.

That feels like it shouldn't be something a simple item is doing, but you know what? I'm good with it.

With that, I took a brief trip back home to rest, change, and resupply.

Fresh, but still in a poor temper, I trudged my way up the road to the sword school, sending the local beasts fleeing with a glower. The optimist in me might have said that they were starting to feel the presence of my spirit earlier than I should have been able to demonstrate my power, but really, I think they just knew who I was at that point, and they could probably tell I wasn't in a great mood.

I hesitated before approaching the sword school itself, uncertain.

What am I even doing here? What's the point?

If I can't even defend Ana in a simple match where I held the advantage . . . is a little more sword training even going to make a difference?

Maybe I'm just going about this fundamentally the wrong way. I could be wasting my time. Should I be trying to broaden my skill set, or maybe just research my opponent and find counters to his skills?

Would any of it be enough?

"Well, *someone* woke up on the wrong side of their grave today."

I spun around just in time to catch a wooden knife aimed at my chest. Well, it *had* been aimed at my back, but, you know, I'd turned around.

I flipped the dagger around in my hand, using it to parry the next few swings from my opponent, but I found myself rapidly falling back, flustered. Daggers weren't my area of specialty, and she was fast, and—

Fade lowered her hand. "Huh. Even getting a beatdown isn't cheering you up. It must be bad. What's wrong? Steal the wrong person's pants?"

I sighed, flipping the wooden dagger back around and tossing it underhanded back to Fade. She caught it deftly, then, with a subtle movement, made it disappear into her sleeve. I would have called it showing off if it was someone else, or a different circumstance, but she didn't even seem to be thinking about it.

Her eyes were on me, sympathetic rather than teasing. Somehow, that made me feel even worse.

"I lost the first round of a duel," I told her.

"Huh." She wrinkled her nose. "When's the second?"

"Three months." I watched as she began to circle around me, looking for an angle to strike, but I didn't respond as usual. Instead, I just kept my eyes on her.

"Three months? Who has a duel with three months between rounds?!" She took a quick jab at me. I stepped to the side, slapping the flat of her knife to deflect it, then flicked at her with a finger. She avoided that, frowning and stepping back.

"I do, obviously. It's a fae thing."

"Explains a bit." She flicked her other wrist, sending a second wooden knife straight at me. I caught it easily, then parried her lunge with the other knife. "Except . . . here's the thing. You can't pout for three months."

"I . . . wasn't planning to." I frowned, hopping back as she took a quick series of slashes at my abdomen. "I'm just sort of—"

"Dwelling on it. Yeah, it happens. Happened to me, too, once. When I was still young." She reached up and wiped at her eyes. "Oh, to be innocent again."

"You're barely older than me!"

"We both know that's not true." She smirked, but there was something sad underlying that. "Can't trick me that easily. Not anymore."

"What do you—"

I barely adjusted my guard in time as she launched into a much longer combination of attacks, ending by throwing a kick at my stomach, then, as I blocked it, throwing something at my face—

"Pocket sand!"

I swept my free hand across the hurled sand, barely keeping it out of my eyes, but there was a knife at my neck when I'd moved my hand out of the way.

"You're learning," Fade told me. "Just focus on that, yeah?"

I frowned. Not because I disagreed with the message, but because I'd just fully processed the fact that the knives we were holding were made of wood.

Real wood, not the phantasmal training weapon.

Fade had made, or otherwise obtained, new weapons for herself. Fade was learning. Learning not just combat, but . . . Thinking about what she'd said about her age, it seemed like she was figuring out something about her true nature, too.

And if she could pick up new tricks simply by understanding herself . . .

Maybe it was time I focused on that a little more, too.

I was feeling a bit better after spending the morning training. I had a plan, at least. I couldn't give up after one round. No student of the Smiling Sword Saint would do such a thing. No student of Red, either.

And definitely not the person who held the legacy of the book I'd found. It was a hint to my past — of that I was certain. Perhaps if I could unlock the answers, I'd get the inspiration I needed.

I continued my translation, pouring myself into it. Hour after hour passed as I focused on the new cipher, rotating and transcribing until my hands were saturated in ink.

Then, I began to read.

There was some elation at first — a joy as I began to wield the sword in a form closer to how it was originally forged, with my mastery growing in incremental steps, just as a swordsman with a new blade might hope for.

But while removing the runestones proved a step forward in some respects, removing the crystals proved too much of a step back.

The crystals were not mere suppression tools — they were formidable artifacts in their own right, each containing complex functions designed to properly harness the Dominion Breaker's abilities. Without them, the sword reverted to a primal state — incredibly potent, but lacking the functions needed to harness that power in useful ways.

When I removed the crystals, my intention was to replace them. At first, I hoped to reverse engineer the crystals and create alternatives to insert into it with new functions that would allow me to bring the sword's full potential forward. I had also begun to study the Empyrean Heart, and I considered modifying it for use with the sword, but I decided that would be of better use in another project.

Before I made my own crystals, I needed to study the weapon itself, without modifications. To learn more about the forces within it — the sae dominion that gave it strength.

Those few who even know of the fathomless dominions often imagine them as being ubiquitous in composition. Four fundamental forces — creation, annihilation, giving, and taking. From years of wielding the sword, I'd already tapped into the weapon's power enough to understand that this was not the case. And, of course, I had a hint of another of the four powers to draw from, but that is beyond the scope of this journal.

The Dominion Breaker was, at its core, simply a vessel for the sae dominion — that which annihilates all things. The potency of this essence was so great that it would cut through any defense with ease, and even strike targets that were on entirely different planes of existence — but that was it. Raw annihilating power, without utility. Aside from the sealed Dominion Breaker function, the only other major function built into the sword's structure was to allow it to recognize itself, preventing the sword from self-destructing.

Kelryssia had made a function within her crystal to expand the weapon's uses, allowing it to be used to detonate mana, but the true genius was not in the technique itself — it was in the realization that the sae dominion could be harnessed toward purposes beyond straightforward annihilation. The flaw, I thought, was that her function was still too limited in usability — too dangerous to deploy against any true opponent.

I was different, or so I thought. A swordsman who knew what functions would be usable in a real combat scenario, not merely as a tool of intimidation and mutually assured destruction. I could redesign the sword to be a useful weapon, one that could be wielded without limitation.

Kelryssia had forged one function — one that opened whole worlds of new destructive possibility.

I began to work on seven.

I paused, taking another break to evaluate what I was reading. I could understand the excitement he must have felt upon realizing the potential of the sae dominion's aspects, and his reason for wishing to harness them. I shared his excitement, my mind racing with ideas for what might constitute other applications — even as I began to work on transcribing the next section. The part where I would, I believed, learn about how he'd failed.

And perhaps, if I was lucky, how the sword had been bonded to me.

Upon analysis of Kelryssia's crystal, I was able to confirm the sae dominion appeared to work largely the same way as other essence types — it had aspects.

It would have been comparatively simple to figure out a set of valid sae aspects, each with a single useful function. Not safe, by any means, but the wielder of the Dominion Breaker was protected from the sword's deleterious effects to some degree, as was the sword itself. Training in isolation on dead planets allowed me a degree of privacy for testing. Ultimately, however, this felt too limited to be considered a form of true mastery of the weapon's potential. I had grander plans.

The fundamental idea behind the revisions was quite straightforward. Rather than having several layers of restriction on the sword that would be perpetually active, as the runestones of the Tae'os Pantheon had been, I would create a new system wherein the sword's powers could be focused in a specific direction through the selective activation and deactivation of different layers of seals.

With practice, I could manage such simple changes, such as limiting the death essence in the composition of the sword's essence, but this wasn't enough. If I wanted fundamentally different functions, I needed a different approach.

So, I began to attempt a novel approach to the problem — rather than purely restricting the sword's power, I began rebuilding with seals that would allow me to focus the sword's abilities, like a lens.

I forged a new layer to the sword, one that would overlap the existing blade and help shape the sword's essence output. With rotations of the pommel, mechanisms within the blade would shift, activating different seals and changing the sword's form and powers.

The default state would involve all seven filters being active — at least, until I mastered each of the others. While limited by all seven seals, the default form of the sword would work similarly to the Sae'kes, but without the weapon's power being as limited by the runestones on the surface.

Each other form would have a single seal removed — and in building the sword in that fashion, all the sword's power would rush through that single opening, allowing for the sword's unbridled power to be used toward a single purpose.

Within that area of focus, the sword's power would be limitless.

Within the sword, I wove seven seals for seven forms. I believed that finishing the sword would be one of my life's greatest victories. Each form cut through the world in ways that even I could not have believed possible.

I never had a chance to celebrate. My next realization came too soon.

I set the journal down, staring at it. Processing. Then, after a brief pause, I stood up, picked up my sword, and unsheathed it.

It can't possibly be as simple as . . .

I put a hand on the pommel.

One heartbeat of hesitation. A breath.

Then I twisted it.

. . . And the pommel didn't budge.

I admit, I exhaled a sigh of relief after that. If I'd missed something as incredibly obvious as just rotating the pommel to turn it on, I'd have been pretty frustrated with myself.

But . . . upon taking that action, I thought back to the story I'd just read. He'd talked about the default state having limitations until he mastered all of them, and he'd need a safety mechanism to keep the sword from flipping forms with any accidental rotation. It was a two-handed sword, and shifting the pommel was too easy to do — a hand on the pommel wasn't an uncommon form of grip.

So, there had to be an extra step. An activation phrase, perhaps, or a secondary physical gesture.

I don't know if it was my own tie to the sword that made it so easy, or if it would have been equally easy for someone else to intuit, but it didn't take me long to sort it out once I had the first step.

There weren't just two requirements to shift the sword—

There were three.

I closed my eyes, holding the sword and focusing inward, on my spirit. I wasn't Hearth-level yet, and didn't have a perfect sense of my spirit's structure, but I still had a lifelong bond to the weapon itself. When I reached out, I could feel the connection that had been unblocked as I broke through the seal to my Spirit Layer. I allowed a hint of my essence to trickle into that layer, and I felt something resonate between the sword and my hand.

And as I felt that subtle tingle in my fingertips, I gripped the pommel and pushed. The pommel slid inward, just a hint. Then, finally, I twisted.

There was a *click*—

Then a burst of power unlike anything I'd ever experienced as a surge of shining silver overtook the blade and blasted upward, piercing straight into the sky.

I panicked just a little, then calmed myself. There was, fortunately, nothing flying straight overhead. And the cloud above . . . well, no one was going to be too worried about a gigantic hole in a cloud, right?

I laughed nervously, then took a breath, examining the sword in my hands. Fortunately, the echoes weren't around at the moment, otherwise Red might have had some questions that I wasn't quite ready to answer.

The weapon's blade had shifted in shape along with the twisting of the hilt. Instead of a colossal greatsword, the blade and hilt had both shortened somewhat, leaving it at about four and a half feet in total length. Still a two-handed sword, but a more conventional one, like a classic knightly longsword. It was, in this form, much less of a monster-hunting weapon and closer to a design for dueling against other sword fighters.

The physical form wasn't the most important part of the change, though it was a useful capability to have. I could feel the essence burning brighter across the blade, infinitely more focused on the Spirit Layer. I could feel the resemblance to a component of my breach essence, but it wasn't quite the same — this was more similar to the raw annihilating essence I'd always sensed within the sword, but put toward a specific purpose.

Unfortunately, I couldn't quite intuit what purpose was.

I spent some time with the sword in that new form. It was surprisingly easy to control the output of the essence that came out of the blade now that I could *feel* the essence. I wasn't going to blow up any more clouds next time I shifted it into this state — I'd simply hold it into a proper shape around the blade.

Once I'd made that decision, I didn't even seem to need to think about it. I wanted the essence restrained, and so, it stayed. I suspected that was a function of our bond, or perhaps something about who I was.

I tinkered with other possibilities as well. The sword worked just fine with my techniques, but I wasn't willing to test them against a real person — not until I had a better idea of what I was dealing with.

I tried changing the sword to other forms, too, of course. Now that I knew there were several aspects, I wasn't going to stop with one. Simply twisting in a different direction didn't get me any results, however — I met with resistance. The same happened when I tried to turn farther to the right.

The reason for this was obvious enough, since it pertained to a component of the activation method I'd already discovered. To turn the sword into its spirit form, I needed to tap into my Spirit Layer and create a connection with the sword on that level.

If I wanted to utilize the sword's other forms — shade, memory, or others — I'd need to be able to tap into the relevant layer of myself first.

Upon realizing that, I took a deep breath and attempted to feel my way through to my dream layer. I'd already cracked the seal to that layer during the fight with my other self, but I hadn't breached it entirely. And, of course, I had a partially completed Destiny Dream and the mark alongside it. If I could tap into that . . .

I closed my eyes, feeling a trickle of essence through that crack. With some effort, I pulled on that essence, trying to feel my way to more without actually breaking the seal open wider — I didn't know what that would do — and tried to twist to the left, intuiting that it would be in that direction to reach toward my extrapolated layers of self, rather than my reflecting ones.

The sword's pommel slipped just a fraction in that direction—

Then yanked back into the original position, resetting the blade to its original greatsword state.

With a groan, I sheathed the sword.

Well, I considered. *At least it's progress. Significant progress. I'm finally getting somewhere, both with the translation and the sword.*

Hopefully the next segment will tell me what the sword actually does.

I took a brief break for food, exercise, and a bit more tinkering with the sword's spirit-aspected form. Then I got back to translating, feeling optimistic.

I wish I'd held on to that feeling just a little bit longer.

The new sword would be a more formidable weapon than I had ever wielded — perhaps enough to match my enemy, if I trained to use it properly.

Seven functions for seven forms. I began to master each of them in turn.

Soulsever, a form to sever spirit arts, spirit bonds, and spirit veins.

Scalesever, a form to cut through all natural defenses, regeneration, and transformation abilities.

Skysever—

I didn't make it that far.

The sword, unbound by the worldmakers' crystals and my own seals, had begun to wake up.

And with that realization, I knew I needed to stop it. At any cost.

No.

My hands tightened in the air. *That's . . .*

I'd known that I was strangely bound to the sword. I'd even considered the possibility that I was a sword spirit of some kind, something like a xiphiad. A cousin to Ana, if not a sibling.

But when the God of Swords had spoken of his wife, I'd considered an alternate line of possibility — that Karasalia had been pregnant when she'd disappeared, and that her child had survived her death, perhaps without Aendaryn's knowledge.

If, for example, Erik Tarren had found Karasalia while she had been dying, and taken her child away to a distant forest so that Vaelien couldn't find him.

Then, perhaps he raised the child as his own grandson, awaiting the day when the child would reclaim his place.

And obviously, I would be the child of the gods.

It was pure hubris on my own part. A fantasy.

But not, apparently, one that I inherited from my parents. Not with that last line.

When Karasalia had disappeared, it had also occurred to me that I might have been a sword spirit after all — perhaps one born through Aendaryn deliberately awakening the sword to help him fight in battle.

That, at least, would have still made me something worthy. A spirit forged to assist him in battle against his greatest foe, to avenge his master and his lost love. To avenge *my own master*, for there was no longer any doubt in my mind that the woman who had trained him was the original version of my own teacher.

I . . . would have had a purpose, then.

A family.

But instead . . .

The God of Swords had not forged me. He had *found* me.

And he had tried to throw me away.

I gripped the manuscript tightly in my hands, and for the first time I could remember, I turned my head toward the sky and screamed.

I hurled the book at a wall, smashed my fists into stone until they bled, and tore apart my shelter with my bare hands.

Only then, with my sword cradled in my arms and tears in my eyes, did I force myself to sleep.

⁂

Crushing pressure. Jagged edges pressing against my skin. The smell of rust.

A moment of panic as I realized that I couldn't see anything. I was in suffocating darkness, restrained on all sides. Not yet fully aware, I acted on instinct. I heard it first — a murmur in the air, as things around me began to shift — then I felt the vibrations in the sharp objects around me.

Then, in an exhalation of breath, I *pushed*.

Hundreds of objects shifted around me, flying or falling, until I was free.

With my head and shoulders exposed, I could see where I was, and what I had done.

I had been lying at the bottom of a pile of broken and battered swords. My muscles trembled as I processed the image around me, emotions surging again in spite of not understanding my situation, and I shoved more blades aside. I felt none of the comforting touch of sword essence here. These swords were inert, lifeless. Junk.

Just like I had been.

I pushed more of the weapons aside with my hands, now that I could use them, and began to climb myself out. The pile of weapons was colossal, improbable, with blades ranging from the size of a pin to a titanic greatsword taller than ancient forest trees.

I ignored all of them, focusing instead on the building that was exposed now. A blacksmith's workplace, the forge still burning. As I watched, I heard a sigh, and then a chute opened in the side of the building.

Another wasted, worthless sword slid down the chute, landing at the bottom of the pile.

I hopped up to my feet, my mind strangely sluggish. When I landed on the ground next to the pile of swords, I realized that the ground and grass were red with rust.

I paid no attention to my other surroundings. They weren't of interest. Instead, as I sensed the lights go dark within the forge, I rushed to the front door. If I could catch the blacksmith, if I could ask him—

I pulled the door open. The room was still and lightless, the forge long cold.

Upon the anvil, incomplete, was a single sword. It was clearly unfinished, with several holes in the blade meant for some kind of crystals. Dust and cobwebs were everywhere within the shop, save for the weapon itself. In spite of its unfinished state, it seemed as if even dust feared to sit upon its surface.

Naturally, despite the state of my mind, I recognized the work. It was my own sword, after all, the two-handed grip seeming to wait for me to grasp it.

And so, I stepped forward, laying a hand on the grip near the blade—

And a second hand, not my own, rested just below it.

I blinked, looking up in sudden surprise.

Dream Girl blinked back at me, equally surprised.

"You!" Her grip tightened below mine. "Hands off, buddy! This sword belongs to me!"

I had no patience for her antics in that moment. I couldn't quite reach back to why I was upset, but my mood wasn't fantastic, and this sword didn't belong to anyone.

I wouldn't let anyone else treat me that way, not again.

"Earn it, then." I yanked the grip toward me.

She snarled and pulled at the same time—

The image of the sword flickered as we both pulled in opposite directions, then fell backward—

Each landing on the ground, several feet away from each other. I was still holding the sword, of course.

Unfortunately, so was she.

We rose slowly together, each holding seemingly identical copies of the sword—

But no, they weren't identical. When I squinted, I could see a difference. It was subtle, but her sword had a hint of a gold hue to it when I looked at it carefully, contrasting the silver of mine.

When I stopped squinting at it, the sword seemed to spring back into the previous color, looking just like mine. I didn't think much of it.

I was much more distracted by the waterfalls surrounding us. Six of them, in a hexagonal shape, maybe a hundred feet away.

There was no shop, now. No junk pile. Solid stone ground, the distant falling of water, and the occasional tree that vanished when I stopped looking at it.

I wiped my nose, clearing the scent of rust, and pushed myself to my feet. Dream Girl stood up at the same time, glaring at me.

"I was *this* close to finally getting my birthright, and now you're here again? What's with you? Are you some kind of sword thief?"

I laughed at the absurdity of that statement, knowing what I knew about the nature of the weapon we both seemed to carry. "I'm not a thief. Think about the fact that you keep finding me near this sword for a second. Have you considered that it might already belong to someone else?"

She put both her hands on the grip as she began to circle me, wary. "I have a hard time believing anyone else could have as good of a claim to it as I do."

"Well," I began, "then you might need to work on your imagination."

I snapped my fingers on my free hand, still holding my sword in my main hand. She flinched, but it wasn't an attack.

Instead, there was a flash as a visible line appeared from my hand, a silver thread showing my connection to the sword — both the version in my hand, and the version she held.

She stepped back instinctively at the sound of my snap, then saw the manifestation and shook her head. "A spirit bond? No. Could be fake. Anything could be fake here. *You* could be fake."

"Fake what, exactly?" I asked her. "What do you think I am?"

"I don't know. You could be a lot of things. Guardian spirit. Agent of the Blackstone, raised the same way I was, but for him. Auntie implied he was doing that with *someone*."

I blinked.

That was . . . a very loaded statement. Enough that I actually lowered my sword for a moment.

"Okay, wow. I am *not* the second one. I mean, probably? I mean, I guess it's technically possible, but that's pretty wild, and I—"

I should have known not to lower my guard. The moment I started to think about the implications of her question, she took a step forward, then she was right next to me, ignoring the space between us.

She planted her rear foot and took a massive swing of her sword, cleaving straight for my chest.

But as bad of an idea as it was for me to lower my guard, it was a worse idea for her to swing at me with that particular sword.

I reacted without even needing to consider it, shifting my stance to parry her strike with one hand. There was no weight in her attack to push me back, not with that sword.

I gripped my own sword with both hands, then shoved, sending her sprawling backward. She slipped on stone that was water-slick now, falling into a seated position. She growled, then punched the floor with one hand, sending tremors through it.

I ignored them, walking forward and lifting my sword to rest it on one shoulder.

Then, I reached down with a free hand. "I'm not in a great mood. I'd rather just talk right now, if it's all the same to you. We can try to kill each other again next time."

She took a look at my hand, staring at it for a moment like it was something completely foreign. Then, finally, she sighed and grabbed my outstretched grip.

I pulled her to her feet, then sheathed my sword on my back. The scabbard probably hadn't been there a moment before, but I didn't need to think about that.

"You've gotten better at adapting to this," she said, watching me.

"I've been practicing." I took a breath. "In dreams, like this one."

"You've been cheating on me?" she asked in a singsong voice, a hand going to the center of her chest. "How could you toy with my heart like this?"

I rolled my eyes. "I'm pretty sure you've been doing some dream training of your own. You were more familiar with this sort of thing from the start."

"That's with family. It's different." She sheathed her own sword on her waist, which didn't make a lot of sense for the size, but it didn't seem to bother her.

Something about her use of the word "family" hit me hard enough that I felt it burn. My breath left me. In that moment, it felt like continuing to struggle for a sword might have been easier. Less painful.

"You good?" She glanced at me. "You look like someone just killed your favorite pet rock."

I shook my head. "I don't have any pet rocks. Honestly, if anyone was killing rocks, it'd probably be me."

"That's so sad." Dream Girl frowned. "You must not have a lot of people to talk to, then."

"I mean, I suppose I do. There's . . . Wait, do you talk to pet rocks?"

Dream Girl took a step forward, taking one of my hands in hers. "Let's focus on the things that make your life terrible and embarrassing, not mine."

"Not really loving that idea, either." I took a breath. "Actually, I'd much rather talk about why you think this sword belongs to you. And, uh, why you think there might be someone working for the Blackstone Assassin looking for it? That . . . seems like it should be concerning, right?"

She shrugged a shoulder. "You get used to that sort of thing in my line of work."

"What is your line of work, exactly?"

Dream Girl chuckled. "The kind of line of work that recognizes when someone is asking a lot of questions but not giving any answers."

She let go of my hand, which was disappointing, and took a step back, spinning around. "You're going to have to give me something if you want to learn more."

"Well, I'm certainly not giving you my sword," I told her.

"You keep saying 'my' sword. You really have a bond to it?" she asked.

I nodded. Then, after a brief moment of hesitation, I volunteered something. "I have the sword in the waking world. Or . . . a part of it, at least, if it's been split into pieces."

She spun back around, facing me, expression serious. "That shouldn't be possible."

"Why?" I asked. "Do you have another part?"

She hesitated, then shook her head. "N . . . not exactly. I mean, you could say that, but . . ." Her expression sank. "You're saying you have, like, an actual, full-on sword?"

I gave her a wry grin. "It's fully functional, and I'm trained in a *variety* of techniques with it."

"I'll bet you are." She winked at me. "But let's not get too off topic. You feel like it's missing something?"

"I know it is." That answer was true. It was part a memory of the story of the sword's construction, and part a feeling of intuition. I knew it was unfinished. I knew *I* was unfinished.

And, perhaps more importantly, I felt like the sword I had just claimed half of in the dream was an actual part of the weapon. Not just an image, not just imagination. The line of glowing light I formed when I'd snapped my finger was showing something real, an actual connection to a thing that was physically present in this dream realm . . . half of which was now in her hands, and half in mine.

I took a breath. "I think this sword we're holding on to here is a fragment representing the sword on the plane of dreams."

"Well, obviously." She frowned. "What do you think happens when I put all the pieces together?"

"Don't think I didn't notice how you phrased that." I folded my arms. "But the answer is that I don't know. I don't even know if it's a good idea, or beneficial. But the sword feels incomplete, and if you were willing to give me the half that you just grabbed—"

"Nice try." She shook her head. "The way I see it, we're both connected to this sword. Even if you think you have a better claim because you have the physical sword, I'm bound to it, too."

With a finger snap of her own, a golden light flashed from her left hand, creating a tether in the air that attached itself to both versions of the sword.

For a moment, my own silvery thread and her gold one met in the air, overlapping. They shimmered as they met, briefly glowing brighter than they did on their own, then drifted apart.

"You see that?" I asked, gesturing toward the threads.

"Was hard to miss. You think that connection is a part of why we keep running into each other here?"

"That, and maybe the fact that I've been doing dream essence training while sitting on top of a breach between worlds, using a fragment of a mirror tied to other layers of reality."

". . . You live an interesting life," she said quietly. Then, after a moment of hesitation, she asked the most important question.

"Who are you, really?"

She stepped in close, her face nearing mine. I could feel her breath on my face.

I hesitated for a critical moment, debating how to answer.

Who was I?

Was I Lien, Ana's rival? The Edge of the Woods, a swordsman who had once saved a princess?

Was I an abandoned sword, now awakened and without purpose?

In that moment of hesitation, she stepped back—

Holding my sword, stolen from its scabbard, in her hands.

"Takes a thief to know a thief." She winked at me. "See you again, Dream Boy."

Then, as I hissed in sudden dismay and stepped forward to grab her, she slammed the sword into the ground. Reality shattered around us, and in an instant, only darkness remained.

⁂

When my eyes opened, I was still angry.

Angry at what I'd read the previous night and the feelings of abandonment it brought.

Angry at the girl in my dream. At her blind entitlement, at her betrayal—

And worst of all that I *liked* her, and liked that she'd outmaneuvered me.

I threw myself into training with wild abandon. The journal lay abandoned where I'd hurled it. More than once, I considered reading the rest. More than that, I considered destroying it.

Instead, I wandered until I found a mountainside, drew my sword, and took out my anger on it.

Ten strokes. Fifty strokes. A hundred strokes. A thousand.

I swung until my arms were exhausted, my muscles burned, and I'd cleaved a furrow deep into the mountain's heart.

Again.

Again.

I cut, and cut, until something implausible happened—

My wrist stopped in midswing, arrested by a strong but gentle hand.

I froze in panic, swinging desperately on instinct with a Sword Hand technique.

The intruder caught the swing just before it brushed against her cheek, blocking my wrist with a book.

I turned to see her face — or, rather, a blur in the place of a face — and I was so startled that I nearly dropped my sword.

"Hey, kid. I think you dropped something important. I don't think that's going to make you feel better," she said, indicating the mountain with a tilt of her head. Even with the blur, I could see the sadness on the edges of her smile.

"Red?" I lowered my sword, then pulled my other arm back self-consciously, dismissing my Sword Hand technique to rub at the corners of my eyes.

"I don't blame you. Can't say I'm particularly happy with everything in here, either." She waved the journal in the air.

My gaze followed it for a moment, then back to her. Not only had she apparently read the journal — or at least my translation of it — but she was . . . away from the school. Not by a lot, maybe, but farther than I'd ever seen her go. And if she wasn't happy about what was in the journal . . .

I frowned. I knew that Green had called her "the first apprentice," but . . .

"Are . . . are you . . . Karasalia? The Impervious Forest Goddess?"

She snorted. "If I had a copper for every time someone made that mistake, I could make myself a sword. Not, like, a good sword. Maybe a dagger. But you get the idea."

"But you're not the sword saint, and . . ."

"No, I'm not." She indicated the journal again. "I'm in there, though. You just didn't get that far. Can't say I blame you — he sure didn't make it easy."

I looked away. "That's not why I stopped."

"Yeah," she said, her tone sympathetic. I couldn't be sure, but I thought she looked down at my sword for a moment before she spoke again. "You want to talk about it?"

I glanced at the journal, then toward her still-blurred face.

". . . Maybe."

"No hurry. For now, let's get back to the school? Maybe do something fun?"

"I could finally steal Fade's pants." I chuckled. "Maybe that'd give her something else to talk about."

"Yeah, don't do that. She'd probably consider it a sign of courtship, and I am absolutely *not* chaperoning you two."

I snorted. "Noted. I'll . . . figure something else out."

"I'm sure you will. For now, though, let's get back home."

"Home?" I pondered at her.

"Home," Red said. "For as long as you want it to be."

I spent another week or so at the sword school, even though it probably wasn't the most efficient way to work on improving my abilities. Having Red around was important for something else. She didn't teach me new techniques for how to use my essence, or new ways to grasp for power beyond what I could normally manage for my level, but she was kind at a time when I truly needed it.

And, from a more practical standpoint, she also continued my lessons in completely essence-free swordplay.

"If you're going to keep lugging around a gigantic sword like that, you need to work on your basic cuts with it. It's impressive you can swing that thing around with as little difficulty as you do, but your strikes aren't clean. When you're repeating the same strike, you should be able to reliably hit the same target at the same angle."

I gave her a little twist of my lips. Not quite a frown, but a hint of disagreement. "Is that really important? If I'm hitting someone with a sword the size of a door, it probably doesn't matter if I'm an inch off target, right?"

She shook her head. "No, in some ways it's more important that you get it right with that kind of weapon. You're not always going to have a clean match with a single opponent. What happens when you're fighting in a line with people at your left and right and your aim isn't fantastic? Even if you don't hit your allies — which you might — there's a good chance you end up, say, hitting one of their weapons if they swing at the same time as you. Or clipping the wrong opponent."

"And if I'm not planning on doing line fighting?" I asked.

She tilted her head. "You're going to be able to plan every fight you're in for the rest of your life?"

I paused.

She continued without making me acknowledge that. "Even if you only ever fight single opponents, there are times when you're going to want to be very precise about where you're hitting someone. Like, you don't want to accidentally cut your opponent's throat when you're aiming for a shoulder."

"That's . . . fair. But I don't think I would be using this kind of sword in a nonlethal tournament or anything. It's not practical for that. I'm honestly hoping to avoid using it even for the duel that's coming up."

Red gave me a quizzical look. "What *would* you be using it for, then?"

"Uh . . ." I took a breath. "Huh. That's . . . a pretty good question, isn't it?"

"I try not to ask any other kind." She smiled at me.

"Right. Okay." I paused, considering. "I guess if it's supposed to be my primary weapon, I should be planning to use it broadly. But . . . assuming I continue to train and have different weapons for different circumstances, the thing this sword is best designed for is fighting gigantic monsters. In which case . . ."

She shook her head, cutting me off before I could draw out that thought completely. "Precision is still a factor, even for that. Even if you're going it alone. You run into a lot of cases where a monster has a small weak point you want to hit, for example, that's surrounded by tough hide or scales."

I nodded. The classic "dragon missing a single scale" example. "In those cases, I'm not sure the sword is even small enough to get into a weak spot like that."

"Maybe not, but in cases like that, you might be able to break through the surrounding area with a sword of that size — provided that you hit the weak spot dead-on. Or, you could develop techniques that project a smaller striking surface, like a thinner extension of your blade, if you really want to prevent hitting the surrounding area for some reason. That requires even greater precision and control to pull off, since you need not only excellent aim for the sword itself, but also your essence."

"That's . . . yeah, okay. Do you know any techniques like that you could teach me?"

She shook her head. "Honestly? You're already better at sword essence than I am."

I stared at her. "But you . . . you're . . ."

"Not much of a sorcerer. Never had a knack for it." She shrugged. "Never needed it much, either."

I couldn't quite wrap my mind around that at the time, but fortunately, that wasn't the focus of the lesson. "Okay. I'll work on trying to be more precise. I don't think that's ever going to be my strength, though."

"Doesn't have to be something you're perfect at. You're clearly more focused on raw power and speed, and that's okay. Met plenty of fighters like that, and it can work. But someday, when you just barely manage to avoid hitting one of your friends, you're going to be really glad you practiced control. Trust me."

I kept training with Red for a while longer, but as wise as she was, repetitive, mundane practice just couldn't keep me engaged indefinitely.

I loved swordplay, and I loved my friends at the sword school. But nothing in the world made me feel more myself than wielding my essence and forming new techniques.

And so, when I'd regained a bit of myself, I returned to the Smiling Sword Saint's arena.

"So," she said, "looks like you made it back alive, kid. How'd it go?"

I told her. She listened carefully, without criticism.

"Two rounds left, then? And a bit under three months until the next one?"

"Yeah. Think it's enough time?"

"To match someone like that? Not even close, kid. But there's a chance it'll be enough time to let you pull off a good trick or two, and I've got a few ideas."

"Another scenario for the circlet?" I couldn't help letting the excitement bleed into my voice, but she shook her head.

"At some point, but no. I've got a different idea for this round."

"What sort of idea?" I asked, leery.

"It's kind of a crazy one, so brace yourself." She raised a single finger. Pillars trembled around her, punctuating the pause.

Then, she exhaled a breath.

"I'm going to teach you one of *my* techniques."

I couldn't see myself, of course, but there's an expression in the Artinian language about someone having stars gleaming in their eyes. I can't imagine I had anything less than a galaxy in my gaze that day.

CHAPTER XXIV

SWORD SKILL

I stood in front of the Smiling Sword Saint, practically bouncing with enthusiasm. We were in the usual arena, but I wasn't wearing the circlet — she was going to teach me something directly this time. I couldn't wait.

"Are you going to teach me the Sword Saint's Smile?"

She laughed outright. "Don't get too cocky, kid. You'd need to learn, like, a dozen prerequisite things for that first."

"Are you going to teach me a dozen—"

"Maybe someday," she cut me off. "But for now, *apparently* you haven't been following my instructions."

I was pretty bad at following instructions sometimes. I wasn't exactly certain which way she meant. "I, uh—"

"Your movement technique. You still tried to use that junk technique, didn't you?"

I winced. "I didn't have a lot of better options. Something was going to fall on top of me, and—"

"Relax. Not here to castigate you." She sighed. "You didn't have a better technique because I failed to teach you one. So, we're going to fix that."

"Then . . . you're going to teach me the Skyward Stride technique?"

I'd heard legends about the Smiling Sword Saint flying on top of a sword. Other members of the Soaring Sword Sect could do it, too, once they reached a more advanced level than the students I'd fought with in her memories.

Flight would be a massive improvement to my capabilities. If I could fly on a sword, avoiding those massive genius loci limbs might have been plausible, or snatching the sword quickly enough to escape into the air . . .

Or even recovering if I did end up falling.

It sounded like a fantastic idea.

"Nope, not teaching you that, either."

I blinked. ". . . Why?"

"Do you remember which essence types I told you I used for the Sword Saint's Smile?"

I blinked. "Of course. Sword essence, aura essence, air essence, and area essence."

"Right. I wouldn't have put them in that order, however. Because the second one our school is expected to learn is air essence."

". . . And that's also what you use to fly?"

"Yep. Sure, some people can fly using other weird stuff like gravity essence, but you pretty much want to have air essence for most normal flight techniques."

I raised an eyebrow. ". . . If you use air essence for it, why bother flying on a sword?"

A dozen swords manifested in the air around her. I braced myself for a sudden attack — I knew my teacher, after all — but instead, they simply rotated in front of her, forming a sort of stairway with their blades. She stepped forward casually onto one blade, then the next, climbing slowly until she stood just above me.

"Aesthetics, kid." She hopped down, flipping over in midair, swords whipping below her. One of the swords flew below her just before she reached the ground and she landed in a sitting position on it. "That, and advanced versions of the technique can serve as a mobile distraction, an extra method of blocking, or even something that can keep me aloft without having to concentrate on it. But it's mostly to show off."

I laughed. "Okay. I can see the appeal. But if I'm not learning that . . ."

"You still need a movement technique. It took me a while to think of one that would work for you, because almost all our techniques for movement require air essence. The one I'm thinking of doesn't require air essence, but it does require something different. Something that usually isn't even possible at your level, or close to it . . . but you've been known to surprise me."

I didn't realize I could still get more excited.

A technique that shouldn't be possible at my level?

"What's this technique called?"

"It's a personal technique, rather than a sect one. The Strategic Side-Step."

I frowned. That didn't sound like a legendary swordsmanship technique. It sounded, in fact, more like . . .

"Yes, my student," she said, apparently reading my mind. "Today, you're going to begin to learn one of the most important lessons in swordsmanship. How to run away."

* * *

In spite of the somewhat less epic nature of learning to run from a fight, I was excited to finally learn a technique directly from my teacher. And one from her personal collection, no less!

I didn't dwell too much on the implications of why my teacher might know a technique for running away. Not at the time, at least.

She stretched out her arms to her side, causing some of her floating swords to fan outward along with her gesture. I had to hop over one to avoid it.

They formed a loose ring around us, smaller than the main arena.

"Your starting goal is going to be to use the technique to be able to move from one of these swords to the next."

I nodded eagerly. "From just standing near one, or standing on top of one?"

"Uh, standing on one sounds good. Good balance exercise."

I shouldn't have asked. That absolutely hadn't been part of the plan. And balancing on a small surface was not my strength. If the swords had been as wide as the one on my back, sure, but the conjured swords were mostly jian size — standing on them was a challenge even when they were still.

I wouldn't complain, however. I didn't want my master to stop wanting to teach me.

So, I stepped over to one of the swords. It took me three solid attempts to even get on top of one properly, then another few before I stopped falling right off.

She waited with something resembling patience.

"What now?" I asked.

"Now," she said, "would normally be where you use aura essence to encompass the area, making it yours to command. This is a fundamental component of how I use my techniques across broad regions — my power is carried through my aura."

That little detail explained *so much*. "And then you use area essence to spread your power farther?"

"Right. Smart. But you don't need area essence for a small place like this."

I nodded . . . then fell right off the sword I was standing on.

It wasn't completely stable, even with the Smiling Sword Saint's magic keeping it aloft. I grimaced, then climbed back up. ". . . Sorry."

"Don't apologize. You're learning. Get steady, then focus."

I nodded, taking a breath, steadying myself. "Okay. I think I'm good for now."

"Great. Now, what were we talking about?"

I didn't know if that was a test or if she'd just forgotten it herself. I answered quickly. "Aura and area essence."

"Right." She nodded. The swords bobbed up and down with her movement, but I managed to remain on mine, barely. "So, I'm going to show you how I do the technique. Then, you do the thing where you, I don't know, somehow manage to fake it without all the parts."

"I . . . uh . . . don't really know if I can fake aura essence. That seems pretty fundamentally different—"

"Oh, right. You don't need to fake that part, exactly. I mean, you do, but not with sword essence. The part you need to fake with your essence somehow is the side-step."

She hopped up to one sword, then stepped forward—

And stood atop a different sword on the other side of the ring.

I blinked. I hadn't seen her move through the intervening distance at all. She was incredibly fast, of course, but that looked more like . . .

"Was that a teleportation technique?" I asked.

"Don't know," she said. "I don't understand how it works."

I stared at her. "But . . . you made the technique."

"Yep! Sure did. Proud of that one, too. It's three parts. Aura essence to control the area. Sword essence to create swords within it. And finally, I use evasion essence — my Retreating Point's essence — to move from sword to sword within my aura. Specifically, side-step aspected evasion essence."

I tried to wrap my head around that. "So . . . you're taking a side-step between things that your aura considers to be 'connected.' And thus, adjacent to each other. Which allows you to . . . dodge the intervening space between them?"

"That sounds right." She nodded confidently.

That doesn't sound right at all.

That definitely shouldn't be how the world works.

And yet . . .

I took a breath, pinching my nose.

When I saw her expression afterward, it looked almost like she was holding back a smile.

Sitting on the top of a nearby pillar, Thane called down, "Now you know how we feel when you use sword essence."

Never before had I simultaneously felt so proud and so frustrated.

I watched the Smiling Sword Saint perform the technique several times.

It still didn't make the slightest bit of sense to me. But I did, through observing it, come to pick up certain basic properties. Not the cause and effect, exactly, but the movements that she took. Where her front foot started for the technique, where it ended on the next sword. The moment where essence wrapped around her, warping my expectations for how she could be adjacent to something that was so far distant.

I couldn't even begin to emulate it, however, because I was missing something fundamental.

"Even if I could skip the dodging part, I need to learn how to make an aura without aura essence," I told her. "What was your idea for that?"

"Every essence sorcerer can make an aura of sorts . . . eventually. Spirit artists can do it even earlier."

I frowned. "You're talking about projecting your spirit?"

"Precisely! You've probably felt it from time to time. The Artinians call it sakki — killing intent. But for an essence sorcerer, projecting your spirit creates a field related to whatever essence type your spirit is invested with. In your case . . ."

"It'd be related to my sword, at least for now. I'm . . . not sure projecting that aura is safe, even if I knew how."

"You're talking about using a sword technique, kid. It's not supposed to be safe."

"Okay, sure, but there are levels—"

"If you don't want to die as a swordsman, you're going to have to accept some risk of doing unintentional harm. There are ways to reduce that risk, but that requires mastery. And mastery requires practice."

. . . I had no way to argue with that. So, I simply moved forward with my questions. "How do I project my spirit?"

"Well, that's the thing. Normally, that's one of the last things you learn in the Spirit Layer. In my time, it was the signature ability for Crown-level. Even then, many Crown-level Skyseekers struggled to learn it."

As a reminder, I was Torch-level at that point. Above that was Hearth-level.

At Hearth-level, someone would gain improved spiritual perception and was expected to form their first spirit bond, either to another person or between two of their own Dianis Points.

I didn't have that kind of spirit perception yet, although I could approximate it by using my Star Shattering Sight. That let me get a rough idea of how to interact with spiritual things, but it wasn't ideal.

Above Hearth-level was Signet-level.

As Signet-level, someone was expected to have formed their first spirit bond. It was only at that point that someone was supposed to start forming bonds with things other than people, like objects. So . . . I guess I was ahead on that, since I'd had a spirit-bonded sword since my birth, and I was finally able to perceive and access the power in it. Unfortunately, that didn't come with any of the prerequisite knowledge.

Above that was Regalia-level.

At Regalia-level, a person was able to incorporate spirit-bonded items into their spirit, either in part or completely. Basically, that meant taking an item in the physical world and shoving it into your spirit. Once stored, you could still benefit from some of the item's passive abilities, or draw from its power directly without the object being physically present on the core plane. You could then manifest your regalia later, either partially — as a sort of spectral item that was half-present in the world — or completely, in order to use it directly.

As a simple example, if I learned how, I could eventually have stored my sword in my spirit, then pulled essence out of it to fuel my abilities without physically lugging the gigantic sword around, or potentially used its power to fuel another sword I was carrying. At higher levels of mastery, you could do some impressive things with stored regalia. A common example among the fae was walking around looking like you were wearing a simple cloth tunic, but having a suit of armor as stored regalia and still benefiting from the object's defensive magic without having it visible. If you needed the defensive power of the physical armor itself, you could manifest the regalia item at any time, or partially manifest it for a lesser benefit.

I had plans for what I wanted to do with my own regalia, but I wasn't there yet. I hadn't even practiced trying to store my sword, since I wasn't sure what exactly what would happen if I did. My weapon was an unusual case, since it was connected with me on several layers of self, and I didn't know what storing an item like that might do to my spirit.

. . . Anyway, all that is Regalia-level stuff.

And, *above* that, was Crown-level.

I wasn't even close. Most people never reached Crown-level. Even Valissar Talis himself wasn't there yet, and he was both years older than myself and a renowned prodigy.

And I was supposed to learn a technique designed for that level?

That sounded . . .

Well, it sounded like a lot of fun.

I cracked my fingers. "How do we start, Master?"

The Smiling Sword Saint looked at me intensely for a moment . . . then shrugged. I felt the mountainside shift slightly. "I have no idea. I cheated and learned aura essence when I was lower level. I never had to learn how to use spirit projection naturally."

"Then . . . what do we even start with?"

"That's simple." The Smiling Sword Saint conjured a half dozen more swords behind her. "I want you to stop these swords from hitting you."

I reached to the sword on my back.

"Without touching them."

I blinked.

". . . But I don't have an aura yet, Master."

"Right." She nodded. "This will encourage you to figure one out quickly."

I gulped.

Then, as if mocking my lack of air essence, the swords began to fly.

* * *

I don't like to be unkind to people, including myself. I think, however, it is fair to say that I was not very good at the Smiling Sword Saint's training exercise.

This is where I'd normally add some kind of dramatic turnaround phrase, like "until I realized" or "until I let go." Nothing like that happened. I stood on a sword. The Smiling Sword Saint hurled floating swords at me. I got hit. I fell off.

This went on for hours, then days.

On the plus side, I had a fantastic new source of sword essence. Without my mysterious sword absorbing all the sword essence in the entire region, I was progressing at absorbing sword essence from the environment any time I took a break, which was regularly. Even when the Smiling Sword Saint switched to blunted swords, I was still getting bruised and battered too much to maintain the exercise for a significant period of time.

I took all that essence and converted it toward my new Dianis Point, which wasn't *exactly* for sword essence. It was sword-aspected and I could convert the sword essence to feed it easily enough, but it had other applications, too. I'd been close to completing the wellspring before the last match and I was confident I could complete it before the next.

From time to time, I'd instinctively use my Rejoinder technique to defend myself before a sword actually hit me, but that was counter to the exercise's purpose. I'd avoid a cut or a bruise, but I wasn't focusing on what I was supposed to — projecting my spirit over the area to take control.

Believe me, I tried that. I tried it a hundred times while standing on a sword, a hundred more while resting. Then a hundred times while standing on a sword once again.

I tried through sheer willpower, thinking about the concept of the area being my domain. That was apparently good enough for some people, but I wasn't a prodigy at spirit manipulation—

And, in fairness to myself, I was four entire levels below where I was supposed to be for this kind of thing. I wasn't even supposed to have access to my Spirit Layer of self yet, and I certainly wasn't expected to be able to impose it on other people or places.

Nevertheless, it was a fantastic idea if I could get it to work. So, I kept trying different approaches, hoping I'd figure something out.

I tried envisioning my connection to my sword, since that was my connection to the spirit dominion. That seemed a logical connection, and when I focused inward, I could sense the specific star veins — spirit veins, technically — that were connecting the Dianis Point in my right hand to my weapon.

I could feel the strange essence flowing from my sword into my body, and when I paid close attention, I could even sense some of my own essence flowing back into the sword as well.

That was, however, about as far as the picture took me. I was trying to look through that connection like a keyhole into the spirit plane, then thinking I could somehow draw out more power through that keyhole into our world. But I couldn't get a clear enough picture to even begin that process.

At Hearth-level, I was supposed to awaken to greater spiritual awareness, much like I'd gained some awareness of my core self at Candle-level. Trying to gaze through that metaphorical keyhole at an earlier stage might have been possible, but I couldn't pull it off through sheer concentration. Not in the time I had available, at least.

Days passed as I experimented. I didn't hate the lack of progress — it gave me something to do. I wasn't focusing on this training exclusively, either.

While I wasn't permitted to use the circlet to play around in the Smiling Sword Saint's memories again yet — she hadn't prepared a new memory for me to experience, and she wanted me focused on "real" sword training for the moment — I had plenty of time to spar with Thane, and even to practice some of my other techniques more.

⊱⊱ ⊰⊰

"Just drawing and sheathing your sword over and over probably isn't the best way to work on drawing essence," Thane told me as he watched my essence-building practice.

"I'm not just doing that. I've been drawing cards out of a deck at night before bed, drawing water from a well, drawing straws—"

"Not what I meant. I was thinking that it made more sense to try to draw your sword quickly in a fight. But wait, you don't think those things are all the same, do you?"

I shrugged. "Probably. I tried drawing pictures, too, but I don't think that's right. For my own form of drawing essence, I think the concept is about 'taking one part of something out of a whole.' Drawing a card, drawing water, and drawing a sword out of a scabbard all meet that requirement."

"Why bother with something that broad instead of just drawing-aspected sword essence?"

"It's a really small efficiency difference, since my drawing essence is going to skew toward swords anyway, and I'll be able to use it with greater flexibility. I'm thinking about using it for more powerful non-sword stuff in the future. Like drawing power out of magical items."

Thane whistled in appreciation. "Not a bad idea. Still, don't get such big ideas that you forget why you were working on this in the first place."

"Don't worry, I'm still working on it for combat, too. Check your belt."

Thane blinked, instinctively reached down to his sword—

And at the same time, I reached out and grabbed the dagger off his belt, sheathing it in an empty sheath on my own side.

"Hey, that was a cheap trick!"

"Misdirection is the father of fortune." I winked at him, then unsheathed and tossed his dagger into the air toward him. And, as he looked up and caught the dagger, I used my new lunging aspect to surge forward, then grabbed the sword hilt on his belt.

"Nice try." He grabbed it at the same time, then kicked me.

I slid backward across the dirt, then cracked my neck and drew my own sword. "Shall we?"

"Finally," he mumbled.

⊱⊱ ⊰⊰

The next few days passed in a similar fashion, while I practiced drawing and sheathing things in unusual — and more typical — ways. I felt like I was making some progress on that, not just in terms of my drawing essence. As that was nearing completion, I was already forming the foundation for my next Dianis Point, too, and some technique ideas along with it.

Still, I had a clear goal, and I wasn't reaching it. So, each day, I'd go back to the Strategic Side-Step training and attempt something new.

One of my earliest near successes was an attempt to saturate the area with my own sword essence, using that as a sort of replacement for aura essence.

When I'd pushed enough essence into the air around me, and I felt a sword flying toward me, I focused on the blade and twisted that essence. For a moment, the sword trembled in midair—

Then the Smiling Sword Saint flicked a finger and the sword flashed forward, cutting a line across my arm.

I grimaced, hopping down to bind the cut. I had more bandages than clothes at this point. If Eliree had been there to help—

I pushed that thought aside, binding my wound, then walking over to the Smiling Sword Saint. "Think I almost had something there until you reasserted control over the sword."

"I *think* you almost had the foundation for a completely different technique that wouldn't have helped you. But hey, if you want to keep getting cut, sure, play with that some more."

I didn't want to keep getting cut, exactly. But I did feel like I was onto something, and so, I pushed on with that strategy for hours. Days.

A week.

Until, finally, I managed to hurl one of the Smiling Sword Saint's swords to the ground. I let out a cheer, which she deigned to allow for just a moment before a second sword tapped me on the shoulder from behind. I turned around comically slowly, then the second sword smacked me in the chest, knocking me off the sword.

"Wonderful work, my student. You've learned the fundamentals of contesting sword essence, a technique that is the foundation of what your opponent, a Sword Lord, will have absolute mastery over. In doing so, you have spent a week on doing something unrelated to the technique that you were trying to work on."

I folded my arms. "You don't think that it'll be useful to be able to fight back when my opponent is controlling all the sword essence around us?"

"Oh, it would be if you had three more years to practice it, no doubt. As it is, it's like he can throw boulders and now you can throw a rock at that boulder. It's not enough to make a difference."

I could see her skepticism, but . . . I thought I was onto something. This was the closest I'd gotten to extending my senses into the area around me and manipulating it—

Although, given what the Smiling Sword Saint had just shown me, that sense was entirely too narrow. She'd managed to get another sword to sneak up behind me, since I had focused so much of my sense forward.

. . . Could I use that against Lord Talis? Would he have the same sensory weakness?

I made a note to consider that option, but for the moment, I needed to apply what I'd learned.

"Master, will you show me the Strategic Side-Step technique again?"

She shrugged. Hills trembled and shifted. "Sure thing, kid."

It was hardly the first time I'd asked that, of course. I'd watched her demonstrate it dozens of times.

But now I tried to feel it, extending my sword essence as widely as I could as she moved from sword to sword—

It didn't help. Not one bit.

I did sense something from each sword as she moved, highlighting her starting point and destination with sword essence in a way I hadn't felt before, but it didn't get me any insight on how to actually move between them. That said, I hadn't really expected it to. It was just step one.

"Again, please, Master."

The second time, I didn't saturate the area with sword essence.

Instead, I saturated the area with my *breach* essence.

This might sound meaningless. In fact, I'd already dismissed the idea early on, because the entire area we were standing on was a breach. It was how the Smiling Sword Saint existed — we were at an area where the lines between the core plane and many other planes had been thinned by the effects of the Sepulcher of Sealed Swords. The greatest breach was between our plane and the plane of memory.

I had tried very early on in the process of watching the Smiling Sword Saint use her technique to look at it with my Star Shattering Sight, but it had been useless. The entire area was so awash with memory-aspected breach essence that I couldn't see anything related to spirit projection. Instead, I'd see an afterimage when the Smiling Sword Saint moved, showing her impact on the plane of memory.

I'd tried to play with my Star Shattering Sight a bit in terms of essence composition, too, but even skewing the aspects I used didn't give me anything meaningful. I could see the Dianis Points within the Smiling Sword Saint, sure, but that wasn't helpful. I was trying to figure out her technique, not hit her weak points.

When I saturated the area with my own breach essence, I made a critical discovery. Much like I could sense the difference between my own sword essence in the environment and that of others, I could sense the breach essence I created.

And, perhaps most importantly, I could sense when the Smiling Sword Saint moved *through* it.

When she stepped forward to activate the Strategic Side-Step, I felt my own breach essence ripple—

And just for a moment, as reality tore to allow a master to dodge the world itself, I had my keyhole.

I looked through the hole she'd torn in my own essence, and I saw into the spirit world for the first time.

There are no words to describe the beauty of that place, nor the feeling of the hairs rising on the back of my neck when I gazed beyond and felt the world itself staring back.

I'd reached an important threshold in my training when I'd manifested the breach essence across the area. Unfortunately, while that gave me a small window to glimpse at what was happening with the Smiling Sword Saint's movement, it didn't give me the slightest improvement in being able to replicate it.

Worse, saturating an area with my breach essence was exhausting. I didn't have that much of it, and while I could draw it back in for an inefficient form of essence compression, I couldn't do it frequently.

If I wanted to copy the Smiling Sword Saint, I needed a breakthrough in manifesting something similar to one of the steps in her process. Understanding each step was the first part, so I tried to break her technique down into understandable components.

Step one was simple: saturate the area with her aura. This was, I was beginning to understand, a mixture of aura essence, area essence, and the manifestation of her spirit that she was trying to get me to copy. I could project enough of my essence to cover an area and sense through it now, but it wasn't my spirit, and that was a problem. I checked, and without the spirit component to the technique, the Smiling Sword Saint couldn't make her own technique work. That was a critical bit of knowledge. The essence types gave her range, but ultimately what she was doing required spirit projection.

Step two was manifesting a set of swords and moving them to different locations, using the aura as a vehicle for their movement and control. I could manifest . . . one sword. Or, with effort, two really shoddy ones. I could not meaningfully move them outside of my grip.

Step three was dodging from one sword to the next. This utilized side-step aspected dodging essence as the mechanism for movement. The swords functioned as doorways to step through on each side. Her aura was the road between the doors.

Essentially, she was creating a pathway through the spirit plane with an opening at each sword, then stepping through and emerging in a place of her choice.

Once I understood this foundation, I could attempt to emulate it with my own meager skills.

I had three main areas I practiced for the following week.

First, arguably the largest gap in my ability to utilize the technique was that I did not have any sort of essence type designed for movement. And, while I technically had the ability to propel myself around with my current movement technique, I'd seen firsthand why that was a bad idea.

So, as a starting point to that particular problem, I followed up on the Smiling Sword Saint's words from when she'd criticized my technique before—

And I had her demonstrate lunging-aspected sword essence for me.

That, at least, was easy enough for me to understand. I could sense the essence as she used it, feel the composition, and attempt to shape it into something usable. It wasn't intuitive for me — what she called lunging-aspected essence contained a significantly greater amount of motion essence than I was used to working with, and that was a direct opposition to my preferred enhancement essence type — but I still was eventually able to batter my sword essence into a similar form.

It took a solid week before I could use it properly, but the final result was promising.

As the Smiling Sword Saint conjured a sword, I built up the new essence type in my body. Then, as she hurled the weapon, I released the built-up essence in my legs like a spring. Her sword flashed right past me as I let out a hoot, hurtling through the air toward another floating sword—

And missed it entirely, crashing into the ground.

Precision took practice. That was what I told myself, at least, as I brushed my knees off and hopped back onto another sword.

"Again."

We drilled with lunging-aspected essence for days. I fiddled with other things in the meantime, building more essence for my new Dianis Points. I also spent more time focusing on my own spirit, gazing into that keyhole.

I thought that maybe, just maybe, I could pull something through that. It felt simple to me, intuitive. But that was Regalia-level stuff, and it wasn't what we were focused on, so I didn't make it a priority.

I did practice it a little. I couldn't resist. But it wasn't my goal.

In addition, I worked on the second part of my technique building.

That was simple practice. I was training at conjuring multiple swords at once, until I could conjure two swords, then plunge them into the ground and keep them stable without physical contact from my hands. This was more difficult than it sounds. Initially, that meant maintain either an aura of sword essence over the entire area, or some kind of smaller conduit of sword essence

— like a thin ribbon of power coming from my body — to maintain the integrity of the sword while I wasn't holding on to it.

Eventually, that proved too prohibitive, so I swapped to making longer-lasting swords by emphasizing hardness-aspected essence in their composition. This would make the swords less functional as weapons, but I didn't need them as weapons at the moment.

I needed doors.

Finally, once I had two stable swords to serve as doorways, I needed a medium to travel through. I asked the Smiling Sword Saint to project her aura repeatedly, feeling the essence composition of what she was using, and then to her slight annoyance, eventually retrieved tools to actually measure it and write it down.

That took a couple days just for the trip back home for tools, but it was worth it. Once I had those measurements, I could adjust my breach essence to a more similar composition and attempt to make a road.

"So, if I end up stepping through here and get stuck on the spirit plane, you'll come get me, right?" I asked her.

"Eh," she replied.

With that wonderous bit of encouragement from my teacher, I drew my sword and brought it down, focusing breach essence through the blade.

For just a moment, I thought I saw my teacher's eyes widen as my sword ripped through reality like paper.

The gash opened just as I'd hoped, showing a visible tear into a world of strange white, like the entire thing was covered in eternal snow. Then, with a loud snap, it shut.

I blinked, turning to the Smiling Sword Saint, who was . . .

Sweating? Panting?

I had never seen her look even the slightest bit winded.

"Never," she said, "*ever* do that again."

"I . . . don't understand. I thought I was supposed to—"

"That wasn't a little breach, kid. The breach we usually sit on is a thinning, a place where the worlds are semipermeable to each other. Like there's only a thin cloth there, and if you pour water on it, some water will drip through . . . but a rock will just sit on top of the cloth. What you made? That wasn't a thin cloth. That was a *hole*."

I processed all that, and it made sense, but I still frowned. "Doesn't that just mean that it would work better for the technique? It'd be easier for me to walk through if I just—"

"Kid, if you start leaving holes in reality every time you want to dodge an attack, you're going to make this world a lot worse. You're not the only thing that can get through a hole like that. There are things *I* would hesitate to fight that could come through those holes."

". . . Okay." I still didn't fully understand, but I could see that she was . . . shaken? That was strange enough that it threw me off.

When she'd seen a vision of her rival — someone who could throw *suns* — she'd been excited, not afraid.

Death didn't scare her. That meant, logically, I'd just done something that was . . . more terrifying than that?

I tried to ponder that, but I didn't get very far. Mostly, I was disappointed.

I'd really thought that was going to work.

For the rest of the week, she watched me very, very closely, and at the time, I wasn't wise enough to understand why.

CHAPTER XXV

SEALED

I continued my training, working further on the technique, but I'd hit a bit of a blocking point when I'd been forced to abandon my whole "cut reality into bits" approach to the problem.

Three weeks later, I was bleeding, broken, and bruised.

That is to say, I was feeling much better.

It wasn't a straight line. Life, I found, rarely offered recovery in straight lines. But I wasn't punishing myself for my loss as much as I had, nor was I stuck obsessing over what I was — or what I wasn't. Or why the one I'd assumed to be my father hadn't wanted me born.

It still wasn't easy, but working through the routine of practicing a new technique was familiar. That familiarity gave me purpose, even if it was a purpose I manufactured for myself, rather than the one I had been made for. Ultimately, it didn't matter what any parent, real or fake, had wanted. I had my own goals, my own desires, and my own methods of achieving them.

I still had a duel to win, and only two more chances to do it. Worse, if I lost in this particular round, Lord Valissar Talis would have the two victories out of three he needed to claim the contest to be over. I couldn't allow that.

Three weeks wasn't enough time to adapt the Strategic Side-Step, but it was enough time that I'd managed to shake myself out of my depressive state a bit. And, with my mind in a clearer place, I could come back to the Strategic Side-Step later. I had unfinished business of a variety of other kinds to deal with, and I hoped that by taking a break and addressing those things, I'd get into a better place for working on the technique as well.

The first was closure.

I found Red training with Grey, who I'd neglected a bit over recent months. His own skill level wasn't improving as much as mine, which I expected to be a combination of his nature as a spirit of memory resisting change, and perhaps the fact that he was still much younger than I was. And, of course, I had unfair advantages — the Smiling Sword Saint's training on top of Red's, as well as my own sword and essence giving me power.

I made a mental note to spend more time training with him once I had a chance, but for the moment, Red was who I was looking for. I waited for them to finish their training round, then I approached Red to talk.

"Hey, hon. You're looking a little more yourself. Feeling better?" she asked.

It helped that someone asked that. As much as the Smiling Sword Saint was a wonderful teacher in some ways, emotional support wasn't in her skill set. "Getting there. I think I'm ready to keep reading."

She nodded, thoughtfully. "Where'd you find it?" she asked.

I paused. Once again, I was concerned about telling her too much about things outside the school — they all thought *I* was the one who was a ghost, and I was worried about the possible repercussions of them finding out the truth. On the other hand, she had apparently already read things in the journal about herself . . . which was partially why I was here.

"In my friend's temple," I said, and quickly moved on. "And . . . I'm realizing that I've been unfair to her. I've got a duel coming up, and I wasn't taking it seriously enough. I have limited time, and I shouldn't be spending it all translating. Can I have your translation?"

"Of course." She put a hand on my shoulder. "I'm proud of you."

I flinched. "Don't be proud of me. I haven't won any matches yet."

"You shouldn't need to win for someone to be proud of you. Sometimes it's important for people to support you just for who you are, you know. And I see your effort."

I didn't really understand her or believe her at the time. But there was something important about that message that I'd need to learn, eventually. Not for myself, not entirely. But to unlearn what I'd taught myself through a life of competition, and the impacts it would have on my relationships with others.

She went and found her own translation, then handed it over to me. "This is just the next section. I'm still working on the last one."

"That's fine — it will help. Thank you."

"Sure thing. And if you want to talk about it, I'm here."

On that, at least, I believed her. And that made things just a little easier, too.

I sat down with the book in front of me. A bit tattered from being hurled, but still very much intact.

I had Red's notes alongside mine, as well as the next part of the translation, completed in Red's flowing script.

Red had used some of my own pen and parchment to continue it. I wondered if she'd known that it would vanish if she'd used materials from the sword school, or if she'd simply continued from where I'd started out of convenience.

Or perhaps to make it feel like we'd done it together. Maybe she'd known what that would mean to me.

Breathe, I told myself.

I'd steeled my resolve to read more and learn. I couldn't deal with another delay. And so, I lifted the pages, and began to read.

I am not known for giving in to fear. There are times, however, when responding to fear is the only rational approach.

It was a stark opening to the next segment, one that struck a tone I had not expected. I continued.

When I realized that the spirit of the Dominion Breaker was developing self-awareness, I had to consider the possibilities.

If the sword developed a consciousness, how would that manifest? Would any spirit that emerged simply assist the wielder, like some rudimentary intelligences were designed to function in conjunction with a master?

I doubted I should be so fortunate.

No, this was a worldmaker-class weapon. To even call it that was to understate the significance of the sword's abilities — no worldmaker could wield it, after all. It was in a class of its own.

Any spirit that awakened would likely be formed from the experiences of those who had held the sword over the years. Those who had drawn the sword out of desperate necessity, each of us failing in our own ways.

If I was a more arrogant man, perhaps I would have assumed that, as the sword's most recent wielder — and perhaps the one who had wielded it longest, interacted with it most — that the emergent entity's spirit would be shaped by my own.

I could ill afford such an assumption. I was one of several who had held the blade, and I could not discount the possibility that the sword's personality and motivations would more closely mirror those of another wielder — including, perhaps, my greatest enemy.

And even that would be a mercy compared to what I truly feared.

A weapon forged with the essence to utterly annihilate anything? What if, like a fire elemental is born with the desire to spread its flames, the spirit of the sword sought to unmake all of reality?

In such a scenario, who could possibly stop it?

I paused, frowning. I could understand, rationally, why one might fear that a newborn spirit would be shaped by the essence of the object that gave it life. But it felt so reductive to assume that annihilation was the core of the sword's purpose.

Perhaps I was operating under my own biases. The writer of that book understood the sword better than I did . . . didn't he?

Could the God of Swords had made a mistake?

Or was it more that he simply feared the mere *possibility* that the presence of that essence would influence the spirit's thoughts?

If that was the case . . .

Could I truly blame him for wanting to prevent that?

What was the *right* degree of fear about an entity that could prove a risk to the entire world? What was the right approach when faced with such a possibility?

I had no easy answers. And, as I read further, it would seem that even a god had no simple solution to offer.

My first response was to delay.

Stasis magic was not my greatest area of strength, but I knew of the great stasis pools utilized by the Warders of the Buried. Immersing the sword in such a pool might destroy the water. I studied the water, then moved on, remembering an area near where I had once trained that contained ancient swords sealed for safety. In that place, I built a platform designed to hold the blade, drawing on a variety of tools and techniques to attempt to delay what was happening.

The concept proved sound, but there was a problem — anything I used to attempt to seal the sword was drained to uselessness in seconds. The sword's power was simply too vast for a simple ritual circle to contain, even when powered by dozens of conventional essence-storage crystals.

I turned toward finding alternate power sources, eventually coming to the conclusion that there was an available resource that I was not drawing upon—

After all, no one else was making use of the swords in the prison above.

I nodded along with the ending of that segment. This part of the story made sense, at least, and conformed to my expectations. The God of Swords had repurposed the sealed weapons of the sepulcher to power a single seal — one designed to suppress the very sword I now carried.

But that obviously was not the end. It was only the beginning of something new.

For years, I kept the sword sealed in that place, studying it further. It was during that time that I realized that I had a responsibility to watch over the weapon, ensuring it was never taken and used until a solution had been found.

All that time, my great enemy had grown in strength, as had his children. I had ignored their threat for as long as I could — left to their own devices, I feared they would conquer Mythralis, and then the world itself.

I could not allow that, but neither could I face my great enemy on equal terms without the sword. Truthfully, I could not face him on equal terms even with it — he had grown too strong.

There was a temptation to throw caution aside and draw the sword, allowing it to awaken and leaving the sword's nature to fate.

But fate was my opponent's game, his power. I could not allow it to guide my decisions.

And so, I left the sword sealed away behind many layers of defenses, knowing I could not abandon the blade long. The danger was too great — I would watch it for eternity if I had to.

But first, I needed someone to take my place. A worthy successor. Someone who could, perhaps, turn the tide of fate without the sword.

I searched for many years before I found her.

My apprentice, forgive me.

Your burden was too much for anyone to carry.

CHAPTER XXVI

SURVIVOR

I set the book aside briefly, returning to my training, but I was too distracted to get much out of it.

For a time, I watched the others at the sword school. Red was leading them in a different routine than usual, and from time to time, she'd come by and invite me to join them as she always did. I waved her off, of course, and she was always polite about accepting my boundaries. It wasn't that I was uninterested, I just wanted to think for a moment.

This, I considered, *is the first apprentice. The successor to the God of Swords.*

And I watched her die to an assassin's blade.

I'd avoided processing it for a while. I still hadn't talked to her about it. But there was something important there, about watching one of my own teachers die and feeling—

Not what Aendaryn had. Not enough, perhaps.

Was there something wrong with me, that I wasn't making elaborate plans for revenge against the Blackstone Assassin?

Or was it simply that Red wasn't truly the same person as the one in the book?

Was it that Red and I hadn't had the kind of emotional closeness that we were moving toward when I'd seen her death scene?

Or . . . was it that I simply didn't have enough of the picture?

There was so much to all this that I still didn't understand. I couldn't process it without more of the picture.

I needed closure. And so, after a brief workout and a meal, I returned to the book.

She was everything I could have hoped for in a student. A true talent, with the best combination of instinct, discipline, and dedication I had ever come across. I often wondered if Therin had felt similarly about me when she had discovered me. I wondered, too, if I could have beaten my apprentice at her own age, with similar training.

My uncertainty about those very questions gave me assurance that I had chosen the right champion to pick up my cause.

For seven years, I would train her. There was to be a grand tournament in my homeland, one where a child of my enemy would compete. My champion would defeat him, and in doing so, declare that she had taken my place in the great saga that my predecessor had begun.

And then I would depart the world to study the sword, for as long as it took to find the answers I needed.

A year into our training, I returned home to find a second apprentice. Apparently, my apprentice had picked her up somewhere in the mountains.

This would become an alarming, yet ultimately endearing, trend.

I wasn't sure it was wise to bring a teenager into our agenda at first, but upon meeting Wrynn and learning her circumstances, I quickly realized that it was at least superior to the alternatives. And, in spite of my initial reservations about disrupting our training regimen, it turned out that my first apprentice learned even more quickly when teaching others than she did from my instruction. I'd like to hope that's not a commentary on my training quality and more a measure of her own skill and character.

Wrynn had different talents than ours, but that had its uses. Her strengths were, it seemed, more akin to those of my great enemy . . . and that had its uses in training.

Wrynn's gifts of shade and spirit were not the same as the vae dominion, but her ability to absorb the magic and techniques were the closest facsimile I had seen to a vae'kes. By training against her, my first apprentice would learn how to deal with such an opponent.

I never expected Wrynn to master my own style. I was shocked by the amount that she learned — and pleased.

Perhaps this plan had some chance of success after all.

I took them around the world, teaching them of each region and the powers there. As they grew older, however, I gave them more space to themselves. Both to allow my apprentices to grow in my absence and because I knew that I had left my other responsibility for too long.

While my apprentices trained in my absence, I continued my studies of the sword. I began to make further changes, experimenting with what might keep the sword stable and render it usable.

I set the book aside, glancing toward the sword school. Fade caught my gaze, gave a comical gasp, then reached up to cover her chest as if she was scandalized by my leering.

I gave her an exaggerated wink. She pretended to faint dead away.

I held my head in my hands and laughed.

Allow me to introduce Wrynn Jaden, the legendary Witch of a Thousand Shadows.

I pushed myself to my feet, setting the book aside, and went over to pick her up.

"Dying . . ." she mumbled. "Wink . . . too strong. Need . . . immediate . . . resuscitation . . ."

I kissed her on the forehead.

Her eyes fluttered open. "Gasp! How forward of you, to make such advances on a young and innocent lady such as myself!"

She actually said, "Gasp," by the way. After her brief speech, she rubbed her nose against mine. I laughed and pulled her to her feet.

"So strong! So manly! I may just faint again."

"Maybe hold off on that, you're already covered in dust," I told her.

"You're right. I *could* use a good bath." She shook her head. "A shame you can't join me, what with ghosts being unable to cross running water and all."

"I'm like . . . ninety percent sure that isn't a thing."

She patted me on the shoulders. "They say that memory is the first thing to go when you're a ghost. Alas. But don't worry, out of pity for your incredibly sad condition, I'll let you work up a sweat with me before I take a bath."

"Are ghosts supposed to sweat?" I asked.

"Let's find out."

Then she jabbed me with a hidden knife and my day got a lot better.

Sparring with Fade — I knew she was likely a young version of the famous Wrynn Jaden now, but she was still Fade to me — did work up a sweat for both of us, but in spite of her obvious flirtations, Fade vanished to go bathe on her own.

After that, I went and spent some time practicing with Red. While I ate and recovered, we talked.

"Finished with my translation?" she asked.

"Not quite," I said. "I got distracted by Wrynn."

She laughed quietly. "Figured her out, hm?"

"I mean, she was the second apprentice. And Green said you were the first, so . . ."

"I was," she agreed. There was something in her tone that gave me pause, though. After a moment, I had it — it was how she'd said "was." Not "am."

"Sounds like he had a lot of respect for you," I said, trying to break the silence.

"Yeah," Red said, "that part was never in doubt."

I raised an eyebrow. "Kind of a loaded response, there."

"Wasn't meant to be," she said, a frown visible even in spite of the blur of her face. "It's just . . . things were complicated."

I blinked. "Wait, were you and he . . ."

I made a particular gesture with my hands.

She stared dead at me for a minute, and I got the impression she was completely taken aback. "Ah . . . *never* do that again."

"You clearly haven't been paying attention to Wrynn if something that minor gets to you."

"It's not about that," she said, recovering her usual composure. "It's weird coming from someone who looks like him."

". . . I look like him?"

"A little. Like . . . an artist's rendering of him, maybe? Not like a good one."

"Oh, wonderful. I'm a bad portrait of a god now."

"Not what I meant, sorry." Red shook her head hastily. "Like, you look normal. Like an ordinary person. It's just that your similarities to him — they're less like family, and more . . ."

"Like a poor reproduction. Yeah, I get that." I tried not to sound how I actually felt about that. I failed completely.

"No, I was going to say . . ." She sighed. "Like someone was trying to draw him from a childhood memory. Beautiful, but without all the details. And there's more than that. I don't think you're all . . . inspired by him. It's more like . . . you've got features from all your other ancestors, too, I think."

I nodded more slowly.

I . . . didn't hate that.

Especially because it meant I was *less* like him. The man who wouldn't be my father.

"Let's talk less about that. More about . . . what was he to you?" I asked.

"My teacher," she said, firmly. "And my friend."

I nodded. "And . . . ?" I didn't make the gesture again, but I tried to imply it with my expression.

"I'm not going to have this conversation with someone who's practically his child."

That was still too close to home, as it were, and I winced.

"I'm *not* his child."

Something in Red's demeanor softened, enough to make me want to explain more.

"I thought I was, for a while. His and Kara's. But that's not possible, if she died when he said she did."

Red looked away, toward the shed I'd made my little shelter.

"Yeah," she said. "About that."

I blinked.

"Keep reading." She gestured toward the shed. "She turned out to be a little less dead than expected."

I blinked.

". . . What?"

⊱ ⊰

I had very mixed feelings about the journal, but Red's approach had worked. I couldn't hear a story hook like that and not pick it back up.

So, I steadied myself as best I could, then sat down in a quiet spot in the shadow of a massive tree to read the next segment.

It happened at the worst possible time.

My first apprentice had nearly finished her training. A new threat was looming on the horizon — someone had begun to summon extradimensional beings to conquer the continent, and we were preparing to battle them. I hoped to bring all my power to bear to stop the invasion before it could truly take hold.

I went to talk to my apprentices, to prepare for us to leave.

Then, I sensed her.

Kara. She was weak, and she was far away, but . . . I was certain it was her.

At first, I thought it was a trick, or a trap.

And so, when I met with my apprentices, I had something different to tell them—

My first apprentice told me she had something to tell me, too, but let me speak first. And so, I told her the news.

Kara was alive. Or, at least, she seemed to be. And I needed to leave, to find her right away.

I had some sense of what my first apprentice was going to tell me.

As I said, it was the worst possible time. And not just because of the threats to the safety of the world.

And so, I simply told her that I needed to go, and that she could tell me the next time we saw each other.

I'd underestimated her bravery, the very characteristic that was rapidly becoming synonymous with her name. Somehow, even after all these years, I'd missed something critical.

I won't write down what she told me. It was something I'd long known, but that was never supposed to be a part of our story. There was little time to discuss it, less time to process.

I felt like a coward, her very opposite, but I had to go.

I left her with one last gift. A sword that I'd forged for her, one worthy of the God of Swords. A blade that shined with the light of the sun. It was my greatest creation, one I hoped would serve her for her entire life.

It wasn't finished, in truth. I'd planned to add a crystal to the pommel, an Empyrean relic held by one of my companions. There were so many stories of the seven Empyrean treasures—

I think we could have spent a lifetime searching for them all. Perhaps a better life.

But we'd never found the time to quest for the others. There was always another disaster.

Wrynn assured me that they'd take care of the invasion without me. In truth, I'd almost forgotten it. Nothing else felt important. Kara was alive, and I was going to find her.

I set the journal down, thinking of the latest twist.

Well, Karasalia being alive would have been a helpful thing to learn when I was still hoping she was my mother. Now, I'm just more confused about the way things turned out, but . . . I might be able to get an answer to one thing, at least.

I went back to Red, pointing at a segment of the journal. "What did you tell him?"

She gave me a sad smile. "I didn't tell him anything. Whatever happens there, it's in my future. Or the future of my other self."

She had obviously figured some things out, but I had too much on my mind to switch topics.

"But you must know, right?" I folded my arms. "It doesn't sound like it's a surprise to him, either."

"It's . . . I could speculate. But I won't. There's no point."

"Even still . . ." I frowned, then I saw the complexity of her expression. And, on that rare occasion, I realized it was time to drop a specific line of a topic. Still, the story was with me, and I couldn't ignore the rest. "He was a jerk," I said. "He left you to fight a war without him."

"Yeah." She shook her head. "I hate it when people do that."

I raised an eyebrow. "You make it sound like that's happened more than once."

Red laughed. "Life can be surprisingly complicated. People can be, too."

"Do you forgive him?" I asked.

She was silent for a minute, then shrugged at me. "I don't know. Do you forgive him for . . . trying not to let you wake up?"

I took a breath.

I had a lot more context, now. His actions were rational. Reasonable, even. They . . . weren't a betrayal. Not really. Because at the time he'd taken them, I hadn't really even existed. Not as a fully conscious being, at least.

Could you betray someone that hadn't yet been born?

"I don't know, either," I concluded.

"That's okay." She reached out for my hand, taking it and squeezing it. "Sometimes there aren't any easy answers."

"Yeah." I took a breath. "How do you deal with the uncertainty?"

"I'm not a philosopher," she told me. "So I deal with it the same way I deal with life's other big problems."

"Swords?" I asked her.

"No. Gods, you have such a one-track mind." Red laughed. "Friends, Edge. I get by because I have *friends*."

CHAPTER XXVII

SUPPORT

I'd like to say that I had some sort of magical epiphany after reading more of the journal and talking to Red about the contents. Nothing like that happened.

Instead, I simply went back with some of my injuries healed, a better frame of mind, and a few new ideas that I'd considered.

I hadn't slacked on my general training while visiting Red, of course, and I was further along with practicing conjuring multiple swords at once, as well as my general sword work. I'd been able to absorb more sword and breach essence while at the sword school, too, so my general power was improving.

I could have rushed my essence consumption and pushed it toward primary essence to try to hit Hearth as quickly as possible, but I didn't think that was a good decision for my overall career. There were always reasons to rush toward a higher form of power. If I made that kind of decision early on in my career, I'd likely be doing the same thing over and over and sacrificing long-term power and stability in the process. So, I maintained a balanced approach, crunching numbers carefully.

If I played my cards just right, hopefully I'd get what I needed without needing to sacrifice my overall strength in the process.

Enough time had passed when I reached the Smiling Sword Saint's school that she seemed a little impatient to see what I'd come up with.

"Go on." She waved a hand. "Distract me."

I showed her the best thing I'd managed to come up with while I was away: I conjured a pair of swords and anchored them in place as doors.

Then, I raised a single hand.

Breach Blade.

My hand flashed with a combination of sword and breach essence — a slight variant on my usual Sword Hand technique, but one that carefully excluded the essence from my sword.

And, ever so slowly, I brought it down and cut a window between worlds.

The Smiling Sword Saint watched carefully. I'd studied my books while I was gone, and while the effect of what I was accomplishing with the Breach Blade technique appeared visually similar to what my sword had done, they were significantly different.

Going back to the Smiling Sword Saint's "cloth and water" analogy, if my personal sword had cut a hole in the cloth, the Breach Blade was *folding* it, creating a point of focus and weakness. Visually, it looked to me like I was tearing a hole because I could see energy passing through that weakness, but the distinction was that the cloth-like fabric between realities would unstretch very quickly, fixing itself. It wasn't truly doing any damage, nor was it creating a great enough weakness for some sort of powerful spirit entity to run through.

Beyond that, I'd also realized that a critical part of what the Smiling Sword Saint had mentioned about my sword's damage was that it wasn't just cutting into the plane of spirits — the strange sealed sword dealt damage across several planar boundaries at the same time. With breach essence, I could target a single plane at a time, simply emphasizing the effect of the existing breaches very briefly.

My new technique was, in many respects, much like how humans had breaches inside their own bodies that connected to other planes. Those weren't tearing holes in reality while we walked — they were thin layers in realities, not gashes.

Anyway, the Smiling Sword Saint nodded in approval, showing none of the fear or dismay she had with my other technique. That was wonderful.

The problem was that making a person-sized fold with my Breach Blade technique took me about five minutes of slowly pulling my conjured weapon downward, then it repaired itself before I could even walk to the other sword to create a second fold.

"It's a good idea," the Smiling Sword Saint noted, "for someone who is, let's say, five levels above you and already able to use their spirit projection to supplement the technique. Making it, you know . . ."

"Useless." I sighed. "Yeah. Back to theory crafting, I guess."

"Hey, it's not so bad!" I jumped at the sound. The Smiling Sword Saint's face showed more alarm than I'd ever seen as swords flashed into existence surrounding . . . a talking log on the side of the arena?

But that voice . . .

There was a poof of smoke as Fade appeared, hands immediately going up in surrender. "So this is where you've been cheating on me and training with someone else! And an older woman, no less!"

The Smiling Sword Saint's eyes narrowed. A tornado of swords narrowed around Fade along with their movement.

"Woah, hold on." I stepped between them. "Master, this is Fade. I've told you about her. She's—"

"My apprentice's *other* apprentice." She wrinkled her nose. The swords retreated just slightly. "You've been watching us in secret?"

"Only for a little." Fade folded her legs in front of her. "And it's not like I'm stealing techniques. I'm technically from your own sword school, you know, Saint Sensei."

"How'd you get through the mist?" I asked.

"What mist?" She blinked. "Oh, you mean the whole thing where reality frays and starts to come apart on the way up the mountainside? Does that look like mist to you?"

". . . Yes?"

"Huh. To me, it looks more like I imagined the afterlife to look, but if time was broken and I was really, really high. So, I navigated it the same way I'd navigate that."

". . . You closed your eyes?" I asked.

"Ooh, good guess, but no! I followed that guy." She pointed at where Thane was hiding behind a tree. "He's been sneaking out to watch our sword school for a while. I thought he was just a run-of-the-mill ghost that was trying to see my underclothes like you, Edge. But after a little while, I realized he was a special ghost that was trying to see that!"

I looked to a cringing Thane, then back to Fade. "I *genuinely* don't know who should be more insulted right now."

"Have my apprentices been behaving inappropriately with you?" The Smiling Sword Saint's blades flashed away from Fade, moving into the air around Thane and myself.

Fade blanched, her usual humor vanishing as the swords moved. "Wait, wait. Sorry, sorry! Wasn't making a real accusation, I'm just teasing. To the best of my knowledge, neither of them has stolen a peek even once." She paused, groaning. "Nor have they even taken one when it's been implied to be available."

"Oh. You're just being children." The swirling swords vanished, and I breathed a sigh of relief. "Good. In my school, taking advantage of anyone without consent is punished severely. If you're consenting . . ." She shrugged, the mountainside shifting. "You're a little young for it. Just make sure no one gets pregnant."

I found this line of conversation a little awkward and unsettling, but at least the danger seemed to be gone.

"Can ghosts get people pregnant?!" Fade's cheerful smile returned, along with a mock gasp and a hand coming up to slowly cover her mouth. "Teacher, please explain!"

. . . On second thought, it was possible the danger had simply *changed*.

Sword training over the next few days was . . . strange. The dynamic at the Smiling Sword Saint's arena had shifted considerably with Fade present, but I had to admit, it actually helped.

Not in an "I found encouragement from a flirtatious girl" sort of way. I suspected that Fade was largely teasing, even then, and I didn't think she was actually interested in me like that. Even if she was, I was too busy to think about it.

Her presence helped because, now that she was outside the school, she was willing to talk to me about her own experience with essence—

And her skill set was a lot closer to my own than I'd suspected. And a lot more, hmm, how do I put this . . .

Overpowered?

"So, in conclusion," Fade finished explaining to me, "my spirit art dedication allows me to copy spirit arts from other dedications."

"That's the most absurd thing I've ever heard. You can copy other powers?"

"Yep!" She clasped her hands together. "They run on my dedication's power, though, and they're less effective than the original. I also can only absorb so many powers at once, or my soul ker-klunks."

"Ker-klunks?"

"That's a technical term for it exploding into a million pieces, dooming me and all of the universe."

"Oh, right. Ker-klunks. I'm sure I have that in a book somewhere." I nodded.

"Definitely should be." Fade nodded vigorously. "Anyway, one of the first techniques I learned was teleportation-adjacent, and it's pretty similar to what you're using. It involves moving from one coin to another in a matched set."

"Huh. Coins are so small . . . you're saying that the doorway doesn't have to be proportionate in size to the object you're using as an anchor?"

"Right! Although I think my coins are making a doorway that is person-sized for me to go through. So, you could reduce the size of your conjured swords, but not the thing where you're focusing the breach."

". . . Which is the hard, time-consuming part."

"Yep! But, hear me out . . . that's only if you're trying to move a person."

I blinked. "I mean, I'm working on a movement technique. What else would I move?"

Fade came very close to me, hand to her chest. "Search yourself, Ghost Edge. What have you been trying to steal this entire time?"

"I'm not making a technique for stealing pants, Fade."

"But what if it was for something . . . pants-adjacent?"

⁂

Weeks passed as I worked on refining my somewhat dubious new technique with the Smiling Sword Saint, Thane, and Fade.

Fade was able to move from place to place now. Thane could, too, and apparently had been for a while. They'd grown beyond the boundaries of the breaches where they'd been born—

And that meant, I knew, that the Smiling Sword Saint could eventually leave, too.

I tried not to think on that eventuality too much. Instead, I refined my technique, and welcomed the fact that now Fade and Thane could walk me to and from the sword school and the arena.

A few weeks in, Fade insisted on introducing Thane to Red, Green, and Grey. That embarrassed him to no end, but Red pretty much adopted him instantly. He clearly didn't know how to handle that, but he stuck around there more and more once he was known to them.

Eventually, I had to bid goodbye to all of them. It was nearly time for my next duel. If my friends could move beyond the limits that existence had imposed upon them, I could move beyond the hesitation in my own mind.

With a day to spare, I made a detour. Not to train or improve my skills further.

The God of Swords may not have truly been my father, nor the Goddess of Protection my mother. It had hurt to hear that, to think on it, but that hadn't been the most important thing I'd learned from my experience. Not the most impactful.

No, when I'd read through the story of a god, the thing that struck me the hardest was his regrets.

Regrets about not having the adventures he wanted. Not letting go of the things he wanted to let go of. And not saying the important things that needed to be said.

I'd learned a great deal from my three months of training, but I think I'd learned something more important from that story.

I stopped by a tree. Not one I'd seen before, but one I'd taken the time and effort to finally ask about.

A tree with bark as dark as night and leaves the color of moonlight, faintly glowing as they rustled in the breeze. The tree was a young one, by the standards of my colossal forest home, but already towering in height and vitality. It stood at the very edge of a cliffside, with a single massive stone in the ground in front of it. It was a breathtaking sight—

And so was she, silhouetted by her own true tree.

"Hey, Elle." I took a few steps closer. "Sorry it took me so long. Can we have a talk?"

Her expression was a complicated combination of confusion and hurt. "About the duel?"

"No," I told her. "About us."

"Okay." She patted the ground next to her tree. "We can talk."

And so, we did.

Too much of that was too personal to share. But we spoke of our first meeting, of our present day, of our futures. Of our goals, shared and different.

And we understood, then, as we spoke, the growing gap between us. The unspoken distance, rendered suddenly visible.

I wanted to see the world. To grow strong enough to learn the full truth about myself. To have adventures.

She wanted a home. A people to belong to. Someone to settle down with.

These were not fundamentally incompatible goals, perhaps, in the long term . . . but we were teenagers. And, in that night, even as we sat side by side, the shining stars above us felt less distant.

And so, with tears in our eyes, we clutched hands—

And we broke up.

It had been a long time coming, by the standards of children.

But when I left, I knew we'd done something important. *I'd* done something important. I'd talked to her, shared my true feelings, and she'd done the same.

And though I lost my first love in speaking the truth to her, I gained something far more important.

In breaking up that night, I truly believe we saved our friendship. One that remains strong to this very day.

When I walked down that mountainside alone at night, it was cold, but I warmed myself with a cloak that Eliree had gifted to me for my journey. I could always sense a bit of her within it, and on that night, that didn't hurt as much as it once had.

When the next day came, and I faced her across the table, it would hurt a little less than it had the last time. And it would hurt less and less every time, until eventually, the hurt was gone, and only the warmth remained.

CHAPTER XXVIII

SECOND

The formalities were largely the same for the second round. We discussed the possibility of ending the conflict, but neither of us was prepared to back down.

And so, it came to a discussion of the challenges.

There were multiple strategies I could use this time, just as the last. I could have focused on trying to preserve my remaining refusals for the last round, but the truth was simple—

I needed a win or the contest would end here. Unfortunately, my opponent knew that.

I didn't like the idea of making suggestions that would feel like automatic wins for me. It wasn't precisely honorable, nor did it feel particularly clever. But this contest wasn't about my honor or cleverness — it was about someone else's freedom. And for that, I'd make whatever choices I needed to.

Valissar had the right to propose the first trial this time, and so, I listened. "For this round, a trial true. Of words spoken and great deeds we'll do, under wise judges' purview."

I'd actually considered something like a literal trial, too. There definitely were advantages to a contest of speaking — in particular, at least two of the judges probably wanted me to win, and as long as I didn't make critical mistakes, I think they'd start out predisposed toward helping me. This was especially true in the second round, since faerie culture tended to skew toward classical storytelling in contests, and giving me a win in the second round would make the story of our duel more interesting.

On the other hand, that same narrative focus among the fae could skew toward a *draw*, allowing for the possibility of the third round being my win and the entire contest being a draw. In some ways, that could work to my advantage, if it resulted in an extra contest and more time to train . . . but I didn't want a draw at this stage.

And I also didn't trust my speaking ability to match someone who had at least one type of essence dedicated toward speech. I still didn't know exactly why he was speaking in rhyming language, but if he had any sort of speech-oriented power, I didn't want him to have the chance to use that to skew our contest. I didn't have any reasonable countermeasures to it. The closest would have probably been attempting to use a Cutting Remark as a counter, but I wasn't confident I could do that, and it very likely would be considered a violation of contest rules even if I managed it.

So, all in all, it was a fair contest to propose, but I refused. "I'll pass."

"Very well, then." Ana spoke for the judges. "That's a refusal for you, for a total of two. What do you propose?"

"A test of knowledge of Ana, the faerie born of the sword Anathema. She is, after all, central to the goal of the contest."

Ana blushed furiously. "Tha . . . that . . . okay, now . . ."

It was a contest that was stacked in my favor, to be certain. And one that, from her reaction, Ana clearly wasn't going to be entirely comfortable with—

But like I said, I needed a win. Or at a minimum to cut down his rejections for the future.

"A clever test of purpose wise, your time well spent to it devise. With more time spent, perhaps such I'd choose, but as it is, I must refuse."

Ana breathed an audible sigh of relief. "And that would be a clear refusal for Lord Valissar Talis, for a total of two. He may choose the next proposal."

Lord Talis nodded. Lord Oloris leaned over and whispered something to him. He blinked, then laughed. "My friend is wise, and liked your test. A novel thought, he does suggest. This time I'll pass, at his behest."

I blinked.

Could he . . . pass?

That would allow him to hold on to more refusals for the next round, rather than being stuck in the back-and-forth rotation.

In short, it ruined my plans.

"Judges, is passing an option?"

The judges took a moment to confer.

After a few minutes, Ana spoke about the decision. "There was nothing in the rules to prevent it. Thus, yes, absolutely, he does not need to propose the next challenge. You may also choose to pass. If you do, we have determined that the judges will determine the contest."

I turned to Darryl and Rusty. ". . . What do you think?"

"The judges want to help you," Rusty noted, "both because of your status here, and because you lost the last round. A judge-determined contest will likely skew at least slightly in your favor. However . . ." She glanced at Darryl.

"It won't necessarily be enough." He shook his head. "No, you've gotta win this one."

"Even though it'll potentially give him an advantage in refusals for next time?"

Darryl nodded. "Even so."

"Rusty?" I asked.

"We're in agreement. You need a contest under your terms now more than you need it later."

". . . Okay." I nodded, turning to Lord Talis. "I propose we flip a coin." I produced a coin from my bag. "This coin. Lord Talis may call his expected side right before the coin is flipped. When it lands, the symbol on the top face determines who wins."

I placed the coin on the table. Lord Talis reached down and picked it up immediately, examining it, then passed it to Lord Oloris, and finally to Eliree.

"A coin of mundane make and mark, without a hint of magic spark." Lord Talis frowned, taking the coin and hefting it in his hand again, flipping it from side to side. "Only a hint uneven weight, not enough to change its fate."

"That is to say we're a bit surprised," Lord Oloris said. "It seems like an ordinary human coin, albeit one from a place I'm not familiar with."

"It is. Just a bit of currency from the Velthryn region on the continent of Mythralis. Sword on one side of the coin, shield on the other."

"Then, what's the contest? Pure destiny to determine the victor?" Oloris asked. "Or did you want to toss the coin, perhaps relying on the slightly greater weight on one side to improve your odds?"

"Oh, no. One of the judges can toss the coin, and I don't expect to leave this to chance." I cracked my knuckles. "I didn't say we couldn't *interfere* with the coin — we just have to wait until it's tossed."

Lord Talis laughed. "A challenge made with purpose clear. A coin we'll flip, its top face steer."

"The challenge is accepted," Ana declared. "On the morrow, you will duel."

In the aftermath of the challenge discussion, Lord Talis and his retinue left the glade. The judges departed, too, save for Ana. Darryl and Rusty exchanged goodbyes with me, then headed off to do their own preparations for the challenge.

I didn't know exactly how they hoped to help me with a coin-flip challenge, but we'd all figure something out.

"So . . ." Ana floated over to me. "A coin?"

I nodded. "Yep."

"Lien, I don't want to ask, but . . . are you taking this seriously?"

I sighed. "I may owe you an apology for leaving as quickly as I did last time. I . . . wasn't doing great. But that's because this means a lot to me, and I don't like the idea of failing you. I have been training all this time, working hard to help you."

"That's great and all, but . . . I'm your friend, too, Lien. If you're having a tough time with this . . ."

"I'd talk to you about it more, but you're one of the judges. Not only would it be inappropriate, I think it genuinely could be a disadvantage if I tell you too much in advance."

"You don't trust me to be objective?" she asked. Not sounding quite offended, but simmering right at the border of it.

"It's not that. I don't trust that there aren't trees, or leaves, or celestial objects watching us right now."

She blinked. "Oh. Yeah, okay, that part makes sense. We could just go chat in the dungeon, then. Much harder to scry on that."

"Wait, what? I'm definitely not allowed to continue work on your dungeon during the competition, Ana. That's, like . . . the whole challenge."

"Of course not, silly! You're specifically not allowed to get any further in my challenges. You could, however, work your way backward a little and talk to me."

". . . Huh. Would that change the place I start when I resume your challenge later?"

Ana shrugged. "It might, it might not. I haven't decided. But I do think it'd be a good idea for us to talk to each other, even if it's just about friend stuff. It's been months, Lien, and I'm worried about you."

"I do have a plan for the coin."

"Uh-huh. Not what I meant. I mean, it's part of what I meant, but . . ."

"Fine, fine." I took a breath. "You're really sure it's okay for me to go in there?"

"Sure. Only fair. Lord Talis has been in the dungeon training almost every day."

". . . Huh. I probably should have been thinking more about that. How's his training going?"

"That's the type of thing I shouldn't tell you, as a judge."

"Okay." I nodded. "Let's go inside."

Ana flapped her way to the door and opened it.

I stared at the entryway of that gigantic tree. It was . . . a thing of great significance to me. Symbolic for passage through my life, and my freedom. It felt strange to walk in for a casual conversation.

Fortunately, that wasn't what was happening.

Ana dropped all pretense of her motivation the moment I appeared inside, within the same crystalline room where I'd left.

"Follow me," she said. "I need your help with something."

I blinked. "In your own dungeon?"

I spent the rest of the day doing dubious things in a dungeon with my dear . . . what's a d-word for friend? "Darling" feels a little off . . .

Disaster. That fits Ana a lot better.

Anyway, my dear disaster and I did daring and dastardly deeds. I won't tell you about them yet, because it's one of those things where I'm just sort of implying something so you can speculate, then I can reveal it later on in the story.

I'll give you a hint. When I left the dungeon, I couldn't remember what had happened inside, but I was relatively confident that the Dreamer's Circlet was in a different pouch than where I'd put it before I'd walked in.

Of course, I come from a fae storytelling tradition, where a hint is often more hindrance than help.

Now, go on. Think on it.

Good. Now, you can feel validated later if you got it right.

⁂

That evening, I went to the Rust River and watered my *tama* necklace for the second time. It wouldn't be ready for this duel — I'd waited too long — but I could sense it growing. The jewel shifted to a red tone as I watered it, which was a little strange, but probably just had something to do with the properties of the water.

Then, I went home for a night of sleepless rest.

The next day, we all met right back in the glade. There was no need for a different locale — we were just flipping a coin, after all. We didn't need a colossal arena.

. . . Or so you'd expect in a human contest, at least. As it was, the area around Ana's tree had drastically changed overnight. I'll let you know now that I was involved with that a bit, but it wasn't the big surprise for later. Just a smaller surprise.

Ana and I had set up a stage of conjured stone, much like the arena where the Smiling Sword Saint resided, but on a much smaller scale. It was only about fifteen feet in any given direction, but that still gave us a clear area to stand, and enough distance from the trees to hopefully prevent any collateral damage.

I'd helped Ana set up a secondary defense for the trees a bit farther out — a hexagonal wall that stood a dozen feet in height, with support pillars at each intersection of the wall. Each pillar had a single crystal set in the top of it, filled with essence.

I couldn't conjure walls, of course. I was *mostly* there to help her with measurements on where to put each of the walls, the angles, that sort of thing. Oh, and the gems. I helped with filling those. I hoped all that preparation would be enough to prevent us from hurting her home.

As the judges took their places on the stage, I met with Darryl and Rusty.

Rusty walked up to me first. "Can I see the coin for a sec?"

"Sure." I pulled it out, handing it off to her.

She pulled a cloth out of one of her sleeves, slipping the coin into it and polishing the surface. "There. Shined it for ya. Nice and glistening now."

That was true. She'd shined it so well, in fact, that it had gone from being a copper coin to a gold one.

I glanced at Lord Talis and winced. I'd very deliberately chosen a copper coin prior to the contest because copper, unlike iron and silver, didn't have a strong significance to fae.

Iron, especially cold-forged iron, was famous for having deleterious effects on many types of fae. Silver, for the most part, was considered a "good" metal to fae, one closely associated with the old moons that once were their allies in the skies.

Gold didn't have a particular significance in my own local faerie culture. It was associated with the sun rather than the moon and effectively neutral as far as the fae were concerned. It wouldn't heal or harm them.

The lost fae were different. They'd been changed by the Ashen Scouring, with the Ashen Scouring robbing them of color and light—

And now, much like the Ashen Lord himself, they were vulnerable to gold.

"Rusty . . . I appreciate you shining the coin, but . . . isn't this going to be a bit of an insult?"

They shrugged a shoulder. "If they didn't want the coin bein' one thing or another, they should'a made a rule."

I still felt terrible about it. Enough that I actually went to talk to the judges about it in advance.

Lord Brine took a look at the coin when I showed it. "Seems reasonable to me. It's the same coin. It's perfectly fair."

"Yeah. Basically the same thing as if you'd poisoned the coin. Nothing to worry about," Master Feather said. Then, belatedly, he added, "Caw."

I raised an eyebrow at that. Felt a little forced, but I wasn't one to say. "Ana?"

"I agree with the others. It's within the rules. They did not specify that the coin could not be modified before the round."

It still didn't sit well with me, so I went to Lord Talis himself. Or, I tried to. Lord Oloris stepped in my way before I could approach.

"Forgive me, young Edge of the Woods, but Lord Talis has requested privacy before the match begins. May I ask what it is that you need?"

I took a breath. "One of my allies has prepared a cunning strategy for the match, but I feel that it may go beyond the bounds of propriety and dip into the realm of insult. I would ask for his approval for it."

Lord Oloris blinked. "My young friend, you are presently losing a contest of potential lifelong significance to you, and you seemingly already have the approval of the judges. And you want to ask your opponent if he feels your strategy is fair?"

I nodded. "Absolutely. My victory would feel hollow if it is built on a foundation of causing a grave insult to someone I respect."

The desert fae rubbed his head, shaking it slowly. "You're a very strange young man. Do you think it's fair to your friend, who you are here to support, that you potentially turn down an advantage because it might cause a slight?"

I turned and looked to Ana. She locked eyes with me, then nodded.

"She understands."

Lord Oloris sighed. "Ancients protect me. You two are entirely too innocent for this world. Give me a moment."

Lord Oloris backed away, going to speak to Lord Talis near the trees.

Eliree walked over to me. "Do you understand what you're doing?"

"Giving him a chance to deny me a potentially critical advantage. I understand."

She smiled at me. "Oh, my once love. You're doing much more than that." She reached out and offered me a hand. I took it and squeezed it. It was just a small gesture of affection, not a trick. She walked away, Lord Oloris coming back a moment later.

"We discussed it. The terms were clear — you will use that coin. Nothing was said to prevent any form of transmutation or glamor of it before the match. However, we must recognize that you have a point. Using a golden coin is an insult to his people, and he would prefer that it not be included in the contest in that form."

I nodded. "Understood, thank you for checking with him."

I returned to my friends and explained the situation. "Rusty, will you be offended if I turn down the advantage you offered?"

"Nah. You're in charge. And I overheard your talk. I think your call is the right one. More than you may realize."

"I'm glad we're in agreement." Then, I lifted the coin and rubbed it on my shirt. The gold melted away from the surface as I disrupted the glamor that had changed it.

"Okay." I nodded to my companions. "Anything else?"

"Drink this," Darryl said, shoving a glass vial into my hand.

"What's it do?" I asked.

"Better to just drink," he said, adjusting his hat. "Trees are listening."

I tossed Eliree a glance. She winked at me, then I was *pretty sure* one of the gigantic trees to my right winked, too.

I sighed. At least we were on better terms now.

I took the glass vial and quaffed the purplish liquid in there—

And the entire world slowed down.

"H . . . o . . . w . . . d . . . oes . . . it . . . ta . . . s . . . te . . . ?" Darryl's voice was strangely slow and stilted.

"Not bad. Very minty." My voice sounded perfectly fine to me.

Rusty and Darryl looked at each other. "M . . . a . . . y . . . be . . . don't . . . ta . . . lk . . . right . . . now . . ."

I nodded. They both winced. Apparently, that was a tell, too.

It's *possible* I should have waited until right before the coin flip to drink the potion. On the other hand, walking in slow motion back to the center of the stage was strange, and it gave me a chance to acclimate.

I listened with some difficulty as the judges reiterated the rules of the challenge, then Master Feather came forward to take the coin from me to inspect it.

Lord Talis, seeing the coin, gave me a look of surprise, then a slow nod of approval.

Then, finally, it was time. Lord Brine accepted the coin, then stepped into the center of the platform and explained a final ruling. I'd acclimated to the slow-motion speech a bit by that point and found it tolerable to listen to. "Lord Talis, you may call the sword or shield side of the coin as your own before it is flipped."

I'd expected this and planned for it.

Then, it was time.

"Three . . . two . . . one."

Valissar Talis spoke a single word. "Sword."

And Lord Brine's thumb sent the coin shooting into the air.

We both moved at once.

Valissar Talis made a drawing motion in the air with a finger. A portal opened in midair just above the coin. Without my accelerated perception, I couldn't have possibly reacted to it.

And even with the potion, I couldn't have done anything if I hadn't prepared the arena ahead of time.

It was a subtle thing. I couldn't have gotten away with infusing the area with too much of my own essence, but Ana's dungeon entrance was very close by, and it was a breach. A hint of breach essence in the six pillars surrounding the arena was not, in itself, all that suspicious.

I wasn't an enchanter. I understood some of the basic theory of magical item creation, but I didn't know how to accomplish true enchanting with only the essence types I had available. Instead, I'd done something far simpler. Ana had created hollow crystals in each of the six pillars, each with a tiny hole in the surface. Then, I'd filled them with some of my breach essence, and she'd sealed the gap, trapping samples of my essence inside.

In doing so, we'd made rudimentary, temporary anchors for my essence that surrounded the entire arena. It allowed me to extend my senses — and my abilities — into those anchors. Not enough to perform most of my techniques, but I didn't need anything fancy for this.

Just a thought to shatter those six crystals and blanket the entire area with breach essence.

The portal flickered out as breach essence reached it, then vanished.

It had taken hours of work to shut down one obvious strategy of my opponent's. I'd bought myself less than a second as he reacted in surprise.

I had to hope it'd be enough.

As the coin continued to soar upward, I activated my body-enhancement technique, Shattering Soul. Not for the usual reasons—

I just needed to be able to jump really, really high.

As I blasted myself upward, Lord Talis did the same, responding to my countermeasure faster than I'd hoped.

Both our hands went out — after all, catching the coin and manually manipulating it before it "landed" had never been disallowed in the rules.

I'd moved first. I'd almost reached it when he flicked a finger, sending a burst of motion into the coin, shooting it horizontally and out of my reach.

So, I swung toward him instead, grabbing at his shirt.

He grinned broadly. And, as we continued to move upward from our technique-enhanced jumps, and the coin flew off to the side of the arena, we exchanged a handful of unarmed attacks at a speed I never could have hoped for under normal circumstances.

I didn't manage to strike him even once.

He was better than me, with three blows landing on my chest and blasting me back down to the arena floor with enough force that the stone shattered where I landed. If I hadn't reinforced my body, my ankles likely would have shattered along with the rock.

But that was the beauty of Shattering Soul—

Not only did his strikes only leave me with bruises, every impact had left a bleeding wound on his hands, and the star veins within them.

I took a moment to steady myself. The coin was still flying sideways, having been launched far beyond the boundaries of the arena itself by Lord Talis's technique. In a moment, it'd be beyond the six pillars surrounding the arena, and thus beyond the reach of the essence I'd released.

And so, before it vanished, I unleashed the technique I'd spent the last three months on, reaching out into the air toward the coin and focusing.

If Lord Talis hadn't been recovering from injuring himself, he almost certainly would have had time for a counter. My technique barely used any sword essence, but he might have sensed it regardless — he was a Sword Lord, after all. As it was, I had to hope that he'd missed it among the noise of other sword essence on the battlefield — my sword on my back, his own sword at his side, and the power that now flowed through my body.

I didn't see him do anything to respond to my technique. In fact, after I grasped at the air, I didn't see him at all.

Not until he reappeared outside the arena, having teleported into the path of the coin.

He caught it in midair, frowned . . .

And then burst into laughter.

"The coin has landed!" Lord Brine pronounced. "The duel is over. Lord Talis, if we might see the coin?"

Lord Talis landed, then strode to the center of the arena. I ended my Shattering Soul technique, walking over, heart slamming in my chest.

We waited a moment for the judges to gather, then Lord Talis opened his hand, revealing the coin—

With neither sword nor shield on the top face.

"How peculiar." Lord Brine blinked. "It would appear to be that this side is blank."

I lifted my own closed hand to the judges and my opponent. "As Talis moved, with speed and grace, I set my grasp upon coin's face. One final move, as you each saw. With sword and match, I made a draw."

I opened my hand to the judges and my opponent, showing the product of three months of work. My movement technique, utilizing my recently formed Advancing Point.

I hadn't managed to finish my Advancing Point prior to our first duel, but I *had* finished it while training for the second. I hadn't originally imagined using it for this sort of scenario—

I'd originally picked drawing essence for my Advancing Point with the idea of quickly drawing my own sword. As it turned out, it worked just as well with other swords, if you built the right technique for it.

I called my first drawing-aspected technique *Sword Steal*. It did exactly what it sounds like.

Within my palm was a thin sliver of metal. I had stolen the coin's sword.

The judges turned to each other, conferring, and then echoed my own declaration. There was no objection from my opponent.

With no sword or shield on the face the coin had landed on, the match was a draw.

INTERLUDE VI

SCRIBE III

SUNSET

As the Dawnfire — or the sun, as they called it locally — descended from the sky, the swordsman slowed his steps. He showed no sign of physical exhaustion but began to travel with greater caution, his eyes occasionally flaring with silvery light.

"So," Scribe asked. "A loss and a draw. That means you'd have to win the third round just to tie. What would happen in that case?"

"A fourth trial as a tiebreaker. That would have to be my objective. I'd have to win both." The swordsman shook his head. "It wasn't an ideal situation."

"Of course not." Scribe paused. "You really stole a sword off the face of a coin?"

"Dream Girl did accuse me of being a sword thief. I didn't think of myself as being one at the time she said it, but it did give me an idea. Between that, and Fade talking about her teleporting coin, I realized that while I couldn't move something as large as a person through a breach, even my own meager power might be enough to move something smaller. I'd considered taking the entire coin, but with my connection to sword essence, and practice at quick-draw techniques, drawing a sword at a distance was closer to my skill set."

"Huh. Did you ever expand that technique?"

The swordsman winked at him. "Keep listening, and maybe you'll find out."

They walked in silence for a time, then the swordsman's eyes flashed silver again briefly. It was the third instance of such an event, so Scribe decided to finally ask about it. "You're using some kind of sensory spell? Or, technique, I suppose they call it?"

"Right. Multiple, actually, although I suppose they wouldn't look distinct to you. Some for identifying threats, others to search for resources. Nothing particularly interesting in the latter case, but I've been dodging a bit of the former. As much as I'd enjoy a chance to stretch my arms, it would be a waste. We don't really want to eat anything from out here, and I haven't seen anything with interesting bones or cores to collect yet."

It was possible that he should have been concerned about the idea of the youth wanting to collect "interesting bones," but in honesty, it was positively mundane compared to some of the things Auntie had said and done in his presence, so he barely paid it any mind. *His* bones were obviously boring and thus not worth being added to the swordsman's collection.

He's likely just thinking in terms of bones that can be harvested for essence, potions, or that sort of thing. Not the type of thing I'd want to drink in a liquid, but I've heard gelatin dishes are more popular in the north, so I might need to get used to it.

He suppressed a shudder at the thought. *Or just . . . not eat. Yeah.*

With the lack of a verbal response from Scribe, the swordsman continued to explain. "I don't anticipate finding anything worthy of concern or collection unless we go significantly farther off the road. This isn't a well-traveled area, but it's close enough to the path that any traveling Skyseekers or Shrineseekers of sufficient level would sense anything truly outstanding in terms of either danger or quality. I don't think Skyseekers come down here often, but it has to happen, and Shrineseekers would be more common. There are bound to be a couple crystal shrines nearby, and I've considered looking myself once I have a bit more familiarity with the region."

"Presumably, shrines that are supposedly lost forever aren't exactly something you're going to stumble upon by wandering a couple miles from town. What would your methodology be?"

The swordsman brightened at the question. "Old maps. I've always loved them, even before I found the one in Ana's shrine. I suppose that should have been a hint, but . . ." He shook his head. "Anyway, I try to get my hands on ancient maps whenever possible. Typically, the really old ones aren't very accurate, so you have to do a bit of work to get anything useful out of them. Also, they're often in older languages — but luckily, those older languages by human standards tend to overlap with the languages still spoken in fae communities. In this case, many of the maps I've found thus far are in Nyn, the primary western fae tongue."

"Meaning that they're hard to read for most people, but they're one of your native languages. That's quite the advantage."

A quick nod from the swordsman. "Not all of them, of course. It's regional — I'm speaking mostly of this area, where humans and fae used to intermix before the war and Nyn was common. As we head farther north, we'll hit areas where any old maps are likely to be in other languages. Ordellar, for example, which is largely used by demibeasts like kitsune and tengu. Er'vahn, if we get into the mountains and start running into des'vahi — although in those cases, they still actively speak the language, so we could find a translator easily enough. That sort of thing."

"I know . . . some of those words you just mentioned." Scribe smiled.

"Ah, apologies, it's easy to forget you're not local. Des'vahi are a powerful mountain people. They tend toward being taller than humans and with larger, more muscular builds. Their Dianis Points are rather fascinating — rather than the conventional layout, they have multiple shield points. That gives them the potential for vastly greater resistance to damage than most species, but less potential for actively using offensive and utility techniques. Tengu are winged, birdlike people who tend to live in mountain ranges and study. They're known for scholarship on a number of esoteric subjects — sacred geometry and knotwork, for example, and specialized breathing techniques. They also have some of the most famous sword fighters in the world, and I've been hoping to train under one of their masters someday."

"And kitsune?"

"A species of people with fox-like characteristics, notably ears and tails. Plural tails for each kitsune, in some cases — they're known to grow more of them over their lifetimes, representing additional power. It's one of the most visible signs any species has of essence development; you can generally guess a kitsune's essence-development level simply by looking at their number of tails. Obviously, some practice illusions specifically to mislead in that regard. They're known for extraordinary spellcasters. There's also a . . . reputation for trickery among kitsune, but I suspect that's largely a cultural thing, rather than anything inherent to the species as a whole."

"Sounds like there's some overlap with fae, in terms of reputation?"

The swordsman nodded. "Absolutely. In fact, there are many tales" — he gave an exaggerated pause, and Scribe groaned at the pun before he continued — "of kitsune and fae having trickery contests, games, and that sort of thing. They usually end in friendship, strangely enough, with the fae and kitsune joining forces to trick some kind of greater threat. Honestly, a lot of it is largely propaganda, but the kind that's designed to *create* unity rather than disrupt it, so I don't really mind."

"I'd be interested in hearing some of those stories at some point, if you wouldn't mind sharing."

The swordsman nodded enthusiastically. "Of course. I'm pleased by your interest. Shall I stop telling my current story to switch, or . . . ?"

"No, no. I'd prefer to hear your story first, but if we're traveling for a while, perhaps there will be time for others."

Edge laughed. "I suppose that depends on how long-winded I get. And how exhausted. And speaking of the latter . . . you're looking a bit worn, and it's getting dark. I'd recommend we find a place to rest soon."

"I wouldn't say no to stopping. I'm used to long hikes, but if we're going to be at this for days . . . some moderation may be wise."

"Agreed. And I'd rather camp while we're relatively safe. Let's find a good spot. I have a tent, do you?"

Scribe shook his head. "I wasn't really planning to camp. I have some supplies, but nothing on that scale."

"I have one, but it's fairly small. We can rotate. That's just as well — we should be taking watch shifts, anyway. I prefer first watch. You?"

"That's fine, no objections on my side." Scribe considered the risks of sleeping in the presence of the swordsman, but they seemed fairly smaller than any available alternatives. Besides, if the swordsman wanted to kill him, he hardly needed to wait until Scribe was asleep. Scribe didn't have any counters to the swordsman's overwhelming speed — not without preparing in advance, and that wouldn't be possible if the swordsman decided to attack suddenly.

They walked on for a bit until Scribe noted a strangely circular gap in the trees. It was about fifteen feet in diameter, perhaps, with flat grassy ground and . . . nothing else. Seemingly no loose rocks, no fallen branches or leaves. He frowned, then lifted a hand to point at it. "That's . . . unusual. Too clear. Too deliberate. Is this—"

"Yes, the sort of thing I was looking for. Maybe not the type we'd want to walk into, though." He ducked down, picking up a rock and tossing it into the center of the grove. Nothing visibly happened.

For about two seconds.

Then the rock simply *vanished*, as if it had never been there in the first place.

"Huh," Edge said.

Scribe turned to him. "Huh? Really? That's it? What is that place?"

Edge shrugged. "No idea. Can't even tell if the rock went invisible or disintegrated. Want to check it out?"

"No! Just . . . no! That's . . . suicidal!"

"Pfft. Nah. I'm very good with disintegration. Going to take a lot more than a little tree barrier to wink me out of existence. You?"

"Obviously not! I'm just a person!" Scribe folded his arms.

Edge laughed. "It's probably just some sort of *kekkai* that hides what's in there. Nothing I'm aware of in nature would disintegrate a rock like that. Dissolve in acid, maybe, or shatter, but not disintegrate. And we didn't see anything like that. It's probably harmless — and possibly useful. Shall we?"

"I'm staying right here." But he *was* curious.

"Suit yourself." Edge took a step forward.

Scribe tapped the side of his own head, narrowing his eyes as he looked beyond the trees . . . and *saw*.

There was a haze in the air between the trees, a distortion not unlike that of heat shimmering in the air. The ground was littered with small objects that he had failed to perceive before — ordinary rocks, sticks, and . . . shards of white sticking out of the ground by the dozens.

The haze in the air shifted, contracted, and he saw something else — something wrought from the smoke and air, focusing into two gleaming points of light that shifted and turned, and a slight curved line in the air below them that twisted into a crescent as it met his own gaze.

Eyes. Eyes the size of a human torso, and a mouth that—

Scribe grabbed Edge's arm before he stepped into the haze. "Monster."

Edge gave him an appraising look. "What do those eyes of yours see?"

"It's big. Partially corporeal, I think. It sees us. And . . ." He gestured at the ground. "There are bones."

There was a rumbling sound as the fragments of the creature's face shifted forward, and he caught a glimpse — just a hint — of tremendous fangs in the monster's mouth. The body must have been huge, too, to cause the tremors it did with its movement.

One step forward, two steps, nearing the boundary of the tree line—

Then it was gone.

"It vanished, I think—"

There was a crack in the air as Edge spun around with an open hand, catching something — a colossal fang — just in front of Scribe's throat.

Scribe intuitively let out an "eep" and stepped back, snapping his fingers in the air on instinct with a "dispel" motion. For an instant, he caught a better look at the creature's bloodstained fangs and pitch-black fur, then Edge was moving.

"*Bad kitty.*" He continued to hold the gigantic beast by a single fang, reaching with his other hand into a pouch and pulling out an herb, waving it in the beast's face.

The monster's eyes widened, then it reared back, breaking his grip . . . and *sneezed.*

Edge took a step forward, waving the herb, and the monster coughed and hacked, then turned its colossal head from side to side . . . and broke into a run.

The beast vanished into the forest. Scribe's heart hammered. He kept his spell active — that thing was quick and it could flank them at any time.

Edge shook his head. "Shame we had to scare her off. She was just defending her home. She'll be back, of course, but this will be an unpleasant evening for her."

"That . . . that's what you're worried about? She nearly ate me!"

Edge shrugged. "Eh, probably not. Most bakeneko don't like the taste of humans. Probably would have used you as a chew toy for a while, though, just to scare you off. And the scent of your blood might have attracted something meaner. Anyway, want to camp here?"

Scribe stared at him. ". . . No? On account of the monster that's coming back later?"

"You sure? I don't think she'll be back tonight, and her *kekkai* will probably be active for a while. The other monsters in the area are likely to know about her lair, so they'll be wary of it. It's a great find, and since I won it in battle, it's reasonable to claim as our own lair — at least for the night."

". . . I was tired before, but I don't think I'm going to be able to sleep anywhere near this."

"Hm. Okay." He paused, then after a moment tore the herb bundle he was holding in half and offered half to Scribe. "Splitpaw. If you're that worried about it coming back, just wear this on your neck for a little while. The scent'll get on you and they won't bite. You . . . might not like the scent yourself much, either, though."

Scribe accepted the herbs and shoved them into his shirt. "That's a price I'm willing to — ugh."

"Yeah."

They walked on.

An hour or so later, they finally found a spot where they were both willing to camp. It was the ruin of what had once been some sort of stone structure, with only fractured remains of stone pillars and other fallen bits of light gray stone visible on the forest's surface. Naturally, Scribe was concerned about what had destroyed the place, but it was so old that he didn't think it was likely they were still present, if they were even alive.

The area was of significant size — maybe sixty feet from front to back and forty feet wide, with evidence of multiple rooms and one large central chamber. From the dimensions and the quality of the stone, Scribe suspected the building might have once been some sort of temple. Which, given that they appeared to be in the middle of nowhere, was a little bit odd.

An entrance to one of those crystal shrines, maybe?

He lifted a hand and made a few gestures while Edge didn't appear to be looking: the hand signs for "reveal" and "secret."

Sense Secret Passages wasn't a spell he used very often, but given the circumstances . . .

He glanced around, hoping to find some evidence of a secret stairway or trapdoor among the wreckage, but he found nothing.

Maybe under the debris, but . . .

There were chunks of stone of varying size everywhere, likely bits of walls, ceilings, and floors. Some were fist-sized, but other half-sunken chunks of pillars were still standing at nearly his height and multiple feet in circumference.

The largest pieces here are going to weigh thousands of pounds. Moving them to search would be impractical, if not impossible.

Upon circling the area, then walking closer, they found no signs of monsters or traps. Edge sounded vaguely disappointed about that, but his interest level when he saw some faded-but-still-visible writing on a few of the stone pieces escalated rapidly into glee. While Scribe began to clear sticks and stones to find a flat spot to sleep on, Edge shrugged off the backpack from under his cloak and removed paper and charcoal to make tracings of the writing on each of the stones. It was a technique that Scribe had heard of but rarely had the need to practice.

After cautiously tucking the charcoal-coated pages into some sort of folder in his backpack, the swordsman washed his hands, wincing when he got to the right — had he been cut by the cat creature's fang? — and then began to walk in a large circle around the structure, drawing a line with a stick.

"Are you putting up some sort of ward?" Scribe asked.

"Only the most basic, unfortunately. I don't have enough salt to surround this whole area. I'm very low on it in general, and even lower on some of the rarer materials I'd use for proper warding. Once I put up the tent, I can make some better wards around that, though. If we put it on one of these stone areas, I can try to chalk it."

Scribe frowned at the ruin. "I don't think any of the individual stone pieces are large or flat enough against the ground to—"

Edge wandered over to one of those stone slabs that Scribe had evaluated to weigh thousands of pounds, grabbed it, and began to drag it across the floor.

Scribe stared blankly for a moment as Edge just . . . walked about, casually dragging things that weighed as much as wagons, occasionally flicking a finger at one and slicing it into smaller pieces.

. . . *Guess he wasn't exaggerating about how much sword essence boosted his strength. If anything, that's . . . way too much. Is he even using a body-enhancement technique right now?*

He considered using a sorcery-detecting sight spell to see if he could get a better look at Edge's essence structure, but that felt a little too intrusive.

After a minute, Edge stood back up, dusted his hands off with another wince, and looked at Scribe. "Better?"

". . . Much. In fact . . ." He glanced around, considering. ". . . What are the odds you could lift each of these up for me to try to search for secret passages underneath?"

Edge's eyes widened for just a moment. "That . . . is . . . a wonderful idea!" He clapped, then winced more seriously. ". . . Maybe in the morning, though. And after I've treated my hand. Giant monster fangs are sharp. Who knew?"

Who . . . knew.

Scribe sighed.

Edge gave him what was probably supposed to be a charming grin. To his chagrin, it kind of worked.

"Tent time!" Edge dropped his backpack again, pulling out a tent that looked suspiciously large for the size of the bag, and began to set it up. "Can you get the other side of this pole . . . ?"

They set up the tent.

Edge marked around it with three circles — chalk, salt, and some of the splitpaw, held in place by bits of rocks. Just in case the big cat decided to catch up and exact revenge on them.

"I'll take first watch. You can use the tent." Edge undid the straps on the front of the tent to open it, then reached into his backpack and pulled out a blanket, which he tossed inside. "Sorry, no pillow."

"It's fine. This is . . . a better accommodation than I expected, thank you."

"It is no difficulty and no repayment is expected," Edge said with a hint of a reminder in the tone. "I'll wake you in six hours?"

". . . That should be fine."

He wasn't going to sleep that long. He'd be lucky if he slept at all, unless . . . yes, drastic measures might be warranted.

He crept into the tent, taking his boots off at the entrance to avoid dirtying it, then closed the flap. He slipped off his own backpack — one with much more meager supplies than the implausible number that Edge seemed to carry — and slipped out his own cloak and blanket to rest with, then, upon further consideration, rolled up Edge's blanket and used it as a pillow.

It wasn't comfortable, but it was much better than being murdered by fake bandits, so there was that.

What a day.

Shutting down proved as impossible as he expected, so after a half hour of false starts, he reached into his bag, withdrew a potion, and took a swig.

Hm. Maybe I should have taken out a cup to measure the . . .

And then he was out.

⊱⊱ ⊰⊰

By the time Scribe woke, the Dawnfire had already taken to the horizon. As he rubbed at his eyes and extracted himself from the tent, he realized that Edge still hadn't taken his own sleep shift. While the young man didn't even mention it, seeming to be willing to simply keep moving without sleep, Scribe ushered the swordsman into the tent to get at least a few hours of rest. "You didn't wake me."

"You seemed like you needed the sleep," Edge said simply, his expression distant.

"I'm not the only one who needs sleep. Go on." He made a sweeping gesture. "Get in there. Sleep."

"You sure?" Edge asked, seeming strangely hesitant.

"I'm fine. I still want to check this place over, anyway, and it'll give me some time to explore."

". . . Good point. Just don't fiddle with the door with all the runes on it." He lifted his hands to reveal a pair of gloves that were blackened with burns.

Scribe snorted. "I pretty much wouldn't have done that, but thanks for the warning. You aren't hurt badly, are you?"

"Not at all, it was just some kind of warning. And I managed to defend myself. But you're not an essence sorcerer yet, you're . . ."

"Much more vulnerable." He sighed. "I know. I'm used to it."

Edge raised an eyebrow at that. "You *could* start working on that, you know."

"I've obviously thought about it, but I haven't made a decision on an essence type yet. I don't know what will be accessible or affordable. I need to get a better idea of what the market looks like."

"Any leanings?" the swordsman asked.

Scribe tilted his head to the side. "Are you just . . . trying to put off sleep by having this conversation now?"

"Yes. But I'm also genuinely curious."

Scribe shook his head. "You really *should* get some rest. But I suppose while we're both up, I could ask you a quick theory question."

"Oh! I love magic theory questions. Please" — Edge gestured enthusiastically — "go ahead."

"You mentioned primary and secondary essences. And you're familiar with Mythralis, so . . . I would presume that what you call secondary essence is the same essence we use for dominion sorcery?"

"Ah!" The youth's face lit up. "Yes, of course. It's been so long since I've spoken to a dominion sorcerer that I didn't think to mention it, but you're absolutely correct."

Scribe considered that. "Is it possible to convert primary essence into secondary essence and vice versa?"

"Already thinking about optimization, are we?" The swordsman smiled. "It's possible, but with caveats. Taking the essence you've started using to form an incomplete Dianis Point and pulling it out to turn it into secondary essence is possible, but then you'll lose the progress you've been making on that Dianis Point. You also have to decompress it, if you've already started the compression process necessary to form a Dianis Point, but that isn't too bad."

"What about the usable essence that's generated by a completed Dianis Point?"

The swordsman nodded. "A much better strategy. If you're thinking about draining a Dianis Point for safer dominion sorcery, that absolutely *does* work. But there are downsides."

"How so?"

"There are three main problems. You probably know this, but when a dominion sorcerer casts spells using secondary essence, their body gradually acclimates to that usage, generating more of it over time, like a form of exercise."

"Ah. I see the issue." Scribe frowned. "If you're using primary essence and your body isn't feeling the cost, there's no potential for growth as a result."

"Precisely. At least, not that type of growth. You'd still be strengthening your star veins by connecting to a dominion, which would improve your long-term efficiency, but if you did that kind of thing exclusively, you'd never be as strong of a sorcerer as someone who uses their secondary essence regularly and carefully. Lower risk, lower reward."

"Understood. What are the other problems?"

"The second is related to the first — it isn't good practice for the Dianis Point itself, either. Since you're pulling the essence out of the Dianis Point and converting it to secondary essence before you use it, you're not exercising the Dianis Point in the same way as using an essence technique. Thus, it isn't helping your development as an essence wielder, either."

"Both of those downsides seem manageable," Scribe mused aloud. "You could primarily train with essence normally, then use dominion sorcery in emergencies."

"Yes, and some people do exactly that. It's a style that Gramps advocated for me to consider when I was older. The main limitation to learning it when I was young was that my first essence type was sword essence, and . . ."

"There is no sword dominion." Scribe nodded. "I see. For complex composite essence types, even if you can convert usable essence into secondary essence, there's no valid dominion to draw from."

"Precisely. I considered training specifically in a prime dominion essence type purely for the purposes of being able to do that — people who mix essence and dominion sorcery are rare, and that's a possible advantage — but completing a Dianis Point is a lot of work, and there are downsides to deviating too heavily from your existing area of specialization."

"You mentioned some of that earlier, yes. But for someone who already practices an essence type related to a prime dominion . . ."

"Or a dominion sorcerer looking to broaden his skill set?" The swordsman smiled knowingly. "Certainly. But you'd need to learn an entirely distinct style of magic, which is a lot of work, and there's a more substantial downside. If you want to use the essence from your Dianis Point, you have to pull it out of the Dianis Point first. After that, you need to convert it into whatever type of essence you want to use for your spell. Primary essence isn't identical to the type of essence your body uses for dominion sorcery. You have to convert essence to some degree for a lot of essence sorcery techniques, too, but this is basically one extra step."

". . . Oh. How long would that process take?"

"That depends on the quantity of essence you need to covert, the composition, and all that. Probably only a few seconds, after you've practiced a bit, but in a fight . . ."

"A few-second-long delay is a death sentence if you're already in close quarters. Yes, I can see how limiting that would be."

For most people, at least. Scribe was a specialist in sight sorcery, and he saw considerable potential in being able to, say, make himself invisible for a while without having to strain his eyesight.

. . . *Glad he mentioned that ordinary carrots won't help build up sight essence, otherwise I might have stumbled into an embarrassing rumor and tried it. I'll have to look into where I can find something to use, presuming I decide I want to match my essence types to my current dominion sorcery abilities. I need more information before I make that kind of decision.*

Of course, he did have another dominion sorcery option to consider . . . but that would require being willing to use it.

Scribe shivered.

It wasn't very cold, but it didn't need to be.

"Any other ideas you're thinking about?" Edge asked.

"Sure," Scribe admitted. "Some. Trying to gain the benefits of an overlapping type with my existing sorcery seems . . . well, hold on. My first point is going to be my Heart Point, isn't it?"

"Right. Assuming you're human?"

"As far as I know." He chuckled, but Edge simply nodded sympathetically. "Pretty sure. And . . . I suppose, thinking in terms of what makes sense for each Dianis Point, sight makes much more sense for a Viewing Point."

"That'd be the more traditional approach, yeah. And in this case, I think it does make sense to go for something else for your Heart Point — maybe something that's still synergistic with sight, but has broader applications. Prime dominions connected to it, like light or deception, would be obvious ones and comparatively easy to pick up. Other deep dominions related to sight, but with broader applications, would also work. And, of course, any of the more complex hybrids or subtypes related to sight."

"What sort of hybrids of sight are there?" Scribe asked.

Edge shrugged. "I'm not an expert at sight essence, but you can extrapolate from the obvious. Anything related to sight conceptually might work, like . . ." He frowned, then pointed straight at Scribe's face.

"What are you . . . oh! Glasses." He nodded. "That one feels a little niche, though. Even more than sight itself."

"Glasses would be. But what about glass?"

Scribe blinked. "Would that really count as conceptually related?"

"Completely depends on who you ask, but I'd imagine that you could find a specific type of glass essence that contains sight essence aspected toward transparency or something similar. Might be a starting point?"

"I'll think about it," Scribe promised. "You should, however, go to sleep."

". . . Fine." Edge took a breath. "Good night, then."

With that, the swordsman finally retired to his tent, and Scribe began his promised look around the ruin.

As interesting as potentially deadly archaeology was, his mind was more focused on the essence conversation, at least at first.

Something related to glass, huh?

It wasn't a terrible match for his existing skill set. He'd apprenticed to a glassblower for a while when he was younger — it was a major part of his primary cover identity — and he was familiar with how flexible glass could be.

And how incredibly dangerous, too.

There was an appeal to that, something that would give him a bit of offensive power if he managed to figure out how to apply it in that fashion. But the mention of glass had given him a clearer picture of something that was an even more obvious option, something more personally connected to his skill set.

He found the door that Edge had mentioned a half hour later, though it was lying flat against the ground among other stones, rather than a classic doorway. And, as he inspected the strange runes from a presumably safe distance, he realized that — as implausible as it sounded — he recognized them.

When I was doing that decryption work when Vee left, some of the documents had runes like this. But that was years ago. Symphony . . . how long have you been planning on sending me here?

He couldn't read them from a safe distance, and given the sheer number — there were thousands and thousands of characters, some more familiar than others — he wouldn't be able to read it in a timely fashion even up close. And that was assuming it wasn't a cipher, which, if it matched his prior experience, it probably was.

What am I getting into here?

There was only one way to find out.

Scribe retrieved an all-too-familiar tool from his bag — a mirror — and carefully placed it to reflect the entire door. Then, he cast a sight spell to create light, improving the image quality, and activated a glyph on the back of the mirror.

The image on the mirror froze, copying the reflection. It would remain that way until he activated the glyph again. Then, he carefully backed away from the dangerous door, retrieved a journal and quill, and got to work at living up to his name.

By the time Edge woke, he had a much better idea of what he was dealing with—

And a much greater idea of how much danger they were in.

"Let's get going," Scribe said after tucking his things away. He worked to break camp while the swordsman ate his own breakfast. Not out of any kindness in his heart, but because, if he was right about the small segment he had managed to translate, he wanted to be as far away from this place as possible before someone came to open the door . . .

From either side.

CHAPTER XXIX

SEASON'S START

After finishing the second round of the duel, I spoke briefly with the judges, then my opponent's team. Valissar himself congratulated me on managing a draw. That was kind.

I wish I'd met him under other circumstances.

Then, I left the glade with my allies to plan how to defeat him.

"You're in a bad spot," Darryl noted, adjusting his gigantic wizard hat as we walked toward my home.

"No kidding. One loss and one draw. That's messy, especially since he's been winning at challenges I've been proposing." I sighed. "Should I have skewed them more in my favor somehow?"

"Tough to do. They have to be thematically aligned with Anathema's shrine. I don't even know why the judges considered a coin flip to count," Darryl noted.

"I can't answer that in detail right now," I told him. "But it's related to my memories of Ana's challenges."

"Ah, got it." He nodded. "Well, we can't be too critical about past rounds. Won't help. What we do know is that each of you has one refusal left, and realistically, you'll both use them. That means that since he goes first . . ."

"I'll refuse once, he'll refuse once, then he'll propose a challenge I can't refuse." I winced. "Meaning the only chance I have is winning at a challenge he proposes. Which seems . . ."

"Unlikely, yeah." Darryl nodded.

"Is it?" Rusty cut in. "Looks like you're good at losin' stuff you suggest. Might be that you're good at winnin' for his ideas."

"I don't think it works like that, but sure, let's hope." I frowned. "No, let's not just hope. Let's plan. What's he going to ask for for the last trial that feels thematically appropriate?"

"I think it's pretty obvious." Darryl shook his head. "Better get that sword sharpened. In three months, your combat by trial is probably going to be an actual duel."

⊱⊰

We walked together awhile longer, south from the shrine to take Darryl back to his house. Then, from there, Rusty walked with me toward my own home.

It wasn't like there was much I needed there in terms of preparation, but I hadn't seen Gramps in a while, and it felt wrong not to at least check in to see if he was back.

While we walked, Rusty stayed close to me, allowing me to make sure they didn't wander into anything particularly dangerous near the house. They were clearly a native fae, but despite being around my age, they seemed less prepared for some of the mundane dangers of the region. That was strange, especially given their general theoretical knowledge, which seemed very high.

They'd managed to get that map for me before the first round, and to glamor a coin for the second. That was an unusual skill set.

I had pieces of knowledge that hinted at who and what I was dealing with, but it wasn't the right time to push that. For the moment, what I needed was direct help for the next match, especially if it was a fight.

"For the first round, you managed to get me a map that gave me a big advantage. Is it fair to say you've got resources somewhere to draw from, like other items?"

"In a sense, sure. What're ya thinkin'?"

"In your capacity as my second, would it be reasonable to ask you to get me a sword to use for the duel?" I asked.

Rusty blinked. "Seems like a pretty classic ask for a second, I'm thinkin'. But I don't know why ye'd need one. Got a honkin' big piece o' metal right there, don't cha?"

"I do." I nodded. "Three problems with that approach. First, I don't really know how to use the magic of it yet, which means both that I can't use it completely and my opponent, with Sword Lord abilities, could potentially use it against me. Second, gigantic swords like this are principally for hunting giant monsters, not personal duels. Third, what little I know about the sword's abilities implies that it's built for highly lethal combat, and I don't want to kill or permanently injure him."

"Thinkin' ye might be worrying too much on account of that last part, since ye've gotta hit him to kill him. But I'm seein' where yer goin', and if you're needin' a duelin' sword . . ." They paused in their step. "Yeah, thinkin' I know where I can find a sword that was made for a duel. Might be needin' your help to go get it, and we're gonna have to be real sneaky-like."

I raised an eyebrow like that. "I don't want to steal anything."

"Oh, it's nae a theft. Don't belong to anyone livin', anyway." They chuckled. "'Course, that's assumin' it's still where I last heard. Gimme some time to look into it, yeah?"

"Sure. How long do you need?"

"One full moon cycle should do it. Use some of that time to practice steppin' light and fast."

"Why?" I asked.

Rusty winked at me. "If you want the sword I'm thinkin' of? Might be that preparin' for your duel is gonna be more dangerous than the duel itself."

When they said that, I could feel my heart beating faster in my chest in excitement. Not just at the words, or the goal, but something else.

Something about that look on Rusty's face, promising danger that we'd face together . . . and perhaps a bit more danger from Rusty, too.

When I reached home, Rusty bade me good night and wandered off into the forest. I watched them leave, frowning as I realized they were heading in the general direction of the Winding Way.

Were they planning for us to go back there for one of the swords from the contest, or the Lady of the Fake? I couldn't be sure. I'd asked directly what they were planning on while we walked home, of course — I'm not shy with questions — but they were a classical faerie and gave me only evasive answers.

I saw light inside the hut as I approached. I blinked in surprise, then rushed to the door.

Gramps was back home.

I swung the door open, finding him sitting at the kitchen table, a cup of tea steaming next to him and an old book in his hands.

"Hm?" He blinked at me as I approached. "Oh, Lien, is it? You're back."

His reaction was a bit strange, but Gramps was always a little unusual if you looked at him through a human lens, so I didn't think much of it at the time. "I could say the same to you. You've been gone for months, so long as I can tell. Where have you been?"

He set his book down, frowning, and then took a draw of his tea. I closed the door behind me, took my boots off, then sat down across from him.

"Well, I went with the queen to a gathering of other courts, as you know," he explained. "Then after that . . . well, you know. Here, there. Nowhere."

"That's a long time to be here, there, and nowhere," I replied.

"Yes." His expression grew dark. "I don't recommend it."

A moment of silence passed between us. I considered prying further, but from the haunted look he wore, it seemed like a bad idea.

". . . Okay." I nodded. "Do you . . . need anything, Grandfather?"

He blinked in surprise at me. "That's an unusual question for you to ask me, b — Grandson." He considered. "No. I don't need anything, strictly, not at this time. But will you tell me what you've been up to?"

"You haven't heard?" I couldn't contain my surprise. Gramps . . . always knew things. He talked to everyone and to no one.

"Perhaps I have." He looked thoughtful. "I don't know. I would like to hear it in your words."

I nodded. "Of course. Let me get myself some tea first. Then, I'll tell you a story."

"Wonderful." He gave me a soft smile. "I've always loved stories."

⊹⊹ ⊹⊹

I told Gramps about what I'd been up to the last few months. He listened patiently, asking questions here and there. The conversation seemed to reinvigorate him a bit, and by the end of it, he seemed a bit more . . . present. Or, at least, I like to think he was.

I hope I helped him just a little, at least.

Then, as my tale concluded, he grew tired. I walked him to his own bed, helped him get into it, and went to my own bed to sleep.

When I woke in the morning, Gramps was gone. On the kitchen table was a note.

I may be away for a while. It's not your fault. Don't look for me. I won't be found, not now.

I frowned at the strange note, tucked it away, and felt a strange melancholy I couldn't quite place. Perhaps I should have taken the time to sort through it, and to search for him, in spite of his words. If my mind had not been so heavily dominated by my pending duel, perhaps I would have.

I'd never been very good at following his instructions.

At that time, however, in that place, I listened, and I moved forward.

I can't say I regret that, exactly. Right choices are hard to find, at times, even in retrospect.

But I do think about it often, and how different things might have been if I'd chosen the right time to disobey.

⊹⊹ ⊹⊹

With no one else around to talk to, I headed off for one moon cycle of training, which was a more classical way of saying about a month.

My first step of that month was to visit Ana again to help her out with one of her plans, as I'd promised. It was the right time window to do it, as Lord Talis was away for a few days on other business, and I needed to go with Ana into her dungeon while he wasn't training inside.

I still didn't understand exactly what she was having me do in there, because unlike my trip that had been interrupted by Lord Talis arriving, I was losing my memories each time I stepped inside to help Ana.

As usual, I tried to judge what might have been going on inside the dungeon by the state of my own body and equipment. I clearly wasn't attempting Ana's trials. I found signs on my clothing of hard work and a couple battles here and there, but I wasn't using my supplies, nor was I acquiring new items.

My best guess was that I was training inside the dungeon, much like Lord Talis was, but in a way that I wouldn't remember. I didn't understand the utility of that, but Ana had asked me to do it, and I'd agreed, so I helped her while I could.

I left a few days later, just before Lord Talis was scheduled to return. Ana told me it was important Lord Talis didn't see what we were up to, and that it was equally important that I didn't remember until the right time. I trusted her, so I helped.

After those few days, I did a few more things in the local area.

I paid a visit to Auntie Temper, bringing her some supplies that we had in surplus that she tended to run out of, since she didn't have full access to the forest like we did.

I went to the healing spring and brewed another elixir for Verthrimax, then brought it to him. I was ashamed of how long I'd left that task to Ana to do by herself.

Then, I paid a visit to Darryl and the Willowbark Witch's family, asking them for advice. They gave me some more supplies for both myself and Gramps, which I brought back home.

After that, I dropped those off, noting that Gramps was still missing, and it was time to go back to the mountains for training.

One month passed in what felt like the blink of an eye. I pushed myself as much as possible, swapping to focusing on acquiring enough primary sword essence to push toward the threshold of Hearth-level. I didn't like the idea of changing my essence ratio significantly, but with a duel pending, I couldn't afford to be stubborn.

I didn't reach Hearth-level before that month was up, but I hoped that with two months remaining, I'd still get there before the day of the duel.

I continued to polish my existing techniques rather than focusing on building new ones. I already had made so many techniques in the last six months that there was no way I was skilled enough to use them all optimally, and I needed to practice their execution before building more.

When the month concluded, I met with Rusty, thinking we would be headed into the Winding Way to retrieve a sword. I knew that there could be danger involved.

I was almost right, but wrong in ways that were critical.

I was right about the danger, but I was wrong about where it was coming from.

CHAPTER XXX

STORY

I found Rusty near my own home, lingering just outside the boundaries of the place. They looked startled at my approach, in spite of obviously having been waiting for me.

"Was startin' to wonder if you were comin'." They wrinkled their nose.

"Am I late?" I asked, suddenly nervous that I'd miscalculated something. As much as I was used to fae culture, time was something that could be hard to grasp with them.

They shook their head. "Not that, exactly. Just was worried you'd forget, with all the folk up in the mountains you like to visit."

I wasn't sure how much I'd told them about that, but I didn't worry about it. Fae had their ways of getting information, and it would have been simple enough just to ask Ana where I usually disappeared to. "I try to keep my obligations when I can."

"Good. That may be important for what comes next."

I raised an eyebrow. "Thought you were just getting me a sword."

"Yep. S'over there." Rusty waved toward the west. I glanced—

And at the border of the tree line, I saw him.

Talisian, in his lacquered wooden armor, a silver sword at his side.

I let out an exhausted sigh as I realized the mistake I'd made.

As you may recall me saying from the first part of my tale, a Talisian is "the sword" of a member of faerie royalty.

"Talisian. It's a pleasure to see you again." I nodded to him respectfully.

He approached without any fanfare, coming to stand before me. "Young Rusty has told me that you are in need of a sword. As you are still owed a favor from the princess, she has deigned to offer you one."

I exhaled a sigh. "I don't think I can justify having you fight on my behalf, even for a favor, Talisian."

A curt nod from him. "Of course not. Instead, I would offer you my services before the duel itself."

"What would . . . oh. Wait. You're going to teach me? Isn't it forbidden to teach the Talisian Order's styles to outsiders?"

Talisian's own face betrayed nothing of his thoughts, but his tone was curt. "I have been *instructed* that your deed in protecting the princess in my absence is sufficient to warrant offering a title that would confer you the full rights of training, should you wish to accept that as a gift."

"... This wouldn't happen to be the same title I already turned down, would it?"

He nodded. "Indeed. One that I believe you are still ill-equipped to accept."

"In that case ... what could you offer me if I didn't accept the title?"

"As Edge of the Woods, and marked as a friend of the court, you are of sufficient standing that I could offer to teach you for one full cycle of the moon's wax and wane. I would teach you of the arts necessary for a duel with one who holds the title 'Talis,' but not any of our hidden techniques."

Was that a wise use of a gift owed by the princess?

I couldn't know for sure, but I immediately understood the utility of the offer.

Even with every bit of training I'd done, I had no chance of matching Talisian's overall power. If I knew his particular combat styles, however, I had a much stronger chance of directly countering his moves, which would hopefully allow me to surprise him. It would likely be a duel for points, and such things allowed for a lower-skill and lower-power person to triumph much more easily than a lethal duel would. Such a thing would still be extraordinarily difficult, but with an understanding of his moves ...

"I don't think I can reasonably refuse that offer," I replied.

"There is something else." Talisian tensed for a moment, his eyes briefly flicking to Rusty, then back to me.

He reached into his right sleeve, retrieving a strip of blood-red cloth bordered with white. It took me a moment to realize what I was looking at — a handkerchief. "Should you accept it, it is within the bounds of tradition for a princess to convey her favor for a knight in training entering in a formal duel."

"I am honored by the offer, of course, but I believe that the princess only owes me one gift at this time, since she has already conferred a title onto me and given me a second favor in taking in a friend as a guest to the court. As such, I could not reasonably accept both your training and the offer of her favor. Unless it is freely given, with no expectation of recompense?"

"It is not." Talisian nodded in acknowledgment. "Should you choose to accept both my training and the princess's favor, you would owe *her* a favor."

I winced. "Would she be insulted if I refuse the handkerchief?"

"I cannot speak to that, though I do suspect she would be disappointed."

I felt my shoulders sink. I really didn't like disappointing people in general, and disappointing a faerie princess who wanted to help me ... well, I was a teenager. I was old enough to know I was being manipulated, but not quite wise enough to fully resist it.

"... I'd like to begin with the training. Perhaps I could make a decision on the princess's token closer to the duel?"

"Of course." Talisian nodded. "Rusty, would you vouchsafe this trinket on behalf of the princess, so that he might choose to accept it at any later time?"

"'Twould be my honor, m'lord." Rusty came forward, knelt, and accepted the handkerchief, tucking it away somewhere.

Talisian turned to me after that was done. "A deal is struck. Follow."

Then he turned and walked deeper into the woods.

I gave one final glance toward Rusty and the danger they carried, then rushed to follow.

⁂

I followed Talisian into the ruins of an ancient city. And there, for a single full cycle of the moon, I trained in the secret arts of the Talisian Order, just as Lord Valissar Talis himself had.

After all, if I was going to fight Lord Talis in a duel, there was no better sword to train with than *his*.

Perhaps Dream Girl was right—

I was, in some sense, a sword thief after all.

⁂

My one month of training with Talisian was not enough to learn to master any of the Talisian Order's techniques myself. Instead, it was more focused around seeing them in use and sparring against them.

The Talisian Order had three different combat styles — one focused on mobility and interception of damage, another designed to cut through weapons, and a third style of deepest secret I will not speak of at all.

Of these, the second style was the one that came most naturally to me. In particular, the *zantetsuken* technique — the Iron Cutting Sword, if translated to Velthryn — was analogous enough to my own style that I could have adapted it for use with my own abilities, given enough time.

But that wasn't the goal. Learning to use the *zantetsuken* would have been little advantage, if any, against an opponent who had mastery over sword essence in his proximity. Instead, I drilled against it, time and time again, to devise how to avoid and counter it.

Mastering it myself would be a future project once my duel was done.

My deal had only bought me a single moon cycle of training, and so, when it was done, I moved on. I had not earned myself the title of a Talis apprentice, not in a mere month, but I had enough knowledge of their abilities that I hoped it would be a critical advantage in the duel ahead.

Upon completing my training, I found Rusty waiting for me.

"C'mon. Time to get us another sword, so you can be ready for some proper stabbin'." They made a hand gesture that I was pretty sure wasn't usually referring to combat, waggled their eyebrows at me, and headed off. I followed.

Before I began that training, however, I needed another weapon to practice with. One that would be more practical for the duel itself.

The first step of that was lifting the mirror that Rusty had given me.

I found my mirror image sitting in a meditative posture, the ice sword still fully intact and lying across his knees.

"Hey, mirror guy. Can you hear me?"

One of his eyes opened. If he hadn't done it so unusually, I might not have noticed that it was bright blue.

That's . . . weird. Something to do with the ice sword?

I shook my head. It wasn't a priority to worry about things like that. I could have asked Rusty, but something told me not to trust Rusty with too much more information about myself.

"I'd like the sword back, please."

He opened his other eye, then sighed silently. A complicated expression passed across my mirror image's face, then he nodded, stood up, and stretched the sword out to me.

"I . . . hesitate to ask this, but do you need the sword for something? Is it important that you keep it?"

The mirror image seemed to consider that, then shook his head. Then he mouthed the words, "It was something to do."

"Huh." I accepted the sword back. "Another idea, then. Time wasn't passing for the sword while you had it, right?"

The mirror image shook a hand in a "so-so" gesture.

"More slowly, then? Or you personally kept it more solid somehow?"

The mirror version of me nodded and mouthed, "Closer."

"Do you think you could hold sword essence in a solid form?" I asked.

"Maybe?" He paused. "Probably?"

"Let's test it." I conjured a phantasmal copy of my own sword using the technique I'd managed when I'd been fighting the nightmare version of myself, who had, of course, also technically been a mirror version of me.

Apparently running weirdly complex mirrors of myself is my lot in life. It's not bad, really, just not what I might have expected.

Anyway, my Sealed Sword Creation technique — that's the improved version of my nonfunctional Ultimate Blade Creation technique, by the way — conjured a phantasmal version of my personal sword. I used it, then handed that through the mirror.

My copy gingerly accepted the conjured sword. "Not bad," he said. Then he walked off to train.

If this works . . . well, that'll be a proof of concept for later. But for the moment, I need to get back to Rusty.

Together we took a trip to the Winding Way. Somehow, Rusty seemed to be able to navigate through the forest without a compass, or even following the wind, at least as far as I could tell.

There, we paid a visit to the Lady of the Fake. And there, we made an exchange. I offered her the ice sword back, in exchange for the first sword she'd offered me.

. . . Which I called "Mug," since, even at the age of fifteen, calling my sword Maximum Ultima Godslayer in public felt like a little too much.

After that, I had two swords to train with, both of which offered significant dangers. I considered retrieving a third from the sepulcher, but it wasn't the right time.

With a single month remaining, I went back to where my training started — the sword school.

And, with the duel fast approaching, I resumed my translation work.

It was time to read the ending of the God of Swords' story and, with it, my own beginning.

⊹⊹ ⊹⊹

To begin my final month of training, I focused on my sword-fighting fundamentals, as well as building up more breach essence, drawing it in from the environment to the best of my ability. I had planned to work on the journal's final cipher during this time, but when I got back to my little shelter after a day of training I found it waiting for me, finished in Red's neat script. I picked it up, closed my eyes, and let myself breathe deeply for a time.

Then, I braced myself and began to read.

I found Kara.

The truth was far from what I had expected.

Kara had been a member of the Warders for many years, predating her ascension. She was one of many who had accepted a grave responsibility, standing in line to hold a seal for Aetor, the Maker of Monsters, should any of the existing sealbearers fail to contain his strength or fall.

It was a dire responsibility, but an important one. One I understood but did not think she would ever need to carry.

When I found the devastated arena where Vaelien had seemingly killed Kara, I assumed that this was because he had come to destroy her, and that he had succeeded.

What Kara told me was a far stranger tale. During her visit to the Grand Conclave, one of the sealbearers had been murdered. And during the chaos, she had been the only one present who had been strong enough to take up the seal.

Her version of the seal had been weak, forged in the heat of battle against an unknown enemy. She had been forced to use much of her personal strength to contain Aetor directly, a feat even I could not have managed.

My great enemy had not been the cause, but he sensed the power of a worldmaker and teleported to the scene. He was attacked by members of the Warders for intruding on their secret gathering, and he defended himself.

Then, when he found Kara, he understood what was happening. He had fought the Sun Eater before, after all, and he understood the threat that any worldmaker represented.

And so, as she began to lose control, he fought her. He forced her into the spring at the base of a stability gateway crystal, freezing her in stasis. This preserved the failing seal on Aetor until the Warders were able to fix it.

When I asked her why she thought Vaelien had concealed this from me, Kara laughed and said it was because he knew me. If I had known that Kara was sealed away with a half-broken seal, I would have tried to fix it and risked the world in the process.

My shame was terrible. I had been deceived by my greatest enemy, but he had not killed my wife — he had saved her, and likely the world in the process.

At least, in the short term.

There was a terrible problem. The seal had been patched while Kara slept, but it was not a complete solution, nor could it be—

The seal was, after all, built for only a single person.

Kara was pregnant. The child was mine, of course. We'd been trying before she disappeared, and—

Well, it seems we'd succeeded, we just hadn't realized it. Ordinarily, anyone who was to be a sealbearer would have been checked for that prior to performing the necessary ritual, but since Kara was responding rapidly to a murder, she hadn't gone through the full process.

And now, Aetor was connected not just to her, but to our child as well.

While the child remains unborn, the seal offers a degree of protection, dubious as it is. When the child is born, however... there will be nothing to stop Aetor from taking them over during the transition.

We must take every possible step to prevent that.

I consulted with Tarren, with the others. It is just as I feared. The seal is not designed to be moved, nor can it easily be expanded to include the child — nor would even a full-sealed child be safe. Even a child of gods does not have the power, seal or no, to resist Aetor.

And so, we came to a deceptively simple solution — the seal must be moved.

But a flawed and patched seal is vulnerable. Even if we were to attempt to use the tae dominion to move it, there is a strong possibility that the seal would fall apart, or otherwise allow Aetor to escape while it is in movement.

There is only one person who I know to have the power and control necessary to move such a thing without risking the loss of my wife and child—

And as I write this, my student is on the way to fight one of his children in a tournament.

I go now to my greatest enemy, carrying an unfinished sword and a desperate plea.

If he helps us, perhaps we can salvage all this and set aside this oldest of grudges. If not . . .

My students, my child, my love—

Forgive me. If you are reading this, I have failed the world one last time.

I set the book down.

This was . . . not the ending I expected. It didn't feel very much like an ending at all.

But it was a journal, not a novel. Perhaps I shouldn't have assumed it would tell a complete story, one with a coherent arc and epilogue.

There was some disappointment at that, I admit, but I did finally have some answers—

Aendaryn and Karasalia, the gods of sword and shield, had a child.

And that child . . .

Wasn't me, was it?

I wondered if the child had survived the ordeal, or if they had been taken over by Aetor. I thought I probably would have heard about it if a worldmaker had been released, but . . .

There was a fragment of Aetor in one of the swords in the sepulcher, wasn't there? Was that related, somehow? A piece that had been drawn out and stored in a weapon?

And my mirror copy . . . he'd talked about me being immune to possession. He'd supposedly claimed all the other swords in the sepulcher and survived.

What did he know that I didn't?

Perhaps the most immediately relevant portion of the tale was a small part — the God of Swords had brought his unfinished weapon with him to his final meeting with his old enemy, Vaelien.

Had things come to blows in that encounter? Had I awakened as a result of it?

I couldn't be sure. But I did know that somehow, in the aftermath, a sword with a piece of Aetor had been sealed in the shrine, as well as the sword that I carried — which was likely the same sword that Aendaryn had been modifying throughout the tale.

In a best-case scenario, the shrine was being used in a similar way to how Karasalia had been kept in stasis in a pool of stability magic. Perhaps a collaborative solution between the two old enemies had resulted in the God of Swords giving up his weapon in exchange for his enemy's help.

But I didn't think so.

No, the strangeness of my existence spoke to a tragedy, one that had not been written on the page. And I knew something else, because I'd seen it—

A vision on the road to the sepulcher, one I didn't have the context for at the time I'd seen it. Red traveling, full of determination, a sword that met the description of the last gift Aendaryn had given her held in her hand.

And her murder at the hands of one of Vaelien's children, the Blackstone Assassin.

After that, while she was dying, her partner had shown up to help. That was a grown-up version of Fade, who I now knew to be Wrynn Jaden, Aendaryn's second student.

That raised questions about what had happened to Green and Grey. It also gave me one possible route to get answers—

So far as I knew, Wrynn Jaden had survived that encounter. I'd been hearing stories about her for years.

And if she'd been there for the death of her partner, perhaps she knew what had happened to her master, and to his child—

And to his sword.

I wasn't going to wait forever to speak to Wrynn Jaden, of course. She was one possible avenue for learning more, but not the only one.

As soon as I finished reading, I brought my finished translation to Red. "It ends a little abruptly."

"Life can be like that." She gave me a sad smile. "It's complicated, and messy, and not always fulfilling in the ways you want."

"That's a little bleak."

"Sorry. It's just . . . hard. Knowing he's gone."

I sat down next to her. "Is he? Do we know for *sure* that he's dead?"

She didn't look at me, instead just gazing out over the mountainside. "Not for certain, no. But you're here, with his journal and that sword, and questions you wouldn't have to ask if he wasn't. And even if he's somehow still alive . . ." She shook her head. "I'm not."

"No," I agreed, reluctantly. "But you're here."

"But I'm not her," she said. "And now I won't be. I'm not . . . real."

"You're real," I told her with sudden necessity. "Anyone who's capable of thinking about themselves like that is."

"You're sweet, but we both know that I'm not the usual kind of real. It's okay. I've seen stranger things than this in my travels. Don't like being incomplete, but I'll get it sorted."

"That's . . . a strangely optimistic attitude to have, considering all this."

"No point in letting little things like being a half-real figment of the past drag me down."

"So, you know what you are?" I asked.

"I've been figuring it out, bit by bit." She gazed fondly toward where the others were training. "They know, too. Some more than others. Wrynn . . . well, she's always been quick. Sprinting ahead of all of us, if we let her. Leaving us all behind."

There was something more to her tone that I didn't understand fully, but I nodded. "Then . . . do you know more about who you were, in life?"

"I remember bits and pieces. The journal helped. I . . . get the impression I'm damaged, somehow. More than the others. Like something is holding me back."

I remembered that in the vision of her death, the Blackstone Assassin had tried to trap her spirit in a stone — perhaps he'd partially succeeded before Wrynn had intercepted him. I debated if it was a good idea to tell her that, then decided she had a right to know what I'd seen.

"What about you?" I asked. "Who were you? I mean, I know you were Aendaryn's first apprentice . . . so, you were, what, a paladin?"

She laughed. "No, not really. I mean, he offered, like . . . a bunch of times. I remember that much. Everyone *thought* I was a paladin. But it never really suited me."

"What do you mean?" I frowned.

"A paladin is a sword in the hands of those who have great power. That was never right for me." Red gave me a soft smile. "The way I see it, the gods already had plenty of swords, especially him. I spent my life striving to be something else. A shield in the hands of the helpless."

A shield in the hands of the helpless.

I felt a shiver run down my spine as I felt something deep within me, a connection to what she said—

It was *almost* perfect.

"What about you?" she asked me. "Who do you want to be?"

It helped that she put the question into words.

"Sometimes," I replied, "I think the helpless could use a sword, too."

Maybe it was just my imagination, but when I spoke those words, the broken mark of destiny on my hand felt just a little bit warm.

⋄⋄⋄

With renewed purpose, I set off to meet with the Smiling Sword Saint.

If I wanted to embrace my intuition about who I was, I needed to start by growing strong enough to protect someone that I loved.

I threw myself into hard training, working until I was exhausted, then resting, eating, and throwing myself straight back into her lessons. I tried desperately to master the Strategic Side-Step — or, at least, my own reverse version, which I'd simply named "Sword Steal."

I didn't get very far with that in such a short time window, but I did make progress with some important things adjacent to it.

First and most importantly, I completed my second new Dianis Point — one I'd started building before the second trial but hadn't finished. It was a very straightforward concept, one I had ample experience with—

Sheathing Essence.

I'd been practicing drawing and sheathing together as complimentary skills, so as soon as I'd finished my Advancing Point for drawing essence, I'd started on a retreating point for sheathing essence. Like my drawing essence, my sheathing essence was sword-aspected. It was actually even easier to train than drawing essence was, since I had a magical scabbard that actively generated sheathing essence, and I was able to slowly use that to fuel my Dianis Point no matter where I was.

As a small note, while I was practicing sheathing and drawing together, I wasn't learning them exactly as opposites — more like two parts of a whole process. This was relevant to making their essence composition complimentary, rather than having versions that would interfere with each other.

There are a lot of different essence compositions you could use to build something called drawing or sheathing essence.

One common way to think about drawing and sheathing would be that they both involve moving an object, so they could be built with an emphasis on motion essence. This would be a way to emphasize speed or transportation, as I'd originally intended, but I'd ended up skewing my essence in a different direction when I had a clearer idea of my longer-term plan for the two complimentary essence wellsprings.

In my case, both of them were built with stability essence as a foundation. In the case of drawing essence, stability is the foundation because it's built around objects, and stability is a huge component of object essences, including swords.

In the case of sheathing essence, the same is also true, but it leans even more heavily in that direction because stability is the essence that is used to keep things the same, in storage, or that sort of thing.

The end result was that these two essence types actually ended up having two very similar compositions, allowing me to build them as two parts of the same cycle, rather than things that would cancel each other out. This would be important for allowing me to incorporate them into techniques.

And, of course, once I had a new essence type to work with, I started practicing my new techniques for it immediately. The first would be something that took my Sword Stealing idea, sheathing essence, and what I'd managed to glean from my spirit practice into a new technique.

Finally, I'd proven that with enough breach essence, I could interfere with Lord Talis's ability to teleport. He probably wouldn't fall for the gems-in-the-pillars trick a second time, however, and I wasn't confident I could push out enough breach essence to interfere with teleportation in a short time without a similar trick.

Without knowing the dueling venue, I worked on making a portable version of the same idea.

With only a couple weeks left of my training time, I paid a visit to Darryl and asked for his expertise in potion making. We worked on making a series of breach potions that I could throw around, creating areas of magical instability that would make it harder to use dimensional travel. Darryl was the potion expert, but to figure out how to interfere with teleportation as efficiently as possible, I needed an expert to train with—

And so, on that rarest of occasions, I found my way back to a small hut, one I had neglected for far too long. And, with a bow, I greeted the sole resident.

"Hello, Grandfather."

"Hm?" Gramps blinked at me from his place at the table. "Oh, hello, Lien. You've been gone for some time, haven't you?"

I gave him a wary expression, then nodded. "I found something. I'd like you to look at it and give me your impressions."

I showed him the journal. I asked him questions.

He frowned at me. "I'm afraid I can't say anything about that, Grandson. But good work on your translation project. I'm glad you're getting a chance to do something with your mind, not just your body."

I wasn't surprised by the lack of answers. And, buoyed by the feeling of warmth I'd gotten from the talk with Red and the mark on my hand, I didn't let it bother me.

"There's something else I wanted to ask you about."

"Oh?" He looked distracted, but interested.

"I have a major duel coming up. Would you assist me with my training?"

I couldn't have possibly expected how much his face lit up when I asked.

And so, the last week of my training was truly back where things began for me—

In and around the small forest glade I had called my childhood home.

CHAPTER XXXI

SUGGESTIONS

Daylight blazed with uncharacteristic intensity above me as I stepped into Anathema's glade, as if she was watching and waiting, as eager as I was to see the results of my final match.

Darryl and Rusty flanked me as I walked in from the glade's western edge. In a way that must have been coordinated without any knowledge of mine, Lord Talis walked in simultaneously from the east, Lord Oloris and Eliree at his own sides. Wordlessly, we met with the three judges in the center of the glade.

Then, with a somber tone, Ana spoke. "It is time to determine your final trial. Unless either duelist wishes to surrender now?"

Ana looked meaningfully in my direction.

"I have no intent to surrender," I told her.

"Nor do I," Lord Talis replied.

"Very well, then." Ana closed her eyes for a moment. "As Lord Talis accepted the last match, it is his choice on what to propose first for the trial."

"Within a sword of weal and woe, a tale of time of long ago. To draw a sword and set it free, one must know its history. We'd speak of this, just you and me."

I blinked. "You want to compete in . . . knowing Anathema's history?"

"The ancient history of the sword prior to Anathema's birth, specifically," Lord Oloris noted.

I blanched.

This was a genuinely appropriate and relevant contest—

And one I absolutely could not compete in. I knew basically nothing about Anathema's past.

If I hadn't been so focused on my own history, maybe I would have taken the time to think about just how relevant Ana's own background — and abilities, too — were to the nature of our contest. It was a tremendous, shameful omission on my part.

I didn't even know if Ana knew her own history. I hadn't really asked.

I took a breath, thinking.

We'd have a day before the actual contest started, as always. Would that be enough time to get ahead in knowledge? I did know some things, including some general esoterica that might be relevant, but . . .

No. If he was proposing this, he had a plan. Or he was much better at bluffing than I was. I couldn't read any trickery in his expression. He seemed perfectly calm.

Which made sense, since he knew that he had me right where he wanted me.

If I refused this, I was out of refusals. He had one left. Meaning that if I didn't pick this challenge, he could pick anything he wanted, as long as it felt reasonable to the judges.

Was this a better option than whatever else he might come up with?

"Allow me to confer with my second and third," I said, finally.

"Of course," Lord Oloris replied on behalf of Lord Talis.

I took a deep breath, trying to steady my nerves. It didn't help.

I turned to Darryl and Rusty. "Do you two happen to have enough secret knowledge of Anathema's pre-incarnation days that you think we should glean an advantage?"

"Not a bit," Darryl replied. "It's not my area of study. I could ask Mother, however. She knew this place long before the sword was here."

That was a good start. "And I could ask Grandfather, if he's around. And Verthrimax, maybe?"

"You would speak to the great dragon?" Rusty blinked at me, seeming uncharacteristically surprised.

"Sure, why not?"

"I was long ago forbidden to tread in his —" Rusty coughed, then made a motion of adjusting their collar. And, at the same time, adjusted their voice a bit. "Was just thinkin' that's quite a risk, yeah? Ol' Iron Breaker isn't one to be trifled with."

I chuckled. "We have a rapport. That won't be a problem."

Rusty gave me the strangest look I'd seen in a while, then just sort of . . . remained silent.

I didn't know how to read that, so I just turned back to Darryl. "Think what we could pick up today would be enough?"

"I think he has some kind of secret about her past he intends to play that we're not going to figure out this rapidly. Unless Rusty has some insight on that?"

"Hm?" Rusty blinked, then shook themselves. "I, uh. No? No. I mean, I know stuff, but not what he's up to."

I took a breath. "How do we balance that against the possibility that he just says 'sword fight' if I refuse?"

"A sword fight is what you've been preparing for," Darryl pointed out. "I think I'd take an improbable contest over an unknown one."

"They're both unknown," I replied. "In fact, this contest is actually more known, since he won't necessarily actually choose a duel."

"But he probably will," Darryl noted. "Hold on, let me actually confer with the other side."

I waited for a bit while Darryl went and discussed. I turned to Rusty while he was gone.

"Are you . . . unwell?"

They rubbed their nose. I saw a brief sparkle of glamor, which wasn't a good sign. "I, uh, it's not that. I'm fine. Just . . . Verthrimax? Huh."

"Wasn't in your calculations for me?" I asked, folding my arms.

They laughed nervously. "Whatever would ye be talkin' about?"

"We can talk about this later." I sighed.

"Technically can, sure." They gave a little whistle. I turned away, waiting for Darryl to return. It didn't take long.

"It'll be a sword contest if you turn this down. Nonlethal, point-based dueling. Might have a theme, might not."

I took a moment, doing a little calculating of my own.

Then I stepped forward. "Though I acknowledge the relevance of the contest, I must respectfully refuse."

Ana nodded. And I saw something else on her face—

Relief?

Was she worried that I'd choose that contest? That was . . . odd.

What did she know that I didn't?

It wasn't the right time to ask, so I waited.

"Edge has refused a challenge, and thus, it is his turn to propose one."

We both knew where this was going, but I still had the obligation to propose something relevant and interesting. "You proposed a challenge related to Anathema's past, before she was born. In a prior round, I proposed a challenge about her present — the Anathema that stands before us now. And so, it is natural that I must now propose a third challenge, one of Ana in a different time. As a trial, we would both speak of what Anathema wishes for her own future."

Ana's eyes widened. "Lien . . . that's . . ."

"A challenge chosen wise and true, but it is one I cannot do," Lord Talis said. "With lifelong bond, you could not lose. That is to say, I must refuse."

I nodded to him, then turned back to Ana—

Who looked even more relieved than before.

That was . . . concerning. It's possible I should have talked my idea out with her in advance. Then again, that wouldn't have been very fair, would it?

Either way, it was decided now.

Ana's expression went somber as she spoke. "Lord Talis has refused the offer, and thus has no more refusals. It is his turn to propose a challenge to Edge — who has no refusals left."

Lord Talis met my gaze directly as he drew in a breath.

"Swords. Tomorrow. Sunrise."

Then he turned and walked away.

As Lord Talis left with his seconds and most of the judges left, I turned to Ana. "You had a stronger reaction to those rejections than I expected. Was there something about those challenges I didn't understand?"

"Ye . . . yeah. But now isn't the time to talk about that. You need to be getting ready for your duel, Lien." She floated over to me, her expression sad. "Do you think you can win?"

I considered that. "*Can* I win? Sure. It's possible. And for you, Ana, I'm going to fight with everything I have."

"Are you really fighting for me?" she asked.

I raised an eyebrow. "Of course I am. What sort of question is that? That's the whole point of this. To let you make a choice."

"It's just . . . we haven't really talked about . . ." She threw her hands up. "Never mind. It's not the time."

I reached out to her. She took a step back.

"I can't. I'm a judge right now. It's not appropriate."

There was clearly a lot going on here that I wasn't seeing. But, instead of arguing, I bowed. "Of course. If that's what you want."

"Not about what I want," she mumbled. Then she waved a hand, as if dismissing me.

I sighed, turned, and walked off with Darryl and Rusty, heading away from the grove.

As we walked out of the area, I turned toward Darryl and Rusty. "Any idea what that was about?"

"Not our business, I suspect," Darryl said. "Think you need to have a long talk with her after this is all over."

"Assumin' you get a chance, before she's, you know, swept off by that noble knight from far away," Rusty added helpfully.

I gave Rusty a hard look. "I have no intention of letting that happen."

"Might be that you should focus on your plans for your opponent, then, seein' as he's still three levels above you and, if we're bein' honest, probably better with a sword."

I frowned at Rusty. "Do you know that he's better with a sword?"

Rusty shrugged. "Can't say what's legend and true, but he's older and more experienced than you."

"Doesn't mean everything." I left it unspoken that it did mean a lot. And that he was a Sword Lord, which meant he could fight against other people with sword essence above their own level. That would significantly limit my options, unless I could use it against him somehow.

I considered for a beat, then shook my head. "What else can I do to prepare?" I asked them.

"Get a good night of sleep. Mom is always talking about how important that is."

"You know I'm not great at sleep. I—"

Darryl reached into his robes, feeling around, then shoved a vial into my hands. "Can't do this often. But drink it tonight, right before you go to bed."

"It'll help me fall asleep?" I asked.

"Probably. Or you'll end up in the Plane of Dreams. One or the other." He shrugged.

"I . . . I'm not sure I should risk that." I'd tapped into my dream self a number of times while asleep, but my meetings with Dream Girl weren't the same thing as my physical body moving to the Plane of Dreams. That'd be orders of magnitude more dangerous.

And fun, of course. But I was short on time.

"Eh, we'd come get you," he said.

I sighed, then accepted the vial. "Rusty? Any last-minute insights?"

"Sure, but none of 'em are *helpful*, exactly." They frowned. "Unless . . ."

"Unless?" I asked.

"Well, there was that thing we met up for before. If you'd be willing to take another trip down there—"

I shook my head. "Can't risk being stuck for days and missing the match."

"That's your objection?" Their eyes flashed. "So, if I wanted to ask you to come out there after this was all over—"

My own eyes narrowed. "I won't have much of a choice after this, would I? Not with the favor I owe."

"What if . . . I didn't want it to be a favor?" Rusty asked.

"Then you shouldn't have put me in a position to owe you one," I told them, perhaps sounding a little harder than I wanted to.

Rusty looked down and away. "This isn't what I wanted."

Darryl stepped between us. "Okay, I don't know exactly what's going on between you two, but I doubt it's immediately relevant. Can you talk out whatever that is another time?"

"Yeah. That's fine," I told him, taking a deep breath. "Rusty, can you do anything to help me prepare for the match that won't cause further delays or favors to be owed?"

They paused, looking a little hurt, then gazed off into the distance. "I'll think on it. Can I visit you in the morning, tomorrow? Very early, maybe waking you?"

I nodded. "Okay."

"Good. Dream well tonight. Tomorrow, I will be your dawn."

CHAPTER XXXII

SWORD STEALER

Darkness was all around me, save for a single distant, flickering candle. I could sense, but not see, walls all around me in other directions. The only way I could see was forward, toward the feeble light.

I didn't care for that.

I drew a sword, then blinked. It wasn't the one I'd expected.

The strange crown-pommeled blade was the one I'd gotten from . . . a lake, somewhere. I couldn't remember exactly where at that moment. It felt more solid than I'd remembered, more tangible for reasons I couldn't properly consider. The blade was a soft, translucent crystal. It reminded me of legends of Ceris, the Song of Harmony, but it wasn't bright blue — it was largely colorless, more like a pane of glass. There was a soft glow within that, but the more I looked at it, the less I could place what color that glow was.

I ignored that incongruity, instead focusing on my predicament. I didn't mind finding myself in strange places, but being stuck on a single path wasn't acceptable.

A hint of essence flashed around my sword. I cut through the wall to my right, making a door.

On the other side, I found a waterfall.

Huh. That looks almost like . . .

I raised my left arm and pushed aside the waterfall, parting it like a curtain. Then, I stepped out, onto the familiar rocks just outside the Hero's Rest.

I'd been here a thousand times, but the company was different than usual this time.

Only three rocks down sat a figure I could never forget, yet she looked different than I'd remembered.

She was a young woman in simple trousers and a rough forest-green tunic. On her waist was a long belt with a half dozen pouches, each holding different materials. Her boots and socks were off, sitting on the shore of the lake nearby, while she dipped her feet into the water by the waterfall. And resting on top of her knees was a sheathed sword. My own sword.

I took a step across the water toward her, my boots forming ice with each step. I didn't think about that at the time, though perhaps I should have. I only had eyes for her.

"It's one thing to steal a sword," I told her, "a rude thing, sure, but understandable in the context of our game. But my clothes? My scabbard?" I shook my head at her.

"Most guys tell me they'd love me to take their clothes," she shot back, barely glancing up toward me. Her tone was half-hearted, distant.

"I think you may misunderstand what guys want out of that equation. Although . . ." I glanced her up and down, paying attention to the way the tunic emphasized her build. "If I'm honest, it's not a bad look for you."

She let out a weak chuckle. "Not your best work, but I'll take it."

"That's what most girls tell me." I winked at her.

She turned up, blinked, and actually let out a real laugh at that one. "That's not your usual style of humor."

"Can't be funny if I'm predictable. Besides," I noted, coming within sword reach of her and sitting down on another large rock, "you're not your usual self right now, either. And I don't mean the clothes."

She wrinkled her nose and sighed. "Is it that obvious?"

"That you're moping? Yeah. Super obvious." I tilted my head to the side. "Do you want to talk about it?"

She sighed. "With you? I don't know. It's stupid."

"Well, if it's enough of an issue that you're worrying about it while you're asleep, it's probably something you should talk to someone about."

She sighed. "You're even more lucid than last time, aren't you?"

I nodded. "Haven't been doing as much training with dreams specifically, but I picked up another sword. Think it's tied to this place."

I tapped my sword, then sheathed it at my waist. I'm not sure I actually had a scabbard there before that moment, but I did when I needed one.

"Another magic sword. And you have it in the real world?"

"This place is just as real as the core plane, but yes, I have it in the waking world." I patted the sword. "I call it Mug."

". . . Mug? Because you're a sword thief?"

I laughed. "No. It's an acronym."

She nodded. "My sword is Gossamer."

I raised an eyebrow. "Wait. You named *my* sword?"

"Looks like my sword to me." She gave me a playful look, patting the hilt. There wasn't as much of a challenge as usual in her glance, but she was trying.

"We'll see about that." I grumbled. "Really? Gossamer? That's a little . . ."

"Girly?" she asked.

"Was going to say 'ephemeral.' Insubstantial."

"Well, it is." She frowned. "At least, to me. Even though I have it here now, it doesn't matter."

"Ahh." I nodded. "You thought you'd get to hold on to it in the physical world if you took my half of it."

She wrinkled her nose. "Maybe."

"Is that what's bothering you, then?"

Dream Girl shook her head. "A little, maybe. But that's not the bigger problem."

"You're right, it isn't. The real problem is that name. Stealing things from me is one thing, but Gossamer? Really?"

She cracked a small smile. "It's an acronym, too."

I raised an eyebrow. "For what, exactly?"

"God-Obliterating Sword Slashing And Murdering Entire Realities."

I paused.

Suddenly, Maximum Ultima Godslayer felt positively mundane, in a way that really shouldn't have been possible.

I raised a finger to say something, opened my mouth, then closed it and put my finger back down. Then, after a breath, I nodded solemnly. "It's a good name, no notes."

"Thank you."

"It's not *that* sword's name — that has a different one. But it's a good name."

She folded her arms. "I don't see why you should get to be the one who decides that. I have the sword."

"Do you?" I asked.

She tensed, as if I was going to attack, but I didn't move. Not yet.

Instead, I simply continued. "The sword isn't yours. I think you understand that, on some level, connection or no."

". . . It should be." She sighed. "It belonged to my family."

"That sword has passed through several hands over the years. It's not the type of thing that's inherited."

"You . . . know where it came from, then?" She sounded more interested then. More focused.

"I have a pretty good idea," I told her. "And . . . I don't remember exactly what I'm doing, but I think I need it right now."

She glanced away. "You can actually use it?"

"To some degree or another, yeah." I took a breath. "And I think it's important that I have it with me when the sun rises. So, from one sword thief to another . . . how about a bargain? I'll tell you a bit about the sword, and you let me hold on to it for a little while."

She turned back toward me. "I don't think I can agree to that. If I hand it off to you now, I don't know if or when I might see it again."

"We seem to be dreaming about each other pretty often. And, as I said, I already have the physical sword. If you really want to claim it, you're going to need to come after me someday either way."

". . . I already know that part." She took a breath. "But I can't agree to this. I can't let go of something else. Not right now. I'm . . . sorry. I . . . think I might need it, too."

"I understand." I reached out to offer her my hand. She hesitated for a moment, then took it. I gave her a gentle squeeze and a soft smile.

Then I pushed her backward into the water.

She hit the liquid with a splash, the sword slipping off her knees. I swiped it as she fell, slipping the scabbard over my shoulder. Logistically, there's no way it should have stayed there, but it did.

She sputtered and pulled herself up from the lake, dripping wet, her expression furious. "You jerk! That's — Hey, that's my sword!"

I stood up. "Not right now, it isn't. I offered you a deal, and you refused. So, I repaid you for the unkindness you did to me last time we met."

She stood up on her own rock, so angry that I could see literal steam rising off her skin. "You can't steal that. Not now. I'm . . . I can't be alone."

I paused, taking her more seriously. "Do you need help? In the waking world? Is that what this is about?"

"It's not like you're thinking. I don't need to be rescued. I'm just . . . Ugh, forget it!" She balled her fists. "We'll settle this the way we started."

Overhead, I could see the very first hints of the sun's light beginning to banish the evening.

"I'd like to do that sometime," I told her, "but unfortunately, I have another date."

"What?"

"I'll see you soon, Dream Girl." I stepped forward, straight toward the water.

She let out a roar, jumping forward in a blur of motion magic, and slammed straight into me. Together, we hit the waterfall and fell back through it—

But as we neared the ground, I commanded the sword on my back to cut. And there, in the world of dreams, there was only one pathway I needed to open.

When we reached what should have been the ground, we continued to fall and fall. Dream Girl's fists flailed against me as the soft light of the sun began to shine around us, and then—

Darkness, then nothing at all.

CHAPTER XXXIII

SUNRISE

I felt something heavy on top of me. My eyes half opened, and I saw someone above me, arm raised.

Purely out of instinct, I grabbed their arm before they could bring down whatever weapon they were carrying, then yanked them down and rolled on top, pinning their arms.

As my heart hammered in my chest, sleep rapidly fleeing from me, I found a wide-eyed and blushing Rusty beneath me.

I met their gaze for just a moment, processing the fact that they weren't holding a weapon in their pinned hands — just a lantern. They must have been reaching to set it down by the bedside, since it was still dark.

I grabbed the now-sideways lantern out of Rusty's hands and set it at the bedside before it could cause a fire — which wasn't really necessary, because on closer examination, there was no fire inside, just some kind of magical light — then went right back to pinning Rusty's hands.

"You can, uh, let me go," they said.

"I could," I agreed. "But you startled me. You could have knocked if you didn't want to alarm me."

"I could have," Rusty said, their expression settling into something more mischievous, "if I didn't want to alarm you, yes."

I brought my head down closer to their ear. "Is this everything you were hoping for in my response?"

". . . Not everything," they whispered, trembling. "But we don't have time for *everything*."

There was a brief pause, then I sighed and sat up, releasing Rusty's hands as I remembered what day it was and that I'd agreed to Rusty visiting me before dawn that morning.

"You have a plan?" I asked.

"Oh," Rusty said, "I always have *several*."

⁂

Rusty and I spent the earliest hours of the predawn morning on a journey to an all-too-familiar waterfall. I had, after all, just seen it the night before.

"You're sure this is wise?" I asked her.

"Not at all. But wisdom is the strength to question your course. The strength of *your* role is to know something is a great personal risk, but to choose to do it anyway, because it is right."

". . . I just meant that the water is going to be really cold at this time of morning."

"Oh, that." She shrugged. "Well, I'm not the one who has to go in there."

I sighed.

Then, setting my equipment to the side, I jumped into the water.

It had been too long since I'd brewed a healing elixir, and this time, it wasn't for someone else. If everything went according to plan, I'd need it very, very soon.

After that, we traveled all the way to the Rust River. There, I watered the *tama* jewel for a third and final time. The jewel grew from the size of a single digit of my finger to a full finger length and shimmered rust red.

I hoped that was a good thing.

Rusty helped me slip the necklace around my neck, then tuck it into my shirt to keep it hidden. I could feel a strange combination of essence types within it, but I couldn't identify anything other than sword essence, which was *definitely* present.

It was a strong magic, but one I didn't understand. I asked Rusty, but they had no better idea. So, with the necklace offering dubious protection, we continued on our way to the trial.

I was shivering all the way to the grove.

Darryl met us just outside the arena and handed me a cup of something hot and steaming. I was immediately grateful for the warmth, and I lifted the cup, then immediately took a sip.

It kicked me like a mule.

It definitely *wasn't* coffee or tea, but it had a similar effect, only magnified . . . and, maybe with a hint of something else I hadn't sensed just yet. As for what it actually was, I wasn't sure I wanted to ask.

We met with Lord Talis, Lord Oloris, and Eliree, as well as the judges.

Then, Ana announced the contest. "The judges have deliberated on the final version of the rules for this trial. This will be a duel of swords for points. Each time you cut your opponent with a sword will be worth a single point, regardless of the severity of the injury. Any form of sword, physical or essence, may be used. This is a nonlethal duel, and as such, striking the opponent in the head, neck, or Heart Point is forbidden."

I was a hint surprised at that last instruction, since attacks to specific Dianis Points were relatively rare — and one of the signatures of my own skill set. I didn't think my breach techniques were lethal, but . . . I supposed it made sense to avoid that kind of risk.

Lord Talis and I nodded at the instructions, then waited as Ana continued.

"This is a duel between opponents of significantly different levels of experience and status, but due to the significance and nature of the contest, there will be no handicaps. Both challengers may rely on outside help for provisions, essence, and morale prior to the start of the duel, but may not accept any help while the duel is in progress. Seconds and thirds may not interfere with the duel while it is in progress. The duel will be paused briefly after each blow is struck for a proper accounting of points. For clarity, seconds and thirds may assist their duelists during this pause, such as treating injuries, but may not interfere with the other team's duelist."

That was a pretty important clarification, and one that was cutting off an obvious loophole. I was surprised to hear it, since fae typically loved allowing loopholes in trials.

Perhaps that one was too obvious?

I had to hope my own tricks wouldn't be cut off quite so easily.

"If there are no further questions, each of the duelists now has three minutes to prepare with their team before the duel begins," Ana finished.

I nodded to Lord Talis, then turned away to approach my team.

"This is it," I told them. "Any last bits of help, material or verbal?"

"Not right now," Darryl told me. "But I do have the antidote for after the duel."

"The . . . what?" I blinked.

Darryl gestured at the cup I still had in my hands. "So, that's going to help even your odds a bit in the fight, assuming I mixed it right. But you're going to want to end the fight quickly, otherwise things are going to get a little weird."

". . . Weird how, exactly?" I asked.

"It helps you tap into your higher layers of self, giving you a small portion of the boost you'd ordinarily get from higher-layer access at greater essence levels. As time passes, the effect grows stronger. Unfortunately, you don't have the control necessary for that kind of power, and, uh, you have breach essence, which I wasn't really thinking about when I made that for you, so . . . yeah, don't take too long. And if any of your imaginary friends show up . . . **kill them**."

That last part definitely hadn't been Darryl's normal voice. I wasn't sure if that was him being extra-serious and throwing some sakki into his voice or if I was already hallucinating.

Great. Reality is going to fall apart while I'm dueling. This seems fine.

I turned to Rusty.

"You have what we brought," Rusty said. "If you want more help, you know the price."

I nodded.

I hoped it wouldn't come to that.

⊹⊹ ⊹⊹

Lord Valissar Talis and I stood across from each other in the center of the arena that had been constructed for the last match. Ana and I had rebuilt the crystals I'd shattered in the pillars, but they were a distraction. I knew I couldn't count on the exact same technique working twice.

. . . I'd try anyway, if I had time, but I couldn't rely on that. Every moment counted against an opponent like Lord Talis. A month of training with a Talisian had shown me that very clearly.

"I'll count down from three to one, then say a word to start the match," Ana explained. "Are both combatants ready?"

"One moment." I went and set my personal sword down against one of the pillars, still sheathed. Lord Talis raised an eyebrow.

Then I walked to Rusty, who produced a different sword — one we'd retrieved from the Lady of the Fake, in exchange for the ice sword — and handed it off to me.

"Changing weapons?" Lord Oloris said.

"My primary sword isn't ideal to use in a duel in its present form," I explained.

"What is this one, then?" he asked.

"I suspect you'll figure it out soon." I was under no obligation to tell him, after all.

Valissar Talis eyed the sword, concentrating for a moment. His eyebrow went up.

He must have realized, at least in part, what I'd sensed when I'd first seen it — the weapon was constructed from the stuff of dreams and desires, not sword essence.

There was a bit of sword essence about it now. This was, I suspected, because I'd been practicing with it before the match, and my own interpretation of the object as a sword had caused it to begin to generate essence of that type. That essence was minimal enough that I hoped he wouldn't be able to shape it, but also significant enough that I could prove it existed, meaning that the weapon counted as a sword for the purposes of the contest.

I was gambling on both of those points, but this match was going to be a series of gambles regardless of what approach I took. It was just about figuring out which bets were the best to place.

"I am ready now," I said, though mentally, I wasn't as sure as I sounded.

Carrying the strange dream sword didn't fill me with confidence, in spite of the weapon's power. I'd practiced with it, but that had been under controlled circumstances.

I hadn't been counting on using a dream sword while under the effects of Darryl's potion. Already, I was beginning to see strange things at the edges of my vision, just beyond clear perception. Hovering blades, echoes of figures from beyond my conscious mind.

Well, at least this won't be boring.

I assumed a generic combat stance. Anything else would give away too much too quickly.

Lord Talis watched me for another moment, assessing, then turned to Ana. "Outside your lair, I stand prepared."

"Good." Ana nodded. "In that case . . . three . . . two . . . one . . ."

Ana clapped her hands.

"Begin!"

INTERLUDE VII

VALISSAR TALIS

SWORD LORD

Valissar Talis stepped straight ahead, his shining blade rising as his enemy fled.

With sword essence flowing, he angled a slash, but a turn of the blade deflected his gash.

With rising suspicion, Lord Talis pressed, finding each of his moves blocked and suppressed.

With what arcane art can he move with such speed?
What strange technique lends him the strength that he needs?
No mere Torch should move as he does,
Nor even I, when I stood as he was.
Yet as he continued, a weakness he saw—
The young swordsman's skill, it came with a flaw.
With each step he took and each movement of blade,
The swordsman retreated toward the back of the glade.
Such predictable moments?
This he forbade.
With a gesture of sword and whisper of breath,
Lord Talis appeared in his enemy's path.
He knew not the nature of the rapid retreat,
But a tactic inlaid, and that he'd defeat.
As the young swordsman's eyes widened, he knew it was done—
A strategy parried, a battle half won.
What move now would his desperate foe make?
Could he rely on a sword that was known to be fake?
With both courage and cunning his opponent resumed,
One technique, then another, rapidly they ensued,
But without power to back them, his methods were doomed.
And so as the young man was backed toward a wall,
Lord Talis knew his opponent would fall.

CHAPTER XXXIV

SPATIAL SHIFT

As the duel began, Lord Talis teleported next to me, as I'd expected. I'd counted on it, in fact.

Teleportation was near instant, accomplished by walking through another plane where space was deeply compressed compared to our own. I did not have the speed to do anything in the passage of time during which a teleportation effect occurred, though I believed that at the absolute peak of power — where the Smiling Sword Saint had once stood, along with her rival — it may have been possible.

I didn't need to accomplish anything during the teleportation, however. I knew from sparring against Talisian that every teleportation technique had a minor effect, one that was so subtle that almost no one took it into account—

Essence senses were very briefly disrupted during the teleportation process. This was a necessity to avoid shattering your mind as you rapidly passed through a space where essence density was vastly different from the real world. For your average person, this was one component of the vertigo that was commonly known as teleportation sickness that occurred after a teleportation spell finished, or when one stepped through a doorway to an extradimensional space. It wasn't just about moving a long distance in a moment — it was about your essence senses being so slammed that they were briefly suppressed.

For a skilled teleporter like Valissar Talis, his essence sense would only be suppressed for an instant, but I timed it perfectly.

In the moment he stepped through space, I took a breath and reached Hearth-level.

In the weeks prior to the match, I'd trained myself to the very threshold of the next essence level.

It wasn't that I'd ever discovered any sort of secret technique for training faster. I'd simply started out with a low estimate of what my current essence value was — it had probably been closer to twenty-four or twenty-five, rather than twenty-two. I'd been training at almost exactly the rate I'd expected, meaning about four and a half essence per month — which meant that I'd brushed up against the thirty-six-essence barrier for Hearth about two months into the season.

I wasn't good enough to sense the exact moment of reaching the next level perfectly, but I had one advantage that virtually no swordsman did—

Gramps, and his immense knowledge of essence theory. He'd used essence-measuring instruments to help me measure out the exact point before I'd reach the next level, then I'd swapped to exclusively focusing my essence into secondary essence production. In order to avoid accidentally generating more primary essence to push over the threshold, I'd only reached the threshold the night before. It helped that I didn't have a Breathing Point yet — if I did, the mathematics behind preventing my accidental leveling would have been much more complex.

Power flooded through me as I reached the next level threshold. I was still two levels behind Valissar Talis himself, but I was compensating with multiple other advantages.

First, Darryl's potion was letting me tap into a fraction of the power of my other selves. With the seals in place, this was minimal, though I could feel more power flowing through my dream layer, both as a result of the cracks I'd caused against my nightmare self in the sepulcher and because of the dream-wrought sword in my hand.

Second, I activated the Shattering Soul technique at the same time I reached Hearth-level. This body-enhancement technique would rapidly drain my essence, but it gave me almost a full tier worth of improved combat ability while it was active. As a secondary effect, this would create a clear manifestation of internal sword essence that my opponent would eventually sense — and one that would, hopefully, cover up the burst of power I was getting from reaching a new level.

Finally, I'd spent a full month studying my opponent's sword styles. I knew his strikes, parries, and counters.

He did not, so far as I knew, have the same advantage.

And so, when he appeared and lashed out with a lightning-quick slash, I parried immediately, stepped in, and countered. His eyes showed momentary surprise, and then we launched into a rapid dance of moves. I fell back out of both strategy and necessity.

Even with the Shattering Soul and Hearth-level, even with knowing his moves, he still had the advantage in raw swordplay. I couldn't hope to match him blow for blow.

So, I was heading back toward where I'd set one of my traps — my sword resting against the pillar.

I was nearly to it when he vanished, then reappeared right behind me, barring my path.

I didn't let myself smile.

I swung around with feigned surprise, barely parried a swing, then snapped the fingers on my free hand.

A burst of sword essence emanated from my own still-sheathed weapon, which was now right behind Lord Talis.

He reacted faster than I'd hoped, reaching backward and grabbing the sword essence out of the air, as if it was solid. It coalesced into the shape of a hiltless blade, which he hurled at me.

I stepped right into it. The blade hit me dead-on in the chest—

And did absolutely nothing. My sword's essence couldn't hurt me. I'd hoped to hit him with it, but this worked almost as well.

I struck at the same time, my borrowed sword of dreams flashing forward as he was recoiling in surprise—

And he was still too fast. He parried my strike, driving my sword into the ground. The grove's floor began to bubble, dream magic shifting and transforming it on contact. I pulled my sword free before anything more deleterious could happen to the area, then stepped backward and threw something of my own—

A vial of breach essence.

As I'd hoped, he sliced it out of the air with a single swipe, which cut the vial in two. From his wince, I saw that he understood his mistake, but it was too late.

It wasn't enough breach essence to stop him from teleporting, but it would interfere, and that was progress for me.

I stepped in, my blade stretching and warping as I swung it. Valissar parried, but the blade's weight suddenly shifted as our swords met, hurling him backward. He slid back a step, offbalance, and countered by stabbing his sword downward, straight toward the ground.

I barely stepped backward in time before a blade pierced upward from beneath me. He blinked in surprise at my rapid response, but I only smiled.

I'd seen that technique before, after all. I'd drilled against it.

I might have telegraphed that fact a little too much, because he swapped strategies immediately, hurling a blast of force straight at me. When that staggered me, he came at me the old-fashioned way, swinging his sword directly at my chest.

I heard a *snap* as the jade on my necklace pulled itself free, interposing itself between us. With a resounding *crunch*, his sword impacted the shimmering jewel. There was a burst of crimson water as the jewel cracked, dripping liquid.

The reddish water drenched his sleeves, and for a moment, his sword hand drooped, seemingly heavier than it should be.

Mentally thanking the whirling jade as it dropped to the ground, spent, I lunged for Lord Talis, hoping to make use of my latest aspect and his moment of weakness. He grimaced as I rushed forward, and a burst of raw motion essence blasted the strange water from his sleeves. I barely adjusted my lunge to avoid being drenched with the strange fluid as he had. My swing went off mark, barely missing his right shoulder.

All those tricks and openings for a miss. Still, I was right next to him, so before he could completely right himself, I threw a kick.

He slid to the side as if the ground was slick with oil, avoiding the attack effortlessly.

I lunged again, desperately focusing my essence. "Shattering—"

Without aiming at me, he stabbed into the air. And a blade appeared on my left, drawing a clear line of crimson across my arm.

"Hold!" The judges called.

I groaned, pausing midstrike. My sword was still flaring with essence, raised at an angle to strike.

"Point for Lord Valissar Talis! Reset!"

I took a breath, then walked back to my place in the center of the platform where we'd begun.

I'd played several tricks, burned through nearly half my essence, and my opponent had still managed to get the first point against me. From any reasonable perspective, I was at a terrible disadvantage.

That is to say, of course, that everything was going according to plan.

CHAPTER XXXV

SECOND SWORD

We reset to our starting positions. I swapped stances this time, choosing to rest in one of the classic stances of the Talisian Iron Cutting style, the only Talisian style I'd had enough time to study in any detail.

He'd surely seen me using the style to counter his own movements in the previous round — this, and my smug smile, would hopefully reinforce that I knew his techniques and lead him to make false assumptions about the scope of my knowledge.

For his part, Lord Talis simply took the same stance as before, his expression thoughtful.

"Three . . . two . . . one . . . begin!"

I flicked my wrist.

A tiny projectile flashed across the ten feet between us.

Lord Talis looked genuinely startled — there was no throwing attack in the Talisian Iron Cutting style. He still effortlessly parried the tiny memento I'd thrown at him—

The sword I'd stolen off the coin in our second round. It flew harmlessly into the distance, where hopefully I'd pick it up later. I wasn't even sure it would have cut him if it hit, but it had served a more important purpose by adjusting his guard just a bit.

A burst of my new lunging-aspected essence carried me forward with such speed that I surprised even myself, then I brought my blade downward, the sword's strange blade flickering like a glass bulb. There was a loud *crack* as Lord Talis barely managed a parry, then cracks spread across my sword, and the world went dark around us, as if someone had put out the sun.

I felt the essence in the air all around us, using that as a guide. It was faster for me, more certain than relying on sound. I caught Lord Talis's retributive slash near the hilt of my blade, then pushed him backward with a burst of strength. I felt him stumble, followed up, and stepped forward with a swing of my off hand, forming a Sword Hand technique—

It might have worked if the light hadn't returned while I was midswing, half blinding me. Lord Talis adjusted faster, just barely avoiding my Sword Hand technique as it tore through his shirt, then vanishing and reappearing to my right.

He thrust at my foot. I kicked his sword, forming a blade along my boot to knock his sword harmlessly aside. He blinked at that in surprise, then vanished again.

I spun around, parrying his predictable swing from my left. Lord Talis was an excellent fighter — a better fighter than I was in general, if I'm honest — but drilling the exact techniques that he'd been trained in for a month had given me a definitive advantage, especially when combined with his uncertainty about my own methods.

I swept both my blades sideways after the parry, aiming for his midsection. He jumped back rather than teleporting, so I released my Sword Hand technique and gripped my dream blade with both hands, then briefly concentrated. The blade flared with light, then I swung it diagonally through the previous swing I'd taken, creating a glowing X of cutting essence that flashed forward.

Lord Talis snapped his fingers. A portal appeared in the attack's path, and another right behind me. As the attack flew into the portal, I acted on instinct, jabbing one hand backward.

Breach Blade.

The exit portal exploded.

When it did, the portal my attack was passing through detonated as well, creating a burst of mixed essence that slammed into Lord Talis's back. It didn't hurt him much, but it burned through his clothes and left welts on his back.

I pulled back my sword for a follow-up—

"Hold!" Lord Feather's voice called out.

I blinked, stopping in my position.

"Lord Talis was injured by that detonation. The judges must confer," Lord Brine explained.

Lord Talis and I waited in our present positions. I considered my next moves, but I didn't have long.

Lord Feather came forward, inspecting Lord Talis's injuries, then returned to where the judges had been standing and talked to the others again.

Ana spoke next. "No point is awarded. While a sword-based attack was involved in the detonation, the principal cause of the explosion was an interaction of teleportation magic and breach essence. We will hold for three minutes for Lord Talis's wounds to be treated."

I released my Shattering Soul technique immediately, conserving what essence I could.

I could have made the argument that my Breach Blade technique used sword essence — it did — but neither the Breach Blade technique nor my X-shaped sword attack had actually hit Lord Talis. If a contest had required hitting a target with fire magic, and I'd hit someone with the rocks from an exploding fireball, the judges wouldn't have counted that — the logic here was the same.

I felt a hint of frustration, but I nodded.

During the three-minute break, Eliree tended to Lord Talis's injuries. I felt a pang of jealousy, but I pushed it aside. I had more important things to worry about.

"Reset positions," Ana called, finally. I frowned. That was unfortunate — I'd had some ideas for where we'd been standing.

Now, I'd drained my essence even more, and—

What was that shadow?

I blinked, and it was gone.

I shook my head. It was probably nothing.

I took another breath, steadying myself. Then, it was time to begin again.

We returned to our starting positions. Something smelled off. I reached up to rub my nose absently and . . .

Was that blood?

Had he hit me in the face at some point? I couldn't remember.

I rubbed the blood on my tunic. A little bit of blood wasn't a major concern.

It was more worrying when I realized, a few moments later, that I couldn't see the blood I'd just wiped off.

I lifted my hand, inspecting it. Clean. There were even some soap suds rising off it, from where I'd washed it.

Wait. That's wrong. I didn't—

"Three . . . two . . ."

The countdown startled me into focus. I shifted my stance back into . . . something stance-like.

Shattering Soul.

Power flooded through me once again, but this time, sparks flew across my skin. That was new.

Lord Talis gave me a quizzical look.

I tried to play it off as best I could, but I was getting . . . a little worried now.

It's possible that playing with powers beyond my control and comprehension was causing some small anomalies in my life experience.

Ah, well. That's how it goes sometimes.

I let out a cheerful whistle, causing Ana to briefly pause her count, blink, then continue.

"One . . ."

"Begin!"

Lord Talis watched me, holding his stance.

I watched him, pretending that I was holding his gaze, when in reality, I was wrestling with the fact that I could, at present, see two additional versions of Lord Talis behind him and slightly overlapping.

Either he'd activated a displacement technique, or, more likely, that not-coffee was really kicking in harder than expected.

Note to self: detonating breach essence portals while holding a dream essence sword and under the effects of experimental layer-perceiving alchemy may not be wise.

Noted, a slightly deeper version of my own voice replied.

I felt a chill down my spine.

My first instinct, when facing fear, was to attack.

In this case, however, I was offbalance enough that I had to go with my second, trustier instinct—

Flagrantly ignoring the intent of a contest in fun and creative ways.

"You're even more formidable than I expected, Lord Talis," I said, walking to the side. We began to circle each other in a classical dueling movement.

He tipped his head in acknowledgment but didn't banter with me. That was fine. I was distracted enough by the ritual circle that was gradually forming on the ground from our movements, like a sword tracing a path along the stone.

I briefly considered invoking the circle for a spell, then I remembered that I was not a ritual spellcaster and, more importantly, that the circle wasn't real.

. . . Or, at least, not real *enough*. Probably. That line was rapidly falling apart.

Instead, I suddenly turned and bolted, running toward the wall where my sword was resting.

Lord Talis appeared in the midst of my path, just as expected. And, in his moment of teleportation disorientation, I stabbed the bottom of my own right boot.

"Hold!" Lord Brine called.

We froze. Which was awkward, of course, because I currently had my sword resting against my boot.

All three judges came over, inspecting my boot. I heard Ana cough out a surprised laugh when she saw it.

The judges conferred briefly.

"One point to Edge," Ana explained. "Return to positions."

Lord Oloris spoke up. "Pardon, judges. I could not see what happened."

Lord Brine turned toward him. "Understandable, given that the lettering is hard to see, even at a distance. Edge had the words 'your opponent' written on the bottom of his boot, which he cut through with a sword. And, in the rules . . ."

"He is awarded a point for cutting 'your opponent.' Very clever." Lord Oloris gave me a nod of acknowledgment. Two other versions of him did the same, although one of them looked into the distance, as if trying to find something.

I blinked at the images of other versions of him.

This time, they didn't go away.

"Return to positions."

Belatedly, I realized I still had my leg raised and my sword pressed against it. Then, I returned to the position I'd started in.

. . . Or, at least, what I thought my position was.

With all the flowers growing, it was getting harder and harder to tell.

INTERLUDE VIII

LORD OLORIS NYSARII

SUPERIOR SUBTLETIES

Lord Oloris Nysarii returned to his waiting position on the sidelines of the battle. He stood alongside his love's former love, which would have been a very powerful statement in itself if this had been a political gathering, but alas, the battle was of a far more mundane kind than those he preferred.

Still, he was finding the whole thing more entertaining than he expected, even if much of the entertainment was (by necessity) of his own creation. Lord Brine would have been more fun to play with if he wasn't in that stuffy guise, but most of the rest of the people involved were mere children and didn't have the sophistication to enjoy proper discourse.

He caught Rusty's eye flashing to him for a moment, then back toward the battle.

Most of the children weren't sophisticated enough, he considered, but there were always exceptions. And that one?

Something about that flick of an eye made his blood run cold. There was something simultaneously friendly and terrifying about that creature, which is to say that they were wondrous. Truly, a reminder of home in this foreign court.

As he turned back toward Lord Talis facing off against the young man known as Edge, Lord Oloris mentally chided the boy for playing his move so soon. A cunning trick to earn a point outside of the typical scoring structure was best used to end a match, not this early. By in doing so at this precise point, and evening the score, he'd played into his opponent's hand.

Before, Lord Talis's body-enhancement technique had hummed quietly within him, subtle and near silent, affording him little benefit. As the match shifted briefly toward giving the boy the narrative focus of a comeback, Lord Talis's technique began to hum a soft internal melody, one that would begin to strengthen his abilities — and grow stronger and stronger, so long as the flow of his Epic was not interrupted.

It was a shame, really. The boy had been doing so well up until this round. Now, unless he had something truly transcendent to play, he would fail to keep up with Lord Talis's continuously growing strength.

And, of course, there was one final twist that could still influence things, no matter what, wasn't there?

Lord Oloris sighed and relaxed, contented.

Everything was going according to plan.

CHAPTER XXXVI

SHARPENED

Even as my essence diminished, I could feel my senses sharpen. Every bit of the arena was feeling crisper, every hint of essence closer—

And beyond all of it, outside the scope of my everyday senses, I could feel something else. Something that smelled . . . purple?

Oh. That's a problem, isn't it?

I blinked away the taste of rainbows, adjusting the windowpane — no, it was a sword, for now — in my right hand.

I glowered at the sword, mentally commanding it to remain stable. My reflection winked at me, his eyes blazing gold.

Don't wink at me like that. I already beat you once, I told him.

Did you? I heard his whisper from behind me. My jaw tightened. *Look, you need to focus up,* my nightmare reflection told me. *You're letting yourself get too distracted by things that might not even be real.*

I don't have to listen to — Wait, are you helping me?

Obviously, my evil voice told me. *Now, he's going to try to get to your boot, since he could pull off the same trick you did with it, and he doesn't want you to do it. You should destroy your boot.*

I'm not sure that's such a—

"Three . . . two . . ." Ana's voice seemed to be counting down slower than usual. Was that actually happening?

I didn't know.

You can take actions before the match starts, the voice told me. *At least get rid of the writing.*

"One . . ."

I lifted my boot a moment, raising a finger that blazed with breach essence, then obliterated the remaining writing on it. I kept the boot itself on. Lord Talis watched me the entire time, but without any obvious reaction.

"Begin!"

Lord Talis walked slowly toward me. He seemed to split apart as he moved, versions of him approaching at other angles. Fortunately, none of them were as solid as the original, so I was *pretty sure* I knew which one was real—

Right up until he vanished, and the others remained.

Not good. Left, my darker voice told me.

I swung around, barely parrying a swing. Sparks flew off my blade, turning into fireflies that danced around us. I ignored the fireflies, lashing out in an immediate counter.

Shattering Sword.

My sword impacted his, mirror copies of my blade exploding outward from the slash. One came so close that it almost cut his arm before freezing at his sleeve, then with a gesture of his off hand, he hurled that phantasmal cut into the distance.

I pulled my sword back to attempt another cut—

Or, at least, I tried to. I blinked as I pulled backward . . . and realized that my sword was stuck.

What?

I tugged at it a couple more times as he reached down to his belt. There was no other visible sword present, but he was clearly going for another weapon.

I slammed breach essence into my own sword, trying to shake it free from whatever technique he was using. It trembled, but remained stuck.

Binding essence, the deeper voice reported. *You haven't learned that one yet. He's too strong to break the sword out, hit him with—*

He pulled another sword out of the air, a thin thing that looked like a pane of glass. He made a casual jab, which I parried with a Sword Hand technique I didn't remember forming.

Then, I released my hand on my sword's grip, letting it fall. He stepped backward, releasing his grip on his own primary sword. Both of our weapons hovered in midair, as if frozen in time.

I formed a second Sword Hand as he maneuvered and lunged in.

No, not that technique, he'll—

My blades came within an inch of his chest before they flexed in midair, twisting and turning backward. They brushed against my own sleeves, but didn't cut me.

Unfortunately, his quick jab from the strange glass side sword did. It was just a trace of blood across my right side, but that was enough—

And it was also enough that my Shattering Soul technique triggered, retributive power shattering the glass of his blade.

As the sword exploded, fragments of glass embedded in my chest and right hand. The defense provided by the same technique prevented anything from sinking deep, but it made a glancing blow a much more severe injury.

I'd miscalculated—

But so had he.

It was only a sliver, but a tiny fragment of glass had pierced one of Lord Talis's own fingertips.

"Hold!"

My legs trembled as I attempted to remain standing where I was and avoid gripping my side.

I barely noticed the judges conferring as blood dripped down my side.

"Both sides have been cut. One point to each combatant. Three-minute pause. See to your injuries."

I blinked.

Pause? Did that mean I could move?

The next thing I remembered, Darryl was standing in front of me, snapping his fingers.

"Not good." He sniffed at the air. "You can move, Edge. Drink this."

He pushed something into my hands.

I didn't question him, slowly sipping at it. It tasted floral, with hints of asparagus and space-time.

"That won't get you quite back to normal, but it should help you sober up a little. Unfortunately, you can't drink a healing potion or elixir right now — too much of a chance of it complicating what you're dealing with on other layers. Rusty, help me get the glass out and bandage him."

"You demand that I help you? That's quite the —" Rusty blinked, then shifted their demeanor. "Right, 'course. Glad to help. Edge, turn off your technique."

I blinked, then realized I still had the Shattering Soul on.

Release Shattering Soul.

I barely remember the next few minutes as they pulled glass out of my side, then wrapped my chest and hand with bandages. At some point, I must have taken off my shirt for that, then put it back on.

Eventually, I was standing back where we'd started. My dream sword was still floating in midair several paces away, entangled with Lord Talis's blade.

He'd found another sword somewhere, one with a pure white blade. It reminded me of something, but I couldn't concentrate enough to place it. My mind was clearing, but slowly.

I did know one thing, however—

I was in very serious trouble.

One last bit of advice before I'm gone, a dark voice whispered to me.

I bristled at the sound, then took a breath.

I'm listening.

CHAPTER XXXVII

SCORE

I'd been struck twice during the duel. Lord Talis had been struck once, and I'd also cut the boot, for two points of my own during the match.

We were nearing the end. Unfortunately, so was my strength.

My use of the Shattering Soul had drained me to the dregs of my essence, even with pausing during each of our three-minute breaks to recover.

Conversely, Lord Talis looked stronger than ever, and I suspected I knew why. Of course, there was a helpful voice there for me to rely on, too.

He's getting stronger because of how his essence works, the voice whispered. *That poetry he's always spouting? He's using Epic essence. Epic as in the poetry style, but also the effect it has on his abilities when the story reaches its peak.*

You need to break his story.

"How?" I whispered into the air.

First off, don't talk to me out loud, I'm talking in your mind, and it looks weird.

Second, I don't know. When I did this, I had all the swords from the sepulcher with me.

I blinked. *You did this?*

Uh, yeah. Alternate you, remember? Anyway, I tricked him into grabbing one of the cursed weapons, which did not work out well for the guy. Don't look at me like that, I broke him free after the duel. I'm not a monster.

I frowned. *I was pretty sure you were a monster.*

I get that a lot. It's the hair, and the evil voice, and the connection with the Maker of Monsters. The voice paused. *Mostly the hair, I think.*

What about the golden eyes and the blackened petals on your face? I asked.

Oh, yeah, he said. *Those, too. Anyway, you're running out of time. You need to do a few things to prepare. First thing? Get your sword.*

I nodded, going over to my scabbard and fastening it to my back, then unsheathing the weapon.

Lord Oloris approached me. "Pardon, but I was under the impression that sword was too dangerous to use in a duel."

I blinked at all three of him. "Right. I did say something like that. Except . . . didn't I also say 'in this form'?"

"You did, indeed." Lord Oloris nodded.

That was good, because I genuinely was sure of very little at that point.

"Right. Well, then, allow me to clarify." I put a hand on the pommel of the sword, sent in a spark of spirit, then pushed and twisted.

. . . In the wrong direction.

I felt the resistance immediately as I pushed the sword toward a form I had not yet unleashed . . . and the resistance was less than it should have been.

I didn't allow myself to react, nor to push through. I simply swapped directions on the twist, shifting my sword into the shape of Soulsever.

The blade flashed as the sword collapsed down to a familiar, gleaming longsword, more appropriate for a duel than the blade's colossal two-handed form. Fortunately, I had practiced with the sword enough at this point to instinctively restrain the burst of essence from the blade as it shifted shapes.

"Marvelous. A shapeshifting sword. I withdraw my objection." Lord Oloris nodded to me, then retreated to speak with Lord Talis.

Rusty stepped up next to me. "Running low on time." They examined my sword closely. "That's an impressive blade, but will it be enough?"

"I'm not sure," I admitted. "I think" — I took a breath, considering all the options available to me, and the words of my darker self — "I may need a favor."

Rusty raised a hand to their chest. "I . . . thought you'd never ask."

⁂

A few moments later, I returned to my starting position, a new sword in hand and a blood-red handkerchief tied around my hand where fragments of glass had pierced it.

I felt it constrict around my fingers as I shifted into a fighting stance. As it did, crimson began to bleed into my shirt and arm, and I felt my strength redoubled.

"A marvelous gift you now wear —" Lord Talis began.

"A favor token from lady fair," I replied.

"Is such a thing a mark of love?"

"I know that not, but I needed a glove."

Lord Talis laughed. "What earned you this, if I may ask?"

"A simple thing, a rescue past."

"A rescue, you say? A noble tale. Perhaps you'll tell me more, after you fail."

I scoffed. "Perhaps I'll tell you, perhaps I'll not. But know this now, before duel is fought. With my true sword and this in hand, with greater strength now I do stand. For one last time, this I demand. Surrender now, before I execute my plan."

"What card is it you think you hold? What makes such a demand so brazen-bold?"

"It's simple, really — I'll tell you true. Through royal grace, my strength forged anew."

Lord Talis actually paused. ". . . Royal?"

My smile twisted as his poetry paused. "I wear now a princess's trust, as potent as a blood-red thrust, for she who stands at palace peak, the scion of the salt and rust."

"Well, now." Lord Oloris stepped forward as Lord Talis's expression faltered. "One noble gift deserves another, doesn't it?"

With a single motion, he removed a necklace from his neck, then clasped it around Lord Talis's throat.

Lord Talis accepted the gift with a nod, and I saw the desert flames burning within the jewels along the necklace.

The object Lord Oloris had bestowed upon his champion was, very likely, a more formidable one in magic than the one that I wore. In truth, I had very little idea of what the strange garment was doing for me, aside from tightening like a hand's grip against mine.

In symbolism, however, I'd robbed him of something, in spite of Lord Oloris's intervention—

By displaying the favor of a princess at a critical moment, I'd successfully deflected the apex of his Epic. Not enough to turn his own power against him, as I'd hoped — Lord Oloris's hasty counter had assured that — but enough to prevent his strength from building toward a greater crescendo as our battle continued.

And with that advantage robbed from him, I thought that, perhaps, I had a chance.

"This has been a fascinating discussion," Lord Brine said, "but perhaps we should return to the match itself?"

"Yes, of course." Ana's voice was oddly numb. "Combatants, ready yourselves."

I nodded. I felt one more squeeze against my hand, bringing me comfort and strength. I turned toward Rusty, who opened their clenched hand to give me a friendly wave. I nodded to them, then to Darryl, and finally turned to Lord Talis.

"Positions."

We assumed our combat stances.

Shattering Soul.

Crimson patches spread across my skin as the technique activated. This was no dream magic at work, no mere spectacle — I could see droplets of red draining out of the handkerchief, turning to a lighter pink shade, as my strength redoubled.

"Three . . . two . . . one . . . begin!"

⊱⊰

There was a heartbeat of silence as the battle raged between us without motion. Our eyes flashed with power as we analyzed targets, movements, possibilities.

And then, as that moment faded, we vanished together in a blur of movement.

Strike. Parry. Riposte.

We were not equally matched, but for a moment, the difference was only the barest margin. Enough to be governed solely by a mistake.

At Hearth-level, I was two full levels below Lord Talis. This was not an impossible margin to conquer, as Lord Talis himself had done it — but it was notable enough that I knew he had done so. It was a part of his reputation and legacy.

I had no illusions that I had the skill level necessary to conquer that gap, but I had three principal advantages.

First, the Shattering Soul technique. A body-enhancement technique, while active, probably accounted for a half level of extra power. That was unusually strong for a body-enhancement technique, but mine was extremely costly, with a maximum usage of minutes.

Lord Talis had the opposite sort of body-enhancement technique — his started off with minimum benefits, then ramped up gradually over a long time period, based on the progression of his Epic. This meant that it was weakest at the start of a battle and strongest at the climax. If I had not interrupted its progress, it might have given him a full level of extra strength here — and it still could, if he wrested the narrative back in the middle of our duel in some way. For the moment, he was at a disadvantage in terms of these techniques, but it would not last long.

Darryl's potion was another advantage to me, but one that was so distracting that it hurt my concentration and technique. Power-wise, I'd say it accounted for another half level of physical ability, but that power waned, even as Lord Talis's power began to wax once again.

And now, finally, I had the gift of the princess wrapped around my hand. The greatest of my advantages in terms of the raw power it provided. I didn't exactly understand how, but I suspected I was getting nearly an entire level worth of extra power out of it. Probably not quite that much, but close.

I also knew it was gradually cutting off the circulation in my sword hand. It's possible I should have wrapped it somewhere else, but I didn't know if that would have worked.

So, two half-level boons, and one worth another nearly an entire level—

Meaning that, at that moment, I had just about the same raw power as Lord Talis. Except, of course, that my power was rapidly declining, while his was increasing.

The clear solution was to strike fast and hope for a victory while I retained strength near to his. The problem was that this method was obvious, and easily countered—

As Lord Talis demonstrated as he vanished from our part of the battlefield, appearing along the opposite wall.

I spun toward him immediately, burning lunging-aspected essence to flash toward him and swing a diagonal cut at his midsection—

Only to cleave straight into the stone wall as he vanished again, appearing far away.

I narrowed my eyes, then took a breath and released a hand from my grip, pulling a vial from my belt and hurling it down to crack against the ground. Breach essence spread from below me, hopefully sealing off this particular spot as a teleportation destination . . . but only briefly.

If he was already teleporting around, that meant the essence I'd used earlier had faded to a point where he considered it safe now, and that meant I only had a matter of minutes before this one would fade, too.

I had the option to stagger my remaining vials between this round and the next, but I couldn't think that way with my strength waning. I began to throw more breach essence around the arena, sealing off spots, and hopefully . . .

He responded, but not in the way I hoped. A flick of his wrist sent one of my vials flying to land right atop another, creating a stronger breach in that spot, but preventing me from denying him more terrain.

Motion essence, rather than travel, or something like it. I've seen him use it before, like with the coin, but he doesn't seem to use it often. Might be because he doesn't need it, or—

Might be because he doesn't want you to know about it, whispered my own voice, but deeper.

Oh, you're still here.

Closer than ever, the voice whispered. *Darryl's reversal potion might be working, but it's slow, and you just dropped a breach underneath you.*

You know, if you throw enough of them, we could go two versus one—

I wrinkled my nose . . . but I did consider it.

No, the other plan was better, I told him.

Then what are you waiting for?

Lord Talis finally began to walk across the arena. Not toward me, but to the two swords that still hovered in midair—

His original sword and, of course, Mug.

That.

I reached through the breach under me, as well as the one I'd just created with the extra breach vials.

Sword Steal.

The two swords, bound together by Lord Talis, vanished as I grabbed my own weapon with a twist of my technique. And, still adhering to each other, they appeared, my own hilt in my hand.

"Nice sword you've got there," I told him. "Hope it isn't too important."

Lord Talis's eyes widened briefly, and for the first time, I saw something resembling alarm in his expression. He shot toward me in a blur — likely a motion-essence technique — but he wasn't quite fast enough for what I had planned.

When I'd failed to learn how to project my spirit before the second duel, I'd learned something important. The Crown-level ability that the Smiling Sword Saint wanted me to learn wasn't just too advanced for me — it was a mismatch for my skill set.

It wasn't that I couldn't learn spirit-layer techniques before I reached the appropriate level. Not exactly. It was that I had a much more natural inclination toward a different type of technique. Not one that involved projecting my power on the environment, but the one that matched a type of essence I already had trained with, and a power that aligned with the nature of my birth.

That is to say, every layer of me was good at both drawing and sheathing swords.

Spirit Sheathe.

With a twist of my spirit, I drew both Mug and Lord Talis's original sword into my spirit.

He froze in midlunge to gawk.

Any Regalia-level essence wielder could absorb their own regalia — that would have been an unusual feat at my level, but not in any way unprecedented. What I'd done was very similar, but I'd done it *without* spirit-bonding the weapons beforehand.

With the Spirit Sheathe technique, I'd drawn two unbonded swords into my soul, then sheathed them there. And, much like a Regalia-level essence wielder could draw power from a spirit-bonded weapon, so could I.

My body flared with stolen essence — dream-forged power from Mug, and something that felt like the familiar touch of silver from Talisian's sword.

And, for the first time, when I leapt forward with Soulsever in my hands to cross edges with Lord Talis, every beat of our exchange felt like I had an advantage.

Strike after strike, he fell back one step, then another. A burst of motion blasted into me from his off hand — I walked straight through it, butterflies flickering into existence as his power touched my skin and Mug's power transformed it.

As his crystal sword met with mine, he detonated it deliberately this time, sending shards into my hand — but the crimson wrap twisted and hardened, guarding my fingers. Not a single piece penetrated my skin.

And then, for just a heartbeat, he was unarmed, and my sword went to his chest.

"Yield," I told him.

"Your strength is certain, your will renewed, but—"

I stabbed him midsentence. Not hard, mind you, but I wasn't going to let him get another line of poetry in.

His necklace flashed brightly as my sword pierced through his shirt. There was a *crack* as a blast of light erupted from his chest, blasting my sword backward and out of position. Then a single gemstone on the necklace cracked and fell to the ground.

I swiped again, but Lord Talis's eyes narrowed in anger as my sword came down—

Then, as he drew in a breath, the world seemed to freeze. My cutting motion moved with glacial slowness as his eyes closed, a warm glow of inner light flowing through Lord Talis as he whispered into the air.

"Your worthy blade cuts quick and true, but of hidden tricks, I have a few. With whispered word and strength of few, I draw new breath and fight anew."

Something in the air around me seemed to *crack* as he spoke his final words. Soft, pale light flowed around him, and in the frozen moment, I could see that they were soft notes of music, gleaming around him and pressing against his skin—

I heard them, then, a whisper of song in the breeze, faintly reaching from his spirit and into the world.

And, with the greatest of ease, he caught my sword between two fingers and stopped it entirely.

Oh, vek.

Lord Talis hadn't grown stronger from recapturing his Epic—

With that breath, he'd hit Crown-level, and utterly shattered my chances of ever matching his strength.

CHAPTER XXXVIII

SHATTERED

Lord Talis twisted his fingers as they gripped my sword, then pushed back. I flew a dozen feet backward as time seemed to reassert itself, my mind flashing through options and abandoning them with every fragment of a moment that passed.

Shattering Sheath? No, too much sword essence involved, he'd counter it.

Another Cutting Remark? Same problem.

Manifest one of the other weapons and fight with two swords? No, I'm not trained in that style, I'd be too sloppy.

Maybe I could—

He caught up to me at a walking pace, even as I shot backward like I'd been fired out of a catapult. He was just that much faster than I was with his Epic active and his new level of power. If I was running at somewhere around Regalia-level with my stolen strength, he was now a level higher to start with, then probably at least one or two levels beyond that with his Epic running at full strength.

Insurmountable. Unstoppable.

I tried to cut him anyway, thrusting in midair and sending a burst of essence along with it. He turned the sword essence aside with a flick of a finger, then conjured another crystalline sword and thrust it casually at my shoulder. He wasn't in a hurry, but he was still so fast that I could barely perceive the thrust.

Rejoinder.

I blasted his sword aside before it brushed against me, hoping that the burst of sword essence that manifested would cut him as well, but he brushed it aside with the fingertips of his free hand without even treating it like an attack.

I swept my own sword down, but Soulsever seemed to move so slowly compared to his own movements that he batted each swing aside without worry.

My right hand was rapidly growing numb, and I could feel the strain of my Shattering Soul technique threatening to tear me apart from the inside.

Three more swings. He turned each aside with his own sword, then responded with three cuts of his own, the last of which I narrowly managed to avoid by lifting my left arm and letting the sword slip under it—

Then, without even thinking, I closed my elbow and trapped his sword between my arm and chest. His sword's blade was in a vertical position, meaning that I'd caught it on the flat and wasn't being cut—

But if he moved it up rapidly enough, he could potentially cut off my entire left arm.

He must have seen that the same moment I did—

But he hesitated. For a moment, we both remained utterly still.

Spirit Sheathe.

For an instant, my spirit reached out to grabble with his hand, trying to wrench the sword from his fingertips—

And in that moment, I felt something invisible slap me across the face. Lord Talis grinned as I stumbled backward, losing my spiritual grip on the blade.

Fortunately, whatever he'd used hadn't made me bleed, but it left me briefly stunned. I tried to throw a quick punch at him, but it was too slow. He shifted to the side, then he raised his other hand, a blade of essence forming along his fingertips, not dissimilar to my own Sword Hand technique. His essence burned bright green with a density that far exceeded anything I could muster. I wasn't strong enough to counter that with a Rejoinder — if he hit me, it would cut through every defense I had.

So, I stepped forward and tried to step on his foot, cutting essence flashing along my boot.

It was a feeble counter, but he responded, disengaging rather than risking the possibility that I'd manage to cut him. His sword slipped out from under my arm without causing harm, and for a moment, we simply watched each other.

"A chance to yield, I offer you," he said. "For one so young, you've battled true."

I shook my head. I wasn't thinking clearly enough to out-rhyme him, and even if I could have, I didn't think it would interrupt his technique now that it had reached this apex. I'd missed my chance to end things in the moment I had superior strength, or at least the appearance of it.

But that wasn't to say I was entirely out of tricks. Now that I had a moment to breathe and observe, I noted something in his movements more clearly—

He wasn't just moving at a casual pace to go easy on me.

Maybe . . .

I kicked a rock at him. There was a pause, then he kicked it out of the air.

I took a few steps to the side—

He took the same number opposite.

I raised my sword into a high stance, preparing to advance.

He lowered his into a different stance a beat later.

Every step he took, every thrust he made, was to the rhythm of a poem's lines that we'd already laid.

When I'd caught his sword, he hadn't hesitated because of mercy, or because I'd moved too quickly for him—

He'd paused because it *wasn't his turn.*

I took a deep breath, exhaling. I was running out of time, rapidly burning through every resource I had—

But when I saw him take a mirrored breath, I knew I'd found a weakness just in time.

Unfortunately, when his eyes narrowed in the next moment, I knew that he knew that I knew. Which is to say that, for the first time, I was ready to fight like a faerie knight.

I didn't need to fight faster than he did, necessarily, or with greater strength.

All I needed to do was to force him into a situation where he could not, under any circumstances, score more points on an exchange than I did.

And so, with that knowledge, we moved into a different dance.

One step forward, one step back.

One step left, one step right.

Faster, slower. Slash after slash, none finding a gash.

Even as I weakened and his strength grew, I found my boldness grow anew—

For in each movement, I found a limit, and every limit was a clue.

Finally, as my fingers failed, it looked as if he had prevailed—

But as I passed my sword to my other hand, he did the same,

Just as I'd planned.

And with a twist of my mind on the grip, I felt my true sword's pommel slip—

A twist of one position, then two,

Then my sword shone as new power grew.

With a final thrust of mind, with a dream sword's power now held inside, I breached a seal on layers three,

Of core, of dreams, and destiny,

And with a final flare of light, my sword transformed, to my delight,

A new blade held in my left hand,

Of rending dreams and shattered plans.

There you are, the voice of my nightmare said into my mind. *Finally.*

Good morning, Somniasever. Help me out here.

I rested the curved, single-edged sword against my shoulder, then gave Lord Talis a wink as he mirrored my movement, looking uncertain.

Then, I lunged.

Lord Talis was still vastly faster than I was, of course — that hadn't changed. But like most people, he wasn't quite as proficient with his off hand as he was with his main hand.

I was no exception to that. I'd trained with two swords on occasion, but as I mentioned, it wasn't my area of expertise. I did use a two-handed sword regularly, so that was an advantage, but it wasn't at all what I was counting on.

No, what I'd relied upon was that I was now drawing from the dream aspect of my sword, and the nightmare version of myself tied to it. A nightmare that had emerged from a mirror.

Which, of course, meant that *he* was left-handed.

I didn't have any of his knowledge or techniques. But when I wielded Somniasever, I had a fraction of his instincts. And so, even as my right hand fell useless at my side, I swept my left hand easily, and Lord Talis struggled to match my finesse.

That wouldn't have been enough on its own, even with the knowledge I'd gleaned about his technique. His speed was simply far too superior for me to hope to cut him—

But I'd trained at something else in my dreams, too. Something my master had long advised me against, but that I'd nevertheless planned for.

As we began a rapid series of exchanges, faster and faster, further and further into a fervor, I feinted—

And as he responded, I left myself entirely open.

He took the opening. Perhaps if he'd still been using the right hand, he could have responded to my plan in time.

But as I'd discovered in the realm of dreams where no consequences applied, where again and again I'd fought and died—

I didn't need to match him speed for speed. Not if I didn't mind letting myself bleed.

His crystalline blade bit into my side the same time I adjusted my feint into a true cut, driving it down into his shoulder.

And, for a moment, all was still, until we heard a familiar word.

"Hold!" Lord Brine's voice rang out.

Blood trickled down my side and his shoulder as we froze in place.

The judges conferred as we watched each other. And, in spite of the command to hold, we both dipped our eyes in acknowledgment to each other.

That exchange had been the most difficult thing I'd managed in my entire life.

And it wasn't without cause. In the moments that followed, and as silence grew, I knew something had not, in fact, gone as I had planned.

"Duelists, separate." Lord Feather spoke.

I blinked at the command, stepped away, careful not to cut my opponent any more. Lord Talis did the same.

"The judges have conferred. Both parties have scored a point. This battle," Ana concluded, "is over."

Lord Talis and I turned toward her.

And, at the same time, we spoke.

". . . What?"

To me, at least, the score was clear.

Lord Talis and I had each scored three points against each other during the match. From his expression, I could see he had made the same assessment.

I felt the crimson cloth around my right hand loosening now that the match was over, but circulation was slow to return, and I could feel a burning through my star veins where too much power had passed.

I released my Shattering Soul, but even that was barely enough to soothe my inner soreness.

I don't know how I could have hoped to strike another point against him, given my condition. I was out of tricks. But . . . I'd expected to need to.

And, at that point, I'd expected to fail.

Ana spoke up as we turned toward her. "Each of you has fought exceptionally, striking three points against each other during the course of today's dueling."

We nodded.

"However, in the preparatory phase for the second round, Edge spoke to his team, the judges, and his opponent about the usage of a golden coin. Though all three times he was told that this was fair within the scope of this contest, he opted not to."

"How is that relevant?" I asked.

"It's setting context. That action itself had no bearing upon this match. However, it was during that discussion that Lord Oloris — speaking for Lord Talis as his second — spoke an important phrase."

Ana opened a notebook, then read a line out loud. "'Nothing was said to prevent any form of transmutation or glamor of it before the match. However, we must recognize that you have a point.'"

I'll admit that my jaw dropped a little.

"That's . . ."

Lord Talis put a hand over his eyes, then exhaled a deep sigh.

Lord Oloris laughed. "Don't worry, darling. It's all according to plan."

I blinked, turning to Lord Oloris, who was smiling, rather than looking ashamed. Instead, he waved at Ana. "Dear, I'd like to interject briefly. You see, when I said, 'You have a point,' that implied he already had one. Thus, it must have referred to a past match, rather than a future one."

"Why, Lord Oloris. What an interesting statement." She glanced at the other judges. "Taking that argument into consideration, we can, perhaps, amend this to consider Edge possessing an extra point for the first round of the competition, rather than this one. Unless anyone disagrees?"

The other judges whispered to each other, then to Ana.

I looked at Lord Talis. He once again looked as confused by this turn of events as I did—

But we seemed like the only ones. Rusty and Darryl were calmly eating apples, as if . . .

As if they'd known this was going to happen, too.

"Good, good." Ana nodded. "It seems we have an agreement. One extra point for Edge in the first round, which . . . oh, I suppose that means that the first trial was actually a draw, not a win for Lord Talis."

Lord Talis stepped forward, as if to say something, but Lord Oloris gave him a curt shake of the head. Lord Talis gave him a quizzical look, but settled himself.

Ana continued. "And . . . well, if the second round was also a draw . . . and I suppose we're at exactly three to three now . . ."

"One more point wins it all cleanly," I said.

"Or," Ana countered, raising a finger, "we could call this whole thing a draw."

I blinked. "Respectfully, if we call a draw now, what would all this have been for?"

"Oh, it accomplished quite a great deal. Lord Oloris, if you please?" Ana gestured toward Lord Oloris, who reached into his tunic and brought out—

A fist-sized, pure-black crystal.

Every person there would have recognized it, in spite of most of us having never seen one. We'd all heard of them in legends and lore, of days forgotten and dragons' hoards.

That item was a dungeon core.

Lord Talis visibly shook, his hand reaching out toward it. "Is that . . ."

"Not the dungeon core that is attached to my sword. But it is a dungeon core — or, at least, a reasonable facsimile of one. Over the course of the last nine months, we worked together to create it. You, by training with me to learn how to master dungeon essence. Lord Oloris, by studying the dungeon core's composition to create a physical facsimile from crystal essence. Edge helped me as well, visiting and testing the new core's abilities to make sure they worked, though he won't remember those experiences . . . or how he let me borrow a fragment of an ancient magic mirror from his pouch as a part of the duplication process. Of course, making a dungeon core is the work of masterful magic, and we could not have accomplished that without the power of an ancient wizard. He is resting now, but Grandfather was of great help."

"Then . . . what are you saying?" Lord Talis asked.

"It's very simple, darling." Lord Oloris stepped forward and offered him the crystal. "This may not be the dungeon core you wanted. It's artificial, and may not work exactly like dear Ana's would have . . . but dungeon cores aren't all the same in any case, and I think we did a good job with this little one. It may not be strong yet, but it will be."

"You all did this? For me?" Lord Talis looked around, water welling at the edges of his eyes, and finally settling on me.

"For what it's worth, I didn't have the slightest idea about this. Everything I did was for Ana. But . . . I'm happy for you. Very happy. Assuming you're willing to accept three draws as the outcome of our trials?"

"Come here, please," he said, tears dripping from his face.

I sheathed my sword, sensing no ill intent in him, and gave him a curious look.

"Edge of the Woods, for this gift you have all given to me . . ." He turned to glance at everyone. "I am, for the first time in my life, completely and utterly defeated. I humbly and gratefully accept your offer. Will you accept one of my own?"

Without another word he turned to me and opened his arms wide.

I felt tears at the edges of my own eyes. I stepped forward to the noble knight I'd fought so hard against.

We embraced each other and wept tears of joy, for we had both earned a greater victory that day than either of us could have possibly hoped for.

CHAPTER XXXIX

SKIP

Lord Talis remained for some time in the grove, saying his goodbyes to each of us in turn and offering his thanks. It was not a faerie's way to express such deep gratitude, but I knew as he carried that crystal in his hands, it was genuine. For the prize that he had taken from our duels was far greater than victory in battle — it was the ability to return to his people in triumph, with both the training and the power necessary to change their lives forever.

We spoke kindly with the others as they departed one by one. Darryl gave me a second reversal potion for the layer-piercing elixir, since the first one still clearly hadn't reversed the effects entirely. Once I felt more or less normal, Rusty gently unwrapped the handkerchief on my hand, tucked it into my shirt, then gently began to apply the healing elixir we'd gathered before the duel.

The crimson that had spread across my body during the Shattering Soul faded, but my right hand still carried a faint red overtone, as if it was stained with blood that had not quite been washed away.

I'd expected to play a sacrifice move like my final point from the start. That was why we'd picked up the healing elixir in advance — I had expected to use it early and often to trade points. I hadn't known Darryl would give me something that would make it unsafe to use, but it was good that he did — without the power that elixir had provided, I never would have stood a chance.

As for the other side effects of the potion, well . . .

I'll be seeing you, kid.

My white-haired counterpart winked at me with a shining golden eye as he stepped backward into a crack in reality, then vanished.

Well, that's not going to be a problem in the future. Nope.

I shook my head, clearing my thoughts as best I could.

With the battle ended, I retrieved the fallen *tama* jewel that had intercepted a hit for me early on. Without it, and so many other small factors, I would have lost. It still dripped rust-red water as I lifted it, and felt far heavier than it should. I looked to Rusty, who had given the jewel to me. "Can it be repaired?"

"Don't know. Probably. Hand it here, I'll see what can be done."

I handed the jewel off to them. Their arm dropped notably when they took it — they hadn't been ready for the weight.

"Huh." They tucked it away in a pouch. "Wasn't expecting that. Figured it'd just do a barrier, like Talisian's necklace."

"Same. The gifts were useful, though. Can I hold on to the mirror and the compass?"

"Sure. Don't have a need for 'em. Will check with Grandma if she needs them back later."

"I couldn't have won without your help as my second." I bowed my head.

"I know." They winked at me. "I'll be seeing you soon."

With that, they wandered off into the woods.

I turned to Darryl. "The potions were a huge help, too. Speaking of, I have another one for you to look at some time soon. Maybe something you can keep, if it's more useful to you."

"Sure thing. Come by soon. The whole family misses you."

I gave Darryl a tight hug, and he headed off, too.

The judges had left, and Lord Oloris whispered something to Lord Talis, then headed off somewhere as well.

That meant nearly everyone had departed, save for Ana . . . and Lord Talis himself, who lingered to speak with us both briefly.

"Before I forget —" I turned to Lord Talis. "Let me return your sword."

I paused at a safe distance, reaching into my spirit to retrieve his silvery sword, which I'd stolen midbattle. I don't know exactly how much power I'd managed to drain from the two swords I'd stowed in my soul, but every little bit had helped. I offered the sword back to him, and he accepted, sheathing it at his side.

"You could have called that a spoil of battle," he remarked.

"Wouldn't have been right. You fought honorably and well. And, if I'm being honest, I'm still trying to learn how to use my own weapon. I should focus on that for a while."

He gave me a nod. "There's wisdom in that, especially with weapons as strange as yours. Still, I am . . . relieved at your decision. I would have missed my little moonlight."

I raised an eyebrow. There was a story in that, but it didn't seem like the right time. "Glad to help. And . . . glad to have met you."

"I feel quite the same, young Edge." He tipped his head to me.

Then, I turned to Ana. She reached out a hand for me. I grabbed her hand and squeezed it tightly. "You outplayed us both."

"I know. And I couldn't have done it without you." She grinned.

"A valuable lesson for us both," Lord Talis said with a smile. "I've been away from courtly life for long enough that it was too easy to forget that it wasn't only my opponent I needed to watch out for. Everyone involved in a contest has an agenda, and of everyone here, you had the strongest reason to make sure the results were what you wished. I can only express my utmost gratitude that what you wished for was everything I could have dreamed."

"Be cautious, my lord," Ana replied. "It also isn't very courtly of you to be so free with thanks."

He nodded immediately. "There is truth in that. I have wandered the human realm for some time now, and though it pains me to admit it, I have acquired a fondness for their custom in this regard. There is . . . a kind of beauty in the expression of thanks, without the expectation that one must expect a shadow of that gratitude as a cost. It is sometimes easier to breathe when not every word is a part of a future game."

"Is that why you didn't have your companions help in the second round?" Ana asked.

I blinked. "What do you mean?"

Ana turned to me. "When you were asking around about the whole gold coin thing, they had other plans. But they never acted on them."

Lord Talis turned to me. "You weren't acting like a proper fae when you insisted on denying yourself that advantage, young Edge. If you were in a faerie court, throwing out a potential advantage like that one would have been seen as confusing at best and most likely a weakness to exploit. But I have seen enough of the world outside to know that there are other forms of honor than those we cherish, and when you displayed that one, I knew it was only appropriate to return the gesture. And so, in that round alone, I denied myself certain advantages."

". . . What would you have done?"

Lord Talis gave me a wry grin. "I'm still a fae, Edge of the Woods. You can't expect me to give away all my secrets for free."

I laughed. "That's true. I fear I don't have any appropriate currency to offer you for such a tale."

"Perhaps later, then, if time permits. But before that, I have something of greater import to say." He took a breath. "You fought far better than I could have expected in every round. I could not have accomplished what you did at your own age."

"You honor me, Lord Talis. I . . . I looked up to you, when I was younger. I still do. Your cause is a noble one, truly. It is only your method—"

"I know. It dishonors me to take any action that would force another away from their own choices. I have seen that from the start. But at times, there do not appear to be good choices." He turned toward Ana. "In most cases, my people are ashamed to admit an error. In this case, I could not be prouder to have been wrong. Your friend's brilliance has exceeded my every expectation, and with her gift, I will return home with only triumph, without the weight of an ignoble choice." He bowed his head. "Without your intervention, she would not have had the time for her wondrous ploy, and this would not have been possible."

"I . . . don't know what to say to that. She played wonderfully. So did you. And I'm sure you're aware I could not have defeated you on equal terms."

He raised his head and laughed. "What are equal terms to one of us? You played your strengths and my weaknesses perfectly. I underestimated you, and I can only express my extreme gratitude for that. For without my weakness, I would not have the strength that you have both given me." He raised his hand, holding the strange crystal that Ana had given him — the half-made dungeon core that he hoped to nurture into a true one to save his people. "It will be a long path to making use of this properly, but a better one. I can live with that."

"I hope that you have a safe journey home and can bring your people the comfort that they need. I wish . . ." I shook my head. It was an idle thought, one that I couldn't speak.

But Lord Talis and I were very much alike. And so, in spite of that, he understood.

"I will not be Lord Talis for much longer." He spoke solemnly. "Your friend saved me from giving up my name early, but soon, it will be time. And when that time comes . . . I will be in need of a squire. One who would be willing to accompany me on my journey home, perhaps. One who has the mark of favor of one court, who may yet earn another."

I blinked. "Is . . . that an offer?"

"It—"

The sound of music, distant and yet all around us, interrupted him midword.

Lord Talis straightened immediately, as did Ana. And though the music was unfamiliar, I understood what it meant.

I turned toward the source of the sound, and I felt my heart thrumming in my chest to the sound of the music.

And, though it was now bound around my belt, I could feel the handkerchief thrum to the beat of the music as well.

Lord Brine re-entered the glade, then fell to a knee as the sound of hoofbeats approached. Ana and Lord Talis hastily followed, falling into formations to kneel.

Pristine white beasts strode first into the glade, the first of their kind that I'd seen. They looked very much like horses, save for the single crimson, metallic point upon their foreheads, and the stains of red across their coats.

Unicorns. Creatures rarely spoken of outside of legends, even among the people of the wood.

Some riders came astride these unicorns — fae wearing resplendent coats of wood and silver, with higher lords wearing armor wrought entirely of scarlet-stained steel or robes of woven salt.

Every fae lord had a presence of spirit about them, their auras shifting the trees and brushing against the power of the wood in ways that I could not have perceived or comprehended save for the lingering effects of Darryl's drinks. Each had a different flavor to their power, of light or dark, of summer or winter, of growth or decay. All were creatures of full-wrought majesty, but none carried a fraction of the beauty of she who rode last into the glade.

"The court kneels in the presence of Discardia, Lady of the Discarded Heart, Princess of Rust and Salt," Lord Brine announced.

I watched in awestruck silence as she appeared at the border of the glade. It had only been a matter of years since I'd last seen her, but we were teenagers now, not children. And even among my people, that brought significant change.

She had been pretty before, in the way that most faeries are, and even beyond it. But now, as a teenager myself, I couldn't help but look upon her and think to myself that she was beyond my former concept of beauty.

This was no longer a frightened girl. When Princess Discardia rode into the glade, she was not astride a unicorn. She rode upon the back of a kelpie, a creature that was known best for dragging anyone who deigned to ride on its back into a watery grave.

For her to sit upon a kelpie without fear was to sit upon the entirety of faerie and make it her own.

No, as a teenager, Discardia was no longer just a princess—

She was a goddess of her people. And a goddess in my own eyes as well, but in a very different way.

Perhaps it was that feeling, that understanding, that made it so that I did not kneel or bow as she approached. I would have knelt before a princess, for such a thing was only polite, and it cost me nothing.

But to bow before a god?

That, even then, I could never do.

As she rode across the glade, one of her perfect eyebrows went up as she saw me standing as others sat or knelt. Then, with a hint of a smile, she rode her kelpie directly to my side. "So gracious of you to stand and wait for me, Edge of the Woods, so as to help me descend gracefully from my mount."

"Of course, m'lady." I reached up, offering my hands. Rather than simply taking my hand with hers, she simply slipped into a sitting position on the saddle, then stepped down on bare feet, directly onto my hands.

I didn't have the balance to hold a person up by just their feet, but I didn't have to. Somehow, she seemed to weigh almost nothing as she stepped down, then seemingly slipped on the blood on my hand, falling directly into my arms.

"How clumsy of me." Her lips parted in a pout. "But you seem to have caught me once again."

I was frozen in that moment for a time, her face so close to my own. "Of course," I managed after a moment, feeling suddenly weak. "Shall I set you down?"

"In a moment, perhaps." She shifted in my grip, leaning closer to whisper in my ear. "We are in public, after all."

I felt a shiver down my spine. For a moment, I simply held her there, paralyzed—

Then, at an "ahem" from Lord Brine, I steeled my resolve and set her down on the forest floor.

For most, it would be dangerous to step bare of foot upon a faerie glade. For her, any dangerous plant would simply duck and hide or pull itself from the ground to run rather than dare to harm her.

And so, she stepped gracefully back, adjusting her pristine dress of crimson and white, and took my hand. "I see that you wore my token, young Edge of the Woods."

"I did. It was of great motivation to me in the duel." I spoke truly, but without the full significance of it, as was expected among my people.

"How wonderful. I am pleased that you accepted my favor, for I hold you in high regard. It is, however, unbecoming of one of my stature to allow a debt to go unpaid for long, in whichever direction it may be owed."

I felt something tighten in my chest, and it wasn't from the gift still tied around my waist. "How may I repay this boon, m'lady?"

"It's a simple thing, really." She raised a hand, seeming to consider it, then lowered her fingers. "As you have aptly proven on more than one occasion, I am a delicate creature, and one prone to flights of fancy. While such a thing is unbecoming of a princess, I am but a girl yet, and one still in the throes of youth. If I am to properly blossom, I require trustworthy companionship, wise friendship, and protection, and you have already proven your capability in these things threefold. And so, though it pains me to take you from your life's path, I must ask this of you, Edge of the Woods. To repay the gift of my boon, will you attend me for a time, and continue your training as a proper princess's protector?"

I took a deep breath, looking to Lord Talis and thinking of the offer he had been just about to give me. The chance to leave, to pursue the destiny I'd always wanted, as squire to a noble knight.

And I turned back to Princess Discardia, thinking of both her beauty and how thoroughly I had been played from the start.

". . . How long?" I whispered.

"It has been a bit more than three years since you first rescued me," the princess said, "and I have been bereft in your absence. And so, in proper symmetry, I must ask you to balance the scale."

"Three years in your service."

"Three years in your capable hands," she teased.

Three years in the service of a young and fickle goddess. That was the price for her favor, the cost of my victory.

I closed my eyes.

A deal was a deal.

And without looking at Lord Talis or Ana, my other paths—

I whispered three words.

“Well played, Princess.”

EPILOGUE

SURPRISE

The swordsman shook his head and chuckled as he finished that section of his story, then mumbled again to himself. "Well played, indeed."

"So . . . wait. You did all that, Lord Talis got to leave with a dungeon core, and you got three years of . . . some kind of indentured service?" Scribe asked.

"It's important when thinking about any fae involved in a situation to remember that they generally have at least three motives. The motive they show you, the hidden motivation beneath that, and their true motivation a layer beyond. I was so focused on the duel that I failed to model what the goals of the princess might be when she offered the handkerchief. I knew there would be consequences, of course. But I only modeled the next, most obvious step — that I would owe her a favor. I thought it would be simple, like playing a potentially deadly game together. You know, kid stuff." He gave a self-deprecating laugh. "But I was thinking of a girl I'd known when we were eleven. And her cunning, power, and ambition had grown even more than her beauty."

"Is that beauty why you called her a goddess?" Scribe found himself asking, realizing only afterward how awkward of a question it might have been.

Fortunately, the swordsman seemed to take the question amiably. "That was a part of it, to be sure. But I meant it in a more literal sense. She was growing into a certain type of power — a bloodline, if you want to call it that. Something I could sense, even then. Perhaps it was the lingering effects of Darryl's potion, but I when I looked at her, I could see something beyond the mere shadows of possibility that I saw when I gazed at others. She was . . ." He paused, seemingly searching for a word. "Glorious. Resplendent. *Transcendent.*"

The emphasis he placed on the final word made it sound as if he was speaking of something beyond the name of a dominion, even an obscure one, but Scribe wasn't sure how to phrase a question about it. "Can you elaborate on that?"

"Perhaps at some point. I shall have to think on how best to articulate certain things . . . especially about her."

Scribe nodded. "Another thing. The dungeon core. I was under the impression they couldn't be replicated."

"So were Lord Talis and myself, of course, otherwise there would have been no point to the duel. But there are few things that are truly impossible when it comes to faerie magic, ancient sorcerers, and a will like Ana's." He paused.

"Also, the fact that she had a piece of the World's Memory to work with probably helped more than she implied."

"Ah." Scribe nodded. "I suppose with a piece of the World's Memory and sufficient control, virtually anything could be duplicated. If the Smiling Sword Saint could use it to make her younger self, why not replicate an item?"

"Right. Thane was fundamentally a memory construct, however, and didn't have immediate access to all his proper essence types. A simple mirror copy of a dungeon core would have probably been the same — just memory essence, not dungeon essence. Thus, it couldn't solve the problem on its own, but I'm guessing Ana and Gramps used the mirror fragment to help create the foundation for a new core. Then, Oloris and Auntie Temper helped her reforge it using their own crystal essence and forge essence to change its nature, while Ana supplied dungeon essence from her own core."

"Could that be done with other things? Like, could you duplicate another magical artifact using the same means? Make infinite copies of something?"

The swordsman shrugged. "I don't know. I'm just speculating on how they did it, to be honest. I wasn't there for the whole process, but in the aftermath, I suspected that was part of why Gramps was missing for such a long period of time. He was likely spending at least part of that time absent in the shrine, working with Ana. It had to be more difficult than it sounds if it took them that much time and effort. Gramps was about as well-versed on magic theory as anyone on our world, after all."

"And his memory loss was because he was losing it after visiting the dungeon, like you often did?" Scribe asked.

The swordsman's expression cracked for just a moment, turning somber. ". . . Not entirely. That may have been a part of it, but . . . ah. If only it was just that."

"Sorry. I didn't mean to—"

"No, it's fine," Lien replied a little too quickly. "Let's move on to another topic."

Scribe took the out, thinking as they walked. As he considered, he could see an opening in the trees up ahead. Before they reached the change in terrain, Scribe offered one last question. "Did you end up serving the princess for the full three years?"

"Perhaps I'll tell you about that at some point. We are, however, coming to the end of one story . . ." He gestured toward the opening in the edge of the woodland. ". . . and the beginning of another."

Scribe looked forward beyond the trees — and in the distance, he could just barely make it out. The walls of a city.

They had finally reached their destination. The city of Larkbridge sprawled before them. He couldn't wait to explore it.

But first, a jingling coin reminded him of an obligation.

⊹⊹ ⊹⊹

Hours later, Scribe stumbled through the doors of the Perfect Stranger tavern. He wasn't surprised to see one within Larkbridge's walls — they were, unfortunately, as common as larceny.

A man with salt-and-pepper hair and a neatly pointed goatee watched him as he stepped in, assessing. Clever ears seemed to perk up as the man heard the jingling of the coin, but he made no other obvious reaction.

"Hello," Scribe mumbled as he approached the counter. "I'm . . . told that I should be asking for Ironthorn."

"Well, well." A wolfish grin spread across the larger man's face. "A referral. And one carrying treasure, at that."

He stepped back, revealing well-muscled arms. "Need a drink? I have a feeling we'll have a great deal to discuss."

Scribe had had water while they traveled, but he was still parched. "Sure. In fact . . . it's been a week. Get me something nice. Something with an *'ess'* on the label, maybe, like mine."

"I've been saving a few choice vintages. What sort of label do you carry?"

"Scribe."

The man gave a low whistle. "Now that's one I've been looking forward to hearing."

Scribe blinked. "Really? Why is that?"

"Got something for you. Aside from the drink, of course." The man opened a bottle of something dark, pouring a cup for each of them, then taking a drink from his own. Presumably to show that it wasn't poisoned, but frankly, Scribe had his own ways to work around that, so it didn't mean much.

Still, he was too tired to argue. If it killed him, eh. That'd be just the life he expected, really.

He raised his own cup, clinked it to the bartender's, and took a drink.

The bartender nodded, then retrieved a small envelope.

With practiced ease, Scribe went through the same personalized method he'd used for the one he'd received at the previous tavern, cutting it open and slipping out the contents.

A note, and something else. His breath caught in his chest when he saw it.

An earring.

He lifted the note.

Jo-jo! You're finally in my part of the woods! It's been too long.

Sent a little something along for you. You already know what it is. Don't lose this one.

I'm so happy that you finally got out of that stuffy old guild office! I can't wait to see what you're up to.

And maybe . . . meet a certain someone, too.
—Vee

Scribe set down the note, breathing heavily, and slipped the earring on his opposite ear.

Then, he took a deep breath, not caring where he was, and rotated the earrings.

"Vee? Can you hear me?"

A brief delay, and then . . .

"Jo-jo! You got my letter!"

His heart hammered. "Vee? Is that really you? It's been—"

A series of jumbled, half-remembered code phrases followed.

Scribe laughed. "Right. Wasn't literally meaning that I needed to authenticate you, but sure."

He whispered a few counterstatements, then frowned. "What's that echo I'm getting? Is this earring different than the old one?"

"Oh, no. Just the acoustics in here. I'm a little tied up at the moment."

". . . Tied up as in busy, or . . . ?"

A cough from Vee's side. "Well, you see, Jo-jo. Sometimes when a woman and a really smoking-hot redhead and a couple friends love each other very much, and also treason—"

"Vee . . . what have you been up to, exactly?"

"Like I was saying, just a little mild treason. You try to overthrow one little god king . . ." Vee sighed.

"It's kind of a long story."

APPENDIX I

ESSENCE SORCERY

A Message from the Pen of a Scribe

As instructed, I've been collecting information on the local style of sorcery for quite some time, but it's only been in recent months that I've managed to find a reliable source. During my travels, I encountered a young swordsman who practices the art of essence sorcery. He is not what the locals call a Skyseeker, exactly, though he appears to pursue power in a similar fashion. The Skyseekers appear to be more of an organization (or perhaps several organizations) that have places of learning called "sects," whereas this swordsman grew up in the wilds, raised primarily by a variety of nonhuman species.

. . . Including wolves, if he is to be believed. Yes, literally raised by wolves. The humor of asking someone who is raised by wolves to teach me complicated sorcerous theory does not escape me, but I assure you, I have taken steps to verify the veracity of his tales. Or, at least, the pertinent portions for this report.

The swordsman refers to himself primarily as Edge — a nickname seemingly derived from the birth name Lien. Yes, Lien, the Liadran word. This Edge might be only a teenager, but his understanding of the functionality of essence is formidable. Much of this information seems to have come from the teachings of his so-called grandfather. I can surmise from the context of the story that Grandfather is a scholar of some repute and one originally of Mythralian origin.

It couldn't be . . . No, I shouldn't make assumptions that grand in scale without more significant evidence. There are many other scholars, after all. It couldn't be *the* scholar, could it?

You would have told me if he was around here, wouldn't you? Never mind, of course not. Question withdrawn.

Continuing on, the local form of sorcery is what we refer to as essence sorcery back in the homeland. Edge uses this term as well, but I'm unclear on if that is actually the local term or if he simply uses it due to his own Mythralian education and heritage.

The basic foundation is that essence sorcerers gather ambient essence from nature and absorb it. Once they have absorbed enough essence of a particular variety, they can compress that essence themselves, creating a container of essence in a set location called a Dianis Point.

Yes, like House Dianis. Noteworthy.

A completed Dianis Point is a crystalline structure that automatically fills itself up over time with the same type of essence that was used to make it. This provides a steady, reusable source of essence, much like how certain dominion-marked items work. A fascinating concept, but one that seems entirely too simple to me.

I can see why building up essence in the body might cause the body to build more of that essence, but these discrete containers seem . . . odd. Artificial. Arbitrary. And things only grow stranger from there.

There are, apparently, a set number of valid Dianis Points . . . and the location of each Dianis Point is relevant to how it functions. And as one completes more Dianis Points, both the points themselves and the person's overall essence can reach higher levels, which grant new abilities.

These parallels to the crystal marks and attunements of the continent of Kaldwyn make me wonder . . . is this essence-progression structure some kind of equivalent to how they work, but one that the residents are born with? If so, is this an organic distinction in the species, or one that comes from the machinations of local gods or other powerful entities?

This bears more investigation, but my sources of reliable information on the deities of this land are minimal. Most seem to believe the gods have moved elsewhere or died. I will continue searching for more information.

In the meantime, I have a few more specific notes that you might find useful.

Firstly, the levels of essence development. There are many of them, but I have made some notes on the first few, which Edge seems most familiar with.

The first three levels are referred to as the Essence Layer or Core Layer, and the levels of this layer of development all have names related to fire. This is, according to my research, a combination of older traditions referring to essence as "inner fire" and because essence sorcerers see the auras of this layer as being either clear, red, or orange, depending on their intensity.

Candle (Clear to Light Red)

- *Reached By:* Completing a first Dianis Point. This appears to be largely an automatic process, as the body processes essence, but it can be guided through attempting to absorb as much essence as possible of a specific type, much as Edge himself did. Some species are born with already completed Dianis Points, and thus, are already at Candle-level from birth.
- *Power Gained:* Internal essence sense. Able to clearly conceptualize and interact with your internal essence structure. In addition, your ability to sense essence in the environment is enhanced.

Torch (Red)

- *Reached By:* Completing three Dianis Points or overloading a smaller number of Dianis Points with essence.
- *Power Gained:* Upon reaching this stage of essence development, the person will undergo a Destiny Dream. Upon waking from the dream, the person will have a destiny mark, which grants different abilities based on the specific mark. For example, destiny marks might be things like Warrior, Wizard, or even Farmer. Once someone has a destiny mark, that mark can also improve over time, but this is a separate and parallel form of progression. Destiny marks are an entire field of study in themselves, and I will write about them more in a separate report. Briefly, however, these destiny marks supposedly draw from alternate versions of the self for power. If true, this is absolutely absurd, and I feel cheated at being stuck with merely a single mediocre self to work with. Ugh.

Hearth (Orange)

- *Reached By:* Completing six Dianis Points or overloading a smaller number of Dianis Points with essence.
- *Power Gained:* People of the Hearth-level gain the ability to form spirit bonds. These can be with other entities, or between two of their own Dianis Points.
    - Forming a spirit bond with another entity has the advantage of allowing the person to get essence of another type, which they can use directly or intermix with the essence in the Dianis Point you linked it to. For example, you could link a Fire Dianis Point to an Air Dianis Point on another entity, allowing you to mix the two to create lightning essence.
    - In addition, spirit-bonded individuals gain a strong sense of each other. As the bond strength progresses, this can allow for remote sensing of the other, telepathy, sensing the health of the other entity, et cetera.
    - My studies have indicated that this is the most common method by a large margin. Among nobles, spirit bonds are formed between partners in marriage ceremonies. This is seen as a means of ensuring loyalty and forming a tangible connection between houses. Ordinary civilians may form spirit bonds with their spouses, parents, grandparents, siblings, or children.
    - Powerful adventurers and Skyseekers often seek out spirit bonds with exotic entities — phoenixes, kitsune, wani, and other legendary beings.
- Binding two Dianis Points together allows for intermixing essence types between separate parts of your own body, rather than just being able

to mix outlying parts with the Heart Point. Basically, this creates a secondary essence route, which allows for direct interaction between two otherwise unrelated Dianis Points.

- This is mostly useful when someone needs to form an additional spirit bond while they're alone, if they are intentionally hiding their power, or have a specific Dianis Point they do not want to link to someone else.
- For example, if someone has an extremely dangerous Dianis Point, or a rare essence type, they might choose this option.
- An essence wielder that is isolated (e.g., someone stuck in prison and planning a prison break) might also try to do this.
- Note that spirit bonds are initially fragile and require time to develop into something permanent. Much like star veins, the amount of essence that can be safely passed through spirit bonds also improves over time.
- Spirit bonds can be removed, but this can apparently be dangerous. I do not have sufficient information on this subject to explore it in detail at this time and will need to do further research.
- I am also currently unaware if spirit bonds persist beyond the death of one bonded individual.

The next layer is the Spirit Layer. These levels all refer to objects or concepts associated with nobility, which makes sense — in most time periods, only nobles could afford the resources necessary to reach these stages. In modern times, many merchants, Skyseekers, and adventurers also reach these stages of development, but the ancient names remain.

Signet (Orange/Yellow)

- *Reached By:* Completing your first spirit bond and solidifying it, similar to how a Dianis Point is completed. Also, continuing to develop your essence in your Dianis Points to a certain level.
- *Power Gained:* Internal spirit sense. Able to clearly conceptualize and interact with your internal spirit structure. In addition, your ability to sense spiritual power in the environment is enhanced.

Regalia (Yellow)

- *Reached By:* Completing three spirit bonds or increasing the level of a smaller number of spirit bonds significantly. Also, as per usual, you must continue to accumulate more essence in your Dianis Point.
- *Power Gained:* Create spirit regalia. This allows you to fuse items into your spirit. This works similar to spirit bonding elsewhere, but it ties the item directly to a component of your spirit. You cannot have both

a spirit bond with a creature and a spirit regalia piece tied to the same Dianis Point (under normal circumstances). Basically, this lets you equip an item on your spirit and incorporate/discorporate it at will, as well as mix essence with it.

Crown Level (Yellow/Green)

- *Reached By:* Completing six spirit bonds or increasing the level of a smaller number of spirit bonds significantly. (Also, more essence.)
- At this stage, I've also heard rumors of something called a Shadow Trial, where one must confront their "inner self." This is not a subject I have studied in great detail, however, and this may be unreliable. It is noteworthy that this might not occur at this level, or another. If it is a parallel to the Destiny Dream, it should occur a level earlier. If it has to do with the shade, it logically should likely occur later, during the Shade Layer.
- *Power Gained:* Create shade weave. This allows you to bind things to your shade, allowing for physical transformations of the body. For example, one could bind their shade to a spirit beast — say, a cat — and gain catlike eyes as a benefit. I'm unclear on the limitations of this, but clearly, this offers significant potential benefits if one is able to find a powerful creature to bind to.
- Upon completing this, a person may then begin to form shade weaves, which allow for physical transformations of the body.

After this, there's a Shade Layer, which is color-coded to green, and a Memory Layer at some point after. There may or may not be other layers between Shade and Memory. I should also make it clear that my information on this subject is what I have gleaned from brief conversations and poorly translated texts; it is not to be taken as perfectly reliable.

I know virtually nothing of the names or powers of specific levels beyond the Spirit Layer at this point in time. I've heard that there is a Sky-level, which appears to be a theoretical maximum, and likely is at least a layer or two beyond the Spirit Layer if it exists. This appears to be one of the possible sources of the Skyseeker name. It may also refer to a physical land that Skyseekers are attempting to find — some kind of divine island in the sky.

Notably, these level titles primarily are used to refer to people, but individual Dianis Points also are sometimes referred to by these level names. In those cases, the level name indicates the expected amount of essence that someone should have in a Dianis Point at that level. A person could have Dianis Points that are lower or higher level than their overall personal power.

Next, the individual Dianis Points.

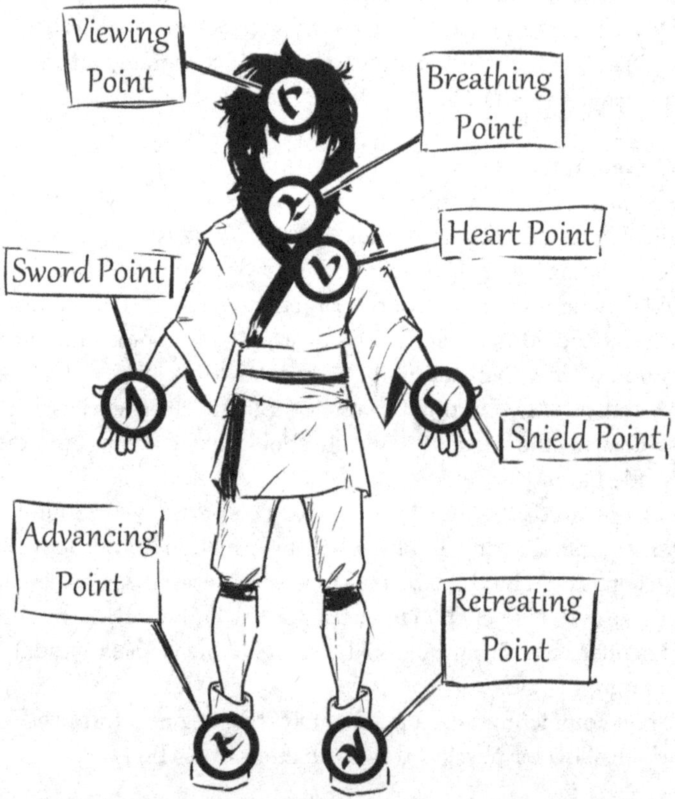

- The Heart Point in the chest is the center of the essence structure, influencing all other points to a limited degree by spreading some of the essence there to every other Dianis Point. In essence (hah!) it seems like the Heart Point can link to other Dianis Points to create the local equivalent of deep dominions from p essence types.
  - It may be more complicated than that . . . Their essence types seem to exceed the variety of dominions. They have complex compound essence types that derive from more than one prime type. I'll write more on this later.
  - The Heart Point is the first Dianis Point humans seem to develop, and the essence chosen for the Heart Point is one of the most integral for long-term development.
- The Viewing Point is in the center of the head. Essence formed in the Viewing Point influences perception.
  - For example, someone who accumulates flame essence in their Viewing Point develops the ability to sense heat, allowing them to perceive people in the dark. Useful, at least for those people who don't have sight sorcery.

- The Breathing Point is in the neck. The Breathing Point determines how a person draws in essence, making it arguably the most important of the Dianis Points.
- The Sword Point in the primary hand allows the essence within it to be used for direct offensive techniques.
- For example, holding ice essence within the Sword Point allows someone to form icicle weapons or hurl shards of ice at their opponents.
- The Shield Point in the off hand is the defensive mirror to the Sword Point, allowing the essence within to be used for defensive purposes.
- The Advancing Point in the primary foot is the principal point for movement techniques, such as increasing speed and agility.
- The Retreating Point in the other foot allows for the essence within to be used for stealth, concealment, and other forms of defensive motion.

Essence manifests in a truly staggering number of varieties in the natural environment here. I am still uncertain about the mechanisms behind this, although Edge has mentioned "breaches" — locations where there is a connection between our world and other dominions — and I believe these may play a critical role. Moreover, I have noted that although elementals exist on this continent, there is a distinct absence of Harvester and Gatherer classifications of elementals. It is possible that essence nodes would manifest naturally in areas of high essence concentration on other continents as well, but that these elemental subtypes prevent that from occurring. This may warrant some experimentation when I return home, or at a minimum, some further research during my stay here.

I intend to see if I'm capable of completing Dianis Points myself, but first . . . I need to make some hard choices.

And on that note, I will leave you in suspense, Auntie. If you want to know what else I find, well, you can send me reinforcements.

Otherwise, hope that I don't die.

Yours in service,
Scribe

APPENDIX II

HIGHER LAYER ADVANCEMENT

From Scribe's Perspective

Lien hasn't gone into higher layers significantly thus far, but I've put together some basic ideas of what to expect, and like him, I've considered some of the positives and negatives of attempting to access the advantages of these layers in some capacity before reaching the typical level.

To begin with, the concept of gaining the advantages of a layer's capabilities ahead of time seems to be well-known to essence sorcerers, at least those with Lien's level of grounding in magic theory. It's generally referred to as "layer breaking," based on the idea that you're breaking into a layer before you would reach it automatically.

Layer breaking does not grant someone all the power that comes from reaching a certain layer, nor all the related abilities. Instead, it simply allows someone to gain access to a single feature that involves interacting with that layer of self: spirit bonds for the Spirit Layer, shade weaves for the Shade Layer, and memory marks for the Memory Layer.

These features are best discussed elsewhere, but I'll provide a very brief overview here for context.

Spirit bonds are connections between an essence sorcerer and someone or something else. Common spirit bonds are to family and spouses, as detailed in my general overview, or less commonly to close friends. Other spirit bonds can be to objects or locations, but these are harder to form and access. Finally, someone can technically bond one of their Dianis Points to another one to create a synergistic bond between them.

Shade weaves involve "weaving" an essence type into the self, creating a permanent physical change related to that essence type. Simply building up secondary essence of stone can make someone stronger and more durable, but a shade weave related to stone might literally transform parts of a person's body into stone. That specific example sounds deeply uncomfortable to me, but I'm certain there are those that would disagree, and other examples sound more palatable, like perhaps turning your body into a partially incorporeal energy type to be resistant to all forms of harm, or a shade weave of shade itself to regenerate from damage rapidly.

Memory marks are the most complex and esoteric, as one might expect from the deepest of the layers of self known to be available through the conventional essence-advancement process. Memory marks involve taking something you've done or experienced and turning it into an anchor. This functions similarly to how an essence sorcerer forms essence for similar essence being gathered in the future, but rather than gathering essence directly, a memory mark anchor serves to gather the power from similar events. In its simplest form, an anchor could be something like, "defeated a monster." This would then gather power from other times the essence sorcerer defeated monsters and provide additional power in a related fashion.

What type of power would you get out of something as general as "defeated a monster"? I genuinely don't know. I suppose it would probably be some sort of general combat enhancement, but it's likely it would also skew toward whatever method was used to defeat the first monster in question. Edge's examples tend to be more hyperspecific, much like he tends to prefer specialized essence types over general ones, and thus, I don't have fantastic examples to work with here.

In each of these cases, the ability to make use of these features early offers significant potential advantage to someone of a lower essence-development level, but with notable long-term ramifications.

First, in order to break into a specific layer, one generally needs to invest in spending the time to build a Dianis Point of that layer's essence type, or a very similar type. Spirit essence for the Spirit Layer, that sort of thing. If someone already intends to invest in spirit essence, this isn't a major downside, but it's a considerable time and power investment, and it may leave someone weaker in the long term if that essence type does not have synergy with the rest of their essence-sorcery composition. Honestly, I don't see this as a tremendous downside, given how flexible most of the layer-specific essence types are, but most people don't seem to share my opinion on the general utility of these essence types (aside from spirit, which is popular).

Second, and much more importantly, choosing spirit bonds, shade weaves, and memory marks early in life means that you're likely to be choosing from a much more limited pool of available options.

This is least pronounced with spirit bonds, because conceivably one could have the best access to people, monsters, items, or locations to bond with at any given point in their lives, not necessarily later (although for most adventurous types, it'll tend toward later, as being more powerful likely leads to more options opening).

With memory marks, you have the clearest downside — as any person ages, accomplishes more things, and experiences more things, they'll have a wider variety of things to choose as anchoring memories. This doesn't mean early events are necessarily poor choices, since my understanding is that memories of difficulties can be just as empowering in some cases as memories of accomplishments. Choosing an anchor like, "The Ashen Lord burned down my humble peasant village" might be a particularly powerful and defining event that leads toward the memory's powers being geared toward empowering the individual against the Ashen Lord and his minions — or so I've been told.

Given that the mechanism behind how memory marks strengthens an individual remains unclear to me, I cannot provide an educated analysis of what memories would be best to choose. Instead, I must extrapolate from what I've heard from a variety of sources.

Factor one: The Memory Layer of self is the last layer known to be reached, and thus, whatever is available at that layer likely has substantial power.

Factor two: Memory sorcery is known to be an emulation-type essence, meaning it can be used to copy other types of essence with varying degrees of efficiency.

Factor three: Edge's stories indicate that memory essence can be used as a major component part in reconstructing entire lifelike individuals (e.g., his version of the Smiling Sword Saint) with apparent sapience.

Given these factors, my best guess is that these memory marks in some way draw from the experience that occurred, emulating a power that would be relevant to victory in that experience, regardless of whether or not victory was actually achieved in the original version of the event.

How would one distinguish between a memory mark coming from a victory and one from a loss? This, at least, Edge did have some guidance on. Memory marks related to losing, survival, or simply experiencing an event tend to be *defensive* in nature. For example, a memory of running from a dragon might involve resistance to the tools that the dragon used in the battle — claws, teeth, fangs, fiery breath. A memory of slaying a dragon might instead reinforce the wielder's power with the tools used to perform the job, helping to crack scales or pierce weak points between them.

As for shade weaves, the largest problem here is not a lack of variety at lower levels of essence development (although that problem does exist), but rather, the ability to survive the processes that enable shade weaves at lower essence-development levels.

In order to form a shade weave, one must immerse their body in a form of essence so significantly that their shade — a reflection of their physical form — begins to reflect that essence as being a core component of them. As one might expect, this is phenomenally dangerous, as immersion in virtually any form of essence type is physically dangerous, especially at lower essence-development levels. One can offset these risks to some degree by immersing one's self in essence types that are theoretically beneficial, but this appears to have a harder time actually forming an anchor for the weave, most likely because the gentle nature of the essence itself helps keep it separate from the components of the body.

So, in summary? Shade weaves are about lighting yourself on fire until you have convinced part of yourself that you are, in fact, fire.

I would advise that no one should ever do this, but with Skyseekers and their Shrineseeking counterparts being what they are, a wide variety of near-suicidal techniques for what they call "body immersion" have been developed. Edge's examples in his own story are naturally themed toward his unnatural sword fixation, but others are equally deadly in different ways.

This is, of course, something sane people can skip entirely by simply reaching the appropriate essence-development level and building a shade weave in a fashion more similar to a conventional essence anchor. I'm told this is the standard method for most essence wielders, but naturally, Edge has no interest in talking about standard methods, and thus, I lack details on the subject.

In conclusion, there is a wide variety of ways to potentially skip ahead in the essence-development process, earning abilities before they develop organically, but each of these methods has risks and potential costs. I would advise against all of them.

And I hope I don't end up having to try any.

—Scribe

APPENDIX III

SWORD TECHNIQUES AND ASPECTS

From Scribe's Perspective

Throughout Lien's story, he's mentioned a wide variety of different sword aspects that he has either utilized himself or discovered others using. I've begun a list of those he's mentioned so far, although I strongly suspect he may know others he has not mentioned.

- **Unaspected** — Basic sword essence without any aspects applied. Notably, there are different compositions of unaspected essence, and they can skew toward one aspect or another. Lien's skews toward cutting-aspected sword essence, for example. It's also noteworthy that different cultures have different default compositions of unaspected sword essence, as they have different concepts of what constitutes a "sword." This is worth noting both due to the implications for Lien's future as a swordsman, since he has an atypical concept on what counts as a sword, and also important for my own uses if I intend to look into other object-oriented essence types with variable essence compositions.
- **Cutting Aspect (Function)** — A sword essence aspect used for cutting things apart. One of Lien's primary essence types, he utilizes both for obvious applications like direct sword enhancement techniques (e.g., Sword Sharpening Shroud) and less intuitive ones like splitting his own attacks into pieces to strike enemies in multiple locations at once.
- **Piercing Aspect (Function)** — A sword aspect used to simulate the piercing tip of a thrusting sword. Useful for augmenting thrusting attacks, as well as piercing through enemy defenses.
- **Deflection Aspect (Function)** — A basic aspect formed around the concept of deflecting a weapon, Lien utilizes this both defensively and for a wide variety of utility purposes, such as deflecting his own essence in different directions.
- **Parrying Aspect (Function)** — A more specialized variant on the Deflection Aspect, the Parrying Aspect is used for defending against

weapon attacks. It lacks the flexibility of the Deflection Aspect, but performs better in its specific role.

- **Beating Aspect (Function)** — Another specialized variant on the Deflection Aspect, a beat is a sword maneuver used to smash an opponent's weapon out of the way to create an opening. While similar to the Parrying Aspect, this is more forceful and has more of an offensive function.
- **Binding Aspect (Function)** — Binding is a technique for trapping an opponent's weapon in position. This advanced aspect is used for a similar function, trapping an opponent's weapon in place against something else.
- **Riposting Aspect (Function)** — An aspect utilized for rapidly countering an opponent's attack.
- **Lunging Aspect (Function)** — A rare sword aspect for body enhancement, sending essence through the body for the purpose of rapidly closing in and striking a distant opponent.
- **Drawing Aspect (Function)** — An aspect focused on drawing a sword out of a sheath. Most swordsmen seem to use this primarily to draw their swords more quickly, as one might intuit from the name, but it also has some less intuitive functions when utilized in conjunction with a scabbard-aspected essence and other forms of seals.
- **Sharpness Aspect (Feature)** — A close cousin of cutting-aspected essence, sharpness-aspected essence improves the cutting ability of a weapon. So far as I can tell, the principal distinction is that cutting-aspected essence conjures a field of essence that can cut through things on its own, while Sharpness Aspect is an enhancement to an existing cutting weapon. They can seemingly be used interchangeably to some degree, but at decreased efficiency, much like Lien uses deflection-aspected sword essence in certain defensive applications where parrying-aspected essence might be more strictly effective.
- **Hardness Aspect (Feature)** — Another weapon-enhancing aspect, the Hardness Aspect lends enhanced durability to an object. Lien's unusual nature and manner of thinking allow him to conceptualize it as an aspect that can also be used for body enhancement, but this appears to be unusual.
- **Greatsword Aspect (Form)** — One of the many weapon aspects, this is largely used for conjuring a weapon in the form of a greatsword, but it can also be used to ascribe greatsword-like qualities to another object.
- **Zanbatou Aspect (Form)** — Near identical to Greatsword Aspect, but more specialized toward the ludicrous-sized weapons that Lien prefers.
- **Scabbard Aspect (Form)** — An aspect that creates a field of essence that can be used to store a sword or a manifestation of sword essence.

Lien uses this essence in several of his techniques in nonstandard ways; this is detailed further in the specific techniques below.

- **Severing Aspect (Function?)** — An unusual sword essence aspect manifested when combining Lien's sword essence with the sealed essence in his right hand. This is a hyperspecialized offensive essence type that has an implausible level of cutting ability, cutting through essence, techniques, and defenses with seemingly no resistance. If this is what Lien can accomplish with only a tiny fraction of his sealed essence, I can only speculate about how terrifying his offensive abilities might be if he unleashed more of the power within his seal.

Lien used many of these aspects, as well as aspects from his other lesser-used essence types, in order to create or learn a wide variety of techniques. While I suspect many of the names he has given to me are false, I have dutifully recorded them as given.

- **Ultimate Blade Creation technique** — A prototechnique for conjuring a sword to use in combat.
- **Sword Hand** — Lien's elementary technique for forming a blade of essence. Rather than just being a raw manifestation of sword essence, he crafts this from a "sandwich" of different sword aspects, creating an approximation of a sword blade that can cut, thrust, and repel other blades.
    - **Sealed Sword Creation technique** — A combination of his Sword Hand technique, his Ultimate Blade Creation technique, and the essence from his sealed hand. Conjures a powerful two-handed sword that mirrors the form of a sword that is familiar to him.
- **Sword Sharpening Shroud** — A technique for wrapping a weapon in a field of cutting energy. Like his Sword Hand technique, this is more complex than it sounds, involving multiple layers, but it's designed not to repel weapons and instead allows both the sword essence and the blade within to deal damage.
    - My strong suspicion is that he has also developed a variation on this technique that heavily emphasizes the hardness aspect of sword essence that he spoke of. This would help explain how I have seen him cut things with seemingly impossible objects, like a strand of wheat — the hardness aspect would theoretically allow the object within the field to remain stable while the cutting field tears through whatever is around it. This is purely speculative on my part based on the abilities he has already explained to me; it's possible that he has an entirely different

technique for that purpose, or that his wheat wielding was simply misdirection for some other type of attack that I was not capable of perceiving.

- **Shattering Sword** — Lien's supposed signature technique, at least for the week he made it. This involves taking a Sword Sharpening Shroud and splitting it into halves deliberately, then using deflection essence just before impact to blast the blades of essence outward. This theoretically creates three or more points of impact for the slash rather than a single one. This sounds useful both for inflicting damage at multiple points in a single attack, which is obviously useful in itself, but also for the potential to strike an opponent's arm when they are parrying your attack or otherwise damaging an opponent from unlikely angles. Given the split nature of the attack, the damage at any individual impact point is more limited than a focused attack would be, but likely still considerable.
    - **Shattering Sheath** — A variation on the Shattering Sword technique. This version of the technique involves Lien creating a layer of scabbard essence to charge up his attack inside, then before impact, he converts it into a slashing aspect. The result is an explosive release of sword essence in several directions simultaneously. If Lien wasn't seemingly immune to his own essence, this probably would have killed him repeatedly. As it is, I'm glad I know he has this, because it means I know to stand very far away from him any time he gets into a fight.
    - **Star Shattering Sword** — A variation of the technique that incorporates forms of breach essence in order to damage a target's star veins and Dianis Points. The effects can range from temporarily reducing a target's ability to utilize essence in that location to being completely debilitating.
- **Draw Sword** — A technique used for converting sword essence flowing through star veins directly into secondary essence used by the body. To do this without causing himself absolutely absurd amounts of pain, he creates a protective barrier of scabbard-aspected sword essence around the rest of the essence, then "draws" it into himself. This is the only technique that Lien has demonstrated that I believe I may be able to learn directly from — not that I intend to use sword essence, but if I begin to develop any analogous essence type, the core concept behind it might be applicable to any form of secondary essence development. Of course, that would require building up a Dianis Point or two first . . .
- **Star Sharpening** — Lien's technique for splitting essence in his star veins into component parts, then eliminating the unwanted essence types. While he claims to have recorded his methodology for doing this, I'm dubious as to how easily it could be replicated by a typical sword

essence wielder. His process appeared to involve the unusual essence type from his strange sword bond, which may or may not be a typical aspect of sword essence. Hm. Perhaps if I had access to that technique scroll, as well as some scrolls demonstrating the composition of standard sword essence, I could compare them to reverse engineer the composition of his more unusual essence type . . . from there . . . yes, there's potential in this idea. But I'm digressing, and that's poor form for a scholar, even a humble scribe.

- **Star Shattering Sight** — A breach essence technique that allows Lien to visualize Dianis Points and star veins in the body. A companion technique to Star Shattering Sword, this is utilized first in order for Lien to see his targets, then he uses the sword technique to strike them.
- **Smashing Sting** — A variant on the Soaring Palm technique from the Soaring Sword Sect. Primarily uses beat-aspected sword essence to launch an opponent backward in an unusual form of knock-back technique.
- **Shattering Soul** — A body-enhancement technique created from reverse engineering an unnamed armor-projection technique from a member of the Soaring Sword Sect (which, though Lien didn't mention it, I suspect to actually be a form of regalia manifestation). Lien's variant mixes a variety of sword aspects, causing his body to be dangerous to touch, as well as breach essence. The latter makes him what he calls "ultracorporeal," meaning simultaneously solid to many different planes (and layers of self), allowing him to strike incorporeal opponents with unarmed attacks — and the essence components of his enemies — while this is active. It also potentially harms opponents who strike him with unarmed attacks, since they're basically punching a wall that is physically present to the Dianis Points and star veins in their bodies.
- **Sundering Stride** — A rudimentary movement technique created by applying similar effects of the Smashing Sting to himself, effectively hurling himself across an area using beat-aspected propulsion. One of his less effective technique experiments, at least at first, as it causes near-immediate motion sickness.
- **Sword Steal** — A technique utilizing drawing essence, breach essence, and sword essence to reach through a breach and steal an opponent's sword from a distance. I'm not entirely certain on the full requirements for using this; he trained in spirit projection prior to learning this technique, but it may or may not be required.

In addition to techniques he created himself, Lien also mentioned a number of other sword techniques used by others, such as the Smiling Sword Saint.

- **Cutting Remark** — A sword essence technique that carries a cutting attack through the air through spoken words. Lien struggles to simulate this technique, as the original version utilizes air essence, a type of essence his own abilities struggle to simulate.
- **Rejoinder** — A variant of the Cutting Remark utilized to rapidly cut an opponent in response to their own attack.
- **Sword Saint's Smile** — The signature technique of the Smiling Sword Saint, said to be able to "divide a nation with her smile." If the stories are literal, as they are believed to be, this is a city-scale cutting attack that she is able to direct simply through the lifting of her lips.
- **Soaring Palm** — A knock-back technique from the Soaring Sword Sect.
- **Strategic Side-Step** — A movement technique used to move between swords on a battlefield.

APPENDIX IV

CHARACTERS

From Lien's Perspective

A list of our intrepid heroes from Part One:

- **Lien**, our protagonist. That's me, although most of the locals call me Edge, or, more formally, Edge of the Woods. That latter part is a title that I earned for my service to the local faerie court. And speaking of faeries, up next we have . . .
- **Ana**, a xiphiad, better known as a sword faerie. Ana is short for Anathema, the name of the sword she was born from. Technically, her name is also Anathema, but no one reasonable calls her that, except for . . .
- **Gramps**, the old man who raised me. He's some kind of weird ancient Skyseeker or something. I don't know his whole deal. I don't think he's my real grandfather, but he raised me after my parents were apparently killed in a suspiciously typical Dark Lord–style murder thing. I'd probably be more upset about it if I remembered them. As it is, well . . . Gramps is my only real family. I suspected he has a close connection of some kind with . . .
- **Erik Tarren**, legendary scholar and world traveler. I grew up with lots of books he wrote. I strongly suspected that he might be in my family, too, or be my grandfather's actual identity. I didn't have any other immediate family, but I was always close to . . .
- **Uncle Eiji**, an ancient shape-changing demi-beast, who basically serves as a second (and much nicer) paternal figure. He's still super old and crochety at times, but at least he brings me stuff from the outside world, like cool trinkets. And, more importantly, news. Oh, and I suppose that means that his kids are family, too, like . . .
- **Hinoka**, the smallest of Eiji's pups. I don't know who her mother is, but it isn't . . .
- **Auntie Temper**, because she isn't actually Eiji's mate — though I'm sure they'd both be hugely amused by *that* idea — but she's still my aunt and my family. She runs the Ghost Forge, a smithy that serves as home to many spirit-bonded weapons that were damaged or

abandoned after a disastrous war between humans and faeries. She's an exile from faerie culture, and thus, she naturally gets along great with other strange people like Eiji and me. She occasionally gets visits from a few other faeries in spite of being banished, like one of my mischievous little friends . . .

- **Lindt**, a faerie with the appearance of a tiny ten-year-old boy, who loves to wander out of where he's supposed to be.
- **Eliree**, my first love. Half dryad, bound to a mysterious tree outside of normal faerie lands. She's also a potent healer.
- **Current**, a naiad, and Flow's twin. Doesn't appear in this story, but I thought about the twins next, so I'm writing them down anyway.
- **Flow**, a naiad, and Current's twin.
- **Verthrimax the Iron Breaker**, a great and powerful dragon who was blinded protecting the forest hundreds of years ago. If the faerie queen is the queen of the forest, he'd be the king. I mean, not in a "they're a married couple" sense. Probably? I don't ask questions about that sort of thing. Anyway, he's ancient. Maybe . . . too ancient. I worry about him.
- **The Willowbark Witch**, a powerful practitioner of foreign magic and alchemy who lives on the eastern side of the woods, along with her children:
- **Belladonna**, the oldest child at roughly twenty and a full witch.
- **Cascade**, a few years my elder and an ocean witch.
- **Darryl**, just a few weeks older than me and a shadow witch. The only male witch in the family.
- **Flare**, a few months younger than me and a fire witch.
- **Root**, eight years old and an earth and crystal witch.
- **Poppy**, a five-year-old with a talent for plant magic.
- **Blink**, the youngest child at three years of age, and possibly a ghost. An actual ghost, though — not an echo, like . . .
- **Gray**, the echo of a small child at an abandoned sword school. Extraordinary talent for his age.
- **Fade**, the echo of a teenaged girl with fading green hair at an abandoned sword school. Dexterity and trickery-based fighting style.
- **Green**, the echo of an adult swordsman at an abandoned sword school. Strength-based combat style, with skill at both swords and unarmed fighting.
- **Red**, the echo of an adult swordswoman at an abandoned sword school. Impossibly skilled, impeccable technique.
- **The Smiling Sword Saint**, a historical master of swordsmanship who died in a legendary duel with her rival hundreds of years ago. I discovered an echo of her at an ancient arena and sought her training, with mixed results. She eventually conjured another echo . . .

- **Thane**, a younger copy of the Smiling Sword Saint, forged from her memories. Manifests as male, since the Sword Saint presented as male when she was younger. Still prefers to be referred to as male at his current age.
- **Lance Rival**, a . . . probably (?) human Skyseeker who came to visit the Sepulcher of Sealed Swords for some kind of pilgrimage. Looks about my age, but he's colossally tall, even without his spiked purple hair. Tremendous strength and speed. Believes I'll one day be his rival, which sounds like it could be pretty exciting, even if it would make Ana jealous.
- **Vantonio**, the ghost of a curator of the Sepulcher of Sealed Swords.
- **Dream Girl**, a young woman who appeared during my Destiny Dream, wielding a strange all-metal spear and wearing armor of green leaves. She had one golden eye and one silver eye in the dream, as well as unnatural blond hair that revealed black or red near the roots. I . . . think I know her somehow, but I don't know how. She seemed to be after my sword. No, not like *that*. Okay, maybe like that, too — she was kind of a flirt. Anyway, I don't know what happened to her after the dream, but I have some ideas, now. And speaking of the present, I just met someone interesting . . .
- **Scribe**, a human from the continent of Mythralis who I met while traveling between human cities. Given that he uses an *Ess* name, has illusion magic, and is from Mythralis, it's incredibly obvious that he has some kind of connection to the legendary . . .
- **Aayara Haven**, the Lady of Thieves. Demigoddess and child of one of the gods of the continent of Mythralis. Also known as Symphony, she famously runs an organized crime syndicate known as the Orchestra with influence on several continents, likely including my own. The fact that cities that are safe from monsters are called Havens has not escaped my notice.

And now, a set of our new cast for our second part of the story:

- **Valissar Talis**, Sword Lord and Knight Errant of a foreign faerie court. Aspirant to the title of Talisian and adventurer. A model swordsman and adventurer, seeking to aid the people of his homeland.
- **Oloris**, Valissar's close companion and partner. A fae of yet another court who has taken up Valissar's cause and joined him in his journeys. Potent magic of fire and purity.
- **Rusty**, a young squire who appears to be a Red Cap, a type of dangerous fae who wears a cap dripping with the blood of their enemies. Definitely a guise of someone I knew, but I won't say quite who.
- **Zeng Wu**, the arrogant young master of the Zeng clan. A, uh, let's say a fictionalized version of a real person from the Smiling Sword Saint's

past, who I encountered using the Dreamer's Circlet. A Hearth-level disciple of the Soaring Sword Sect and capable fighter.

- **Xiao Qin, also known as Minion A**, one of Zeng Wu's lackeys and an outer disciple of the Soaring Sword Sect. Uses flame essence with gunpowder to produce explosive results. Also a fan of poison needles and backstabbing.
- **Xiao Min, Disciple of the Threefold Blade, also known as Minion B**, a disciple of the Soaring Sword Sect and follower of Zeng Wu. Capable of multiplying his sword into three and/or conjuring swords out of nothing. His style is like a rudimentary version of what I've seen the Smiling Sword Saint and Thane use on numerous occasions.
- **Liao Yun**, a server at a tavern in one of the Smiling Sword Saint's memories.

ACKNOWLEDGMENTS

I'd like to get this one started by thanking my parents, Chris and Bruce Rowe, for their constant support of my writing career from my childhood onward. I often write about characters without supportive parent figures — because, let's face it, orphans are a classic fantasy tradition — but I had exactly the opposite. My parents have always been absolutely fantastic about supporting me, including beta reading the vast majority of my books and often giving me copious notes.

(No, Mom, gerunds are not always a grammatical mistake.)

Thank you both for your constant love and support.

Mallory Reaves was a huge help on this one, providing me with hundreds of notes on the book — and not *just* because Red is one of her personal characters. (But she is, and I can't wait for us to show you more of Red in future books.)

Aside from Red, Mallory is the principal inspiration for Ana. Our own childhood antics inspired many of the interactions in the story, and both Red and Ana draw from our years of role-playing together in different ways.

Jess Richards has also been a tremendous help for all my books, from providing direct editing in many earlier books to simply providing ideas and advice in later ones. Jess also played a major role in introducing me to a broader variety of fiction, including many web serials and novels that have helped inspire my own style, such as pointing me toward *Mother of Learning* many years ago. Without Jess, it's much more likely that I'd still be writing very generic medieval fantasy without many of the more creative elements that have helped define my works.

Thank you as always to my literary agent, Paul Lucas, for helping make this book possible.

I'd also like to thank my publisher, Podium Entertainment, for picking up this series and working to help make my writing and publishing process easier. In particular, Victoria has been a tireless champion of my books as a whole, and I truly appreciate her help.

This book continues to draw obvious inspiration from *The Legend of Zelda* and *Peter Pan*, two of the most iconic stories of my youth. In addition, there are more nods to classical faerie stories in this one, with some direct nods to Celtic mythology, as well as some non-Celtic myths, like Little Red Riding Hood. The Lady of the Fake is an obvious nod to the Lady of the Lake and Arthurian myth. Lien and Valissar both use strategies and have visual imagery based around classical mythological heroes from

Celtic, Germanic, and Greek traditions. (Notably, the gray pallor of Valissar Talis isn't a direct nod to Arawn's depiction in the Mabinogi, but there might have been some subconscious inspiration.)

There's also some clear inspiration from *The Faerie Queene* here, in that I have a knightly faerie who speaks (and acts) largely in verse. While I considered writing these segments in actual Spenserian verse, using that structure would have made Lord Valissar Talis's dialogue too clunky, so I stuck with a simpler (and less structured) rhyme scheme.

Thank you to my fellow progression fantasy writers, especially those who have been constantly pushing the envelope and definition of what is accepted in our genre. Also, double thank-you for those who I've managed to steal for beta reading at one point or another, such as Will Wight, John Bierce, Tobias Begley, and Lorne Ryburn.

Thank you to all my beta readers in general, including Carly (the problem child), John Bierce, Baird Bedient, Eli Brandt, Tobias Begley, Doug Driggs, Yvonne Etzkorn, Markus Kemppainen, Sarah Lin, Jonah L. L., James L. M. Wolter, Anthony Mulder, Andrew Ritchie, Mallory Reaves, Rebecca Reeves, Bruce Rowe, and Brandon Yee.

An extra thank-you to the people who inspired the characters in this story, largely through the tabletop games and LARPs that I played in and ran as a youth. The Willowbark Witch's family, for example, are in many ways inspired by the Noel family, who ran many of the games I played in as a child. Auntie Temper draws heavily from them, too. Eliree is one of many characters inspired by Carly Thomas, most famous for playing the original character that Wrynn Jaden is based off.

Valissar Talis is one of my own characters, created as one of the several people tied to the Talisian Order in my role-playing games. Several other people played Talisian, including Dani Lee Collins and Michael Kelly.

Oloris Nysarii is based on a character played by Michael Corr. As always, I've made changes for the book version, but I hope he finds my depiction of the character worthy.

Rusty is based on a number of people, as well as mythological and gaming inspirations. Player-wise, some of Rusty's elements are based on characters played by Carly Thomas and Heather Crosthwaite. They also take clear inspiration from faerie stories about Red Caps — and, of course, Little Red Riding Hood, who is also known as Little Red Cap. Riding Grandmother Wolf can be seen as a take on Little Red Riding Hood, but imagery-wise, I also picture it as being a nod to San in *Princess Mononoke*. And, as you may have noticed, there's a bit of an *Ocarina of Time* nod from Rusty, too.

As previously noted, Mallory Reaves is my model for both Ana and Red, the latter of which is related to the longest-standing player character in my universe, and someone I can't wait for us to show you more of someday.

And finally, thank you to all my fans for reading this book. I hope you enjoyed it!

ABOUT THE AUTHOR

Andrew Rowe was once a professional game designer for awesome companies like Blizzard Entertainment, Cryptic Studios, and Obsidian Entertainment. Nowadays, he's writing full time.

When he's not crunching numbers for game balance, he runs live-action role-playing games set in the same universe as his books. In addition, he writes for pen-and-paper role-playing games.

Aside from game design and writing, Andrew watches a lot of anime, reads a metric ton of fantasy books, and plays every role-playing game he can get his hands on.

Interested in following Andrew's books releases, or discussing them with other people? You can find more info, updates, and discussions in a few places online:

Andrew's Blog: andrewkrowe.wordpress.com
Mailing List: andrewkrowe.wordpress.com/mailing-list
Facebook: Facebook.com/Arcane-Ascension-378362729189084
Reddit: Reddit.com/r/ClimbersCourt